Between the Gothic and the Plague:

Why We Can't Have Nice Things

T0336360

Edited By Jan Kostka

ZMOK
BOOKS

Between the Gothic and the Plague: Why We Can't Have Nice Things
Cover from *The Sleep of Reason Produces Monsters* by Francisco Goya, 1799
Edited by Jan Kostka
This edition published in 2020

Zmok Books is an imprint of

Winged Hussar Publishing, LLC
1525 Hulse Rd, Unit 1
Point Pleasant, NJ 08742

Copyright © Zmok Books
ISBN 978-1-950423-38-5 Paperback
ISBN 978-1-950423-39-2 Ebook
LCN 2020937068

Bibliographical References and Index
1.Horror. 2. Dark Fantasy. 3. Plague

Winged Hussar Publishing, LLC All rights reserved
For more information
visit us at www.wingedhussarpublishing.com

Twitter: WingHusPubLLC
Facebook: Winged Hussar Publishing LLC

CONTENTS

Introduction

The Castle of Ontarato (1764)
        by Horace Walpole

Vathek, An Arabian Tale (1782)
        by William Beckford

The Last Man (1826)
        by Mary Shelley

The Masque of the Red Death (1842)
        by Edgar Allen Poe

The Scarlet Plague (1912)
        by Jack London

INTRODUCTION

This volume contains five stories – some short, some long. Each that builds upon the heritage of the other. It starts with *The Castle of Ontarato* (1764) by Horace Walpole which is considered the first, "Gothic Novel"; *Vathek, An Arabian Tale* (1782) by William Beckford, was influenced by Walpole and Arabian Nights; *The Last Man* (1826) by Mary Shelley carries on the theme of the previous works, but could be viewed as one of the first science fiction post-apocalyptic novels; *The Masque of the Red Death* (1842) by Edgar Allen Poe also focuses on apocalyptic forces and society's efforts (or lack thereof) to deal with it. Finally, *The Scarlet Plague* (1912) by Jack London describes a world-wide pandemic that humanity cannot control. Even the cover illustration, *The Sleep of Reason Produces Monsters*, by Goya is influenced by the Gothic art and forms a sort of double-entendre of monsters made in our mind and by doing nothing.

In creating this collection, we have not edited the language, feeling that they are best presented in their original form, but knowing that they are products of their age. We have, updated spelling from the original form to make it more readable. As you read these stories, you can see the development of novels and short stories in the modern tradition. Each is a tale of horror – not supernatural, but as the result of nature and perhaps people looking out for themselves rather than what should be done. They are studies in action and reaction. I hope you enjoy them.

The Castle of Otranto

By Horace Walpole

ABOUT THE AUTHOR

Horace Walpole (1717 - 1797) was the youngest son of Sir Robert Walpole, the great statesman, who died Earl of Orford. He was born in 1717, the year in which his father resigned office, remaining in opposition for almost three years before his return to a long tenure of power. Horace Walpole was educated at Eton, where he formed a school friendship with Thomas Gray, who was but a few months older. In 1739 Gray was travelling companion with Walpole in France and Italy until they differed and parted; but the friendship was afterwards renewed and remained firm to the end. Horace Walpole went from Eton to King's College, Cambridge, and entered Parliament in 1741, the year before his father's final resignation and acceptance of an earldom. His way of life was made easy to him. As Usher of the Exchequer, Comptroller of the Pipe, and Clerk of the Estreats in the Exchequer, he received nearly two thousand a year for doing nothing, lived with his father, and amused himself.

Horace Walpole's father died in 1745. The eldest son, who succeeded to the earldom, died in 1751, and left a son, George, who was for a time insane, and lived until 1791. As George left no child, the title and estates passed to Horace Walpole, then seventy-four years old, and the only uncle who survived. Horace Walpole thus became Earl of Orford, during the last six years of his life. As to the title, he said that he felt himself being called names in his old age. He died unmarried, in the year 1797, at the age of eighty.

He had turned his house at Strawberry Hill, by the Thames, near Twickenham, into a Gothic villa - eighteenth-century Gothic - and amused himself by spending freely upon its adornment with such things as were then fashionable as objects of taste. But he delighted also in his flowers and his trellises of roses, and the quiet Thames. When confined by gout to his London house in Arlington Street, flowers from Strawberry Hill and a bird were necessary consolations. He set up also a private printing press at Strawberry Hill, where he printed his friend Gray's poems, as well as his own "Catalogue of the Royal and Noble Authors of England" in 1758, and five volumes of "Anecdotes of Painting in England," between 1762 and 1771.

Horace Walpole produced, *The Castle of Otranto in 1765*, at the mature age of forty-eight. It was suggested by a dream from which he said he waked one morning, and of which "all I could recover was, that I had thought myself in an ancient castle (a very natural dream for a head like mine, filled with Gothic story), and that on the uppermost banister of a great staircase I saw a gigantic hand in armor. In the evening I sat down and began to write, without knowing in the least what I intended to say or relate." So began the tale which professed to be translated by "William Marshal, gentleman, from the Italian of Onuphro Muralto, canon of the Church of St. Nicholas, at Otranto." It was written in two months. Walpole's friend Gray reported to him that at Cambridge the book made "some of them cry a little, and all in general afraid to go to bed o' nights." The Castle of

Otranto was, in its own way, an early sign of the reaction towards romance in the latter part of the last century. This gives it interest. But it has had many followers, and the hardy modern reader, when he read's Gray's note from Cambridge, needs to be reminded of its date.

PREFACE TO THE FIRST EDITION

The following work was found in the library of an ancient Catholic family in the north of England. It was printed at Naples, in the black letter, in the year 1529. How much sooner it was written does not appear. The principal incidents are such as were believed in the darkest ages of Christianity; but the language and conduct have nothing that savors of barbarism. The style is the purest Italian.

If the story was written near the time when it is supposed to have happened, it must have been between 1095, the era of the first Crusade, and 1243, the date of the last, or not long afterwards. There is no other circumstance in the work that can lead us to guess at the period in which the scene is laid: the names of the actors are evidently fictitious, and probably disguised on purpose: yet the Spanish names of the domestics seem to indicate that this work was not composed until the establishment of the Aragon Kings in Naples had made Spanish appellations familiar in that country. The beauty of the diction, and the zeal of the author (moderated, however, by singular judgment) concur to make me think that the date of the composition was little antecedent to that of the impression. Letters were then in their most flourishing state in Italy, and contributed to dispel the empire of superstition, at that time so forcibly attacked by the reformers. It is not unlikely that an artful priest might endeavor to turn their own arms on the innovators and might avail himself of his abilities as an author to confirm the populace in their ancient errors and superstitions. If this was his view, he has certainly acted with signal address. Such a work as the following would enslave a hundred vulgar minds beyond half the books of controversy that have been written from the days of Luther to the present hour.

This solution of the author's motives is, however, offered as a mere conjecture. Whatever his views were, or whatever effects the execution of them might have, his work can only be laid before the public at present as a matter of entertainment. Even as such, some apology for it is necessary. Miracles, visions, necromancy, dreams, and other preternatural events are exploded now even from romances. That was not the case when our author wrote, much less when the story itself is supposed to have happened. Belief in every kind of prodigy was so established in those dark ages, that an author would not be faithful to the manners of the times, who should omit all mention of them. He is not bound to believe them himself, but he must represent his actors as believing them.

If this air of the miraculous is excused, the reader will find nothing else unworthy of his perusal. Allow the possibility of the facts, and all the actors comport themselves as persons would do in their situation. There is no bombast, no similes, flowers, digressions, or unnecessary descriptions. Everything tends directly to the catastrophe. Never is the reader's attention relaxed. The rules of the drama are almost observed throughout the conduct of the piece. The characters are well drawn, and still better maintained. Terror, the author's principal engine, prevents the story from ever languishing; and it is so often contrasted by pity, that the mind is kept up in a constant vicissitude of interesting passions.

Some persons may perhaps think the characters of the domestics too little serious for the general cast of the story; but besides their opposition to the principal personages, the art of the author is very observable in his conduct of the subalterns. They discover many passages essential to the story, which could not be well brought to light but by their naïveté and simplicity. In particular, the womanish terror and foibles of Bianca, in the last chapter, conduce essentially towards advancing the catastrophe.

It is natural for a translator to be prejudiced in favor of his adopted work. More impartial readers may not be so much struck with the beauties of this piece as I was. Yet I am not blind to my author's defects. I could wish he had grounded his plan on a more useful moral than this: that "the sins of fathers are visited on their children to the third and fourth generation." I doubt whether, in his time, any more than at present, ambition curbed its appetite of dominion from the dread of so remote a punishment. And yet this moral is weakened by that less direct insinuation, that even such anathema may be diverted by devotion to St. Nicholas. Here the interest of the Monk plainly gets the better of the judgment of the author. However, with all its faults, I have no doubt, but the English reader will be pleased with a sight of this performance. The piety that reigns throughout, the lessons of virtue that are inculcated, and the rigid purity of the sentiments, exempt this work from the censure to which romances are but too liable. Should it meet with the success I hope for, I may be encouraged to reprint the original Italian, though it will tend to depreciate my own labor.

Our language falls far short of the charms of the Italian, both for variety and harmony. The latter is peculiarly excellent for simple narrative. It is difficult in English to relate without falling too low or rising too high; a fault obviously occasioned by the little care taken to speak pure language in common conversation. Every Italian or Frenchman of any rank piques himself on speaking his own tongue correctly and with choice. I cannot flatter myself with having done justice to my author in this respect: his style is as elegant as his conduct of the passions is masterly. It is a pity that he did not apply his talents to what they were evidently proper for - the theatre.

I will detain the reader no longer, but to make one short remark. Though the machinery is invention, and the names of the actor's imaginary, I cannot but believe that the groundwork of the story is founded on truth. The scene is undoubtedly laid in some real castle. The author seems frequently, without design, to describe particular parts. "The chamber," says he, "on the right hand;" "the door on the left hand;" "the distance from the chapel to Conrad's apartment:" these and other passages are strong presumptions that the author had some certain building in his eye. Curious persons, who have leisure to employ in such researches, may possibly discover in the Italian writers the foundation on which our author has built. If a catastrophe, at all resembling that which he describes, is believed to have given rise to this work, it will contribute to interest the reader, and will make the, Castle of Otranto, a still more moving story.

SONNET TO THE RIGHT HONOURABLE LADY MARY COKE

The gentle maid, whose hapless tale
These melancholy pages speak.
Say, gracious lady, shall she fail
To draw the tear adown thy cheek?

No; never was thy pitying breast
Insensible to human woes.
Tender, tho' firm, it melts distress
For weaknesses it never knows.

Oh! guard the marvels I relate
Of fell ambition scourg'd by fate,
From reason's peevish blame.
Blest with thy smile, my dauntless sail
I dare expand to Fancy's gale,
For sure thy smiles are Fame.

H. W.

CHAPTER I

Manfred, Prince of Otranto, had one son and one daughter: the latter, a most beautiful virgin, aged eighteen, was called Matilda. Conrad, the son, was three years younger, a homely youth, sickly, and of no promising disposition; yet he was the darling of his father, who never showed any symptoms of affection to Matilda. Manfred had contracted a marriage for his son with the Marquis of Vicenza's daughter, Isabella; and she had already been delivered by her guardians into the hands of Manfred, that he might celebrate the wedding as soon as Conrad's infirm state of health would permit.

Manfred's impatience for this ceremonial was remarked by his family and neighbors. The former, indeed, apprehending the severity of their Prince's disposition, did not dare to utter their surmises on this precipitation. Hippolita, his wife, an amiable lady, did sometimes venture to represent the danger of marrying their only son so early, considering his great youth, and greater infirmities; but she never received any other answer than reflections on her own sterility, who had given him but one heir. His tenants and subjects were less cautious in their discourses. They attributed this hasty wedding to the Prince's dread of seeing accomplished an ancient prophecy, which was said to have pronounced that the castle and lordship of Otranto "should pass from the present family, whenever the real owner should be grown too large to inhabit it." It was difficult to make any sense of this prophecy; and still less easy to conceive what it had to do with the marriage in question. Yet these mysteries, or contradictions, did not make the populace adhere the less to their opinion.

Young Conrad's birthday was fixed for his espousals. The company was assembled in the chapel of the Castle, and everything ready for beginning the divine office, when Conrad himself was missing. Manfred, impatient of the least delay, and who had not observed his son retire, dispatched one of his attendants to summon the young Prince. The servant, who had not stayed long enough to have crossed the court to Conrad's apartment, came running back breathless, in a frantic manner, his eyes staring, and foaming at the mouth. He said nothing but pointed to the court.

The company were struck with terror and amazement. The Princess Hippolita, without knowing what the matter was, but anxious for her son, swooned away. Manfred, less apprehensive than enraged at the procrastination of the nuptials, and at the folly of his domestic, asked imperiously what was the matter? The fellow made no answer but continued pointing towards the courtyard; and at last, after repeated questions put to him, cried out, "Oh! the helmet! the helmet!"

In the meantime, some of the company had run into the court, from whence was heard a confused noise of shrieks, horror, and surprise. Manfred, who began to be alarmed at not seeing his son, went himself to get information of what occasioned this strange confusion. Matilda remained endeavoring to assist her mother, and

Isabella stayed for the same purpose, and to avoid showing any impatience for the bridegroom, for whom, in truth, she had conceived little affection.

The first thing that struck Manfred's eyes was a group of his servants endeavoring to raise something that appeared to him a mountain of sable plumes. He gazed without believing his sight.

"What are ye doing?" cried Manfred, wrathfully; "where is my son?"

A volley of voices replied, "Oh! my Lord! the Prince! the Prince! the helmet! the helmet!"

Shocked with these lamentable sounds, and dreading he knew not what, he advanced hastily, - but what a sight for a father's eyes! - he beheld his child dashed to pieces, and almost buried under an enormous helmet, an hundred times more large than any casque ever made for human being, and shaded with a proportionable quantity of black feathers.

The horror of the spectacle, the ignorance of all around how this misfortune had happened, and above all, the tremendous phenomenon before him, took away the Prince's speech. Yet his silence lasted longer than even grief could occasion. He fixed his eyes on what he wished in vain to believe a vision; and seemed less attentive to his loss, than buried in meditation on the stupendous object that had occasioned it. He touched; he examined the fatal casque; nor could even the bleeding mangled remains of the young Prince divert the eyes of Manfred from the portent before him.

All who had known his partial fondness for young Conrad, were as much surprised at their Prince's insensibility, as thunderstruck themselves at the miracle of the helmet. They conveyed the disfigured corpse into the hall, without receiving the least direction from Manfred. As little as he was attentive to the ladies who remained in the chapel. On the contrary, without mentioning the unhappy princesses, his wife and daughter, the first sounds that dropped from Manfred's lips were, "Take care of the Lady Isabella."

The domestics, without observing the singularity of this direction, were guided by their affection to their mistress, to consider it as peculiarly addressed to her situation, and flew to her assistance. They conveyed her to her chamber more dead than alive, and indifferent to all the strange circumstances she heard, except the death of her son.

Matilda, who doted on her mother, smothered her own grief and amazement, and thought of nothing but assisting and comforting her afflicted parent. Isabella, who had been treated by Hippolita like a daughter, and who returned that tenderness with equal duty and affection, was scarce less assiduous about the Princess; at the same time endeavoring to partake and lessen the weight of sorrow which she saw Matilda strove to suppress, for whom she had conceived the warmest sympathy of friendship. Yet her own situation could not help finding its place in her thoughts. She felt no concern for the death of young Conrad, except commiseration; and she was not sorry to be delivered from a marriage which had promised her little felicity, either from her destined bridegroom, or from the severe temper of Manfred, who, though he had distinguished her by great indulgence, had imprinted her mind with terror, from his causeless rigor to such amiable princesses as Hippolita and Matilda.

While the ladies were conveying the wretched mother to her bed, Manfred remained in the court, gazing on the ominous casque, and regardless of the crowd which the strangeness of the event had now assembled around him. The few words he articulated, tended solely to inquiries, whether any man knew from whence it could have come? Nobody could give him the least information. However, as it seemed to be the sole object of his curiosity, it soon became so to the rest of the spectators, whose conjectures were as absurd and improbable, as the catastrophe itself was unprecedented. In the midst of their senseless guesses, a young peasant, whom rumor had drawn thither from a neighboring village, observed that the miraculous helmet was exactly like that on the figure in black marble of Alfonso the Good, one of their former princes, in the church of St. Nicholas. "Villain! What sayest thou?" cried Manfred, starting from his trance in a tempest of rage, and seizing the young man by the collar; "how darest thou utter such treason? Thy life shall pay for it."

The spectators, who as little comprehended the cause of the Prince's fury as all the rest they had seen, were at a loss to unravel this new circumstance. The young peasant himself was still more astonished, not conceiving how he had offended the Prince. Yet recollecting himself, with a mixture of grace and humility, he disengaged himself from Manfred's grip, and then with an obeisance, which discovered more jealousy of innocence than dismay, he asked, with respect, of what he was guilty? Manfred, more enraged at the vigor, however decently exerted, with which the young man had shaken off his hold, than appeased by his submission, ordered his attendants to seize him, and, if he had not been withheld by his friends whom he had invited to the nuptials, would have poniarded the peasant in their arms.

During this altercation, some of the vulgar spectators had run to the great church, which stood near the castle, and came back open-mouthed, declaring that the helmet was missing from Alfonso's statue. Manfred, at this news, grew perfectly frantic; and, as if he sought a subject on which to vent the tempest within him, he rushed again on the young peasant, crying:

"Villain! Monster! Sorcerer! 'tis thou hast done this! 'tis thou hast slain my son!"

The mob, who wanted some object within the scope of their capacities, on whom they might discharge their bewildered reasoning, caught the words from the mouth of their lord, and re-echoed:

"Ay, ay; 'tis he, 'tis he: he has stolen the helmet from good Alfonso's tomb, and dashed out the brains of our young Prince with it," never reflecting how enormous the disproportion was between the marble helmet that had been in the church, and that of steel before their eyes; nor how impossible it was for a youth seemingly not twenty, to wield a piece of armor of so prodigious a weight.

The folly of these ejaculations brought Manfred to himself: yet whether provoked at the peasant having observed the resemblance between the two helmets, and thereby led to the farther discovery of the absence of that in the church, or wishing to bury any such rumor under so impertinent a supposition, he gravely pronounced that the young man was certainly a necromancer, and that till the Church could take cognizance of the affair, he would have the Magician, whom they had thus detected, kept prisoner under the helmet itself, which he ordered his attendants to raise, and place the young man under it; declaring he should be kept there without food, with which his own infernal art might furnish him.

It was in vain for the youth to represent against this preposterous sentence: in vain did Manfred's friends endeavor to divert him from this savage and ill-grounded resolution. The generality were charmed with their lord's decision, which, to their apprehensions, carried great appearance of justice, as the Magician was to be punished by the very instrument with which he had offended: nor were they struck with the least compunction at the probability of the youth being starved, for they firmly believed that, by his diabolic skill, he could easily supply himself with nutriment.

Manfred thus saw his commands even cheerfully obeyed; and appointing a guard with strict orders to prevent any food being conveyed to the prisoner, he dismissed his friends and attendants, and retired to his own chamber, after locking the gates of the castle, in which he suffered none but his domestics to remain.

In the meantime, the care and zeal of the young Ladies had brought the Princess Hippolita to herself, who amidst the transports of her own sorrow frequently demanded news of her lord, would have dismissed her attendants to watch over him, and at last enjoined Matilda to leave her, and visit and comfort her father. Matilda, who wanted no affectionate duty to Manfred, though she trembled at his austerity, obeyed the orders of Hippolita, whom she tenderly recommended to Isabella; and inquiring of the domestics for her father, was informed that he was retired to his chamber, and had commanded that nobody should have admittance to him. Concluding that he was immersed in sorrow for the death of her brother, and fearing to renew his tears by the sight of his sole remaining child, she hesitated whether she should break in upon his affliction; yet solicitude for him, backed by the commands of her mother, encouraged her to venture disobeying the orders he had given; a fault she had never been guilty of before.

The gentle timidity of her nature made her pause for some minutes at his door. She heard him traverse his chamber backwards, and forwards with disordered steps; a mood which increased her apprehensions. She was, however, just going to beg admittance, when Manfred suddenly opened the door; and as it was now twilight, concurring with the disorder of his mind, he did not distinguish the person, but asked angrily, who it was? Matilda replied, trembling:

"My dearest father, it is I, your daughter."

Manfred, stepping back hastily, cried, "Begone! I do not want a daughter;" and flinging back abruptly, clapped the door against the terrified Matilda.

She was too well acquainted with her father's impetuosity to venture a second intrusion. When she had a little recovered the shock of so bitter a reception, she wiped away her tears to prevent the additional stab that the knowledge of it would give to Hippolita, who questioned her in the most anxious terms on the health of Manfred, and how he bore his loss. Matilda assured her he was well and supported his misfortune with manly fortitude.

"But will he not let me see him?" said Hippolita mournfully; "will he not permit me to blend my tears with his, and shed a mother's sorrows in the bosom of her Lord? Or do you deceive me, Matilda? I know how Manfred doted on his son: is not the stroke too heavy for him? has he not sunk under it? You do not answer me — alas! I dread the worst! - Raise me, my maidens; I will, I will see my Lord. Bear me to him instantly: he is dearer to me even than my children."

Matilda made signs to Isabella to prevent Hippolita's rising; and both those lovely young women were using their gentle violence to stop and calm the

Princess, when a servant, on the part of Manfred, arrived and told Isabella that his Lord demanded to speak with her.

"With me!" cried Isabella.

"Go," said Hippolita, relieved by a message from her Lord: "Manfred cannot support the sight of his own family. He thinks you less disordered than we are and dreads the shock of my grief. Console him, dear Isabella, and tell him I will smother my own anguish rather than add to his."

As it was now evening the servant who conducted Isabella bore a torch before her. When they came to Manfred, who was walking impatiently about the gallery, he started, and said hastily,

"Take away that light, and begone."

Then shutting the door impetuously, he flung himself upon a bench against the wall, and bade Isabella sit by him. She obeyed trembling.

"I sent for you, Lady," said he—and then stopped under great appearance of confusion.

"My Lord!"

"Yes, I sent for you on a matter of great moment," resumed he. "Dry your tears, young Lady—you have lost your bridegroom. Yes, cruel fate! and I have lost the hopes of my race! But Conrad was not worthy of your beauty."

"How, my Lord!" said Isabella; "sure you do not suspect me of not feeling the concern I ought: my duty and affection would have always—"

"Think no more of him," interrupted Manfred; "he was a sickly, puny child, and Heaven has perhaps taken him away, that I might not trust the honors of my house on so frail a foundation. The line of Manfred calls for numerous supports. My foolish fondness for that boy blinded the eyes of my prudence—but it is better as it is. I hope, in a few years, to have reason to rejoice at the death of Conrad."

Words cannot paint the astonishment of Isabella. At first, she apprehended that grief had disordered Manfred's understanding. Her next thought suggested that this strange discourse was designed to ensnare her: she feared that Manfred had perceived her indifference for his son: and in consequence of that idea she replied—

"Good my Lord, do not doubt my tenderness: my heart would have accompanied my hand. Conrad would have engrossed all my care; and wherever fate shall dispose of me, I shall always cherish his memory, and regard your Highness and the virtuous Hippolita as my parents."

"Curse on Hippolita!" cried Manfred. "Forget her from this moment, as I do. In short, Lady, you have missed a husband undeserving of your charms: they shall now be better disposed of. Instead of a sickly boy, you shall have a husband in the prime of his age, who will know how to value your beauties, and who may expect a numerous offspring."

"Alas, my Lord!" said Isabella, "my mind is too sadly engrossed by the recent catastrophe in your family to think of another marriage. If ever my father returns, and it shall be his pleasure, I shall obey, as I did when I consented to give my hand to your son: but until his return, permit me to remain under your hospitable roof, and employ the melancholy hours in assuaging yours, Hippolita's, and the fair Matilda's affliction."

"I desired you once before," said Manfred angrily, "not to name that woman: from this hour she must be a stranger to you, as she must be to me. In short, Isabella, since I cannot give you my son, I offer you myself."

"Heavens!" cried Isabella, waking from her delusion, "what do I hear? You! my Lord! You! My father-in-law! the father of Conrad! the husband of the virtuous and tender Hippolita!"

"I tell you," said Manfred imperiously, "Hippolita is no longer my wife; I divorce her from this hour. Too long has she cursed me by her unfruitfulness. My fate depends on having sons, and this night I trust will give a new date to my hopes."

At those words he seized the cold hand of Isabella, who was half dead with fright and horror. She shrieked, and started from him, Manfred rose to pursue her, when the moon, which was now up, and gleamed in at the opposite casement, presented to his sight the plumes of the fatal helmet, which rose to the height of the windows, waving backwards and forwards in a tempestuous manner, and accompanied with a hollow and rustling sound. Isabella, who gathered courage from her situation, and who dreaded nothing so much as Manfred's pursuit of his declaration, cried:

"Look, my Lord! see, Heaven itself declares against your impious intentions!"

"Heaven nor Hell shall impede my designs," said Manfred, advancing again to seize the Princess.

At that instant the portrait of his grandfather, which hung over the bench where they had been sitting, uttered a deep sigh, and heaved its breast.

Isabella, whose back was turned to the picture, saw not the motion, nor knew whence the sound came, but started, and said:

"Hark, my Lord! What sound was that?" and at the same time made towards the door.

Manfred, distracted between the flight of Isabella, who had now reached the stairs, and yet unable to keep his eyes from the picture, which began to move, had, however, advanced some steps after her, still looking backwards on the portrait, when he saw it quit its panel, and descend on the floor with a grave and melancholy air.

"Do I dream?" cried Manfred, returning; "or are the devils themselves in league against me? Speak, internal specter! Or, if thou art my grandsire, why dost thou too conspire against thy wretched descendant, who too dearly pays for—" Ere he could finish the sentence, the vision sighed again, and made a sign to Manfred to follow him.

"Lead on!" cried Manfred; "I will follow thee to the gulf of perdition."

The specter marched sedately, but dejected, to the end of the gallery, and turned into a chamber on the right hand. Manfred accompanied him at a little distance, full of anxiety and horror, but resolved. As he would have entered the chamber, the door was clapped to with violence by an invisible hand. The Prince, collecting courage from this delay, would have forcibly burst open the door with his foot, but found that it resisted his utmost efforts.

"Since Hell will not satisfy my curiosity," said Manfred, "I will use the human means in my power for preserving my race; Isabella shall not escape me."

The lady, whose resolution had given way to terror the moment she had quitted Manfred, continued her flight to the bottom of the principal staircase. There she stopped, not knowing whither to direct her steps, nor how to escape from the impetuosity of the Prince. The gates of the castle, she knew, were locked, and guards placed in the court. Should she, as her heart prompted her, go and prepare Hippolita for the cruel destiny that awaited her, she did not doubt but Manfred would seek her there, and that his violence would incite him to double the injury he meditated, without leaving room for them to avoid the impetuosity of his passions. Delay might give him time to reflect on the horrid measures he had conceived, or produce some circumstance in her favor, if she could — for that night, at least — avoid his odious purpose. Yet where conceal herself? How avoid the pursuit he would infallibly make throughout the castle?

As these thoughts passed rapidly through her mind, she recollected a subterraneous passage which led from the vaults of the castle to the church of St. Nicholas. Could she reach the altar before she was overtaken, she knew even Manfred's violence would not dare to profane the sacredness of the place; and she determined, if no other means of deliverance offered, to shut herself up for ever among the holy virgins whose convent was contiguous to the cathedral. In this resolution, she seized a lamp that burned at the foot of the staircase and hurried towards the secret passage.

The lower part of the castle was hollowed into several intricate cloisters; and it was not easy for one under so much anxiety to find the door that opened into the cavern. An awful silence reigned throughout those subterraneous regions, except now and then some blasts of wind that shook the doors she had passed, and which, grating on the rusty hinges, were re-echoed through that long labyrinth of darkness. Every murmur struck her with new terror; yet more she dreaded to hear the wrathful voice of Manfred urging his domestics to pursue her.

She trod as softly as impatience would give her leave, yet frequently stopped and listened to hear if she was followed. In one of those moments she thought she heard a sigh. She shuddered and recoiled a few paces. In a moment she thought she heard the step of some person. Her blood curdled; she concluded it was Manfred. Every suggestion that horror could inspire rushed into her mind. She condemned her rash flight, which had thus exposed her to his rage in a place where her cries were not likely to draw anybody to her assistance. Yet the sound seemed not to come from behind. If Manfred knew where she was, he must have followed her. She was still in one of the cloisters, and the steps she had heard were too distinct to proceed from the way she had come. Cheered with this reflection, and hoping to find a friend in whoever was not the Prince, she was going to advance, when a door that stood ajar, at some distance to the left, was opened gently: but ere her lamp, which she held up, could discover who opened it, the person retreated precipitately on seeing the light.

Isabella, whom every incident was sufficient to dismay, hesitated whether she should proceed. Her dread of Manfred soon outweighed every other terror. The very circumstance of the person avoiding her gave her a sort of courage. It could only be, she thought, some domestic belonging to the castle. Her gentleness had never raised her an enemy, and conscious innocence made her hope that, unless sent by the Prince's order to seek her, his servants would rather assist than prevent her flight. Fortifying herself with these reflections, and believing by what she could observe that she was near the mouth of the subterraneous cavern, she approached the door that had been opened; but a sudden gust of wind that met her at the door extinguished her lamp, and left her in total darkness.

Words cannot paint the horror of the Princess's situation. Alone in so dismal a place, her mind imprinted with all the terrible events of the day, hopeless of escaping, expecting every moment the arrival of Manfred, and far from tranquil on knowing she was within reach of somebody, she knew not whom, who for some cause seemed concealed thereabouts; all these thoughts crowded on her distracted mind, and she was ready to sink under her apprehensions. She addressed herself to every saint in heaven, and inwardly implored their assistance. For a considerable time, she remained in an agony of despair.

At last, as softly as was possible, she felt for the door, and having found it, entered trembling into the vault from whence she had heard the sigh and steps. It gave her a kind of momentary joy to perceive an imperfect ray of clouded moonshine gleam from the roof of the vault, which seemed to be fallen in, and from whence hung a fragment of earth or building, she could not distinguish which, that appeared to have been crushed inwards. She advanced eagerly towards this chasm, when she discerned a human form standing close against the wall.

She shrieked, believing it the ghost of her betrothed Conrad. The figure, advancing, said, in a submissive voice -

"Be not alarmed, Lady; I will not injure you."

Isabella, a little encouraged by the words and tone of voice of the stranger, and recollecting that this must be the person who had opened the door, recovered her spirits enough to reply—

"Sir, whoever you are, take pity on a wretched Princess, standing on the brink of destruction. Assist me to escape from this fatal castle, or in a few moments I may be made miserable forever."

"Alas!" said the stranger, "what can I do to assist you? I will die in your defense; but I am unacquainted with the castle, and want -"

"Oh!" said Isabella, hastily interrupting him; "help me but to find a trapdoor that must be hereabout, and it is the greatest service you can do me, for I have not a minute to lose."

Saying these words, she felt about on the pavement, and directed the stranger to search likewise, for a smooth piece of brass enclosed in one of the stones.

"That," said she, "is the lock, which opens with a spring, of which I know the secret. If we can find that, I may escape - if not, alas! courteous stranger, I fear I shall have involved you in my misfortunes: Manfred will suspect you for the accomplice of my flight, and you will fall a victim to his resentment."

"I value not my life," said the stranger, "and it will be some comfort to lose it in trying to deliver you from his tyranny."

"Generous youth," said Isabella, "how shall I ever requite -"

As she uttered those words, a ray of moonshine, streaming through a cranny of the ruin above, shone directly on the lock they sought.

"Oh! transport!" said Isabella; "here is the trap-door!" and, taking out the key, she touched the spring, which, starting aside, discovered an iron ring. "Lift up the door," said the Princess.

The stranger obeyed, and beneath appeared some stone steps descending into a vault totally dark.

"We must go down here," said Isabella. "Follow me; dark and dismal as it is, we cannot miss our way; it leads directly to the church of St. Nicholas. But, perhaps," added the Princess modestly, "you have no reason to leave the castle, nor have I farther occasion for your service; in a few minutes I shall be safe from Manfred's rage - only let me know to whom I am so much obliged."

"I will never quit you," said the stranger eagerly, "until I have placed you in safety - nor think me, Princess, more generous than I am, though you are my principal care -"

The stranger was interrupted by a sudden noise of voices that seemed approaching, and they soon distinguished these words -

"Talk not to me of necromancers; I tell you she must be in the castle; I will find her in spite of enchantment."

"Oh, heavens!" cried Isabella; "it is the voice of Manfred! Make haste, or we are ruined! and shut the trap-door after you."

Saying this, she descended the steps precipitately; and as the stranger hastened to follow her, he let the door slip out of his hands: it fell, and the spring closed over it. He tried in vain to open it, not having observed Isabella's method of touching the spring; nor had he many moments to make an essay. The noise of the falling door had been heard by Manfred, who, directed by the sound, hastened thither, attended by his servants with torches.

"It must be Isabella," cried Manfred, before he entered the vault. "She is escaping by the subterraneous passage, but she cannot have got far."

What was the astonishment of the Prince when, instead of Isabella, the light of the torches discovered to him the young peasant whom he thought confined under the fatal helmet!

"Traitor!" said Manfred; "how camest thou here? I thought thee in durance above in the court."

"I am no traitor," replied the young man boldly, "nor am I answerable for your thoughts."

"Presumptuous villain!" cried Manfred; "dost thou provoke my wrath? Tell me, how hast thou escaped from above? Thou hast corrupted thy guards, and their lives shall answer it."

"My poverty," said the peasant calmly, "will not blame them: though the ministers of a tyrant's wrath, to thee they are faithful, and but too willing to execute the orders which you unjustly imposed upon them."

"Art thou so hardy as to dare my vengeance?" said the Prince; "but tortures shall force the truth from thee. Tell me; I will know thy accomplices."

"There was my accomplice!" said the youth, smiling, and pointing to the roof.

Manfred ordered the torches to be held up, and perceived that one of the cheeks of the enchanted casque had forced its way through the pavement of the court, as his servants had let it fall over the peasant, and had broken through into the vault, leaving a gap, through which the peasant had pressed himself some minutes before he was found by Isabella.

"Was that the way by which thou didst descend?" said Manfred.

"It was," said the youth.

"But what noise was that" said Manfred, "which I heard as I entered the cloister?"

"A door clapped," said the peasant; "I heard it as well as you."

"What door?" said Manfred hastily.

"I am not acquainted with your castle," said the peasant; "this is the first time I ever entered it, and this vault the only part of it within which I ever was."

"But I tell thee," said Manfred (wishing to find out if the youth had discovered the trapdoor), "it was this way I heard the noise. My servants heard it too."

"My Lord," interrupted one of them officiously, "to be sure it was the trap-door, and he was going to make his escape."

"Peace, blockhead!" said the Prince angrily; "if he was going to escape, how should he come on this side? I will know from his own mouth what noise it was I heard. Tell me truly; thy life depends on thy veracity."

"My veracity is dearer to me than my life," said the peasant; "nor would I purchase the one by forfeiting the other."

"Indeed, young philosopher!" said Manfred contemptuously; "tell me, then, what was the noise I heard?"

"Ask me what I can answer," said he, "and put me to death instantly if I tell you a lie."

Manfred, growing impatient at the steady valor and indifference of the youth, cried -

"Well, then, thou man of truth, answer! Was it the fall of the trap-door that I heard?"

"It was," said the youth.

"It was!" said the Prince; "and how didst thou come to know there was a trap-door here?"

"I saw the plate of brass by a gleam of moonshine," replied he.

"But what told thee it was a lock?" said Manfred. "How didst thou discover the secret of opening it?"

"Providence, that delivered me from the helmet, was able to direct me to the spring of a lock," said he.

"Providence should have gone a little farther and have placed thee out of the reach of my resentment," said Manfred. "When Providence had taught thee to open the lock, it abandoned thee for a fool, who did not know how to make use of its favors. Why didst thou not pursue the path pointed out for thy escape? Why didst thou shut the trap-door before thou hadst descended the steps?"

"I might ask you, my Lord," said the peasant, "how I, totally unacquainted with your castle, was to know that those steps led to any outlet? but I scorn to evade your questions. Wherever those steps lead to, perhaps I should have explored the way - I could not be in a worse situation than I was. But the truth is, I let the trap-door fall: your immediate arrival followed. I had given the alarm — what imported it to me whether I was seized a minute sooner or a minute later?"

"Thou art a resolute villain for thy years," said Manfred; "yet on reflection I suspect thou dost but trifle with me. Thou hast not yet told me how thou didst open the lock."

"That I will show you, my Lord," said the peasant; and, taking up a fragment of stone that had fallen from above, he laid himself on the trapdoor, and began to beat on the piece of brass that covered it, meaning to gain time for the escape of the Princess. This presence of mind, joined to the frankness of the youth, staggered Manfred. He even felt a disposition towards pardoning one who had been guilty of no crime. Manfred was not one of those savage tyrants who wanton in cruelty unprovoked. The circumstances of his fortune had given an asperity to his temper, which was naturally humane; and his virtues were always ready to operate, when his passions did not obscure his reason.

While the Prince was in this suspense, a confused noise of voices echoed through the distant vaults. As the sound approached, he distinguished the clamors of some of his domestics, whom he had dispersed through the castle in search of Isabella, calling out:

"Where is my Lord? where is the Prince?"

"Here I am," said Manfred, as they came nearer; "have you found the Princess?"

The first that arrived, replied, "Oh, my Lord! I am glad we have found you."

"Found me!" said Manfred; "have you found the Princess?"

"We thought we had, my Lord," said the fellow, looking terrified, "but -"

"But, what?" cried the Prince; "has she escaped?"

"Jaquez and I, my Lord -"

"Yes, I and Diego," interrupted the second, who came up in still greater consternation.

"Speak one of you at a time," said Manfred; "I ask you, where is the Princess?"

"We do not know," said they both together; "but we are frightened out of our wits."

"So I think, blockheads," said Manfred; "what is it has scared you thus?"

"Oh! my Lord," said Jaquez, "Diego has seen such a sight! your Highness would not believe our eyes."

"What new absurdity is this?" cried Manfred; "give me a direct answer, or, by Heaven -"

"Why, my Lord, if it please your Highness to hear me," said the poor fellow, "Diego and I -"

"Yes, I and Jaquez," cried his comrade.

"Did not I forbid you to speak both at a time?" said the Prince: "you, Jaquez, answer; for the other fool seems more distracted than thou art; what is the matter?"

"My gracious Lord," said Jaquez, "if it please your Highness to hear me; Diego and I, according to your Highness's orders, went to search for the young Lady; but being comprehensive that we might meet the ghost of my young Lord, your Highness's son, God rest his soul, as he has not received Christian burial..."

"Sot!" cried Manfred in a rage; "is it only a ghost, then, that thou hast seen?"

"Oh! worse! worse! my Lord," cried Diego: "I had rather have seen ten whole ghosts."

"Grant me patience!" said Manfred; "these blockheads distract me. Out of my sight, Diego! and thou, Jaquez, tell me in one word, art thou sober? art thou raving? thou wast wont to have some sense: has the other sot frightened himself and thee too? Speak; what is it he fancies he has seen?"

"Why, my Lord," replied Jaquez, trembling, "I was going to tell your Highness, that since the calamitous misfortune of my young Lord, God rest his precious soul! not one of us your Highness's faithful servants - indeed we are, my Lord, though poor men - I say, not one of us has dared to set a foot about the castle, but two together: so Diego and I, thinking that my young Lady might be in the great gallery, went up there to look for her, and tell her your Highness wanted something to impart to her."

"O blundering fools!" cried Manfred; "and in the meantime, she has made her escape, because you were afraid of goblins! - Why, thou knave! she left me in the gallery; I came from thence myself."

"For all that, she may be there still for aught I know," said Jaquez; "but the devil shall have me before I seek her there again - poor Diego! I do not believe he will ever recover it."

"Recover what?" said Manfred; "am I never to learn what it is has terrified these rascals? - but I lose my time; follow me, slave; I will see if she is in the gallery."

"For Heaven's sake, my dear, good Lord," cried Jaquez, "do not go to the gallery. Satan himself I believe is in the chamber next to the gallery."

Manfred, who hitherto had treated the terror of his servants as an idle panic, was struck at this new circumstance. He recollected the apparition of the portrait, and the sudden closing of the door at the end of the gallery. His voice faltered, and he asked with disorder:

"What is in the great chamber?"

"My Lord," said Jaquez, "when Diego and I came into the gallery, he went first, for he said he had more courage than I. So, when we came into the gallery, we found nobody. We looked under every bench and stool; and still we found nobody."

"Were all the pictures in their places?" said Manfred.

"Yes, my Lord," answered Jaquez; "but we did not think of looking behind them."

"Well, well!" said Manfred; "proceed."

"When we came to the door of the great chamber," continued Jaquez, "we found it shut."

"And could not you open it?" said Manfred.

"Oh! yes, my Lord; would to Heaven we had not!" replied he - "nay, it was not I neither; it was Diego: he was grown foolhardy, and would go on, though I advised him not - if ever I open a door that is shut again - "

"Trifle not," said Manfred, shuddering, "but tell me what you saw in the great chamber on opening the door."

"I! my Lord!" said Jaquez; "I was behind Diego; but I heard the noise."

"Jaquez," said Manfred, in a solemn tone of voice; "tell me, I adjure thee by the souls of my ancestors, what was it thou sawest? what was it thou heardest?"

"It was Diego saw it, my Lord, it was not I," replied Jaquez; "I only heard the noise. Diego had no sooner opened the door, than he cried out, and ran back. I ran back too, and said, 'Is it the ghost?' 'The ghost! no, no,' said Diego, and his hair stood on end - 'it is a giant, I believe; he is all clad in armor, for I saw his foot and part of his leg, and they are as large as the helmet below in the court.' As he said these words, my Lord, we heard a violent motion and the rattling of armor, as if the giant was rising, for Diego has told me since that he believes the giant was lying down, for the foot and leg were stretched at length on the floor. Before we could get to the end of the gallery, we heard the door of the great chamber clap behind us, but we did not dare turn back to see if the giant was following us - yet, now I think on it, we must have heard him if he had pursued us — but for Heaven's sake, good my Lord, send for the chaplain, and have the castle exorcised, for, for certain, it is enchanted."

"Ay, pray do, my Lord," cried all the servants at once, "or we must leave your Highness's service."

"Peace, dotards!" said Manfred, "and follow me; I will know what all this means."

"We! my Lord!" cried they with one voice; "we would not go up to the gallery for your Highness's revenue." The young peasant, who had stood silent, now spoke.

"Will your Highness," said he, "permit me to try this adventure? My life is of consequence to nobody; I fear no bad angel and have offended no good one."

"Your behavior is above your seeming," said Manfred, viewing him with surprise and admiration - "hereafter I will reward your bravery - but now," continued he with a sigh, "I am so circumstanced, that I dare trust no eyes but my own. However, I give you leave to accompany me."

Manfred, when he first followed Isabella from the gallery, had gone directly to the apartment of his wife, concluding the Princess had retired thither. Hippolita, who knew his step, rose with anxious fondness to meet her Lord, whom she had not seen since the death of their son. She would have flown in a transport mixed of joy and grief to his bosom, but he pushed her rudely off, and said -

"Where is Isabella?"

"Isabella! my Lord!" said the astonished Hippolita.

"Yes, Isabella," cried Manfred imperiously; "I want Isabella."

"My Lord," replied Matilda, who perceived how much his behavior had shocked her mother, "she has not been with us since your Highness summoned her to your apartment."

"Tell me where she is," said the Prince; "I do not want to know where she has been."

"My good Lord," says Hippolita, "your daughter tells you the truth: Isabella left us by your command, and has not returned since; - but, my good Lord, compose yourself: retire to your rest: this dismal day has disordered you. Isabella shall wait your orders in the morning."

"What, then, you know where she is!" cried Manfred. "Tell me directly, for I will not lose an instant - and you, woman," speaking to his wife, "order your chaplain to attend me forthwith."

"Isabella," said Hippolita calmly, "is retired, I suppose, to her chamber: she is not accustomed to watch at this late hour. Gracious my Lord," continued she, "let me know what has disturbed you. Has Isabella offended you?"

"Trouble me not with questions," said Manfred, "but tell me where she is."

"Matilda shall call her," said the Princess. "Sit down, my Lord, and resume your wonted fortitude."

"What, art thou jealous of Isabella?" replied he, "that you wish to be present at our interview!"

"Good heavens! my Lord," said Hippolita, "what is it your Highness means?"

"Thou wilt know ere many minutes are passed," said the cruel Prince. "Send your chaplain to me and wait my pleasure here."

At these words he flung out of the room in search of Isabella, leaving the amazed ladies thunderstruck with his words and frantic deportment, and lost in vain conjectures on what he was meditating.

Manfred was now returning from the vault, attended by the peasant and a few of his servants whom he had obliged to accompany him. He ascended the staircase without stopping till he arrived at the gallery, at the door of which he met Hippolita and her chaplain. When Diego had been dismissed by Manfred, he had gone directly to the Princess's apartment with the alarm of what he had seen. That excellent Lady, who no more than Manfred doubted of the reality of the vision yet affected to treat it as a delirium of the servant. Willing, however, to save her Lord from any additional shock, and prepared by a series of griefs not to tremble at any accession to it, she determined to make herself the first sacrifice, if fate had marked the present hour for their destruction. Dismissing the reluctant Matilda to her rest, who in vain sued for leave to accompany her mother, and attended only by her chaplain, Hippolita had visited the gallery and great chamber; and now with more serenity of soul than she had felt for many hours, she met her Lord, and assured him that the vision of the gigantic leg and foot was all a fable; and no doubt an impression made by fear, and the dark and dismal hour of the night, on the minds of his servants. She and the chaplain had examined the chamber and found everything in the usual order.

Manfred, though persuaded, like his wife, that the vision had been no work of fancy, recovered a little from the tempest of mind into which so many strange events had thrown him. Ashamed, too, of his inhuman treatment of a Princess who returned every injury with new marks of tenderness and duty, he felt returning love forcing itself into his eyes; but not less ashamed of feeling remorse towards one against whom he was inwardly meditating a yet more bitter outrage, he curbed the yearnings of his heart, and did not dare to lean even towards pity. The next transition of his soul was to exquisite villainy.

Presuming on the unshaken submission of Hippolita, he flattered himself that she would not only acquiesce with patience to a divorce, but would obey, if it was his pleasure, in endeavoring to persuade Isabella to give him her hand—but ere he could indulge his horrid hope, he reflected that Isabella was not to be found. Coming to himself, he gave orders that every avenue to the castle should be strictly guarded and charged his domestics on pain of their lives to suffer nobody to pass out. The young peasant, to whom he spoke favorably, he ordered to remain in a small chamber on the stairs, in which there was a pallet-bed, and the key of which he took away himself, telling the youth he would talk with him in the morning. Then dismissing his attendants and bestowing a sullen kind of half-nod on Hippolita, he retired to his own chamber.

CHAPTER II

Matilda, who by Hippolita's order had retired to her apartment, was ill-disposed to take any rest. The shocking fate of her brother had deeply affected her. She was surprised at not seeing Isabella; but the strange words which had fallen from her father, and his obscure menace to the Princess his wife, accompanied by the most furious behavior, had filled her gentle mind with terror and alarm. She waited anxiously for the return of Bianca, a young damsel that attended her, whom she had sent to learn what was become of Isabella. Bianca soon appeared and informed her mistress of what she had gathered from the servants, that Isabella was nowhere to be found. She related the adventure of the young peasant who had been discovered in the vault, though with many simple additions from the incoherent accounts of the domestics; and she dwelt principally on the gigantic leg and foot which had been seen in the gallery-chamber. This last circumstance had terrified Bianca so much, that she was rejoiced when Matilda told her that she would not go to rest but would watch till the Princess should rise.

The young Princess wearied herself in conjectures on the flight of Isabella, and on the threats of Manfred to her mother. "But what business could he have so urgent with the chaplain?" said Matilda, "Does he intend to have my brother's body interred privately in the chapel?"

"Oh, Madam!" said Bianca, "now, I guess. As you are become his heiress, he is impatient to have you married: he has always been raving for more sons; I warrant he is now impatient for grandsons. As sure as I live, Madam, I shall see you a bride at last. - Good madam, you won't cast off your faithful Bianca: you won't put Donna Rosara over me now you are a great Princess."

"My poor Bianca," said Matilda, "how fast your thoughts amble! I a great princess! What hast thou seen in Manfred's behavior since my brother's death that bespeaks any increase of tenderness to me? No, Bianca; his heart was ever a stranger to me - but he is my father, and I must not complain. Nay, if Heaven shuts my father's heart against me, it overpays my little merit in the tenderness of my mother - O that dear mother! yes, Bianca, 'tis there I feel the rugged temper of Manfred. I can support his harshness to me with patience; but it wounds my soul when I am witness to his causeless severity towards her."

"Oh! Madam," said Bianca, "all men use their wives so, when they are weary of them."

"And yet you congratulated me but now," said Matilda, "when you fancied my father intended to dispose of me!"

"I would have you a great Lady," replied Bianca, "come what will. I do not wish to see you moped in a convent, as you would be if you had your will, and if my Lady, your mother, who knows that a bad husband is better than no husband at all, did not hinder you. - Bless me! what noise is that! St. Nicholas forgive me! I was but in jest."

"It is the wind," said Matilda, "whistling through the battlements in the tower above: you have heard it a thousand times."

"Nay," said Bianca, "there was no harm neither in what I said: it is no sin to talk of matrimony - and so, Madam, as I was saying, if my Lord Manfred should offer you a handsome young Prince for a bridegroom, you would drop him a curtsey, and tell him you would rather take the veil?"

"Thank Heaven! I am in no such danger," said Matilda: "you know how many proposals for me he has rejected -"

"And you thank him, like a dutiful daughter, do you, Madam? But come, Madam; suppose, to-morrow morning, he was to send for you to the great council chamber, and there you should find at his elbow a lovely young Prince, with large black eyes, a smooth white forehead, and manly curling locks like jet; in short, Madam, a young hero resembling the picture of the good Alfonso in the gallery, which you sit and gaze at for hours together —"

"Do not speak lightly of that picture," interrupted Matilda sighing; "I know the adoration with which I look at that picture is uncommon - but I am not in love with a colored panel. The character of that virtuous Prince, the veneration with which my mother has inspired me for his memory, the orisons which, I know not why, she has enjoined me to pour forth at his tomb, all have concurred to persuade me that somehow or other my destiny is linked with something relating to him."

"Lord, Madam! how should that be?" said Bianca; "I have always heard that your family was in no way related to his: and I am sure I cannot conceive why my Lady, the Princess, sends you in a cold morning or a damp evening to pray at his tomb: he is no saint by the almanack. If you must pray, why does she not bid you address yourself to our great St. Nicholas? I am sure he is the saint I pray to for a husband."

"Perhaps my mind would be less affected," said Matilda, "if my mother would explain her reasons to me: but it is the mystery she observes, that inspires me with this - I know not what to call it. As she never acts from caprice, I am sure there is some fatal secret at bottom - nay, I know there is: in her agony of grief for my brother's death she dropped some words that intimated as much."

"Oh! dear Madam," cried Bianca, "what were they?"

"No," said Matilda, "if a parent lets fall a word, and wishes it recalled, it is not for a child to utter it."

"What! was she sorry for what she had said?" asked Bianca; "I am sure, Madam, you may trust me -"

"With my own little secrets when I have any, I may," said Matilda; "but never with my mother's: a child ought to have no ears or eyes but as a parent directs."

"Well! to be sure, Madam, you were born to be a saint," said Bianca, "and there is no resisting one's vocation: you will end in a convent at last. But there is my Lady Isabella would not be so reserved to me: she will let me talk to her of young men: and when a handsome cavalier has come to the castle, she has owned to me that she wished your brother Conrad resembled him."

"Bianca," said the Princess, "I do not allow you to mention my friend disrespectfully. Isabella is of a cheerful disposition, but her soul is pure as virtue itself. She knows your idle babbling humor, and perhaps has now and then encouraged it, to divert melancholy, and enliven the solitude in which my father keeps us -"

"Blessed Mary!" said Bianca, starting, "there it is again! Dear Madam, do you hear nothing? this castle is certainly haunted!"

"Peace!" said Matilda, "and listen! I did think I heard a voice—but it must be fancy: your terrors, I suppose, have infected me."

"Indeed! indeed! Madam," said Bianca, half-weeping with agony, "I am sure I heard a voice."

"Does anybody lie in the chamber beneath?" said the Princess.

"Nobody has dared to lie there," answered Bianca, "since the great astrologer, that was your brother's tutor, drowned himself. For certain, Madam, his ghost and the young Prince's are now met in the chamber below—for Heaven's sake let us fly to your mother's apartment!"

"I charge you not to stir," said Matilda. "If they are spirits in pain, we may ease their sufferings by questioning them. They can mean no hurt to us, for we have not injured them—and if they should, shall we be safer in one chamber than in another? Reach me my beads; we will say a prayer, and then speak to them."

"Oh! dear Lady, I would not speak to a ghost for the world!" cried Bianca. As she said those words, they heard the casement of the little chamber below Matilda's open. They listened attentively, and in a few minutes thought they heard a person sing but could not distinguish the words.

"This can be no evil spirit," said the Princess, in a low voice; "it is undoubtedly one of the family—open the window, and we shall know the voice."

"I dare not, indeed, Madam," said Bianca.

"Thou art a very fool," said Matilda, opening the window gently herself. The noise the Princess made was, however, heard by the person beneath, who stopped; and they concluded had heard the casement open.

"Is anybody below?" said the Princess; "if there is, speak."

"Yes," said an unknown voice.

"Who is it?" said Matilda.

"A stranger," replied the voice.

"What stranger?" said she; "and how didst thou come there at this unusual hour, when all the gates of the castle are locked?"

"I am not here willingly," answered the voice. "But pardon me, Lady, if I have disturbed your rest; I knew not that I was overheard. Sleep had forsaken me; I left a restless couch and came to waste the irksome hours with gazing on the fair approach of morning, impatient to be dismissed from this castle."

"Thy words and accents," said Matilda, "are of melancholy cast; if thou art unhappy, I pity thee. If poverty afflicts thee, let me know it; I will mention thee to the Princess, whose beneficent soul ever melts for the distressed, and she will relieve thee."

"I am indeed unhappy," said the stranger; "and I know not what wealth is. But I do not complain of the lot which Heaven has cast for me; I am young and healthy and am not ashamed of owing my support to myself - yet think me not proud, or that I disdain your generous offers. I will remember you in my orisons and will pray for blessings on your gracious self and your noble mistress - if I sigh, Lady, it is for others, not for myself."

"Now I have it, Madam," said Bianca, whispering the Princess; "this is certainly the young peasant; and, by my conscience, he is in love - Well! this is a charming adventure! - do, Madam, let us sift him. He does not know you but takes you for one of my Lady Hippolita's women."

"Art thou not ashamed, Bianca!" said the Princess. "What right have us to pry into the secrets of this young man's heart? He seems virtuous and frank and tells us he is unhappy. Are those circumstances that authorize us to make a property of him? How are we entitled to his confidence?"

"Lord, Madam! how little you know of love!" replied Bianca; "why, lovers have no pleasure equal to talking of their mistress."

"And would you have me become a peasant's confidante?" said the Princess.

"Well, then, let me talk to him," said Bianca; "though I have the honor of being your Highness's maid of honor, I was not always so great. Besides, if love levels rank, it raises them too; I have a respect for any young man in love."

"Peace, simpleton!" said the Princess. "Though he said he was unhappy, it does not follow that he must be in love. Think of all that has happened to-day, and tell me if there are no misfortunes but what love causes. —Stranger," resumed the Princess, "if thy misfortunes have not been occasioned by thy own fault, and are within the compass of the Princess Hippolita's power to redress, I will take upon me to answer that she will be thy protectress. When thou art dismissed from this castle, repair to holy father Jerome, at the convent adjoining to the church of St. Nicholas, and make thy story known to him, as far as thou thinkest meet. He will not fail to inform the Princess, who is the mother of all that want her assistance. Farewell: it is not seemly for me to hold farther converse with a man at this unwonted hour."

"May the saints guard thee, gracious Lady!" replied the peasant; "but oh! if a poor and worthless stranger might presume to beg a minute's audience farther; am I so happy? the casement is not shut; might I venture to ask -"

"Speak quickly," said Matilda; "the morning dawns apace: should the laborer's come into the fields and perceive us - What wouldst thou ask?"

"I know not how, I know not if I dare," said the Young stranger, faltering; "yet the humanity with which you have spoken to me emboldens—Lady! dare I trust you?"

"Heavens!" said Matilda, "what dost thou mean? With what wouldst thou trust me? Speak boldly, if thy secret is fit to be entrusted to a virtuous breast."

"I would ask," said the peasant, recollecting himself, "whether what I have heard from the domestics is true, that the Princess is missing from the castle?"

"What imports it to thee to know?" replied Matilda. "Thy first words bespoke a prudent and becoming gravity. Dost thou come hither to pry into the secrets of Manfred? Adieu. I have been mistaken in thee." Saying these words, she shut the casement hastily, without giving the young man time to reply.

"I had acted more wisely," said the Princess to Bianca, with some sharpness, "if I had let thee converse with this peasant; his inquisitiveness seems of a piece with thy own."

"It is not fit for me to argue with your Highness," replied Bianca; "but perhaps the questions I should have put to him would have been more to the purpose than those you have been pleased to ask him."

"Oh! no doubt," said Matilda; "you are a very discreet personage! May I know what you would have asked him?"

"A bystander often sees more of the game than those that play," answered Bianca. "Does your Highness think, Madam, that this question about my Lady Isabella was the result of mere curiosity? No, no, Madam, there is more in it than you great folks are aware of. Lopez told me that all the servants believe this young fellow contrived my Lady Isabella's escape; now, pray, Madam, observe you and I both know that my Lady Isabella never much fancied the Prince your brother. Well! he is killed just in a critical minute - I accuse nobody. A helmet falls from the moon—so, my Lord, your father says; but Lopez and all the servants say that this young spark is a magician, and stole it from Alfonso's tomb."

"Have done with this rhapsody of impertinence," said Matilda.

"Nay, Madam, as you please," cried Bianca; "yet it is very particular though, that my Lady Isabella should be missing the very same day, and that this young sorcerer should be found at the mouth of the trap-door. I accuse nobody; but if my young Lord came honestly by his death -"

"Dare not on thy duty," said Matilda, "to breathe a suspicion on the purity of my dear Isabella's fame."

"Purity, or not purity," said Bianca, "gone she is - a stranger is found that nobody knows; you question him yourself; he tells you he is in love, or unhappy, it is the same thing - nay, he owned he was unhappy about others; and is anybody unhappy about another, unless they are in love with them? and at the very next word, he asks innocently, pour soul! if my Lady Isabella is missing."

"To be sure," said Matilda, "thy observations are not totally without foundation - Isabella's flight amazes me. The curiosity of the stranger is very particular; yet Isabella never concealed a thought from me."

"So, she told you," said Bianca, "to fish out your secrets; but who knows, Madam, but this stranger may be some Prince in disguise? Do, Madam, let me open the window, and ask him a few questions."

"No," replied Matilda, "I will ask him myself, if he knows aught of Isabella; he is not worthy I should converse farther with him." She was going to open the casement, when they heard the bell ring at the postern-gate of the castle, which is on the right hand of the tower, where Matilda lay. This prevented the Princess from renewing the conversation with the stranger.

After continuing silent for some time, "I am persuaded," said she to Bianca, "that whatever be the cause of Isabella's flight it had no unworthy motive. If this stranger was accessory to it, she must be satisfied with his fidelity and worth. I observed, did not you, Bianca? that his words were tinctured with an uncommon infusion of piety. It was no ruffian's speech; his phrases were becoming a man of gentle birth."

"I told you, Madam," said Bianca, "that I was sure he was some Prince in disguise."

"Yet," said Matilda, "if he was privy to her escape, how will you account for his not accompanying her in her flight? why expose himself unnecessarily and rashly to my father's resentment?"

"As for that, Madam," replied she, "if he could get from under the helmet, he will find ways of eluding your father's anger. I do not doubt but he has some talisman or other about him."

"You resolve everything into magic," said Matilda; "but a man who has any intercourse with infernal spirits, does not dare to make use of those tremendous and holy words which he uttered. Didst thou not observe with what fervor he vowed to remember me to heaven in his prayers? Yes, Isabella was undoubtedly convinced of his piety."

"Commend me to the piety of a young fellow and a damsel that consult to elope!" said Bianca. "No, no, Madam, my Lady Isabella is of another guess mould than you take her for. She used indeed to sigh and lift up her eyes in your company, because she knows you are a saint; but when your back was turned—"

"You wrong her," said Matilda; "Isabella is no hypocrite; she has a due sense of devotion, but never affected a call she has not. On the contrary, she always combated my inclination for the cloister; and though I own the mystery she has made to me of her flight confounds me; though it seems inconsistent with the friendship between us; I cannot forget the disinterested warmth with which she always opposed my taking the veil. She wished to see me married, though my dower would have been a loss to her and my brother's children. For her sake I will believe well of this young peasant."

"Then you do think there is some liking between them," said Bianca. While she was speaking, a servant came hastily into the chamber and told the Princess that the Lady Isabella was found.

"Where?" said Matilda.

"She has taken sanctuary in St. Nicholas's church," replied the servant; "Father Jerome has brought the news himself; he is below with his Highness."

"Where is my mother?" said Matilda.

"She is in her own chamber, Madam, and has asked for you."

Manfred had risen at the first dawn of light, and gone to Hippolita's apartment, to inquire if she knew aught of Isabella. While he was questioning her, word was brought that Jerome demanded to speak with him. Manfred, little suspecting the cause of the Friar's arrival, and knowing he was employed by Hippolita in her charities, ordered him to be admitted, intending to leave them together, while he pursued his search after Isabella.

"Is your business with me or the Princess?" said Manfred.

"With both," replied the holy man. "The Lady Isabella—"

"What of her?" interrupted Manfred, eagerly.

"Is at St. Nicholas's altar," replied Jerome.

"That is no business of Hippolita," said Manfred with confusion; "let us retire to my chamber, Father, and inform me how she came thither."

"No, my Lord," replied the good man, with an air of firmness and authority, that daunted even the resolute Manfred, who could not help revering the saint-like virtues of Jerome; "my commission is to both, and with your Highness's good-liking, in the presence of both I shall deliver it; but first, my Lord, I must interrogate the Princess, whether she is acquainted with the cause of the Lady Isabella's retirement from your castle."

"No, on my soul," said Hippolita; "does Isabella charge me with being privy to it?"

"Father," interrupted Manfred, "I pay due reverence to your holy profession; but I am sovereign here and will allow no meddling priest to interfere in the affairs of my domestic. If you have ought to say attend me to my chamber; I do not use to let my wife be acquainted with the secret affairs of my state; they are not within a woman's province."

"My Lord," said the holy man, "I am no intruder into the secrets of families. My office is to promote peace, to heal divisions, to preach repentance, and teach mankind to curb their headstrong passions. I forgive your Highness's uncharitable apostrophe; I know my duty and am the minister of a mightier prince than Manfred. Hearken to him who speaks through my organs."

Manfred trembled with rage and shame. Hippolita's countenance declared her astonishment and impatience to know where this would end. Her silence more strongly spoke her observance of Manfred.

"The Lady Isabella," resumed Jerome, "commends herself to both your Highnesses; she thanks both for the kindness with which she has been treated in your castle: she deplores the loss of your son, and her own misfortune in not becoming the daughter of such wise and noble Princes, whom she shall always respect as Parents; she prays for uninterrupted union and felicity between you" [Manfred's color changed]: "but as it is no longer possible for her to be allied to you, she entreats your consent to remain in sanctuary, till she can learn news of her father, or, by the certainty of his death, be at liberty, with the approbation of her guardians, to dispose of herself in suitable marriage."

"I shall give no such consent," said the Prince, "but insist on her return to the castle without delay: I am answerable for her person to her guardians, and will not brook her being in any hands but my own."

"Your Highness will recollect whether that can any longer be proper," replied the Friar.

"I want no monitor," said Manfred, coloring; "Isabella's conduct leaves room for strange suspicions - and that young villain, who was at least the accomplice of her flight, if not the cause of it -"

"The cause!" interrupted Jerome; "was a young man the cause?"

"This is not to be borne!" cried Manfred. "Am I to be bearded in my own palace by an insolent Monk? Thou art privy, I guess, to their amours."

"I would pray to heaven to clear up your uncharitable surmises," said Jerome, "if your Highness were not satisfied in your conscience how unjustly you accuse me. I do pray to heaven to pardon that uncharitableness: and I implore your Highness to leave the Princess at peace in that holy place, where she is not liable to be disturbed by such vain and worldly fantasies as discourses of love from any man."

"Cant not to me," said Manfred, "but return and bring the Princess to her duty."

"It is my duty to prevent her return hither," said Jerome. "She is where orphans and virgins are safest from the snares and wiles of this world; and nothing but a parent's authority shall take her thence."

"I am her parent," cried Manfred, "and demand her."

"She wished to have you for her parent," said the Friar; "but Heaven that forbad that connection has forever dissolved all ties betwixt you: and I announce to your Highness -"

"Stop! audacious man," said Manfred, "and dread my displeasure."

"Holy Father," said Hippolita, "it is your office to be no respecter of persons: you must speak as your duty prescribes: but it is my duty to hear nothing that it pleases not my Lord I should hear. Attend the Prince to his chamber. I will retire to my oratory and pray to the blessed Virgin to inspire you with her holy counsels, and to restore the heart of my gracious Lord to its wonted peace and gentleness."

"Excellent woman!" said the Friar. "My Lord, I attend your pleasure."

Manfred, accompanied by the Friar, passed to his own apartment, where shutting the door, "I perceive, Father," said he, "that Isabella has acquainted you with my purpose. Now hear my resolve and obey. Reasons of state, most urgent reasons, my own and the safety of my people, demand that I should have a son. It is in vain to expect an heir from Hippolita. I have made choice of Isabella. You must bring her back; and you must do more. I know the influence you have with Hippolita: her conscience is in your hands. She is, I allow, a faultless woman: her soul is set on heaven and scorns the little grandeur of this world: you can withdraw her from it entirely. Persuade her to consent to the dissolution of our marriage, and to retire into a monastery - she shall endow one if she will; and she shall have the means of being as liberal to your order as she or you can wish. Thus, you will divert the calamities that are hanging over our heads and have the merit of saying the principality of Otranto from destruction. You are a prudent man, and though the warmth of my temper betrayed me into some unbecoming expressions, I honor your virtue, and wish to be indebted to you for the repose of my life and the preservation of my family."

"The will of heaven be done!" said the Friar. "I am but its worthless instrument. It makes use of my tongue to tell thee, Prince, of thy unwarrantable designs. The injuries of the virtuous Hippolita have mounted to the throne of pity. By me thou art reprimanded for thy adulterous intention of repudiating her: by me thou art warned not to pursue the incestuous design on thy contracted daughter. Heaven that delivered her from thy fury, when the judgments so recently fallen on thy house ought to have inspired thee with other thoughts, will continue to watch over her. Even I, a poor and despised Friar, am able to protect her from thy violence - I, sinner as I am, and uncharitably reviled by your Highness as an accomplice of I know not what amours, scorn the allurements with which it has pleased thee to tempt mine honesty. I love my order; I honor devout souls; I respect the piety of thy Princess - but I will not betray the confidence she reposes in me, nor serve even the cause of religion by foul and sinful compliances - but forsooth! the welfare of the state depends on your Highness having a son! Heaven mocks the short-sighted views of man. But yester-morn, whose house was so great, so flourishing as Manfred's? - where is young Conrad now? - My Lord, I respect your tears - but I mean not to check them - let them flow, Prince! They will weigh more with heaven toward the welfare of thy subjects, than a marriage, which, founded on lust or policy, could never prosper. The scepter, which passed from the race of Alfonso to thine, cannot be preserved by a match which the church will never allow. If it is the will of the Most High that Manfred's name must perish, resign yourself, my Lord, to its decrees; and thus, deserve a crown that can never pass away. Come, my Lord; I like this sorrow — let us return to the Princess: she is not apprised of your cruel intentions; nor did I mean more than to alarm you. You saw with what gentle patience, with what efforts of love, she heard, she rejected hearing, the extent of your guilt. I know she longs to fold you in her arms and assure you of her unalterable affection."

"Father," said the Prince, "you mistake my compunction: true, I honor Hippolita's virtues; I think her a Saint; and wish it were for my soul's health to tie faster the knot that has united us - but alas! Father, you know not the bitterest of my pangs! it is some time that I have had scruples on the legality of our union: Hippolita is related to me in the fourth degree - it is true, we had a dispensation: but I have been informed that she had also been contracted to another. This it is that sits heavy at my heart: to this state of unlawful wedlock I impute the visitation that has fallen on me in the death of Conrad! - ease my conscience of this burden: dissolve our marriage, and accomplish the work of godliness - which your divine exhortations have commenced in my soul."

How cutting was the anguish which the good man felt, when he perceived this turn in the wily Prince! He trembled for Hippolita, whose ruin he saw was determined; and he feared if Manfred had no hope of recovering Isabella, that his impatience for a son would direct him to some other object, who might not be equally proof against the temptation of Manfred's rank. For some time, the holy man remained absorbed in thought. At length, conceiving some hopes from delay, he thought the wisest conduct would be to prevent the Prince from despairing of recovering Isabella. Her the Friar knew he could dispose, from her affection to Hippolita, and from the aversion she had expressed to him for Manfred's addresses, to second his views, till the censures of the church could be fulminated against a divorce. With this intention, as if struck with the Prince's scruples, he at length said:

> *"My Lord, I have been pondering on what your Highness has said; and if in truth it is delicacy of conscience that is the real motive of your repugnance to your virtuous Lady, far be it from me to endeavor to harden your heart. The church is an indulgent mother: unfold your griefs to her: she alone can administer comfort to your soul, either by satisfying your conscience, or upon examination of your scruples, by setting you at liberty, and indulging you in the lawful means of continuing your lineage. In the latter case, if the Lady Isabella can be brought to consent -"*

Manfred, who concluded that he had either over-reached the good man, or that his first warmth had been but a tribute paid to appearance, was overjoyed at this sudden turn, and repeated the most magnificent promises, if he should succeed by the Friar's mediation. The well-meaning priest suffered him to deceive himself, fully determined to traverse his views, instead of seconding them.

"Since we now understand one another," resumed the Prince, "I expect, Father, that you satisfy me in one point. Who is the youth that I found in the vault? He must have been privy to Isabella's flight: tell me truly, is he her lover? or is he an agent for another's passion? I have often suspected Isabella's indifference to my son: a thousand circumstances crowd on my mind that confirm that suspicion. She herself was so conscious of it, that while I discoursed her in the gallery, she outran my suspicious, and endeavored to justify herself from coolness to Conrad."

The Friar, who knew nothing of the youth, but what he had learnt occasionally from the Princess, ignorant what was become of him, and not sufficiently reflecting on the impetuosity of Manfred's temper, conceived that it might not be amiss to sow the seeds of jealousy in his mind: they might be turned to some use hereafter, either by prejudicing the Prince against Isabella, if he persisted in that union or by diverting his attention to a wrong scent, and employing his thoughts on a visionary intrigue, prevent his engaging in any new pursuit. With this unhappy policy, he answered in a manner to confirm Manfred in the belief of some connection between Isabella and the youth. The Prince, whose passions wanted little fuel to throw them into a blaze, fell into a rage at the idea of what the Friar suggested.

"I will fathom to the bottom of this intrigue," cried he; and quitting Jerome abruptly, with a command to remain there till his return, he hastened to the great hall of the castle, and ordered the peasant to be brought before him.

"Thou hardened young impostor!" said the Prince, as soon as he saw the youth; "what becomes of thy boasted veracity now? it was Providence, was it, and the light of the moon, that discovered the lock of the trap-door to thee? Tell me, audacious boy, who thou art, and how long thou hast been acquainted with the Princess - and take care to answer with less equivocation than thou didst last night, or tortures shall wring the truth from thee."

The young man, perceiving that his share in the flight of the Princess was discovered, and concluding that anything he should say could no longer be of any service or detriment to her, replied -

"I am no impostor, my Lord, nor have I deserved opprobrious language. I answered to every question your Highness put to me last night with the same veracity that I shall speak now: and that will not be from fear of your tortures, but because my soul abhors a falsehood. Please to repeat your questions, my Lord; I am ready to give you all the satisfaction in my power."

"You know my questions," replied the Prince, "and only want time to prepare an evasion. Speak directly; who art thou? and how long hast thou been known to the Princess?"

"I am a laborer at the next village," said the peasant; "my name is Theodore. The Princess found me in the vault last night: before that hour I never was in her presence."

"I may believe as much or as little as I please of this," said Manfred; "but I will hear thy own story before I examine into the truth of it. Tell me, what reason did the Princess give thee for making her escape? thy life depends on thy answer."

"She told me," replied Theodore, "that she was on the brink of destruction, and that if she could not escape from the castle, she was in danger in a few moments of being made miserable forever."

"And on this slight foundation, on a silly girl's report," said Manfred, "thou didst hazard my displeasure?"

"I fear no man's displeasure," said Theodore, "when a woman in distress puts herself under my protection."

During this examination, Matilda was going to the apartment of Hippolita. At the upper end of the hall, where Manfred sat, was a boarded gallery with latticed windows, through which Matilda and Bianca were to pass. Hearing her father's voice, and seeing the servants assembled round him, she stopped to learn the occasion. The prisoner soon drew her attention: the steady and composed manner in which he answered, and the gallantry of his last reply, which were the first words she heard distinctly, interested her in his flavor. His person was noble, handsome, and commanding, even in that situation: but his countenance soon engrossed her whole care.

"Heavens! Bianca," said the Princess softly, "do I dream? or is not that youth the exact resemblance of Alfonso's picture in the gallery?"

She could say no more, for her father's voice grew louder at every word.

"This bravado," said he, "surpasses all thy former insolence. Thou shalt experience the wrath with which thou darest to trifle. Seize him," continued Manfred, "and bind him - the first news the Princess hears of her champion shall be, that he has lost his head for her sake."

"The injustice of which thou art guilty towards me," said Theodore, "convinces me that I have done a good deed in delivering the Princess from thy tyranny. May she be happy, whatever becomes of me!"

"This is a lover!" cried Manfred in a rage: "a peasant within sight of death is not animated by such sentiments. Tell me, tell me, rash boy, who thou art, or the rack shall force thy secret from thee."

"Thou hast threatened me with death already," said the youth, "for the truth I have told thee: if that is all the encouragement I am to expect for sincerity, I am not tempted to indulge thy vain curiosity farther."

"Then thou wilt not speak?" said Manfred.

"I will not," replied he.

"Bear him away into the courtyard," said Manfred; "I will see his head this instant severed from his body."

Matilda fainted at hearing those words. Bianca shrieked, and cried -

"Help! help! the Princess is dead!" Manfred started at this ejaculation and demanded what was the matter! The young peasant, who heard it too, was struck with horror, and asked eagerly the same question; but Manfred ordered him to be hurried into the court, and kept there for execution, till he had informed himself of the cause of Bianca's shrieks. When he learned the meaning, he treated it as a womanish panic, and ordering Matilda to be carried to her apartment, he rushed into the court, and calling for one of his guards, bade Theodore kneel down, and prepare to receive the fatal blow.

The undaunted youth received the bitter sentence with a resignation that touched every heart but Manfred's. He wished earnestly to know the meaning of the words he had heard relating to the Princess; but fearing to exasperate the tyrant more against her, he desisted. The only boon he deigned to ask was, that he might be permitted to have a confessor, and make his peace with heaven. Manfred, who hoped by the confessor's means to come at the youth's history, readily granted his request; and being convinced that Father Jerome was now in his interest, he ordered him to be called and shrive the prisoner. The holy man, who had little foreseen the catastrophe that his imprudence occasioned, fell on his knees to the Prince, and adjured him in the most solemn manner not to shed innocent blood. He accused himself in the bitterest terms for his indiscretion, endeavored to disculpate the youth, and left no method untried to soften the tyrant's rage. Manfred, more incensed than appeased by Jerome's intercession, whose retraction now made him suspect he had been imposed upon by both, commanded the Friar to do his duty, telling him he would not allow the prisoner many minutes for confession.

"Nor do I ask many, my Lord," said the unhappy young man. "My sins, thank heaven, have not been numerous; nor exceed what might be expected at my years. Dry your tears, good Father, and let us dispatch. This is a bad world; nor have I had cause to leave it with regret."

"Oh, wretched youth!" said Jerome; "how canst thou bear the sight of me with patience? I am thy murderer! it is I have brought this dismal hour upon thee!"

"I forgive thee from my soul," said the youth, "as I hope heaven will pardon me. Hear my confession, Father; and give me thy blessing."

"How can I prepare thee for thy passage as I ought?" said Jerome. "Thou canst not be saved without pardoning thy foes - and canst thou forgive that impious man there?"

"I can," said Theodore; "I do."

"And does not this touch thee, cruel Prince?" said the Friar.

"I sent for thee to confess him," said Manfred, sternly; "not to plead for him. Thou didst first incense me against him - his blood be upon thy head!"

"It will! it will!" said the good man, in an agony of sorrow. "Thou and I must never hope to go where this blessed youth is going!"

"Dispatch!" said Manfred; "I am no more to be moved by the whining of priests than by the shrieks of women."

"What!" said the youth; "is it possible that my fate could have occasioned what I heard! Is the Princess then again in thy power?"

"Thou dost but remember me of my wrath," said Manfred. "Prepare thee, for this moment is thy last."

The youth, who felt his indignation rise, and who was touched with the sorrow which he saw he had infused into all the spectators, as well as into the Friar, suppressed his emotions, and putting off his doublet, and unbuttoning, his collar, knelt down to his prayers. As he stooped, his shirt slipped down below his shoulder, and discovered the mark of a bloody arrow.

"Gracious heaven!" cried the holy man, starting; "what do I see? It is my child! my Theodore!"

The passions that ensued must be conceived; they cannot be painted. The tears of the assistants were suspended by wonder, rather than stopped by joy. They seemed to inquire in the eyes of their Lord what they ought to feel. Surprise, doubt, tenderness, respect, succeeded each other in the countenance of the youth. He received with modest submission the effusion of the old man's tears and embraces. Yet afraid of giving a loose to hope, and suspecting from what had passed the inflexibility of Manfred's temper, he cast a glance towards the Prince, as if to say, canst thou be unmoved at such a scene as this?

Manfred's heart was capable of being touched. He forgot his anger in his astonishment; yet his pride forbad his owning himself affected. He even doubted whether this discovery was not a contrivance of the Friar to save the youth.

"What may this mean?" said he. "How can he be thy son? Is it consistent with thy profession or reputed sanctity to avow a peasant's offspring for the fruit of thy irregular amours!"

"Oh, God!" said the holy man, "dost thou question his being mine? Could I feel the anguish I do if I were not his father? Spare him! good Prince! spare him! and revile me as thou pleasest."

"Spare him! spare him!" cried the attendants; "for this good man's sake!"

"Peace!" said Manfred, sternly. "I must know more ere I am disposed to pardon. A Saint's bastard may be no saint himself."

"Injurious Lord!" said Theodore, "add not insult to cruelty. If I am this venerable man's son, though no Prince, as thou art, know the blood that flows in my veins -"

"Yes," said the Friar, interrupting him, "his blood is noble; nor is he that abject thing, my Lord, you speak him. He is my lawful son, and Sicily can boast of few houses more ancient than that of Falconara. But alas! my Lord, what is blood! what is nobility! We are all reptiles, miserable, sinful creatures. It is piety alone that can distinguish us from the dust whence we sprung, and whither we must return."

"Truce to your sermon," said Manfred; "you forget you are no longer Friar Jerome, but the Count of Falconara. Let me know your history; you will have time to moralize hereafter, if you should not happen to obtain the grace of that sturdy criminal there."

"Mother of God!" said the Friar, "is it possible my Lord can refuse a father the life of his only, his long-lost, child! Trample me, my Lord, scorn, afflict me, accept my life for his, but spare my son!"

"Thou canst feel, then," said Manfred, "what it is to lose an only son! A little hour ago thou didst preach up resignation to me: my house, if fate so pleased, must perish - but the Count of Falconara -"

"Alas! my Lord," said Jerome, "I confess I have offended; but aggravate not an old man's sufferings! I boast not of my family, nor think of such vanities - it is nature, that pleads for this boy; it is the memory of the dear woman that bore him. Is she, Theodore, is she dead?"

"Her soul has long been with the blessed," said Theodore.

"Oh! how?" cried Jerome, "tell me – no - she is happy! Thou art all my care now! - Most dread Lord! will you — will you grant me my poor boy's life?"

"Return to thy convent," answered Manfred; "conduct the Princess hither; obey me in what else thou knowest; and I promise thee the life of thy son."

"Oh! my Lord," said Jerome, "is my honesty the price I must pay for this dear youth's safety?"

"For me!" cried Theodore. "Let me die a thousand deaths, rather than stain thy conscience. What is it the tyrant would exact of thee? Is the Princess still safe from his power? Protect her, thou venerable old man; and let all the weight of his wrath fall on me."

Jerome endeavored to check the impetuosity of the youth; and ere Manfred could reply, the trampling of horses was heard, and a brazen trumpet, which hung without the gate of the castle, was suddenly sounded. At the same instant the sable plumes on the enchanted helmet, which remained at the other end of the court, were tempestuously agitated, and nodded thrice, as if bowed by some invisible wearer.

CHAPTER III

Manfred's heart misgave him when he beheld the plumage on the miraculous casque shaken in concert with the sounding of the brazen trumpet.

"Father!" said he to Jerome, whom he now ceased to treat as Count of Falconara, "what mean these portents? If I have offended -" the plumes were shaken with greater violence than before.

"Unhappy Prince that I am," cried Manfred. "Holy Father! will you not assist me with your prayers?"

"My Lord," replied Jerome, "heaven is no doubt displeased with your mockery of its servants. Submit yourself to the church; and cease to persecute her ministers. Dismiss this innocent youth; and learn to respect the holy character I wear. Heaven will not be trifled with: you see -" the trumpet sounded again.

"I acknowledge I have been too hasty," said Manfred. "Father, do you go to the wicket, and demand who is at the gate."

"Do you grant me the life of Theodore?" replied the Friar.

"I do," said Manfred; "but inquire who is without!"

Jerome, falling on the neck of his son, discharged a flood of tears, that spoke the fulness of his soul.

"You promised to go to the gate," said Manfred.

"I thought," replied the Friar, "your Highness would excuse my thanking you first in this tribute of my heart."

"Go, dearest Sir," said Theodore; "obey the Prince. I do not deserve that you should delay his satisfaction for me."

Jerome, inquiring who was without, was answered, "A Herald."

"From whom?" said he.

"From the Knight of the Gigantic Sabre," said the Herald; "and I must speak with the usurper of Otranto."

Jerome returned to the Prince and did not fail to repeat the message in the very words it had been uttered. The first sounds struck Manfred with terror; but when he heard himself styled usurper, his rage rekindled, and all his courage revived.

"Usurper! - insolent villain!" cried he; "who dares to question my title? Retire, Father; this is no business for Monks: I will meet this presumptuous man myself. Go to your convent and prepare the Princess's return. Your son shall be a hostage for your fidelity: his life depends on your obedience."

"Good heaven! my Lord," cried Jerome, "your Highness did but this instant freely pardon my child - have you so soon forgot the interposition of heaven?"

"Heaven," replied Manfred, "does not send Heralds to question the title of a lawful Prince. I doubt whether it even notifies its will through Friars - but that is your affair, not mine. At present you know my pleasure; and it is not a saucy Herald that shall save your son, if you do not return with the Princess."

It was in vain for the holy man to reply. Manfred commanded him to be conducted to the postern-gate and shut out from the castle. And he ordered some of his attendants to carry Theodore to the top of the black tower, and guard him strictly; scarce permitting the father and son to exchange a hasty embrace at parting. He then withdrew to the hall, and seating himself in princely state, ordered the Herald to be admitted to his presence.

"Well! thou insolent!" said the Prince, "what wouldst thou with me?"

"I come," replied he, "to thee, Manfred, usurper of the principality of Otranto, from the renowned and invincible Knight, the Knight of the Gigantic Sabre: in the name of his Lord, Frederic, Marquis of Vicenza, he demands the Lady Isabella, daughter of that Prince, whom thou hast basely and traitorously got into thy power, by bribing her false guardians during his absence; and he requires thee to resign the principality of Otranto, which thou hast usurped from the said Lord Frederic, the nearest of blood to the last rightful Lord, Alfonso the Good. If thou dost not instantly comply with these just demands, he defies thee to single combat to the last extremity." And so, saying the Herald cast down his warder.

"And where is this braggart who sends thee?" said Manfred.

"At the distance of a league," said the Herald: "he comes to make good his Lord's claim against thee, as he is a true knight, and thou a usurper and ravisher."

Injurious as this challenge was, Manfred reflected that it was not his interest to provoke the Marquis. He knew how well founded the claim of Frederic was; nor was this the first time he had heard of it. Frederic's ancestors had assumed the style of Princes of Otranto, from the death of Alfonso the Good without issue; but Manfred, his father, and grandfather, had been too powerful for the house of Vicenza to dispossess them. Frederic, a martial and amorous young Prince, had married a beautiful young lady, of whom he was enamored, and who had died in childbed of Isabella. Her death affected him so much that he had taken the cross and gone to the Holy Land, where he was wounded in an engagement against the infidels, made prisoner, and reported to be dead. When the news reached Manfred's ears, he bribed the guardians of the Lady Isabella to deliver her up to him as a bride for his son Conrad, by which alliance he had proposed to unite the claims of the two houses. This motive, on Conrad's death, had co-operated to make him so suddenly resolve on espousing her himself; and the same reflection determined him now to endeavor at obtaining the consent of Frederic to this marriage. A like policy inspired him with the thought of inviting Frederic's champion into the castle, lest he should be informed of Isabella's flight, which he strictly enjoined his domestics not to disclose to any of the Knight's retinue.

"Herald," said Manfred, as soon as he had digested these reflections, "return to thy master, and tell him, ere we liquidate our differences by the sword, Manfred would hold some converse with him. Bid him welcome to my castle, whereby my faith, as I am a true Knight, he shall have courteous reception, and full security for himself and followers. If we cannot adjust our quarrel by amicable means, I swear he shall depart in safety, and shall have full satisfaction according to the laws of arms: So help me God and His holy Trinity!"

The Herald made three obeisance's and retired.

During this interview Jerome's mind was agitated by a thousand contrary passions. He trembled for the life of his son, and his first thought was to persuade Isabella to return to the castle. Yet he was scarce less alarmed at the thought of her union with Manfred. He dreaded Hippolita's unbounded submission to the will of her Lord; and though he did not doubt but he could alarm her piety not to consent to a divorce, if he could get access to her; yet should Manfred discover that the obstruction came from him, it might be equally fatal to Theodore. He was impatient to know whence came the Herald, who with so little management had questioned the title of Manfred: yet he did not dare absent himself from the convent, lest Isabella should leave it, and her flight be imputed to him. He returned disconsolately to the monastery, uncertain on what conduct to resolve. A Monk, who met him in the porch and observed his melancholy air, said -

"Alas! brother, is it then true that we have lost our excellent Princess Hippolita?"

The holy man started, and cried, "What meanest thou, brother? I come this instant from the castle and left her in perfect health."

"Martelli," replied the other Friar, "passed by the convent but a quarter of an hour ago on his way from the castle and reported that her Highness was dead. All our brethren are gone to the chapel to pray for her happy transit to a better life and willed me to wait thy arrival. They know thy holy attachment to that good Lady and are anxious for the affliction it will cause in thee - indeed we have all reason to weep; she was a mother to our house. But this life is but a pilgrimage; we must not murmur — we shall all follow her! May our end be like hers!"

"Good brother, thou dreamest," said Jerome. "I tell thee I come from the castle and left the Princess well. Where is the Lady Isabella?"

"Poor Gentlewoman!" replied the Friar; "I told her the sad news and offered her spiritual comfort. I reminded her of the transitory condition of mortality and advised her to take the veil: I quoted the example of the holy Princess Sanchia of Arragon."

"Thy zeal was laudable," said Jerome, impatiently; "but at present it was unnecessary: Hippolita is well - at least I trust in the Lord she is; I heard nothing to the contrary - yet, methinks, the Prince's earnestness - Well, brother, but where is the Lady Isabella?"

"I know not," said the Friar; "she wept much, and said she would retire to her chamber."

Jerome left his comrade abruptly, and hastened to the Princess, but she was not in her chamber. He inquired of the domestics of the convent but could learn no news of her. He searched in vain throughout the monastery and the church, and dispatched messengers round the neighborhood, to get intelligence if she had been seen, but to no purpose. Nothing could equal the good man's perplexity. He judged that Isabella, suspecting Manfred of having precipitated his wife's death, had taken the alarm, and withdrawn herself to some more secret place of concealment. This new flight would probably carry the Prince's fury to the height. The report of Hippolita's death, though it seemed almost incredible, increased his consternation; and though Isabella's escape bespoke her aversion of Manfred for a husband, Jerome could feel no comfort from it, while it endangered the life of his son. He determined to return to the castle and made several of his brethren accompany him to attest his innocence to Manfred, and, if necessary, join their intercession with his for Theodore.

The Prince, in the meantime, had passed into the court, and ordered the gates of the castle to be flung open for the reception of the stranger Knight and his train. In a few minutes the cavalcade arrived. First came two harbingers with wands. Next a herald, followed by two pages and two trumpets. Then a hundred foot-guards. These were attended by as many horses. After them fifty footmen, clothed in scarlet and black, the colors of the Knight. Then a led horse. Two heralds on each side of a gentleman on horseback bearing a banner with the arms of Vicenza and Otranto quarterly - a circumstance that much offended Manfred - but he stifled his resentment. Two more pages. The Knight's confessor telling his beads. Fifty more footmen clad as before. Two Knights habited in complete armor, their beavers down, comrades to the principal Knight. The squires of the two Knights, carrying their shields and devices. The Knight's own squire. A hundred gentlemen bearing an enormous sword and seeming to faint under the weight of it. The Knight himself on a chestnut steed, in complete armor, his lance in the rest, his face entirely concealed by his vizor, which was surmounted by a large plume of scarlet and black feathers. Fifty foot-guards with drums and trumpets closed the procession, which wheeled off to the right and left to make room for the principal Knight.

As soon as he approached the gate he stopped; and the herald advancing, read again the words of the challenge. Manfred's eyes were fixed on the gigantic sword, and he scarce seemed to attend to the cartel: but his attention was soon diverted by a tempest of wind that rose behind him. He turned and beheld the Plumes of the enchanted helmet agitated in the same extraordinary manner as before. It required intrepidity like Manfred's not to sink under a concurrence of circumstances that seemed to announce his fate. Yet scorning in the presence of strangers to betray the courage he had always manifested, he said boldly -

"Sir Knight, whoever thou art, I bid thee welcome. If thou art of mortal mould, thy valor shall meet its equal: and if thou art a true Knight, thou wilt scorn to employ sorcery to carry thy point. Be these omens from heaven or hell, Manfred trusts to the righteousness of his cause and to the aid of St. Nicholas, who has ever protected his house. Alight, Sir Knight, and repose thyself. To-morrow thou shalt have a fair field, and heaven befriend the juster side!"

The Knight made no reply, but dismounting, was conducted by Manfred to the great hall of the castle. As they traversed the court, the Knight stopped to gaze on the miraculous casque; and kneeling down, seemed to pray inwardly for some minutes. Rising, he made a sign to the Prince to lead on. As soon as they entered the hall, Manfred proposed to the stranger to disarm, but the Knight shook his head in token of refusal.

"Sir Knight," said Manfred, "this is not courteous, but by my good faith I will not cross thee, nor shalt thou have cause to complain of the Prince of Otranto. No treachery is designed on my part; I hope none is intended on thine; here take my gage" (giving him his ring): "your friends and you shall enjoy the laws of hospitality. Rest here until refreshments are brought. I will but give orders for the accommodation of your train and return to you." The three Knights bowed as accepting his courtesy. Manfred directed the stranger's retinue to be conducted to an adjacent hospital, founded by the Princess Hippolita for the reception of pilgrims. As they made the circuit of the court to return towards the gate, the gigantic sword burst from the supporters, and falling to the ground opposite to the helmet, remained immovable. Manfred, almost hardened to preternatural appearances, surmounted the shock of this new prodigy; and returning to the hall, whereby this time the feast was ready, he invited his silent guests to take their places. Manfred, however ill his heart was at ease, endeavored to inspire the company with mirth. He put several questions to them but was answered only by signs. They raised their vizors but sufficiently to feed themselves, and that sparingly.

"Sirs" said the Prince, "ye are the first guests I ever treated within these walls who scorned to hold any intercourse with me: nor has it oft been customary, I ween, for princes to hazard their state and dignity against strangers and mutes. You say you come in the name of Frederic of Vicenza; I have ever heard that he was a gallant and courteous Knight; nor would he, I am bold to say, think it beneath him to mix in social converse with a Prince that is his equal, and not unknown by deeds in arms. Still ye are silent - well! be it as it may - by the laws of hospitality and chivalry ye are masters under this roof: ye shall do your pleasure. But come, give me a goblet of wine; ye will not refuse to pledge me to the health of your fair mistresses."

The principal Knight sighed and crossed himself and was rising from the board.

"Sir Knight," said Manfred, "what I said was but in sport. I shall constrain you in nothing: use your good liking. Since mirth is not your mood, let us be sad. Business may hit your fancies better. Let us withdraw and hear if what I have to unfold may be better relished than the vain efforts I have made for your pastime." Manfred then conducting the three Knights into an inner chamber, shut the door, and inviting them to be seated, began thus, addressing himself to the chief personage: -

"You come, Sir Knight, as I understand, in the name of the Marquis of Vicenza, to re-demand the Lady Isabella, his daughter, who has been contracted in the face of Holy Church to my son, by the consent of her legal guardians; and to require me to resign my dominions to your Lord, who gives himself for the nearest of blood to Prince Alfonso, whose soul God rest! I shall speak to the latter article of your demands first. You must know, your Lord knows, that I enjoy the principality of Otranto from my father, Don Manuel, as he received it from his father, Don Ricardo. Alfonso, their predecessor, dying childless in the Holy Land, bequeathed his estates to my grandfather, Don Ricardo, in consideration of his faithful services." The stranger shook his head.

"Sir Knight," said Manfred, warmly, "Ricardo was a valiant and upright man; he was a pious man; witness his munificent foundation of the adjoining church and two convents. He was peculiarly patronized by St. Nicholas - my grandfather was incapable - I say, Sir, Don Ricardo was incapable - excuse me, your interruption has disordered me. I venerate the memory of my grandfather. Well, Sirs, he held this estate; he held it by his good sword and by the favor of St. Nicholas - so did my father; and so, Sirs, will I, come what come will. But Frederic, your Lord, is nearest in blood. I have consented to put my title to the issue of the sword. Does that imply a vicious title? I might have asked, where is Frederic your Lord? Report speaks him dead in captivity. You say, your actions say, he lives - I question it not - I might, Sirs, I might - but I do not. Other Princes would bid Frederic take his inheritance by force, if he can: they would not stake their dignity on a single combat: they would not submit it to the decision of unknown mutes! — pardon me, gentlemen, I am too warm: but suppose yourselves in my situation: as ye are stout Knights, would it not move your choler to have your own and the honor of your ancestors called in question?"

"But to the point. Ye require me to deliver up the Lady Isabella. Sirs, I must ask if ye are authorized to receive her?"

The Knight nodded.

"Receive her," continued Manfred; "well, you are authorized to receive her, but, gentle Knight, may I ask if you have full powers?"

The Knight nodded.

"'Tis well," said Manfred; "then hear what I have to offer. Ye see, gentlemen, before you, the most unhappy of men!" (he began to weep); "afford me your compassion; I am entitled to it, indeed I am. Know, I have lost my only hope, my joy, the support of my house—Conrad died yester morning."

The Knights discovered signs of surprise.

"Yes, Sirs, fate has disposed of my son. Isabella is at liberty."

"Do you then restore her?" cried the chief Knight, breaking silence.

"Afford me your patience," said Manfred. "I rejoice to find, by this testimony of your goodwill, that this matter may be adjusted without blood. It is no interest of mine dictates what little I have farther to say. Ye behold in me a man disgusted with the world: the loss of my son has weaned me from earthly cares. Power and greatness have no longer any charms in my eyes. I wished to transmit the scepter I had received from my ancestors with honor to my son - but that is over! Life itself is so indifferent to me, that I accepted your defiance with joy. A good Knight cannot go to the grave with more satisfaction than when falling in his vocation: whatever is the will of heaven, I submit; for alas! Sirs, I am a man of many sorrows. Manfred is no object of envy, but no doubt you are acquainted with my story."

The Knight made signs of ignorance and seemed curious to have Manfred proceed.

"Is it possible, Sirs," continued the Prince, "that my story should be a secret to you? Have you heard nothing relating to me and the Princess Hippolita?"

They shook their heads.

"No! Thus, then, Sirs, it is. You think me ambitious: ambition, alas! is composed of more rugged materials. If I were ambitious, I should not for so many years have been a prey to all the hell of conscientious scruples. But I weary your patience: I will be brief. Know, then, that I have long been troubled in mind on my union with the Princess Hippolita. Oh! Sirs, if ye were acquainted with that excellent woman! if ye knew that I adore her like a mistress and cherish her as a friend - but man was not born for perfect happiness! She shares my scruples, and with her consent I have brought this matter before the church, for we are related within the forbidden degrees. I expect every hour the definitive sentence that must separate us forever - I am sure you feel for me - I see you do - pardon these tears!"

The Knights gazed on each other, wondering where this would end.

Manfred continued:

"The death of my son betiding while my soul was under this anxiety, I thought of nothing but resigning my dominions, and retiring forever from the sight of mankind. My only difficulty was to fix on a successor, who would be tender of my people, and to dispose of the Lady Isabella, who is dear to me as my own blood. I was willing to restore the line of Alfonso, even in his most distant kindred. And though, pardon me, I am satisfied it was his will that Ricardo's lineage should take place of his own relations; yet where was I to search for those relations? I knew of none but Frederic, your Lord; he was a captive to the infidels, or dead; and were he living, and at home, would he quit the flourishing State of Vicenza for the inconsiderable principality of Otranto? If he would not, could I bear the thought of seeing a hard, unfeeling, Viceroy set over my poor faithful people? for, Sirs, I love my people, and thank heaven am beloved by them. But ye will ask whither tends this long discourse? Briefly, then, thus, Sirs. Heaven in your arrival seems to point out a remedy for these difficulties and my misfortunes. The Lady Isabella is at liberty; I shall soon be so. I would submit to anything for the good of my people. Were it not the best, the only way to extinguish the feuds between our families, if I was to take the Lady Isabella to wife? You start. But though Hippolita's virtues will ever be dear to me, a Prince must not consider himself; he is born for his people." A servant at that instant entering the chamber apprised Manfred that Jerome and several of his brethren demanded immediate access to him.

The Prince, provoked at this interruption, and fearing that the Friar would discover to the strangers that Isabella had taken sanctuary, was going to forbid Jerome's entrance. But recollecting that he was certainly arrived to notify the Princess's return, Manfred began to excuse himself to the Knights for leaving them for a few moments but was prevented by the arrival of the Friars. Manfred angrily reprimanded them for their intrusion and would have forced them back from the chamber; but Jerome was too much agitated to be repulsed. He declared aloud the flight of Isabella, with protestations of his own innocence.

Manfred, distracted at the news, and not less at its coming to the knowledge of the strangers, uttered nothing but incoherent sentences, now upbraiding the Friar, now apologizing to the Knights, earnest to know what was become of Isabella, yet equally afraid of their knowing; impatient to pursue her, yet dreading to have them join in the pursuit. He offered to dispatch messengers in quest of her, but the chief Knight, no longer keeping silence, reproached Manfred in bitter terms for his dark and ambiguous dealing and demanded the cause of Isabella's first absence from the castle. Manfred, casting a stern look at Jerome, implying a command of silence, pretended that on Conrad's death he had placed her in sanctuary until he could determine how to dispose of her. Jerome, who trembled for his son's life, did not dare contradict this falsehood, but one of his brethren, not under the same anxiety, declared frankly that she had fled to their church in the preceding night. The Prince in vain endeavored to stop this discovery, which overwhelmed him with shame and confusion. The principal stranger, amazed at the contradictions he heard, and more than half persuaded that Manfred had secreted the Princess, notwithstanding the concern he expressed at her flight, rushing to the door, said:

"Thou traitor Prince! Isabella shall be found."

Manfred endeavored to hold him, but the other Knights assisting their comrade, he broke from the Prince, and hastened into the court, demanding his attendants. Manfred, finding it vain to divert him from the pursuit, offered to accompany him and summoning his attendants, and taking Jerome and some of the Friars to guide them, they issued from the castle; Manfred privately giving orders to have the Knight's company secured, while to the knight he affected to dispatch a messenger to require their assistance.

The company had no sooner quitted the castle than Matilda, who felt herself deeply interested for the young peasant, since she had seen him condemned to death in the hall, and whose thoughts had been taken up with concerting measures to save him, was informed by some of the female attendants that Manfred had dispatched all his men various ways in pursuit of Isabella. He had in his hurry given this order in general terms, not meaning to extend it to the guard he had set upon Theodore but forgetting it. The domestics, officious to obey so peremptory a Prince, and urged by their own curiosity and love of novelty to join in any precipitate chase, had to a man left the castle. Matilda disengaged herself from her women, stole up to the black tower, and unbolting the door, presented herself to the astonished Theodore.

"Young man," said she, "though filial duty and womanly modesty condemn the step I am taking, yet holy charity, surmounting all other ties, justifies this act. Fly: the doors of thy prison are open: my father and his domestics are absent; but they may soon return. Be gone in safety; and may the angels of heaven direct thy course!"

"Thou art surely one of those angels!" said the enraptured Theodore: "none but a blessed saint could speak, could act — could look — like thee. May I not know the name of my divine protectress? Methought thou namedst thy father. Is it possible? Can Manfred's blood feel holy pity! Lovely Lady, thou answerest not. But how art thou here thyself? Why dost thou neglect thy own safety, and waste a thought on a wretch like Theodore? Let us fly together: the life thou bestowest shall be dedicated to thy defense."

"Alas! thou mistakest," said Matilda, signing: "I am Manfred's daughter, but no dangers await me."

"Amazement!" said Theodore; "but last night I blessed myself for yielding thee the service thy gracious compassion so charitably returns me now."

"Still thou art in an error," said the Princess; "but this is no time for explanation. Fly, virtuous youth, while it is in my power to save thee: should my father return, thou and I both should indeed have cause to tremble."

"How!" said Theodore; "thinkest thou, charming maid, that I will accept of life at the hazard of aught calamitous to thee? Better I endured a thousand deaths."

"I run no risk," said Matilda, "but by thy delay. Depart; it cannot be known that I have assisted thy flight."

"Swear by the saints above," said Theodore, "that thou canst not be suspected; else here I vow to await whatever can befall me."

"Oh! thou art too generous," said Matilda; "but rest assured that no suspicion can alight on me."

"Give me thy beauteous hand in token that thou dost not deceive me," said Theodore; "and let me bathe it with the warm tears of gratitude."

"Forbear!" said the Princess; "this must not be."

"Alas!" said Theodore, "I have never known but calamity until this hour — perhaps shall never know other fortune again: suffer the chaste raptures of holy gratitude: 'tis my soul would print its effusions on thy hand."

"Forbear, and be gone," said Matilda. "How would Isabella approve of seeing thee at my feet?"

"Who is Isabella?" said the young man with surprise.

"Ah, me! I fear," said the Princess, "I am serving a deceitful one. Hast thou forgot thy curiosity this morning?"

"Thy looks, thy actions, all thy beauteous self seem an emanation of divinity," said Theodore; "but thy words are dark and mysterious. Speak, Lady; speak to thy servant's comprehension."

"Thou understandest but too well!" said Matilda; "but once more I command thee to be gone: thy blood, which I may preserve, will be on my head, if I waste the time in vain discourse."

"I go, Lady," said Theodore, "because it is thy will, and because I would not bring the grey hairs of my father with sorrow to the grave. Say but, adored Lady, that I have thy gentle pity."

"Stay," said Matilda; "I will conduct thee to the subterraneous vault by which Isabella escaped; it will lead thee to the church of St. Nicholas, where thou mayst take sanctuary."

"What!" said Theodore, "was it another, and not thy lovely self that I assisted to find the subterraneous passage?"

"It was," said Matilda; "but ask no more; I tremble to see thee still abide here; fly to the sanctuary."

"To sanctuary," said Theodore; "no, Princess; sanctuaries are for helpless damsels, or for criminals. Theodore's soul is free from guilt, nor will wear the appearance of it. Give me a sword, Lady, and thy father shall learn that Theodore scorns an ignominious flight."

"Rash youth!" said Matilda; "thou wouldst not dare to lift thy presumptuous arm against the Prince of Otranto?"

"Not against thy father; indeed, I dare not," said Theodore. "Excuse me, Lady; I had forgotten. But could I gaze on thee and remember thou art sprung from the tyrant Manfred! But he is thy father, and from this moment my injuries are buried in oblivion."

A deep and hollow groan, which seemed to come from above, startled the Princess and Theodore.

"Good heaven! we are overheard!" said the Princess. They listened; but perceiving no further noise, they both concluded it the effect of pent-up vapors. And the Princess, preceding Theodore softly, carried him to her father's armory, where, equipping him with a complete suit, he was conducted by Matilda to the postern-gate.

"Avoid the town," said the Princess, "and all the western side of the castle. 'Tis there the search must be making by Manfred and the strangers; but hie thee to the opposite quarter. Yonder behind that forest to the east is a chain of rocks, hollowed into a labyrinth of caverns that reach to the seacoast. There thou mayst lie concealed, till thou canst make signs to some vessel to put on shore and take thee off. Go! heaven be thy guide! - and sometimes in thy prayers remember - Matilda!"

Theodore flung himself at her feet, and seizing her lily hand, which with struggles she suffered him to kiss, he vowed on the earliest opportunity to get himself knighted, and fervently entreated her permission to swear himself eternally her knight. Ere the Princess could reply, a clap of thunder was suddenly heard that shook the battlements. Theodore, regardless of the tempest, would have urged his suit: but the Princess, dismayed, retreated hastily into the castle, and commanded the youth to be gone with an air that would not be disobeyed. He sighed, and retired, but with eyes fixed on the gate, until Matilda, closing it, put an end to an interview, in which the hearts of both had drunk so deeply of a passion, which both now tasted for the first time.

Theodore went pensively to the convent, to acquaint his father with his deliverance. There he learned the absence of Jerome, and the pursuit that was making after the Lady Isabella, with some particulars of whose story he now first became acquainted. The generous gallantry of his nature prompted him to wish to assist her; but the Monks could lend him no lights to guess at the route she had taken. He was not tempted to wander far in search of her, for the idea of Matilda had imprinted itself so strongly on his heart, that he could not bear to absent himself at much distance from her abode. The tenderness Jerome had expressed for him concurred to confirm this reluctance; and he even persuaded himself that filial affection was the chief cause of his hovering between the castle and monastery.

Until Jerome should return at night, Theodore at length determined to repair to the forest that Matilda had pointed out to him. Arriving there, he sought the gloomiest shades, as best suited to the pleasing melancholy that reigned in his mind. In this mood he roved insensibly to the caves which had formerly served as a retreat to hermits and were now reported round the country to be haunted by evil spirits. He recollected to have heard this tradition; and being of a brave and adventurous disposition, he willingly indulged his curiosity in exploring the secret recesses of this labyrinth. He had not penetrated far before he thought he heard the steps of some person who seemed to retreat before him.

Theodore, though firmly grounded in all our holy faith enjoins to be believed, had no apprehension that good men were abandoned without cause to the malice of the powers of darkness. He thought the place more likely to be infested by robbers than by those infernal agents who are reported to molest and bewilder travelers. He had long burned with impatience to approve his valor. Drawing his sabre, he marched sedately onwards, still directing his steps as the imperfect rustling sound before him led the way. The armor he wore was a like indication to the person who avoided him. Theodore, now convinced that he was not mistaken, redoubled his pace, and evidently gained on the person that fled, whose haste increasing, Theodore came up just as a woman fell breathless before him. He hasted to raise her, but her terror was so great that he apprehended she would faint in his arms. He used every gentle word to dispel her alarms, and assured her that far from injuring, he would defend her at the peril of his life. The Lady recovering her spirits from his courteous demeanor, and gazing on her protector, said:

"Sure, I have heard that voice before!"

"Not to my knowledge," replied Theodore; "unless, as I conjecture, thou art the Lady Isabella."

"Merciful heaven!" cried she. "Thou art not sent in quest of me, art thou?" And saying those words, she threw herself at his feet, and besought him not to deliver her up to Manfred.

"To Manfred!" cried Theodore - "no, Lady; I have once already delivered thee from his tyranny, and it shall fare hard with me now, but I will place thee out of the reach of his daring."

"Is it possible," said she, "that thou shouldst be the generous unknown whom I met last night in the vault of the castle? Sure, thou art not a mortal, but my guardian angel. On my knees, let me thank -"

"Hold! gentle Princess," said Theodore, "nor demean thyself before a poor and friendless young man. If heaven has selected me for thy deliverer, it will accomplish its work, and strengthen my arm in thy cause. But come, Lady, we are too near the mouth of the cavern; let us seek its inmost recesses. I can have no tranquility till I have placed thee beyond the reach of danger."

"Alas! what mean you, sir?" said she. "Though all your actions are noble, though your sentiments speak the purity of your soul, is it fitting that I should accompany you alone into these perplexed retreats? Should we be found together, what would a censorious world think of my conduct?"

"I respect your virtuous delicacy," said Theodore; "nor do you harbor a suspicion that wounds my honor. I meant to conduct you into the most private cavity of these rocks, and then at the hazard of my life to guard their entrance against every living thing. Besides, Lady," continued he, drawing a deep sigh, "beauteous and all perfect as your form is, and though my wishes are not guiltless of aspiring, know, my soul is dedicated to another; and although -" A sudden noise prevented Theodore from proceeding. They soon distinguished these sounds -

"Isabella! what, ho! Isabella!" The trembling Princess relapsed into her former agony of fear. Theodore endeavored to encourage her, but in vain. He assured her he would die rather than suffer her to return under Manfred's power; and begging her to remain concealed, he went forth to prevent the person in search of her from approaching.

At the mouth of the cavern he found an armed Knight, discoursing with a peasant, who assured him he had seen a lady enter the passes of the rock. The Knight was preparing to seek her, when Theodore, placing himself in his way, with his sword drawn, sternly forbad him at his peril to advance.

"And who art thou, who darest to cross my way?" said the Knight, haughtily.

"One who does not dare more than he will perform," said Theodore.

"I seek the Lady Isabella," said the Knight, "and understand she has taken refuge among these rocks. Impede me not, or thou wilt repent having provoked my resentment."

"Thy purpose is as odious as thy resentment is contemptible," said Theodore. "Return whence thou camest, or we shall soon know whose resentment is most terrible."

The stranger, who was the principal Knight that had arrived from the Marquis of Vicenza, had galloped from Manfred as he was busied in getting information of the Princess, and giving various orders to prevent her falling into the power of the three Knights. Their chief had suspected Manfred of being privy to the Princess's absconding, and this insult from a man, who he concluded was stationed by that Prince to secrete her, confirming his suspicions, he made no reply, but discharging a blow with his sabre at Theodore, would soon have removed all obstruction, if Theodore, who took him for one of Manfred's captains, and who had no sooner given the provocation than prepared to support it, had not received the stroke on his shield. The valor that had so long been smothered in his breast broke forth at once; he rushed impetuously on the Knight, whose pride and wrath were not less powerful incentives to hardy deeds. The combat was furious, but not long. Theodore wounded the Knight in three several places, and at last disarmed him as he fainted by the loss of blood.

The peasant, who had fled on the first onset, had given the alarm to some of Manfred's domestics, who, by his orders, were dispersed through the forest in pursuit of Isabella. They came up as the Knight fell, whom they soon discovered to be the noble stranger. Theodore, notwithstanding his hatred to Manfred, could not behold the victory he had gained without emotions of pity and generosity. But he was more touched when he learned the quality of his adversary, and was informed that he was no retainer, but an enemy, of Manfred. He assisted the servants of the latter in disarming the Knight, and in endeavoring to stanch the blood that flowed from his wounds. The Knight recovering his speech, said, in a faint and faltering voice -

"Generous foe, we have both been in an error. I took thee for an instrument of the tyrant; I perceive thou hast made the like mistake. It is too late for excuses. I faint. If Isabella is at hand - call her - I have important secrets to -"

"He is dying!" said one of the attendants; "has nobody a crucifix about them? Andrea, do thou pray over him."

"Fetch some water," said Theodore, "and pour it down his throat, while I hasten to the Princess."

Saying this, he flew to Isabella, and in few words told her modestly that he had been so unfortunate by mistake as to wound a gentleman from her father's court, who wished, ere he died, to impart something of consequence to her.

The Princess, who had been transported at hearing the voice of Theodore, as he called to her to come forth, was astonished at what she heard. Suffering herself to be conducted by Theodore, the new proof of whose valor recalled her dispersed spirits, she came where the bleeding Knight lay speechless on the ground. But her fears returned when she beheld the domestics of Manfred. She would again have fled if Theodore had not made her observe that they were unarmed and had not threatened them with instant death if they should dare to seize the Princess.

The stranger, opening his eyes, and beholding a woman, said, "Art thou - pray tell me truly - art thou Isabella of Vicenza?"

"I am," said she: "good heaven restore thee!"

"Then thou - then thou" - said the Knight, struggling for utterance - "seest - thy father. Give me one -"

"Oh! amazement! horror! what do I hear! what do I see!" cried Isabella. "My father! You my father! How came you here, Sir? For heaven's sake, speak! Oh! run for help, or he will expire!"

"'Tis most true," said the wounded Knight, exerting all his force; "I am Frederic thy father. Yes, I came to deliver thee. It will not be. Give me a parting kiss, and take—"

"Sir," said Theodore, "do not exhaust yourself; suffer us to convey you to the castle."

"To the castle!" said Isabella. "Is there no help nearer than the castle? Would you expose my father to the tyrant? If he goes thither, I dare not accompany him; and yet, can I leave him!"

"My child," said Frederic, "it matters not for me whither I am carried. A few minutes will place me beyond danger; but while I have eyes to dote on thee, forsake me not, dear Isabella! This brave Knight—I know not who he is—will protect thy innocence. Sir, you will not abandon my child, will you?"

Theodore, shedding tears over his victim, and vowing to guard the Princess at the expense of his life, persuaded Frederic to suffer himself to be conducted to the castle. They placed him on a horse belonging to one of the domestics, after binding up his wounds as well as they were able. Theodore marched by his side; and the afflicted Isabella, who could not bear to quit him, followed mournfully behind.

CHAPTER IV

The sorrowful troop no sooner arrived at the castle, than they were met by Hippolita and Matilda, whom Isabella had sent one of the domestics before to advertise of their approach. The ladies causing Frederic to be conveyed into the nearest chamber, retired, while the surgeons examined his wounds. Matilda blushed at seeing Theodore and Isabella together; but endeavored to conceal it by embracing the latter, and condoling with her on her father's mischance. The surgeons soon came to acquaint Hippolita that none of the Marquis's wounds were dangerous; and that he was desirous of seeing his daughter and the Princesses.

Theodore, under pretense of expressing his joy at being freed from his apprehensions of the combat being fatal to Frederic, could not resist the impulse of following Matilda. Her eyes were so often cast down on meeting his, that Isabella, who regarded Theodore as attentively as he gazed on Matilda, soon divined who the object was that he had told her in the cave engaged his affections. While this mute scene passed, Hippolita demanded of Frederic the cause of his having taken that mysterious course for reclaiming his daughter; and threw in various apologies to excuse her Lord for the match contracted between their children.

Frederic, however incensed against Manfred, was not insensible to the courtesy and benevolence of Hippolita: but he was still more struck with the lovely form of Matilda. Wishing to detain them by his bedside, he informed Hippolita of his story. He told her that, while prisoner to the infidels, he had dreamed that his daughter, of whom he had learned no news since his captivity, was detained in a castle, where she was in danger of the most dreadful misfortunes: and that if he obtained his liberty, and repaired to a wood near Joppa, he would learn more. Alarmed at this dream, and incapable of obeying the direction given by it, his chains became more grievous than ever. But while his thoughts were occupied on the means of obtaining his liberty, he received the agreeable news that the confederate Princes who were warring in Palestine had paid his ransom. He instantly set out for the wood that had been marked in his dream.

For three days he and his attendants had wandered in the forest without seeing a human form: but on the evening of the third they came to a cell, in which they found a venerable hermit in the agonies of death. Applying rich cordials, they brought the fainting man to his speech.

"My sons," said he, "I am bounden to your charity - but it is in vain - I am going to my eternal rest - yet I die with the satisfaction of performing the will of heaven. When first I repaired to this solitude, after seeing my country become a prey to unbelievers - it is alas! above fifty years since I was witness to that dreadful scene! St. Nicholas appeared to me, and revealed a secret, which he bade me never disclose to mortal man, but on my deathbed. This is that tremendous hour, and ye are no doubt the chosen warriors to whom I was ordered to reveal my trust. As soon as ye have done the last offices to this wretched course, dig under the seventh tree on the left hand of this poor cave, and your pains will - Oh! good heaven receive my soul!" With those words the devout man breathed his last.

"By break of day," continued Frederic, "when we had committed the holy relics to earth, we dug according to direction. But what was our astonishment when about the depth of six feet we discovered an enormous sabre — the very weapon yonder in the court. On the blade, which was then partly out of the scabbard, though since closed by our efforts in removing it, were written the following lines — no; excuse me, Madam," added the Marquis, turning to Hippolita; "if I forbear to repeat them: I respect your sex and rank, and would not be guilty of offending your ear with sounds injurious to aught that is dear to you."

He paused. Hippolita trembled. She did not doubt but Frederic was destined by heaven to accomplish the fate that seemed to threaten her house. Looking with anxious fondness at Matilda, a silent tear stole down her cheek: but recollecting herself, she said -

"Proceed, my Lord; heaven does nothing in vain; mortals must receive its divine behests with lowliness and submission. It is our part to deprecate its wrath or bow to its decrees. Repeat the sentence, my Lord; we listen resigned."

Frederic was grieved that he had proceeded so far. The dignity and patient firmness of Hippolita penetrated him with respect, and the tender silent affection with which the Princess and her daughter regarded each other, melted him almost to tears. Yet apprehensive that his forbearance to obey would be more alarming, he repeated in a faltering and low voice the following lines:

"Where'er a casque that suits this sword is found,
With perils is thy daughter compass'd round.
Alfonso's blood alone can save the maid,
And quiet a long restless Prince's shade."

"What is there in these lines," said Theodore impatiently, "that affects these Princesses? Why were they to be shocked by a mysterious delicacy, that has so little foundation?"

"Your words are rude, young man," said the Marquis; "and though fortune has favored you once…"

"My honored Lord," said Isabella, who resented Theodore's warmth, which she perceived was dictated by his sentiments for Matilda, "discompose not yourself for the glozing of a peasant's son: he forgets the reverence he owes you; but he is not accustomed -"

Hippolita, concerned at the heat that had arisen, checked Theodore for his boldness, but with an air acknowledging his zeal; and changing the conversation, demanded of Frederic where he had left her Lord? As the Marquis was going to reply, they heard a noise without, and rising to inquire the cause, Manfred, Jerome, and part of the troop, who had met an imperfect rumor of what had happened, entered the chamber. Manfred advanced hastily towards Frederic's bed to condole with him on his misfortune, and to learn the circumstances of the combat, when starting in an agony of terror and amazement, he cried:

"Ha! what art thou? thou dreadful specter! Is my hour come?"

"My dearest, gracious Lord," cried Hippolita, clasping him in her arms, "what is it you see! Why do you fix your eye-balls thus?"

"What!" cried Manfred breathless; "dost thou see nothing, Hippolita? Is this ghastly phantom sent to me alone—to rue, who did not—"

"For mercy's sweetest self, my Lord," said Hippolita, "resume your soul, command your reason. There is none here, but us, your friends."

"What, is not that Alfonso?" cried Manfred. "Dost thou not see him? can it be my brain's delirium?"

"This! my Lord," said Hippolita; "this is Theodore, the youth who has been so unfortunate."

"Theodore!" said Manfred mournfully, and striking his forehead; "Theodore or a phantom, he has unhinged the soul of Manfred. But how comes he here? and how comes he in armor?"

"I believe he went in search of Isabella," said Hippolita.

"Of Isabella!" said Manfred, relapsing into rage; "yes, yes, that is not doubtful - . But how did he escape from durance in which I left him? Was it Isabella, or this hypocritical old Friar, that procured his enlargement?"

"And would a parent be criminal, my Lord," said Theodore, "if he meditated the deliverance of his child?"

Jerome, amazed to hear himself in a manner accused by his son, and without foundation, knew not what to think. He could not comprehend how Theodore had escaped, how he came to be armed, and to encounter Frederic. Still he would not venture to ask any questions that might tend to inflame Manfred's wrath against his son. Jerome's silence convinced Manfred that he had contrived Theodore's release.

"And is it thus, thou ungrateful old man," said the Prince, addressing himself to the Friar, "that thou repayest mine and Hippolita's bounties? And not content with traversing my heart's nearest wishes, thou armest thy bastard, and bringest him into my own castle to insult me!"

"My Lord," said Theodore, "you wrong my father: neither he nor I are capable of harboring a thought against your peace. Is it insolence thus to surrender myself to your Highness's pleasure?" added he, laying his sword respectfully at Manfred's feet. "Behold my bosom; strike, my Lord, if you suspect that a disloyal thought is lodged there. There is not a sentiment engraven on my heart that does not venerate you and yours."

The grace and fervor with which Theodore uttered these words interested every person present in his favor. Even Manfred was touched - yet still possessed with his resemblance to Alfonso, his admiration was dashed with secret horror.

"Rise," said he; "thy life is not my present purpose. But tell me thy history, and how thou camest connected with this old traitor here."

"My Lord," said Jerome eagerly.

"Peace! impostor!" said Manfred; "I will not have him prompted."

"My Lord," said Theodore, "I want no assistance; my story is very brief. I was carried at five years of age to Algiers with my mother, who had been taken by corsairs from the coast of Sicily. She died of grief in less than a twelvemonth;" the tears gushed from Jerome's eyes, on whose countenance a thousand anxious passions stood expressed. "Before she died," continued Theodore, "she bound a writing about my arm under my garments, which told me I was the son of the Count Falconara."

"It is most true," said Jerome; "I am that wretched father."

"Again, I enjoin thee silence," said Manfred: "proceed."

"I remained in slavery," said Theodore, "until within these two years, when attending on my master in his cruises, I was delivered by a Christian vessel, which overpowered the pirate; and discovering myself to the captain, he generously put me on shore in Sicily; but alas! instead of finding a father, I learned that his estate, which was situated on the coast, had, during his absence, been laid waste by the Rover who had carried my mother and me into captivity: that his castle had been burnt to the ground, and that my father on his return had sold what remained, and was retired into religion in the kingdom of Naples, but where no man could inform me. Destitute and friendless, hopeless almost of attaining the transport of a parent's embrace, I took the first opportunity of setting sail for Naples, from whence, within these six days, I wandered into this province, still supporting myself by the labor of my hands; nor until yester-morn did I believe that heaven had reserved any lot for me but peace of mind and contented poverty. This, my Lord, is Theodore's story. I am blessed beyond my hope in finding a father; I am unfortunate beyond my desert in having incurred your Highness's displeasure."

He ceased. A murmur of approbation gently arose from the audience.

"This is not all," said Frederic; "I am bound in honor to add what he suppresses. Though he is modest, I must be generous; he is one of the bravest youths on Christian ground. He is warm too; and from the short knowledge I have of him, I will pledge myself for his veracity: if what he reports of himself were not true, he would not utter it - and for me, youth, I honor a frankness which becomes thy birth; but now, and thou didst offend me: yet the noble blood which flows in thy veins, may well be allowed to boil out, when it has so recently traced itself to its source. Come, my Lord," (turning to Manfred), "if I can pardon him, surely you may; it is not the youth's fault, if you took him for a specter."

This bitter taunt galled the soul of Manfred.

"If beings from another world," replied he haughtily, "have power to impress my mind with awe, it is more than living man can do; nor could a stripling's arm."

"My Lord," interrupted Hippolita, "your guest has occasion for repose: shall we not leave him to his rest?" Saying this, and taking Manfred by the hand, she took leave of Frederic, and led the company forth.

The Prince, not sorry to quit a conversation which recalled to mind the discovery he had made of his most secret sensations, suffered himself to be conducted to his own apartment, after permitting Theodore, though under engagement to return to the castle on the morrow (a condition the young man gladly accepted), to retire with his father to the convent. Matilda and Isabella were too much occupied with their own reflections, and too little content with each other, to wish for farther converse that night. They separated each to her chamber, with more expressions of ceremony and fewer of affection than had passed between them since their childhood.

If they parted with small cordiality, they did but meet with greater impatience, as soon as the sun was risen. Their minds were in a situation that excluded sleep, and each recollected a thousand questions which she wished she had put to the other overnight. Matilda reflected that Isabella had been twice delivered by Theodore in very critical situations, which she could not believe accidental. His eyes, it was true, had been fixed on her in Frederic's chamber; but that might have been to disguise his passion for Isabella from the fathers of both. It were better to clear this up. She wished to know the truth, lest she should wrong her friend by entertaining a passion for Isabella's lover. Thus, jealousy prompted, and at the same time borrowed an excuse from friendship to justify its curiosity.

Isabella, not less restless, had better foundation for her suspicions. Both Theodore's tongue and eyes had told her his heart was engaged; it was true - yet, perhaps, Matilda might not correspond to his passion; she had ever appeared insensible to love: all her thoughts were set on heaven.

"Why did I dissuade her?" said Isabella to herself; "I am punished for my generosity; but when did they meet? where? It cannot be; I have deceived myself; perhaps last night was the first time they ever beheld each other; it must be some other object that has prepossessed his affections - if it is, I am not so unhappy as I thought; if it is not my friend Matilda - how! Can I stoop to wish for the affection of a man, who rudely and unnecessarily acquainted me with his indifference? and that at the very moment in which common courtesy demanded at least expressions of civility. I will go to my dear Matilda, who will confirm me in this becoming pride. Man is false - I will advise with her on taking the veil: she will rejoice to find me in this disposition; and I will acquaint her that I no longer oppose her inclination for the cloister."

In this frame of mind, and determined to open her heart entirely to Matilda, she went to that Princess's chamber, whom she found already dressed, and leaning pensively on her arm. This attitude, so correspondent to what she felt herself, revived Isabella's suspicions, and destroyed the confidence she had purposed to place in her friend. They blushed at meeting and were too much novices to disguise their sensations with address. After some unmeaning questions and replies, Matilda demanded of Isabella the cause of her flight? The latter, who had almost forgotten Manfred's passion, so entirely was she occupied by her own, concluding that Matilda referred to her last escape from the convent, which had occasioned the events of the preceding evening, replied -

"Martelli brought word to the convent that your mother was dead."

"Oh!" said Matilda, interrupting her, "Bianca has explained that mistake to me: on seeing me faint, she cried out, 'The Princess is dead!' and Martelli, who had come for the usual dole to the castle -"

"And what made you faint?" said Isabella, indifferent to the rest. Matilda blushed and stammered:

"My father - he was sitting in judgment on a criminal -"

"What criminal?" said Isabella eagerly.

"A young man," said Matilda; "I believe -"

"I think it was that young man that..."

"What, Theodore?" said Isabella.

"Yes," answered she; "I never saw him before; I do not know how he had offended my father, but as he has been of service to you, I am glad my Lord has pardoned him."

"Served me!" replied Isabella; "do you term it serving me, to wound my father, and almost occasion his death? Though it is but since yesterday that I am blessed with knowing a parent, I hope Matilda does not think I am such a stranger to filial tenderness as not to resent the boldness of that audacious youth, and that it is impossible for me ever to feel any affection for one who dared to lift his arm against the author of my being. No, Matilda, my heart abhors him; and if you still retain the friendship for me that you have vowed from your infancy, you will detest a man who has been on the point of making me miserable forever."

Matilda held down her head and replied: "I hope my dearest Isabella does not doubt her Matilda's friendship: I never beheld that youth until yesterday; he is almost a stranger to me: but as the surgeons have pronounced your father out of danger, you ought not to harbor uncharitable resentment against one, who I am persuaded did not know the Marquis was related to you."

"You plead his cause very pathetically," said Isabella, "considering he is so much a stranger to you! I am mistaken, or he returns your charity."

"What mean you?" said Matilda.

"Nothing," said Isabella, repenting that she had given Matilda a hint of Theodore's inclination for her. Then changing the discourse, she asked Matilda what occasioned Manfred to take Theodore for a specter?

"Bless me," said Matilda, "did not you observe his extreme resemblance to the portrait of Alfonso in the gallery? I took notice of it to Bianca even before I saw him in armor; but with the helmet on, he is the very image of that picture."

"I do not much observe pictures," said Isabella: "much less have I examined this young man so attentively as you seem to have done. Ah? Matilda, your heart is in danger, but let me warn you as a friend, he has owned to me that he is in love; it cannot be with you, for yesterday was the first time you ever met—was it not?"

"Certainly," replied Matilda; "but why does my dearest Isabella conclude from anything I have said, that" - she paused - then continuing: "he saw you first, and I am far from having the vanity to think that my little portion of charms could engage a heart devoted to you; may you be happy, Isabella, whatever is the fate of Matilda!"

"My lovely friend," said Isabella, whose heart was too honest to resist a kind expression, "it is you that Theodore admires; I saw it; I am persuaded of it; nor shall a thought of my own happiness suffer me to interfere with yours."

This frankness drew tears from the gentle Matilda; and jealousy that for a moment had raised a coolness between these amiable maidens soon gave way to the natural sincerity and candor of their souls. Each confessed to the other the impression that Theodore had made on her; and this confidence was followed by a struggle of generosity, each insisting on yielding her claim to her friend. At length the dignity of Isabella's virtue reminding her of the preference which Theodore had almost declared for her rival, made her determine to conquer her passion, and cede the beloved object to her friend.

During this contest of amity, Hippolita entered her daughter's chamber.

"Madam," said she to Isabella, "you have so much tenderness for Matilda, and interest yourself so kindly in whatever affects our wretched house, that I can have no secrets with my child which are not proper for you to hear."

The princesses were all attention and anxiety.

"Know then, Madam," continued Hippolita, "and you my dearest Matilda, that being convinced by all the events of these two last ominous days, that heaven purposes the scepter of Otranto should pass from Manfred's hands into those of the Marquis Frederic, I have been perhaps inspired with the thought of averting our total destruction by the union of our rival houses. With this view I have been proposing to Manfred, my lord, to tender this dear, dear child to Frederic, your father."

"Me to Lord Frederic!" cried Matilda; "good heavens! my gracious mother - and have you named it to my father?"

"I have," said Hippolita; "he listened benignly to my proposal and is gone to break it to the Marquis."

"Ah! wretched princess!" cried Isabella; "what hast thou done! what ruin has thy inadvertent goodness been preparing for thyself, for me, and for Matilda!"

"Ruin from me to you and to my child!" said Hippolita "what can this mean?"

"Alas!" said Isabella, "the purity of your own heart prevents your seeing the depravity of others. Manfred, your lord, that impious man -"

"Hold," said Hippolita; "you must not in my presence, young lady, mention Manfred with disrespect: he is my lord and husband, and -"

"Will not long be so," said Isabella, "if his wicked purposes can be carried into execution."

"This language amazes me," said Hippolita. "Your feeling, Isabella, is warm; but until this hour I never knew it betray you into intemperance. What deed of Manfred authorizes you to treat him as a murderer, an assassin?"

"Thou virtuous, and too credulous Princess!" replied Isabella; "it is not thy life he aims at—it is to separate himself from thee! to divorce thee! To -"

"To divorce me!" "To divorce my mother!" cried Hippolita and Matilda at once.

"Yes," said Isabella; "and to complete his crime, he meditates - I cannot speak it!"

"What can surpass what thou hast already uttered?" said Matilda.

Hippolita was silent. Grief choked her speech; and the recollection of Manfred's late ambiguous discourses confirmed what she heard.

"Excellent, dear lady! madam! mother!" cried Isabella, flinging herself at Hippolita's feet in a transport of passion; "trust me, believe me, I will die a thousand deaths sooner than consent to injure you, than yield to so odious - oh! -

"This is too much!" cried Hippolita: "What crimes does one crime suggest! Rise, dear Isabella; I do not doubt your virtue. Oh! Matilda, this stroke is too heavy for thee! weep not, my child; and not a murmur, I charge thee. Remember, he is thy father still!"

"But you are my mother too," said Matilda fervently; "and you are virtuous, you are guiltless! - Oh! must not I, must not I complain?"

"You must not," said Hippolita - "come, all will yet be well. Manfred, in the agony for the loss of thy brother, knew not what he said; perhaps Isabella misunderstood him; his heart is good - and, my child, thou knowest not all! There is a destiny hangs over us; the hand of Providence is stretched out; oh! could I but save thee from the wreck! Yes," continued she in a firmer tone, "perhaps the sacrifice of myself may atone for all; I will go and offer myself to this divorce - it boots not what becomes of me. I will withdraw into the neighboring monastery and waste the remainder of life in prayers and tears for my child and - the Prince!"

"Thou art as much too good for this world," said Isabella, "as Manfred is execrable; but think not, lady, that thy weakness shall determine for me. I swear, hear me all ye angels..."

"Stop, I adjure thee," cried Hippolita: "remember thou dost not depend on thyself; thou hast a father."

"My father is too pious, too noble," interrupted Isabella, "to command an impious deed. But should he command it; can a father enjoin a cursed act? I was contracted to the son, can I wed the father? No, madam, no; force should not drag me to Manfred's hated bed. I loathe him, I abhor him: divine and human laws forbid - and my friend, my dearest Matilda! would I wound her tender soul by injuring her adored mother? my own mother—I never have known another"

"Oh! she is the mother of both!" cried Matilda: "can we, can we, Isabella, adore her too much?"

"My lovely children," said the touched Hippolita, "your tenderness over-powers me - but I must not give way to it. It is not ours to make election for our-selves: heaven, our fathers, and our husbands must decide for us. Have patience until you hear what Manfred and Frederic have determined. If the Marquis ac-cepts Matilda's hand, I know she will readily obey. Heaven may interpose and prevent the rest. What means my child?" continued she, seeing Matilda fall at her feet with a flood of speechless tears - "But no; answer me not, my daughter: I must not hear a word against the pleasure of thy father."

"Oh! doubt not my obedience, my dreadful obedience to him and to you!" said Matilda. "But can I, most respected of women, can I experience all this tender-ness, this world of goodness, and conceal a thought from the best of mothers?"

"What art thou going to utter?" said Isabella trembling. "Recollect thyself, Matilda."

"No, Isabella," said the Princess, "I should not deserve this incomparable parent, if the inmost recesses of my soul harbored a thought without her permis-sion - nay, I have offended her; I have suffered a passion to enter my heart without her avowal - but here I disclaim it; here I vow to heaven and her."

"My child! my child;" said Hippolita, "what words are these! what new calamities has fate in store for us! Thou, a passion? Thou, in this hour of destruc-tion -"

"Oh! I see all my guilt!" said Matilda. "I abhor myself, if I cost my mother a pang. She is the dearest thing I have on earth - Oh! I will never, never behold him more!"

"Isabella," said Hippolita, "thou art conscious to this unhappy secret, whatever it is. Speak!"

"What!" cried Matilda, "have I so forfeited my mother's love, that she will not permit me even to speak my own guilt? oh! wretched, wretched Matilda!"

"Thou art too cruel," said Isabella to Hippolita: "canst thou behold this anguish of a virtuous mind, and not commiserate it?"

"Not pity my child!" said Hippolita, catching Matilda in her arms - "Oh! I know she is good; she is all virtue, all tenderness, and duty. I do forgive thee, my excellent, my only hope!"

The princesses then revealed to Hippolita their mutual inclination for Theodore, and the purpose of Isabella to resign him to Matilda. Hippolita blamed their imprudence and showed them the improbability that either father would consent to bestow his heiress on so poor a man, though nobly born. Some comfort it gave her to find their passion of so recent a date, and that Theodore had had but little cause to suspect it in either. She strictly enjoined them to avoid all corre-spondence with him. This Matilda fervently promised: but Isabella, who flattered herself that she meant no more than to promote his union with her friend, could not determine to avoid him; and made no reply.

"I will go to the convent," said Hippolita, "and order new masses to be said for a deliverance from these calamities."

"Oh! my mother," said Matilda, "you mean to quit us: you mean to take sanctuary, and to give my father an opportunity of pursuing his fatal intention. Alas! on my knees I supplicate you to forbear; will you leave me a prey to Frederic? I will follow you to the convent."

"Be at peace, my child," said Hippolita: "I will return instantly. I will never abandon thee, until I know it is the will of heaven, and for thy benefit."

"Do not deceive me," said Matilda. "I will not marry Frederic until thou commandest it. Alas! what will become of me?"

"Why that exclamation?" said Hippolita. "I have promised thee to re-turn—"

"Ah! my mother," replied Matilda, "stay and save me from myself. A frown from thee can do more than all my father's severity. I have given away my heart, and you alone can make me recall it."

"No more," said Hippolita; "thou must not relapse, Matilda."

"I can quit Theodore," said she, "but must I wed another? let me attend thee to the altar and shut myself from the world forever."

"Thy fate depends on thy father," said Hippolita; "I have ill-bestowed my tenderness, if it has taught thee to revere aught beyond him. Adieu! my child: I go to pray for thee."

Hippolita's real purpose was to demand of Jerome, whether in conscience she might not consent to the divorce. She had oft urged Manfred to resign the principality, which the delicacy of her conscience rendered an hourly burthen to her. These scruples concurred to make the separation from her husband appear less dreadful to her than it would have seemed in any other situation.

Jerome, at quitting the castle overnight, had questioned Theodore severe-ly why he had accused him to Manfred of being privy to his escape. Theodore owned it had been with design to prevent Manfred's suspicion from alighting on Matilda; and added, the holiness of Jerome's life and character secured him from the tyrant's wrath. Jerome was heartily grieved to discover his son's inclination for that princess; and leaving him to his rest, promised in the morning to acquaint him with important reasons for conquering his passion.

Theodore, like Isabella, was too recently acquainted with parental author-ity to submit to its decisions against the impulse of his heart. He had little curi-osity to learn the Friar's reasons, and less disposition to obey them. The lovely Matilda had made stronger impressions on him than filial affection. All night he pleased himself with visions of love; and it was not till late after the morning-of-fice, that he recollected the Friar's commands to attend him at Alfonso's tomb.

"Young man," said Jerome, when he saw him, "this tardiness does not please me. Have a father's commands already so little weight?"

Theodore made awkward excuses and attributed his delay to having overslept himself.

"And on whom were thy dreams employed?" said the Friar sternly. His son blushed. "Come, come," resumed the Friar, "inconsiderate youth, this must not be eradicating this guilty passion from thy breast -"

"Guilty passion!" cried Theodore: "Can guilt dwell with innocent beauty and virtuous modesty?"

"It is sinful," replied the Friar, "to cherish those whom heaven has doomed to destruction. A tyrant's race must be swept from the earth to the third and fourth generation."

"Will heaven visit the innocent for the crimes of the guilty?" said Theodore. "The fair Matilda has virtues enough -"

"To undo thee:" interrupted Jerome. "Hast thou so soon forgotten that twice the savage Manfred has pronounced thy sentence?"

"Nor have I forgotten, sir," said Theodore, "that the charity of his daughter delivered me from his power. I can forget injuries, but never benefits."

"The injuries thou hast received from Manfred's race," said the Friar, "are beyond what thou canst conceive. Reply not but view this holy image! Beneath this marble monument rest the ashes of the good Alfonso; a prince adorned with every virtue: the father of his people! the delight of mankind! Kneel, headstrong boy, and list, while a father unfolds a tale of horror that will expel every sentiment from thy soul, but sensations of sacred vengeance — Alfonso! much injured prince! let thy unsatisfied shade sit awful on the troubled air, while these trembling lips - ha! who comes there? -"

"The most wretched of women!" said Hippolita, entering the choir. "Good Father, art thou at leisure? - but why this kneeling youth? what means the horror imprinted on each countenance? why at this venerable tomb - alas! hast thou seen aught?"

"We were pouring forth our orisons to heaven," replied the Friar, with some confusion, "to put an end to the woes of this deplorable province. Join with us, Lady! thy spotless soul may obtain an exemption from the judgments which the portents of these days but too speakingly denounce against thy house."

"I pray fervently to heaven to divert them," said the pious Princess. "Thou knowest it has been the occupation of my life to wrest a blessing for my Lord and my harmless children. - One alas! is taken from me! would heaven but hear me for my poor Matilda! Father! intercede for her!"

"Every heart will bless her," cried Theodore with rapture.

"Be dumb, rash youth!" said Jerome. "And thou, fond Princess, contend not with the Powers above! the Lord giveth, and the Lord taketh away: bless His holy name, and submit to his decrees."

"I do most devoutly," said Hippolita; "but will He not spare my only comfort? must Matilda perish too? - ah! Father, I came - but dismiss thy son. No ear but thine must hear what I have to utter."

"May heaven grant thy every wish, most excellent Princess!" said Theodore retiring. Jerome frowned.

Hippolita then acquainted the Friar with the proposal she had suggested to Manfred, his approbation of it, and the tender of Matilda that he was gone to make to Frederic. Jerome could not conceal his dislike of the notion, which he covered under pretense of the improbability that Frederic, the nearest of blood to Alfonso, and who was come to claim his succession, would yield to an alliance with the usurper of his right. But nothing could equal the perplexity of the Friar, when Hippolita confessed her readiness not to oppose the separation and demanded his opinion on the legality of her acquiescence. The Friar caught eagerly at her request of his advice, and without explaining his aversion to the proposed marriage of Manfred and Isabella, he painted to Hippolita in the most alarming colors the sinfulness of her consent, denounced judgments against her if she complied, and enjoined her in the severest terms to treat any such proposition with every mark of indignation and refusal.

Manfred, in the meantime, had broken his purpose to Frederic, and proposed the double marriage. That weak Prince, who had been struck with the charms of Matilda, listened but too eagerly to the offer. He forgot his enmity to Manfred, whom he saw but little hope of dispossessing by force; and flattering himself that no issue might succeed from the union of his daughter with the tyrant, he looked upon his own succession to the principality as facilitated by wedding Matilda. He made faint opposition to the proposal; affecting, for form only, not to acquiesce unless Hippolita should consent to the divorce. Manfred took that upon himself.

Transported with his success, and impatient to see himself in a situation to expect sons, he hastened to his wife's apartment, determined to extort her compliance. He learned with indignation that she was absent at the convent. His guilt suggested to him that she had probably been informed by Isabella of his purpose. He doubted whether her retirement to the convent did not import an intention of remaining there, until she could raise obstacles to their divorce; and the suspicions he had already entertained of Jerome, made him apprehend that the Friar would not only traverse his views, but might have inspired Hippolita with the resolution of talking sanctuary. Impatient to unravel this clue, and to defeat its success, Manfred hastened to the convent, and arrived there as the Friar was earnestly exhorting the Princess never to yield to the divorce.

"Madam," said Manfred, "what business drew you hither? why did you not await my return from the Marquis?"

"I came to implore a blessing on your councils," replied Hippolita.

"My councils do not need a Friar's intervention," said Manfred; "and of all men living is that hoary traitor the only one whom you delight to confer with?"

"Profane Prince!" said Jerome; "is it at the altar that thou choosest to insult the servants of the altar? - but, Manfred, thy impious schemes are known. Heaven and this virtuous lady know them — nay, frown not, Prince. The Church despises thy menaces. Her thunders will be heard above thy wrath. Dare to proceed in thy cursed purpose of a divorce, until her sentence be known, and here I lance her anathema at thy head."

"Audacious rebel!" said Manfred, endeavoring to conceal the awe with which the Friar's words inspired him. "Dost thou presume to threaten thy lawful Prince?"

"Thou art no lawful Prince," said Jerome; "thou art no Prince - go, discuss thy claim with Frederic; and when that is done -"

"It is done," replied Manfred; "Frederic accepts Matilda's hand, and is content to waive his claim, unless I have no male issue" - as he spoke those words three drops of blood fell from the nose of Alfonso's statue. Manfred turned pale, and the Princess sank on her knees.

"Behold!" said the Friar; "mark this miraculous indication that the blood of Alfonso will never mix with that of Manfred!"

"My gracious Lord," said Hippolita, "let us submit ourselves to heaven. Think not thy ever-obedient wife rebels against thy authority. I have no will but that of my Lord and the Church. To that revered tribunal let us appeal. It does not depend on us to burst the bonds that unite us. If the Church shall approve the dissolution of our marriage, be it so - I have but few years, and those of sorrow, to pass. Where can they be worn away so well as at the foot of this altar, in prayers for thine and Matilda's safety?"

"But thou shalt not remain here until then," said Manfred. "Repair with me to the castle, and there I will advise on the proper measures for a divorce; - but this meddling Friar comes not thither; my hospitable roof shall never more harbor a traitor - and for thy Reverence's offspring," continued he, "I banish him from my dominions. He, I ween, is no sacred personage, nor under the protection of the Church. Whoever weds Isabella, it shall not be Father Falconara's started-up son."

"They start up," said the Friar, "who are suddenly beheld in the seat of lawful Princes; but they wither away like the grass, and their place knows them no more."

Manfred, casting a look of scorn at the Friar, led Hippolita forth; but at the door of the church whispered one of his attendants to remain concealed about the convent, and bring him instant notice, if any one from the castle should repair thither.

CHAPTER V

Every reflection which Manfred made on the Friar's behavior, conspired to persuade him that Jerome was privy to an amour between Isabella and Theodore. But Jerome's new presumption, so dissonant from his former meekness, suggested still deeper apprehensions. The Prince even suspected that the Friar depended on some secret support from Frederic, whose arrival, coinciding with the novel appearance of Theodore, seemed to bespeak a correspondence. Still more was he troubled with the resemblance of Theodore to Alfonso's portrait. The latter he knew had unquestionably died without issue. Frederic had consented to bestow Isabella on him. These contradictions agitated his mind with numberless pangs. He saw but two methods of extricating himself from his difficulties. The one was to resign his dominions to the Marquis - pride, ambition, and his reliance on ancient prophecies, which had pointed out a possibility of his preserving them to his posterity, combated that thought. The other was to press his marriage with Isabella. After long ruminating on these anxious thoughts, as he marched silently with Hippolita to the castle, he at last discoursed with that Princess on the subject of his disquiet, and used every insinuating and plausible argument to extract her consent to, even her promise of promoting the divorce. Hippolita needed little persuasions to bend her to his pleasure. She endeavored to win him over to the measure of resigning his dominions; but finding her exhortations fruitless, she assured him, that as far as her conscience would allow, she would raise no opposition to a separation, though without better founded scruples than what he yet alleged, she would not engage to be active in demanding it.

This compliance, though inadequate, was sufficient to raise Manfred's hopes. He trusted that his power and wealth would easily advance his suit at the court of Rome, whither he resolved to engage Frederic to take a journey on purpose. That Prince had discovered so much passion for Matilda, that Manfred hoped to obtain all he wished by holding out or withdrawing his daughter's charms, according as the Marquis should appear more or less disposed to co-operate in his views. Even the absence of Frederic would be a material point gained, until he could take further measures for his security.

Dismissing Hippolita to her apartment, he repaired to that of the Marquis; but crossing the great hall through which he was to pass he met Bianca. The damsel he knew was in the confidence of both the young ladies. It immediately occurred to him to sift her on the subject of Isabella and Theodore. Calling her aside into the recess of the oriel window of the hall, and soothing her with many fair words and promises, he demanded of her whether she knew aught of the state of Isabella's affections.

"I! my Lord! no my Lord - yes my Lord - poor Lady! she is wonderfully alarmed about her father's wounds; but I tell her he will do well; don't your Highness think so?"

"I do not ask you," replied Manfred, "what she thinks about her father; but you are in her secrets. Come, be a good girl and tell me; is there any young man - ha! - you understand me."

"Lord bless me! understand your Highness? no, not I. I told her a few vulnerary herbs and repose…"

"I am not talking," replied the Prince, impatiently, "about her father; I know he will do well."

"Bless me, I rejoice to hear your Highness say so; for though I thought it not right to let my young Lady despond, methought his greatness had a wan look, and a something - I remember when young Ferdinand was wounded by the Venetian -"

"Thou answerest from the point," interrupted Manfred; "but here, take this jewel, perhaps that may fix thy attention - nay, no reverences; my favor shall not stop here - come, tell me truly; how stands Isabella's heart?"

"Well! your Highness has such a way!" said Bianca, "to be sure—but can your Highness keep a secret? if it should ever come out of your lips -"

"It shall not, it shall not," cried Manfred.

"Nay, but swear, your Highness."

"By my halidame, if it should ever be known that I said it -"

"Why, truth is truth, I do not think my Lady Isabella ever much affectioned my young Lord your son; yet he was a sweet youth as one should see; I am sure, if I had been a Princess - but bless me! I must attend my Lady Matilda; she will marvel what is become of me."

"Stay," cried Manfred; "thou hast not satisfied my question. Hast thou ever carried any message, any letter?"

"I! good gracious!" cried Bianca; "I carry a letter? I would not to be a Queen. I hope your Highness thinks, though I am poor, I am honest. Did your Highness never hear what Count Marsigli offered me, when he came a wooing to my Lady Matilda?"

"I have not leisure," said Manfred, "to listen to thy tale. I do not question thy honesty. But it is thy duty to conceal nothing from me. How long has Isabella been acquainted with Theodore?"

"Nay, there is nothing can escape your Highness!" said Bianca; "not that I know any thing of the matter. Theodore, to be sure, is a proper young man, and, as my Lady Matilda says, the very image of good Alfonso. Has not your Highness remarked it?"

"Yes, yes, - No - thou torturest me," said Manfred. "Where did they meet? when?"

"Who! my Lady Matilda?" said Bianca.

"No, no, not Matilda: Isabella; when did Isabella first become acquainted with this Theodore!"

"Virgin Mary!" said Bianca, "how should I know?"

"Thou dost know," said Manfred; "and I must know; I will -"

"Lord! your Highness is not jealous of young Theodore!" said Bianca.

"Jealous! no, no. Why should I be jealous? perhaps I mean to unite them - If I were sure Isabella would have no repugnance."

"Repugnance! no, I'll warrant her," said Bianca; "he is as comely a youth as ever trod on Christian ground. We are all in love with him; there is not a soul in the castle but would be rejoiced to have him for our Prince - I mean, when it shall please heaven to call your Highness to itself."

"Indeed!" said Manfred, "has it gone so far! oh! this cursed Friar! - but I must not lose time - go, Bianca, attend Isabella; but I charge thee, not a word of what has passed. Find out how she is affected towards Theodore; bring me good news, and that ring has a companion. Wait at the foot of the winding staircase: I am going to visit the Marquis and will talk further with thee at my return."

Manfred, after some general conversation, desired Frederic to dismiss the two Knights, his companions, having to talk with him on urgent affairs.

As soon as they were alone, he began in artful guise to sound the Marquis on the subject of Matilda; and finding him disposed to his wish, he let drop hints on the difficulties that would attend the celebration of their marriage, unless - At that instant Bianca burst into the room with a wildness in her look and gestures that spoke the utmost terror.

"Oh! my Lord, my Lord!" cried she; "we are all undone! it is come again! it is come again!"

"What is come again?" cried Manfred amazed.

"Oh! the hand! the Giant! the hand! - support me! I am terrified out of my senses," cried Bianca. "I will not sleep in the castle to-night. Where shall I go? my things may come after me to-morrow — would I had been content to wed Frances-co! this comes of ambition!"

"What has terrified thee thus, young woman?" said the Marquis. "Thou art safe here; be not alarmed."

"Oh! your Greatness is wonderfully good," said Bianca, "but I dare not— no, pray let me go - I had rather leave everything behind me, than stay another hour under this roof."

"Go to, thou hast lost thy senses," said Manfred. "Interrupt us not; we were communing on important matters - My Lord, this wench is subject to fits - Come with me, Bianca."

"Oh! the Saints! No," said Bianca, "for certain it comes to warn your Highness; why should it appear to me else? I say my prayers morning and eve-ning - oh! if your Highness had believed Diego! 'Tis the same hand that he saw the foot to in the gallery-chamber - Father Jerome has often told us the prophecy would be out one of these days - 'Bianca,' said he, 'mark my words -'"

"Thou ravest," said Manfred, in a rage; "be gone, and keep these fooleries to frighten thy companions."

"What! my Lord," cried Bianca, "do you think I have seen nothing? go to the foot of the great stairs yourself - as I live, I saw it."

"Saw what? tell us, fair maid, what thou hast seen," said Frederic.

"Can your Highness listen," said Manfred, "to the delirium of a silly wench, who has heard stories of apparitions until she believes them?"

"This is more than fancy," said the Marquis; "her terror is too natural and too strongly impressed to be the work of imagination. Tell us, fair maiden, what it is has moved thee thus?"

"Yes, my Lord, thank your Greatness," said Bianca; "I believe I look very pale; I shall be better when I have recovered myself - I was going to my Lady Isa-bella's chamber, by his Highness's order."

"We do not want the circumstances," interrupted Manfred. "Since his Highness will have it so, proceed; but be brief."

"Lord! your Highness thwarts one so!" replied Bianca; "I fear my hair - I am sure I never in my life - well! as I was telling your Greatness, I was going by his Highness's order to my Lady Isabella's chamber; she lies in the watchet-colored chamber, on the right hand, one pair of stairs: so when I came to the great stairs - I was looking on his Highness's present here -"

"Grant me patience!" said Manfred, "will this wench never come to the point? what imports it to the Marquis, that I gave thee a bauble for thy faithful attendance on my daughter? we want to know what thou sawest."

"I was going to tell your Highness," said Bianca, "if you would permit me. So as I was rubbing the ring - I am sure I had not gone up three steps, but I heard the rattling of armor; for all the world such a clatter as Diego says he heard when the Giant turned him about in the gallery-chamber."

"What Giant is this, my Lord?" said the Marquis; "is your castle haunted by giants and goblins?"

"Lord! what, has not your Greatness heard the story of the Giant in the gallery-chamber?" cried Bianca. "I marvel his Highness has not told you; mayhap you do not know there is a prophecy -"

"This trifling is intolerable," interrupted Manfred. "Let us dismiss this silly wench, my Lord! we have more important affairs to discuss."

"By your favor," said Frederic, "these are no trifles. The enormous sabre I was directed to in the wood, yon casque, its fellow - are these visions of this poor maiden's brain?"

"So, Jaquez thinks, may it please your Greatness," said Bianca. "He says this moon will not be out without our seeing some strange revolution. For my part, I should not be surprised if it was to happen to-morrow; for, as I was saying, when I heard the clattering of armor, I was all in a cold sweat. I looked up, and, if your Greatness will believe me, I saw upon the uppermost banister of the great stairs a hand in armor as big as big. I thought I should have swooned. I never stopped until I came hither - would I were well out of this castle. My Lady Matilda told me but yester-morning that her Highness Hippolita knows something."

"Thou art an insolent!" cried Manfred. "Lord Marquis, it much misgives me that this scene is concerted to affront me. Are my own domestics suborned to spread tales injurious to my honor? Pursue your claim by manly daring; or let us bury our feuds, as was proposed, by the intermarriage of our children. But trust me, it ill becomes a Prince of your bearing to practice on mercenary wenches."

"I scorn your imputation," said Frederic. "Until this hour I never set eyes on this damsel: I have given her no jewel. My Lord, my Lord, your conscience, your guilt accuses you, and would throw the suspicion on me; but keep your daughter and think no more of Isabella. The judgments already fallen on your house forbid me matching into it."

Manfred, alarmed at the resolute tone in which Frederic delivered these words, endeavored to pacify him. Dismissing Bianca, he made such submissions to the Marquis, and threw in such artful encomiums on Matilda, that Frederic was once more staggered. However, as his passion was of so recent a date, it could not at once surmount the scruples he had conceived. He had gathered enough from Bianca's discourse to persuade him that heaven declared itself against Manfred.

The proposed marriages too removed his claim to a distance; and the principality of Otranto was a stronger temptation than the contingent reversion of it with Matilda. Still he would not absolutely recede from his engagements; but purposing to gain time, he demanded of Manfred if it was true in fact that Hippolita consented to the divorce. The Prince, transported to find no other obstacle, and depending on his influence over his wife, assured the Marquis it was so, and that he might satisfy himself of the truth from her own mouth.

As they were thus discoursing, word was brought that the banquet was prepared. Manfred conducted Frederic to the great hall, where they were received by Hippolita and the young Princesses. Manfred placed the Marquis next to Matilda and seated himself between his wife and Isabella. Hippolita comported herself with an easy gravity; but the young ladies were silent and melancholy. Manfred, who was determined to pursue his point with the Marquis in the remainder of the evening, pushed on the feast until it waxed late, affecting unrestrained gaiety, and plying Frederic with repeated goblets of wine. The latter, more upon his guard than Manfred wished, declined his frequent challenges, on pretense of his late loss of blood; while the Prince, to raise his own disordered spirits, and to counterfeit unconcern, indulged himself in plentiful draughts, though not to the intoxication of his senses.

The evening being far advanced, the banquet concluded. Manfred would have withdrawn with Frederic; but the latter pleading weakness and want of repose, retired to his chamber, gallantly telling the Prince that his daughter should amuse his Highness until himself could attend him. Manfred accepted the party, and to the no small grief of Isabella, accompanied her to her apartment. Matilda waited on her mother to enjoy the freshness of the evening on the ramparts of the castle.

Soon as the company were dispersed their several ways, Frederic, quitting his chamber, inquired if Hippolita was alone, and was told by one of her attendants, who had not noticed her going forth, that at that hour she generally withdrew to her oratory, where he probably would find her. The Marquis, during the repast, had beheld Matilda with increase of passion. He now wished to find Hippolita in the disposition her Lord had promised. The portents that had alarmed him were forgotten in his desires. Stealing softly and unobserved to the apartment of Hippolita, he entered it with a resolution to encourage her acquiescence to the divorce, having perceived that Manfred was resolved to make the possession of Isabella an unalterable condition, before he would grant Matilda to his wishes.

The Marquis was not surprised at the silence that reigned in the Princess's apartment. Concluding her, as he had been advertised, in her oratory, he passed on. The door was ajar; the evening gloomy and overcast. Pushing open the door gently, he saw a person kneeling before the altar. As he approached nearer, it seemed not a woman, but one in a long woolen weed, whose back was towards him. The person seemed absorbed in prayer. The Marquis was about to return, when the figure, rising, stood some moments fixed in meditation, without regarding him. The Marquis, expecting the holy person to come forth, and meaning to excuse his uncivil interruption, said,

"Reverend Father, I sought the Lady Hippolita."

"Hippolita!" replied a hollow voice; "camest thou to this castle to seek Hippolita?" and then the figure, turning slowly round, discovered to Frederic the fleshless jaws and empty sockets of a skeleton, wrapped in a hermit's cowl.

"Angels of grace protect me!" cried Frederic, recoiling.

"Deserve their protection!" said the Specter. Frederic, falling on his knees, adjured the phantom to take pity on him.

"Dost thou not remember me?" said the apparition. "Remember the wood of Joppa!"

"Art thou that holy hermit?" cried Frederic, trembling. "Can I do aught for thy eternal peace?"

"Wast thou delivered from bondage," said the specter, "to pursue carnal delights? Hast thou forgotten the buried sabre, and the behest of Heaven engraved on it?"

"I have not, I have not," said Frederic; "but say, blest spirit, what is thy errand to me? What remains to be done?"

"To forget Matilda!" said the apparition; and vanished.

Frederic's blood froze in his veins. For some minutes he remained motionless. Then falling prostrate on his face before the altar, he besought the intercession of every saint for pardon. A flood of tears succeeded to this transport; and the image of the beauteous Matilda rushing in spite of him on his thoughts, he lay on the ground in a conflict of penitence and passion. Ere he could recover from this agony of his spirits, the Princess Hippolita with a taper in her hand entered the oratory alone. Seeing a man without motion on the floor, she gave a shriek, concluding him dead. Her fright brought Frederic to himself. Rising suddenly, his face bedewed with tears, he would have rushed from her presence; but Hippolita stopping him, conjured him in the most plaintive accents to explain the cause of his disorder, and by what strange chance she had found him there in that posture.

"Ah, virtuous Princess!" said the Marquis, penetrated with grief, and stopped.

"For the love of Heaven, my Lord," said Hippolita, "disclose the cause of this transport! What mean these doleful sounds, this alarming exclamation on my name? What woes has heaven still in store for the wretched Hippolita? Yet silent! By every pitying angel, I adjure thee, noble Prince," continued she, falling at his feet, "to disclose the purport of what lies at thy heart. I see thou feelest for me; thou feelest the sharp pangs that thou inflictest - speak, for pity! Does aught thou knowest concern my child?"

"I cannot speak," cried Frederic, bursting from her. "Oh, Matilda!"

Quitting the Princess thus abruptly, he hastened to his own apartment. At the door of it he was accosted by Manfred, who flushed by wine and love had come to seek him, and to propose to waste some hours of the night in music and reveling. Frederic, offended at an invitation so dissonant from the mood of his soul, pushed him rudely aside, and entering his chamber, flung the door intemperately against Manfred, and bolted it inwards. The haughty Prince, enraged at this unaccountable behavior, withdrew in a frame of mind capable of the most fatal excesses. As he crossed the court, he was met by the domestic whom he had planted at the convent as a spy on Jerome and Theodore. This man, almost breathless with the haste he had made, informed his Lord that Theodore, and some lady from the castle were, at that instant, in private conference at the tomb of Alfonso in St. Nicholas's church. He had dogged Theodore thither, but the gloominess of the night had prevented his discovering who the woman was.

Manfred, whose spirits were inflamed, and whom Isabella had driven from her on his urging his passion with too little reserve, did not doubt but the inquietude she had expressed had been occasioned by her impatience to meet Theodore. Provoked by this conjecture, and enraged at her father, he hastened secretly to the great church. Gliding softly between the aisles and guided by an imperfect gleam of moonshine that shone faintly through the illuminated windows, he stole towards the tomb of Alfonso, to which he was directed by indistinct whispers of the persons he sought. The first sounds he could distinguish were—

"Does it, alas! depend on me? Manfred will never permit our union."

"No, this shall prevent it!" cried the tyrant, drawing his dagger, and plunging it over her shoulder into the bosom of the person that spoke.

"Ah, me, I am slain!" cried Matilda, sinking. "Good heaven, receive my soul!"

"Savage, inhuman monster, what hast thou done!" cried Theodore, rushing on him, and wrenching his dagger from him.

"Stop, stop thy impious hand!" cried Matilda; "it is my father!"

Manfred, waking as from a trance, beat his breast, twisted his hands in his locks, and endeavored to recover his dagger from Theodore to dispatch himself. Theodore, scarce less distracted, and only mastering the transports of his grief to assist Matilda, had now by his cries drawn some of the monks to his aid. While part of them endeavored, in concert with the afflicted Theodore, to stop the blood of the dying Princess, the rest prevented Manfred from laying violent hands on himself.

Matilda, resigning herself patiently to her fate, acknowledged with looks of grateful love the zeal of Theodore. Yet oft as her faintness would permit her speech its way, she begged the assistants to comfort her father. Jerome, by this time, had learnt the fatal news, and reached the church. His looks seemed to reproach Theodore, but turning to Manfred, he said,

"Now, tyrant! behold the completion of woe fulfilled on thy impious and devoted head! The blood of Alfonso cried to heaven for vengeance; and heaven has permitted its altar to be polluted by assassination, that thou mightest shed thy own blood at the foot of that Prince's sepulcher!"

"Cruel man!" cried Matilda, "to aggravate the woes of a parent; may heaven bless my father and forgive him as I do! My Lord, my gracious Sire, dost thou forgive thy child? Indeed, I came not hither to meet Theodore. I found him praying at this tomb, whither my mother sent me to intercede for thee, for her - dearest father, bless your child, and say you forgive her."

"Forgive thee! Murderous monster!" cried Manfred, "can assassins forgive? I took thee for Isabella; but heaven directed my bloody hand to the heart of my child. Oh, Matilda! - I cannot utter it - canst thou forgive the blindness of my rage?"

"I can, I do; and may heaven confirm it!" said Matilda; "but while I have life to ask it - oh! my mother! what will she feel? Will you comfort her, my Lord? Will you not put her away? Indeed, she loves you! Oh, I am faint! bear me to the castle. Can I live to have her close my eyes?"

Theodore and the monks besought her earnestly to suffer herself to be borne into the convent; but her instances were so pressing to be carried to the castle, that placing her on a litter, they conveyed her thither as she requested.

Theodore, supporting her head with his arm, and hanging over her in an agony of despairing love, still endeavored to inspire her with hopes of life. Jerome, on the other side, comforted her with discourses of heaven, and holding a crucifix before her, which she bathed with innocent tears, prepared her for her passage to immortality. Manfred, plunged in the deepest affliction, followed the litter in despair.

Ere they reached the castle, Hippolita, informed of the dreadful catastrophe, had flown to meet her murdered child; but when she saw the afflicted procession, the mightiness of her grief deprived her of her senses, and she fell lifeless to the earth in a swoon. Isabella and Frederic, who attended her, were overwhelmed in almost equal sorrow. Matilda alone seemed insensible to her own situation: every thought was lost in tenderness for her mother.

Ordering the litter to stop, as soon as Hippolita was brought to herself, she asked for her father. He approached, unable to speak. Matilda, seizing his hand and her mother's, locked them in her own, and then clasped them to her heart. Manfred could not support this act of pathetic piety. He dashed himself on the ground and cursed the day he was born. Isabella, apprehensive that these struggles of passion were more than Matilda could support, took upon herself to order Manfred to be borne to his apartment, while she caused Matilda to be conveyed to the nearest chamber. Hippolita, scarce more alive than her daughter, was regardless of everything but her; but when the tender Isabella's care would have likewise removed her, while the surgeons examined Matilda's wound, she cried,

"Remove me! never, never! I lived but in her and will expire with her."

Matilda raised her eyes at her mother's voice but closed them again without speaking. Her sinking pulse and the damp coldness of her hand soon dispelled all hopes of recovery. Theodore followed the surgeons into the outer chamber and heard them pronounce the fatal sentence with a transport equal to frenzy.

"Since she cannot live mine," cried he, "at least she shall be mine in death! Father! Jerome! will you not join our hands?" cried he to the Friar, who, with the Marquis, had accompanied the surgeons.

"What means thy distracted rashness?" said Jerome. "Is this an hour for marriage?"

"It is, it is," cried Theodore. "Alas! there is no other!"

"Young man, thou art too unadvised," said Frederic. "Dost thou think we are to listen to thy fond transports in this hour of fate? What pretensions hast thou to the Princess?"

"Those of a Prince," said Theodore; "of the sovereign of Otranto. This reverend man, my father, has informed me who I am."

"Thou ravest," said the Marquis. "There is no Prince of Otranto but myself, now Manfred, by murder, by sacrilegious murder, has forfeited all pretensions."

"My Lord," said Jerome, assuming an air of command, "he tells you true. It was not my purpose the secret should have been divulged so soon, but fate presses onward to its work. What his hot-headed passion has revealed, my tongue confirms. Know, Prince, that when Alfonso set sail for the Holy Land..."

"Is this a season for explanations?" cried Theodore. "Father, come and unite me to the Princess; she shall be mine! In every other thing I will dutifully obey you. My life! my adored Matilda!" continued Theodore, rushing back into the inner chamber, "will you not be mine? Will you not bless your..."

Isabella made signs to him to be silent, apprehending the Princess was near her end.

"What, is she dead?" cried Theodore; "is it possible!"

The violence of his exclamations brought Matilda to herself. Lifting up her eyes, she looked round for her mother.

"Life of my soul, I am here!" cried Hippolita; "think not I will quit thee!"

"Oh! you are too good," said Matilda. "But weep not for me, my mother! I am going where sorrow never dwells - Isabella, thou hast loved me; wouldst thou not supply my fondness to this dear, dear woman? Indeed, I am faint!"

"Oh! my child! my child!" said Hippolita in a flood of tears, "can I not withhold thee a moment?"

"It will not be," said Matilda; "commend me to heaven - Where is my father? forgive him, dearest mother - forgive him my death; it was an error. Oh! I had forgotten - dearest mother, I vowed never to see Theodore more - perhaps that has drawn down this calamity - but it was not intentional - can you pardon me?"

"Oh! wound not my agonizing soul!" said Hippolita; "thou never couldst offend me - Alas! she faints! help! help!"

"I would say something more," said Matilda, struggling, "but it cannot be – Isabella – Theodore - for my sake - Oh! -" she expired.

Isabella and her women tore Hippolita from the course; but Theodore threatened destruction to all who attempted to remove him from it. He printed a thousand kisses on her clay-cold hands and uttered every expression that despairing love could dictate.

Isabella, in the meantime, was accompanying the afflicted Hippolita to her apartment; but, in the middle of the court, they were met by Manfred, who, distracted with his own thoughts, and anxious once more to behold his daughter, was advancing to the chamber where she lay. As the moon was now at its height, he read in the countenances of this unhappy company the event he dreaded.

"What! is she dead?" cried he in wild confusion. A clap of thunder at that instant shook the castle to its foundations; the earth rocked, and the clank of more than mortal armor was heard behind. Frederic and Jerome thought the last day was at hand. The latter, forcing Theodore along with them, rushed into the court. The moment Theodore appeared, the walls of the castle behind Manfred were thrown down with a mighty force, and the form of Alfonso, dilated to an immense magnitude, appeared in the center of the ruins.

"Behold in Theodore the true heir of Alfonso!" said the vision: And having pronounced those words, accompanied by a clap of thunder, it ascended solemnly towards heaven, where the clouds parting asunder, the form of St. Nicholas was seen, and receiving Alfonso's shade, they were soon wrapped from mortal eyes in a blaze of glory.

The beholders fell prostrate on their faces, acknowledging the divine will. The first that broke silence was Hippolita.

"My Lord," said she to the desponding Manfred, "behold the vanity of human greatness! Conrad is gone! Matilda is no more! In Theodore we view the true Prince of Otranto. By what miracle he is so I know not - suffice it to us, our doom is pronounced! shall we not, can we but dedicate the few deplorable hours we have to live, in deprecating the further wrath of heaven? heaven ejects us - whither can we fly, but to yon holy cells that yet offer us a retreat."

"Thou guiltless but unhappy woman! unhappy by my crimes!" replied Manfred, "my heart at last is open to thy devout admonitions. Oh! Could - but it cannot be - ye are lost in wonder - let me at last do justice on myself! To heap shame on my own head is all the satisfaction I have left to offer to offended heaven. My story has drawn down these judgments: Let my confession atone - but, ah! what can atone for usurpation and a murdered child? a child murdered in a consecrated place? List, sirs, and may this bloody record be a warning to future tyrants!"

"Alfonso, ye all know, died in the Holy Land - ye would interrupt me; ye would say he came not fairly to his end - it is most true - why else this bitter cup which Manfred must drink to the dregs. Ricardo, my grandfather, was his chamberlain - I would draw a veil over my ancestor's crimes - but it is in vain! Alfonso died by poison. A fictitious will declared Ricardo his heir. His crimes pursued him - yet he lost no Conrad, no Matilda! I pay the price of usurpation for all! A storm overtook him. Haunted by his guilt he vowed to St. Nicholas to found a church and two convents, if he lived to reach Otranto. The sacrifice was accepted: the saint appeared to him in a dream, and promised that Ricardo's posterity should reign in Otranto until the rightful owner should be grown too large to inhabit the castle, and as long as issue male from Ricardo's loins should remain to enjoy it - alas! alas! nor male nor female, except myself, remains of all his wretched race! I have done - the woes of these three days speak the rest. How this young man can be Alfonso's heir I know not - yet I do not doubt it. His are these dominions; I resign them - yet I knew not Alfonso had an heir - I question not the will of heaven - poverty and prayer must fill up the woeful space, until Manfred shall be summoned to Ricardo."

"What remains is my part to declare," said Jerome. "When Alfonso set sail for the Holy Land he was driven by a storm to the coast of Sicily. The other vessel, which bore Ricardo and his train, as your Lordship must have heard, was separated from him."

"It is most true," said Manfred; "and the title you give me is more than an outcast can claim - well! be it so - proceed."

Jerome blushed, and continued. "For three months Lord Alfonso was wind-bound in Sicily. There he became enamored of a fair virgin named Victoria. He was too pious to tempt her to forbidden pleasures. They were married. Yet deeming this amour incongruous with the holy vow of arms by which he was bound, he determined to conceal their nuptials until his return from the Crusade, when he purposed to seek and acknowledge her for his lawful wife. He left her pregnant. During his absence she was delivered of a daughter. But scarce had she felt a mother's pangs ere she heard the fatal rumor of her Lord's death, and the succession of Ricardo. What could a friendless, helpless woman do? Would her testimony avail? - yet, my lord, I have an authentic writing -"

"It needs not," said Manfred; "the horrors of these days, the vision we have but now seen, all corroborate thy evidence beyond a thousand parchments. Matilda's death and my expulsion -"

"Be composed, my Lord," said Hippolita; "this holy man did not mean to recall your griefs." Jerome proceeded.

"I shall not dwell on what is needless. The daughter of which Victoria was delivered, was at her maturity bestowed in marriage on me. Victoria died; and the secret remained locked in my breast. Theodore's narrative has told the rest."

The Friar ceased. The disconsolate company retired to the remaining part of the castle. In the morning Manfred signed his abdication of the principality, with the approbation of Hippolita, and each took on them the habit of religion in the neighboring convents. Frederic offered his daughter to the new Prince, which Hippolita's tenderness for Isabella concurred to promote. But Theodore's grief was too fresh to admit the thought of another love; and it was not until after frequent discourses with Isabella of his dear Matilda, that he was persuaded he could know no happiness but in the society of one with whom he could forever indulge the melancholy that had taken possession of his soul.

THE END

VATHEK: AN ARABIAN TALE

BY WILLIAM BECKFORD, ESQ.

ABOUT THE AUHTOR

William Beckford (1760 – 1844), was born in 1760, and died in the spring of 1844, at the age of eighty-four years. His great-great-grandfather was lieutenant-governor and commander of the forces in Jamaica, and his grandfather president of the council in the same island. His father was a large landed proprietor, both in England and the West Indies, was lord mayor of London, and distinguished himself in presenting an address to the king, George the Third. When his grandfather died in 1770, he was the wealthiest commoner in England.

Besides Latin and Greek, he spoke five modern languages, read Persian and Arabic, and studied music under the great Mozart.

At the age of eighteen he visited Paris and was introduced to Voltaire. "On taking leave of me," said Beckford, "he placed his hand on my head, saying, 'There, young Englishman, I give you the blessing of a very old man.' Voltaire was a mere skeleton - a bony anatomy. His countenance I shall never forget."

Vathek, which Lord Byron so much admired, and on which he so frequently complimented the author, - Vathek, the finest of Oriental romances, as "Lallah Rookh" is the first of Oriental poems, by the pen of a "Frank," was written and published before our author had completed his twentieth year, it having been composed at a single sitting!

Vathek, was originally written in French and published in 1786. For splendor of description, exquisite humor, and supernatural interest and grandeur, it stands without a rival in romance. In as thoroughly Oriental keeping, Hope's, Anastasius, or Memoirs of a Modern Greek, which Beckford himself highly admired, can alone be compared with it.

Fonthill Abbey, which had been destroyed by fire, and re-built during the life-time of the elder Beckford, was demolished, and re-built again under the superintendence of our author himself, assisted by James Wyatt, Esq. at great expense for the time

The distinguishing architectural peculiarity of Fonthill Abbey, was a lofty tower, 280 feet in height. This tower was prominently shadowed forth in "Vathek," and shows how strong a hold the idea had upon his mind. During the progress of the building, the tower caught fire, and was partly destroyed. The owner, however, was present, and enjoyed the magnificent burning spectacle. It was soon restored; but a radical fault in laying the foundation, caused it eventually to fall down, and leave Fonthill a ruin in the lifetime of its founder.

Nearly fifty years after the publication of "Vathek," in 1835, Mr. Beckford published his, Recollections of an Excursion to the Monasteries of Alcobaca and Batalha, which he wrote in 1795, together with an epistolary record of his observations in Italy, Spain and Portugal, between the years 1780 and 1794.

After the sale of Fonthill, our author lived a considerable time in Portugal, and hence Lord Byron, who was fond of casting the shadow of his own imagination over every object, penned the well-known lines at Cintra:

There thou, too, Vathek, England's wealthiest son,
Once formed thy paradise; as not aware
Where wanton wealth her mightiest deeds hath done,
Meek peace, voluptuous lures, was ever wont to shun.
Here didst thou dwell; here scenes of pleasure plan,
Beneath yon mountain's ever beauteous brow;
But now, as if a thing unblest by man,
Thy fairy dwelling is as lone as thou!
Here giant weeds a passage scarce allow
To halls deserted; portals gaping wide
Fresh lessons to the thinking bosom; how
Vain are the pleasances on earth supplied,
Swept into wrecks anon by time's ungentle tide.

Vathek

The original of the following story, with some others of a similar kind, collected in the east by a man of letters, was communicated to the editor above three years ago. The pleasure he received from the perusal of it induced him at that time to transcribe, and since to translate it. How far the copy may be a just representation it becomes not him to determine. He presumes however to hope that if the difficulty of accommodating our English idioms to the Arabic, preserving the correspondent tones of a diversified narration, and discriminating the nicer touches of character through the shades of foreign manners be p. duly considered, a failure in some points will not preclude him from all claim to indulgence; especially if those images, sentiments, and passions, which being independent of local peculiarities, may be expressed in every language, shall be found to retain their native energy in our own.

Vathek, ninth Caliph of the race of the Abbasside's, was the son of Motassem, and the grandson of Haroun Al Raschid. From an early accession to the throne, and the talents he possessed to adorn it, his subjects were induced to expect that his reign would be long and happy. His figure was pleasing and majestic; but when he was angry, one of his eyes became so terrible that no person could bear to behold it; and the wretch upon whom it was fixed instantly fell backward, and sometimes expired. For fear, however, of depopulating his dominions, and making his palace desolate, he but rarely gave way to his anger.

Being much addicted to women, and the pleasures of the table, he sought by his affability to procure agreeable companions; and he succeeded the better, as his generosity was unbounded and his indulgences unrestrained; for he was by no means scrupulous: nor did he think, with the Caliph Omar Ben Abdalaziz, that it was necessary to make a hell of this world to enjoy Paradise in the next.

He surpassed in magnificence all his predecessors. The palace of Alkoremmi, which his father Motassem had erected on the hill of Pied Horses, and which commanded the whole city of Samarah, [8b] was in his idea far too scanty: he added, therefore, five wings, or rather other palaces, which he destined for the particular gratification of each of his senses.

In the first of these were tables continually covered with the most exquisite dainties, which were supplied both by night and by day according to their constant consumption; whilst the most delicious wines, and the choicest cordials, flowed forth from a hundred fountains, that were never exhausted. This palace was called "The Eternal, or Unsatiating Banquet."

The second was styled "The Temple of Melody, or the Nectar of the Soul." It was inhabited by the most skillful musicians and admired poets of the time, who not only displayed their talents within, but dispersing in bands without, caused every surrounding scene to reverberate their songs, which were continually varied in the most delightful succession.

The palace named "The Delight of the Eyes, or the Support of Memory," was one entire enchantment. Rarities collected from every corner of the earth were there found in such profusion as to dazzle and confound, but for the order in which they were arranged. One gallery exhibited the pictures of the celebrated Mani; and statues that seemed to be alive. Here a well-managed perspective attracted the sight; there, the magic of optics agreeably deceived it; whilst the naturalist, on his part, exhibited in their several classes the various gifts that heaven had bestowed on our globe. In a word, Vathek omitted nothing in this particular that might gratify the curiosity of those who resorted to it, although he was not able to satisfy his own; for he was, of all men, the most curious.

"The Palace of Perfumes," which was termed likewise, "The Incentive to Pleasure," consisted of various halls, where the different perfumes which the earth produces were kept perpetually burning in censers of gold. Flambeaus and aromatic lamps were here lighted in open day; but the too powerful effects of this agreeable delirium might be avoided by descending into an immense garden, where an assemblage of every fragrant flower diffused through the air the purest odors.

The fifth palace, denominated "The Retreat of Joy, or the Dangerous," was frequented by troops of young females, beautiful as the Houris, and not less seducing, who never failed to receive with caresses all whom the Caliph allowed to approach them; for he was by no means disposed to be jealous, as his own women were secluded within the palace he inhabited himself.

Notwithstanding the sensuality in which Vathek indulged, he experienced no abatement in the love of his people, who thought that a sovereign immersed in pleasure was not less tolerable to his subjects than one that employed himself in creating them foes. But the unquiet and impetuous disposition of the Caliph would not allow him to rest there: he had studied so much for his amusement in the life-time of his father as to acquire a great deal of knowledge, though not a sufficiency to satisfy himself; for he wished to know everything; even sciences that did not exist. He was fond of engaging in disputes with the learned but liked them not to push their opposition with warmth. He stopped the mouths of those with presents, whose mouths could be stopped; whilst others, whom his liberality was unable to subdue, he sent to prison to cool their blood; a remedy that often succeeded.

Vathek discovered also a predilection for theological controversy; but it was not with the orthodox that he usually held. By this means he induced the zealots to oppose him, and then persecuted them in return; for he resolved, at any rate, to have reason on his side.

The great prophet Mahomet, whose vicars the Caliphs are, beheld with indignation from his abode in the seventh heaven the irreligious conduct of such a vicegerent.

"Let us leave him to himself," said he to the Genii, who are always ready to receive his commands; "let us see to what lengths his folly and impiety will carry him; if he run into excess we shall know how to chastise him. Assist him, therefore, to complete the tower which, in imitation of Nimrod, he hath begun; not, like that great warrior, to escape being drowned, but from the insolent curiosity of penetrating the secrets of heaven: he will not divine the fate that awaits him."

The Genii obeyed; and when the workmen had raised their structure a cubit in the daytime, two cubits more were added in the night. The expedition with which the fabric arose was not a little flattering to the vanity of Vathek. He fancied that even insensible matter showed forwardness to subserve his designs; not considering that the successes of the foolish and wicked form the first rod of their chastisement.

His pride arrived at its height when, having ascended, for the first time, the eleven thousand stairs of his tower, he cast his eyes below and beheld men not larger than pismires; mountains than shells; and cities than beehives. The idea which such an elevation inspired of his own grandeur completely bewildered him; he was almost ready to adore himself; till lifting his eyes upwards, he saw the stars as high above him as they appeared when he stood on the surface of the earth. He consoled himself, however, for this transient perception of his littleness with the thought of being great in the eyes of the others, and flattered himself that the light of his mind would extend beyond the reach of his sight, and transfer to the stars the decrees of his destiny.

With this view the inquisitive prince passed most of his nights on the summit of his tower, till he became an adept in the mysteries of astrology, and imagined that the planets had disclosed to him the most marvelous adventures, which were to be accomplished by an extraordinary personage, from a country altogether unknown. Prompted by motives of curiosity, he had always been courteous to strangers; but from this instant he redoubled his attention, and ordered it to be announced by sound of trumpet, through all the streets of Samarah, that no one of his subjects, on peril of his displeasure, should either lodge or detain a traveler, but forthwith bring him to the palace.

Not long after this proclamation, there arrived in his metropolis, a man so hideous that the very guards who arrested him were forced to shut their eyes as they led him along. The Caliph himself appeared startled at so horrible a visage; but joy succeeded to this emotion of terror when the stranger displayed to his view such rarities as he had never before seen, and of which he had no conception.

In reality, nothing was ever so extraordinary as the merchandise this stranger produced. Most of his curiosities, which were not less admirable for their workmanship than their splendor, had besides, their several virtues described on a parchment fastened to each. There were slippers which enabled the feet to walk; knives that cut without the motion of a hand; sabers which dealt the blow at the person they were wished to strike; and the whole enriched with gems that were hitherto unknown.

The sabers, whose blades emitted a dazzling radiance, fixed more than all the Caliph's attention, who promised himself to decipher at his leisure the uncouth characters engraved on their sides. Without, therefore, demanding their price, he ordered all the coined gold to be brought from his treasury, and commanded the merchant to take what he pleased. The stranger complied with modesty and silence.

Vathek, imagining that the merchant's taciturnity was occasioned by the awe which his presence inspired, encouraged him to advance, and asked him, with an air of condescension, "Who he was? whence he came? and where he obtained such beautiful commodities?"

The man, or rather monster, instead of making a reply, thrice rubbed his forehead, which, as well as his body, was blacker than ebony; four times clapped his paunch, the projection of which was enormous; opened wide his huge eyes, which glowed like firebrands; began to laugh with a hideous noise, and discovered his long amber colored teeth bestreaked with green.

The Caliph, though a little startled, renewed his enquiries, but without being able to procure a reply. At which, beginning to be ruffled, he exclaimed, "knowest thou, varlet, who I am? and at whom thou art aiming thy gibes?" Then addressing his guards, "have ye heard him speak? is he dumb?"

"He hath spoken," they replied, "though but little."

"Let him speak then again," said Vathek, "and tell me who he is, from whence he came, and where he procured these singular curiosities, or I swear, by the ass of Balaam, that I will make him rue his pertinacity."

This menace was accompanied by the Caliph with one of his angry and perilous glances, which the stranger sustained without the slightest emotion, although his eyes were fixed on the terrible eye of the prince.

No words can describe the amazement of the courtiers, when they beheld this rude merchant withstand the encounter unshocked. They all fell prostrate with their faces on the ground, to avoid the risk of their lives, and continued in the same abject posture till the Caliph exclaimed in a furious tone:

> Up, cowards! seize the miscreant! see that he be committed to prison and guarded by the best of my soldiers! Let him, however, retain the money I gave him; it is not my intent to take from him his property, I only want him to speak.

No sooner had he uttered these words than the stranger was surrounded, pinioned with strong fetters, and hurried away to the prison of the great tower, which was encompassed by seven implements of iron bars, and armed with spikes in every direction, longer and sharper than spits.

The Caliph, nevertheless, remained in the most violent agitation. He sat down indeed to eat, but of the three hundred covers that were daily placed before him, could taste of no more than thirty-two.

A diet to which he had been so little accustomed, was sufficient of itself to prevent him from sleeping, what then must be its effect when joined to the anxiety that prayed upon his spirits? At the first glimpse of dawn he hastened to the prison, again to importune this intractable stranger; but the rage of Vathek exceeded all bounds on finding the prison empty, the gates burst asunder, and his guards lying lifeless around him. In the paroxysm of his passion he fell furiously on the poor carcasses and kicked them till evening without intermission. His courtiers and viziers exerted their efforts to soothe his extravagance, but finding every expedient ineffectual, they all united in one vociferation:

> The Caliph is gone mad! the Caliph is out of his senses!

This outcry, which was soon resounded through the streets of Samarah, at length reached the ears of Carathis, his mother: she flew in the utmost consternation to try her ascendency on the mind of her son. Her tears and caresses called off his attention; and he was prevailed upon by her entreaties to be brought back to the palace.

Carathis, apprehensive of leaving Vathek to himself, caused him to be put to bed; and seating herself by him, endeavored by her conversation to heal and compose him. Nor could anyone have attempted it with better success; for the Caliph not only loved her as a mother but respected her as a person of superior genius. It was she who had induced him, being a Greek herself, to adopt all the sciences and systems of her country, which good Mussulmans hold in such thorough abhorrence.

Judicial astrology was one of those systems in which Carathis was a perfect adept. She began, therefore, with reminding her son of the promise which the stars had made him; and intimated an intention of consulting them again.

"Alas!" sighed the Caliph, as soon as he could speak, "what a fool have I been! not for the kicks bestowed on my guards, who so tamely submitted to death, but for never considering that this extraordinary man was the same the planets had foretold; whom, instead of ill-treating, I should have conciliated by all the arts of persuasion."

"The past," said Carathis, "cannot be recalled; but it behooves us to think of the future: perhaps you may again see the object you so much regret: it is possible the inscriptions on the sabers will afford information. Eat, therefore, and take thy repose, my dear son. We will consider, to-morrow, in what manner to act."

Vathek yielded to her counsel as well as he could and arose in the morning with a mind more at ease. The sabers he commanded to be instantly brought; and poring upon them through a green glass, that their glittering might not dazzle, he set himself in earnest to decipher the inscriptions; but his reiterated attempts were all of them nugatory: in vain did he beat his head and bite his nails; not a letter of the whole was he able to ascertain. So unlucky a disappointment would have undone him again, had not Carathis, by good fortune, entered the apartment.

"Have patience, son!" said she. "You certainly are possessed of every important science, but the knowledge of languages is a trifle, at best; and the accomplishment of none but a pedant. Issue forth a proclamation that you will confer such rewards as become your greatness upon anyone that shall interpret what you do not understand, and what it is beneath you to learn. You will soon find your curiosity gratified."

"That may be," said the Caliph; "but in the mean time I shall be horribly disgusted by a crowd of smatterers, who will come to the trial as much for the pleasure of retailing their jargon as from the hope of gaining the reward. To avoid this evil, it will be proper to add that I will put every candidate to death who shall fail to give satisfaction; for, thank heaven, I have skill enough to distinguish between one that translates and one that invents."

"Of that I have no doubt," replied Carathis, "but to put the ignorant to death is somewhat severe and may be productive of dangerous effects. Content yourself with commanding their beards to be burnt beards, in a state, are not quite so essential as men."

The Caliph submitted to the reasons of his mother, and sending for Morakanabad, his prime vizier, said:

Let the common criers proclaim, not only in Samarah, but throughout every city
in my empire, that whosoever will repair hither, and decipher certain characters
which appear to be inexplicable, shall experience the liberality for which I am re-

nowned; but that all who fail upon trial shall have their beards burnt off to the last hair. Let them add also, that I will bestow fifty beautiful slaves, and as many jars of apricots from the isle of Kirmith, upon any man that shall bring me intelligence of the stranger.

The subjects of the Caliph, like their sovereign, being great admirers of women, and apricots from Kirmith, felt their mouths water at these promises, but were totally unable to gratify their hankering, for no one knew which way the stranger had gone.

As to the Caliph's other requisition the result was different: the learned, the half-learned, and those who were neither, but fancied themselves equal to both, came boldly to hazard their beards, and all shamefully lost them.

The exaction of these forfeitures, which found sufficient employment for the Eunuchs, gave them such a smell of singed hair as greatly to disgust the ladies of the seraglio, and make it necessary that this new occupation of their guardians should be transferred into other hands.

At length, however, an old man presented himself, whose beard was a cubit-and-a-half longer than any that had appeared before him. The officers of the palace whispered to each other, as they ushered him in:

What a pity such a beard should be burnt!

Even the Caliph, when he saw it, concurred with them in opinion; but his concern was entirely needless. This venerable personage read the characters with facility, and explained them verbatim, as follows:

"We were made where everything good is made; we are the least of the wonders of a place where all is wonderful; and deserving the sight of the first potentate on earth."

"You translate admirably!" cried Vathek. "I know to what these marvelous characters allude. Let him receive as many robes of honor, and thousands of sequins of gold, as he hath spoken words. I am in some measure relieved from the perplexity that embarrassed me!"

Vathek invited the old man to dine, and even to remain some days in the palace. Unluckily for him, he accepted the offer; for the Caliph having ordered him next morning to be called, said:

"Read again to me what you have read already; I cannot hear too often the promise that is made me, the completion of which I languish to obtain."

The old man forthwith put on his green spectacles; but they instantly dropped from his nose, on perceiving that the characters he had read the day preceding, had given place to others of different import.

"What ails you?" asked the Caliph; "and why these symptoms of wonder?"

"Sovereign of the world," replied the old man, "these sabers hold another language to-day, from that they yesterday held."

"How say you?" returned Vathek. "But it matters not! tell me, if you can, what they mean."

"It is this, my lord," rejoined the old man: "'Woe to the rash mortal who seeks to know that of which he should remain ignorant and to undertake that which surpasseth his power!'"

"And woe to thee!" cried the Caliph, in a burst of indignation: "to-day thou art void of understanding: begone from my presence, they shall burn but the half of thy beard, because thou wert yesterday fortunate in guessing. My gifts I never resume."

The old man, wise enough to perceive he had luckily escaped, considering the folly of disclosing so disgusting a truth, immediately withdrew, and appeared not again.

But it was not long before Vathek discovered abundant reason to regret his precipitation; for though he could not decipher the characters himself, yet, by constantly poring upon them, he plainly perceived that they every day changed; and unfortunately no other candidate offered to explain them. This perplexing occupation inflamed his blood, dazzled his sight, and brought on a giddiness and debility that he could not support. He failed not, however, though in so reduced a condition, to be often carried to his tower, as he flattered himself that he might there read in the stars, which he went to consult, something more congruous to his wishes. But in this his hopes were deluded; for his eyes, dimmed by the vapors of his head, began to subserve his curiosity so ill, that he beheld nothing but a thick dun cloud, which he took for the most direful of omens.

Agitated with so much anxiety, Vathek entirely lost all firmness; a fever seized him, and his appetite failed. Instead of being one of the greatest eaters, he became as distinguished for drinking. So insatiable was the thirst which tormented him, that his mouth, like a funnel, was always open to receive the various liquors that might be poured into it and especially cold water, which calmed him more than every other.

This unhappy prince being thus incapacitated for the enjoyment of any pleasure, commanded the palaces of the five senses to be shut up; forbore to appear in public, either to display his magnificence or administer justice; and retired to the inmost apartment of his harem. As he had ever been an indulgent husband, his wives, overwhelmed with grief at his deplorable situation, incessantly offered their prayers for his health, and unremittingly supplied him with water.

In the meantime, the Princess Carathis, whose affliction no words can describe, instead of restraining herself to sobbing and tears, was closeted daily with the Vizier Morakanabad, to find out some cure or mitigation of the Caliph's disease. Under the persuasion that it was caused by enchantment, they turned over together leaf by leaf, all the books of magic that might point out a remedy; and caused the horrible stranger, whom they accused as the enchanter, to be everywhere sought for with the strictest diligence.

At the distance of a few miles from Samarah stood a high mountain, whose sides were covered with wild thyme and basil, and its summit overspread with so delightful a plain that it might be taken for the Paradise destined for the faithful. Upon it grew a hundred thickets of eglantine and other fragrant shrubs; a hundred arbors of roses, jessamine, and honeysuckle; as many clumps of orange trees, cedar, and citron; whose branches, interwoven with the palm, the pomegranate, and the vine, presented every luxury that could regale the eye or the taste. The ground was strewed with violets, harebells, and pansies; in the midst of which sprung forth tufts of jonquils, hyacinths, and carnations, with every other perfume that impregnates the air. Four fountains, not less clear than deep, and so abundant as to slake the thirst of ten armies, seemed purposely placed here to make the scene more resemble the garden of Eden, which was watered by the four sacred rivers. Here the nightingale sang the birth of the rose, her well-beloved, and at the same time lamented its short-lived beauty; whilst the turtle deplored the loss of more substantial pleasures and the wakeful lark hailed the rising light that reanimates the whole creation. Here, more than anywhere, the mingled melodies of birds expressed the various passions they inspired; as if the exquisite fruits, which they pecked at pleasure, had given them a double energy.

To this mountain Vathek was sometimes brought, for the sake of breathing a purer air; and especially, to drink at will of the four fountains, which were reputed in the highest degree salubrious, and sacred to himself. His attendants were his mother, his wives, and some eunuchs, who assiduously employed themselves in filling capacious bowls of rock crystal, and emulously presenting them to him. But it frequently happened that his avidity exceeded their zeal; insomuch that he would prostrate himself upon the ground to lap up the water, of which he could never have enough.

One day when this unhappy prince had been long lying in so debasing a posture, a voice, hoarse but strong, thus addressed him:

"Why assumest thou the function of a dog, oh Caliph, so proud of thy dignity and power?"

At this apostrophe he raised up his head and beheld the stranger that had caused him so much affliction. Inflamed with anger at the sight, he exclaimed:

"Accursed Giaour! what comest thou hither to do? is it not enough to have transformed a prince, remarkable for his agility, into one of those leather barrels which the Bedouin Arabs carry on their camels when they traverse the deserts? Perceivest thou not that I may perish by drinking to excess, no less than by a total abstinence?"

"Drink then this draught," said the stranger, as he presented to him a phial of a red and yellow mixture; "and to satiate the thirst of thy soul as well as of thy body, know that I am an Indian, but from a region of India which is wholly unknown."

The Caliph, delighted to see his desires accomplished in part, and flattering himself with the hope of obtaining their entire fulfilment, without a moment's hesitation swallowed the potion, and instantaneously found his health restored, his thirst appeased, and his limbs as agile as ever.

In the transports of his joy, Vathek leaped upon the neck of the frightful Indian, and kissed his horrid mouth and hollow cheeks, as though they had been the coral lips, and the lilies and roses of his most beautiful wives; whilst they, less terrified than jealous at the sight, dropped their veils to hide the blush of mortification that suffused their foreheads.

Nor would the scene have closed here, had not Carathis, with all the art of insinuation, a little repressed the raptures of her son. Having prevailed upon him to return to Samarah, she caused a herald to precede him, whom she commanded to proclaim as loudly as possible:

"The wonderful stranger hath appeared again; he hath healed the Caliph; he hath spoken! he hath spoken!"

Forthwith all the inhabitants of this vast city quitted their habitations, and ran together in crowds to see the procession of Vathek and the Indian, whom they now blessed as much as they had before execrated, incessantly shouting,

"He hath healed our sovereign; he hath spoken! he hath spoken!"

Nor were these words forgotten in the public festivals, which were celebrated the same evening to testify the general joy, for the poets applied them as a chorus to all the songs they composed.

The Caliph, in the mean while caused the palaces of the senses to be again set open, and as he found himself prompted to visit that of taste, in preference to the rest, immediately ordered a splendid entertainment, to which his great officers and favorite courtiers were all invited. The Indian, who was placed near the prince, seemed to think that as a proper acknowledgment of so distinguished a privilege, he could neither eat, drink, nor talk too much. The various dainties were no sooner served up than they vanished, to the great mortification of Vathek, who piqued himself on being the greatest eater alive, and at this time in particular had an excellent appetite.

The rest of the company looked round at each other in amazement, but the Indian without appearing to observe it, quaffed large bumpers to the health of each of them: sung in a style altogether extravagant; related stories at which he laughed immoderately; and poured forth extemporaneous verses which would not have been thought bad, but for the strange grimaces with which they were uttered. In a word, his loquacity was equal to that of a hundred astrologers; he ate as much as a hundred porters and caroused in proportion.

The Caliph, notwithstanding the table had been thirty times covered, found himself incommoded by the voraciousness of his guest, who was now considerably declined in the prince's esteem. Vathek, however, being unwilling to betray the chagrin he could hardly disguise, said in a whisper to Bababalouk, the chief of his eunuchs:

"You see how enormous his performances in every way are; what would be the consequence should he get at my wives? Go! redouble your vigilance, and be sure look well to my Circassians, who would be more to his taste than all of the rest."

The bird of the morning had thrice renewed his song, when the hour of the divan sounded. Vathek, in gratitude to his subjects, having promised to attend, immediately arose from table and repaired thither leaning upon his vizier, who could scarcely support him, so disordered was the poor prince by the wine he had drank, and still more by the extravagant vagaries of his boisterous guest.

The viziers, the officers of the crown, and of the law, arranged themselves in a semi-circle about their sovereign, and preserved a respectful silence, whilst the Indian, who looked as cool as if come from a fast, sat down without ceremony on a step of the throne, laughing in his sleeve at the indignation with which his temerity had filled the spectators.

The Caliph, however, whose ideas were confused and his head embarrassed, went on administering justice at hap-hazard, till at length the prime vizier perceiving his situation, hit upon a sudden expedient to interrupt the audience, and rescue the honor of his master, to whom he said in a whisper:

"My lord, the princess Carathis, who hath passed the night in consulting the planets, informs you that they portend you evil; and the danger is urgent. Beware, lest this stranger whom you have so lavishly recompensed for his magical gewgaws, should make some attempt on your life: his liquor, which at first had the appearance of effecting your cure, may be no more than a poison of a sudden operation. Slight not this surmise; ask him, at least, of what it was compounded; whence he procured it; and mention the sabers, which you seem to have forgotten."

Vathek, to whom the insolent airs of the stranger became every moment less supportable, intimated to his vizier by a wink of acquiescence, that he would adopt his advice, and at once turning towards the Indian, said:

"Get up and declare in full divan of what drugs the liquor was compounded you enjoined me to take, for it is suspected to be poison; add also the explanation I have so earnestly desired concerning the sabers you sold me, and thus show your gratitude for the favors heaped on you."

Having pronounced these words in as moderate a tone as a Caliph well could, he waited in silent expectation for an answer; but the Indian, still keeping his seat, began to renew his loud shouts of laughter, and exhibit the same horrid grimaces he had shown them before, without vouchsafing a word in reply. Vathek, no longer able to brook such insolence, immediately kicked him from the steps, instantly descending repeated his blow, and persisted with such assiduity, as incited all who were present to follow his example. Every foot was aimed at the Indian, and no sooner had anyone given him a kick than he felt himself constrained to reiterate the stroke.

The stranger afforded them no small entertainment; for being both short and plump, he collected himself into a ball and rolled round on all sides at the blows of his assailants, who pressed after him wherever he turned, with an eagerness beyond conception, whilst their numbers were every moment increasing. The ball, indeed, in passing from one apartment to another, drew every person after it that came in its way, insomuch that the whole palace was thrown into confusion, and resounded with a tremendous clamor. The women of the harem, amazed at the uproar, flew to their blinds to discover the cause, but no sooner did they catch a glimpse of the ball than feeling themselves unable to refrain, they broke from the clutches of their eunuchs, who to stop their flight pinched them till they bled, but in vain; whilst themselves, though trembling with terror at the escape of their charge, were as incapable of resisting the attraction.

The Indian, after having traversed the halls, galleries, chambers, kitchens, gardens, and stables of the palace, at last took his course through the courts, whilst the Caliph, pursuing him closer than the rest, bestowed as many kicks as he possibly could, yet not without receiving now and then one, which his competitors, in their eagerness, designed for the ball.

Carathis, Morakanabad, and two or three old viziers whose wisdom had hitherto withstood the attraction, wishing to prevent Vathek from exposing himself in the presence of his subjects, fell down in his way to impede the pursuit, but he, regardless of their obstruction, leaped over their heads, and went on as before. They then ordered the muezzins to call the people to prayers, both for the sake of getting them out of the way, and of endeavoring by their petitions to avert the calamity; but neither of these expedients was a whit more successful. The sight of this fatal ball was alone sufficient to draw after it every beholder. The muezzins themselves, though they saw it but at a distance, hastened down from their minarets and mixed with the crowd, which continued to increase in so surprising a manner, that scarce an inhabitant was left in Samarah, except the aged, the sick confined to their beds, and infants at the breast, whose nurses could run more nimbly without them. Even Carathis, Morakanabad, and the rest, were all become of the party.

The shrill screams of the females who had broken from their apartments, and were unable to extricate themselves from the pressure of the crowd, together with those of the eunuchs jostling after them, terrified lest their charge should escape from their sight, increased by the execrations of husbands urging forward and menacing both, kicks given and received, stumbling and falling at every step, in a word, the confusion that universally prevailed, rendered Samarah like a city taken by storm, and devoted to absolute plunder.

At last the cursed Indian, who still preserved his rotundity of figure, after passing through all the streets and public places, and leaving them empty, rolled onwards to the plain of Catoul, and traversed the valley at the foot of the mountain of the four fountains.

As a continual fall of water had excavated an immense gulph in the valley, whose opposite side was closed in by a steep acclivity, the Caliph and his attendants were apprehensive lest the ball should bound into the chasm, and to prevent it, redoubled their efforts, but in vain. The Indian persevered in his onward direction, and as had been apprehended, glancing from the precipice with the rapidity of lightning, was lost in the gulph below.

Vathek would have followed the perfidious Giaour, had not an invisible agency arrested his progress. The multitude that pressed after him were at once checked in the same manner, and a calm instantaneously ensued. They all gazed at each other with an air of astonishment; and notwithstanding that the loss of veils and turbans, together with torn habits, and dust blended with sweat, presented a most laughable spectacle, there was not one smile to be seen; on the contrary, all with looks of confusion and sadness returned in silence to Samarah, and retired to their inmost apartments, without ever reflecting that they had been impelled by an invisible power into the extravagance for which they reproached themselves: for it is but just, that men who so often arrogate to their own merit the good of which they are but instruments, should attribute to themselves the absurdities which they could not prevent.

The Caliph was the only person that refused to leave the valley. He commanded his tents to be pitched there, and stationed himself on the very edge of the precipice, in spite of the representations of Carathis and Morakanabad, who pointed out the hazard of its brink giving way, and the vicinity to the magician that had so severely tormented him. Vathek derided all their remonstrances; and having ordered a thousand flambeaus to be lighted, and directed his attendants to proceed in lighting more, lay down on the slippery margin, and attempted, by the help of this artificial splendor, to look through that gloom which all the fires of the empyrean had been insufficient to pervade. One while he fancied to himself voices arising from the depth of the gulph, at another he seemed to distinguish the accents of the Indian, but all was no more than the hollow murmur of waters, and the din of the cataracts that rushed from steep to steep, down the sides of the mountain.

Having passed the night in this cruel perturbation, the Caliph at day-break retired to his tent, where, without taking the least sustenance, he continued to doze till the dusk of evening began to come on; he then resumed his vigils as before, and persevered in observing them for many nights together. At length, fatigued with so successless an employment, he sought relief from change. To this end he sometimes paced with hasty strides across the plain; and as he wildly gazed at the stars, reproached them with having deceived him; but lo! on a sudden the clear blue sky appeared streaked over with streams of blood, which reached from the valley even to the city of Samarah. As this awful phenomenon seemed to touch his tower, Vathek at first thought of repairing thither to view it more distinctly, but feeling himself unable to advance, and being overcome with apprehension, he muffled up his face in his robe.

Terrifying as these prodigies were, this impression upon him was no more than momentary, and served only to stimulate his love of the marvelous. Instead, therefore, of returning to his palace, he persisted in the resolution of abiding where the Indian vanished from his view. One night, however, while he was walking as usual on the plain, the moon and the stars at once were eclipsed, and a total darkness ensued. The earth trembled beneath him, and a voice came forth, the voice of the Giaour, who in accents more sonorous than thunder, thus addressed him: "Would'st thou devote thyself to me? adore then the terrestrial influences and abjure Mahomet. On these conditions I will bring thee to the palace of subterranean fire: there shalt thou behold, in immense depositories, the treasures which the stars have promised thee, and which will be conferred by those intelligences whom thou shalt thus render propitious. It was from thence I brought my sabers; and it is there that Soliman Ben Daoud reposes, surrounded by the talismans that control the world."

The astonished Caliph trembled as he answered, yet in a style that showed him to be no novice in preternatural adventures:

"Where art thou? Be present to my eyes; dissipate the gloom that perplexes me, and of which I deem thee the cause. After the many flambeaus I have burnt to discover thee, thou mayest at least grant a glimpse of thy horrible visage."

"Abjure then Mahomet," replied the Indian, "and promise me full proofs of thy sincerity; otherwise thou shalt never behold me again."

The unhappy Caliph, instigated by insatiable curiosity, lavished his promises in the utmost profusion. The sky immediately brightened; and by the light of the planets, which seemed almost to blaze, Vathek beheld the earth open, and at the extremity of a vast black chasm a portal of ebony, before which stood the Indian, still blacker, holding in his hand a golden key, that caused the lock to resound.

"How," cried Vathek, "can I descend to thee, without the certainty of breaking my neck? Come take me, and instantly open the portal."

"Not so fast," replied the Indian, "impatient Caliph! Know that I am parched with thirst and cannot open this door till my thirst be thoroughly appeased. I require the blood of fifty of the most beautiful sons of thy viziers and great men, or neither can my thirst nor thy curiosity be satisfied. Return to Samarah; procure for me this necessary libation; come back hither; throw it thyself into this chasm; and then shalt thou see!"

Having thus spoken, the Indian turned his back on the Caliph, who, incited by the suggestion of demons, resolved on the direful sacrifice. He now pretended to have regained his tranquility and set out for Samarah amidst the acclamations of a people who still loved him and forbore not to rejoice when they believed him to have recovered his reason. So successfully did he conceal the emotion of his heart, that even Carathis and Morakanabad were equally deceived with the rest. Nothing was heard of but festivals and rejoicings. The ball, which no tongue had hitherto ventured to mention, was again brought on the tapis. A general laugh went round; though many, still smarting under the hands of the surgeon, from the hurts received in that memorable adventure, had no great reason for mirth.

The prevalence of this gay humor was not a little grateful to Vathek, as perceiving how much it conduced to his project. He put on the appearance of affability to every one; but especially to his viziers, and the grandees of his court, whom he failed not to regale with a sumptuous banquet, during which he insensibly inclined the conversation to the children of his guests. Having asked, with a good-natured air, who of them were blessed with the handsomest boys, every father at once asserted the pretensions of his own; and the contest imperceptibly grew so warm, that nothing could have with-holden them from coming to blows but their profound reverence for the person of the Caliph. Under the pretense, therefore, of reconciling the disputants, Vathek took upon him to decide; and with this view commanded the boys to be brought.

It was not long before a troop of these poor children made their appearance, all equipped by their fond mothers with such ornaments as might give the greatest relief to their beauty, or most advantageously display the graces of their age. But whilst this brilliant assemblage attracted the eyes and hearts of everyone besides, the Caliph scrutinized each in his turn with a malignant avidity that passed for attention and selected from their number the fifty whom he judged the Giaour would prefer.

With an equal show of kindness as before, he proposed to celebrate a festival on the plain, for the entertainment of his young favorites, who he said ought to rejoice still more than all at the restoration of his health, on account of the favors he intended for them.

The Caliph's proposal was received with the greatest delight, and soon published through Samarah. Litters, camels, and horses were prepared. Women and children, old men and young - everyone placed himself in the station he chose. The cavalcade set forward, attended by all the confectioners in the city and its precincts. The populace, following on foot, composed an amazing crowd, and occasioned no little noise. All was joy; nor did any one call to mind what most of them had suffered when they first travelled the road they were now passing so gaily.

The evening was serene, the air refreshing, the sky clear, and the flowers exhaled their fragrance. The beams of the declining sun, whose mild splendor reposed on the summit of the mountain, shed a glow of ruddy light over its green declivity, and the white flocks sporting upon it. No sounds were audible, save the murmurs of the four fountains, and the reeds and voices of shepherds, calling to each other from different eminences.

The lovely innocents, proceeding to the destined sacrifice, added not a little to the hilarity of the scene. They approached the plain full of sportiveness; some coursing butterflies, others culling flowers, or picking up the shining little pebbles that attracted their notice. At intervals, they nimbly started from each other, for the sake of being caught again, and mutually imparting a thousand caresses.

The dreadful chasm, at whose bottom the portal of ebony was placed, began to appear at a distance. It looked like a black streak that divided the plain. Morakanabad and his companions took it for some work which the Caliph had ordered. Unhappy men! little did they surmise for what it was destined.

Vathek, not liking that they should examine it too nearly, stopped the procession, and ordered a spacious circle to be formed on this side, at some distance from the accursed chasm. The bodyguard of eunuchs was detached, to measure out the lists intended for the games, and prepare ringles for the lines to keep off the crowd. The fifty competitors were soon stripped and presented to the admiration of the spectators the suppleness and grace of their delicate limbs. Their eyes sparkled with a joy which those of their fond parents reflected. Everyone offered wishes for the little candidate nearest his heart and doubted not of his being victorious. A breathless suspense awaited the contest of these amiable and innocent victims.

The Caliph, availing himself of the first moment to retire from the crowd, advanced towards the chasm, and there heard, yet not without shuddering, the voice of the Indian, who, gnashing his teeth, eagerly demanded:

"Where are they? Where are they? perceivest thou not how my mouth waters?"

"Relentless Giaour!" answered Vathek, with emotion, "can nothing content thee but the massacre of these lovely victims? Ah! wert thou to behold their beauty, it must certainly move thy compassion."

"Perdition on thy compassion, babbler!" cried the Indian. "Give them me! instantly give them, or my portal shall be closed against thee forever!"

"Not so loudly," replied the Caliph, blushing.

"I understand thee," returned the Giaour, with the grin of an ogre: "thou wantest to summon up more presence of mind. I will for a moment forbear."

During this exquisite dialogue the games went forward with all alacrity, and at length concluded, just as the twilight began to overcast the mountains. Vathek, who was still standing on the edge of the chasm, called out with all his might:

"Let my fifty little favorites approach me, separately; and let them come in the order of their success. To the first I will give my diamond bracelet; to the second my collar of emeralds; to the third my aigret of rubies; to the fourth my girdle of topazes; and to the rest, each a part of my dress, even down to my slippers."

This declaration was received with reiterated acclamations; and all extolled the liberality of a prince who would thus strip himself for the amusement of his subjects and the encouragement of the rising generation.

The Caliph in the mean while undressed himself by degrees; and raising his arm as high as he was able, made each of the prizes glitter in the air; but, whilst he delivered it with one hand to the child, who sprang forward to receive it, he with the other pushed the poor innocent into the gulph, where the Giaour, with a sullen muttering, incessantly repeated "More! more!"

This dreadful device was executed with so much dexterity, that the boy who was approaching him remained unconscious of the fate of his forerunner; and as to the spectators, the shades of evening, together with their distance, precluded them from perceiving any object distinctly. Vathek, having in this manner thrown in the last of the fifty, and expecting that the Giaour on receiving him would have presented the key, already fancied himself as great as Soliman, and consequently above being amenable for what he had done; when, to his utter amazement, the chasm closed, and the ground became as entire as the rest of the plain.

No language could express his rage and despair. He execrated the perfidy of the Indian; loaded him with the most infamous invectives; and stamped with his foot as resolving to be heard. He persisted in this demeanor till his strength failed him, and then fell on the earth like one void of sense. His viziers and grandees, who were nearer than the rest, supposed him at first to be sitting on the grass at play with their amiable children; but at length, prompted by doubt, they advanced towards the spot, and found the Caliph alone, who wildly demanded what they wanted.

"Our children! our children!" cried they.

"It is assuredly pleasant," said he, "to make me accountable for accidents. Your children, while at play, fell from the precipice that was here; and I should have experienced their fate had I not been saved by a sudden start back."

At these words, the fathers of the fifty boys cried out aloud: the mothers repeated their exclamations an octave higher; whilst the rest, without knowing the cause, soon drowned the voices of both, with still louder lamentations of their own.

"Our Caliph," said they, and the report soon circulated, "Our Caliph has played us this trick, to gratify his accursed Giaour. Let us punish him for his perfidy! let us avenge ourselves! let us avenge the blood of the innocent! let us throw this cruel Prince into the gulph that is near, and let his name be mentioned no more!"

At this rumor, and these menaces, Carathis, full of consternation, hastened to Morakanabad, and said:

"Vizier, you have lost two beautiful boys, and must necessarily be the most afflicted of fathers; but you are virtuous; save your master!"

"I will brave every hazard," replied the Vizier, "to rescue him from his present danger; but afterwards will abandon him to his fate. Bababalouk," continued he, "put yourself at the head of your Eunuchs, disperse the mob, and if possible, bring back this unhappy Prince to his palace."

Bababalouk and his fraternity, felicitating each other in a low voice on their disability of ever being fathers, obeyed the mandate of the Vizier; who, seconding their exertions to the utmost of his power, at length accomplished his generous enterprise, and retired, as he resolved, to lament at his leisure.

No sooner had the Caliph re-entered his palace, than Carathis commanded the doors to be fastened; but perceiving the tumult to be still violent, and hearing the imprecations which resounded from all quarters, she said to her son:

"Whether the populace be right or wrong, it behooves you to provide for your safety: let us retire to your own apartment, and from thence, through the subterranean passage known only to ourselves, into your tower; there, with the assistance of the mutes who never leave it, we may be able to make some resistance. Bababalouk, supposing us to be still in the palace, will guard its avenues for his own sake; and we shall soon find, without the counsels of that blubberer Morakanabad, what expedient may be the best to adopt."

Vathek, without making the least reply, acquiesced in his mother's proposal, and repeated as he went:

"Nefarious Giaour! where art thou? hast thou not yet devoured those poor children? where are thy sabers? thy golden key? thy talismans?"

Carathis, who guessed from these interrogations a part of the truth, had no difficulty to apprehend in getting at the whole, as soon as he should be a little composed in his tower. This Princess was so far from being influenced by scruples that she was as wicked as woman could be, which is not saying a little, for the sex pique themselves on their superiority in every competition. The recital of the Caliph therefore occasioned neither terror nor surprise to his mother; she felt no emotion but from the promises of the Giaour; and said to her son:

"This Giaour, it must be confessed, is somewhat sanguinary in his taste, but the terrestrial powers are always terrible: nevertheless, what the one has promised, and the others can confer, will prove a sufficient indemnification. No crimes should be thought too dear for such a reward. Forbear then to revile the Indian: you have not fulfilled the conditions to which his services are annexed. For instance, is not a sacrifice to the subterranean Genii required? and should we not be prepared to offer it as soon as the tumult is subsided? This charge I will take on myself and have no doubt of succeeding by means of your treasures, which, as there are now so many others in store, may without fear be exhausted."

Accordingly, the Princess, who possessed the most consummate skill in the art of persuasion, went immediately back through the subterranean passage, and presenting herself to the populace from a window of the palace, began to harangue them with all the address of which she was mistress, whilst Bababalouk showered money from both hands amongst the crowd, who by these united means were soon appeased. Every person retired to his home, and Carathis returned to the tower.

Prayer at break of day was announced, when Carathis and Vathek ascended the steps which led to the summit of the tower, where they remained for some time, though the weather was lowering and wet. This impending gloom corresponded with their malignant dispositions; but when the sun began to break through the clouds, they ordered a pavilion to be raised as a screen from the intrusion of his beams. The Caliph, overcome with fatigue, sought refreshment from repose, at the same time hoping that significant dreams might attend on his slumbers; whilst the indefatigable Carathis, followed by a party of her mutes, descended to prepare whatever she judged proper for the oblation of the approaching night.

By secret stairs, known only to herself and her son, she first repaired to the mysterious recesses in which were deposited the mummies that had been brought from the catacombs of the ancient Pharaohs. Of these she ordered several to be taken. From thence she resorted to a gallery, where, under the guard of fifty female negroes, mute, and blind of the right eye, were preserved the oil of the most venomous serpents, rhinoceros' horns, and woods of a subtle and penetrating odor, procured from the interior of the Indies, together with a thousand other horrible rarities. This collection had been formed for a purpose like the present, by Carathis herself, from a presentiment that she might one day enjoy some intercourse with the infernal powers, to whom she had ever been passionately attached, and to whose taste she was no stranger.

To familiarize herself the better with the horrors in view, the Princess remained in the company of her negresses, who squinted in the most amiable manner from the only eye they had, and leered with exquisite delight at the skulls and skeletons which Carathis had drawn forth from her cabinets, whose key she entrusted to no one; all of them making contortions, and uttering a frightful jargon, but very amusing to the Princess till at last, being stunned by their gibbering, and suffocated by the potency of their exhalations, she was forced to quit the gallery, after stripping it of a part of its treasures.

Whilst she was thus occupied, the Caliph, who instead of the visions he expected, had acquired in these insubstantial regions a voracious appetite, was greatly provoked at the negresses: for, having totally forgotten their deafness, he had impatiently asked them for food; and seeing them regardless of his demand, he began to cuff, pinch, and push them, till Carathis arrived to terminate a scene so indecent, to the great content of these miserable creatures, who having been brought up by her, understood all her signs, and communicated in the same way their thoughts in return.

"Son! what means all this?" said she, panting for breath. "I thought I heard as I came up, the shrieks of a thousand bats, tearing from their crannies in the recesses of a cavern, and it was the outcry only of these poor mutes, whom you were so unmercifully abusing. In truth you but ill deserve the admirable provision I have brought you."

"Give it me instantly!" exclaimed the Caliph: "I am perishing for hunger!"

"As to that," answered she, "you must have an excellent stomach if it can digest what I have been preparing."

"Be quick," replied the Caliph. "But oh, heavens! what horrors! What do you intend?"

"Come, come," returned Carathis, "be not so squeamish, but help me to arrange everything properly, and you shall see that what you reject with such symptoms of disgust will soon complete your felicity. Let us get ready the pile for the sacrifice of tonight and think not of eating till that is performed. Know you not that all solemn rites are preceded by a rigorous abstinence?"

The Caliph, not daring to object, abandoned himself to grief, and the wind that ravaged his entrails, whilst his mother went forward with the requisite operations. Phials of serpents' oil, mummies, and bones were soon set in order on the balustrade of the tower. The pile began to rise; and in three hours was as many cubits high. At length, darkness approached, and Carathis having stripped herself to her inmost garment, clapped her hands in an impulse of ecstasy, and struck light with all her force. The mutes followed her example: but Vathek, extenuated with hunger and impatience, was unable to support himself, and fell down in a swoon. The sparks had already kindled the dry wood; the venomous oil burst into a thousand blue flames; the mummies, dissolving, emitted a thick dun vapor; and the rhinoceros' horns beginning to consume; all together diffused such a stench, that the Caliph, recovering, started from his trance and gazed wildly on the scene in full blaze around him. The oil gushed forth in a plentitude of streams; and the negresses, who supplied it without intermission, united their cries to those of the Princess. At last the fire became so violent, and the flames reflected from the polished marble so dazzling, that the Caliph, unable to withstand the heat and the blaze, effected his escape, and clambered up the imperial standard.

In the meantime, the inhabitants of Samarah, scared at the light which shone over the city, arose in haste, ascended their roofs, beheld the tower on fire, and hurried half-naked to the square. Their love to their sovereign immediately awoke; and apprehending him in danger of perishing in his tower, their whole thoughts were occupied with the means of his safety. Morakanabad flew from his retirement, wiped away his tears, and cried out for water like the rest. Bababa-louk, whose olfactory nerves were more familiarized to magical odors, readily conjecturing that Carathis was engaged in her favorite amusements, strenuously exhorted them not to be alarmed. Him, however, they treated as an old poltroon; and forbore not to style him a rascally traitor. The camels and dromedaries were advancing with water, but no one knew by which way to enter the tower. Whilst the populace was obstinate in forcing the doors, a violent east wind drove such a volume of flame against them, as at first forced them off; but afterwards, rekindled their zeal. At the p. 47same time, the stench of the horns and mummies increasing, most of the crowd fell backward in a state of suffocation. Those that kept their feet mutually wondered at the cause of the smell and admonished each other to retire. Morakanabad, sicker than the rest, remained in a piteous condition. Holding his nose with one hand, he persisted in his efforts with the other to burst open the doors and obtain admission. A hundred and forty of the strongest and most res-olute at length accomplished their purpose. Having gained the staircase by their violent exertions, they attained a great height in a quarter of an hour.

Carathis, alarmed at the signs of her mutes, advanced to the staircase, went down a few steps, and heard several voices calling out from below:

"You shall in a moment have water!"

Being rather alert, considering her age, she presently regained the top of the tower, and bade her son suspend the sacrifice for some minutes, adding:

"We shall soon be enabled to render it more grateful. Certain dolts of your subjects, imagining, no doubt, that we were on fire, have been rash enough to break through those doors, which had hitherto remained inviolate, for the sake of bringing up water. They are very kind, you must allow, so soon to forget the wrongs you have done them: but that is of little moment. Let us offer them to the Giaour. Let them come up: our mutes, who neither want strength nor experience, will soon dispatch them, exhausted as they are with fatigue."

"Be it so," answered the Caliph, "provided we finish, and I dine."

In fact, these good people, out of breath from ascending eleven thousand stairs in such haste, and chagrined at having spilt, by the way, the water they had taken, were no sooner arrived at the top than the blaze of the flames and the fumes of the mummies at once overpowered their senses. It was a pity! for they beheld not the agreeable smile with which the mutes and the negresses adjusted the cord to their necks: these amiable personages rejoiced, however, no less at the scene. Never before had the ceremony of strangling been performed with so much facility. They all fell without the least resistance or struggle; so that Vathek, in the space of a few moments, found himself surrounded by the dead bodies of his most faithful subjects, all of which were thrown on the top of the pile.

Carathis, whose presence of mind never forsook her, perceiving that she had carcasses sufficient to complete her oblation, commanded the chains to be stretched across the staircase, and the iron doors barricaded, that no more might come up.

No sooner were these orders obeyed, than the tower shook; the dead bodies vanished in the flames; which at once changed from a swarthy crimson to a bright rose color. An ambient vapor emitted the most exquisite fragrance; the marble columns rang with harmonious sounds, and the liquefied horns diffused a delicious perfume. Carathis, in transports, anticipated the success of her enterprise; whilst the mutes and negresses, to whom these sweets had given the cholic, retired to their cells grumbling.

Scarcely were they gone, when, instead of the pile, horns, mummies, and ashes, the Caliph both saw and felt, with a degree of pleasure which he could not express, a table, covered with the most magnificent repast: flagons of wine, and vases of exquisite sherbet, floating on snow. He availed himself, without scruple, of such an entertainment; and had already laid hands on a lamb stuffed with pistachios, whilst Carathis was privately drawing from a filigreed urn, a parchment that seemed to be endless; and which had escaped the notice of her son. Totally occupied, in gratifying an importunate appetite, he left her to peruse it, without interruption, which having finished, she said to him, in an authoritative tone,

"Put an end to your gluttony and hear the splendid promises with which you are favored!" She then read, as follows:

Vathek, my well-beloved, thou hast surpassed my hopes: my nostrils have been regaled by the savor of thy mummies, thy horns; and, still more, by the lives devoted on the pile. At the full of the moon, cause the bands of thy musicians, and thy tymbals, to be heard; depart from thy palace surrounded by all the pageants of majesty; thy most faithful slaves, thy best beloved wives; thy most magnificent litters; thy richest laden camels; and set forward on thy way to Istakar. There await I thy coming. That is the region of wonders. There shalt thou receive the diadem of Gian Ben Gian, the talismans of Soliman, and the treasures of the pre-Adamite Sultans: there shalt thou be solaced with all kinds of delight. But beware how thou enterest any dwelling on thy route, or thou shalt feel the effects of my anger.

The Caliph, who, notwithstanding his habitual luxury, had never before dined with so much satisfaction, gave full scope to the joy of these golden tidings, and betook himself to drinking anew. Carathis, whose antipathy to wine was by no means insuperable, failed not to supply a reason for every bumper, which they ironically quaffed to the health of Mahomet. This infernal liquor completed their impious temerity and prompted them to utter a profusion of blasphemies. They gave a loose to their wit, at the expense of the ass of Balaam, the dog of the seven sleepers, and the other animals admitted into the paradise of Mahomet. In this sprightly humor they descended the eleven thousand stairs, diverting themselves as they went at the anxious faces they saw on the square, through the oilets of the tower, and at length arrived at the royal apartments by the subterranean passage. Bababalouk was parading to and fro and issuing his mandates with great pomp to the eunuchs, who were snuffing the lights and painting the eyes of the Circassians. No sooner did he catch sight of the Caliph and his mother than he exclaimed,

Hah! you have then, I perceive, escaped from the flames; I was not, however, altogether out of doubt.

"Of what moment is it to us what you thought or think?" cried Carathis "go, speed, tell Morakanabad that we immediately want him; and take care how you stop by the way to make your insipid reflections."

Morakanabad delayed not to obey the summons and was received by Vathek and his mother with great solemnity. They told him with an air of composure and commiseration that the fire at the top of the tower was extinguished, but that it had cost the lives of the brave people who sought to assist them.

"Still more misfortunes!" cried Morakanabad with a sigh. "Ah, commander of the faithful, our holy prophet is certainly irritated against us! it behooves you to appease him."

"We will appease him hereafter," replied the Caliph, with a smile that augured nothing of good. "You will have leisure sufficient for your supplications during my absence; for this country is the bane of my health. I am disgusted with the mountain of the Four Fountains and am resolved to go and drink of the stream of Rocnabad. I long to refresh myself in the delightful valleys which it waters. Do you, with the advice of my mother, govern my dominions; and take care to supply whatever her experiments may demand; for you well know that our tower abounds in materials for the advancement of science."

The tower but ill-suited Morakanabad's taste. Immense treasures had been lavished upon it and nothing had he ever seen carried thither but female negroes, mutes, and abominable drugs. Nor did he know well what to think of Carathis, who like a chameleon could assume all possible colors. Her cursed eloquence had often driven the poor Mussulman to his last shifts. He considered, however, that if she possessed but few good qualities, her son had still fewer, and that the alternative, on the whole, would be in her favor. Consoled, therefore, with this reflection, he went in good spirits to soothe the populace, and make the proper arrangements for his master's journey.

Vathek, to conciliate the spirits of the subterranean palace, resolved that his expedition should be uncommonly splendid. With this view he confiscated on all sides the property of his subjects, whilst his worthy mother stripped the seraglios, she visited of the gems they contained. She collected all the seamstresses and embroiderers of Samarah, and other cities, to the distance of sixty leagues, to prepare pavilions, palanquins, sofas, canopies, and litters, for the train of the monarch. There was not left in Masulipatan a single piece of chintz; and so much muslin had been bought up to dress out Bababalouk and the other black eunuchs, that there remained not an ell in the whole Irak of Babylon.

During these preparations, Carathis, who never lost sight of her great object, which was to obtain favor with the powers of darkness, made select parties of the fairest and most delicate ladies of the city; but in the midst of their gaiety she contrived to introduce serpents amongst them, and to break pots of scorpions under the table. They all bit to a wonder, and Carathis would have left them to bite, were it not that to fill up the time, she now and then amused herself in curing their wounds with an excellent anodyne of her own invention; for this good princess abhorred being indolent.

Vathek, who was not altogether so active as his mother, devoted his time to the sole gratification of his senses, in the palaces which were severally dedicated to them. He disgusted himself no more with the divan or the mosque. One half of Samarah followed his example, whilst the other lamented the progress of corruption.

In the midst of these transactions, the embassy returned which had been sent in pious times to Mecca. It consisted of the most reverend mullahs, who had fulfilled their commission, and brought back one of those precious besoms which are used to sweep the sacred Kaaba; a present truly worthy of the greatest potentate on earth!

The Caliph happened at this instant to be engaged in an apartment by no means adapted to the reception of embassies, though adorned with a certain magnificence, not only to render it agreeable, but also because he resorted to it frequently, and staid a considerable time together. Whilst occupied in this retreat, he heard the voice of Bababalouk calling out from between the door and the tapestry that hung before it:

Here are the excellent Mahomet Ebn Edris al Shafei, and the seraphic Al Mou-hadethin, who have brought the besom from Mecca, and with tears of joy entreat they may present it to your majesty in person.

"Let them bring the besom hither, it may be of use," said Vathek, who was still employed, not having quite racked off his wine.

"How!" answered Bababalouk, half aloud and amazed.

"Obey," replied the Caliph, "for it is my sovereign will; go instantly! vanish! for here will I receive the good folk who have thus filled thee with joy."

The eunuch departed muttering, and bade the venerable train attend him. A sacred rapture was diffused amongst these reverend old men. Though fatigued with the length of their expedition, they followed Bababalouk with an alertness almost miraculous, and felt themselves highly flattered as they swept along the stately porticos, that the Caliph would not receive them like ambassadors in ordinary, in his hall of audience. Soon reaching the interior of the harem (where, through blinds of Persian they perceived large soft eyes, dark and blue, that went and came like lightning) penetrated with respect and wonder, and full of their celestial mission, they advanced in procession towards the small corridors that appeared to terminate in nothing, but nevertheless led to the cell where the Caliph expected their coming.

"What! is the commander of the faithful sick?" said Ebn Edris al Shafei, in a low voice to his companion.

"I rather think he is in his oratory," answered Al Mouhadethin.

Vathek, who heard the dialogue, cried out "What imports it you how I am employed? approach without delay."

They advanced, and Bababalouk almost sunk with confusion, whilst the Caliph, without showing himself, put forth his hand from behind the tapestry that hung before the door, and demanded of them the besom.

Having prostrated themselves as well as the corridor would permit, and even in a tolerable semi-circle, the venerable Al Shafei, drawing forth the besom from the embroidered and perfumed scarfs in which it had been enveloped, and secured from the profane gaze of vulgar eyes, arose from his associates and advanced with an air of the most awful solemnity towards the supposed oratory; but with what astonishment! with what horror was he seized!

Vathek, bursting out into a villainous laugh, snatched the besom from his trembling hand, and fixing upon it some cobwebs that hung suspended from the ceiling, gravely brushed away till not a single one remained.

The old men, overpowered with amazement, were unable to lift their beards from the ground; for as Vathek had carelessly left the tapestry between them half drawn, they were witnesses to the whole transaction. Their tears gushed forth on the marble. Al Mouhadethin swooned through mortification and fatigue, whilst the Caliph, throwing himself backward on his seat, shouted and clapped his hands without mercy. At last, addressing himself to Bababalouk:

"My dear black," said he, "go, regale these pious poor souls with my good wine from Shiraz; and as they can boast of having seen more of my palace than any one besides, let them also visit my office courts, and lead them out by the back steps that go to my stables." Having said this, he threw the besom in their face, and went to enjoy the laugh with Carathis.

Bababalouk did all in his power to console the ambassadors, but the two most infirm expired on the spot; the rest were carried to their beds, from whence, being heart-broken with sorrow and shame, they never arose.

The succeeding night, Vathek, attended by his mother, ascended the tower to see if everything were ready for his journey, for he had great faith in the influence of the stars. The planets appeared in their most favorable aspects. The Caliph, to enjoy so flattering a sight, supped gaily on the roof, and fancied that he heard, during his repast, loud shouts of laughter resound through the sky, in a manner that inspired the fullest assurance.

All was in motion at the palace; lights were kept burning through the whole of the night; the sound of implements, and of artisans finishing their work; the voices of women and their guardians who sung at their embroidery; all conspired to interrupt the stillness of nature, and infinitely delight the heart of Vathek, who imagined himself going in triumph to sit upon the throne of Soliman.

The people were not less satisfied than himself; all assisted to accelerate the moment which should rescue them from the wayward caprices of so extravagant a master.

The day preceding the departure of this infatuated prince was employed by Carathis in repeating to him the decrees of the mysterious parchment, which she had thoroughly gotten by heart; and in recommending him not to enter the habitation of any one by the way; "for well thou knowest," added she, "how liquorish thy taste is after good dishes and young damsels; let me therefore enjoin thee to be content with thy old cooks, who are the best in the world; and not to forget that in thy ambulatory seraglio there are three dozen pretty faces, which Bababalouk hath not yet unveiled. I, myself, have a great desire to watch over thy conduct, and visit the subterranean palace, which no doubt contains whatever can interest persons like us. There is nothing so pleasing as retiring to caverns; my taste for dead bodies and everything like mummy is decided; and I am confident thou wilt see the most exquisite of their kind. Forget me not then, but the moment thou art in possession of the talismans which are to open to thee the mineral kingdoms, and the center of the earth itself, fail not to dispatch some trusty genius to take me and my cabinet, for the oil of the serpents I have pinched to death will be a pretty present to the Giaour, who cannot but be charmed with such dainties."

Scarcely had Carathis ended this edifying discourse, when the sun, setting behind the mountain of the Four Fountains, gave place to the rising moon. This planet being that evening at full, appeared of unusual beauty and magnitude in the eyes of the women, the eunuchs, and the pages, who were all impatient to set forward. The city re-echoed with shouts of joy and flourishing of trumpets. Nothing was visible but plumes nodding on pavilions, and aigrettes shining in the mild luster of the moon. The spacious square resembled an immense parterre, variegated with the most stately tulips of the east.

Arrayed in the robes which were only worn at the most distinguished ceremonials, and supported by his vizier and Bababalouk, the Caliph descended the grand staircase of the tower in the sight of all his people. He could not forbear pausing at intervals to admire the superb appearance which everywhere courted his view, whilst the whole multitude, even to the camels with their sumptuous burdens, knelt down before him. For some time, a general stillness prevailed, which nothing happened to disturb, but the shrill screams of some eunuchs in the rear. These vigilant guards having remarked certain cages of the ladies swaging somewhat awry and discovered that a few adventurous gallants had contrived to get in, soon dislodged the enraptured culprits, and consigned them with good commendations, to the surgeons of the serail. The majesty of so magnificent a spectacle was not, however, violated by incidents like these. Vathek, meanwhile, saluted the moon with an idolatrous air, that neither pleased Morakanabad nor the doctors of the law, any more than the viziers and grandees of his court, who were all assembled to enjoy the last view of their sovereign.

At length the clarions and trumpets from the top of the tower announced the prelude of departure. Though the instruments were in unison with each other, yet a singular dissonance was blended with their sounds. This proceeded from Carathis, who was singing her direful orisons to the Giaour, whilst the negresses and mutes supplied thorough bass without articulating a word. The good Mussulmans fancied that they heard the sullen hum of those nocturnal insects which presage evil, and importuned Vathek to beware how he ventured his sacred person.

On a given signal the great standard of the Caliphate was displayed; twenty thousand lances shone around it; and the Caliph, treading royally on the cloth of gold which had been spread for his feet, ascended his litter amidst the general awe that possessed his subjects.

The expedition commenced with the utmost order, and so entire a silence, that even the locusts were heard from the thickets on the plain of Catoul. Gaiety and good humor prevailing, six good leagues were past before the dawn; and the morning star was still glittering in the firmament when the whole of this numerous train had halted on the banks of the Tigris, where they encamped to repose for the rest of the day.

The three days that followed were spent in the same manner, but on the fourth the heavens looked angry, lightnings broke forth in frequent flashes, re-echoing peals of thunder succeeded, and the trembling Circassians clung with all their might to their ugly guardians. The Caliph himself was greatly inclined to take shelter in the large town of Gulchissar, the governor of which came forth to meet him, and tendered every kind of refreshment the place could supply. But having examined his tablets, he suffered the rain to soak him almost to the bone, notwithstanding the importunity of his first favorites. Though he began to regret the palace of the senses, yet he lost not sight of his enterprise, and his sanguine expectations confirmed his resolution. His geographers were ordered to attend him, but the weather proved so terrible, that these poor people exhibited a lamentable appearance; and as no long journeys had been undertaken since the time of Haroun al Raschid, their maps of the different countries were in a still worse plight than themselves. Everyone was ignorant which way to turn; for Vathek, though well versed in the course of the heavens, no longer knew his situation on earth. He thundered even louder than the elements and muttered forth certain hints of the bowstring which were not very soothing to literary ears. Disgusted at the toilsome weariness of the way, he determined to cross over the craggy heights, and follow the guidance of a peasant, who undertook to bring him, in four days, to Rocnabad. Remonstrances were all to no purpose, his resolution was fixed, and an invasion commenced on the province of the goats, who sped away in large troops before them. It was curious to view on these half-calcined rocks camels richly caparisoned, and pavilions of gold and silk waving on their summits, which till then had never been covered, but with sapless thistles and fern.

The females and eunuchs uttered shrill wailings at the sight of the precipices below them, and the dreary prospects that opened in the vast gorges of the mountains. Before they could reach the ascent of the steepest rock night overtook them, and a boisterous tempest arose, which having rent the awnings of the palanquins and cages, exposed to the raw gusts the poor ladies within, who had never before felt so piercing a cold. The dark clouds that overcast the face of the sky deepened the horrors of this disastrous night, insomuch that nothing could be heard distinctly but the mewling of pages, and lamentations of sultanas.

To increase the general misfortune, the frightful uproar of wild beasts resounded at a distance, and there were soon perceived in the forest they were skirting the glaring of eyes which could belong only to devils or tigers. The pioneers, who as well as they could, had marked out a track, and a part of the advanced guard were devoured before they had been in the least apprised of their danger. The confusion that prevailed was extreme. Wolves, tigers, and other carnivorous animals, invited by the howling of their companions, flocked together from every quarter. The crushing of bones was heard on all sides, and a fearful rush of wings overhead, for now vultures also began to be of the party.

The terror at length reached the main body of the troops which surrounded the monarch and his harem, at the distance of two leagues from the scene. Vathek (voluptuously reposed in his capacious litter upon cushions of silk, with two little pages beside him, of complexions more fair than the enamel of Franguestan, who were occupied in keeping off flies) was soundly asleep, and contemplating in his dreams the treasures of Soliman. The shrieks, however, of his wives awoke him with a start, and instead of the Giaour with his key of gold, he beheld Bababalouk full of consternation.

"Sire," exclaimed this good servant of the most potent of monarchs, "misfortune has arrived at its height; wild beasts, who entertain no more reverence for your sacred person than for that of a dead ass, have beset your camels and their drivers: thirty of the richest laden are already become their prey, as well as all your confectioners, your cooks, and purveyors, and unless our holy prophet should protect us, we shall have all eaten our last meal."

At the mention of eating, the Caliph lost all patience. He began to bellow, and even beat himself, for there was no seeing in the dark. The rumor every instant increased, and Bababalouk finding no good could be done with his master stopped both his ears against the hurly-burly of the harem, and called out aloud:

"Come, ladies and brothers! all hands to work! strike light in a moment! never shall it be said that the commander of the faithful served to regale these infidel brutes."

Though there wanted not in this bevy of beauties a sufficient number of capricious and wayward, yet, on the present occasion they were all compliance. Fires were visible in a twinkling in all their cages. Ten thousand torches were lighted at once. The Caliph himself seized a large one of wax; every person followed his example; and by kindling ropes ends dipped in oil and fastened on poles, an amazing blaze was spread. The rocks were covered with the splendor of sunshine. The trails of sparks wafted by the wind, communicated to the dry fern, of which there was plenty. Serpents were observed to crawl forth from their retreats with amazement and hissings, whilst the horses snorted, stamped the ground, tossed their noses in the air, and plunged about without mercy.

One of the forests of cedar that bordered their way took fire, and the branches that overhung the path extending their flames to the muslins and chintzes which covered the cages of the ladies, obliged them to jump out at the peril of their necks. Vathek, who vented on the occasion a thousand blasphemies, was himself compelled to touch with his sacred feet the naked earth.

Never had such an incident happened before. Full of mortification, shame and despondence, and not knowing how to walk, the ladies fell into the dirt.

"Must I go on foot," said one.

"Must I wet my feet," cried another.

"Must I soil my dress," asked a third.

"Execrable Bababalouk," exclaimed all; "Outcast of hell! what hadst thou to do with torches? Better were it to be eaten by tigers than to fall into our present condition; we are forever undone. Not a porter is there in the army, nor a currier of camels but hath seen some part of our bodies, and what is worse, our very faces!"

On saying this, the most bashful amongst them hid their foreheads on the ground, whilst such as had more boldness flew at Bababalouk, but he, well apprised of their humor, and not wanting in shrewdness, betook himself to his heels along with his comrades, all dropping their torches and striking their tymbals.

It was not less light than in the brightest of the dogdays, and the weather was hot in proportion; but how degrading was the spectacle, to behold the Caliph bespattered like an ordinary mortal! As the exercise of his faculties seemed to be suspended, one of his Ethiopian wives (for he delighted in variety) clasped him in her arms, threw him upon her shoulder like a sack of dates, and finding that the fire was hemming them in, set off with no small expedition, considering the weight of her burden. The other ladies who had just learned the use of their feet followed her; their guards galloped after; and the camel drivers brought up the rear as fast as their charge would permit.

They soon reached the spot where the wild beasts had commenced the carnage, and which they had too much spirit to leave, notwithstanding the approaching tumult, and the luxurious supper they had made. Bababalouk nevertheless seized on a few of the plumpest, which were unable to budge from the place, and began to flay them with admirable adroitness. The cavalcade being got so far from the conflagration as that the heat felt rather grateful than violent, it was immediately resolved on to halt. The tattered chintzes were picked up; the scraps left by the wolves and tigers interred; and vengeance was taken on some dozens of vultures that were too much glutted to rise on the wing. The camels which had been left unmolested to make sal-ammoniac being numbered, and the ladies once more enclosed in their cages, the imperial tent was pitched on the level ground they could find.

Vathek, reposing upon a mattress of down, and tolerably recovered from the jolting of the Ethiopian, who, to his feelings seemed the roughest trotting jade he had hitherto mounted, called out for something to eat; but alas! those delicate cakes which had been baked in silver ovens for his royal mouth, those rich manchets, amber comfits, flagons of Shiraz wine, porcelain vases of snow, and grapes from the banks of the Tigris, were all irremediably lost; and nothing had Bababalouk to present in their stead, but a roasted wolf, vultures à la daube, aromatic herbs of the most acrid poignancy, rotten truffles, boiled thistles, and such other wild plants as must ulcerate the throat and parch up the tongue. Nor was he better provided in the article of drink, for he could procure nothing to accompany these irritating viands but a few phials of abominable brandy, which had been secreted by the scullions in their slippers.

Vathek made wry faces at so savage a repast, and Bababalouk answered them with shrugs and contortions. The Caliph however ate with tolerable appetite and fell into a nap that lasted six hours. The splendor of the sun, reflected from the white cliffs of the mountains in spite of the curtains that enclosed him, at length disturbed his repose. He awoke terrified and stung to the quick by those wormwood-colored flies which emit from their wings a suffocating stench. The miserable monarch was perplexed how to act, though his wits were not idle in seeking expedients, whilst Bababalouk lay snoring amidst a swarm of those insects, that busily thronged to pay court to his nose. The little pages, famished with hunger, had dropped their fans on the ground, and exerted their dying voices in bitter reproaches on the Caliph, who now for the first time heard the language of truth. Thus stimulated, he renewed his imprecations against the Giaour, and bestowed upon Mahomet some soothing expressions.

"Where am I?" cried he; "What are these dreadful rocks; these valleys of darkness? Are we arrived at the horrible Kaf? Is the Simurgh coming to pluck out my eyes as a punishment for undertaking this impious enterprise?"

Having said this, he bellowed like a calf, and turned himself towards an outlet in the side of his pavilion. But alas! what objects occurred to his view! on one side a plain of black sand that appeared to be unbounded, and on the other perpendicular crags bristled over with those abominable thistles which had so severely lacerated his tongue. He fancied, however, that he perceived amongst the brambles and briars some gigantic flowers, but was mistaken, for these were only the dangling palampores and variegated tatters of his gay retinue. As there were several clefts in the rock from whence water seemed to have flowed, Vathek applied his ear with the hope of catching the sound of some latent runnel, but could only distinguish the low murmurs of his people, who were repining at their journey, and complaining for the want of water.

"To what purpose," asked they, "have we been brought hither? Hath our Caliph another tower to build? or have the relentless Afrits whom Carathis so much loves, fixed in this place their abode?"

At the name of Carathis, Vathek recollected the tablets he had received from his mother, who assured him they were fraught with preternatural qualities, and advised him to consult them as emergencies might require. Whilst he was engaged in turning them over, he heard a shout of joy, and a loud clapping of hands. The curtains of his pavilion were soon drawn back, and he beheld Bababalouk, followed by a troop of his favorites, conducting two dwarfs, each a cubit high, who brought between them a large basket of melons, oranges, and pomegranates. They were singing in the sweetest tones the words that follow:

"We dwell on the top of these rocks, in a cabin of rushes and canes; the eagles envy us our nest; a small spring supplies us with abdest, and we daily repeat prayers which the prophet approves. We love you, O commander of the faithful! our master, the good emir Fakhreddin, loves you also; he reveres in your person the vicegerent of Mahomet. Little as we are, in us he confides; he knows our hearts to be good, as our bodies are contemptible, and hath placed us here to aid those who are bewildered on these dreary mountains. Last night, whilst we were occupied within our cell in reading the holy Koran, a sudden hurricane blew out our lights and rocked our habitation. For two whole hours a palpable darkness prevailed: but we heard sounds at a distance which we conjectured to proceed from the bells of a cafila, passing over the rocks. Our ears were soon filled with deplorable shrieks, frightful roaring, and the sound of tymbals. Chilled with terror, we concluded that the Deggial with his exterminating angels had sent forth their plagues on the earth. In the midst of these melancholy reflections, we perceived flames of the deepest red glow in the horizon and found ourselves in a few moments covered with flakes of fire. Amazed at so strange an appearance, we took up the volume dictated by the blessed intelligence, and kneeling by the light of the fire that surrounded us, we recited the verse which says: 'Put no trust in anything but the mercy of heaven; there is no help save in the holy prophet; the mountain of Kaf itself may tremble; it is the power of Allah only that cannot be moved.' After having pronounced these words, we felt consolation, and our minds were hushed into a sacred repose. Silence ensued, and our ears clearly distinguished a voice in the air, saying: 'Servants of my faithful servant, go down to the happy valley of Fakhreddin; tell him that an illustrious opportunity now offers to satiate the thirst of his hospitable heart. The commander of true believers is this day bewildered amongst these mountains and stands in need of thy aid.' We obeyed with joy the angelic mission, and our master, filled with pious zeal, hath culled with his own hands these melons, oranges, and pomegranates. He is following us with a hundred dromedaries laden with the purest waters of his fountains, and is coming to kiss the fringe of your consecrated robe, and implore you to enter his humble habitation, which, placed amidst these barren wilds, resembles an emerald set in lead."

The dwarfs having ended their address, remained still standing, and with hands crossed upon their bosoms, preserved a respectful silence.

Vathek, in the midst of this curious harangue seized the basket, and long before it was finished, the fruits had dissolved in his mouth. As he continued to eat, his piety increased, and in the same breath which recited his prayers, he called for the Koran and sugar.

Such was the state of his mind when the tablets, which were thrown by at the approach of the dwarfs, again attracted his eye. He took them up but was ready to drop on the ground when he beheld, in large red characters, these words inscribed by Carathis, which were indeed enough to make him tremble.

"Beware of thy old doctors, and their puny messengers of but one cubit high; distrust their pious frauds; and instead of eating their melons, impale on a spit the bearers of them. Shouldst thou be such a fool as to visit them, the portal of the subterranean palace will be shut in thy face, and with such force as shall shake thee asunder; thy body shall be spit upon, and bats will engender in thy belly."

"To what tends this ominous rhapsody?" cries the Caliph; "and must I then perish in these deserts with thirst, whilst I may refresh myself in the valley of melons and cucumbers? Accursed be the Giaour with his portal of ebony! he hath made me dance attendance too long already. Besides, who shall prescribe laws to me? I, forsooth, must not enter any one's habitation! Be it so, but what one can I enter that is not my own."

Bababalouk, who lost not a syllable of this soliloquy, applauded it with all his heart; and the ladies, for the first time, agreed with him in opinion. The dwarfs were entertained, caressed, and seated with great ceremony on little cushions of satin. The symmetry of their persons was the subject of criticism; not an inch of them was suffered to pass unexamined. Nick-knacks and dainties were offered in profusion, but all were declined with respectful gravity. They clambered up the sides of the Caliph's seat, and placing themselves each on one of his shoulders, began to whisper prayers in his ears. Their tongues quivered like the leaves of a poplar, and the patience of Vathek was almost exhausted, when the acclamations of the troops announced the approach of Fakhreddin, who was come with a hundred old grey-beards, and as many Koran's and dromedaries. They instantly set about their ablutions and began to repeat the Bismillah. Vathek, to get rid of these officious monitors, followed their example, for his hands were burning.

The good Emir, who was punctiliously religious, and likewise a great dealer in compliments, made a harangue five times more prolix and insipid than his harbingers had already delivered. The Caliph, unable any longer to refrain, exclaimed:

"For the love of Mahomet, my dear Fakhreddin, have done! let us proceed to your valley, and enjoy the fruits that heaven hath vouchsafed you." The hint of proceeding put all into motion. The venerable attendants of the emir set forward somewhat slowly, but Vathek having ordered his little pages, in private, to goad on the dromedaries, loud fits of laughter broke forth from the cages, for the unwieldy curvetting of these poor beasts, and the ridiculous distress of their superannuated riders afforded the ladies no small entertainment.

They descended, however, unhurt into the valley, by the large steps which the emir had cut in the rock; and already the murmuring of streams and the rustling of leaves began to catch their attention. The cavalcade soon entered a path, which was skirted by flowering shrubs, and extended to a vast wood of palm-trees whose branches overspread a building of hewn stone. This edifice was crowned with nine domes, and adorned with as many portals of bronze, on which was engraven the following inscription:

"This is the asylum of pilgrims, the refuge of travelers, and the depository of secrets for all parts of the world."

Nine pages beautiful as the day, and clothed in robes of Egyptian linen, very long and very modest, were standing at each door. They received the whole retinue with an easy and inviting air. Four of the most amiable placed the Caliph on a magnificent taktrevan; four others, somewhat less graceful, took charge of Bababalouk, who capered for joy at the snug little cabin that fell to his share; the pages that remained, waited on the rest of the train.

When everything masculine was gone out of sight, the gate of a large enclosure on the right turned on its harmonious hinges, and a young female of a slender form came forth. Her light brown hair floated in the hazy breeze of the twilight. A troop of young maidens, like the Pleiades, attended her on tiptoe. They hastened to the pavilions that contained the sultanas; and the young lady gracefully bending said to them:

"Charming princesses, everything is ready; we have prepared beds for your repose and strewed your apartments with jasmine; no insects will keep off slumber from visiting your eyelids; we will dispel them with a thousand plumes. Come then, amiable ladies! refresh your delicate feet and your ivory limbs in baths of rose water, and by the light of perfumed lamps your servants will amuse you with tales."

The sultanas accepted with pleasure these obliging offers, and followed the young lady to the emir's harem, where we must for a moment leave them and return to the Caliph.

Vathek found himself beneath a vast dome illuminated by a thousand lamps of rock crystal, as many vases of the same material filled with excellent sherbet sparkled on a large table, where a profusion of viands were spread. Amongst others were sweetbreads stewed in milk of almonds, saffron soups, and lamb à la crême, of all of which the Caliph was amazingly fond. He took of each as much as he was able; testified his sense of the emir's friendship by the gaiety of his heart; and made the dwarfs dance against their will; for these little devotees durst not refuse the commander of the faithful. At last he spread himself on the sofa and slept sounder than he had ever before.

Beneath this dome a general silence prevailed, for there was nothing to disturb it but the jaws of Bababalouk, who had untrussed himself to eat with greater advantage, being anxious to make amends for his fast in the mountains. As his spirits were too high to admit of his sleeping, and not loving to be idle, he proposed with himself to visit the harem, and repair to his charge of the ladies, to examine if they had been properly lubricated with the balm of Mecca, if their eye-brows and tresses were in order, and in a word, to perform all the little offices they might need. He sought for a long time together, but without being able to find out the door. He durst not speak aloud for fear of disturbing the Caliph, and not a soul was stirring in the precincts of the palace. He almost despaired of effecting his purpose, when a low whispering just reached his ear: it came from the dwarfs, who were returned to their old occupation, and for the nine hundred and ninety-ninth time in their lives were reading over the Koran. They very politely invited Bababalouk to be of their party, but his head was full of other concerns. The dwarfs, though scandalized at his dissolute morals, directed him to the apartments he wanted to find. His way thither lay through a hundred dark corridors, along which he groped as he went, and at last began to catch, from the extremity of a passage, the charming gossiping of women, which not a little delighted his heart.

"Ah, ah! what not yet asleep?" cried he, and taking long strides as he spoke, "did you not suspect me of abjuring my charge? I stayed but to finish what my master had left."

Two of the black eunuchs on hearing a voice so loud detached a party in haste, sabre in hand, to discover the cause, but presently was repeated on all sides:

"'Tis only Bababalouk, no one but Bababalouk!"

This circumspect guardian having gone up to a thin veil of carnation color silk that hung before the doorway, distinguished by means of a softened splendor that shone through it, an oval bath of dark porphyry surrounded by curtains festooned in large folds. Through the apertures between them, as they were not drawn close, groups of young slaves were visible, amongst whom Bababalouk perceived his pupils indulgingly expanding their arms, as if to embrace the perfumed water, and refresh themselves after their fatigues. The looks of tender languor, their confidential whispers, and the enchanting smiles with which they were imparted, the exquisite fragrance of the roses, all combined to inspire a voluptuousness which even Bababalouk himself was scarce able to withstand.

He summoned up, however, his usual solemnity, and in the peremptory tone of authority commanded the ladies instantly to leave the bath. Whilst he was issuing these mandates, the young Nouronihar, daughter of the emir, who was sprightly as an antelope, and full of wanton gaiety, beckoned one of her slaves to let down the great swing, which was suspended to the ceiling by cords of silk, and whilst this was doing winked to her companions in the bath, who chagrined to be forced from so soothing a state of indolence, began to twist it round Bababalouk, and tease him with a thousand vagaries.

When Nouronihar perceived that he was exhausted with fatigue, she accosted him with an arch air of respectful concern, and said:

"My lord, it is not by any means decent that the chief eunuch of the Caliph our sovereign should thus continue standing, deign but to recline your graceful person upon this sofa, which will burst with vexation if it have not the honor to receive you."

Caught by these flattering accents, Bababalouk gallantly replied:

"Delight of the apple of my eye! I accept the invitation of thy honied lips, and to say truth, my senses are dazzled with the radiance that beams from thy charms."

"Repose, then, at your ease," replied the beauty, and placed him on the pretended sofa, which, quicker than lightning, gave way all at once. The rest of the women having aptly conceived her design, sprang naked from the bath and plied the swing with such unmerciful jerks, that it swept through the whole compass of a very lofty dome, and took from the poor victim all power of respiration. Sometimes his feet raised the surface of the water, and at others the skylight almost flattened his nose. In vain did he pierce the air with the cries of a voice that resembled the ringing of a cracked basin, for their peals of laughter were still more predominant.

Nouronihar in the inebriety of youthful spirits being used only to eunuchs of ordinary harems and having never seen anything so royal and disgusting, was far more diverted than all of the rest. She began to parody some Persian verses, and sung with an accent most demurely piquant:

O gentle white dove as thou soar'st through the air,
Vouchsafe one kind glance on the mate of thy love:
Melodious Philomel I am thy rose;
Warble some couplet to ravish my heart!

The sultanas and their slaves stimulated by these pleasantries persevered at the swing with such unremitted assiduity, that at length the cord which had secured it snapped suddenly asunder, and Bababalouk fell floundering like a turtle to the bottom of the bath. This accident occasioned a universal shout. Twelve little doors till now unobserved flew open at once, and the ladies in an instant made their escape, after throwing all the towels on his head, and putting out the lights that remained.

The deplorable animal, in water to the chin, overwhelmed with darkness, and unable to extricate himself from the warp that embarrassed him, was still doomed to hear for his further consolation, the fresh bursts of merriment his disaster occasioned. He bustled but in vain to get from the bath, for the margin was become so slippery with the oil spilt in breaking the lamps, that at every effort he slid back with a plunge, which resounded aloud through the hollow of the dome.

These cursed peals of laughter at every relapse were redoubled, and he, who thought the place infested rather by devils than women, resolved to cease groping, and abide in the bath, where he amused himself with soliloquies interspersed with imprecations, of which his malicious neighbors, reclining on down, suffered not an accent to escape. In this delectable plight the morning surprised him. The Caliph, wondering at his absence, had caused him to be everywhere sought for. At last he was drawn forth almost smothered from the whisp of linen, and wet even to the marrow. Limping, and chattering his teeth, he appeared before his master, who inquired what was the matter, and how he came soused in so strange a pickle.

"And why did you enter this cursed lodge?"answered Bababalouk, gruffly. "Ought a monarch like you to visit with his harem the abode of a grey bearded emir who knows nothing of life? And with what gracious damsels does the place too abound! Fancy to yourself how they have soaked me like a burnt crust and made me dance like a jack-pudding the live-long night through on their damnable swing. What an excellent lesson for your sultanas to follow, into whom I have instilled such reserve and decorum!"

Vathek, comprehending not a syllable of all this invective, obliged him to relate minutely the transaction; but instead of sympathizing with the miserable sufferer, he laughed immoderately at the device of the swing, and the figure of Bababalouk mounting upon it. The stung eunuch could scarcely preserve the semblance of respect.

"Aye, laugh my lord! laugh," said he, "but I wish this Nouronihar would play some trick on you; she is too wicked to spare even majesty itself."

These words made for the present but a slight impression on the Caliph, but they not long after recurred to his mind.

This conversation was cut short by Fakhreddin, who came to request that Vathek would join in the prayers and ablutions to be solemnized on a spacious meadow, watered by innumerable streams. The Caliph found the waters refreshing, but the prayers abominably irksome. He diverted himself however with the

multitude of Calendars, Santons, and Dervishes who were continually coming
and going, but especially with the Brahmins, Faquirs, and other enthusiasts, who
had travelled from the heart of India, and halted on their way with the emir. These
latter had each of them some mummery peculiar to himself. One dragged a huge
chain wherever he went, another an orangutan, whilst a third was furnished with
scourges, and all performed to a charm. Some clambered up trees, holding one
foot in the air; others poised themselves over a fire, and without mercy filliped
their noses. There were some amongst them that cherished vermin, which were
not ungrateful in requiting their caresses. These rambling fanatics revolted the
hearts of the Dervishes, the Calendars, and Santons; however, the vehemence of
their aversion soon subsided under the hope that the presence of the Caliph would
cure their folly, and convert them to the Mussulman faith. But alas! how great was
their disappointment! for Vathek, instead of preaching to them, treated them as
buffoons; bade them present his compliments to Visnow and Ixhora, and discovered a predilection for a squat old man from the Isle of Serendib, who was more
ridiculous than any of the rest.

"Come," said he, "for the love of your gods, bestow a few slaps on your
chops to amuse me."

The old fellow offended at such an address began loudly to weep; but as
he betrayed a villainous driveling in his tears, the Caliph turned his back and listened to Bababalouk, who whispered, whilst he held the umbrella over him:

"Your majesty should be cautious of this odd assembly, which hath been
collected I know not for what. Is it necessary to exhibit such spectacles to a mighty
potentate, with interludes of talapoins mangier than dogs? Were I you, I would
command a fire to be kindled, and at once purge the earth of the emir, his harem,
and all his menagerie."

"Tush, dolt," answered Vathek, "and know that all this infinitely charms
me. Nor shall I leave the meadow till I have visited every hive of these pious men-
dicants."

Where ever the Caliph directed his course, objects of pity were sure to
swarm round him: the blind, the purblind, smarts without noses, damsels without
ears, each to extol the munificence of Fakhreddin, who, as well as his attendant
grey-beards, dealt about gratis plasters and cataplasms to all that applied. At
noon a superb corps of cripples made its appearance; and soon after advanced
by platoons on the plain the completest association of invalids that had ever been
embodied till then. The blind went groping with the blind; the lame limped on
together; and the maimed made gestures to each other with the only arm that remained. The sides of a considerable waterfall were crowded by the deaf, amongst
whom were some from Pegu, with ears uncommonly handsome and large, but
were still less able to hear than the rest. Nor were there wanting others in abundance with hump backs, wenny necks, and even horns of an exquisite polish.

The emir, to aggrandize the solemnity of the festival in honor of his illustrious visitant, ordered the turf to be spread on all sides with skins and table
cloths, upon which were served up for the good mussulmans pilaus of every hue,
with other orthodox dishes, and by the express order of Vathek, who was shamefully tolerant, small plates of abominations for regaling the rest. This prince on
seeing so many mouths put in motion began to think it time for employing his
own. In spite, therefore, of every remonstrance from the chief of his eunuchs, he

resolved to have a dinner dressed on the spot. The complaisant emir immediately gave orders for a table to be placed in the shade of the willows. The first service consisted of fish, which they drew from a river flowing over sands of gold, at the foot of a lofty hill: these were broiled as fast as taken, and served up with a sauce of vinegar and small herbs that grew on Mount Sinai; for everything with the emir was excellent and pious.

The dessert was not quite set on when the sound of lutes from the hill was repeated by the echoes of the neighboring mountains. The Caliph with an emotion of pleasure and surprise, had no sooner raised up his head than a handful of jasmine dropped on his face. An abundance of tittering succeeded this frolic, and instantly appeared through the bushes the elegant forms of several young females, skipping and bounding like roes. The fragrance diffused from their hair struck the sense of Vathek, who in an ecstasy, suspending his repast, said to Bababalouk:

"Are the Peries come down from their spheres? Note her in particular whose form is so perfect, venturously running on the brink of the precipice, and turning back her head as regardless of nothing but the graceful flow of her robe. With what captivating impatience doth she contend with the bushes for her veil? Could it be she who threw the jasmine at me?"

"Aye, she it was; and you too would she throw from the top of the rock," answered Bababalouk, "for that is my good friend Nouronihar, who so kindly lent me her swing. My dear lord and master," added he, twisting a twig that hung by the rind from a willow, "let me correct her for her want of respect: the emir will have no reason to complain, since (bating what I owe to his piety) he is much to be censured for keeping a troop of girls on the mountains, whose sharp air gives their blood too brisk a circulation."

"Peace, blasphemer!" said the Caliph: "speak not thus of her who over her mountains leads my heart a willing captive. Contrive, rather, that my eyes may be fixed upon hers — that I may respire her sweet breath, as she bounds panting along these delightful wilds!"

On saying these words, Vathek extended his arms towards the hill, and directing his eyes with an anxiety unknown to him before, endeavored to keep within view the object that enthralled his soul; but her course was as difficult to follow as the flight of one of those beautiful blue butterflies of Cachmere, which are at once so volatile and rare.

The Caliph, not satisfied with seeing, wished also to hear Nouronihar, and eagerly turned to catch the sound of her voice. At last he distinguished her whispering to one of her companions behind the thicket from whence she had thrown the jasmine:

"A Caliph, it must be owned, is a fine thing to see, but my little Gulchenrouz is much more amiable; one lock of his hair is of more value to me than the richest embroidery of the Indies. I had rather that his teeth should mischievously press my finger, than the richest ring of the imperial treasure. Where have you left him, Sutlememe? and why is he now not here?"

The agitated Caliph still wished to hear more, but she immediately retired with all her attendants. The fond monarch pursued her with his eyes till she was gone out of sight, and then continued like a bewildered and benighted traveler, from whom the clouds had obscured the constellation that guided his way. The curtain of night seemed dropped before him - everything appeared discolored.

The falling waters filled his soul with dejection, and his tears trickled down the jasmines he had caught from Nouronihar, and placed in his inflamed bosom. He snatched up a shining pebble to remind him of the scene where he felt the first tumults of love. Two hours were elapsed, and evening drew on before he could resolve to depart from the place. He often, but in vain, attempted to go: a soft languor enervated the powers of his mind. Extending himself on the brink of the stream, he turned his eyes towards the blue summits of the mountain, and exclaimed:

"What concealest thou behind thee? what is passing in thy solitudes? Whither is she gone? O heaven! perhaps she is now wandering in the grottoes with her happy Gulchenrouz!"

In the meantime, the damps began to descend, and the emir, solicitous for the health of the Caliph, ordered the imperial litter to be brought. Vathek, absorbed in his reveries, was imperceptibly removed and conveyed back to the saloon that received him the evening before.

But let us leave the Caliph immersed in his new passion, and attend Nouronihar beyond the rocks, where she had again joined her beloved Gulchenrouz. This Gulchenrouz was the son of Ali Hassan, brother to the emir, and the most delicate and lovely creature in the world. Ali Hassan, who had been absent ten years on a voyage to the unknown seas, committed at his departure this child, the only survivor of many, to the care and protection of his brother. Gulchenrouz could write in various characters with precision, and paint upon vellum the most elegant arabesques that fancy could devise. His sweet voice accompanied the lute in the most enchanting manner; and when he sung the loves of Megnoun and Leileh, or some unfortunate lovers of ancient days, tears insensibly overflowed the cheeks of his auditors. The verses he composed (for like Megnoun, he too was a poet) inspired that unresisting languor so frequently fatal to the female heart. The women all doted upon him, for though he had passed his thirteenth year, they still detained him in the harem. His dancing was light as the gossamer waved by the zephyrs of spring; but his arms which twined so gracefully with those of the young girls in the dance, could neither dart the lance in the chase, nor curb the steeds that pastured his uncle's domains. The bow, however, he drew with a certain aim, and would have excelled his competitors in the race, could he have broken the ties that bound him to Nouronihar.

The two brothers had mutually engaged their children to each other; and Nouronihar loved her cousin more than her eyes. Both had the same tastes and amusements; the same long languishing looks; the same tresses; the same fair complexions; and when Gulchenrouz appeared in the dress of his cousin, he seemed to be more feminine than even herself. If at any time he left the harem to visit Fakhreddin, it was with all the bashfulness of a fawn that consciously ventures from the lair of its dam; he was however wanton enough to mock the solemn old grey-beards to whom he was subject, though sure to be rated without mercy in return. Whenever this happened, he would plunge into the recesses of the harem, and sobbing take refuge in the arms of Nouronihar, who loved even his faults beyond the virtues of others.

It fell out this evening that after leaving the Caliph in the meadow, she ran with Gulchenrouz over the green sward of the mountain that sheltered the vale, where Fakhreddin had chosen to reside. The sun was dilated on the edge of the horizon; and the young people, whose fancies were lively and inventive, imagined they beheld in the gorgeous clouds of the west the domes of Shadukiam and Ambreabad, where the Peries have fixed their abode. Nouronihar, sitting on the slope of the hill, supported on her knees the perfumed head of Gulchenrouz. The air was calm, and no sound stirred but the voices of other young girls who were drawing cool water from the streams below. The unexpected arrival of the Caliph, and the splendor that marked his appearance, had already filled with emotion the ardent soul of Nouronihar. Her vanity irresistibly prompted her to pique the prince's attention, and this she before took good care to effect whilst he picked up the jasmine, she had thrown upon him. But when Gulchenrouz asked after the flowers he had culled for her bosom, Nouronihar was all in confusion. She hastily kissed his forehead, arose in a flutter, and walked with unequal steps on the border of the precipice. Night advanced, and the pure gold of the setting sun had yielded to a sanguine red, the glow of which, like the reflection of a burning furnace, flushed Nouronihar's animated countenance. Gulchenrouz alarmed at the agitation of his cousin, said to her with a supplicating accent:

"Let us be gone; the sky looks portentous: the tamarisks tremble more than common; and the raw wind chills my very heart. Come, let us be gone, 'tis a melancholy night."

Then taking hold of her hand he drew it towards the path he besought her to go. Nouronihar unconsciously followed the attraction, for a thousand strange imaginations occupied her spirit. She passed the large round of honeysuckles, her favorite resort, without ever vouchsafing it a glance, yet Gulchenrouz could not help snatching off a few shoots in his way, though he ran as if a wild beast were behind.

The young females seeing him approach in such haste, and according to custom expecting a dance, instantly assembled in a circle and took each other by the hand, but Gulchenrouz coming up out of breath, fell down at once on the grass. This accident struck with consternation the whole of this frolicsome party, whilst Nouronihar, half distracted, and overcome both by the violence of her exercise and the tumult of her thoughts, sunk feebly down at his side, cherished his cold hands in her bosom, and chafed his temples with a fragrant unguent. At length he came to himself and wrapping up his head in the robe of his cousin, entreated that she would not return to the harem. He was afraid of being snapped at by Shaban his tutor, a wrinkled old eunuch of a surly disposition, for having interrupted the stated walk of Nouronihar, he dreaded lest the churl should take it amiss. The whole of this sprightly group, sitting round upon a mossy knoll, began to entertain themselves with various pastimes, whilst their superintendents the eunuchs were gravely conversing at a distance. The nurse of the emir's daughter observing her pupil sit ruminating with her eyes on the ground, endeavored to amuse her with diverting tales, to which Gulchenrouz, who had already forgotten his inquietudes, listened with a breathless attention. He laughed; he clapped his hands; and passed a hundred little tricks on the whole of the company, without omitting the eunuchs, whom he provoked to run after him, in spite of their age and decrepitude.

During these occurrences the moon arose, the wind subsided, and the evening became so serene and inviting that a resolution was taken to sup on the spot. Sutlememe, who excelled in dressing a salad, having filled large bowls of porcelain with eggs of small birds, curds turned with citron juice, slices of cucumber, and the inmost leaves of delicate herbs, handed it round from one to another, and gave each their shares in a large spoon of Cocknos. Gulchenrouz nestling as usual in the bosom of Nouronihar, pouted out his vermillion little lips against the offer of Sutlememe, and would take it only from the hand of his cousin, on whose mouth he hung like a bee inebriated with the quintessence of flowers. One of the eunuchs ran to fetch melons, whilst others were employed in showering down almonds from the branches that overhung this amiable party.

In the midst of this festive scene there appeared a light on the top of the highest mountain, which attracted the notice of every eye. This light was not less bright than the moon when at full and might have been taken for her had it not been that the moon was already risen. The phenomenon occasioned a general surprise, and no one could conjecture the cause. It could not be a fire, for the light was clear and bluish; nor had meteors ever been seen of that magnitude or splendor. This strange light faded for a moment, and immediately renewed its brightness. It first appeared motionless at the foot of the rock, whence it darted in an instant to sparkle in a thicket of palm trees, from thence it glided along the torrent, and at last fixed in a glen that was narrow and dark. The moment it had taken its direction, Gulchenrouz, whose heart always trembled at anything sudden or rare, drew Nouronihar by the robe, and anxiously requested her to return to the harem. The women were importunate in seconding the entreaty, but the curiosity of the emir's daughter prevailed. She not only refused to go back but resolved at all hazards to pursue the appearance. Whilst they were debating what was best to be done, the light shot forth so dazzling a blaze that they all fled away shrieking. Nouronihar followed them a few steps but coming to the turn of a little bye path stopped and went back alone. As she ran with an alertness peculiar to herself, it was not long before she came to the place where they had just been supping. The globe of fire now appeared stationary in the glen and burned in majestic stillness. Nouronihar compressing her hands upon her bosom, hesitated for some moments to advance. The solitude of her situation was new; the silence of the night awful; and every object inspired sensations which till then she never had felt. The affright of Gulchenrouz recurred to her mind; and she a thousand times turned to go back, but this luminous appearance was always before her. Urged on by an irresistible impulse, she continued to approach it in defiance of every obstacle that opposed her progress.

At length she arrived at the opening of the glen, but instead of coming up to the light, she found herself surrounded by darkness, except that at a considerable distance a faint spark glimmered by fits. She stopped a second time: the sound of waterfalls mingling their murmurs, the hollow rustlings amongst the palm branches, and the funereal screams of the birds from their rifted trunks, all conspired to fill her with terror. She imagined every moment that she trod on some venomous reptile. All the stories of malignant Dives, and dismal Ghouls thronged into her memory, but her curiosity was notwithstanding more predominant than her fears. She therefore firmly entered a winding track that led towards the spark, but being a stranger to the path, she had not gone far till she began to repent of her rashness.

"Alas!" said she, "that I were but in those secure and illuminated apartments where my evenings glided on with Gulchenrouz! Dear child, how would thy heart flutter with terror wert thou wandering in these wild solitudes like me."

At the close of this apostrophe she regained her road and coming to steps hewn out in the rock ascended them undismayed. The light, which was now gradually enlarging, appeared above her on the summit of the mountain. At length she distinguished a plaintive and melodious union of voices proceeding from a sort of cavern, that resembled the dirges which are sung over tombs. A sound likewise like that which arises from the filling of baths, at the same time struck her ear. She continued ascending and discovered large wax torches in full blaze planted here and there in the fissures of the rock. This preparation filled her with fear, whilst the subtle and potent odor which the torches exhaled caused her to sink almost lifeless at the entrance of the grot.

Casting her eyes within in this kind of trance, she beheld a large cistern of gold filled with a water, whose vapor distilled on her face a dew of the essence of roses. A soft symphony resounded through the grot. On the sides of the cistern she noticed appendages of royalty; diadems and feathers of the heron, all sparkling with carbuncles. Whilst her attention was fixed on this display of magnificence, the music ceased, and a voice instantly demanded:

"For what monarch were these torches kindled, this bath prepared, and these habiliments? which belong not only to the sovereigns of the earth, but even to the talismanic powers!"

To which a second voice answered:

"They are for the charming daughter of the emir Fakhreddin."

"What," replied the first, "for that trifler who consumes her time with a giddy child, immersed in softness, and who at best can make but an enervated husband?"

"And can she," rejoined the other voice, "be amused with such empty trifles, whilst the Caliph, the sovereign of the world, he who is destined to enjoy the treasures of the pre-Adamite sultans, a prince six feet high, and whose eyes pervade the inmost soul of a female, is inflamed with the love of her? no, she will be wise enough to answer that passion alone that can aggrandize her glory. No doubt she will and despise the puppet of her fancy; then all the riches this place contains, as well as the carbuncle of Giamschid shall be hers."

"You judge right," returned the first voice, "and I haste to Istakar to prepare the palace of subterranean fire for the reception of the bridal pair."

The voices ceased, the torches were extinguished, the most entire darkness succeeded, and Nouronihar recovering with a start, found herself reclined on a sofa in the harem of her father. She clapped her hands, and immediately came together Gulchenrouz and her women, who, in despair at having lost her, had dispatched eunuchs to seek her in every direction. Shaban appeared with the rest, and began to reprimand her with an air of consequence:

"Little impertinent," said he, "whence got you false keys? or are you beloved of some genius that hath given you a picklock? I will try the extent of your power; come, to your chamber! through the two skylights and expect not the company of Gulchenrouz. Be expeditious! I will shut you up in the double tower."

At these menaces Nouronihar indignantly raised her head, opened on Shaban her black eyes, which since the important dialogue of the enchanted grot were considerably enlarged, and said:

"Go, speak thus to slaves! but learn to reverence her who is born to give laws, and subject all to her power."

She was proceeding in the same style, but was interrupted by a sudden exclamation of,

"The Caliph! the Caliph!"

The curtains at once were thrown open, and the slaves prostrate in double rows, whilst poor little Gulchenrouz hid himself beneath the elevation of a sofa. At first appeared a file of black eunuchs trailing after them long trains of muslin embroidered with gold, and holding in their hand's censers, which dispensed as they passed the grateful perfume of the wood of aloes. Next marched Bababalouk with a solemn strut, and tossing his head as not over pleased at the visit. Vathek came close after superbly robed; his gait was unembarrassed and noble, and his presence would have engaged admiration, though he had not been the sovereign of the world. He approached Nouronihar with a throbbing heart and seemed enraptured at the full effulgence of her radiant eyes, of which he had before caught but a few glimpses; but she instantly depressed them, and her confusion augmented her beauty.

Bababalouk, who was a thorough adept in coincidences of this nature, and knew that the worst game should be played with the best face, immediately made a signal for all to retire, and no sooner did he perceive beneath the sofa the little one's feet, than he drew him forth without ceremony, set him upon his shoulders, and lavished on him as he went off a thousand odious caresses. Gulchenrouz cried out and resisted till his cheeks became the color of the blossom of the pomegranate, and the tears that started into his eyes shot forth a gleam of indignation. He cast a significant glance at Nouronihar, which the Caliph noticing, asked:

"Is that then your Gulchenrouz?"

"Sovereign of the world," answered she, "spare my cousin, whose innocence and gentleness deserve not your anger!"

"Take comfort," said Vathek with a smile, "he is in good hands. Bababalouk is fond of children, and never goes without sweetmeats and comfits."

The daughter of Fakhreddin was abashed; and suffered Gulchenrouz to be borne away without adding a word. The tumult of her bosom betrayed her confusion; and Vathek becoming still more impassioned, gave a loose to his frenzy, which had only not subdued the last faint struggling of reluctance, when the emir suddenly bursting in, threw his face upon the ground at the feet of the Caliph, and said:

"Commander of the faithful, abase not yourself to the meanness of your slave."

"No, emir," replied Vathek, "I raise her to an equality with myself; I declare her my wife; and the glory of your race shall extend from one generation to another."

"Alas! my lord," said Fakhreddin, as he plucked off the honors of his beard, "cut short the days of your faithful servant rather than force him to depart from his word. Nouronihar, as her hands evince, is solemnly promised to Gulchenrouz, the son of my brother, Ali Hassan; they are united also in heart; their faith is mutually plighted, and affiances so sacred cannot be broken."

"What, then," replied the Caliph bluntly, "would you surrender this divine beauty to a husband more womanish than herself? And can you imagine that

I will suffer her charms to decay in hands so inefficient and nerveless? No! she is destined to live out her life within my embraces: such is my will: retire and disturb not the night I devote to the homage of her charms."

The irritated emir drew forth his sabre, presented it to Vathek, and stretching out his neck, said in a firm tone of voice:

"Strike your unhappy host my lord! he has lived long enough, since he hath seen the prophet's vicegerent violate the rights of hospitality."

At his uttering these words, Nouronihar unable to support any longer the conflict of her passions, sunk down in a swoon. Vathek, both terrified for her life, and furious at an opposition to his will, bade Fakhreddin assist his daughter, and withdrew, darting his terrible look at the unfortunate emir, who suddenly fell backward bathed in a sweat, cold as the damp of death.

Gulchenrouz, who had escaped from the hands of Bababalouk, and was that instant returned, called out for help as loudly as he could, not having strength to afford it himself. Pale and panting, the poor child attempted to revive Nouronihar by caresses, and it happened that the thrilling warmth of his lips restored her to life. Fakhreddin beginning also to recover from the look of the Caliph, with difficulty tottered to a seat, and after warily casting round his eye to see if this dangerous prince were gone, sent for Shaban and Sutlememe, and said to them apart:

My friends, violent evils require as violent remedies; the Caliph has brought desolation and horror into my family, and how shall we resist his power? Another of his looks will send me to my grave. Fetch then that narcotic powder which the Dervise brought me from Aracan. A dose of it, the effect of which will continue three days, must be administered to each of these children. The Caliph will believe them to be dead, for they will have all the appearance of death. We shall go as if to inter them in the cave of Meimoune, at the entrance of the great desert of sand, and near the cabin of my dwarfs. When all the spectators shall be withdrawn, you, Shaban, and four select eunuchs shall convey them to the lake, where provision shall be ready to support them a month; for, one day allotted to the surprise this event will occasion, five to the tears, a fortnight to reflection, and the rest to prepare for renewing his progress, will, according to my calculation, fill up the whole time that Vathek will tarry, and I shall then be freed from his intrusion.

"Your plan," said Sutlememe, "is a good one, if it can but be effected. I have remarked that Nouronihar is well able to support the glances of the Caliph, and that he is far from being sparing of them to her; be assured therefore, notwithstanding her fondness for Gulchenrouz, she will never remain quiet while she knows him to be here, unless we can persuade her that both herself and Gulchenrouz are really dead, and that they were conveyed to those rocks for a limited season to expiate the little faults of which their love was the cause. We will add that we killed ourselves in despair, and that your dwarfs whom they never yet saw will preach to them delectable sermons. I will engage that everything shall succeed to the bent of your wishes."

"Be it so," said Fakhreddin; "I approve your proposal; let us lose not a moment to give it effect." They forthwith hastened to seek for the powder, which being mixed in a sherbet was immediately drunk by Gulchenrouz and Nouronihar. Within the space of an hour both were seized with violent palpitations, and a general numbness gradually ensued. They arose from the floor, where they had remained ever since the Caliph's departure, and ascending to the sofa, reclined themselves at full length upon it, clasped in each other's embraces.

"Cherish me, my dear Nouronihar," said Gulchenrouz; "put thy hand upon my heart, for it feels as if it were frozen. Alas! thou art as cold as myself! hath the Caliph murdered us both with his terrible look?"

"I am dying," cried she in a faltering voice; "press me closer, I am ready to expire!"

"Let us die then together," answered the little Gulchenrouz, whilst his breast labored with a convulsive sigh; "let me at least breathe forth my soul on thy lips."

They spoke no more and became as dead.

Immediately the most piercing cries were heard through the harem, whilst Shaban and Sutlememe personated with great adroitness the parts of persons in despair. The emir, who was sufficiently mortified to be forced into such untoward expedients and had now for the first time made a trial of his powder, was under no necessity of counterfeiting grief. The slaves, who had flocked together from all quarters, stood motionless at the spectacle before them. All lights were extinguished save two lamps, which shed a wan glimmering over the faces of these lovely flowers, that seemed to be faded in the springtime of life. Funeral vestments were prepared; their bodies were washed with rose water; their beautiful tresses were braided and incensed; and they were wrapped in symars whiter than alabaster. At the moment that their attendants were placing two wreaths of their favorite jasmines on their brows, the Caliph, who had just heard the tragical catastrophe, arrived. He looked not less pale and haggard than the ghouls that wander at night among graves. Forgetful of himself and everyone else, he broke through the midst of the slaves, fell prostrate at the foot of the sofa, beat his bosom, called himself "atrocious murderer," and invoked upon his head a thousand imprecations. With a trembling hand he raised the veil that covered the countenance of Nouronihar, and uttering a loud shriek fell lifeless on the floor. The chief of the eunuchs dragged him off with horrible grimaces, and repeated as he went:

"Aye, I foresaw she would play you some ungracious turn."

No sooner was the Caliph gone than the emir commanded biers to be brought and forbade that anyone should enter the harem. Every window was fastened; all instruments of music were broken; and the Imams began to recite their prayers. Towards the close of this melancholy day Vathek sobbed in silence, for they had been forced to compose with anodynes his convulsions of rage and desperation.

At the dawn of the succeeding morning the wide folding doors of the palace were set open, and the funeral procession moved forward for the mountain. The wailful cries of "La Ilah illa Alla," reached to the Caliph, who was eager to cicatrize himself and attend the ceremonial; nor could he have been dissuaded, had not his excessive weakness disabled him from walking. At the few first steps, he fell on the ground, and his people were obliged to lay him on a bed, where he remained many days in such a state of insensibility as excited compassion in the emir himself.

When the procession was arrived at the grot of Meimoune, Shaban and Sutlememe dismissed the whole of the train excepting the four confidential eunuchs who were appointed to remain. After resting some moments near the biers which had been left in the open air, they caused them to be carried to the brink of a small lake whose banks were overgrown with a hoary moss. This was the great resort of herons and storks, which preyed continually on little blue fishes. The dwarfs, instructed by the emir, soon repaired thither, and with the help of the eunuchs began to construct cabins of rushes and reeds, a work in which they had admirable skill. A magazine also was contrived for provisions, with a small oratory for themselves, and a pyramid of wood neatly piled, to furnish the necessary fuel, for the air was bleak in the hollows of the mountains.

At evening two fires were kindled on the brink of the lake, and the two lovely bodies taken from their biers were carefully deposited upon a bed of dried leaves within the same cabin. The dwarfs began to recite the Koran with their clear shrill voices, and Shaban and Sutlememe stood at some distance anxiously waiting the effects of the powder. At length Nouronihar and Gulchenrouz faintly stretched out their arms, and gradually opening their eyes began to survey with looks of increasing amazement every object around them. They even attempted to rise, but for want of strength fell back again. Sutlememe on this administered a cordial which the emir had taken care to provide.

Gulchenrouz thoroughly aroused sneezed out aloud and raising himself with an effort that expressed his surprise, left the cabin, and inhaled the fresh air with the greatest avidity.

"Yes," said he, "I breathe again! again do I exist! I hear sounds! I behold a firmament spangled over with stars!"

Nouronihar catching these beloved accents extricated herself from the leaves and ran to clasp Gulchenrouz to her bosom. The first objects she remarked were their long symars, their garlands of flowers, and their naked feet: she hid her face in her hands to reflect. The vision of the enchanted bath, the despair of her father, and more vividly than both, the majestic figure of Vathek recurred to her memory. She recollected also, that herself and Gulchenrouz had been sick and dying; but all these images bewildered her mind. Not knowing where she was, she turned her eyes on all sides, as if to recognize the surrounding scene. This singular lake, those flames reflected from its glassy surface, the pale hues of its banks, the romantic cabins, the bull-rushes that sadly waved their drooping heads, the storks whose melancholy cries blended with the shrill voices of the dwarfs, everything conspired to persuade them that the angel of death had opened the portal of some other world.

Gulchenrouz on his part, lost in wonder, clung to the neck of his cousin. He believed himself in the region of phantoms and was terrified at the silence she preserved. At length addressing her:

"Speak," said he; "where are we! do you not see those specters that are stirring the burning coals? Are they the Monker and Nakir, come to throw us into them? Does the fatal bridge cross this lake, whose solemn stillness perhaps conceals from us an abyss, in which for whole ages we shall be doomed incessantly to sink?"

"No my children," said Sutlememe going towards them; "take comfort, the exterminating angel who conducted our souls hither after yours, hath assured us that the chastisement of your indolent and voluptuous life shall be restricted to a certain series of years, which you must pass in this dreary abode, where the sun is scarcely visible, and where the soil yields neither fruits nor flowers. These," continued she, pointing to the dwarfs, "will provide for our wants; for souls so mundane as ours retain too strong a tincture of their earthly extraction. Instead of meats, your food will be nothing but rice, and your bread shall be moistened in the fogs that brood over the surface of the lake."

At this desolating prospect the poor children burst into tears, and prostrated themselves before the dwarfs, who perfectly supported their characters, and delivered an excellent discourse of a customary length upon the sacred camel, which after a thousand years was to convey them to the paradise of the faithful.

The sermon being ended, and ablutions performed, they praised Allah and the prophet, supped very indifferently, and retired to their withered leaves. Nouronihar and her little cousin consoled themselves on finding that, though dead, they yet lay in one cabin. Having slept well before, the remainder of the night was spent in conversation on what had befallen them; and both, from a dread of apparitions, betook themselves for protection to one another's arms.

In the morning, which was lowering and rainy, the dwarfs mounted high poles like minarets, and called them to prayers. The whole congregation, which consisted of Sutlememe, Shaban, the four eunuchs, and some storks, were already assembled. The two children came forth from their cabin with a slow and dejected pace. As their minds were in a tender and melancholy mood, their devotions were performed with fervor. No sooner were they finished than Gulchenrouz demanded of Sutlememe and the rest, "how they happened to die so opportunely for his cousin and himself."

"We killed ourselves," returned Sutlememe, "in despair at your death."

On this, said Nouronihar, who notwithstanding what was past, had not yet forgotten her vision:

"And the Caliph, is he also dead of his grief? and will he likewise come hither?"

The dwarfs, who were prepared with an answer, most demurely replied:

"Vathek is damned beyond all redemption!"

"I readily believe so," said Gulchenrouz; "and am glad from my heart to hear it, for I am convinced it was his horrible look that sent us hither, to listen to sermons and mess upon rice."

One week passed away on the side of the lake unmarked by any variety; Nouronihar ruminating on the grandeur of which death had deprived her, and Gulchenrouz applying to prayers and to panniers along with the dwarfs, who infinitely pleased him. Whilst this scene of innocence was exhibiting in the mountains, the Caliph presented himself to the emir in a new light. The instant he recovered the use of his senses, with a voice that made Bababalouk quake, he thundered out:

"Perfidious Giaour! I renounce thee forever! it is thou who hast slain my beloved Nouronihar! and I supplicate the pardon of Mahomet, who would have preserved her to me had I been wiser. Let water be brought to perform my ablutions and let the pious Fakhreddin be called to offer up his prayers with mine and reconcile me to him. Afterwards we will go together and visit the sepulcher of the unfortunate Nouronihar. I am resolved to become a hermit and consume the residue of my days on this mountain, in hope of expiating my crimes."

Nouronihar was not altogether so content, for though she felt a fondness for Gulchenrouz, who to augment the attachment, had been left at full liberty with her, yet she still regarded him as but a bauble that bore no competition with the carbuncle of Giamschid. At times she indulged doubts on the mode of her being, and scarcely could believe that the dead had all the wants and the whims of the living. To gain satisfaction, however, on so perplexing a topic, she arose one morning whilst all were asleep with a breathless caution from the side of Gulchenrouz, and after having given him a soft kiss, began to follow the windings of the lake till it terminated with a rock whose top was accessible though lofty. This she clambered up with considerable toil, and having reached the summit, set forward in a run like a doe that unwittingly follows her hunter. Though she skipped along with the alertness of an antelope, yet at intervals she was forced to desist, and rest beneath the tamarisks to recover her breath. Whilst she, thus reclined, was occupied with her little reflections on the apprehension that she had some knowledge of the place, Vathek, who finding himself that morning but ill at ease, had gone forth before the dawn, presented himself on a sudden to her view. Motionless with surprise, he durst not approach the figure before him, which lay shrouded up in a symar extended on the ground, trembling and pale, but yet lovely to behold. At length Nouronihar, with a mixture of pleasure and affliction, raising her fine eyes to him, said:

"My lord, are you come hither to eat rice and hear sermons with me?"

"Beloved phantom!" cried Vathek, "dost thou speak? hast thou the same graceful form? the same radiant features? art thou palpable likewise?" and eagerly embracing her he added, "here are limbs and a bosom animated with a gentle warmth! what can such a prodigy mean?"

Nouronihar with diffidence answered:

"You know my lord that I died on the night you honored me with your visit; my cousin maintains it was from one of your glances, but I cannot believe him, for to me they seem not so dreadful. Gulchenrouz died with me, and we were both brought into a region of desolation, where we are fed with a wretched diet. If you be dead also, and are come hither to join us, I pity your lot, for you will be stunned with the clang of the dwarfs and the storks. Besides, it is mortifying in the extreme that you as well as myself should have lost the treasures of the subterranean palace."

At the mention of the subterranean palace, the Caliph suspended his caresses, which indeed had proceeded pretty far, to seek from Nouronihar an explanation of her meaning. She then recapitulated her vision - what immediately followed - and the history of her pretended death; adding also a description of the palace of expiation from whence she had fled; and all in a manner that would have extorted his laughter, had not the thoughts of Vathek been too deeply engaged. No sooner, however, had she ended, than he again clasped her to his bosom, and said:

"Light of my eyes! the mystery is unraveled; we both are alive! Your father is a cheat, who for the sake of dividing hath deluded us both; and the Giaour, whose design, as far as I can discover, is that we shall proceed together, seems scarce a whit better. It shall be some time at least before he finds us in his palace of fire. Your lovely little person in my estimation is far more precious than all the treasures of the pre-Adamite sultans, and I wish to possess it at pleasure, and in open day for many a moon, before I go to burrow underground like a mole."

"Forget this little trifler Gulchenrouz, and" -

"Ah, my lord," interposed Nouronihar, "let me entreat that you do him no evil."

"No, no," replied Vathek, "I have already bid you forbear to alarm yourself for him. He has been brought up too much on milk and sugar to stimulate my jealousy. We will leave him with the dwarfs, who by the bye are my old acquaintances; their company will suit him far better than yours. As to other matters, I will return no more to your father's. I want not to have my ears dinned by him and his dotards with the violation of the rights of hospitality; as if it were less an honor for you to espouse the sovereign of the world, than a girl dressed up like a boy."

Nouronihar could find nothing to oppose in a discourse so eloquent. She only wished the amorous monarch had discovered more ardor for the carbuncle of Giamschid; but flattered herself it would gradually increase, and therefore yielded to his will with the most bewitching submission.

When the Caliph judged it proper he called for Bababalouk, who was asleep in the cave of Meimoune, and dreaming that the phantom of Nouronihar having mounted him once more on her swing, had just given him such a jerk that he one moment soared above the mountains, and the next sunk into the abyss. Starting from his sleep at the voice of his master, he ran gasping for breath, and had nearly fallen backward at the sight, as he believed, of the specter, by whom he had so lately been haunted in his dream.

"Ah my lord," cried he, recoiling ten steps, and covering his eyes with both hands, "do you then perform the office of a ghoul? 'Tis true you have dug up the dead yet hope not to make her your prey; for after all she hath caused me to suffer, she is even wicked enough to prey upon you."

"Cease thy folly," said Vathek, "and thou shalt soon be convinced that it is Nouronihar herself, alive and well, whom I clasp to my breast. Go only and pitch my tents in the neighboring valley. There will I fix my abode with this beautiful tulip, whose colors I soon shall restore. There exert thy best endeavors to procure whatever can augment the enjoyments of life, till I shall disclose to thee more of my will."

The news of so unlucky an event soon reached the ears of the emir, who abandoned himself to grief and despair, and began, as did all his old greybeards, to begrime his visage with ashes. A total supineness ensued; travelers were no longer entertained, no more plasters were spread, and instead of the charitable activity that had distinguished this asylum, the whole of its inhabitants exhibited only faces of a half cubit long, and uttered groans that accorded with their forlorn situation.

Though Fakhreddin bewailed his daughter as lost to him forever, yet Gulchenrouz was not forgotten. He dispatched immediate instruction to Sutlememe, Shaban, and the dwarfs, enjoining them not to undeceive the child in respect to his state, but under some pretense to convey him far from the lofty rock at the extremity of the lake, to a place which he should appoint, as safer from danger; for he suspected that Vathek intended him evil.

Gulchenrouz in the meanwhile was filled with amazement at not finding his cousin; nor were the dwarfs at all less surprised; but Sutlememe, who had more penetration, immediately guessed what had happened. Gulchenrouz was amused with the delusive hope of once more embracing Nouronihar in the interior recesses of the mountains, where the ground, strewed over with orange blossoms and jasmines, offered beds much more inviting than the withered leaves in their cabin, where they might accompany with their voices the sounds of their lutes, and chase butterflies in concert. Sutlememe was far gone in this sort of description when one of the four eunuchs beckoned her aside to apprise her of the arrival of a messenger from their fraternity, who had explained the secret of the flight of Nouronihar, and brought the commands of the emir. A council with Shaban and the dwarfs was immediately held. Their baggage being stowed in consequence of it, they embarked in a shallop and quietly sailed with the little one, who acquiesced in all their proposals. Their voyage proceeded in the same manner, till they came to the place where the lake sinks beneath the hollow of the rock, but as soon as the bark had entered it, and Gulchenrouz found himself surrounded with darkness, he was seized with a dreadful consternation, and incessantly uttered the most piercing outcries; for he now was persuaded he should actually be damned for having taken too many little freedoms in his life-time with his cousin.

But let us return to the Caliph, and her who ruled over his heart. Bababalouk had pitched the tents and closed up the extremities of the valley with magnificent screens of India cloth, which were guarded by Ethiopian slaves with their drawn sabers. To preserve the verdure of this beautiful enclosure in its natural freshness, the white eunuchs went continually round it with their red water vessels. The waving of fans was heard near the imperial pavilion, whereby the voluptuous light that glowed through the muslins, the Caliph enjoyed at full view all the attractions of Nouronihar. Inebriated with delight, he was all ear to her charming voice which accompanied the lute; while she was not less captivated with his descriptions of Samarah and the tower full of wonders, but especially with his relation of the adventure of the ball, and the chasm of the Giaour with its ebony portal.

In this manner they conversed for a day and a night; they bathed together in a basin of black marble, which admirably relieved the fairness of Nouronihar. Bababalouk, whose good graces this beauty had regained, spared no attention that their repasts might be served up with the minutest exactness: some exquisite rarity was ever placed before them; and he sent even to Shiraz for that fragrant and delicious wine which had been hoarded up in bottles prior to the birth of Mahomet. He had excavated little ovens in the rock to bake the nice manchets which were prepared by the hands of Nouronihar, from whence they had derived a flavor so grateful to Vathek, that he regarded the ragouts of his other wives as entirely maukish; whilst they would have died at the emir's of chagrin at finding themselves so neglected, if Fakhreddin, notwithstanding his resentment, had not taken pity upon them.

The sultana Dilara, who till then had been the favorite, took this dereliction of the Caliph to heart with a vehemence natural to her character; for during her continuance in favor she had imbibed from Vathek many of his extravagant fancies, and was fired with impatience to behold the superb tombs of Istakar, and the palace of forty columns; besides, having been brought up amongst the magi, she had fondly cherished the idea of the Caliph's devoting himself to the worship of fire; thus his voluptuous and desultory life with her rival was to her a double source of affliction. The transient piety of Vathek had occasioned her some serious alarms, but the present was an evil of far greater magnitude. She resolved therefore without hesitation to write to Carathis, and acquaint her that all things went ill; that they had eaten, slept, and reveled at an old emir's, whose sanctity was very formidable, and that after all the prospect of possessing the treasures of the pre-Adamite sultans was no less remote than before. This letter was entrusted to the care of two woodmen who were at work on one of the great forests of the mountains, and being acquainted with the shortest cuts, arrived in ten days at Samarah.

The princess Carathis was engaged at chess with Morakanabad, when the arrival of these wood-fellers was announced. She, after some weeks of Vathek's absence, had forsaken the upper regions of her tower, because everything appeared in confusion among the stars, whom she consulted relative to the fate of her son. In vain did she renew her fumigations and extend herself on the roof to obtain mystic visions, nothing more could she see in her dreams than pieces of brocade, nosegays of flowers, and other unmeaning gewgaws. These disappointments had thrown her into a state of dejection which no drug in her power was sufficient to remove. Her only resource was in Morakanabad, who was a good man, and endowed with a decent share of confidence, yet whilst in her company he never thought himself on roses.

No person knew aught of Vathek, and a thousand ridiculous stories were propagated at his expense. The eagerness of Carathis may be easily guessed at receiving the letter, as well as her rage at reading the dissolute conduct of her son.

"Is it so," said she; "either I will perish, or Vathek shall enter the palace of fire. Let me expire in flames, provided he may reign on the throne of Soliman!"

Having said this, and whirled herself round in a magical manner, which struck Morakanabad with such terror as caused him to recoil, she ordered her great camel Alboufaki to be brought, and the hideous Nerkes with the unrelenting Cafour to attend.

"I require no other retinue," said she to Morakanabad: "I am going on affairs of emergency, a truce therefore to parade! Take you care of the people, fleece them well in my absence, for we shall expend large sums, and one knows not what may betide."

The night was uncommonly dark, and a pestilential blast ravaged the plain of Catoul that would have deterred any other traveler however urgent the call; but Carathis enjoyed most whatever filled others with dread. Nerkes concurred in opinion with her, and Cafour had a particular predilection for a pestilence. In the morning this accomplished caravan, with the wood-fellers who directed their route, halted on the edge of an extensive marsh, from whence so noxious a vapor arose as would have destroyed any animal but Alboufaki, who naturally inhaled these malignant fogs. The peasants entreated their convoy not to sleep in this place.

"To sleep," cried Carathis, "what an excellent thought! I never sleep but for visions; and as to my attendants, their occupations are too many to close the only eye they each have."

The poor peasants, who were not over pleased with their party, remained open-mouthed with surprise.

Carathis alighted as well as her negresses, and severally stripping off their outer garments, they all ran in their drawers to cull from those spots where the sun shone fiercest, the venomous plants that grew on the marsh. This provision was made for the family of the emir, and whoever might retard the expedition to Istakar. The woodmen were overcome with fear when they beheld these three horrible phantoms run, and not much relishing the company of Alboufaki, stood aghast at the command of Carathis to set forward, notwithstanding it was noon, and the heat fierce enough to calcine even rocks. In spite, however, of every remonstrance, they were forced implicitly to submit.

Alboufaki, who delighted in solitude, constantly snorted whenever he perceived himself near a habitation, and Carathis, who was apt to spoil him with indulgence, as constantly turned him aside; so that the peasants were precluded from procuring subsistence; for the milk goats and ewes which Providence had sent towards the district they traversed, to refresh travelers with their milk, all fled at the sight of the hideous animal and his strange riders. As to Carathis, she needed no common aliment; for her invention had previously furnished her with an opiate to stay her stomach, some of which she imparted to her mutes.

At the fall of night Alboufaki making a sudden stop, stamped with his foot, which to Carathis, who understood his paces, was a certain indication that she was near the confines of some cemetery. The moon shed a bright light on the spot, which served to discover a long wall with a large door in it standing a-jar, and so high that Alboufaki might easily enter. The miserable guides, who perceived their end approaching, humbly implored Carathis, as she had now so good an opportunity, to inter them, and immediately gave up the ghost. Nerkes and Cafour, whose wit was of a style peculiar to themselves, were by no means parsimonious of it on the folly of these poor people, nor could anything have been found more suited to their taste than the site of the burying ground, and the sepulchers which its precincts contained. There were at least two thousand of them on the declivity of a hill; some in the form of pyramids, others like columns, and in short, the variety of their shapes was endless. Carathis was too much immersed in her sublime contemplations to stop at the view, charming as it appeared in her eyes. Pondering the advantages that might accrue from her present situation, she could not forbear to exclaim:

"So beautiful a cemetery must be haunted by Ghouls, and they want not for intelligence! having heedlessly suffered my guides to expire, I will apply for directions to them, and as an inducement, will invite them to regale on these fresh corpses."

After this short soliloquy, she beckoned to Nerkes and Cafour, and made signs with her fingers, as much as to say:

"Go, knock against the sides of the tombs, and strike up your delightful warbling's, that are so like to those of the guests whose company I wish to obtain."

The negresses, full of joy at the behests of their mistress, and promising themselves much pleasure from the society of the Ghouls, went with an air of conquest, and began their knockings at the tombs. As their strokes were repeated, a hollow noise was heard in the earth, the surface hove up into heaps, and the Ghouls on all sides protruded their noses to inhale the effluvia which the carcasses of the woodmen began to emit.

They assembled before a sarcophagus of white marble, where Carathis was seated between the bodies of her miserable guides. The princess received her visitants with distinguished politeness, and when supper was ended, proceeded with them to business. Having soon learnt from them everything she wished to discover, it was her intention to set forward forthwith on her journey, but her negresses, who were forming tender connections with the Ghouls, importuned her with all their fingers to wait, at least till the dawn. Carathis, however, being chastity in the abstract, and an implacable enemy to love and repose, at once rejected their prayer, mounted Alboufaki, and commanded them to take their seats in a moment. Four days and four nights she continued her route, without turning to the right hand or left; on the fifth she traversed the mountains and half-burnt forests, and arrived on the sixth before the beautiful screens which concealed from all eyes the voluptuous wanderings of her son.

It was daybreak, and the guards were snoring on their posts in careless security, when the rough trot of Alboufaki awoke them in consternation. Imagining that a group of specters ascended from the abyss was approaching, they all without ceremony took to their heels. Vathek was at that instant with Nouronihar in the bath, hearing tales and laughing at Bababalouk who related them; but no sooner did the outcry of his guards reach him, than he flounced from the water like a carp, and as soon threw himself back at the sight of Carathis, who advancing with her negresses upon Alboufaki, broke through the muslin awnings and veils of the pavilion. At this sudden apparition Nouronihar (for she was not at all times free from remorse) fancied that the moment of celestial vengeance was come and clung about the Caliph in amorous despondence.

Carathis, still seated on her camel, foamed with indignation at the spectacle which obtruded itself on her chaste view. She thundered forth without check or mercy:

"Thou double-headed and four-legged monster! What means all this winding and writhing? art thou not ashamed to be seen grasping this limber sapling, in preference to the scepter of the pre-Adamite sultans? Is it then for this paltry doxy that thou hast violated the conditions in the parchment of our Giaour? Is it on her thou hast lavished thy precious moments? Is this the fruit of the knowledge I have taught thee? Is this the end of thy journey? Tear thyself from the arms of this little simpleton; drown her in the water before me, and instantly follow my guidance."

In the first ebullition of his fury, Vathek resolved to make a skeleton of Alboufaki, and to stuff the skins of Carathis and her blacks; but the ideas of the Giaour, the palace of Istakar, the sabers, and the talismans, flashing before his imagination with the simultaneousness of lightning, he became more moderate, and said to his mother in a civil but decisive tone:

"Dread lady, you shall be obeyed; but I will not drown Nouronihar; she is sweeter to me than a Myrobalan comfit, and is enamored of carbuncles, especially that of Giamschid, which hath also been promised to be conferred upon her; she therefore shall go along with us, for I intend to repose with her beneath the canopies of Soliman; I can sleep no more without her."

"Be it so," replied Carathis alighting, and at the same time committing Alboufaki to the charge of her women.

Nouronihar, who had not yet quitted her hold, began to take courage, and said with an accent of fondness to the Caliph:

"Dear sovereign of my soul! I will follow thee, if it be thy will beyond the Kaf, in the land of the Afrits. I will not hesitate to climb for thee the nest of the

Simurgh, who, this lady excepted, is the most awful of created existences."

"We have here then," subjoined Carathis, "a girl both of courage and science."

Nouronihar had certainly both; but notwithstanding all her firmness, she could not help casting back a look of regret upon the graces of her little Gulchenrouz, and the days of tenderness she had participated with him. She even dropped a few tears, which Carathis observed, and inadvertently breathed out with a sigh:

"Alas! my gentle cousin, what will become of him!"

Vathek at this apostrophe knitted up his brows, and Carathis enquired what it could mean.

"She is preposterously sighing after a stripling with languishing eyes and soft hair who loves her," said the Caliph.

"Where is he?" asked Carathis. "I must be acquainted with this pretty child; for," added she, lowering her voice, "I design before I depart to regain the favor of the Giaour. There is nothing so delicious in his estimation as the heart of a delicate boy, palpitating with the first tumults of love."

Vathek as he came from the bath commanded Bababalouk to collect the women and other movables of his harem, embody his troops, and hold himself in readiness to march in three days; whilst Carathis retired alone to a tent, where the Giaour solaced her with encouraging visions; but at length waking, she found at her feet Nerkes and Cafour, who informed her by their signs, that having led Alboufaki to the borders of a lake, to browse on some moss that looked tolerably venomous, they had discovered certain blue fishes of the same kind with those in the reservoir on the top of the tower.

"Ah, ah," said she, "I will go thither to them. These fish are past doubt of a species that by a small operation I can render oracular. They may tell me where this little Gulchenrouz is, whom I am bent upon sacrificing."

Having thus spoken, she immediately set out with her swarthy retinue.

It being but seldom that time is lost in the accomplishment of a wicked enterprise, Carathis and her negresses soon arrived at the lake, where, after burning the magical drugs with which they were always provided, they, stripping themselves naked, waded to their chins, Nerkes and Cafour waving torches around them, and Carathis pronouncing her barbarous incantations. The fishes with one accord thrust forth their heads from the water, which was violently rippled by the flutter of their fins, and at length finding themselves constrained by the potency of the charm, they opened their piteous mouths, said:

"From gills to tail we are yours; what seek ye to know?"

"Fishes," answered she, "I conjure you by your glittering scales, tell me where now is Gulchenrouz?"

"Beyond the rock," replied the shoal in full chorus: "will this content you? for we do not delight in expanding our mouths."

"It will," returned the princess: "I am not to learn that you like not long conversations; I will leave you therefore to repose, though I had other questions to propound."

The instant she had spoken the water became smooth, and the fishes at once disappeared.

Carathis, inflated with the venom of her projects, strode hastily over the rock, and found the amiable Gulchenrouz asleep in an arbor, whilst the two dwarfs were watching at his side, and ruminating their accustomed prayers. These diminutive personages possessed the gift of divining whenever an enemy to good Mussulmans approached; thus, they anticipated the arrival of Carathis, who stopping short, said to herself:

"How placidly doth he reclines his lovely little head! how pale and languishing are his looks! it is just the very child of my wishes!"

The dwarfs interrupted this delectable soliloquy by leaping instantly upon her and scratching her face with their utmost zeal. But Nerkes and Cafour be taking themselves to the succor of their mistress, pinched the dwarfs so severely in return, that they both gave up the ghost, imploring Mahomet to inflict his sorest vengeance upon this wicked woman and all her household.

At the noise which this strange conflict occasioned in the valley, Gulchenrouz awoke, and bewildered with terror sprung impetuously upon an old fig-tree that rose against the acclivity of the rocks, from thence gained their summits, and ran for two hours without once looking back. At last, exhausted with fatigue, he fell as if dead into the arms of a good old Genius, whose fondness for the company of children had made it his sole occupation to protect them, and who, whilst performing his wonted rounds through the air, happening on the cruel Giaour at the instant of his growling in the horrible chasm, rescued the fifty little victims which the impiety of Vathek had devoted to his maw. These the Genius brought up in nests still higher than the clouds, and himself fixed his abode in a nest more capacious than the rest, from which he had expelled the possessors that had built it.

These inviolable asylums were defended against the Dives and the Afrits by waving streamers, on which were inscribed in characters of gold that flashed like lightning, the names of Allah and the prophet. It was there that Gulchenrouz, who as yet remained undeceived with respect to his pretended death, thought himself in the mansions of eternal peace. He admitted without fear the congratulations of his little friends, who were all assembled in the nest of the venerable Genius and vied with each other in kissing his serene forehead and beautiful eyelids. This he found to be the state congenial to his soul—remote from the inquietudes of earth - the impertinence of harems - the brutality of eunuchs - and the lubricity of women. In this peaceable society his days, months, and years glided on, nor was he less happy than the rest of his companions, for the Genius, instead of burdening his pupils with perishable riches, and the vain sciences of the world, conferred upon them the boon of perpetual childhood.

Carathis, unaccustomed to the loss of her prey, vented a thousand execrations on her negresses for not seizing the child, instead of amusing themselves with pinching to death the dwarfs, from which they could gain no advantage. She returned into the valley murmuring and finding that her son was not risen from the arms of Nouronihar, discharged her ill-humor upon both. The idea, however, of departing next day for Istakar, and cultivating, through the good offices of the Giaour, an intimacy with Eblis himself, at length consoled her chagrin: but fate had ordained it otherwise.

In the evening, as Carathis was conversing with Dilara, who through her contrivance had become of the party, and whose taste resembled her own, Bababalouk came to acquaint her "that the sky towards Samarah looked of a fiery red, and seemed to portend some alarming disaster." Immediately recurring to her astrolabes and instruments of magic, she took the altitude of the planets, and discovered by her calculations, to her great mortification, that a formidable revolt had taken place at Samarah; that Motavakel, availing himself of the disgust which was inveterate against his brother had incited commotions amongst the populace, made himself master of the palace, and actually invested the great tower, to which Morakanabad had retired with a handful of the few that still remained faithful to Vathek.

"What," exclaimed she, "must I lose then my tower, my mutes, my negresses, my mummies, and worse than all, the laboratory, in which I have spent so many a night, without knowing, at least, if my hair-brained son will complete his adventure? No! I will not be the dupe! Immediately will I speed to support Morakanabad. By my formidable art the clouds shall sleet hailstones in the faces of the assailants, and shafts of red-hot iron on their heads. I will spring mines of serpents and torpedoes from beneath them, and we shall soon see the stand they will make against such an explosion!"

Having thus spoken, Carathis hasted to her son, who was tranquilly banqueting with Nouronihar in his superb carnation colored tent.

"Glutton that thou art," cried she, "were it not for me, thou wouldst soon find thyself the commander only of pies. Thy faithful subjects have abjured the faith they swore to thee. Motavakel thy brother now reigns on the hill of pied horses; and had I not some slight resources in the tower, would not be easily persuaded to abdicate. But that time may not be lost, I shall only add four words: strike tent to-night; set forward; and beware how thou loiterest again by the way. Though thou hast forfeited the conditions of the parchment, I am not yet without hope; for it cannot be denied that thou hast violated to admiration the laws of hospitality by seducing the daughter of the emir, after having partaken of his bread and his salt. Such a conduct cannot but be delightful to the Giaour; and if on thy march thou canst signalize thyself by an additional crime, all will still go well, and thou shalt enter the palace of Soliman in triumph. Adieu! Alboufaki and my negresses are waiting."

The Caliph had nothing to offer in reply: he wished his mother a prosperous journey and eat on till he had finished his supper. At midnight the camp broke up, amidst the flourishing of trumpets and other martial instruments; but loud indeed must have been the sound of the tymbals, to overpower the blubbering of the emir and his long-beards, who by an excessive profusion of tears had so far exhausted the radical moisture, that their eyes shriveled up in their sockets, and their hairs dropped off by the roots. Nouronihar, to whom such a symphony was painful, did not grieve to get out of hearing. She accompanied the Caliph in the imperial litter, where they amused themselves with imagining the splendor which was soon to surround them. The other women, overcome with dejection, were dolefully rocked in their cages, whilst Dilara consoled herself with anticipating the joy of celebrating the rites of fire on the stately terraces of Istakar.

In four days, they reached the spacious valley of Rocnabad. The season of spring was in all its vigor, and the grotesque branches of the almond trees in full blossom fantastically checkered the clear blue sky. The earth, variegated with hyacinths and jonquils, breathed forth a fragrance which diffused through the soul a divine repose. Myriads of bees, and scarce fewer of Santons had there taken up their abode. On the banks of the stream hives and oratories were alternately ranged, and their neatness and whiteness were set off by the deep green of the cypresses that spired up amongst them. These pious personages amused themselves with cultivating little gardens that abounded with flowers and fruits, especially muskmelons of the best flavor that Persia could boast. Sometimes dispersed over the meadow they entertained themselves with feeding peacocks whiter than snow, and turtles more blue than the sapphire. In this manner were they occupied when the harbingers of the imperial procession began to proclaim:

"Inhabitants of Rocnabad, prostrate yourselves on the brink of your pure waters, and tender your thanksgivings to heaven that vouchsafeth to shew you a ray of its glory; for lo! the commander of the faithful draws near."

The poor Santons, filled with holy energy, having bustled to light up wax torches in their oratories, and expand the Koran on their ebony desks, went forth to meet the Caliph with baskets of honeycomb, dates, and melons. But whilst they were advancing in solemn procession and with measured steps, the horses, camels, and guards wantoned over their tulips and other flowers, and made a terrible havoc amongst them. The Santons could not help casting from one eye a look of pity on the ravages committing around them, whilst the other was fixed upon the Caliph and heaven. Nouronihar, enraptured with the scenery of a place which brought back to her remembrance the pleasing solitudes where her infancy had passed, entreated Vathek to stop, but he, suspecting that each oratory might be deemed by the Giaour a distinct habitation, commanded his pioneers to level them all. The Santons stood motionless with horror at the barbarous mandate, and at last broke out into lamentations, but these were uttered with so ill a grace, that Vathek bade his eunuchs to kick them from his presence. He then descended from the litter with Nouronihar. They sauntered together in the meadow, and amused themselves with culling flowers, and passing a thousand pleasantries on each other. But the bees, who were staunch Mussulmans, thinking it their duty to revenge the insult on their dear masters the Santons, assembled so zealously to do it with effect, that the Caliph and Nouronihar were glad to find their tents prepared to receive them.

Bababalouk, who in capacity of purveyor, had acquitted himself with applause, as to peacocks and turtles, lost no time in consigning some dozens to the spit, and as many more to be fricasseed. Whilst they were feasting, laughing, carousing, and blaspheming at pleasure on the banquet so liberally furnished, the Mullahs, the Sheiks, the Cadis, and Iman's of Shiraz (who seemed not to have met the Santons) arrived, leading by bridles of ribband, inscribed from the Koran, a train of asses which were loaded with the choicest fruits the country could boast. Having presented their offerings to the Caliph, they petitioned him to honor their city and mosques with his presence.

"Fancy not," said Vathek, "that you can detain me. Your presents I condescend to accept, but beg you will let me be quiet, for I am not over fond of resisting temptation. Retire then. Yet, as it is not decent for personages so reverend to return on foot, and as you have not the appearance of expert riders, my eunuchs shall tie you on your asses with the precaution that your backs be not turned towards me, for they understand etiquette."

In this deputation were some high-stomached Shoiks, who taking Vathek for a fool, scrupled not to speak their opinion. These Bababalouk girded with double cords; and having well-disciplined their asses with nettles behind, they all started with a preternatural alertness, plunging, kicking, and running afoul of each other in the most ludicrous manner imaginable.

Nouronihar and the Caliph mutually contended who should most enjoy so degrading a sight. They burst out in volleys of laughter to see the old men and their asses fall into the stream. The leg of one was fractured, the shoulder of another dislocated, the teeth of a third dashed out, and the rest suffered still worse.

Two days more, undisturbed by fresh embassies, having been devoted to the pleasures of Rocnabad, the expedition proceeded, leaving Shiraz on the right, and verging towards a large plain, from whence were discernible on the edge of the horizon the dark summits of the mountains of Istakar.

At this prospect the Caliph and Nouronihar were unable to repress their transports. They bounded from their litter to the ground and broke forth into such wild exclamations as amazed all within hearing. Interrogating each other, they shouted,

"Are we not approaching the radiant palace of light, or gardens more delightful than those of Sheddad?"

Infatuated mortals! they thus indulged delusive conjecture, unable to fathom the decrees of the Most High!

The good Genii who had not totally relinquished the superintendence of Vathek, repairing to Mahomet in the seventh heaven, said:

"Merciful Prophet! stretch forth thy propitious arms towards thy vicegerent, who is ready to fall irretrievably into the snare which his enemies the Dives have prepared to destroy him. The Giaour is awaiting his arrival in the abominable palace of fire, where if he once set his foot his perdition will be inevitable."

Mahomet answered with an air of indignation:

"He hath too well deserved to be resigned to himself; but I permit you to try if one effort more will be effectual to divert him from pursuing his ruin."

One of these beneficent Genii, assuming without delay the exterior of a shepherd, more renowned for his piety than all the Dervishes and Santons of the region, took his station near a flock of white sheep on the slope of a hill, and began to pour forth from his flute such airs of pathetic melody, as subdued the very soul; and awakening remorse, drove far from it every frivolous fancy. At these energetic sounds, the sun hid himself beneath a gloomy cloud; and the waters of two little lakes, that were naturally clearer than crystal, became a color like blood. The whole of this superb assembly was involuntarily drawn towards the declivity of the hill. With downcast eyes, they all stood abashed; each upbraiding himself with the evil he had done. The heart of Dilara palpitated; and the chief of the eunuchs, with a sigh of contrition, implored pardon of the women, whom, for his own satisfaction, he had so often tormented.

Vathek and Nouronihar turned pale in their litter; and, regarding each other with haggard looks, reproached themselves—the one with a thousand of the blackest crimes, a thousand projects of impious ambition; the other, with the desolation of her family, and the perdition of the amiable Gulchenrouz. Nouronihar persuaded herself that she heard in the fatal music the groans of her dying father; and Vathek, the sobs of the fifty children he had sacrificed to the Giaour. Amidst these complicated pangs of anguish, they perceived themselves impelled towards the shepherd, whose countenance was so commanding, that Vathek, for the first time, felt overawed; whilst Nouronihar concealed her face with her hands. The music paused, and the Genius, addressing the Caliph, said:

"Deluded Prince! to whom Providence hath confided the care of innumerable subjects, is it thus that thou fulfillest thy mission? Thy crimes are already completed; and art thou now hastening towards thy punishment? Thou knowest, that beyond these mountains, Eblis and his accursed Dives hold their infernal empire; and seduced by a malignant phantom, thou art proceeding to surrender thyself to them! This moment is the last of grace allowed thee! Abandon thy atrocious purpose. Return. Give back Nouronihar to her father, who still retains a few sparks of life. Destroy thy tower, with all its abominations. Drive Carathis from thy councils. Be just to thy subjects. Respect the ministers of the Prophet. Compensate for thy impieties by an exemplary life; and, instead of squandering thy days in voluptuous indulgence, lament thy crimes on the sepulchers of thy ancestors. Thou beholdest the clouds that obscure the sun; at the instant he recovers his splendor, if thy heart be not changed, the time of mercy assigned thee will be past forever."

Vathek, depressed with fear, was on the point of prostrating himself at the feet of the shepherd, whom he perceived to be of a nature superior to man, but his pride prevailing, he audaciously lifted his head, and glancing at him one of his terrible looks, said:

"Whoever thou art, withhold thy useless admonitions. Thou wouldst either delude me, or art thyself deceived. If what I have done be so criminal as thou pretendest, there remains not for me a moment of grace. I have traversed a sea of blood, to acquire a power which will make thy equals tremble; deem not that I shall retire when in view of the port; or that I will relinquish her who is dearer to me than either my life or thy mercy. Let the sun appear! Let him illumine my career! It matters not where it may end."

On uttering these words, which made even the Genius shudder, Vathek threw himself into the arms of Nouronihar, and commanded that his horses should be forced back to the road.

There was no difficulty in obeying these orders, for the attraction had ceased, the sun shone forth in all his glory, and the shepherd vanished with a lamentable scream.

The fatal impression of the music of the Genius remained, notwithstanding, in the hearts of Vathek's attendants. They viewed each other with looks of consternation. At the approach of night, almost all of them escaped; and, of this numerous assemblage, there only remained the chief of the eunuchs, some idolatrous slaves, Dilara, and a few other women, who, like herself, were votaries of the religion of the Magi.

The Caliph, fired with the ambition of prescribing laws to the Intelligences of Darkness, was but little embarrassed at this dereliction. The impetuosity of his blood prevented him from sleeping; nor did he encamp any more as before. Nouronihar, whose impatience, if possible, exceeded his own, importuned him to hasten his march, and lavished on him a thousand caresses, to beguile all reflection. She fancied herself already more potent than Balkis; and pictured to her imagination the Genii falling prostrate at the foot of her throne. In this manner they advanced by moonlight, till they came within view of the two towering rocks, that form a kind of portal to the valley, at whose extremity rose the vast ruins of Istakar. Aloft on the mountain, glimmered the fronts of various royal mausoleums, the horror of which was deepened by the shadows of night. They passed through two villages, almost deserted; the only inhabitants remaining being a few feeble old men, who at the sight of horses and litters fell upon their knees, and cried out:

"O heaven! is it then by these phantoms that we have been for six months tormented! Alas! it was from the terror of these specters, and the noise beneath the mountains, that our people have fled, and left us at the mercy of maleficent spirits!"

The Caliph, to whom these complaints were but unpromising auguries, drove over the bodies of these wretched old men, and at length arrived at the foot of the terrace of black marble. There he descended from his litter, handing down Nouronihar; both, with beating hearts, stared wildly around them, and expected, with an apprehensive shudder, the approach of the Giaour. But nothing as yet announced his appearance.

A deathlike stillness reigned over the mountain, and through the air. The moon dilated, on a vast platform, the shades of the lofty columns, which reached from the terrace almost to the clouds. The gloomy watch-towers, whose number could not be counted, were veiled by no roof: and their capitals, of an architecture unknown in the records of the earth, served as an asylum for the birds of darkness, which, alarmed at the approach of such visitants, fled away croaking.

The chief of the eunuchs, trembling with fear, besought Vathek that a fire might be kindled.

"No!" replied he, "there is no time left to think of such trifles; abide where thou art and expect my commands."

Having thus spoken, he presented his hand to Nouronihar, and ascending the steps of a vast staircase, reached the terrace, which was flagged with squares of marble, and resembled a smooth expanse of water, upon whose surface not a leaf ever dared to vegetate. On the right rose the watchtowers, ranged before the ruins of an immense palace, whose walls were embossed with various figures. In front stood forth the colossal forms of four creatures, composed of the leopard and the griffin: and though but of stone, inspired emotions of terror. Near these were distinguished by the splendor of the moon, which streamed full on the place, characters like those on the sabers of the Giaour, that possessed the same virtue of changing every moment. These, after vacillating for some time, at last fixed in Arabic letters, and prescribed to the Caliph the following words:

"Vathek! thou hast violated the conditions of my parchment, and deservest to be sent back; but in favor to thy companion, and as the need for what thou hast done to obtain it, Eblis permitteth that the portal of his palace shall be opened, and the subterranean fire will receive thee into the number of its adorers." He scarcely had read these words before the mountain, against which the terrace was reared, trembled; and the watchtowers were ready to topple headlong upon them. The rock yawned, and disclosed within it a staircase of polished marble, that seemed to approach the abyss. Upon each stair were planted two large torches, like those Nouronihar had seen in her vision, the camphorated vapor ascending from which gathered into a cloud under the hollow of the vault.

This appearance, instead of terrifying, gave new courage to the daughter of Fakhreddin. Scarcely deigning to bid adieu to the moon and the firmament, she abandoned without hesitation the pure atmosphere, to plunge into these infernal exhalations. The gait of those impious personages was haughty and determined.

As they descended, by the effulgence of the torches, they gazed on each other with mutual admiration, and both appeared so resplendent, that they already esteemed themselves spiritual intelligences. The only circumstance that perplexed them, was they're not arriving at the bottom of the stairs. On hastening their descent, with an ardent impetuosity, they felt their steps accelerated to such a degree, that they seemed not walking, but falling from a precipice. Their progress, however, was at length impeded by a vast portal of ebony, which the Caliph without difficulty recognized. Here the Giaour awaited them, with the key in his hand,

"Ye are welcome!" said he to them, with a ghastly smile, "in spite of Mahomet, and all his dependents. I will now admit you into that palace, where you have so highly merited a place."

Whilst he was uttering these words, he touched the enameled lock with his key, and the doors at once expanded with a noise still louder than the thunder of mountains, and as suddenly recoiled the moment they had entered.

The Caliph and Nouronihar beheld each other with amazement, at finding themselves in a place which, though roofed with a vaulted ceiling, was so spacious and lofty, that at first, they took it for an immeasurable plain. But their eyes at length growing to the grandeur of the objects at hand, they extended their view to those at a distance, and discovered rows of columns and arcades, which gradually diminished, till they terminated in a point, radiant as the sun, when he darts his last beams athwart the ocean. The pavement, strewed over with gold dust and saffron, exhaled so subtle an odor, as almost overpowered them. They, however, went on, and observed an infinity of censers, in which ambergris and the wood of aloes were continually burning. Between the several columns were placed tables, each spread with a profusion of viands, and wines of every species, sparkling in vases of crystal. A throng of Genii, and other fantastic spirits, of each sex, danced lasciviously in troops, at the sound of music which issued from beneath.

In the midst of this immense hall, a vast multitude was incessantly passing, who severally kept their right hands on their hearts, without once regarding any thing around them. They had all the livid paleness of death. Their eyes, deep sank in their sockets, resembled those phosphoric meteors, that glimmer by night in places of interment. Some stalked slowly on, absorbed in profound reverie; some shrieking with agony, ran furiously about, like tigers wounded with poisoned arrows; whilst others, grinding their teeth in rage, foamed along, more frantic than the wildest maniac. They all avoided each other, and though surrounded by a multitude that no one could number, each wandered at random unheedful of the rest, as if alone on a desert which no foot had trodden.

Vathek and Nouronihar, frozen with terror at a sight so baleful, demanded of the Giaour what these appearances might mean, and why these ambulating specters never withdrew their hands from their hearts.

"Perplex not yourselves," replied he bluntly, "with so much at once, you will soon be acquainted with all; let us haste and present you to Eblis."

They continued their way through the multitude, but notwithstanding their confidence at first, they were not sufficiently composed to examine with attention the various perspectives of halls, and of galleries, that opened on the right hand and left, which were all illuminated by torches and braziers, whose flames rose in pyramids, to the center of the vault. At length they came to a place where long curtains, brocaded with crimson and gold, fell from all parts, in striking confusion. Here the choirs and dances were heard no longer. The light which glimmered came from afar.

After some time Vathek and Nouronihar perceived a gleam brightening through the drapery, and entered a vast tabernacle, carpeted with the skins of leopards. An infinity of elders, with streaming beards, and afrits, in complete armor, had prostrated themselves before the ascent of a lofty eminence, on the top of which, upon a globe of fire, sat the formidable Eblis. His person was that of a young man, whose noble and regular features seemed to have been tarnished by malignant vapors. In his large eyes appeared both pride and despair; his flowing hair retained some resemblance to that of an angel of light. In his hand, which thunder had blasted, he swayed the iron scepter, that causes the monster Ouranabad, the afrits, and all the powers of the abyss to tremble. At his presence the heart of the Caliph sank within him, and, for the first time, he fell prostrate on his face. Nouronihar, however, though greatly dismayed, could not help admiring the person of Eblis, for she expected to have seen some stupendous giant. Eblis, with a voice milder than might be imagined, but such as transfused through the soul the deepest melancholy, said:

"Creatures of clay, I receive you into mine empire. Ye are numbered amongst my adorers. Enjoy whatever this palace affords - the treasures of the pre-Adamite sultans, their bickering sabers, and those talismans that compel the Dives to open the subterranean expanses of the mountain of Kaf, which communicate with these. There, insatiable as your curiosity may be, shall you find sufficient to gratify it. You shall possess the exclusive privilege of entering the fortress of Akerman, and the halls of Argenk, where are portrayed all creatures endowed with intelligence, and the various animals that inhabited the earth prior to the creation of that contemptible being, whom ye denominate the Father of Mankind."

Vathek and Nouronihar feeling themselves revived and encouraged by this harangue, eagerly said to the Giaour:

"Bring us instantly to the place which contains these precious talismans."

"Come," answered this wicked Dive, with his malignant grin, "come, and possess all that my sovereign hath promised, and more."

He then conducted them into a long aisle adjoining the tabernacle, preceding them with hasty steps, and followed by his disciples with the utmost alacrity. They reached at length a hall of great extent, and covered with a lofty dome, around which appeared fifty portals of bronze, secured with as many fastenings of iron. A funereal gloom prevailed over the whole scene. Here, upon two beds of incorruptible cedar, lay recumbent the fleshless forms of the pre-Adamite kings, who had been monarchs of the whole earth. They still possessed enough of life to be conscious of their deplorable condition. Their eyes retained a melancholy motion; they regarded each other with looks of the deepest dejection, each holding his right hand motionless on his heart. At their feet were inscribed the events of their several reigns, their power, their pride, and their crimes. Soliman Raad, Soliman Daki, and Soliman Di Gian Ben Gian, who, after having chained up the Dives in the dark caverns of Kaf, became so presumptuous, as to doubt of the Supreme Power. All these maintained great states, though not to be compared with the eminence of Soliman Ben Daoud.

This king, so renowned for his wisdom, was on the loftiest elevation, and placed immediately under the dome. He appeared to possess more animation than the rest, though, from time to time, he labored with profound sighs, and, like his companions, kept his right hand on his heart; yet his countenance was more composed, and he seemed to be listening to the sullen roar of a vast cataract, visible in part through the grated portals. This was the only sound that intruded on the silence of these doleful mansions. A range of brazen vases surrounded the elevation.

"Remove the covers from these cabalistic depositaries," said the Giaour to Vathek, "and avail thyself of the talismans, which will break asunder all these gates of bronze, and not only render thee master of the treasures contained within them, but also of the spirits by which they are guarded."

The Caliph, whom this ominous preliminary had entirely disconcerted, approached the vases with faltering footsteps, and was ready to sink with terror, when he heard the groans of Soliman. As he proceeded, a voice from the livid lips of the prophet articulated these words:

"In my lifetime, I filled a magnificent throne, having on my right hand twelve thousand seats of gold, where the patriarchs and prophets heard my doctrines; on my left the sages and doctors, upon as many thrones of silver, were present at all my decisions. Whilst I thus administered justice to innumerable multitudes, the birds of the air liberating over me, served as a canopy from the rays of the sun. My people flourished, and my palace rose to the clouds. I erected a temple to the Most High, which was the wonder of the universe; but I basely suffered myself to be seduced by the love of women, and a curiosity that could not be restrained by sub-lunary things. I listened to the counsels of Aherman, and the daughter of Pharaoh, and adored fire, and the host of heaven. I forsook the holy city and commanded the Genii to rear the stupendous palace of Istakar, and the terrace of the watchtowers, each of which was consecrated to a star. There for a while I enjoyed myself in the zenith of glory and pleasure. Not only men, but supernatural existences were subject also to my will. I began to think, as these unhappy monarchs around had already thought, that the vengeance of heaven was asleep, when at once the thunder burst my structures asunder, and precipitated me hither; where, however, I do not remain like the other inhabitants totally destitute of hope, for an angel of light hath revealed, that in consideration of the piety of my early youth, my woes shall come to an end when this cataract shall forever cease to flow. Till then I am in torments, ineffable torments, an unrelenting fire preys on my heart."

Having uttered this exclamation, Soliman raised his hands towards heaven, in token of supplication, and the Caliph discerned through his bosom, which was transparent as crystal, his heart enveloped in flames. At a sight so full of horror, Nouronihar fell back like one petrified, into the arms of Vathek, who cried out with a convulsive sob:

"O Giaour! whither hast thou brought us! Allow us to depart, and I will relinquish all thou hast promised. O Mahomet! remains there no more mercy!"

"None! none!" replied the malicious Dive. "Know, miserable prince, thou art now in the abode of vengeance, and despair. Thy heart, also, will be kindled, like those of the other votaries of Eblis. A few days are allotted thee previous to this fatal period; employ them as thou wilt. Recline on these heaps of gold: command the Infernal Potentates: range at thy pleasure through these immense subterranean domains. No barrier shall be shut against thee. As for me, I have fulfilled my mission. I now leave thee to thyself."

At these words he vanished.

The Caliph and Nouronihar remained in the most abject affliction. Their tears unable to flow, scarcely could they support themselves. At length, taking each other despondingly by the hand, they went faltering from this fatal hall, indifferent which way they turned their steps. Every portal opened at their approach. The Dives fell prostrate before them. Every reservoir of riches was disclosed to their view, but they no longer felt the incentives of curiosity, pride, or avarice. With like apathy they heard the chorus of Genii, and saw the stately banquets prepared to regale them. They went wandering on from chamber to chamber, hall to hall, and gallery to gallery; all without bounds or limit; all distinguishable by the same lowering gloom; all adorned with the same awful grandeur; all traversed by persons in search of repose and consolation, but who sought them in vain, for every one carried within him a heart tormented in flames. Shunned by these various sufferers, who seemed by their looks to be upbraiding the partners of their guilt, they withdrew from them, to wait in direful suspense the moment which should render them to each other the like objects of terror.

"What," exclaimed Nouronihar, "will the time come, when I shall snatch my hand from thine!"

"Ah!" said Vathek, "and shall my eyes ever cease to drink from thine long draughts of enjoyment! Shall the moments of our reciprocal ecstasies be reflected on with horror! It was not thou that broughtest me hither; the principles by which Carathis perverted my youth have been the sole cause of my perdition!"

Having given vent to these painful expressions, he called to an Afrit, who was stirring up one of the braziers, and bade him fetch the Princess Carathis from the palace of Samarah.

After issuing these orders, the Caliph and Nouronihar continued walking amidst the silent crowd, till they heard voices at the end of the gallery. Presuming them to proceed from some unhappy beings, who like themselves were awaiting their final doom, they followed the sound, and found it to come from a small square chamber, where they discovered sitting on sofas, five young men of goodly figure, and a lovely female, who were all holding a melancholy conversation, by the glimmering of a lonely lamp. Each had a gloomy and forlorn air, and two of them were embracing each other with great tenderness. On seeing the Caliph and the daughter of Fakhreddin enter they arose, saluted, and gave them place. Then he who had appeared the most considerable of the group, addressed himself thus to Vathek:

"Strangers! who doubtless are in the same state of suspense as ourselves, as you do not yet bear your hand on your heart, if you are come hither to pass the interval allotted previous to the infliction of our common punishment, condescend to relate the adventures that have brought you to this fatal place; and we in return will acquaint you with ours; which deserves but too well to be heard. We will trace back our crimes to their source, though we are not permitted to repent. This is the only employment suited to wretches like us."

The Caliph and Nouronihar assented to the proposal, and Vathek began, not without tears and lamentations, a sincere recital of every circumstance that had passed. When the afflicting narrative was closed, the young man entered on his own. Each person proceeded in order, and when the fourth prince had reached the midst of his adventures, a sudden noise interrupted him, which caused the vault to tremble, and to open.

Immediately a cloud descended, which gradually dissipating, discovered Carathis, on the back of an Afrit, who grievously complained of his burden. She, instantly springing to the ground, advanced towards her son, and said:

"What dost thou here, in this little square chamber? As the Dives are become subject to thy beck, I expected to have found thee on the throne of the pre-Adamite kings."

"Execrable woman!" answered the Caliph; "cursed be the day thou gavest me birth! Go! follow this Afrit; let him conduct thee to the hall of the Prophet Soliman; there thou wilt learn to what these palaces are destined, and how much I ought to abhor the impious knowledge thou hast taught me."

"The height of power to which thou art arrived, has certainly turned thy brain," answered Carathis; "but I ask no more, than permission to show my respect for the prophet. It is, however, proper thou shouldst know, that, as the Afrit has informed me neither of us shall return to Samarah, I requested his permission to arrange my affairs, and he politely consented. Availing myself, therefore, of the few moments allowed me, I set fire to the tower, and consumed in it the mutes, negresses, and serpents, which have rendered me so much good service; nor should I have been less kind to Morakanabad, had he not prevented me, by deserting at last to thy brother. As for Bababalouk, who had the folly to return to Samarah, and all the good brotherhood to provide husbands for thy wives, I undoubtedly would have put them to the torture, could I but have allowed them the time. Being, however, in a hurry, I only hung him, after having caught him in a snare with thy wives; whilst them I buried alive by the help of my negresses, who thus spent their last moments, greatly to their satisfaction. With respect to Dilara, whoever stood high in my favor, she hath evinced the greatness of her mind, by fixing herself near, in the service of one of the Magi, and, I think, will soon be our own."

Vathek, too much cast down to express the indignation excited by such a discourse, ordered the Afrit to remove Carathis from his presence, and continued immersed in thought, which his companions durst not disturb.

Carathis, however, eagerly entered the dome of Soliman, and, without regarding in the least the groans of the Prophet, undauntedly removed the covers of the vases, and violently seized on the talismans. Then, with a voice more loud than had hitherto been heard in these mansions, she compelled the Dives to disclose to her the most secret treasures, the most profound stores, which the Afrit himself had not seen. She passed by rapid descents known only to Eblis and his most favored Potentates, and thus penetrated the very entrails of the earth, where breathes the Sansar, or icy wind of death. Nothing appalled her dauntless soul. She perceived, however, in all the inmates who bore their hands on their heart, a little singularity not much to her taste. As she was emerging from one of the abysses, Eblis stood forth to her view, but, notwithstanding he displayed the full effulgence of his infernal majesty, she preserved her countenance unaltered, and even paid her compliments with considerable firmness.

This superb monarch thus answered:

"Princess, whose knowledge and whose crimes have merited a conspicuous rank in my empire, thou doest well to employ the leisure that remains, for the flames and torments which are ready to seize on thy heart, will not fail to provide thee with full employment."

He said this and was lost in the curtains of his tabernacle.

Carathis paused for a moment with surprise, but resolved to follow the advice of Eblis, she assembled all the choirs of Genii, and all the Dives, to pay her homage. Thus, marched she in triumph through a vapor of perfumes, amidst the acclamations of all the malignant spirits; with most of whom she had formed a previous acquaintance. She even attempted to dethrone one of the Solimans, for the purpose of usurping his place, when a voice, proceeding from the Abyss of Death, proclaimed:

"All is accomplished!"

Instantaneously, the haughty forehead of the intrepid princess became corrugated with agony; she uttered a tremendous yell, and fixed - no more to be withdrawn - her right hand upon her heart, which was become a receptacle of eternal fire.

In this delirium, forgetting all ambitious projects, and her thirst for that knowledge which should ever be hidden from mortals, she overturned the offerings of the Genii; and, having execrated the hour she was begotten, and the womb that had borne her, glanced off in a whirl that rendered her invisible, and continued to revolve without intermission.

At almost the same instant, the same voice announced to the Caliph, Nouronihar, the five princes, and the princess, the awful and irrevocable decree. Their hearts immediately took fire, and they at once lost the most precious of the gifts of heaven - hope. These unhappy beings recoiled, with looks of the most furious distraction. Vathek beheld in the eyes of Nouronihar nothing but rage and vengeance; nor could she discern ought in his but aversion and despair. The two princes who were friends, and till that moment had preserved their attachment, shrunk back, gnashing their teeth with mutual and unchangeable hatred. Kalilah and his sister made reciprocal gestures of imprecation; whilst the two other princes testified their horror for each other by the most ghastly convulsions, and screams that could not be smothered. All severally plunged themselves into the accursed multitude, there to wander in an eternity of unabating anguish.

Such was, and such should be, the punishment of unrestrained passions, and atrocious actions. Such is, and such should be, the chastisement of blind ambition, that would transgress those bounds which the Creator hath prescribed to human knowledge, and by aiming at discoveries reserved for pure intelligence, acquire that infatuated pride, which perceives not the condition appointed to man is, to be ignorant and humble.

Thus the Caliph Vathek who, for the sake of empty pomp and forbidden power, hath sullied himself with a thousand crimes, became a prey to grief without end, and remorse without mitigation; whilst the humble and despised Gulchenrouz passed whole ages in undisturbed tranquility, and the pure happiness of childhood.

THE END

The Last Man

By Mary W. Shelley

The Last Man

By Mary W. Shelley

ABOUT THE AUTHOR

Mary Wollstonecraft Shelley (1797 – 1851) was an English novelist who is most famous for writing the Gothic novel Frankenstein; or, The Modern Prometheus (1818). She also edited and promoted the works of her husband, the Romantic poet and philosopher Percy Bysshe Shelley. Her father was the political philosopher William Godwin and her mother was the philosopher and feminist Mary Wollstonecraft.

Shelley's mother died less than a month after giving birth to her. She was raised by her father who was able to provide her with a rich if informal education, encouraging her to adhere to his own anarchist political theories. When she was four, her father married a neighbor with whom Shelley came to have a troubled relationship.

In 1814, Shelley began a romance with one of her father's political followers, Percy Bysshe Shelley, who was already married. Together with her stepsister, Claire Clairmont, she and Percy left for France and travelled through Europe. Upon their return to England, Shelley was pregnant with Percy's child. Over the next two years, she and Percy faced ostracism, constant debt and the death of their prematurely born daughter. They married in late 1816, after the suicide of Percy Shelley's first wife, Harriet.

In 1816, the couple famously spent a summer with Lord Byron, John William Polidori and Claire Clairmont near Geneva, Switzerland, where Shelley conceived the idea for her novel Frankenstein. The Shelley's left Britain in 1818 for Italy, where their second and third children died before Shelley gave birth to her last and only surviving child, Percy Florence Shelley. In 1822, her husband drowned when his sailing boat sank during a storm near Viareggio. A year later, Shelley returned to England and from then on devoted herself to the upbringing of her son and a career as a professional author. The last decade of her life was dogged by illness, most likely caused by the brain tumor which killed her at age fifty-three.

The Last Man is a post-apocalyptic science fiction novel by Mary Shelley, which was first published in 1826. The book tells of a future world that has been ravaged by a plague. The novel was harshly reviewed at the time and was virtually unknown – having been eclipsed by Shelley's more popular works – until a scholarly revival in the 1960s. It contains semi-biographical portraits of Romantic figures in Shelley's circle, particularly Shelley's late husband Percy Bysshe Shelley and Lord Byron.

VOL. I.

INTRODUCTION

I visited Naples in the year 1818. On the 8th of December of that year, my companion and I crossed the Bay, to visit the antiquities which are scattered on the shores of Baiae. The translucent and shining waters of the calm sea covered fragments of old Roman villas, which were interlaced by sea-weed, and received diamond tints from the checking of the sun-beams; the blue and pellucid element was such as Galatea might have skimmed in her car of mother of pearl; or Cleopatra, more fitly than the Nile, have chosen as the path of her magic ship. Though it was winter, the atmosphere seemed more appropriate to early spring; and its genial warmth contributed to inspire those sensations of placid delight, which are the portion of every traveler, as he lingers, loath to quit the tranquil bays and radiant promontories of Baiae.

We visited the so-called Elysian Fields and Avernus: and wandered through various ruined temples, baths, and classic spots; at length we entered the gloomy cavern of the Cumaean Sibyl. Our Lazzarone bore flaring torches, which shone red, and almost dusky, in the murky subterranean passages, whose darkness thirstily surrounding them, seemed eager to imbibe more and more of the element of light. We passed by a natural archway, leading to a second gallery, and enquired, if we could not enter there also. The guides pointed to the reflection of their torches on the water that paved it, leaving us to form our own conclusion; but adding it was a pity, for it led to the Sibyl's Cave. Our curiosity and enthusiasm were excited by this circumstance, and we insisted upon attempting the passage. As is usually the case in the prosecution of such enterprises, the difficulties decreased on examination. We found, on each side of the humid pathway, "dry land for the sole of the foot."

At length we arrived at a large, desert, dark cavern, which the Lazzarone assured us was the Sibyl's Cave. We were sufficiently disappointed — Yet we examined it with care, as if its blank, rocky walls could still bear trace of celestial visitant. On one side was a small opening. Whither does this lead? we asked: can we enter here? - Questo poi, no, - said the wild looking savage, who held the torch; "you can advance but a short distance, and nobody visits it."

"Nevertheless, I will try it," said my companion; "it may lead to the real cavern. Shall I go alone, or will you accompany me?"

I signified my readiness to proceed, but our guides protested against such a measure. With great volubility, in their native Neapolitan dialect, with which we were not very familiar, they told us that there were specters, that the roof would fall in, that it was too narrow to admit us, that there was a deep hole within, filled with water, and we might be drowned. My friend shortened the harangue, by taking the man's torch from him; and we proceeded alone.

The passage, which at first scarcely admitted us, quickly grew narrower and lower; we were almost bent double; yet still we persisted in making our way through it. At length we entered a wider space, and the low roof heightened; but, as we congratulated ourselves on this change, our torch was extinguished by a current of air, and we were left in utter darkness. The guides bring with them materials for renewing the light, but we had none - our only resource was to return as we came. We groped round the widened space to find the entrance, and after a time fancied that we had succeeded. This proved however to be a second passage, which evidently ascended. It terminated like the former; though something approaching to a ray, we could not tell whence, shed a very doubtful twilight in the space. By degrees, our eyes grew somewhat accustomed to this dimness, and we perceived that there was no direct passage leading us further; but that it was possible to climb one side of the cavern to a low arch at top, which promised a more easy path, from whence we now discovered that this light proceeded. With considerable difficulty we scrambled up, and came to another passage with still more of illumination, and this led to another ascent like the former.

After a succession of these, which our resolution alone permitted us to surmount, we arrived at a wide cavern with an arched dome-like roof. An aperture in the midst let in the light of heaven; but this was overgrown with brambles and underwood, which acted as a veil, obscuring the day, and giving a solemn religious hue to the apartment. It was spacious, and nearly circular, with a raised seat of stone, about the size of a Grecian couch, at one end. The only sign that life had been here, was the perfect snow-white skeleton of a goat, which had probably not perceived the opening as it grazed on the hill above and had fallen headlong. Ages perhaps had elapsed since this catastrophe; and the ruin it had made above, had been repaired by the growth of vegetation during many hundred summers.

The rest of the furniture of the cavern consisted of piles of leaves, fragments of bark, and a white filmy substance, resembling the inner part of the green hood which shelters the grain of the unripe Indian corn. We were fatigued by our struggles to attain this point, and seated ourselves on the rocky couch, while the sounds of tinkling sheep-bells, and shout of shepherd-boy, reached us from above.

At length my friend, who had taken up some of the leaves strewed about, exclaimed, "This is the Sibyl's cave; these are Sibylline leaves." On examination, we found that all the leaves, bark, and other substances, were traced with written characters. What appeared to us more astonishing, was that these writings were expressed in various languages: some unknown to my companion, ancient Chaldea, and Egyptian hieroglyphics, old as the Pyramids. Stranger still, some were in modern dialects, English and Italian. We could make out little by the dim light, but they seemed to contain prophecies, detailed relations of events but lately passed; names, now well known, but of modern date; and often exclamations of exultation or woe, of victory or defeat, were traced on their thin scant pages. This was certainly the Sibyl's Cave; not indeed exactly as Virgil describes it, but the whole of this land had been so convulsed by earthquake and volcano, that the change was not wonderful, though the traces of ruin were effaced by time; and we probably owed the preservation of these leaves, to the accident which had closed the mouth of the cavern, and the swift-growing vegetation which had rendered its sole opening impervious to the storm. We made a hasty selection of such of the leaves, whose writing one at least of us could understand; and then, laden with our treasure, we bade adieu to the dim hypaethralic cavern, and after much difficulty succeeded in rejoining our guides.

During our stay at Naples, we often returned to this cave, sometimes alone, skimming the sun-lit sea, and each time added to our store. Since that period, whenever the world's circumstance has not imperiously called me away, or the temper of my mind impeded such study, I have been employed in deciphering these sacred remains. Their meaning, wondrous and eloquent, has often repaid my toil, soothing me in sorrow, and exciting my imagination to daring flights, through the immensity of nature and the mind of man. For a while my labors were not solitary; but that time is gone; and, with the selected and matchless companion of my toils, their dearest reward is also lost to me—

> *Di mie tenere frondi altro lavoro*
> *Credea mostrarte; e qual fero pianeta*
> *Ne' nvidio insieme, o mio nobil tesoro?*
>
> *(Of my tender fronds of other work*
> *Thoughts showing you; and what a savage planet*
> *Neither do I envy together, my noble treasure?)*

I present the public with my latest discoveries in the slight Sibylline pages. Scattered and unconnected as they were, I have been obliged to add links, and model the work into a consistent form. But the main substance rests on the truths contained in these poetic rhapsodies, and the divine intuition which the Cumaean damsel obtained from heaven.

I have often wondered at the subject of her verses, and at the English dress of the Latin poet. Sometimes I have thought, that, obscure and chaotic as they are, they owe their present form to me, their decipherer. As if we should give to another artist, the painted fragments which form the mosaic copy of Raphael's Transfiguration in St. Peter's; he would put them together in a form, whose mode would be fashioned by his own peculiar mind and talent. Doubtless the leaves of the Cumaean Sibyl have suffered distortion and diminution of interest and excellence in my hands. My only excuse for thus transforming them, is that they were unintelligible in their pristine condition.

My labors have cheered long hours of solitude, and taken me out of a world, which has averted its once benignant face from me, to one glowing with imagination and power. Will my readers ask how I could find solace from the narration of misery and woeful change? This is one of the mysteries of our nature, which holds full sway over me, and from whose influence I cannot escape. I confess, that I have not been unmoved by the development of the tale; and that I have been depressed, nay, agonized, at some parts of the recital, which I have faithfully transcribed from my materials. Yet such is human nature, that the excitement of mind was dear to me, and that the imagination, painter of tempest and earthquake, or, worse, the stormy and ruin-fraught passions of man, softened my real sorrows and endless regrets, by clothing these fictitious ones in that ideality, which takes the mortal sting from pain.

I hardly know whether this apology is necessary. For the merits of my adaptation and translation must decide how far I have well bestowed my time and imperfect powers, in giving form and substance to the frail and attenuated Leaves of the Sibyl.

CHAPTER I

I am the native of a sea-surrounded nook, a cloud-enshrouded land, which, when the surface of the globe, with its shoreless ocean and trackless continents, presents itself to my mind, appears only as an inconsiderable speck in the immense whole; and yet, when balanced in the scale of mental power, far outweighed countries of larger extent and more numerous population. So true it is, that man's mind alone was the creator of all that was good or great to man, and that Nature herself was only his first minister. England, seated far north in the turbid sea, now visits my dreams in the semblance of a vast and well-manned ship, which mastered the winds and rode proudly over the waves. In my boyish days she was the universe to me. When I stood on my native hills, and saw plain and mountain stretch out to the utmost limits of my vision, speckled by the dwellings of my countrymen, and subdued to fertility by their labors, the earth's very center was fixed for me in that spot, and the rest of her orb was as a fable, to have forgotten which would have cost neither my imagination nor understanding an effort.

My fortunes have been, from the beginning, an exemplification of the power that mutability may possess over the varied tenor of man's life. With regard to myself, this came almost by inheritance. My father was one of those men on whom nature had bestowed to prodigality the envied gifts of wit and imagination, and then left his bark of life to be impelled by these winds, without adding reason as the rudder, or judgment as the pilot for the voyage. His extraction was obscure; but circumstances brought him early into public notice, and his small paternal property was soon dissipated in the splendid scene of fashion and luxury in which he was an actor. During the short years of thoughtless youth, he was adored by the high-bred triflers of the day, nor least by the youthful sovereign, who escaped from the intrigues of party, and the arduous duties of kingly business, to find never-failing amusement and exhilaration of spirit in his society. My father's impulses, never under his own control, perpetually led him into difficulties from which his ingenuity alone could extricate him; and the accumulating pile of debts of honor and of trade, which would have bent to earth any other, was supported by him with a light spirit and tameless hilarity; while his company was so necessary at the tables and assemblies of the rich, that his derelictions were considered venial, and he himself received with intoxicating flattery.

This kind of popularity, like every other, is evanescent: and the difficulties of every kind with which he had to contend, increased in a frightful ratio compared with his small means of extricating himself. At such times the king, in his enthusiasm for him, would come to his relief, and then kindly take his friend to task; my father gave the best promises for amendment, but his social disposition, his craving for the usual diet of admiration, and more than all, the fiend of gambling, which fully possessed him, made his good resolutions transient, his promises vain. With the quick sensibility peculiar to his temperament, he perceived his power in the brilliant circle to be on the wane. The king married; and the haughty princess of Austria, who became, as queen of England, the head of fashion, looked with harsh eyes on his defects, and with contempt on the affection her royal husband entertained for him. My father felt that his fall was near; but so far from profiting by this last calm before the storm to save himself, he sought to forget anticipated evil by making still greater sacrifices to the deity of pleasure, deceitful and cruel arbiter of his destiny.

The king, who was a man of excellent dispositions, but easily led, had now become a willing disciple of his imperious consort. He was induced to look with extreme disapprobation, and at last with distaste, on my father's imprudence and follies. It is true that his presence dissipated these clouds; his warm-hearted frankness, brilliant sallies, and confiding demeanor were irresistible: it was only when at a distance, while still renewed tales of his errors were poured into his royal friend's ear, that he lost his influence. The queen's dexterous management was employed to prolong these absences and gather together accusations. At length the king was brought to see in him a source of perpetual disquiet, knowing that he should pay for the short-lived pleasure of his society by tedious homilies, and more painful narrations of excesses, the truth of which he could not disprove. The result was that he would make one more attempt to reclaim him, and in case of ill success, cast him off forever.

Such a scene must have been one of deepest interest and high-wrought passion. A powerful king, conspicuous for a goodness which had heretofore made him meek, and now lofty in his admonitions, with alternate entreaty and reproof, besought his friend to attend to his real interests, resolutely to avoid those fascinations which in fact were fast deserting him, and to spend his great powers on a worthy field, in which he, his sovereign, would be his prop, his stay, and his pioneer. My father felt this kindness; for a moment ambitious dreams floated before him; and he thought that it would be well to exchange his present pursuits for nobler duties. With sincerity and fervor, he gave the required promise: as a pledge of continued favor, he received from his royal master a sum of money to defray pressing debts and enable him to enter under good auspices his new career. That very night, while yet full of gratitude and good resolves, this whole sum, and its amount doubled, was lost at the gaming-table. In his desire to repair his first losses, my father risked double stakes, and thus incurred a debt of honor he was wholly unable to pay. Ashamed to apply again to the king, he turned his back upon London, its false delights and clinging miseries; and, with poverty for his sole companion, buried himself in solitude among the hills and lakes of Cumberland. His wit, his bon mots, the record of his personal attractions, fascinating manners, and social talents, were long remembered and repeated from mouth to mouth. Ask where now was this favorite of fashion, this companion of the noble, this excelling beam, which gilt with alien splendor the assemblies of the courtly and the gay - you heard that he was under a cloud, a lost man; not one thought it belonged to him to repay pleasure by real services, or that his long reign of brilliant wit deserved a pension on retiring. The king lamented his absence; he loved to repeat his sayings, relate the adventures they had had together, and exalt his talents - but here ended his reminiscence.

Meanwhile my father, forgotten, could not forget. He repined for the loss of what was more necessary to him than air or food - the excitements of pleasure, the admiration of the noble, the luxurious and polished living of the great. A nervous fever was the consequence; during which he was nursed by the daughter of a poor cottager, under whose roof he lodged. She was lovely, gentle, and, above all, kind to him; nor can it afford astonishment, that the late idol of high-bred beauty should, even in a fallen state, appear a being of an elevated and wondrous nature to the lowly cottage-girl. The attachment between them led to the ill-fated marriage, of which I was the offspring. Notwithstanding the tenderness and sweetness of my mother, her husband still deplored his degraded state. Unaccustomed to industry, he knew not in what way to contribute to the support of his increasing family. Sometimes he thought of applying to the king; pride and shame for a while withheld him; and, before his necessities became so imperious as to compel him to some kind of exertion, he died. For one brief interval before this catastrophe, he looked forward to the future, and contemplated with anguish the desolate situation in which his wife and children would be left. His last effort was a letter to the king, full of touching eloquence, and of occasional flashes of that brilliant spirit which was an integral part of him. He bequeathed his widow and orphans to the friendship of his royal master, and felt satisfied that, by this means, their prosperity was better assured in his death than in his life. This letter was enclosed to the care of a nobleman, who, he did not doubt, would perform the last and inexpensive office of placing it in the king's own hand.

He died in debt, and his little property was seized immediately by his creditors. My mother, penniless and burthened with two children, waited week after week, and month after month, in sickening expectation of a reply, which never came. She had no experience beyond her father's cottage; and the mansion of the lord of the manor was the chiefest type of grandeur she could conceive. During my father's life, she had been made familiar with the name of royalty and the courtly circle; but such things, ill according with her personal experience, appeared, after the loss of him who gave substance and reality to them, vague and fantastical. If, under any circumstances, she could have acquired sufficient courage to address the noble persons mentioned by her husband, the ill success of his own application caused her to banish the idea. She saw therefore no escape from dire penury: perpetual care, joined to sorrow for the loss of the wondrous being, whom she continued to contemplate with ardent admiration, hard labor, and naturally delicate health, at length released her from the sad continuity of want and misery.

The condition of her orphan children was peculiarly desolate. Her own father had been an emigrant from another part of the country, and had died long since: they had no one relation to take them by the hand; they were outcasts, paupers, unfriended beings, to whom the most scanty pittance was a matter of favor, and who were treated merely as children of peasants, yet poorer than the poorest, who, dying, had left them, a thankless bequest, to the close-handed charity of the land.

I, the elder of the two, was five years old when my mother died. A remembrance of the discourses of my parents, and the communications which my mother endeavored to impress upon me concerning my father's friends, in slight hope that I might one day derive benefit from the knowledge, floated like an indistinct dream through my brain. I conceived that I was different and superior to my protectors and companions, but I knew not how or wherefore. The sense of injury, associated with the name of king and noble, clung to me; but I could draw no conclusions from such feelings, to serve as a guide to action. My first real knowledge of myself was as an unprotected orphan among the valleys and fells of Cumberland. I was in the service of a farmer; and with crook in hand, my dog at my side, I shepherded a numerous flock on the near uplands. I cannot say much in praise of such a life; and its pains far exceeded its pleasures. There was freedom in it, a companionship with nature, and a reckless loneliness; but these, romantic as they were, did not accord with the love of action and desire of human sympathy, characteristic of youth. Neither the care of my flock, nor the change of seasons, were sufficient to tame my eager spirit; my out-door life and unemployed time were the temptations that led me early into lawless habits. I associated with others friendless like myself; I formed them into a band, I was their chief and captain. All shepherd-boys alike, while our flocks were spread over the pastures, we schemed and executed many a mischievous prank, which drew on us the anger and revenge of the rustics. I was the leader and protector of my comrades, and as I became distinguished among them, their misdeeds were usually visited upon me. But while I endured punishment and pain in their defense with the spirit of a hero, I claimed as my reward their praise and obedience.

In such a school my disposition became rugged, but firm. The appetite for admiration and small capacity for self-control which I inherited from my father, nursed by adversity, made me daring and reckless. I was rough as the elements and unlearned as the animals I tended. I often compared myself to them, and finding that my chief superiority consisted in power, I soon persuaded myself that it was in power only that I was inferior to the chiefest potentates of the earth. Thus, untaught in refined philosophy, and pursued by a restless feeling of degradation from my true station in society, I wandered among the hills of civilized England as uncouth a savage as the wolf-bred founder of old Rome. I owned but one law, it was that of the strongest, and my greatest deed of virtue was never to submit.

Yet let me a little retract from this sentence I have passed on myself. My mother, when dying, had, in addition to her other half-forgotten and misapplied lessons, committed, with solemn exhortation, her other child to my fraternal guardianship; and this one duty I performed to the best of my ability, with all the zeal and affection of which my nature was capable. My sister was three years younger than myself; I had nursed her as an infant, and when the difference of our sexes, by giving us various occupations, in a great measure divided us, yet she continued to be the object of my careful love. Orphans, in the fullest sense of the term, we were poorest among the poor, and despised among the unhonored. If my daring and courage obtained for me a kind of respectful aversion, her youth and sex, since they did not excite tenderness, by proving her to be weak, were the causes of numberless mortifications to her; and her own disposition was not so constituted as to diminish the evil effects of her lowly station.

She was a singular being, and, like me, inherited much of the peculiar disposition of our father. Her countenance was all expression; her eyes were not dark, but impenetrably deep; you seemed to discover space after space in their intellectual glance, and to feel that the soul which was their soul, comprehended an universe of thought in its ken. She was pale and fair, and her golden hair clustered on her temples, contrasting its rich hue with the living marble beneath. Her coarse peasant-dress, little consonant apparently with the refinement of feeling which her face expressed, yet in a strange manner accorded with it. She was like one of Guido's saints, with heaven in her heart and in her look, so that when you saw her you only thought of that within, and costume and even feature were secondary to the mind that beamed in her countenance.

Yet though lovely and full of noble feeling, my poor Perdita (for this was the fanciful name my sister had received from her dying parent), was not altogether saintly in her disposition. Her manners were cold and repulsive. If she had been nurtured by those who had regarded her with affection, she might have been different; but unloved and neglected, she repaid want of kindness with distrust and silence. She was submissive to those who held authority over her, but a perpetual cloud dwelt on her brow; she looked as if she expected enmity from everyone who approached her, and her actions were instigated by the same feeling. All the time she could command she spent in solitude. She would ramble to the most unfrequented places, and scale dangerous heights, that in those unvisited spots she might wrap herself in loneliness. Often she passed whole hours walking up and down the paths of the woods; she wove garlands of flowers and ivy, or watched the flickering of the shadows and glancing of the leaves; sometimes she sat beside a stream, and as her thoughts paused, threw flowers or pebbles into the waters, watching how those swam and these sank; or she would set afloat boats formed of bark of trees or leaves, with a feather for a sail, and intensely watch the navigation of her craft among the rapids and shallows of the brook. Meanwhile her active fancy wove a thousand combinations; she dreamt "of moving accidents by flood and field" — she lost herself delightedly in these self-created wanderings and returned with unwilling spirit to the dull detail of common life. Poverty was the cloud that veiled her excellencies, and all that was good in her seemed about to perish from want of the genial dew of affection. She had not even the same advantage as I in the recollection of her parents; she clung to me, her brother, as her only friend, but her alliance with me completed the distaste that her protectors felt for her; and every error was magnified by them into crimes. If she had been bred in that sphere of life to which by inheritance the delicate framework of her mind and person was adapted, she would have been the object almost of adoration, for her virtues were as eminent as her defects. All the genius that ennobled the blood of her father illustrated hers; a generous tide flowed in her veins; artifice, envy, or meanness, were at the antipodes of her nature; her countenance, when enlightened by amiable feeling, might have belonged to a queen of nations; her eyes were bright; her look fearless.

Although by our situation and dispositions we were almost equally cut off from the usual forms of social intercourse, we formed a strong contrast to each other. I always required the stimulants of companionship and applause. Perdita was all-sufficient to herself. Notwithstanding my lawless habits, my disposition was sociable; her's recluse. My life was spent among tangible realities, hers was a dream. I might be said even to love my enemies, since by exciting me they in a sort bestowed happiness upon me; Perdita almost disliked her friends, for they interfered with her visionary moods. All my feelings, even of exultation and triumph, were changed to bitterness, if unparticipated; Perdita, even in joy, fled to loneliness, and could go on from day to day, neither expressing her emotions, nor seeking a fellow-feeling in another mind. Nay, she could love and dwell with tenderness on the look and voice of her friend, while her demeanor expressed the coldest reserve. A sensation with her became a sentiment, and she never spoke until she had mingled her perceptions of outward objects with others which were the native growth of her own mind. She was like a fruitful soil that imbibed the airs and dews of heaven, and gave them forth again to light in loveliest forms of fruits and flowers; but then she was often dark and rugged as that soil, raked up, and new sown with unseen seed.

She dwelt in a cottage whose trim grass-plat sloped down to the waters of the lake of Ullswater; a beech wood stretched up the hill behind, and a purling brook gently falling from the acclivity ran through poplar-shaded banks into the lake. I lived with a farmer whose house was built higher up among the hills: a dark crag rose behind it, and exposed to the north, the snow lay in its crevices the summer through. Before dawn I led my flock to the sheep-walks and guarded them through the day. It was a life of toil; for rain and cold were more frequent than sunshine; but it was my pride to condemn the elements. My trusty dog watched the sheep as I slipped away to the rendezvous of my comrades, and thence to the accomplishment of our schemes. At noon we met again, and we threw away in contempt our peasant fare, as we built our fireplace and kindled the cheering blaze destined to cook the game stolen from the neighboring preserves. Then came the tale of hairbreadth escapes, combats with dogs, ambush and flight, as gypsy-like we encompassed our pot. The search after a stray lamb, or the devices by which we elude or endeavored to elude punishment, filled up the hours of afternoon; in the evening my flock went to its fold, and I to my sister.

It was seldom indeed that we escaped, to use an old-fashioned phrase, scot free. Our dainty fare was often exchanged for blows and imprisonment. Once, when thirteen years of age, I was sent for a month to the county jail. I came out, my morals unimproved, my hatred to my oppressors increased tenfold. Bread and water did not tame my blood, nor solitary confinement inspire me with gentle thoughts. I was angry, impatient, miserable; my only happy hours were those during which I devised schemes of revenge; these were perfected in my forced solitude, so that during the whole of the following season, and I was freed early in September, I never failed to provide excellent and plenteous fare for myself and my comrades. This was a glorious winter. The sharp frost and heavy snows tamed the animals and kept the country gentlemen by their firesides; we got more game than we could eat, and my faithful dog grew sleek upon our refuse.

Thus, years passed on; and years only added fresh love of freedom, and contempt for all that was not as wild and rude as me. At the age of sixteen I had shot up in appearance to man's estate; I was tall and athletic; I was practiced to feats of strength and inured to the inclemency of the elements. My skin was embrowned by the sun; my step was firm with conscious power. I feared no man and loved none. In after life I looked back with wonder to what I then was; how utterly worthless I should have become if I had pursued my lawless career. My life was like that of an animal, and my mind was in danger of degenerating into that which informs brute nature. Until now, my savage habits had done me no radical mischief; my physical powers had grown up and flourished under their influence, and my mind, undergoing the same discipline, was imbued with all the hardy virtues. But now my boasted independence was daily instigating me to acts of tyranny, and freedom was becoming licentiousness. I stood on the brink of manhood; passions, strong as the trees of a forest, had already taken root within me, and were about to shadow with their noxious overgrowth, my path of life.

I panted for enterprises beyond my childish exploits and formed distempered dreams of future action. I avoided my ancient comrades, and I soon lost them. They arrived at the age when they were sent to fulfil their destined situations in life; while I, an outcast, with none to lead or drive me forward, paused. The old began to point at me as an example, the young to wonder at me as a being distinct from themselves; I hated them, and began, last and worst degradation, to hate myself. I clung to my ferocious habits, yet half despised them; I continued my war against civilization, and yet entertained a wish to belong to it.

I revolved again and again all that I remembered my mother to have told me of my father's former life; I contemplated the few relics I possessed belonging to him, which spoke of greater refinement than could be found among the mountain cottages; but nothing in all this served as a guide to lead me to another and pleasanter way of life. My father had been connected with nobles, but all I knew of such connection was subsequent neglect. The name of the king, - he to whom my dying father had addressed his latest prayers, and who had barbarously slighted them, was associated only with the ideas of unkindness, injustice, and consequent resentment. I was born for something greater than I was - and greater I would become; but greatness, at least to my distorted perceptions, was no necessary associate of goodness, and my wild thoughts were unchecked by moral considerations when they rioted in dreams of distinction. Thus I stood upon a pinnacle, a sea of evil rolled at my feet; I was about to precipitate myself into it, and rush like a torrent over all obstructions to the object of my wishes - when a stranger influence came over the current of my fortunes, and changed their boisterous course to what was in comparison like the gentle meanderings of a meadow-encircling streamlet.

CHAPTER II

I lived far from the busy haunts of men, and the rumor of wars or political changes came worn to a mere sound, to our mountain abodes. England had been the
scene of momentous struggles, during my early boyhood. In the year 2073, the
last of its kings, the ancient friend of my father, had abdicated in compliance with
the gentle force of the remonstrances of his subjects, and a republic was instituted.
Large estates were secured to the dethroned monarch and his family; he received
the title of Earl of Windsor, and Windsor Castle, an ancient royalty, with its wide
demesnes were a part of his allotted wealth. He died soon after, leaving two children, a son and a daughter.

The ex-queen, a princess of the house of Austria, had long impelled her
husband to withstand the necessity of the times. She was haughty and fearless; she
cherished a love of power, and a bitter contempt for him who had despoiled himself of a kingdom. For her children's sake alone she consented to remain, shorn of
regality, a member of the English republic. When she became a widow, she turned
all her thoughts to the educating her son Adrian, second Earl of Windsor, so as to
accomplish her ambitious ends; and with his mother's milk he imbibed, and was
intended to grow up in the steady purpose of re-acquiring his lost crown. Adrian
was now fifteen years of age. He was addicted to study and imbued beyond his
years with learning and talent: report said that he had already begun to thwart
his mother's views, and to entertain republican principles. However, this might
be, the haughty Countess entrusted none with the secrets of her family-tuition.
Adrian was bred up in solitude and kept apart from the natural companions of
his age and rank. Some unknown circumstance now induced his mother to send
him from under her immediate tutelage; and we heard that he was about to visit
Cumberland. A thousand tales were rife, explanatory of the Countess of Windsor's
conduct; nontrue probably; but each day it became more certain that we should
have the noble scion of the late regal house of England among us.

There was a large estate with a mansion attached to it, belonging to this
family, at Ullswater. A large park was one of its appendages, laid out with great
taste, and plentifully stocked with game. I had often made depredations on these
preserves; and the neglected state of the property facilitated my incursions. When
it was decided that the young Earl of Windsor should visit Cumberland, workmen
arrived to put the house and grounds in order for his reception. The apartments
were restored to their pristine splendor, and the park, all disrepairs restored, was
guarded with unusual care.

I was beyond measure disturbed by this intelligence. It roused all my dor-
mant recollections, my suspended sentiments of injury, and gave rise to the new
one of revenge. I could no longer attend to my occupations; all my plans and devices were forgotten; I seemed about to begin life anew, and that under no good
auspices. The tug of war, I thought, was now to begin. He would come triumphantly to the district to which my parent had fled broken-hearted; he would find

the ill-fated offspring, bequeathed with such vain confidence to his royal father, miserable paupers. That he should know of our existence, and treat us, near at hand, with the same contumely which his father had practiced in distance and absence, appeared to me the certain consequence of all that had gone before. Thus, then I should meet this titled stripling—the son of my father's friend. He would be hedged in by servants; nobles, and the sons of nobles, were his companions; all England rang with his name; and his coming, like a thunderstorm, was heard from far: while I, unlettered and unfashioned, should, if I came in contact with him, in the judgment of his courtly followers, bear evidence in my very person to the propriety of that ingratitude which had made me the degraded being I appeared.

With my mind fully occupied by these ideas, I might be said as if fascinated, to haunt the destined abode of the young Earl. I watched the progress of the improvements, and stood by the unlading wagons, as various articles of luxury, brought from London, were taken forth and conveyed into the mansion. It was part of the Ex-Queen's plan, to surround her son with princely magnificence. I beheld rich carpets and silken hangings, ornaments of gold, richly embossed metals, emblazoned furniture, and all the appendages of high rank arranged, so that nothing but what was regal in splendor should reach the eye of one of royal descent. I looked on these; I turned my gaze to my own mean dress. - Whence sprung this difference? Whence but from ingratitude, from falsehood, from a dereliction on the part of the prince's father, of all noble sympathy and generous feeling. Doubtless, he also, whose blood received a mingling tide from his proud mother - he, the acknowledged focus of the kingdom's wealth and nobility, had been taught to repeat my father's name with disdain, and to scoff at my just claims to protection. I strove to think that all this grandeur was but more glaring infamy, and that, by planting his gold-enwoven flag beside my tarnished and tattered banner, he proclaimed not his superiority, but his debasement. Yet I envied him. His stud of beautiful horses, his arms of costly workmanship, the praise that attended him, the adoration, ready servitor, high place and high esteem, - I considered them as forcibly wrenched from me, and envied them all with novel and tormenting bitterness.

To crown my vexation of spirit, Perdita, the visionary Perdita, seemed to awake to real life with transport, when she told me that the Earl of Windsor was about to arrive.

"And this pleases you?" I observed, moodily.

"Indeed it does, Lionel," she replied; "I quite long to see him; he is the descendant of our kings, the first noble of the land: every one admires and loves him, and they say that his rank is his least merit; he is generous, brave, and affable."

"You have learnt a pretty lesson, Perdita," said I, "and repeat it so literally, that you forget the while the proofs we have of the Earl's virtues; his generosity to us is manifest in our plenty, his bravery in the protection he affords us, his affability in the notice he takes of us. His rank his least merit, do you say? Why, all his virtues are derived from his station only; because he is rich, he is called generous; because he is powerful, brave; because he is well served, he is affable. Let them call him so, let all England believe him to be thus - we know him - he is our enemy - our penurious, dastardly, arrogant enemy; if he were gifted with one particle of the virtues you call his, he would do justly by us, if it were only to shew, that if he must strike, it should not be a fallen foe. His father injured my father - his father, unassailable on his throne, dared despise him who only stooped beneath himself, when he deigned to associate with the royal ingrate. We, descendants from the one and the other, must be enemies also. He shall find that I can feel my injuries; he shall learn to dread my revenge!"

A few days after he arrived. Every inhabitant of the most miserable cottage, went to swell the stream of population that poured forth to meet him: even Perdita, in spite of my late philippic, crept near the highway, to behold this idol of all hearts. I, driven half mad, as I met party after party of the country people, in their holiday best, descending the hills, escaped to their cloud-veiled summits, and looking on the sterile rocks about me, exclaimed - "They do not cry, long live the Earl!" Nor, when night came, accompanied by drizzling rain and cold, would I return home; for I knew that each cottage rang with the praises of Adrian; as I felt my limbs grow numb and chill, my pain served as food for my insane aversion; nay, I almost triumphed in it, since it seemed to afford me reason and excuse for my hatred of my unheeding adversary. All was attributed to him, for I confounded so entirely the idea of father and son, that I forgot that the latter might be wholly unconscious of his parent's neglect of us; and as I struck my aching head with my hand, I cried: "He shall hear of this! I will be revenged! I will not suffer like a spaniel! He shall know, beggar and friendless as I am, that I will not tamely submit to injury!" Each day, each hour added to these exaggerated wrongs. His praises were so many adder's stings infixed in my vulnerable breast. If I saw him at a distance, riding a beautiful horse, my blood boiled with rage; the air seemed poisoned by his presence, and my very native English was changed to a vile jargon, since every phrase I heard was coupled with his name and honor. I panted to relieve this painful heart-burning by some misdeed that should rouse him to a sense of my antipathy. It was the height of his offending, that he should occasion in me such intolerable sensations, and not deign himself to afford any demonstration that he was aware that I even lived to feel them.

It soon became known that Adrian took great delight in his park and preserves. He never sported but spent hours in watching the tribes of lovely and almost tame animals with which it was stocked and ordered that greater care should be taken of them than ever. Here was an opening for my plans of offence, and I made use of it with all the brute impetuosity I derived from my active mode of life. I proposed the enterprise of poaching on his demesne to my few remaining comrades, who were the most determined and lawless of the crew; but they all shrunk from the peril; so, I was left to achieve my revenge myself. At first my exploits were unperceived; I increased in daring; footsteps on the dewy grass, torn boughs, and marks of slaughter, at length betrayed me to the gamekeepers. They kept better watch; I was taken and sent to prison. I entered its gloomy walls in a fit of triumphant extasy: "He feels me now," I cried, "and shall, again and again!" - I passed but one day in confinement; in the evening I was liberated, as I was told, by the order of the Earl himself. This news precipitated me from my self-raised pinnacle of honor. He despises me, I thought; but he shall learn that I despise him and hold in equal contempt his punishments and his clemency. On the second night after my release, I was again taken by the gamekeepers - again imprisoned, and again released; and again, such was my pertinacity, did the fourth night find me in the forbidden park. The gamekeepers were more enraged than their lord by my obstinacy. They had received orders that if I were again taken, I should be brought to the Earl; and his lenity made them expect a conclusion which they considered ill befitting my crime. One of them, who had been from the first the leader among those who had seized me, resolved to satisfy his own resentment, before he made me over to the higher powers.

The late setting of the moon, and the extreme caution I was obliged to use in this my third expedition, consumed so much time, that something like a qualm of fear came over me when I perceived dark night yield to twilight. I crept along by the fern, on my hands and knees, seeking the shadowy coverts of the under-wood, while the birds awoke with unwelcome song above, and the fresh morning wind, playing among the boughs, made me suspect a footfall at each turn. My heart beat quick as I approached the palings; my hand was on one of them, a leap would take me to the other side, when two keepers sprang from an ambush upon me: one knocked me down, and proceeded to inflict a severe horse-whipping. I started up - a knife was in my grasp; I made a plunge at his raised right arm, and inflicted a deep, wide wound in his hand. The rage and yells of the wounded man, the howling execrations of his comrade, which I answered with equal bitterness and fury, echoed through the dell; morning broke more and more, ill accordant in its celestial beauty with our brute and noisy contest. I and my enemy were still struggling, when the wounded man exclaimed, "The Earl!" I sprang out of the herculean hold of the keeper, panting from my exertions; I cast furious glances on my persecutors, and placing myself with my back to a tree, resolved to defend myself to the last. My garments were torn, and they, as well as my hands, were stained with the blood of the man I had wounded; one hand grasped the dead birds - my hard-earned prey, the other held the knife; my hair was matted; my face besmeared with the same guilty signs that bore witness against me on the dripping instrument I clenched; my whole appearance was haggard and squalid. Tall and muscular as I was in form, I must have looked like, what indeed I was, the merest ruffian that ever trod the earth.

The name of the Earl startled me, and caused all the indignant blood that warmed my heart to rush into my cheeks; I had never seen him before; I figured to myself a haughty, assuming youth, who would take me to task, if he deigned to speak to me, with all the arrogance of superiority. My reply was ready; a reproach I deemed calculated to sting his very heart. He came up the while; and his appearance blew aside, with gentle western breath, my cloudy wrath: a tall, slim, fair boy, with a physiognomy expressive of the excess of sensibility and refinement stood before me; the morning sunbeams tinged with gold his silken hair, and spread light and glory over his beaming countenance. "How is this?" he cried. The men eagerly began their defense; he put them aside, saying, "Two of you at once on a mere lad - for shame!" He came up to me: "Verney," he cried, "Lionel Verney, do we meet thus for the first time? We were born to be friends to each other; and though ill fortune has divided us, will you not acknowledge the hereditary bond of friendship which I trust will hereafter unite us?"

As he spoke, his earnest eyes, fixed on me, seemed to read my very soul: my heart, my savage revengeful heart, felt the influence of sweet benignity sink upon it; while his thrilling voice, like sweetest melody, awoke a mute echo within me, stirring to its depths the life-blood in my frame. I desired to reply, to acknowl-edge his goodness, accept his proffered friendship; but words, fitting words, were not afforded to the rough mountaineer; I would have held out my hand, but its guilty stain restrained me. Adrian took pity on my faltering mien: "Come with me," he said, "I have much to say to you; come home with me—you know who I am?"

"Yes," I exclaimed, "I do believe that I now know you, and that you will pardon my mistakes - my crime."

Adrian smiled gently; and after giving his orders to the gamekeepers, he came up to me; putting his arm in mine, we walked together to the mansion.

It was not his rank - after all that I have said, surely it will not be suspected that it was Adrian's rank, that, from the first, subdued my heart of hearts, and laid my entire spirit prostrate before him. Nor was it I alone who felt thus intimately his perfections. His sensibility and courtesy fascinated everyone. His vivacity, intelligence, and active spirit of benevolence completed the conquest. Even at this early age, he was deep read and imbued with the spirit of high philosophy. This spirit gave a tone of irresistible persuasion to his intercourse with others, so that he seemed like an inspired musician, who struck, with unerring skill, the "lyre of mind," and produced thence divine harmony. In person, he hardly appeared of this world; his slight frame was overinformed by the soul that dwelt within; he was all mind; "Man but a rush against" his breast, and it would have conquered his strength; but the might of his smile would have tamed an hungry lion, or caused a legion of armed men to lay their weapons at his feet.

I spent the day with him. At first, he did not recur to the past, or indeed to any personal occurrences. He wished probably to inspire me with confidence and give me time to gather together my scattered thoughts. He talked of general subjects and gave me ideas I had never before conceived. We sat in his library, and he spoke of the old Greek sages, and of the power which they had acquired over the minds of men, through the force of love and wisdom only. The room was decorated with the busts of many of them, and he described their characters to me. As he spoke, I felt subject to him; and all my boasted pride and strength were subdued by the honeyed accents of this blue-eyed boy. The trim and paled demesne of civilization, which I had before regarded from my wild jungle as inaccessible, had its wicket opened by him; I stepped within, and felt, as I entered, that I trod my native soil.

As evening came on, he reverted to the past. "I have a tale to relate," he said, "and much explanation to give concerning the past; perhaps you can assist me to curtail it. Do you remember your father? I had never the happiness of seeing him, but his name is one of my earliest recollections: he stands written in my mind's tablets as the type of all that was gallant, amiable, and fascinating in man. His wit was not more conspicuous than the overflowing goodness of his heart, which he poured in such full measure on his friends, as to leave, alas! small remnant for himself."

Encouraged by this encomium, I proceeded, in answer to his inquiries, to relate what I remembered of my parent; and he gave an account of those circumstances which had brought about a neglect of my father's testamentary letter. When, in after times, Adrian's father, then king of England, felt his situation become more perilous, his line of conduct more embarrassed, again and again he wished for his early friend, who might stand a mound against the impetuous anger of his queen, a mediator between him and the parliament. From the time that he had quitted London, on the fatal night of his defeat at the gaming-table, the king had received no tidings concerning him; and when, after the lapse of years, he exerted himself to discover him, every trace was lost. With fonder regret than ever, he clung to his memory; and gave it in charge to his son, if ever he should meet this valued friend, in his name to bestow every succor, and to assure him that, to the last, his attachment survived separation and silence.

A short time before Adrian's visit to Cumberland, the heir of the nobleman to whom my father had confided his last appeal to his royal master, put this letter, its seal unbroken, into the young Earl's hands. It had been found cast aside with a mass of papers of old date, and accident alone brought it to light. Adrian read it with deep interest; and found there that living spirit of genius and wit he had so often heard commemorated. He discovered the name of the spot whither my father had retreated, and where he died; he learnt the existence of his orphan children; and during the short interval between his arrival at Ullswater and our meeting in the park, he had been occupied in making inquiries concerning us, and arranging a variety of plans for our benefit, preliminary to his introducing himself to our notice.

The mode in which he spoke of my father was gratifying to my vanity; the veil which he delicately cast over his benevolence, in alleging a duteous fulfilment of the king's latest will, was soothing to my pride. Other feelings, less ambiguous, were called into play by his conciliating manner and the generous warmth of his expressions, respect rarely before experienced, admiration, and love - he had touched my rocky heart with his magic power, and the stream of affection gushed forth, imperishable and pure. In the evening we parted; he pressed my hand: "We shall meet again; come to me to-morrow." I clasped that kind hand; I tried to answer; a fervent "God bless you!" was all my ignorance could frame of speech, and I darted away, oppressed by my new emotions.

I could not rest. I sought the hills; a west wind swept them, and the stars glittered above. I ran on, careless of outward objects, but trying to master the struggling spirit within me by means of bodily fatigue. "This," I thought, "is power! Not to be strong of limb, hard of heart, ferocious, and daring; but kind compassionate and soft." - Stopping short, I clasped my hands, and with the fervor of a new proselyte, cried, "Doubt me not, Adrian, I also will become wise and good!" and then quite overcome, I wept aloud.

As this gust of passion passed from me, I felt more composed. I lay on the ground, and giving the reins to my thoughts, repassed in my mind my former life; and began, fold by fold, to unwind the many errors of my heart, and to discover how brutish, savage, and worthless I had hitherto been. I could not however at that time feel remorse, for methought I was born anew; my soul threw off the burthen of past sin, to commence a new career in innocence and love. Nothing harsh or rough remained to jar with the soft feelings which the transactions of the day had inspired; I was as a child lisping its devotions after its mother, and my plastic soul was remolded by a master hand, which I neither desired nor was able to resist.

This was the first commencement of my friendship with Adrian, and I must commemorate this day as the most fortunate of my life. I now began to be human. I was admitted within that sacred boundary which divides the intellectual and moral nature of man from that which characterizes animals. My best feelings were called into play to give fitting responses to the generosity, wisdom, and amenity of my new friend. He, with a noble goodness all his own, took infinite delight in bestowing to prodigality the treasures of his mind and fortune on the long-neglected son of his father's friend, the offspring of that gifted being whose excellencies and talents he had heard commemorated from infancy.

After his abdication the late king had retreated from the sphere of politics, yet his domestic circle afforded him small content. The ex-queen had none of the virtues of domestic life, and those of courage and daring which she possessed were rendered null by the secession of her husband: she despised him and did not care to conceal her sentiments. The king had, in compliance with her exactions, cast off his old friends, but he had acquired no new ones under her guidance. In this dearth of sympathy, he had recourse to his almost infant son; and the early development of talent and sensibility rendered Adrian no unfitting depository of his father's confidence. He was never weary of listening to the latter's often re-peated accounts of old times, in which my father had played a distinguished part; his keen remarks were repeated to the boy, and remembered by him; his wit, his fascinations, his very faults were hallowed by the regret of affection; his loss was sincerely deplored. Even the queen's dislike of the favorite was ineffectual to de-prive him of his son's admiration: it was bitter, sarcastic, contemptuous - but as she bestowed her heavy censure alike on his virtues as his errors, on his devoted friendship and his ill-bestowed loves, on his disinterestedness and his prodigality, on his pre-possessing grace of manner, and the facility with which he yielded to temptation, her double shot proved too heavy, and fell short of the mark. Nor did her angry dislike prevent Adrian from imaging my father, as he had said, the type of all that was gallant, amiable, and fascinating in man. It was not strange there-fore, that when he heard of the existence of the offspring of this celebrated person, he should have formed the plan of bestowing on them all the advantages his rank made him rich to afford. When he found me a vagabond shepherd of the hills, a poacher, an unlettered savage, still his kindness did not fail. In addition to the opinion he entertained that his father was to a degree culpable of neglect towards us, and that he was bound to every possible reparation, he was pleased to say that under all my ruggedness there glimmered forth an elevation of spirit, which could be distinguished from mere animal courage, and that I inherited a similarity of countenance to my father, which gave proof that all his virtues and talents had not died with him. Whatever those might be which descended to me, my noble young friend resolved should not be lost for want of culture.

Acting upon this plan in our subsequent intercourse, he led me to wish to participate in that cultivation which graced his own intellect. My active mind, when once it seized upon this new idea, fastened on it with extreme avidity. At first it was the great object of my ambition to rival the merits of my father and render myself worthy of the friendship of Adrian. But curiosity soon awoke, and an earnest love of knowledge, which caused me to pass days and nights in reading and study. I was already well acquainted with what I may term the panorama of nature, the change of seasons, and the various appearances of heaven and earth. But I was at once startled and enchanted by my sudden extension of vision, when the curtain, which had been drawn before the intellectual world, was withdrawn, and I saw the universe, not only as it presented itself to my outward senses, but as it had appeared to the wisest among men. Poetry and its creations, philosophy and its researches and classifications, alike awoke the sleeping ideas in my mind, and gave me new ones.

I felt as the sailor, who from the topmast first discovered the shore of America; and like him I hastened to tell my companions of my discoveries in unknown regions. But I was unable to excite in any breast the same craving appetite for knowledge that existed in mine. Even Perdita was unable to understand me. I had lived in what is generally called the world of reality, and it was awakening to a new country to find that there was a deeper meaning in all I saw, besides that which my eyes conveyed to me. The visionary Perdita beheld in all this only a new gloss upon an old reading, and her own was sufficiently inexhaustible to content her. She listened to me as she had done to the narration of my adventures, and sometimes took an interest in this species of information; but she did not, as I did, look on it as an integral part of her being, which having obtained, I could no more put off than the universal sense of touch.

We both agreed in loving Adrian: although she not having yet escaped from childhood could not appreciate as I did the extent of his merits or feel the same sympathy in his pursuits and opinions. I was forever with him. There was a sensibility and sweetness in his disposition, that gave a tender and unearthly tone to our converse. Then he was gay as a lark caroling from its skiey tower, soaring in thought as an eagle, innocent as the mild-eyed dove. He could dispel the seriousness of Perdita and take the sting from the torturing activity of my nature. I looked back to my restless desires and painful struggles with my fellow beings as to a troubled dream, and felt myself as much changed as if I had transmigrated into another form, whose fresh sensorium and mechanism of nerves had altered the reflection of the apparent universe in the mirror of mind. But it was not so; I was the same in strength, in earnest craving for sympathy, in my yearning for active exertion. My manly virtues did not desert me, for the witch Urania spared the locks of Sampson, while he reposed at her feet; but all was softened and humanized. Nor did Adrian instruct me only in the cold truths of history and philosophy. At the same time that he taught me by their means to subdue my own reckless and uncultured spirit, he opened to my view the living page of his own heart and gave me to feel and understand its wondrous character.

The ex-queen of England had, even during infancy, endeavored to implant daring and ambitious designs in the mind of her son. She saw that he was endowed with genius and surpassing talent; these she cultivated for the sake of afterwards using them for the furtherance of her own views. She encouraged his craving for knowledge and his impetuous courage; she even tolerated his tameless love of freedom, under the hope that this would, as is too often the case, lead to a passion for command. She endeavored to bring him up in a sense of resentment towards, and a desire to revenge himself upon, those who had been instrumental in bringing about his father's abdication. In this she did not succeed. The accounts furnished him, however distorted, of a great and wise nation asserting its right to govern itself, excited his admiration: in early days he became a republican from principle. Still his mother did not despair. To the love of rule and haughty pride of birth she added determined ambition, patience, and self-control. She devoted herself to the study of her son's disposition. By the application of praise, censure, and exhortation, she tried to seek and strike the fitting chords; and though the melody that followed her touch seemed discord to her, she built her hopes on his talents, and felt sure that she would at last win him. The kind of banishment he now experienced arose from other causes.

The ex-queen had also a daughter, now twelve years of age; his fairy sister, Adrian was wont to call her; a lovely, animated, little thing, all sensibility and truth. With these, her children, the noble widow constantly resided at Windsor; and admitted no visitors, except her own partisans, travelers from her native Germany, and a few of the foreign ministers. Among these, and highly distinguished by her, was Prince Zaimi, ambassador to England from the free States of Greece; and his daughter, the young Princess Evadne, passed much of her time at Windsor Castle. In company with this sprightly and clever Greek girl, the Countess would relax from her usual state. Her views with regard to her own children, placed all her words and actions relative to them under restraint: but Evadne was a plaything she could in no way fear; nor were her talents and vivacity slight alleviations to the monotony of the Countess's life.

Evadne was eighteen years of age. Although they spent much time together at Windsor, the extreme youth of Adrian prevented any suspicion as to the nature of their intercourse. But he was ardent and tender of heart beyond the common nature of man, and had already learnt to love, while the beauteous Greek smiled benignantly on the boy. It was strange to me, who, though older than Adrian, had never loved, to witness the whole heart's sacrifice of my friend. There was neither jealousy, inquietude, or mistrust in his sentiment; it was devotion and faith. His life was swallowed up in the existence of his beloved; and his heartbeat only in unison with the pulsations that vivified hers. This was the secret law of his life—he loved and was beloved. The universe was to him a dwelling, to inhabit with his chosen one; and not either a scheme of society or an enchainment of events, that could impart to him either happiness or misery. What, though life and the system of social intercourse were a wilderness, a tiger-haunted jungle! Through the midst of its errors, in the depths of its savage recesses, there was a disentangled and flowery pathway, through which they might journey in safety and delight. Their track would be like the passage of the Red Sea, which they might traverse with unwet feet, though a wall of destruction were impending on either side.

Alas! why must I record the hapless delusion of this matchless specimen of humanity? What is there in our nature that is forever urging us on towards pain and misery? We are not formed for enjoyment; and, however we may be attuned to the reception of pleasurable emotion, disappointment is the never-failing pilot of our life's bark, and ruthlessly carries us on to the shoals. Who was better framed than this highly gifted youth to love and be beloved, and to reap unalienable joy from an unblamed passion? If his heart had slept but a few years longer, he might have been saved; but it awoke in its infancy; it had power, but no knowledge; and it was ruined, even as a too early-blowing bud is nipped by the killing frost.

I did not accuse Evadne of hypocrisy or a wish to deceive her lover; but the first letter that I saw of hers convinced me that she did not love him; it was written with elegance, and, foreigner as she was, with great command of language. The handwriting itself was exquisitely beautiful; there was something in her very paper and its folds, which even I, who did not love, and was withal unskilled in such matters, could discern as being tasteful. There was much kindness, gratitude, and sweetness in her expression, but no love. Evadne was two years older than Adrian; and who, at eighteen, ever loved one so much their junior? I compared her placid epistles with the burning ones of Adrian. His soul seemed to distil itself into the words he wrote, and they breathed on the paper, bearing with them a portion of the life of love, which was his life. The very writing used to exhaust him; and he would weep over them, merely from the excess of emotion they awakened in his heart.

Adrian's soul was painted in his countenance, and concealment or deceit were at the antipodes to the dreadless frankness of his nature. Evadne made it her earnest request that the tale of their loves should not be revealed to his mother; and after for a while contesting the point, he yielded it to her. A vain concession: his demeanor quickly betrayed his secret to the quick eyes of the ex-queen. With the same wary prudence that characterized her whole conduct, she concealed her discovery, but hastened to remove her son from the sphere of the attractive Greek. He was sent to Cumberland; but the plan of correspondence between the lovers, arranged by Evadne, was effectually hidden from her. Thus, the absence of Adrian, concerted for the purpose of separating, united them in firmer bonds than ever. To me he discoursed ceaselessly of his beloved Ionian. Her country, its ancient annals, its late memorable struggles, were all made to partake in her glory and excellence. He submitted to be away from her, because she commanded this submission; but for her influence, he would have declared his attachment before all England, and resisted, with unshaken constancy, his mother's opposition. Evadne's feminine prudence perceived how useless any assertion of his resolves would be, till added years gave weight to his power. Perhaps there was besides a lurking dislike to bind herself in the face of the world to one whom she did not love - not love, at least, with that passionate enthusiasm which her heart told her she might one day feel towards another. He obeyed her injunctions and passed a year in exile in Cumberland.

CHAPTER III.

Happy, thrice happy, were the months, and weeks, and hours of that year. Friendship, hand in hand with admiration, tenderness and respect, built a bower of delight in my heart, late rough as an untrod wild in America, as the homeless wind or herbless sea. Insatiate thirst for knowledge, and boundless affection for Adrian, combined to keep both my heart and understanding occupied, and I was consequently happy. What happiness is so true and unclouded, as the overflowing and talkative delight of young people. In our boat, upon my native lake, beside the streams and the pale bordering poplars - in valley and over hill, my crook thrown aside, a nobler flock to tend than silly sheep, even a flock of new-born ideas, I read or listened to Adrian; and his discourse, whether it concerned his love or his theories for the improvement of man, alike entranced me. Sometimes my lawless mood would return, my love of peril, my resistance to authority; but this was in his absence; under the mild sway of his dear eyes, I was obedient and good as a boy of five years old, who does his mother's bidding.

After a residence of about a year at Ullswater, Adrian visited London, and came back full of plans for our benefit. You must begin life, he said: you are seventeen, and longer delay would render the necessary apprenticeship more and more irksome. He foresaw that his own life would be one of struggle, and I must partake his labors with him. The better to fit me for this task, we must now separate. He found my name a good passport to preferment, and he had procured for me the situation of private secretary to the Ambassador at Vienna, where I should enter on my career under the best auspices. In two years, I should return to my country, with a name well known and a reputation already founded.

And Perdita? - Perdita was to become the pupil, friend and younger sister of Evadne. With his usual thoughtfulness, he had provided for her independence in this situation. How refuse the offers of this generous friend? - I did not wish to refuse them; but in my heart of hearts, I made a vow to devote life, knowledge, and power, all of which, in as much as they were of any value, he had bestowed on me - all, all my capacities and hopes, to him alone I would devote.

Thus, I promised myself, as I journeyed towards my destination with roused and ardent expectation: expectation of the fulfilment of all that in boyhood we promise ourselves of power and enjoyment in maturity. Methought the time was now arrived, when, childish occupations laid aside, I should enter into life. Even in the Elysian fields, Virgil describes the souls of the happy as eager to drink of the wave which was to restore them to this mortal coil. The young are seldom in Elysium, for their desires, outstripping possibility, leave them as poor as a moneyless debtor. We are told by the wisest philosophers of the dangers of the world, the deceits of men, and the treason of our own hearts: but not the less fearlessly does each put off his frail bark from the port, spread the sail, and strain his oar, to attain the multitudinous streams of the sea of life. How few in youth's prime, moor their vessels on the "golden sands," and collect the painted shells that strew them. But all at close of day, with riven planks and rent canvas make for shore, and are either wrecked ere they reach it, or find some wave-beaten haven, some desert strand, whereon to cast themselves and die unmourned.

A truce to philosophy! - Life is before me, and I rush into possession. Hope, glory, love, and blameless ambition are my guides, and my soul knows no dread. What has been, though sweet, is gone; the present is good only because it is about to change, and the to come is all my own. Do I fear, that my heart palpitates? high aspirations cause the flow of my blood; my eyes seem to penetrate the cloudy midnight of time, and to discern within the depths of its darkness, the fruition of all my soul desires.

Now pause! - During my journey I might dream, and with buoyant wings reach the summit of life's high edifice. Now that I am arrived at its base, my pinions are furled, the mighty stairs are before me, and step by step I must ascend the wondrous fane.

Speak! - What door is opened?

Behold me in a new capacity. A diplomatist: one among the pleasure-seeking society of a gay city; a youth of promise; favorite of the Ambassador. All was strange and admirable to the shepherd of Cumberland. With breathless amaze I entered on the gay scene, whose actors were -the lilies glorious as Solomon, who toil not, neither do they spin.

Soon, too soon, I entered the giddy whirl, forgetting my studious hours, and the companionship of Adrian. Passionate desire of sympathy, and ardent pursuit for a wished-for object still characterized me. The sight of beauty entranced me, and attractive manners in man or woman won my entire confidence. I called it rapture, when a smile made my heartbeat; and I felt the life's blood tingle in my frame, when I approached the idol which for a while I worshipped. The mere flow of animal spirits was Paradise, and at night's close I only desired a renewal of the intoxicating delusion. The dazzling light of ornamented rooms; lovely forms arrayed in splendid dresses; the motions of a dance, the voluptuous tones of exquisite music, cradled my senses in one delightful dream.

And is not this in its kind happiness? I appeal to moralists and sages. I ask if in the calm of their measured reveries, if in the deep meditations which fill their hours, they feel the extasy of a youthful tyro in the school of pleasure? Can the calm beams of their heaven-seeking eyes equal the flashes of mingling passion which blind his, or does the influence of cold philosophy steep their soul in a joy equal to his, engaged

In this dear work of youthful revelry.

But in truth, neither the lonely meditations of the hermit, nor the tumultuous raptures of the reveler, are capable of satisfying man's heart. From the one we gather unquiet speculation, from the other satiety. The mind flags beneath the weight of thought, and droops in the heartless intercourse of those whose sole aim is amusement. There is no fruition in their vacant kindness, and sharp rocks lurk beneath the smiling ripples of these shallow waters.

Thus, I felt, when disappointment, weariness, and solitude drove me back upon my heart, to gather thence the joy of which it had become barren. My flagging spirits asked for something to speak to the affections; and not finding it, I drooped. Thus, notwithstanding the thoughtless delight that waited on its commencement, the impression I have of my life at Vienna is melancholy. Goethe has said, that in youth we cannot be happy unless we love. I did not love; but I was devoured by a restless wish to be something to others. I became the victim of ingratitude and cold coquetry - then I desponded and imagined that my discontent gave me a right to hate the world. I receded to solitude; I had recourse to my books, and my desire again to enjoy the society of Adrian became a burning thirst.

Emulation, that in its excess almost assumed the venomous properties of envy, gave a sting to these feelings. At this period the name and exploits of one of my countrymen filled the world with admiration. Relations of what he had done, conjectures concerning his future actions, were the never-failing topics of the hour. I was not angry on my own account, but I felt as if the praises which this idol received were leaves torn from laurels destined for Adrian. But I must enter into some account of this darling of fame - this favorite of the wonder-loving world.

Lord Raymond was the sole remnant of a noble but impoverished family. From early youth he had considered his pedigree with complacency, and bitterly lamented his want of wealth. His first wish was aggrandizement; and the means that led towards this end were secondary considerations. Haughty, yet trembling to every demonstration of respect; ambitious, but too proud to shew his ambition; willing to achieve honor, yet a votary of pleasure, - he entered upon life. He was met on the threshold by some insult, real or imaginary; some repulse, where he least expected it; some disappointment, hard for his pride to bear. He writhed beneath an injury he was unable to revenge; and he quitted England with a vow not to return, till the good time should arrive, when she might feel the power of him, she now despised.

He became an adventurer in the Greek wars. His reckless courage and comprehensive genius brought him into notice. He became the darling hero of this rising people. His foreign birth, and he refused to throw off his allegiance to his native country, alone prevented him from filling the first offices in the state. But though others might rank higher in title and ceremony, Lord Raymond held a station above and beyond all this. He led the Greek armies to victory; their triumphs were all his own. When he appeared, whole towns poured forth their population to meet him; new songs were adapted to their national airs, whose themes were his glory, valor, and munificence. A truce was concluded between the Greeks and Turks. At the same time, Lord Raymond, by some unlooked-for chance, became the possessor of an immense fortune in England, whither he returned, crowned with glory, to receive the meed of honor and distinction before denied to his pretensions. His proud heart rebelled against this change. In what was the despised Raymond not the same? If the acquisition of power in the shape of wealth caused this alteration, that power should they feel as an iron yoke. Power therefore was the aim of all his endeavors; aggrandizement the mark at which he forever shot. In open ambition or close intrigue, his end was the same - to attain the first station in his own country.

This account filled me with curiosity. The events that in succession followed his return to England, gave me keener feelings. Among his other advantages, Lord Raymond was supremely handsome; everyone admired him; of women he was the idol. He was courteous, honey-tongued - an adept in fascinating arts. What could not this man achieve in the busy English world? Change succeeded to change; the entire history did not reach me; for Adrian had ceased to write, and Perdita was a laconic correspondent. The rumor went that Adrian had become - how write the fatal word - mad: that Lord Raymond was the favorite of the ex-queen, her daughter's destined husband. Nay, more, that this aspiring noble revived the claim of the house of Windsor to the crown, and that, on the event of Adrian's incurable disorder and his marriage with the sister, the brow of the ambitious Raymond might be encircled with the magic ring of regality.

Such a tale filled the trumpet of many voiced fame; such a tale rendered my longer stay at Vienna, away from the friend of my youth, intolerable. Now I must fulfil my vow; now range myself at his side and be his ally and support till death. Farewell to courtly pleasure; to politic intrigue; to the maze of passion and folly! All hail, England! Native England receive thy child! thou art the scene of all my hopes, the mighty theatre on which is acted the only drama that can, heart and soul, bear me along with it in its development. A voice most irresistible, a power omnipotent, drew me thither. After an absence of two years I landed on its shores, not daring to make any inquiries, fearful of every remark. My first visit would be to my sister, who inhabited a little cottage, a part of Adrian's gift, on the borders of Windsor Forest. From her I should learn the truth concerning our protector; I should hear why she had withdrawn from the protection of the Princess Evadne, and be instructed as to the influence which this overtopping and towering Raymond exercised over the fortunes of my friend.

I had never before been in the neighborhood of Windsor; the fertility and beauty of the country around now struck me with admiration, which increased as I approached the antique wood. The ruins of majestic oaks which had grown, flourished, and decayed during the progress of centuries, marked where the limits of the forest once reached, while the shattered palings and neglected underwood shewed that this part was deserted for the younger plantations, which owed their birth to the beginning of the nineteenth century, and now stood in the pride of maturity. Perdita's humble dwelling was situated on the skirts of the most ancient portion; before it was stretched Bishopgate Heath, which towards the east appeared interminable, and was bounded to the west by Chapel Wood and the grove of Virginia Water. Behind, the cottage was shadowed by the venerable fathers of the forest, under which the deer came to graze, and which for the most part hollow and decayed, formed fantastic groups that contrasted with the regular beauty of the younger trees. These, the offspring of a later period, stood erect and seemed ready to advance fearlessly into coming time; while those out worn stragglers, blasted and broke, clung to each other, their weak boughs sighing as the wind buffeted them—a weather-beaten crew.

A light railing surrounded the garden of the cottage, which, low-roofed, seemed to submit to the majesty of nature, and cower amidst the venerable remains of forgotten time. Flowers, the children of the spring, adorned her garden and casements; in the midst of lowliness there was an air of elegance which spoke the graceful taste of the inmate. With a beating heart I entered the enclosure; as I stood at the entrance, I heard her voice, melodious as it had ever been, which before I saw her assured me of her welfare.

A moment more and Perdita appeared; she stood before me in the fresh bloom of youthful womanhood, different from and yet the same as the mountain girl I had left. Her eyes could not be deeper than they were in childhood, nor her countenance more expressive; but the expression was changed and improved; intelligence sat on her brow; when she smiled her face was embellished by the softest sensibility, and her low, modulated voice seemed tuned by love. Her person was formed in the most feminine proportions; she was not tall, but her mountain life had given freedom to her motions, so that her light step scarce made her footfall heard as she tripped across the hall to meet me. When we had parted, I had clasped her to my bosom with unrestrained warmth; we met again, and new feelings were awakened; when each beheld the other, childhood passed, as full-grown actors on this changeful scene. The pause was but for a moment; the flood of association and natural feeling which had been checked, again rushed in full tide upon our hearts, and with tenderest emotion we were swiftly locked in each other's embrace.

This burst of passionate feeling over, with calmed thoughts we sat together, talking of the past and present. I alluded to the coldness of her letters; but the few minutes we had spent together sufficiently explained the origin of this. New feelings had arisen within her, which she was unable to express in writing to one whom she had only known in childhood; but we saw each other again, and our intimacy was renewed as if nothing had intervened to check it. I detailed the incidents of my sojourn abroad, and then questioned her as to the changes that had taken place at home, the causes of Adrian's absence, and her secluded life.

The tears that suffused my sister's eyes when I mentioned our friend, and her heightened color seemed to vouch for the truth of the reports that had reached me. But their import was too terrible for me to give instant credit to my suspicion. Was there indeed anarchy in the sublime universe of Adrian's thoughts, did madness scatter the well-appointed legions, and was he no longer the lord of his own soul? Beloved friend, this ill world was no clime for your gentle spirit; you delivered up its governance to false humanity, which stripped it of its leaves ere winter-time, and laid bare its quivering life to the evil ministration of roughest winds. Have those gentle eyes, those "channels of the soul" lost their meaning, or do they only in their glare disclose the horrible tale of its aberrations? Does that voice no longer "discourse excellent music?" Horrible, most horrible! I veil my eyes in terror of the change, and gushing tears bear witness to my sympathy for this unimaginable ruin.

In obedience to my request Perdita detailed the melancholy circumstances that led to this event.

The frank and unsuspicious mind of Adrian, gifted as it was by every natural grace, endowed with transcendent powers of intellect, unblemished by the shadow of defect (unless his dreadless independence of thought was to be construed into one), was devoted, even as a victim to sacrifice, to his love for Evadne. He entrusted to her keeping the treasures of his soul, his aspirations after excellence, and his plans for the improvement of mankind. As manhood dawned upon him, his schemes and theories, far from being changed by personal and prudential motives, acquired new strength from the powers he felt arise within him; and his love for Evadne became deep-rooted, as he each day became more certain that the path he pursued was full of difficulty, and that he must seek his reward, not in the applause or gratitude of his fellow creatures, hardly in the success of his plans, but in the approbation of his own heart, and in her love and sympathy, which was to lighten every toil and recompence every sacrifice.

In solitude, and through many wanderings afar from the haunts of men, he matured his views for the reform of the English government, and the improvement of the people. It would have been well if he had concealed his sentiments, until he had come into possession of the power which would secure their practical development. But he was impatient of the years that must intervene, he was frank of heart and fearless. He gave not only a brief denial to his mother's schemes, but published his intention of using his influence to diminish the power of the aristocracy, to effect a greater equalization of wealth and privilege, and to introduce a perfect system of republican government into England. At first his mother treated his theories as the wild ravings of inexperience. But they were so systematically arranged, and his arguments so well supported, that though still in appearance incredulous, she began to fear him. She tried to reason with him, and finding him inflexible, learned to hate him.

Strange to say, this feeling was infectious. His enthusiasm for good which did not exist; his contempt for the sacredness of authority; his ardor and imprudence were all at the antipodes of the usual routine of life; the worldly feared him; the young and inexperienced did not understand the lofty severity of his moral views, and disliked him as a being different from themselves. Evadne entered but coldly into his systems. She thought he did well to assert his own will, but she wished that will to have been more intelligible to the multitude. She had none of the spirit of a martyr and did not incline to share the shame and defeat of a fallen patriot. She was aware of the purity of his motives, the generosity of his disposition, his true and ardent attachment to her; and she entertained a great affection for him. He repaid this spirit of kindness with the fondest gratitude and made her the treasure-house of all his hopes.

At this time Lord Raymond returned from Greece. No two persons could be more opposite than Adrian and him. With all the incongruities of his character, Raymond was emphatically a man of the world. His passions were violent; as these often obtained the mastery over him, he could not always square his conduct to the obvious line of self-interest, but self-gratification at least was the paramount object with him. He looked on the structure of society as but a part of the machinery which supported the web on which his life was traced. The earth was spread out as a highway for him; the heavens built up as a canopy for him.

Adrian felt that he made a part of a great whole. He owned affinity not only with mankind, but all nature was akin to him; the mountains and sky were his friends; the winds of heaven and the offspring of earth his playmates; while he the focus only of this mighty mirror, felt his life mingle with the universe of existence. His soul was sympathy and dedicated to the worship of beauty and excellence. Adrian and Raymond now came into contact, and a spirit of aversion rose between them. Adrian despised the narrow views of the politician, and Raymond held in supreme contempt the benevolent visions of the philanthropist.

With the coming of Raymond was formed the storm that laid waste at one fell blow the gardens of delight and sheltered paths which Adrian fancied that he had secured to himself, as a refuge from defeat and contumely. Raymond, the deliverer of Greece, the graceful soldier, who bore in his mien a tinge of all that, peculiar to her native clime, Evadne cherished as most dear - Raymond was loved by Evadne. Overpowered by her new sensations, she did not pause to examine them, or to regulate her conduct by any sentiments except the tyrannical one which suddenly usurped the empire of her heart. She yielded to its influence, and the too natural consequence in a mind unattuned to soft emotions was, that the attentions of

Adrian became distasteful to her. She grew capricious; her gentle conduct towards him was exchanged for asperity and repulsive coldness. When she perceived the wild or pathetic appeal of his expressive countenance, she would relent, and for a while resume her ancient kindness. But these fluctuations shook to its depths the soul of the sensitive youth; he no longer deemed the world subject to him, because he possessed Evadne's love; he felt in every nerve that the dire storms of the mental universe were about to attack his fragile being, which quivered at the expectation of its advent.

Perdita, who then resided with Evadne, saw the torture that Adrian endured. She loved him as a kind elder brother; a relation to guide, protect, and instruct her, without the too frequent tyranny of parental authority. She adored his virtues, and with mixed contempt and indignation she saw Evadne pile drear sorrow on his head, for the sake of one who hardly marked her. In his solitary despair Adrian would often seek my sister, and in covered terms express his misery, while fortitude and agony divided the throne of his mind. Soon, alas! was one to conquer. Anger made no part of his emotion. With whom should he be angry? Not with Raymond, who was unconscious of the misery he occasioned; not with Evadne, for her his soul wept tears of blood — poor, mistaken girl, slave not tyrant was she, and amidst his own anguish he grieved for her future destiny. Once a writing of his fell into Perdita's hands; it was blotted with tears - well might any blot it with the like -

"Life" - it began thus -"is not the thing romance writers describe it; going through the measures of a dance, and after various evolutions arriving at a conclusion, when the dancers may sit down and repose. While there is life there is action and change. We go on, each thought linked to the one which was its parent, each act to a previous act. No joy or sorrow dies barren of progeny, which forever generated and generating, weaves the chain that make our life:

Un dia llama a otro dia y assi llama, y encadena llanto a llanto, y pena a pena.
(One day he calls another day and so he calls, and in chains crying to crying, and grief to grief.)

Truly disappointment is the guardian deity of human life; she sits at the threshold of unborn time and marshals the events as they come forth. Once my heart sat lightly in my bosom; all the beauty of the world was doubly beautiful, irradiated by the sunlight shed from my own soul. O wherefore are love and ruin forever joined in this our mortal dream? So that when we make our hearts a lair for that gently seeming beast, its companion enters with it, and pitilessly lays waste what might have been a home and a shelter."

By degrees his health was shaken by his misery, and then his intellect yielded to the same tyranny. His manners grew wild; he was sometimes ferocious, sometimes absorbed in speechless melancholy. Suddenly Evadne quitted London for Paris; he followed, and overtook her when the vessel was about to sail; none knew what passed between them, but Perdita had never seen him since; he lived in seclusion, no one knew where, attended by such persons as his mother selected for that purpose.

CHAPTER IV

The next day Lord Raymond called at Perdita's cottage, on his way to Windsor Castle. My sister's heightened color and sparkling eyes half revealed her secret to me. He was perfectly self-possessed; he accosted us both with courtesy, seemed immediately to enter into our feelings, and to make one with us. I scanned his physiognomy, which varied as he spoke, yet was beautiful in every change. The usual expression of his eyes was soft, though at times he could make them even glare with ferocity; his complexion was colorless; and every trait spoke predominate self-will; his smile was pleasing, though disdain too often curled his lips - lips which to female eyes were the very throne of beauty and love. His voice, usually gentle, often startled you by a sharp discordant note, which shewed that his usual low tone was rather the work of study than nature. Thus full of contradictions, unbending yet haughty, gentle yet fierce, tender and again neglectful, he by some strange art found easy entrance to the admiration and affection of women; now caressing and now tyrannizing over them according to his mood, but in every change a despot.

At the present time Raymond evidently wished to appear amiable. Wit, hilarity, and deep observation were mingled in his talk, rendering every sentence that he uttered as a flash of light. He soon conquered my latent distaste; I endeavored to watch him and Perdita, and to keep in mind everything I had heard to his disadvantage. But all appeared so ingenuous, and all was so fascinating, that I forgot everything except the pleasure his society afforded me. Under the idea of initiating me in the scene of English politics and society, of which I was soon to become a part, he narrated a number of anecdotes, and sketched many characters; his discourse, rich and varied, flowed on, pervading all my senses with pleasure. But for one thing he would have been completely triumphant. He alluded to Adrian and spoke of him with that disparagement that the worldly wise always attach to enthusiasm. He perceived the cloud gathering, and tried to dissipate it; but the strength of my feelings would not permit me to pass thus lightly over this sacred subject; so I said emphatically, "Permit me to remark, that I am devotedly attached to the Earl of Windsor; he is my best friend and benefactor. I reverence his goodness, I accord with his opinions, and bitterly lament his present, and I trust temporary, illness. That illness, from its peculiarity, makes it painful to me beyond words to hear him mentioned, unless in terms of respect and affection."

Raymond replied, but there was nothing conciliatory in his reply. I saw that in his heart he despised those dedicated to any but worldly idols. "Every man," he said, "dreams about something, love, honor, and pleasure; you dream of friendship, and devote yourself to a maniac; well, if that be your vocation, doubtless you are in the right to follow it."

Some reflection seemed to sting him, and the spasm of pain that for a moment convulsed his countenance, checked my indignation. "Happy are dreamers," he continued, "so that they be not awakened! Would I could dream! but 'broad and garish day' is the element in which I live; the dazzling glare of reality inverts the scene for me. Even the ghost of friendship has departed, and love..." He broke off; nor could I guess whether the disdain that curled his lip was directed against the passion, or against himself for being its slave.

This account may be taken as a sample of my intercourse with Lord Raymond. I became intimate with him, and each day afforded me occasion to admire more and more his powerful and versatile talents, that together with his eloquence, which was graceful and witty, and his wealth now immense, caused him to be feared, loved, and hated beyond any other man in England.

My descent, which claimed interest, if not respect, my former connection with Adrian, the favor of the ambassador, whose secretary I had been, and now my intimacy with Lord Raymond, gave me easy access to the fashionable and political circles of England. To my inexperience we at first appeared on the eve of a civil war; each party was violent, acrimonious, and unyielding. Parliament was divided by three factions, aristocrats, democrats, and royalists. After Adrian's declared predeliction to the republican form of government, the latter party had nearly died away, chiefless, guideless; but, when Lord Raymond came forward as its leader, it revived with redoubled force. Some were royalists from prejudice and ancient affection, and there were many moderately inclined who feared alike the capricious tyranny of the popular party, and the unbending despotism of the aristocrats. More than a third of the members ranged themselves under Raymond, and their number was perpetually increasing. The aristocrats built their hopes on their preponderant wealth and influence; the reformers on the force of the nation itself; the debates were violent, more violent the discourses held by each knot of politicians as they assembled to arrange their measures. Opprobrious epithets were bandied about, resistance even to the death threatened; meetings of the populace disturbed the quiet order of the country; except in war, how could all this end? Even as the destructive flames were ready to break forth, I saw them shrink back; allayed by the absence of the military, by the aversion entertained by everyone to any violence, save that of speech, and by the cordial politeness and even friendship of the hostile leaders when they met in private society. I was from a thousand motives induced to attend minutely to the course of events and watch each turn with intense anxiety.

I could not but perceive that Perdita loved Raymond; methought also that he regarded the fair daughter of Verney with admiration and tenderness. Yet I knew that he was urging forward his marriage with the presumptive heiress of the Earldom of Windsor, with keen expectation of the advantages that would thence accrue to him. All the ex-queen's friends were his friends; no week passed that he did not hold consultations with her at Windsor.

I had never seen the sister of Adrian. I had heard that she was lovely, amiable, and fascinating. Wherefore should I see her. There are times when we have an indefinable sentiment of impending change for better or for worse, to arise from an event; and be it for better or for worse, we fear the change, and shun the event. For this reason, I avoided this high-born damsel. To me she was everything and nothing; her very name mentioned by another made me start and tremble; the endless discussion concerning her union with Lord Raymond was real agony to me. Methought that, Adrian withdrawn from active life, and this beauteous Idris, a victim probably to her mother's ambitious schemes, I ought to come forward to protect her from undue influence, guard her from unhappiness, and secure to her freedom of choice, the right of every human being. Yet how was I to do this? She herself would disdain my interference. Since then I must be an object of indifference or contempt to her, better, far better avoid her, nor expose myself before her and the scornful world to the chance of playing the mad game of a fond, foolish Icarus. One day, several months after my return to England, I quitted London to visit my sister. Her society was my chief solace and delight; and my spirits always rose at the expectation of seeing her. Her conversation was full of pointed remark and discernment; in her pleasant alcove, redolent with sweetest flowers, adorned by magnificent casts, antique vases, and copies of the finest pictures of Raphael, Correggio, and Claude, painted by herself, I fancied myself in a fairy retreat untainted by and inaccessible to the noisy contentions of politicians and the frivolous pursuits of fashion. On this occasion, my sister was not alone; nor could I fail to recognize her companion: it was Idris, the till now unseen object of my mad idolatry.

In what fitting terms of wonder and delight, in what choice expression and soft flow of language, can I usher in the loveliest, wisest, best? How in poor assemblage of words convey the halo of glory that surrounded her, the thousand graces that waited unwearied on her. The first thing that struck you on beholding that charming countenance was its perfect goodness and frankness; candor sat upon her brow, simplicity in her eyes, heavenly benignity in her smile. Her tall slim figure bent gracefully as a poplar to the breezy west, and her gait, goddess-like, was as that of a winged angel new alit from heaven's high floor; the pearly fairness of her complexion was stained by a pure suffusion; her voice resembled the low, subdued tenor of a flute. It is easiest perhaps to describe by contrast. I have detailed the perfections of my sister; and yet she was utterly unlike Idris. Perdita, even where she loved, was reserved and timid; Idris was frank and confiding. The one recoiled to solitude, that she might there entrench herself from disappointment and injury; the other walked forth in open day, believing that none would harm her. Wordsworth has compared a beloved female to two fair objects in nature; but his lines always appeared to me rather a contrast than a similitude:

> *A violet by a mossy stone*
> *Half hidden from the eye,*
> *Fair as a star when only one*
> *Is shining in the sky.*

Such a violet was sweet Perdita, trembling to entrust herself to the very air, cowering from observation, yet betrayed by her excellences; and repaying with a thousand graces the labor of those who sought her in her lonely bye-path. Idris was as the star, set in single splendor in the dim anadem of balmy evening; ready to enlighten and delight the subject world, shielded herself from every taint by her unimagined distance from all that was not like herself akin to heaven.

I found this vision of beauty in Perdita's alcove, in earnest conversation with its inmate. When my sister saw me, she rose, and taking my hand, said, "He is here, even at our wish; this is Lionel, my brother." Idris arose also, and bent on me her eyes of celestial blue, and with grace peculiar said - "You hardly need an introduction; we have a picture, highly valued by my father, which declares at once your name. Verney, you will acknowledge this tie, and as my brother's friend, I feel that I may trust you."

Then, with lids humid with a tear and trembling voice, she continued - "Dear friends, do not think it strange that now, visiting you for the first time, I ask your assistance, and confide my wishes and fears to you. To you alone do I dare speak; I have heard you commended by impartial spectators; you are my brother's friends, therefore you must be mine. What can I say? if you refuse to aid me, I am lost indeed!" She cast up her eyes, while wonder held her auditors mute; then, as if carried away by her feelings, she cried — "My brother! beloved, ill-fated Adrian! how speak of your misfortunes? Doubtless you have both heard the current tale; perhaps believe the slander; but he is not mad! Were an angel from the foot of God's throne to assert it, never, never would I believe it. He is wronged, betrayed, imprisoned - save him! Verney, you must do this; seek him out in whatever part of the island he is immured; find him, rescue him from his persecutors, restore him to himself, to me - on the wide earth I have none to love but only him!"

Her earnest appeal, so sweetly and passionately expressed, filled me with wonder and sympathy; and, when she added, with thrilling voice and look, "Do you consent to undertake this enterprise?" I vowed, with energy and truth, to devote myself in life and death to the restoration and welfare of Adrian. We then conversed on the plan I should pursue and discussed the probable means of discovering his residence. While we were in earnest discourse, Lord Raymond entered unannounced: I saw Perdita tremble and grow deadly pale, and the cheeks of Idris glow with purest blushes. He must have been astonished at our conclave, disturbed by it I should have thought; but nothing of this appeared; he saluted my companions, and addressed me with a cordial greeting. Idris appeared suspended for a moment, and then with extreme sweetness, she said, "Lord Raymond, I confide in your goodness and honor."

Smiling haughtily, he bent his head, and replied, with emphasis, "Do you indeed confide, Lady Idris?"

She endeavored to read his thought, and then answered with dignity, "As you please. It is certainly best not to compromise oneself by any concealment."

"Pardon me," he replied, "if I have offended. Whether you trust me or not, rely on my doing my utmost to further your wishes, whatever they may be."

Idris smiled her thanks and rose to take leave. Lord Raymond requested permission to accompany her to Windsor Castle, to which she consented, and they quitted the cottage together. My sister and I were left—truly like two fools, who fancied that they had obtained a golden treasure, till daylight shewed it to be lead—two silly, luckless flies, who had played in sunbeams and were caught in a spider's web. I leaned against the casement, and watched those two glorious creatures, till they disappeared in the forest-glades; and then I turned. Perdita had not moved; her eyes fixed on the ground, her cheeks pale, her very lips white, motionless and rigid, every feature stamped by woe, she sat. Half frightened, I would have taken her hand; but she shudderingly withdrew it and strove to collect herself. I entreated her to speak to me: "Not now," she replied, "nor do you speak to me, my dear Lionel; you can say nothing, for you know nothing. I will see you to-morrow; in the meantime, adieu!" She rose and walked from the room; but pausing at the door, and leaning against it, as if her over-busy thoughts had taken from her the power of supporting herself, she said, "Lord Raymond will probably return. Will you tell him that he must excuse me to-day, for I am not well. I will see him to-morrow if he wishes it, and you also. You had better return to London with him; you can there make the enquiries agreed upon, concerning the Earl of Windsor and visit me again to-morrow, before you proceed on your journey - till then, farewell!"

She spoke falteringly and concluded with a heavy sigh. I gave my assent to her request; and she left me. I felt as if, from the order of the systematic world, I had plunged into chaos, obscure, contrary, unintelligible. That Raymond should marry Idris was more than ever intolerable; yet my passion, though a giant from its birth, was too strange, wild, and impracticable, for me to feel at once the misery I perceived in Perdita. How should I act? She had not confided in me; I could not demand an explanation from Raymond without the hazard of betraying what was perhaps her most treasured secret. I would obtain the truth from her the following day - in the meantime - But, while I was occupied by multiplying reflections, Lord Raymond returned. He asked for my sister; and I delivered her message. After musing on it for a moment, he asked me if I were about to return to London, and if I would accompany him: I consented. He was full of thought, and remained silent during a considerable part of our ride; at length he said, "I must apologize to you for my abstraction; the truth is, Ryland's motion comes on to-night, and I am considering my reply."

Ryland was the leader of the popular party, a hard-headed man, and in his way eloquent; he had obtained leave to bring in a bill making it treason to endeavor to change the present state of the English government and the standing laws of the republic. This attack was directed against Raymond and his machinations for the restoration of the monarchy.

Raymond asked me if I would accompany him to the House that evening. I remembered my pursuit for intelligence concerning Adrian; and, knowing that my time would be fully occupied, I excused myself. "Nay," said my companion, "I can free you from your present impediment. You are going to make enquiries concerning the Earl of Windsor. I can answer them at once, he is at the Duke of Athol's seat at Dunkeld. On the first approach of his disorder, he travelled about from one place to another; until, arriving at that romantic seclusion he refused to quit it, and we made arrangements with the Duke for his continuing there."

I was hurt by the careless tone with which he conveyed this information and replied coldly: "I am obliged to you for your intelligence and will avail myself of it."

"You shall, Verney," said he, "and if you continue of the same mind, I will facilitate your views. But first witness, I beseech you, the result of this night's contest, and the triumph I am about to achieve, if I may so call it, while I fear that victory is to me defeat. What can I do? My dearest hopes appear to be near their fulfilment. The ex-queen gives me Idris; Adrian is totally unfitted to succeed to the earldom, and that earldom in my hands becomes a kingdom. By the reigning God it is true; the paltry earldom of Windsor shall no longer content him, who will inherit the rights which must forever appertain to the person who possesses it. The Countess can never forget that she has been a queen, and she disdains to leave a diminished inheritance to her children; her power and my wit will rebuild the throne, and this brow will be clasped by a kingly diadem. - I can do this - I can marry Idris." -

He stopped abruptly, his countenance darkened, and its expression changed again and again under the influence of internal passion. I asked, "Does Lady Idris love you?"

"What a question," replied he laughing. "She will of course, as I shall her, when we are married."

"You begin late," said I, ironically, "marriage is usually considered the grave, and not the cradle of love. So you are about to love her, but do not already?"

"Do not catechize me, Lionel; I will do my duty by her, be assured. Love! I must steel my heart against that; expel it from its tower of strength, barricade it out: the fountain of love must cease to play, its waters be dried up, and all passionate thoughts attendant on it die - that is to say, the love which would rule me, not that which I rule. Idris is a gentle, pretty, sweet little girl; it is impossible not to have an affection for her, and I have a very sincere one; only do not speak of love - love, the tyrant and the tyrant-queller; love, until now my conqueror, now my slave; the hungry fire, the untamable beast, the fanged snake – no -no - I will have nothing to do with that love. Tell me, Lionel, do you consent that I should marry this young lady?"

He bent his keen eyes upon me, and my uncontrollable heart swelled in my bosom. I replied in a calm voice—but how far from calm was the thought imaged by my still words - "Never! I can never consent that Lady Idris should be united to one who does not love her."

"Because you love her yourself."

"Your Lordship might have spared that taunt; I do not, dare not love her."

"At least," he continued haughtily, "she does not love you. I would not marry a reigning sovereign, were I not sure that her heart was free. But, O, Lionel! a kingdom is a word of might, and gently sounding are the terms that compose the style of royalty. Were not the mightiest men of the olden times kings? Alexander was a king; Solomon, the wisest of men, was a king; Napoleon was a king; Caesar died in his attempt to become one, and Cromwell, the puritan and king-killer, aspired to regality. The father of Adrian yielded up the already broken scepter of England; but I will rear the fallen plant, join its dismembered frame, and exalt it above all the flowers of the field.

"You need not wonder that I freely discover Adrian's abode. Do not suppose that I am wicked or foolish enough to found my purposed sovereignty on a fraud, and one so easily discovered as the truth or falsehood of the Earl's insanity. I am just come from him. Before I decided on my marriage with Idris, I resolved to see him myself again, and to judge of the probability of his recovery. - He is irrecoverably mad."

I gasped for breath—

"I will not detail to you," continued Raymond, "the melancholy particulars. You shall see him, and judge for yourself; although I fear this visit, useless to him, will be insufferably painful to you. It has weighed on my spirits ever since. Excellent and gentle as he is even in the downfall of his reason, I do not worship him as you do, but I would give all my hopes of a crown and my right hand to boot, to see him restored to himself."

His voice expressed the deepest compassion. "Thou most unaccountable being," I cried, "whither will thy actions tend, in all this maze of purpose in which thou seemest lost?"

"Whither indeed? To a crown, a golden be-gemmed crown, I hope; and yet I dare not trust and though I dream of a crown and wake for one, ever and anon a busy devil whispers to me, that it is but a fool's cap that I seek, and that were I wise, I should trample on it, and take in its stead, that which is worth all the crowns of the east and presidentship's of the west."

"And what is that?"

"If I do make it my choice, then you shall know; at present I dare not speak, even think of it."

Again, he was silent, and after a pause turned to me laughingly. When scorn did not inspire his mirth, when it was genuine gaiety that painted his features with a joyous expression, his beauty became super-eminent, divine. "Verney," said he, "my first act when I become King of England, will be to unite with the Greeks, take Constantinople, and subdue all Asia. I intend to be a warrior, a conqueror; Napoleon's name shall vail to mine; and enthusiasts, instead of visiting his rocky grave, and exalting the merits of the fallen, shall adore my majesty, and magnify my illustrious achievements."

I listened to Raymond with intense interest. Could I be other than all ear, to one who seemed to govern the whole earth in his grasping imagination, and who only quailed when he attempted to rule himself. Then on his word and will depended my own happiness — the fate of all dear to me. I endeavored to divine the concealed meaning of his words. Perdita's name was not mentioned; yet I could not doubt that love for her caused the vacillation of purpose that he exhibited. And who was so worthy of love as my noble-minded sister? Who deserved the hand of this self-exalted king more than she whose glance belonged to a queen of nations? who loved him, as he did her; notwithstanding that disappointment quelled her passion, and ambition held strong combat with his.

We went together to the House in the evening. Raymond, while he knew that his plans and prospects were to be discussed and decided during the expected debate, was gay and careless. A hum, like that of ten thousand hives of swarming bees, stunned us as we entered the coffee-room. Knots of politicians were assembled with anxious brows and loud or deep voices. The aristocratical party, the richest and most influential men in England, appeared less agitated than the others, for the question was to be discussed without their interference. Near the fire was Ryland and his supporters. Ryland was a man of obscure birth and of immense wealth, inherited from his father, who had been a manufacturer. He had witnessed, when a young man, the abdication of the king, and the amalgamation of the two houses of Lords and Commons; he had sympathized with these popular encroachments, and it had been the business of his life to consolidate and increase them. Since then, the influence of the landed proprietors had augmented; and at first Ryland was not sorry to observe the machinations of Lord Raymond, which drew off many of his opponent's partisans. But the thing was now going too far. The poorer nobility hailed the return of sovereignty, as an event which would restore them to their power and rights, now lost. The half extinct spirit of royalty roused itself in the minds of men; and they, willing slaves, self-constituted subjects, were ready to bend their necks to the yoke. Some erect and manly spirits still remained, pillars of state; but the word republic had grown stale to the vulgar ear; and many - the event would prove whether it was a majority - pined for the tinsel and show of royalty. Ryland was roused to resistance; he asserted that his sufferance alone had permitted the increase of this party; but the time for indulgence was passed, and with one motion of his arm he would sweep away the cobwebs that blinded his countrymen.

When Raymond entered the coffee-room, his presence was hailed by his friends almost with a shout. They gathered round him, counted their numbers, and detailed the reasons why they were now to receive an addition of such and such members, who had not yet declared themselves. Some trifling business of the House having been gone through, the leaders took their seats in the chamber; the clamor of voices continued, till Ryland arose to speak, and then the slightest whispered observation was audible. All eyes were fixed upon him as he stood — ponderous of frame, sonorous of voice, and with a manner which, though not graceful, was impressive. I turned from his marked, iron countenance to Raymond, whose face, veiled by a smile, would not betray his care; yet his lips quivered somewhat, and his hand clasped the bench on which he sat, with a convulsive strength that made the muscles start again.

Ryland began by praising the present state of the British empire. He recalled past years to their memory; the miserable contentions which in the time of our fathers arose almost to civil war, the abdication of the late king, and the foundation of the republic. He described this republic; shewed how it gave privilege to each individual in the state, to rise to consequence, and even to temporary sovereignty. He compared the royal and republican spirit; shewed how the one tended to enslave the minds of men, while all the institutions of the other served to raise even the meanest among us to something great and good. He shewed how England had become powerful, and its inhabitants valiant and wise, by means of the freedom they enjoyed. As he spoke, every heart swelled with pride, and every cheek glowed with delight to remember, that each one there was English, and that each supported and contributed to the happy state of things now commemorated. Ryland's fervor increased - his eyes lighted up - his voice assumed the tone of passion. There was one man, he continued, who wished to alter all this, and bring us back to our days of impotence and contention: - one man, who would dare arrogate the honor which was due to all who claimed England as their birthplace, and set his name and style above the name and style of his country. I saw at this juncture that Raymond changed color; his eyes were withdrawn from the orator, and cast on the ground; the listeners turned from one to the other; but in the meantime the speaker's voice filled their ears - the thunder of his denunciations influenced their senses. The very boldness of his language gave him weight; each knew that he spoke truth - a truth known, but not acknowledged. He tore from reality the mask with which she had been clothed; and the purposes of Raymond, which before had crept around, ensnaring by stealth, now stood a hunted stag - even at bay - as all perceived who watched the irrepressible changes of his countenance. Ryland ended by moving, that any attempt to re-erect the kingly power should be declared treason, and he a traitor who should endeavor to change the present form of government. Cheers and loud acclamations followed the close of his speech.

After his motion had been seconded, Lord Raymond rose, - his countenance bland, his voice softly melodious, his manner soothing, his grace and sweetness came like the mild breathing of a flute, after the loud, organ-like voice of his adversary. He rose, he said, to speak in favor of the honorable member's motion, with one slight amendment subjoined. He was ready to go back to old times, and commemorate the contests of our fathers, and the monarch's abdication. Nobly and greatly, he said, had the illustrious and last sovereign of England sacrificed himself to the apparent good of his country, and divested himself of a power which could only be maintained by the blood of his subjects - these subjects named so no more, these, his friends and equals, had in gratitude conferred certain favors and distinctions on him and his family forever. An ample estate was allotted to them, and they took the first rank among the peers of Great Britain. Yet it might be conjectured that they had not forgotten their ancient heritage; and it was hard that his heir should suffer alike with any other pretender, if he attempted to regain what by ancient right and inheritance belonged to him. He did not say that he should favor such an attempt; but he did say that such an attempt would be venial; and, if the aspirant did not go so far as to declare war, and erect a standard in the kingdom, his fault ought to be regarded with an indulgent eye. In his amendment he proposed that an exception should be made in the bill in favor of any person who claimed the sovereign power in right of the earls of Windsor. Nor did Raymond make an end without drawing in vivid and glowing colors, the splendor of a kingdom, in opposition to the commercial spirit of republicanism. He asserted, that each individual under the English monarchy, was then as now, capable of attaining high rank and power - with one only exception, that of the function of chief magistrate; higher and nobler rank, than a bartering, timorous commonwealth could afford. And for this one exception, to what did it amount? The nature of riches and influence forcibly confined the list of candidates to a few of the wealthiest; and it was much to be feared, that the ill-humor and contention generated by this triennial struggle, would counterbalance its advantages in impartial eyes. I can ill record the flow of language and graceful turns of expression, the wit and easy raillery that gave vigor and influence to his speech. His manner, timid at first, became firm - his changeful face was lit up to superhuman brilliancy; his voice, various as music, was like that enchanting.

It was useless to record the debate that followed this harangue. Party speeches were delivered, which clothed the question in cant, and veiled its simple meaning in a woven wind of words. The motion was lost; Ryland withdrew in rage and despair; and Raymond, gay and exulting, retired to dream of his future kingdom.

CHAPTER IV

Is there such a feeling as love at first sight? And if there be, in what does its nature differ from love founded in long observation and slow growth? Perhaps its effects are not so permanent; but they are, while they last, as violent and intense. We walk the pathless mazes of society, vacant of joy, till we hold this clue, leading us through that labyrinth to paradise. Our nature dim, like to an unlighted torch, sleeps in formless blank till the fire attain it; this life of life, this light to moon, and glory to the sun. What does it matter, whether the fire be struck from flint and steel, nourished with care into a flame, slowly communicated to the dark wick, or whether swiftly the radiant power of light and warmth passes from a kindred power, and shines at once the beacon and the hope. In the deepest fountain of my heart the pulses were stirred; around, above, beneath, the clinging Memory as a cloak enwrapped me. In no one moment of coming time did I feel as I had done in time gone by. The spirit of Idris hovered in the air I breathed; her eyes were ever and forever bent on mine; her remembered smile blinded my faint gaze, and caused me to walk as one, not in eclipse, not in darkness and vacancy - but in a new and brilliant light, too novel, too dazzling for my human senses. On every leaf, on every small division of the universe, (as on the hyacinth ai is engraved) was imprinted the talisman of my existence - *SHE LIVES! SHE IS!* - I had not time yet to analyze my feeling, to take myself to task, and leash in the tameless passion; all was one idea, one feeling, one knowledge - it was my life!

But the die was cast - Raymond would marry Idris. The merry marriage bells rung in my ears; I heard the nation's gratulation which followed the union; the ambitious noble uprose with swift eagle-flight, from the lowly ground to regal supremacy - and to the love of Idris. Yet not so! She did not love him; she had called me her friend; she had smiled on me; to me she had entrusted her heart's dearest hope, the welfare of Adrian. This reflection thawed my congealing blood, and again the tide of life and love flowed impetuously onward, again to ebb as my busy thoughts changed.

The debate had ended at three in the morning. My soul was in tumults; I traversed the streets with eager rapidity. Truly, I was mad that night— love— which I have named a giant from its birth, wrestled with despair! My heart, the field of combat, was wounded by the iron heel of the one, watered by the gushing tears of the other. Day, hateful to me, dawned; I retreated to my lodgings—I threw myself on a couch—I slept—was it sleep?—for thought was still alive—love and despair struggled still, and I writhed with unendurable pain.

I awoke half stupefied; I felt a heavy oppression on me, but knew not wherefore; I entered, as it were, the council-chamber of my brain, and questioned the various ministers of thought therein assembled; too soon I remembered all; too soon my limbs quivered beneath the tormenting power; soon, too soon, I knew myself a slave!

Suddenly, unannounced, Lord Raymond entered my apartment. He came in gaily, singing the Tyrolese song of liberty; noticed me with a gracious nod, and threw himself on a sofa opposite the copy of a bust of the Apollo Belvidere. After one or two trivial remarks, to which I sullenly replied, he suddenly cried, looking at the bust, "I am called like that victor! Not a bad idea; the head will serve for my new coinage and be an omen to all dutiful subjects of my future success."

He said this in his most gay, yet benevolent manner, and smiled, not disdainfully, but in playful mockery of himself. Then his countenance suddenly darkened, and in that shrill tone peculiar to himself, he cried, "I fought a good battle last night; higher conquest the plains of Greece never saw me achieve. Now I am the first man in the state, burthen of every ballad, and object of old women's mumbled devotions. What are your meditations? You, who fancy that you can read the human soul, as your native lake reads each crevice and folding of its surrounding hills—say what you think of me; king-expectant, angel or devil, which?"

This ironical tone was discord to my bursting, over-boiling-heart; I was nettled by his insolence and replied with bitterness; "There is a spirit, neither angel or devil, damned to limbo merely." I saw his cheeks become pale, and his lips whiten and quiver; his anger served but to enkindle mine, and I answered with a determined look his eyes which glared on me; suddenly they were withdrawn, cast down, a tear, I thought, wetted the dark lashes; I was softened, and with involuntary emotion added, "Not that you are such, my dear lord."

I paused, even awed by the agitation he evinced; "Yes," he said at length, rising and biting his lip, as he strove to curb his passion; "Such am I! You do not know me, Verney; neither you, nor our audience of last night, nor does universal England know aught of me. I stand here, it would seem, an elected king; this hand is about to grasp a scepter; these brows feel in each nerve the coming diadem. I appear to have strength, power, victory; standing as a dome-supporting column stands; and I am - a reed! I have ambition, and that attains its aim; my nightly dreams are realized, my waking hopes fulfilled; a kingdom awaits my acceptance, my enemies are overthrown. But here," and he struck his heart with violence, "here is the rebel, here the stumbling-block; this over-ruling heart, which I may drain of its living blood; but, while one fluttering pulsation remains, I am its slave."

He spoke with a broken voice, then bowed his head, and, hiding his face in his hands, wept. I was still smarting from my own disappointment; yet this scene oppressed me even to terror, nor could I interrupt his access of passion. It subsided at length; and, throwing himself on the couch, he remained silent and motionless, except that his changeful features shewed a strong internal conflict. At last he rose, and said in his usual tone of voice, "The time grows on us, Verney, I must away. Let me not forget my chiefest errand here. Will you accompany me to Windsor to-morrow? You will not be dishonored by my society, and as this is probably the last service, or disservice you can do me, will you grant my request?"

He held out his hand with almost a bashful air. Swiftly I thought - Yes, I will witness the last scene of the drama. Beside which, his mien conquered me, and an affectionate sentiment towards him, again filled my heart - I bade him command me. "Aye, that I will," said he gaily, "that's my cue now; be with me to-morrow morning by seven, be secret and faithful; and you shall be groom of the stole ere long."

So, saying, he hastened away, vaulted on his horse, and with a gesture as if he gave me his hand to kiss, bade me another laughing adieu. Left to myself, I strove with painful intensity to divine the motive of his request and foresee the events of the coming day. The hours passed on unperceived; my head ached with thought, the nerves seemed teeming with the over full fraught - I clasped my burning brow, as if my fevered hand could medicine its pain. I was punctual to the appointed hour on the following day and found Lord Raymond waiting for me. We got into his carriage and proceeded towards Windsor. I had tutored myself and was resolved by no outward sign to disclose my internal agitation.

"What a mistake Ryland made," said Raymond, "when he thought to over-power me the other night. He spoke well, very well; such a harangue would have succeeded better addressed to me singly, than to the fools and knaves assembled yonder. Had I been alone, I should have listened to him with a wish to hear reason, but when he endeavored to vanquish me in my own territory, with my own weapons, he put me on my mettle, and the event was such as all might have expected."

I smiled incredulously, and replied: "I am of Ryland's way of thinking, and will, if you please, repeat all his arguments; we shall see how far you will be induced by them, to change the royal for the patriotic style."

"The repetition would be useless," said Raymond, "since I well remember them, and have many others, self-suggested, which speak with unanswerable persuasion."

He did not explain himself, nor did I make any remark on his reply. Our silence endured for some miles, till the country with open fields, or shady woods and parks, presented pleasant objects to our view. After some observations on the scenery and seats, Raymond said: "Philosophers have called man a microcosm of nature and find a reflection in the internal mind for all this machinery visibly at work around us. This theory has often been a source of amusement to me; and many an idle hour have I spent, exercising my ingenuity in finding resemblances. Does not Lord Bacon say that, 'the falling from a discord to a concord, which maketh great sweetness in music, hath an agreement with the affections, which are re-integrated to the better after some dislikes?' What a sea is the tide of passion, whose fountains are in our own nature! Our virtues are the quicksand, which shew themselves at calm and low water; but let the waves arise and the winds buffet them, and the poor devil whose hope was in their durability, finds them sink from under him. The fashions of the world, its exigencies, educations and pursuits, are winds to drive our wills, like clouds all one way; but let a thunderstorm arise in the shape of love, hate, or ambition, and the rack goes backward, stemming the opposing air in triumph."

"Yet," replied I, "nature always presents to our eyes the appearance of a patient: while there is an active principle in man which is capable of ruling fortune, and at least of tacking against the gale, till it in some mode conquers it."

"There is more of what is specious than true in your distinction," said my companion. "Did we form ourselves, choosing our dispositions, and our powers? I find myself, for one, as a stringed instrument with chords and stops - but I have no power to turn the pegs or pitch my thoughts to a higher or lower key."

"Other men," I observed, "may be better musicians."

"I talk not of others, but myself," replied Raymond, "and I am as fair an example to go by as another. I cannot set my heart to a particular tune or run voluntary changes on my will. We are born; we choose neither our parents, nor our station; we are educated by others, or by the world's circumstance, and this cultivation, mingling with our innate disposition, is the soil in which our desires, passions, and motives grow."

"There is much truth in what you say," said I, "and yet no man ever acts upon this theory. Who, when he makes a choice, says, Thus I choose, because I am necessitated? Does he not on the contrary feel a freedom of will within him, which, though you may call it fallacious, still actuates him as he decides?"

"Exactly so," replied Raymond, "another link of the brakeless chain. Were I now to commit an act which would annihilate my hopes, and pluck the regal garment from my mortal limbs, to clothe them in ordinary weeds, would this, think you, be an act of free-will on my part?"

As we talked thus, I perceived that we were not going the ordinary road to Windsor, but through Englefield Green, towards Bishopgate Heath. I began to divine that Idris was not the object of our journey, but that I was brought to witness the scene that was to decide the fate of Raymond - and of Perdita. Raymond had evidently vacillated during his journey, and irresolution was marked in every gesture as we entered Perdita's cottage. I watched him curiously, determined that, if this hesitation should continue, I would assist Perdita to overcome herself, and teach her to disdain the wavering love of him, who balanced between the possession of a crown, and of her, whose excellence and affection transcended the worth of a kingdom.

We found her in her flower-adorned alcove; she was reading the newspaper report of the debate in parliament, that apparently doomed her to hopelessness. That heart-sinking feeling was painted in her sunk eyes and spiritless attitude; a cloud was on her beauty, and frequent sighs were tokens of her distress. This sight had an instantaneous effect on Raymond; his eyes beamed with tenderness, and remorse clothed his manners with earnestness and truth. He sat beside her; and, taking the paper from her hand, said, "Not a word more shall my sweet Perdita read of this contention of madmen and fools. I must not permit you to be acquainted with the extent of my delusion, lest you despise me; although, believe me, a wish to appear before you, not vanquished, but as a conqueror, inspired me during my wordy war."

Perdita looked at him like one amazed; her expressive countenance shone for a moment with tenderness; to see him only was happiness. But a bitter thought swiftly shadowed her joy; she bent her eyes on the ground, endeavoring to master the passion of tears that threatened to overwhelm her. Raymond continued, "I will not act a part with you, dear girl, or appear other than what I am, weak and unworthy, more fit to excite your disdain than your love. Yet you do love me; I feel and know that you do, and thence I draw my most cherished hopes. If pride guided you, or even reason, you might well reject me. Do so; if your high heart, incapable of my infirmity of purpose, refuses to bend to the lowness of mine. Turn from me, if you will, - if you can. If your whole soul does not urge you to forgive me - if your entire heart does not open wide its door to admit me to its very center, forsake me, never speak to me again. I, though sinning against you almost beyond remission, I also am proud, there must be no reserve in your pardon - no drawback to the gift of your affection."

Perdita looked down, confused, yet pleased. My presence embarrassed her; so that she dared not turn to meet her lover's eye, or trust her voice to assure him of her affection; while a blush mantled her cheek, and her disconsolate air was exchanged for one expressive of deep-felt joy. Raymond encircled her waist with his arm, and continued, "I do not deny that I have balanced between you and the highest hope that mortal men can entertain; but I do so no longer. Take me - mould me to your will, possess my heart and soul to all eternity. If you refuse to contribute to my happiness, I quit England to-night, and will never set foot in it again.

"Lionel, you hear. Witness for me: persuade your sister to forgive the injury I have done her; persuade her to be mine."

"There needs no persuasion," said the blushing Perdita, "except your own dear promises, and my ready heart, which whispers to me that they are true."

That same evening, we all three walked together in the forest, and, with the garrulity which happiness inspires, they detailed to me the history of their loves. It was pleasant to see the haughty Raymond and reserved Perdita changed through happy love into prattling, playful children, both losing their characteristic dignity in the fulness of mutual contentment. A night or two ago Lord Raymond, with a brow of care, and a heart oppressed with thought, bent all his energies to silence or persuade the legislators of England that a scepter was not too weighty for his hand, while visions of dominion, war, and triumph floated before him; now, frolicsome as a lively boy sporting under his mother's approving eye, the hopes of his ambition were complete, when he pressed the small fair hand of Perdita to his lips; while she, radiant with delight, looked on the still pool, not truly admiring herself, but drinking in with rapture the reflection there made of the form of herself and her lover, shewn for the first time in dear conjunction.

I rambled away from them. If the rapture of assured sympathy was theirs, I enjoyed that of restored hope. I looked on the regal towers of Windsor. High is the wall and strong the barrier that separate me from my Star of Beauty. But not impassible. She will not be his. A few more years dwell in thy native garden, sweet flower, till I by toil and time acquire a right to gather thee. Despair not, nor bid me despair! What must I do now? First, I must seek Adrian, and restore him to her. Patience, gentleness, and untired affection shall recall him, if it be true, as Raymond says, that he is mad; energy and courage shall rescue him, if he be unjustly imprisoned.

After the lovers again joined me, we supped together in the alcove. Truly it was a fairy's supper; for though the air was perfumed by the scent of fruits and wine, we none of us either ate or drank - even the beauty of the night was unobserved; their extasy could not be increased by outward objects, and I was wrapped in reverie. At about midnight Raymond and I took leave of my sister, to return to town. He was all gaiety; scraps of songs fell from his lips; every thought of his mind - every object about us, gleamed under the sunshine of his mirth. He accused me of melancholy, of ill-humor and envy.

"Not so," said I, "though I confess that my thoughts are not occupied as pleasantly as yours are. You promised to facilitate my visit to Adrian; I conjure you to perform your promise. I cannot linger here; I long to soothe —perhaps to cure the malady of my first and best friend. I shall immediately depart for Dunkeld."

"Thou bird of night," replied Raymond, "what an eclipse do you throw across my bright thoughts, forcing me to call to mind that melancholy ruin, which stands in mental desolation, more irreparable than a fragment of a carved column in a weed-grown field. You dream that you can restore him? Daedalus never wound so inextricable an error round Minotaur, as madness has woven about his imprisoned reason. Nor you, nor any other Theseus, can thread the labyrinth, to which perhaps some unkind Ariadne has the clue."

"You allude to Evadne Zaimi: but she is not in England."

"And were she," said Raymond, "I would not advise her seeing him. Better to decay in absolute delirium, than to be the victim of the methodical unreason of ill-bestowed love. The long duration of his malady has probably erased from his mind all vestige of her; and it were well that it should never again be imprinted. You will find him at Dunkeld; gentle and tractable he wanders up the hills, and through the wood, or sits listening beside the waterfall. You may see him - his hair stuck with wild flowers - his eyes full of untraceable meaning - his voice broken - his person wasted to a shadow. He plucks flowers and weeds, and weaves chaplets of them, or sails yellow leaves and bits of bark on the stream, rejoicing in their safety, or weeping at their wreck. The very memory half unmans me. By Heaven! the first tears I have shed since boyhood rushed scalding into my eyes when I saw him."

It needed not this last account to spur me on to visit him. I only doubted whether or not I should endeavor to see Idris again, before I departed. This doubt was decided on the following day. Early in the morning Raymond came to me; intelligence had arrived that Adrian was dangerously ill, and it appeared impossible that his failing strength should surmount the disorder. "To-morrow," said Raymond, "his mother and sister set out for Scotland to see him once again."

"And I go to-day," I cried; "this very hour I will engage a sailing balloon; I shall be there in forty-eight hours at furthest, perhaps in less, if the wind is fair. Farewell, Raymond; be happy in having chosen the better part in life. This turn of fortune revives me. I feared madness, not sickness - I have a presentiment that Adrian will not die; perhaps this illness is a crisis, and he may recover."

Everything favored my journey. The balloon rose about half a mile from the earth, and with a favorable wind it hurried through the air, its feathered vans cleaving the unimposing atmosphere. Notwithstanding the melancholy object of my journey, my spirits were exhilarated by reviving hope, by the swift motion of the airy pinnace, and the balmy visitation of the sunny air. The pilot hardly moved the plumed steerage, and the slender mechanism of the wings, wide unfurled, gave forth a murmuring noise, soothing to the sense. Plain and hill, stream and cornfield, were discernible below, while we unimpeded sped on swift and secure, as a wild swan in his spring-tide flight. The machine obeyed the slightest motion of the helm; and, the wind blowing steadily, there was no let or obstacle to our course. Such was the power of man over the elements; a power long sought, and lately won; yet foretold in by-gone time by the prince of poets, whose verses I quoted much to the astonishment of my pilot, when I told him how many hundred years ago they had been written: —

Oh! human wit, thou can'st invent much ill,
Thou searchest strange arts: who would think by skill,
An heavy man like a light bird should stray,
And through the empty heavens find a way?

I alighted at Perth; and, though much fatigued by a constant exposure to the air for many hours, I would not rest, but merely altering my mode of conveyance, I went by land instead of air, to Dunkeld. The sun was rising as I entered the opening of the hills. After the revolution of ages Birnam hill was again covered with a young forest, while more aged pines, planted at the very commencement of the nineteenth century by the then Duke of Athol, gave solemnity and beauty to the scene. The rising sun first tinged the pine tops; and my mind, rendered through my mountain education deeply susceptible of the graces of nature, and now on the eve of again beholding my beloved and perhaps dying friend, was strangely influenced by the sight of those distant beams: surely they were ominous, and as such I regarded them, good omens for Adrian, on whose life my happiness depended.

Poor fellow! he lay stretched on a bed of sickness, his cheeks glowing with the hues of fever, his eyes half closed, his breath irregular and difficult. Yet it was less painful to see him thus, than to find him fulfilling the animal functions uninterruptedly, his mind sick the while. I established myself at his bedside; I never quitted it day or night. Bitter task was it, to behold his spirit waver between death and life: to see his warm cheek, and know that the very fire which burned too fiercely there, was consuming the vital fuel; to hear his moaning voice, which might never again articulate words of love and wisdom; to witness the ineffectual motions of his limbs, soon to be wrapped in their mortal shroud. Such for three days and nights appeared the consummation which fate had decreed for my labors, and I became haggard and specter-like, through anxiety and watching. At length his eyes unclosed faintly, yet with a look of returning life; he became pale and weak; but the rigidity of his features was softened by approaching convalescence. He knew me. What a brimful cup of joyful agony it was, when his face first gleamed with the glance of recognition - when he pressed my hand, now more fevered than his own, and when he pronounced my name! No trace of his past insanity remained, to dash my joy with sorrow.

This same evening his mother and sister arrived. The Countess of Windsor was by nature full of energetic feeling; but she had very seldom in her life permitted the concentrated emotions of her heart to shew themselves on her features. The studied immovability of her countenance; her slow, equable manner, and soft but unmelodious voice, were a mask, hiding her fiery passions, and the impatience of her disposition. She did not in the least resemble either of her children; her black and sparkling eye, lit up by pride, was totally unlike the blue luster, and frank, benignant expression of either Adrian or Idris. There was something grand and majestic in her motions, but nothing persuasive, nothing amiable. Tall, thin, and strait, her face still handsome, her raven hair hardly tinged with grey, her forehead arched and beautiful, had not the eye-brows been somewhat scattered - it was impossible not to be struck by her, almost to fear her. Idris appeared to be the only being who could resist her mother, notwithstanding the extreme mildness of her character. But there was a fearlessness and frankness about her, which said that she would not encroach on another's liberty but held her own sacred and un-assailable.

The Countess cast no look of kindness on my worn-out frame, though afterwards she thanked me coldly for my attentions. Not so Idris; her first glance was for her brother; she took his hand, she kissed his eye-lids, and hung over him with looks of compassion and love. Her eyes glistened with tears when she thanked me, and the grace of her expressions was enhanced, not diminished, by the fervor, which caused her almost to falter as she spoke. Her mother, all eyes and ears, soon interrupted us; and I saw, that she wished to dismiss me quietly, as one whose services, now that his relatives had arrived, were of no use to her son. I was harassed and ill, resolved not to give up my post, yet doubting in what way I should assert it; when Adrian called me, and clasping my hand, bade me not leave him. His mother, apparently inattentive, at once understood what was meant, and seeing the hold we had upon her, yielded the point to us.

The days that followed were full of pain to me; so that I sometimes regretted that I had not yielded at once to the haughty lady, who watched all my motions, and turned my beloved task of nursing my friend to a work of pain and irritation. Never did any woman appear so entirely made of mind, as the Countess of Windsor. Her passions had subdued her appetites, even her natural wants; she slept little, and hardly ate at all; her body was evidently considered by her as a mere machine, whose health was necessary for the accomplishment of her schemes, but whose senses formed no part of her enjoyment. There is something fearful in one who can thus conquer the animal part of our nature, if the victory be not the effect of consummate virtue; nor was it without a mixture of this feeling, that I beheld the figure of the Countess awake when others slept, fasting when I, abstemious naturally, and rendered so by the fever that preyed on me, was forced to recruit myself with food. She resolved to prevent or diminish my opportunities of acquiring influence over her children, and circumvented my plans by a hard, quiet, stubborn resolution, that seemed not to belong to flesh and blood. War was at last tacitly acknowledged between us. We had many pitched battles, during which no word was spoken, hardly a look was interchanged, but in which each resolved not to submit to the other. The Countess had the advantage of position; so I was vanquished, though I would not yield.

I became sick at heart. My countenance was painted with the hues of ill health and vexation. Adrian and Idris saw this; they attributed it to my long watching and anxiety; they urged me to rest, and take care of myself, while I most truly assured them, that my best medicine was their good wishes; those, and the assured convalescence of my friend, now daily more apparent. The faint rose again blushed on his cheek; his brow and lips lost the ashy paleness of threatened dissolution; such was the dear reward of my unremitting attention - and bounteous heaven added overflowing recompence, when it gave me also the thanks and smiles of Idris.

After the lapse of a few weeks, we left Dunkeld. Idris and her mother returned immediately to Windsor, while Adrian and I followed by slow journeys and frequent stoppages, occasioned by his continued weakness. As we traversed the various counties of fertile England, all wore an exhilarating appearance to my companion, who had been so long secluded by disease from the enjoyments of weather and scenery. We passed through busy towns and cultivated plains. The husbandmen were getting in their plenteous harvests, and the women and children, occupied by light rustic toils, formed groups of happy, healthful persons, the very sight of whom carried cheerfulness to the heart. One evening, quitting our inn, we strolled down a shady lane, then up a grassy slope, till we came to an eminence, that commanded an extensive view of hill and dale, meandering rivers, dark woods, and shining villages. The sun was setting; and the clouds, straying, like new-shorn sheep, through the vast fields of sky, received the golden color of his parting beams; the distant uplands shone out, and the busy hum of evening came, harmonized by distance, on our ear. Adrian, who felt all the fresh spirit infused by returning health, clasped his hands in delight, and exclaimed with transport:

"O happy earth, and happy inhabitants of earth! A stately palace has God built for you, O man! and worthy are you of your dwelling! Behold the verdant carpet spread at our feet, and the azure canopy above; the fields of earth which generate and nurture all things, and the track of heaven, which contains and clasps all things. Now, at this evening hour, at the period of repose and refection, methinks all hearts breathe one hymn of love and thanksgiving, and we, like priests of old on the mountain-tops, give a voice to their sentiment.

Assuredly a most benignant power built up the majestic fabric we inhabit and framed the laws by which it endures. If mere existence, and not happiness, had been the final end of our being, what need of the profuse luxuries which we enjoy? Why should our dwelling place be so lovely, and why should the instincts of nature minister pleasurable sensations? The very sustaining of our animal machine is made delightful; and our sustenance, the fruits of the field, is painted with transcendent hues, endued with grateful odors, and palatable to our taste. Why should this be, if HE were not good? We need houses to protect us from the seasons, and behold the materials with which we are provided; the growth of trees with their adornment of leaves; while rocks of stone piled above the plains variegate the prospect with their pleasant irregularity.

Nor are outward objects alone the receptacles of the Spirit of Good. Look into the mind of man, where wisdom reigns enthroned; where imagination, the painter, sits, with his pencil dipped in hues lovelier than those of sunset, adorning familiar life with glowing tints. What a noble boon, worthy the giver, is the imagination! it takes from reality its leaden hue: it envelopes all thought and sensation in a radiant veil, and with an hand of beauty beckons us from the sterile seas of life, to her gardens, and bowers, and glades of bliss. And is not love a gift of the divinity? Love, and her child, Hope, which can bestow wealth on poverty, strength on the weak, and happiness on the sorrowing.

My lot has not been fortunate. I have consorted long with grief, entered the gloomy labyrinth of madness, and emerged, but half alive. Yet I thank God that I have lived! I thank God, that I have beheld his throne, the heavens, and earth, his footstool. I am glad that I have seen the changes of his day; to behold the sun, fountain of light, and the gentle pilgrim moon; to have seen the fire bearing flowers of the sky, and the flowery stars of earth; to have witnessed the sowing and the harvest. I am glad that I have loved and have experienced sympathetic joy and sorrow with my fellow-creatures. I am glad now to feel the current of thought flow through my mind, as the blood through the articulations of my frame; mere existence is pleasure; and I thank God that I live!

And all ye happy nurslings of mother-earth, do ye not echo my words? Ye who are linked by the affectionate ties of nature, companions, friends, lovers! fathers, who toil with joy for their offspring; women, who while gazing on the living forms of their children, forget the pains of maternity; children, who neither toil nor spin, but love and are loved!

Oh, that death and sickness were banished from our earthly home! that hatred, tyranny, and fear could no longer make their lair in the human heart! that each man might find a brother in his fellow, and a nest of repose amid the wide plains of his inheritance! that the source of tears were dry, and that lips might no longer form expressions of sorrow. Sleeping thus under the beneficent eye of heaven, can evil visit thee, O Earth, or grief cradle to their graves thy luckless children? Whisper it not, let the demons hear and rejoice! The choice is with us; let us will it, and our habitation becomes a paradise. For the will of man is omnipotent, blunting the arrows of death, soothing the bed of disease, and wiping away the tears of agony. And what is each human being worth, if he do not put forth his strength to aid his fellow-creatures? My soul is a fading spark, my nature frail as a spent wave; but I dedicate all of intellect and strength that remains to me, to that one work, and take upon me the task, as far as I am able, of bestowing blessings on my fellow-men!"

His voice trembled, his eyes were cast up, his hands clasped, and his fragile person was bent, as it were, with excess of emotion. The spirit of life seemed to linger in his form, as a dying flame on an altar flickers on the embers of an accepted sacrifice.

CHAPTER V

When we arrived at Windsor, I found that Raymond and Perdita had departed for the continent. I took possession of my sister's cottage and blessed myself that I lived within view of Windsor Castle. It was a curious fact, that at this period, when by the marriage of Perdita I was allied to one of the richest individuals in England, and was bound by the most intimate friendship to its chiefest noble, I experienced the greatest excess of poverty that I had ever known. My knowledge of the worldly principles of Lord Raymond, would have ever prevented me from applying to him, however deep my distress might have been. It was in vain that I repeated to myself with regard to Adrian, that his purse was open to me; that one in soul, as we were, our fortunes ought also to be common. I could never, while with him, think of his bounty as a remedy to my poverty; and I even put aside hastily his offers of supplies, assuring him of a falsehood, that I needed them not. How could I say to this generous being, "Maintain me in idleness. You who have dedicated your powers of mind and fortune to the benefit of your species, shall you so misdirect your exertions, as to support in uselessness the strong, healthy, and capable?"

And yet I dared not request him to use his influence that I might obtain an honorable provision for myself - for then I should have been obliged to leave Windsor. I hovered forever around the walls of its Castle, beneath its unshadowing thickets; my sole companions were my books and my loving thoughts. I studied the wisdom of the ancients and gazed on the happy walls that sheltered the beloved of my soul. My mind was nevertheless idle. I pored over the poetry of old times; I studied the metaphysics of Plato and Berkeley. I read the histories of Greece and Rome, and of England's former periods, and I watched the movements of the lady of my heart. At night I could see her shadow on the walls of her apartment; by day I viewed her in her flower-garden or riding in the park with her usual companions. Methought the charm would be broken if I were seen, but I heard the music of her voice and was happy. I gave to each heroine of whom I read, her beauty and matchless excellences — such was Antigone, when she guided the blind Oedipus to the grove of the Eumenides, and discharged the funeral rites of Polynices; such was Miranda in the unvisited cave of Prospero; such Hades, on the sands of the Ionian island. I was mad with excess of passionate devotion; but pride, tameless as fire, invested my nature, and prevented me from betraying myself by word or look.

In the meantime, while I thus pampered myself with rich mental repasts, a peasant would have disdained my scanty fare, which I sometimes robbed from the squirrels of the forest. I was, I own, often tempted to recur to the lawless feats of my boyhood and knock down the almost tame pheasants that perched upon the trees and bent their bright eyes on me. But they were the property of Adrian, the nurslings of Idris; and so, although my imagination rendered sensual by privation, made me think that they would better become the spit in my kitchen, than the green leaves of the forest.

Nevertheless,

I checked my haughty will, and did not eat; but supped upon sentiment, and dreamt vainly of "such morsels sweet," as I might not waking attain.

But, at this period, the whole scheme of my existence was about to change. The orphan and neglected son of Verney, was on the eve of being linked to the mechanism of society by a golden chain, and to enter into all the duties and affections of life. Miracles were to be wrought in my favor; the machine of social life pushed with vast effort backward. Attend, O reader! while I narrate this tale of wonders!

One day as Adrian and Idris were riding through the forest, with their mother and accustomed companions, Idris, drawing her brother aside from the rest of the cavalcade, suddenly asked him, "What had become of his friend, Lionel Verney?"

"Even from this spot," replied Adrian, pointing to my sister's cottage, "you can see his dwelling."

"Indeed!" said Idris, "and why, if he be so near, does he not come to see us, and make one of our society?"

"I often visit him," replied Adrian; "but you may easily guess the motives, which prevent him from coming where his presence may annoy any one among us."

"I do guess them," said Idris, "and such as they are, I would not venture to combat them. Tell me, however, in what way he passes his time; what he is doing and thinking in his cottage retreat?"

"Nay, my sweet sister," replied Adrian, "you ask me more than I can well answer; but if you feel interest in him, why not visit him? He will feel highly honored, and thus you may repay a part of the obligation I owe him and compensate for the injuries fortune has done him."

"I will most readily accompany you to his abode," said the lady, "not that I wish that either of us should unburthen ourselves of our debt, which, being no less than your life, must remain unpayable ever. But let us go; to-morrow we will arrange to ride out together, and proceeding towards that part of the forest, call upon him."

The next evening, therefore, though the autumnal change had brought on cold and rain, Adrian and Idris entered my cottage. They found me Curious-like, feasting on sorry fruits for supper; but they brought gifts richer than the golden bribes of the Sabines, nor could I refuse the invaluable store of friendship and delight which they bestowed. Surely the glorious twins of Latona were not more welcome, when, in the infancy of the world, they were brought forth to beautify and enlighten this "sterile promontory," than were this angelic pair to my lowly dwelling and grateful heart. We sat like one family round my hearth. Our talk was on subjects, unconnected with the emotions that evidently occupied each; but we each divined the other's thought, and as our voices spoke of indifferent matters, our eyes, in mute language, told a thousand things no tongue could have uttered.

They left me in an hour's time. They left me happy - how unspeakably happy. It did not require the measured sounds of human language to syllable the story of my extasy. Idris had visited me; Idris I should again and again see - my imagination did not wander beyond the completeness of this knowledge. I trod air; no doubt, no fear, no hope even, disturbed me; I clasped with my soul the fulness of contentment, satisfied, undesiring, beatified.

For many days Adrian and Idris continued to visit me thus. In this dear intercourse, love, in the guise of enthusiastic friendship, infused more and more of his omnipotent spirit. Idris felt it. Yes, divinity of the world, I read your characters in her looks and gesture; I heard your melodious voice echoed by her - you prepared for us a soft and flowery path, all gentle thoughts adorned it—your name, O Love, was not spoken, but you stood the Genius of the Hour, veiled, and time, but no mortal hand, might raise the curtain. Organs of articulate sound did not proclaim the union of our hearts; for untoward circumstance allowed no opportunity for the expression that hovered on our lips. Oh, my pen! haste thou to write what was, before the thought of what is, arrests the hand that guides thee. If I lift up my eyes and see the desert earth and feel that those dear eyes have spent their mortal luster, and that those beauteous lips are silent, their "crimson leaves" faded, forever I am mute!

But you live, my Idris, even now you move before me! There was a glade, O reader! a grassy opening in the wood; the retiring trees left its velvet expanse as a temple for love; the silver Thames bounded it on one side, and a willow bending down dipped in the water its Naiad hair, disheveled by the wind's viewless hand. The oaks around were the home of a tribe of nightingales - there am I now; Idris, in youth's dear prime, is by my side - remember, I am just twenty-two, and seventeen summers have scarcely passed over the beloved of my heart. The river swollen by autumnal rains, deluged the lowlands, and Adrian in his favorite boat is employed in the dangerous pastime of plucking the topmost bough from a submerged oak. Are you weary of life, O Adrian, that you thus play with danger? -

He has obtained his prize, and he pilots his boat through the flood; our eyes were fixed on him fearfully, but the stream carried him away from us; he was forced to land far lower down, and to make a considerable circuit before he could join us. "He is safe!" said Idris, as he leapt on shore, and waved the bough over his head in token of success; "we will wait for him here."

We were alone together; the sun had set; the song of the nightingales began; the evening star shone distinct in the flood of light, which was yet unfaded in the west. The blue eyes of my angelic girl were fixed on this sweet emblem of herself: "How the light palpitates," she said, "which is that star's life. Its vacillating effulgence seems to say that its state, even like ours upon earth, is wavering and inconstant; it fears, methinks, and it loves."

"Gaze not on the star, dear, generous friend," I cried, "read not love in its trembling rays; look not upon distant worlds; speak not of the mere imagination of a sentiment. I have long been silent; long even to sickness have I desired to speak to you, and submit my soul, my life, my entire being to you. Look not on the star, dear love, or do, and let that eternal spark plead for me; let it be my witness and my advocate, silent as it shines - love is to me as light to the star; even so long as that is uneclipsed by annihilation, so long shall I love you."

Veiled forever to the world's callous eye must be the transport of that moment. Still do I feel her graceful form press against my full-fraught heart - still does sight, and pulse, and breath sicken and fail, at the remembrance of that first kiss. Slowly and silently we went to meet Adrian, whom we heard approaching.

I entreated Adrian to return to me after he had conducted his sister home. And that same evening, walking among the moon-lit forest paths, I poured forth my whole heart, its transport and its hope, to my friend. For a moment he looked disturbed - "I might have foreseen this," he said, "what strife will now ensue! Pardon me, Lionel, nor wonder that the expectation of contest with my mother should jar me, when else I should delightedly confess that my best hopes are fulfilled, in confiding my sister to your protection. If you do not already know it, you will soon learn the deep hate my mother bears to the name Verney. I will converse with Idris; then all that a friend can do, I will do; to her it must belong to play the lover's part, if she be capable of it."

While the brother and sister were still hesitating in what manner they could best attempt to bring their mother over to their party, she, suspecting our meetings, taxed her children with them; taxed her fair daughter with deceit, and an unbecoming attachment for one whose only merit was being the son of the profligate favorite of her imprudent father; and who was doubtless as worthless as he from whom he boasted his descent. The eyes of Idris flashed at this accusation; she replied, "I do not deny that I love Verney; prove to me that he is worthless; and I will never see him more."

"Dear Madam," said Adrian, "let me entreat you to see him, to cultivate his friendship. You will wonder then, as I do, at the extent of his accomplishments, and the brilliancy of his talents." (Pardon me, gentle reader, this is not futile vanity; - not futile, since to know that Adrian felt thus, brings joy even now to my lone heart).

"Mad and foolish boy!" exclaimed the angry lady, "you have chosen with dreams and theories to overthrow my schemes for your own aggrandizement; but you shall not do the same by those I have formed for your sister. I but too well understand the fascination you both labor under; since I had the same struggle with your father, to make him cast off the parent of this youth, who hid his evil propensities with the smoothness and subtlety of a viper. In those days how often did I hear of his attractions, his widespread conquests, his wit, his refined manners. It is well when flies only are caught by such spiders' webs; but is it for the high-born and powerful to bow their necks to the flimsy yoke of these unmeaning pretensions? Were your sister indeed the insignificant person she deserves to be, I would willingly leave her to the fate, the wretched fate, of the wife of a man, whose very person, resembling as it does his wretched father, ought to remind you of the folly and vice it typifies - but remember, Lady Idris, it is not alone the once royal blood of England that colors your veins, you are a Princess of Austria, and every life-drop is akin to emperors and kings. Are you then a fit mate for an uneducated shepherd-boy, whose only inheritance is his father's tarnished name?"

"I can make but one defense," replied Idris, "the same offered by my brother; see Lionel, converse with my shepherd-boy" - The Countess interrupted her indignantly - "Yours!" - she cried: and then, smoothing her impassioned features to a disdainful smile, she continued - "We will talk of this another time. All I now ask, all your mother, Idris, requests are, that you will not see this upstart during the interval of one month."

"I dare not comply," said Idris, "it would pain him too much. I have no right to play with his feelings, to accept his proffered love, and then sting him with neglect."

"This is going too far," her mother answered, with quivering lips, and eyes again instinct by anger.

"Nay, Madam," said Adrian, "unless my sister consent never to see him again, it is surely a useless torment to separate them for a month."

"Certainly," replied the ex-queen, with bitter scorn, "his love, and her love, and both their childish flutterings, are to be put in fit comparison with my years of hope and anxiety, with the duties of the offspring of kings, with the high and dignified conduct which one of her descent ought to pursue. But it is unworthy of me to argue and complain. Perhaps you will have the goodness to promise me not to marry during that interval?"

This was asked only half ironically; and Idris wondered why her mother should extort from her a solemn vow not to do, what she had never dreamed of doing - but the promise was required and given.

All went on cheerfully now; we met as usual and talked without dread of our future plans. The Countess was so gentle, and even beyond her wont, amiable with her children, that they began to entertain hopes of her ultimate consent. She was too unlike them, too utterly alien to their tastes, for them to find delight in her society, or in the prospect of its continuance, but it gave them pleasure to see her conciliating and kind. Once even, Adrian ventured to propose her receiving me. She refused with a smile, reminding him that for the present his sister had promised to be patient.

One day, after the lapse of nearly a month, Adrian received a letter from a friend in London, requesting his immediate presence for the furtherance of some important object. Guileless himself, Adrian feared no deceit. I rode with him as far as Staines: he was in high spirits; and, since I could not see Idris during his absence, he promised a speedy return. His gaiety, which was extreme, had the strange effect of awakening in me contrary feelings; a presentiment of evil hung over me; I loitered on my return; I counted the hours that must elapse before I saw Idris again. Wherefore should this be? What evil might not happen in the meantime? Might not her mother take advantage of Adrian's absence to urge her beyond her sufferance, perhaps to entrap her? I resolved, let what would befall, to see and converse with her the following day. This determination soothed me. To-morrow, loveliest and best, hope and joy of my life, to-morrow I will see thee - Fool, to dream of a moment's delay!

I went to rest. At past midnight I was awaked by a violent knocking. It was now deep winter; it had snowed, and was still snowing; the wind whistled in the leafless trees, despoiling them of the white flakes as they fell; its drear moaning, and the continued knocking, mingled wildly with my dreams - at length I was wide awake; hastily dressing myself, I hurried to discover the cause of this disturbance, and to open my door to the unexpected visitor. Pale as the snow that showered about her, with clasped hands, Idris stood before me. "Save me!" she exclaimed and would have sunk to the ground had I not supported her. In a moment however she revived, and, with energy, almost with violence, entreated me to saddle horses, to take her away, away to London - to her brother - at least to save her. I had no horses — she wrung her hands. "What can I do?" she cried, "I am lost - we are both for ever lost! But come - come with me, Lionel; here I must not stay, - we can get a chaise at the nearest post-house; yet perhaps we have time! come, O come with me to save and protect me!"

When I heard her piteous demands, while with disordered dress, disheveled hair, and aghast looks, she wrung her hands - the idea shot across me is she also mad? - "Sweet one," and I folded her to my heart, "better repose than wander further; - rest - my beloved, I will make a fire - you are chill."

"Rest!" she cried, "repose! you rave, Lionel! If you delay, we are lost; come, I pray you, unless you would cast me off forever."

That Idris, the princely born, nursling of wealth and luxury, should have come through the tempestuous winter-night from her regal abode, and standing at my lowly door, conjure me to fly with her through darkness and storm - was surely a dream - again her plaintive tones, the sight of her loveliness assured me that it was no vision. Looking timidly around, as if she feared to be overheard, she whispered: "I have discovered - tomorrow - that is, to-day - already the to-morrow is come - before dawn, foreigners, Austrians, my mother's hirelings, are to carry me off to Germany, to prison, to marriage - to anything, except you and my brother - take me away, or soon they will be here!"

I was frightened by her vehemence and imagined some mistake in her incoherent tale; but I no longer hesitated to obey her. She had come by herself from the Castle, three long miles, at midnight, through the heavy snow; we must reach Englefield Green, a mile and a half further, before we could obtain a chaise. She told me, that she had kept up her strength and courage till her arrival at my cottage, and then both failed. Now she could hardly walk. Supporting her as I did, still she lagged: and at the distance of half a mile, after many stoppages, shivering fits, and half-fainting, she slipped from my supporting arm on the snow, and with a torrent of tears averred that she must be taken, for that she could not proceed. I lifted her up in my arms; her light form rested on my breast. - I felt no burthen, except the internal one of contrary and contending emotions. Brimming delight now invested me. Again, her chill limbs touched me as a torpedo; and I shuddered in sympathy with her pain and fright. Her head lay on my shoulder, her breath waved my hair, her heart beat near mine, transport made me tremble, blinded me, annihilated me - till a suppressed groan, bursting from her lips, the chattering of her teeth, which she strove vainly to subdue, and all the signs of suffering she evinced, recalled me to the necessity of speed and succor. At last I said to her, "There is Englefield Green; there the inn. But, if you are seen thus strangely circumstanced, dear Idris, even now your enemies may learn your flight too soon: were it not better that I hired the chaise alone? I will put you in safety meanwhile and return to you immediately."

She answered that I was right and might do with her as I pleased. I observed the door of a small out-house a-jar. I pushed it open; and, with some hay strewed about, I formed a couch for her, placing her exhausted frame on it, and covering her with my cloak. I feared to leave her, she looked so wan and faint - but in a moment she reacquired animation, and, with that, fear; and again, she implored me not to delay. To call up the people of the inn, and obtain a conveyance and horses, even though I harnessed them myself, was the work of many minutes; minutes, each freighted with the weight of ages. I caused the chaise to advance a little, waited till the people of the inn had retired, and then made the post-boy draw up the carriage to the spot where Idris, impatient, and now somewhat recovered, stood waiting for me. I lifted her into the chaise; I assured her that with our four horses we should arrive in London before five o'clock, the hour when she would be sought and missed. I besought her to calm herself; a kindly shower of tears relieved her, and by degrees she related her tale of fear and peril.

That same night after Adrian's departure, her mother had warmly expostulated with her on the subject of her attachment to me. Every motive, every
threat, every angry taunt was urged in vain. She seemed to consider that through
me she had lost Raymond; I was the evil influence of her life; I was even accused of
increasing and confirming the mad and base apostacy of Adrian from all views of
advancement and grandeur; and now this miserable mountaineer was to steal her
daughter. Never, Idris related, did the angry lady deign to recur to gentleness and
persuasion; if she had, the task of resistance would have been exquisitely painful.
As it was, the sweet girl's generous nature was roused to defend, and ally herself
with, my despised cause. Her mother ended with a look of contempt and covert
triumph, which for a moment awakened the suspicions of Idris. When they parted
for the night, the Countess said, "To-morrow I trust your tone will be changed: be
composed; I have agitated you; go to rest; and I will send you a medicine I always
take when unduly restless - it will give you a quiet night."

By the time that she had with uneasy thoughts laid her fair cheek upon
her pillow, her mother's servant brought a draught; a suspicion again crossed her
at this novel proceeding, sufficiently alarming to determine her not to take the
potion; but dislike of contention, and a wish to discover whether there was any
just foundation for her conjectures, made her, she said, almost instinctively, and in
contradiction to her usual frankness, pretend to swallow the medicine. Then, agitated as she had been by her mother's violence, and now by unaccustomed fears,
she lay unable to sleep, starting at every sound. Soon her door opened softly, and
on her springing up, she heard a whisper, "Not asleep yet," and the door again
closed. With a beating heart she expected another visit, and when after an interval her chamber was again invaded, having first assured herself that the intruders were her mother and an attendant, she composed herself to feigned sleep. A
step approached her bed, she dared not move, she strove to calm her palpitations,
which became more violent, when she heard her mother say mutteringly, "Pretty
simpleton, little do you think that your game is already at an end forever."

For a moment the poor girl fancied that her mother believed that she had
drank poison: she was on the point of springing up; when the Countess, already
at a distance from the bed, spoke in a low voice to her companion, and again Idris
listened: "Hasten," said she, "there is no time to lose - it is long past eleven; they
will be here at five; take merely the clothes necessary for her journey, and her jew-
el-casket." The servant obeyed; few words were spoken on either side; but those
were caught at with avidity by the intended victim. She heard the name of her own
maid mentioned; - "No, no," replied her mother, "she does not go with us; Lady
Idris must forget England, and all belonging to it." And again, she heard, "She will
not wake till late to-morrow, and we shall then be at sea." - "All is ready," at length
the woman announced. The Countess again came to her daughter's bedside: "In
Austria at least," she said, "you will obey. In Austria, where obedience can be enforced, and no choice left but between an honorable prison and a fitting marriage."
Both then withdrew; though, as she went, the Countess said, "Softly; all sleep;
though all have not been prepared for sleep, like her. I would not have any one
suspect, or she might be roused to resistance, and perhaps escape. Come with me
to my room; we will remain there till the hour agreed upon." They went. Idris,
panic-struck, but animated and strengthened even by her excessive fear, dressed
herself hurriedly, and going down a flight of back-stairs, avoiding the vicinity of

her mother's apartment, she contrived to escape from the castle by a low window, and came through snow, wind, and obscurity to my cottage; nor lost her courage, until she arrived, and, depositing her fate in my hands, gave herself up to the desperation and weariness that overwhelmed her.

I comforted her as well as I might. Joy and exultation were mine, to possess, and to save her. Yet not to excite fresh agitation in her, *per non turbar quel bel viso sereno*, I curbed my delight. I strove to quiet the eager dancing of my heart; I turned from her my eyes, beaming with too much tenderness, and proudly, to dark night, and the inclement atmosphere, murmured the expressions of my transport. We reached London, methought, all too soon; and yet I could not regret our speedy arrival, when I witnessed the extasy with which my beloved girl found herself in her brother's arms, safe from every evil, under his unblamed protection.

Adrian wrote a brief note to his mother, informing her that Idris was under his care and guardianship. Several days elapsed, and at last an answer came, dated from Cologne. "It was useless," the haughty and disappointed lady wrote, "for the Earl of Windsor and his sister to address again the injured parent, whose only expectation of tranquility must be derived from oblivion of their existence. Her desires had been blasted; her schemes overthrown. She did not complain; in her brother's court she would find, not compensation for their disobedience (filial unkindness admitted of none), but such a state of things and mode of life, as might best reconcile her to her fate. Under such circumstances, she positively declined any communication with them."

Such were the strange and incredible events, that finally brought about my union with the sister of my best friend, with my adored Idris. With simplicity and courage, she set aside the prejudices and opposition which were obstacles to my happiness, nor scrupled to give her hand, where she had given her heart. To be worthy of her, to raise myself to her height through the exertion of talents and virtue, to repay her love with devoted, unwearied tenderness, were the only thanks I could offer for the matchless gift.

CHAPTER VI

And now let the reader, passing over some short period of time, be introduced to our happy circle. Adrian, Idris and I, were established in Windsor Castle; Lord Raymond and my sister, inhabited a house which the former had built on the borders of the Great Park, near Perdita's cottage, as was still named the low-roofed abode, where we two, poor even in hope, had each received the assurance of our felicity. We had our separate occupations and our common amusements. Sometimes we passed whole days under the leafy covert of the forest with our books and music. This occurred during those rare days in this country, when the sun mounts his ethereal throne in unclouded majesty, and the windless atmosphere is as a bath of pellucid and grateful water, wrapping the senses in tranquility. When the clouds veiled the sky, and the wind scattered them there and here, rending their woof, and strewing its fragments through the aerial plains — then we rode out, and sought new spots of beauty and repose. When the frequent rains shut us within doors, evening recreation followed morning study, ushered in by music and song. Idris had a natural musical talent; and her voice, which had been carefully cultivated, was full and sweet. Raymond and I made a part of the concert, and Adrian and Perdita were devout listeners. Then we were as gay as summer insects, playful as children; we ever met one another with smiles and read content and joy in each other's countenances. Our prime festivals were held in Perdita's cottage; nor were we ever weary of talking of the past or dreaming of the future. Jealousy and disquiet were unknown among us; nor did a fear or hope of change ever disturb our tranquility. Others said, "We might be happy" - we said – "We are".

When any separation took place between us, it generally so happened, that Idris and Perdita would ramble away together, and we remained to discuss the affairs of nations, and the philosophy of life. The very difference of our dispositions gave zest to these conversations. Adrian had the superiority in learning and eloquence; but Raymond possessed a quick penetration, and a practical knowledge of life, which usually displayed itself in opposition to Adrian, and thus kept up the ball of discussion. At other times we made excursions of many days' duration and crossed the country to visit any spot noted for beauty or historical association. Sometimes we went up to London and entered into the amusements of the busy throng; sometimes our retreat was invaded by visitors from among them. This change made us only the more sensible to the delights of the intimate intercourse of our own circle, the tranquility of our divine forest, and our happy evenings in the halls of our beloved Castle.

The disposition of Idris was peculiarly frank, soft, and affectionate. Her temper was unalterably sweet; and although firm and resolute on any point that touched her heart, she was yielding to those she loved. The nature of Perdita was less perfect; but tenderness and happiness improved her temper and softened her natural reserve. Her understanding was clear and comprehensive, her imagination vivid; she was sincere, generous, and reasonable. Adrian, the matchless brother of my soul, the sensitive and excellent Adrian, loving all, and beloved by all, yet seemed destined not to find the half of himself, which was to complete his happiness. He often left us, and wandered by himself in the woods, or sailed in his little skiff, his books his only companions. He was often the gayest of our party, at the same time that he was the only one visited by fits of despondency; his slender frame seemed overcharged with the weight of life, and his soul appeared rather to inhabit his body than unite with it. I was hardly more devoted to my Idris than to her brother, and she loved him as her teacher, her friend, the benefactor who had secured to her the fulfilment of her dearest wishes. Raymond, the ambitious, restless Raymond, reposed midway on the great high road of life, and was content to give up all his schemes of sovereignty and fame, to make one of us, the flowers of the field. His kingdom was the heart of Perdita, his subjects her thoughts; by her he was loved, respected as a superior being, obeyed, waited on. No office, no devotion, no watching was irksome to her, as it regarded him. She would sit apart from us and watch him; she would weep for joy to think that he was hers. She erected a temple for him in the depth of her being, and each faculty was a priestess vowed to his service. Sometimes she might be wayward and capricious; but her repentance was bitter, her return entire, and even this inequality of temper suited him who was not formed by nature to float idly down the stream of life.

During the first year of their marriage, Perdita presented Raymond with a lovely girl. It was curious to trace in this miniature model the very traits of its father. The same half-disdainful lips and smile of triumph, the same intelligent eyes, the same brow and chestnut hair; her very hands and taper fingers resembled his. How very dear she was to Perdita! In progress of time, I also became a father, and our little darlings, our playthings and delights, called forth a thousand new and delicious feelings.

Years passed thus, - even years. Each month brought forth its successor, each year one like to that gone by; truly, our lives were a living comment on that beautiful sentiment of Plutarch, that "our souls have a natural inclination to love, being born as much to love, as to feel, to reason, to understand and remember." We talked of change and active pursuits, but still remained at Windsor, incapable of violating the charm that attached us to our secluded life.

> *Parliamo aver qui tutto il ben raccolto*
> *Che fra mortali in piu parte si rimembra*
> *(We speak of having all the well-collected here*
> *Which among mortals in most parts is remembered)*

Now also that our children gave us occupation, we found excuses for our idleness, in the idea of bringing them up to a more splendid career. At length our tranquility was disturbed, and the course of events, which for five years had flowed on in hushing tranquility, was broken by breakers and obstacles, that woke us from our pleasant dream.

A new Lord Protector of England was to be chosen; and, at Raymond's request, we removed to London, to witness, and even take a part in the election. If Raymond had been united to Idris, this post had been his stepping-stone to higher dignity; and his desire for power and fame had been crowned with fullest measure. He had exchanged a scepter for a lute, a kingdom for Perdita.

Did he think of this as we journeyed up to town? I watched him but could make but little of him. He was particularly gay, playing with his child, and turning to sport every word that was uttered. Perhaps he did this because he saw a cloud upon Perdita's brow. She tried to rouse herself, but her eyes every now and then filled with tears, and she looked wistfully on Raymond and her girl, as if fearful that some evil would betide them. And so, she felt. A presentiment of ill hung over her. She leaned from the window looking on the forest, and the turrets of the Castle, and as these became hid by intervening objects, she passionately ex-claimed - "Scenes of happiness! scenes sacred to devoted love, when shall I see you again! and when I see ye, shall I be still the beloved and joyous Perdita, or shall I, heart-broken and lost, wander among your groves, the ghost of what I am!"

"Why, silly one," cried Raymond, "what is your little head pondering upon, that of a sudden you have become so sublimely dismal? Cheer up, or I shall make you over to Idris, and call Adrian into the carriage, who, I see by his gesture, sympathizes with my good spirits."

Adrian was on horseback; he rode up to the carriage, and his gaiety, in ad-dition to that of Raymond, dispelled my sister's melancholy. We entered London in the evening and went to our several abodes near Hyde Park.

The following morning Lord Raymond visited me early. "I come to you," he said, "only half assured that you will assist me in my project, but resolved to go through with it, whether you concur with me or not. Promise me secrecy; howev-er, for if you will not contribute to my success, at least you must not baffle me."

"Well, I promise. And now -"

"And now, my dear fellow, for what are we come to London? To be pres-ent at the election of a Protector, and to give our yea or nay for his shuffling Grace of -? or for that noisy Ryland? Do you believe, Verney, that I brought you to town for that? No, we will have a Protector of our own. We will set up a candidate and ensure his success. We will nominate Adrian and do our best to bestow on him the power to which he is entitled by his birth, and which he merits through his virtues.

"Do not answer; I know all your objections and will reply to them in order. First, whether he will or will not consent to become a great man? Leave the task of persuasion on that point to me; I do not ask you to assist me there. Secondly, whether he ought to exchange his employment of plucking blackberries, and nurs-ing wounded partridges in the forest, for the command of a nation? My dear Lio-nel, we are married men, and find employment sufficient in amusing our wives, and dancing our children. But Adrian is alone, wifeless, childless, unoccupied. I have long observed him. He pines for want of some interest in life. His heart, exhausted by his early sufferings, reposes like a new-healed limb, and shrinks from all excitement. But his understanding, his charity, his virtues, want a field for exercise and display; and we will procure it for him. Besides, is it not a shame, that the genius of Adrian should fade from the earth like a flower in an untrod mountain-path, fruitless? Do you think Nature composed his surpassing machine for no purpose? Believe me, he was destined to be the author of infinite good to his native England. Has she not bestowed on him every gift in prodigality? - birth, wealth, talent, goodness? Does not everyone love and admire him? and does he not delight singly in such efforts as manifest his love to all? Come, I see that you are already persuaded, and will second me when I propose him to-night in parlia-ment."

"You have got up all your arguments in excellent order," I replied, "and, if Adrian consent, they are unanswerable. One only condition I would make, - that you do nothing without his concurrence."

"I believe you are in the right," said Raymond; "although I had thought at first to arrange the affair differently. Be it so. I will go instantly to Adrian; and, if he inclines to consent, you will not destroy my labor by persuading him to return and turn squirrel again in Windsor Forest. Idris, you will not act the traitor towards me?"

"Trust me," replied she, "I will preserve a strict neutrality."

"For my part," said I, "I am too well convinced of the worth of our friend, and the rich harvest of benefits that all England would reap from his Protectorship, to deprive my countrymen of such a blessing, if he consent to bestow it on them."

In the evening Adrian visited us. - "Do you cabal also against me," said he, laughing; "and will you make common cause with Raymond, in dragging a poor visionary from the clouds to surround him with the fire-works and blasts of earthly grandeur, instead of heavenly rays and airs? I thought you knew me better."
"I do know you better," I replied "than to think that you would be happy in such a situation; but the good you would do to others may be an inducement, since the time is probably arrived when you can put your theories into practice, and you may bring about such reformation and change, as will conduce to that perfect system of government which you delight to portray."

"You speak of an almost-forgotten dream," said Adrian, his countenance slightly clouding as he spoke; "the visions of my boyhood have long since faded in the light of reality; I know now that I am not a man fitted to govern nations; sufficient for me, if I keep in wholesome rule the little kingdom of my own mortality.

"But do not you see, Lionel, the drift of our noble friend; a drift, perhaps, unknown to himself, but apparent to me. Lord Raymond was never born to be a drone in the hive, and to find content in our pastoral life. He thinks that he ought to be satisfied; he imagines that his present situation precludes the possibility of aggrandizement; he does not therefore, even in his own heart, plan change for himself. But do you not see, that, under the idea of exalting me, he is chalking out a new path for himself; a path of action from which he has long wandered?

"Let us assist him. He, the noble, the warlike, the great in every quality that can adorn the mind and person of man; he is fitted to be the Protector of England. If I - that is, if we propose him, he will assuredly be elected, and will find, in the functions of that high office, scope for the towering powers of his mind. Even Perdita will rejoice. Perdita, in whom ambition was a covered fire until she married Raymond, which event was for a time the fulfilment of her hopes; Perdita will rejoice in the glory and advancement of her lord - and, coyly and prettily, not be discontented with her share. In the meantime, we, the wise of the land, will return to our Castle, and, Cincinnatus-like, take to our usual labors, until our friend shall require our presence and assistance here."

The more Adrian reasoned upon this scheme, the more feasible it appeared. His own determination never to enter into public life was insurmountable, and the delicacy of his health was a sufficient argument against it. The next step was to induce Raymond to confess his secret wishes for dignity and fame. He entered while we were speaking. The way in which Adrian had received his project for setting him up as a candidate for the Protectorship, and his replies, had already awakened in his mind, the view of the subject which we were now discussing. His countenance and manner betrayed irresolution and anxiety; but the anxiety arose from a fear that we should not prosecute, or not succeed in our idea; and his irresolution, from a doubt whether we should risk a defeat. A few words from us decided him, and hope and joy sparkled in his eyes; the idea of embarking in a career, so congenial to his early habits and cherished wishes, made him as before energetic and bold. We discussed his chances, the merits of the other candidates, and the dispositions of the voters.

After all we miscalculated. Raymond had lost much of his popularity and was deserted by his peculiar partisans. Absence from the busy stage had caused him to be forgotten by the people; his former parliamentary supporters were principally composed of royalists, who had been willing to make an idol of him when he appeared as the heir of the Earldom of Windsor; but who were indifferent to him, when he came forward with no other attributes and distinctions than they conceived to be common to many among themselves. Still he had many friends, admirers of his transcendent talents; his presence in the house, his eloquence, address and imposing beauty, were calculated to produce an electric effect. Adrian also, notwithstanding his recluse habits and theories, so adverse to the spirit of party, had many friends, and they were easily induced to vote for a candidate of his selection.

The Duke of --, and Mr. Ryland, Lord Raymond's old antagonist, were the other candidates. The Duke was supported by all the aristocrats of the republic, who considered him their proper representative. Ryland was the popular candidate; when Lord Raymond was first added to the list, his chance of success appeared small. We retired from the debate which had followed on his nomination: we, his nominators, mortified; he dispirited to excess. Perdita reproached us bitterly. Her expectations had been strongly excited; she had urged nothing against our project, on the contrary, she was evidently pleased by it; but its evident ill success changed the current of her ideas. She felt, that, once awakened, Raymond would never return unrepiningly to Windsor. His habits were unhinged; his restless mind roused from its sleep, ambition must now be his companion through life; and if he did not succeed in his present attempt, she foresaw that unhappiness and cureless discontent would follow. Perhaps her own disappointment added a sting to her thoughts and words; she did not spare us, and our own reflections added to our disquietude.

It was necessary to follow up our nomination, and to persuade Raymond to present himself to the electors on the following evening. For a long-time he was obstinate. He would embark in a balloon; he would sail for a distant quarter of the world, where his name and humiliation were unknown. But this was useless; his attempt was registered; his purpose published to the world; his shame could never be erased from the memories of men. It was as well to fail at last after a struggle, as to fly now at the beginning of his enterprise.

From the moment that he adopted this idea, he was changed. His depression and anxiety fled; he became all life and activity. The smile of triumph shone on his countenance; determined to pursue his object to the uttermost, his manner and expression seem ominous of the accomplishment of his wishes. Not so Perdita. She was frightened by his gaiety, for she dreaded a greater revulsion at the end. If his appearance even inspired us with hope, it only rendered the state of her mind more painful. She feared to lose sight of him; yet she dreaded to remark any change in the temper of his mind. She listened eagerly to him yet tantalized herself by giving to his words a meaning foreign to their true interpretation, and adverse to her hopes. She dared not be present at the contest; yet she remained at home a prey to double solicitude. She wept over her little girl; she looked, she spoke, as if she dreaded the occurrence of some frightful calamity. She was half mad from the effects of uncontrollable agitation.

Lord Raymond presented himself to the house with fearless confidence and insinuating address. After the Duke of -- and Mr. Ryland had finished their speeches, he commenced. Assuredly he had not conned his lesson; and at first, he hesitated, pausing in his ideas, and in the choice of his expressions. By degrees he warmed; his words flowed with ease, his language was full of vigor, and his voice of persuasion. He reverted to his past life, his successes in Greece, his favor at home. Why should he lose this, now that added years, prudence, and the pledge which his marriage gave to his country, ought to increase, rather than diminish his claims to confidence? He spoke of the state of England; the necessary measures to be taken to ensure its security and confirm its prosperity. He drew a glowing picture of its present situation. As he spoke, every sound was hushed, every thought suspended by intense attention. His graceful elocution enchained the senses of his hearers. In some degree also he was fitted to reconcile all parties. His birth pleased the aristocracy; his being the candidate recommended by Adrian, a man intimately allied to the popular party, caused a number, who had no great reliance either on the Duke or Mr. Ryland, to range on his side.

The contest was keen and doubtful. Neither Adrian nor myself would have been so anxious, if our own success had depended on our exertions; but we had egged our friend on to the enterprise, and it became us to ensure his triumph. Idris, who entertained the highest opinion of his abilities, was warmly interested in the event: and my poor sister, who dared not hope, and to whom fear was misery, was plunged into a fever of disquietude.

Day after day passed while we discussed our projects for the evening, and each night was occupied by debates which offered no conclusion. At last the crisis came: the night when parliament, which had so long delayed its choice, must decide: as the hour of twelve passed, and the new day began, it was by virtue of the constitution dissolved, its power extinct.

We assembled at Raymond's house, we and our partisans. At half past five o'clock we proceeded to the House. Idris endeavored to calm Perdita; but the poor girl's agitation deprived her of all power of self-command. She walked up and down the room, - gazed wildly when anyone entered, fancying that they might be the announcers of her doom. I must do justice to my sweet sister: it was not for herself that she was thus agonized. She alone knew the weight which Raymond attached to his success. Even to us he assumed gaiety and hope, and assumed them so well, that we did not divine the secret workings of his mind. Sometimes a nervous trembling, a sharp dissonance of voice, and momentary fits of absence revealed to Perdita the violence he did himself; but we, intent on our plans, observed only his ready laugh, his joke intruded on all occasions, the flow of his spirits which seemed incapable of ebb. Besides, Perdita was with him in his retirement; she saw the moodiness that succeeded to this forced hilarity; she marked his disturbed sleep, his painful irritability - once she had seen his tears - hers had scarce ceased to flow, since she had beheld the big drops which disappointed pride had caused to gather in his eye, but which pride was unable to dispel. What wonder then that her feelings were wrought to this pitch! I thus accounted to myself for her agitation; but this was not all, and the sequel revealed another excuse.

One moment we seized before our departure, to take leave of our beloved girls. I had small hope of success, and entreated Idris to watch over my sister. As I approached the latter, she seized my hand, and drew me into another apartment; she threw herself into my arms and wept and sobbed bitterly and long. I tried to soothe her; I bade her hope; I asked what tremendous consequences would ensue even on our failure. "My brother," she cried, "protector of my childhood, dear, most dear Lionel, my fate hangs by a thread. I have you all about me now - you, the companion of my infancy; Adrian, as dear to me as if bound by the ties of blood; Idris, the sister of my heart, and her lovely offspring. This, O this may be the last time that you will surround me thus!"

Abruptly she stopped, and then cried: "What have I said? - foolish false girl that I am!" She looked wildly on me, and then suddenly calming herself, apologized for what she called her unmeaning words, saying that she must indeed be insane, for, while Raymond lived, she must be happy; and then, though she still wept, she suffered me tranquilly to depart. Raymond only took her hand when he went and looked on her expressively; she answered by a look of intelligence and assent.

Poor girl! what she then suffered! I could never entirely forgive Raymond for the trials he imposed on her, occasioned as they were by a selfish feeling on his part. He had schemed, if he failed in his present attempt, without taking leave of any of us, to embark for Greece, and never again to revisit England. Perdita acceded to his wishes; for his contentment was the chief object of her life, the crown of her enjoyment; but to leave us all, her companions, the beloved partners of her happiest years, and in the interim to conceal this frightful determination, was a task that almost conquered her strength of mind. She had been employed in arranging for their departure; she had promised Raymond during this decisive evening, to take advantage of our absence, to go one stage of the journey, and he, after his defeat was ascertained, would slip away from us, and join her.

Although, when I was informed of this scheme, I was bitterly offended by the small attention which Raymond paid to my sister's feelings, I was led by reflection to consider, that he acted under the force of such strong excitement, as to take from him the consciousness, and, consequently, the guilt of a fault. If he had permitted us to witness his agitation, he would have been more under the guidance of reason; but his struggles for the shew of composure, acted with such violence on his nerves, as to destroy his power of self-command. I am convinced that, at the worst, he would have returned from the seashore to take leave of us, and to make us the partners of his council. But the task imposed on Perdita was not the less painful. He had extorted from her a vow of secrecy; and her part of the drama, since it was to be performed alone, was the most agonizing that could be devised. But to return to my narrative.

The debates had hitherto been long and loud; they had often been protracted merely for the sake of delay. But now each seemed fearful lest the fatal moment should pass, while the choice was yet undecided. Unwonted silence reigned in the house, the members spoke in whispers, and the ordinary business was transacted with celerity and quietness. During the first stage of the election, the Duke of -- had been thrown out; the question therefore lay between Lord Raymond and Mr. Ryland. The latter had felt secure of victory, until the appearance of Raymond; and, since his name had been inserted as a candidate, he had canvassed with eagerness. He had appeared each evening, impatience and anger marked in his looks, scowling on us from the opposite side of St. Stephen's, as if his mere frown would cast eclipse on our hopes.

Everything in the English constitution had been regulated for the better preservation of peace. On the last day, two candidates only were allowed to remain; and to obviate, if possible, the last struggle between these, a bribe was offered to him who should voluntarily resign his pretensions; a place of great emolument and honor was given him, and his success facilitated at a future election. Strange to say however, no instance had yet occurred, where either candidate had had recourse to this expedient; in consequence the law had become obsolete, nor had been referred to by any of us in our discussions. To our extreme surprise, when it was moved that we should resolve ourselves into a committee for the election of the Lord Protector, the member who had nominated Ryland, rose and informed us that this candidate had resigned his pretensions. His information was at first received with silence; a confused murmur succeeded; and, when the chairman declared Lord Raymond duly chosen, it amounted to a shout of applause and victory. It seemed as if, far from any dread of defeat even if Mr. Ryland had not resigned, every voice would have been united in favor of our candidate. In fact, now that the idea of contest was dismissed, all hearts returned to their former respect and admiration of our accomplished friend. Each felt that England had never seen a Protector so capable of fulfilling the arduous duties of that high office. One voice made of many voices, resounded through the chamber; it syllabled the name of Raymond.

He entered. I was on one of the highest seats and saw him walk up the passage to the table of the speaker. The native modesty of his disposition conquered the joy of his triumph. He looked round timidly; a mist seemed before his eyes. Adrian, who was beside me, hastened to him, and jumping down the benches, was at his side in a moment. His appearance re-animated our friend; and, when he came to speak and act, his hesitation vanished, and he shone out supreme in majesty and victory. The former Protector tendered him the oaths, and presented him with the insignia of office, performing the ceremonies of installation. The house then dissolved. The chief members of the state crowded round the new magistrate and conducted him to the palace of government. Adrian suddenly vanished; and, by the time that Raymond's supporters were reduced to our intimate friends merely, returned leading Idris to congratulate her friend on his success.

But where was Perdita? In securing solicitously an unobserved retreat in case of failure, Raymond had forgotten to arrange the mode by which she was to hear of his success; and she had been too much agitated to revert to this circumstance. When Idris entered, so far had Raymond forgotten himself, that he asked for my sister; one word, which told of her mysterious disappearance, recalled him. Adrian it is true had already gone to seek the fugitive, imagining that her tameless anxiety had led her to the purlieus of the House, and that some sinister event detained her. But Raymond, without explaining himself, suddenly quitted us, and in another moment, we heard him gallop down the street, in spite of the wind and rain that scattered tempest over the earth. We did not know how far he had to go, and soon separated, supposing that in a short time he would return to the palace with Perdita, and that they would not be sorry to find themselves alone.

Perdita had arrived with her child at Dartford, weeping and inconsolable. She directed everything to be prepared for the continuance of their journey, and placing her lovely sleeping charge on a bed, passed several hours in acute suffering. Sometimes she observed the war of elements, thinking that they also declared against her, and listened to the pattering of the rain in gloomy despair. Sometimes she hung over her child, tracing her resemblance to the father, and fearful lest in after life she should display the same passions and uncontrollable impulses, that rendered him unhappy. Again, with a gush of pride and delight, she marked in the features of her little girl, the same smile of beauty that often-irradiated Raymond's countenance. The sight of it soothed her. She thought of the treasure she possessed in the affections of her lord; of his accomplishments, surpassing those of his contemporaries, his genius, his devotion to her. - Soon she thought that all she possessed in the world, except him, might well be spared, nay, given with delight, a propitiatory offering, to secure the supreme good she retained in him. Soon she imagined that fate demanded this sacrifice from her, as a mark she was devoted to Raymond, and that it must be made with cheerfulness. She figured to herself their life in the Greek isle he had selected for their retreat; her task of soothing him; her cares for the beauteous Clara, her rides in his company, her dedication of herself to his consolation. The picture then presented itself to her in such glowing colors, that she feared the reverse, and a life of magnificence and power in London; where Raymond would no longer be hers only, nor she the sole source of happiness to him. So far as she merely was concerned, she began to hope for defeat; and it was only on his account that her feelings vacillated, as she heard him gallop into the courtyard of the inn. That he should come to her alone, wetted by the storm, careless of everything except speed, what else could it mean, than that, vanquished and solitary, they were to take their way from native England, the scene of shame, and hide themselves in the myrtle groves of the Grecian isles?

In a moment she was in his arms. The knowledge of his success had become so much a part of himself, that he forgot that it was necessary to impart it to his companion. She only felt in his embrace a dear assurance that while he possessed her, he would not despair. "This is kind," she cried; "this is noble, my own beloved! O fear not disgrace or lowly fortune, while you have your Perdita; fear not sorrow, while our child lives and smiles. Let us go even where you will; the love that accompanies us will prevent our regrets."

Locked in his embrace, she spoke thus, and cast back her head, seeking an assent to her words in his eyes - they were sparkling with ineffable delight. "Why, my little Lady Protectress," said he, playfully, "what is this you say? And what pretty scheme have you woven of exile and obscurity, while a brighter web, a gold-enwoven tissue, is that which, in truth, you ought to contemplate?"

He kissed her brow - but the wayward girl, half sorry at his triumph, agitated by swift change of thought, hid her face in his bosom and wept. He comforted her; he instilled into her his own hopes and desires; and soon her countenance beamed with sympathy. How very happy were they that night! How full even to bursting was their sense of joy!

CHAPTER VII

Having seen our friend properly installed in his new office, we turned our eyes towards Windsor. The nearness of this place to London was such, as to take away the idea of painful separation, when we quitted Raymond and Perdita. We took leave of them in the Protectoral Palace. It was pretty enough to see my sister enter as it were into the spirit of the drama, and endeavor to fill her station with becoming dignity. Her internal pride and humility of manner were now more than ever at war. Her timidity was not artificial but arose from that fear of not being properly appreciated, that slight estimation of the neglect of the world, which also characterized Raymond. But then Perdita thought more constantly of others than he; and part of her bashfulness arose from a wish to take from those around her a sense of inferiority; a feeling which never crossed her mind. From the circumstances of her birth and education, Idris would have been better fitted for the formulae of ceremony; but the very ease which accompanied such actions with her, arising from habit, rendered them tedious; while, with every drawback, Perdita evidently enjoyed her situation. She was too full of new ideas to feel much pain when we departed; she took an affectionate leave of us and promised to visit us soon; but she did not regret the circumstances that caused our separation. The spirits of Raymond were unbounded; he did not know what to do with his new got power; his head was full of plans; he had as yet decided on none - but he promised himself, his friends, and the world, that the aera of his Protectorship should be signalized by some act of surpassing glory. Thus, we talked of them, and moralized, as with diminished numbers we returned to Windsor Castle. We felt extreme delight at our escape from political turmoil and sought our solitude with redoubled zest. We did not want for occupation; but my eager disposition was now turned to the field of intellectual exertion only; and hard study I found to be an excellent medicine to allay a fever of spirit with which in indolence, I should doubtless have been assailed. Perdita had permitted us to take Clara back with us to Windsor; and she and my two lovely infants were perpetual sources of interest and amusement.

The only circumstance that disturbed our peace, was the health of Adrian. It evidently declined, without any symptom which could lead us to suspect his disease, unless indeed his brightened eyes, animated look, and flustering cheeks, made us dread consumption; but he was without pain or fear. He betook himself to books with ardor, and reposed from study in the society he best loved, that of his sister and myself. Sometimes he went up to London to visit Raymond and watch the progress of events. Clara often accompanied him in these excursions; partly that she might see her parents, partly because Adrian delighted in the prattle, and intelligent looks of this lovely child.

Meanwhile all went on well in London. The new elections were finished; parliament met, and Raymond was occupied in a thousand beneficial schemes. Canals, aqueducts, bridges, stately buildings, and various edifices for public utility, were entered upon; he was continually surrounded by projectors and projects, which were to render England one scene of fertility and magnificence; the state of poverty was to be abolished; men were to be transported from place to place almost with the same facility as the Princes Hussain, Ali, and Ahmed, in the Arabian Nights. The physical state of man would soon not yield to the beatitude of angels; disease was to be banished; labor lightened of its heaviest burden. Nor did this seem extravagant. The arts of life, and the discoveries of science had augmented in a ratio which left all calculation behind; food sprung up, so to say, spontaneously - machines existed to supply with facility every want of the population. An evil direction still survived; and men were not happy, not because they could not, but because they would not rouse themselves to vanquish self-raised obstacles. Raymond was to inspire them with his beneficial will, and the mechanism of society, once systematized according to faultless rules, would never again swerve into disorder. For these hopes he abandoned his long-cherished ambition of being enregistered in the annals of nations as a successful warrior; laying aside his sword, peace and its enduring glories became his aim - the title he coveted was that of the benefactor of his country.

Among other works of art in which he was engaged, he had projected the erection of a national gallery for statues and pictures. He possessed many himself, which he designed to present to the Republic; and, as the edifice was to be the great ornament of his Protectorship, he was very fastidious in his choice of the plan on which it would be built. Hundreds were brought to him and rejected. He sent even to Italy and Greece for drawings; but, as the design was to be characterized by originality as well as by perfect beauty, his endeavors were for a time without avail. At length a drawing came, with an address where communications might be sent, and no artist's name affixed. The design was new and elegant, but faulty; so faulty, that although drawn with the hand and eye of taste, it was evidently the work of one who was not an architect. Raymond contemplated it with delight; the more he gazed, the more pleased he was and yet the errors multiplied under inspection. He wrote to the address given, desiring to see the draughtsman, that such alterations might be made, as should be suggested in a consultation between him and the original conceiver.

A Greek came. A middle-aged man, with some intelligence of manner, but with so commonplace a physiognomy, that Raymond could scarcely believe that he was the designer. He acknowledged that he was not an architect; but the idea of the building had struck him, though he had sent it without the smallest hope of its being accepted. He was a man of few words. Raymond questioned him; but his reserved answers soon made him turn from the man to the drawing. He pointed out the errors, and the alterations that he wished to be made; he offered the Greek a pencil that he might correct the sketch on the spot; this was refused by his visitor, who said that he perfectly understood, and would work at it at home. At length Raymond suffered him to depart.

The next day he returned. The design had been re-drawn; but many defects still remained, and several of the instructions given had been misunderstood. "Come," said Raymond, "I yielded to you yesterday, now comply with my request - take the pencil."

The Greek took it, but he handled it in no artist-like way; at length he said: "I must confess to you, my Lord, that I did not make this drawing. It is impossible for you to see the real designer; your instructions must pass through me. Condescend therefore to have patience with my ignorance, and to explain your wishes to me; in time I am certain that you will be satisfied."

Raymond questioned vainly; the mysterious Greek would say no more. Would an architect be permitted to see the artist? This also was refused. Raymond repeated his instructions, and the visitor retired. Our friend resolved however not to be foiled in his wish. He suspected that unaccustomed poverty was the cause of the mystery, and that the artist was unwilling to be seen in the garb and abode of want. Raymond was only the more excited by this consideration to discover him; impelled by the interest he took in obscure talent, he therefore ordered a person skilled in such matters, to follow the Greek the next time he came, and observe the house in which he should enter. His emissary obeyed and brought the desired intelligence. He had traced the man to one of the most penurious streets in the metropolis. Raymond did not wonder, that, thus situated, the artist had shrunk from notice, but he did not for this alter his resolve.

On the same evening, he went alone to the house named to him. Poverty, dirt, and squalid misery characterized its appearance. Alas! thought Raymond, I have much to do before England becomes a Paradise. He knocked; the door was opened by a string from above - the broken, wretched staircase was immediately before him, but no person appeared; he knocked again, vainly - and then, impatient of further delay, he ascended the dark, creaking stairs. His main wish, more particularly now that he witnessed the abject dwelling of the artist, was to relieve one, possessed of talent, but depressed by want. He pictured to himself a youth, whose eyes sparkled with genius, whose person was attenuated by famine. He half feared to displease him; but he trusted that his generous kindness would be administered so delicately, as not to excite repulse. What human heart is shut to kindness? and though poverty, in its excess, might render the sufferer unapt to submit to the supposed degradation of a benefit, the zeal of the benefactor must at last relax him into thankfulness. These thoughts encouraged Raymond, as he stood at the door of the highest room of the house. After trying vainly to enter the other apartments, he perceived just within the threshold of this one, a pair of small Turkish slippers; the door was ajar, but all was silent within. It was probable that the inmate was absent, but secure that he had found the right person, our adventurous Protector was tempted to enter, to leave a purse on the table, and silently depart. In pursuance of this idea, he pushed open the door gently - but the room was inhabited.

Raymond had never visited the dwellings of want, and the scene that now presented itself struck him to the heart. The floor was sunk in many places; the walls ragged and bare - the ceiling weather-stained - a tattered bed stood in the corner; there were but two chairs in the room, and a rough broken table, on which was a light in a tin candlestick; - yet in the midst of such drear and heart sickening poverty, there was an air of order and cleanliness that surprised him. The thought was fleeting; for his attention was instantly drawn towards the inhabitant of this wretched abode. It was a female. She sat at the table; one small hand shaded her eyes from the candle; the other held a pencil; her looks were fixed on a drawing before her, which Raymond recognized as the design presented to him. Her whole appearance awakened his deepest interest. Her dark hair was braided and twined in thick knots like the head-dress of a Grecian statue; her garb was mean, but her attitude might have been selected as a model of grace. Raymond had a confused remembrance that he had seen such a form before; he walked across the room; she did not raise her eyes, merely asking in Romaic, who is there? "A friend," replied Raymond in the same dialect. She looked up wondering, and he saw that it was Evadne Zaimi. Evadne, once the idol of Adrian's affections; and who, for the sake of her present visitor, had disdained the noble youth, and then, neglected by him she loved, with crushed hopes and a stinging sense of misery, had returned to her native Greece. What revolution of fortune could have brought her to England, and housed her thus?

Raymond recognized her; and his manner changed from polite beneficence to the warmest protestations of kindness and sympathy. The sight of her, in her present situation, passed like an arrow into his soul. He sat by her, he took her hand, and said a thousand things which breathed the deepest spirit of compassion and affection. Evadne did not answer; her large dark eyes were cast down, at length a tear glimmered on the lashes. "Thus," she cried, "kindness can do, what no want, no misery ever effected; I weep." She shed indeed many tears; her head sunk unconsciously on the shoulder of Raymond; he held her hand: he kissed her sunken tear-stained cheek. He told her, that her sufferings were now over: no one possessed the art of consoling like Raymond; he did not reason or declaim, but his look shone with sympathy; he brought pleasant images before the sufferer; his caresses excited no distrust, for they arose purely from the feeling which leads a mother to kiss her wounded child; a desire to demonstrate in every possible way the truth of his feelings, and the keenness of his wish to pour balm into the lacerated mind of the unfortunate. As Evadne regained her composure, his manner became even gay; he sported with the idea of her poverty. Something told him that it was not its real evils that lay heavily at her heart, but the debasement and disgrace attendant on it; as he talked, he divested it of these; sometimes speaking of her fortitude with energetic praise; then, alluding to her past state, he called her his Princess in disguise. He made her warm offers of service; she was too much occupied by more engrossing thoughts, either to accept or reject them; at length he left her, making a promise to repeat his visit the next day. He returned home, full of mingled feelings, of pain excited by Evadne's wretchedness, and pleasure at the prospect of relieving it. Some motive for which he did not account, even to himself, prevented him from relating his adventure to Perdita.

The next day he threw such disguise over his person as a cloak afforded, and revisited Evadne. As he went, he bought a basket of costly fruits, such as were natives of her own country, and throwing over these various beautiful flowers, bore it himself to the miserable garret of his friend. "Behold," cried he, as he entered, "what bird's food I have brought for my sparrow on the house-top."

Evadne now related the tale of her misfortunes. Her father, though of high rank, had in the end dissipated his fortune, and even destroyed his reputation and influence through a course of dissolute indulgence. His health was impaired beyond hope of cure; and it became his earnest wish, before he died, to preserve his daughter from the poverty which would be the portion of her orphan state. He therefore accepted for her, and persuaded her to accede to, a proposal of marriage, from a wealthy Greek merchant settled at Constantinople. She quitted her native Greece; her father died; by degrees she was cut off from all the companions and ties of her youth.

The war, which about a year before the present time had broken out between Greece and Turkey, brought about many reverses of fortune. Her husband became bankrupt, and then in a tumult and threatened massacre on the part of the Turks, they were obliged to fly at midnight, and reached in an open boat an English vessel under sail, which brought them immediately to this island. The few jewels they had saved, supported them awhile. The whole strength of Evadne's mind was exerted to support the failing spirits of her husband. Loss of property, hopelessness as to his future prospects, the inoccupation to which poverty condemned him, combined to reduce him to a state bordering on insanity. Five months after their arrival in England, he committed suicide.

"You will ask me," continued Evadne, "what I have done since; why I have not applied for succor to the rich Greeks resident here; why I have not returned to my native country? My answer to these questions must needs appear to you unsatisfactory, yet they have sufficed to lead me on, day after day, enduring every wretchedness, rather than by such means to seek relief. Shall the daughter of the noble, though prodigal Zaimi, appear a beggar before her compeers or inferiors - superiors she had none. Shall I bow my head before them, and with servile gesture sell my nobility for life? Had I a child, or any tie to bind me to existence, I might descend to this - but, as it is - the world has been to me a harsh step-mother; fain would I leave the abode she seems to grudge, and in the grave forget my pride, my struggles, my despair. The time will soon come; grief and famine have already sapped the foundations of my being; a very short time, and I shall have passed away; unstained by the crime of self-destruction, unstung by the memory of degradation, my spirit will throw aside the miserable coil, and find such recompense as fortitude and resignation may deserve. This may seem madness to you, yet you also have pride and resolution; do not then wonder that my pride is tameless, my resolution unalterable."

Having thus finished her tale, and given such an account as she deemed fit, of the motives of her abstaining from all endeavor to obtain aid from her countrymen, Evadne paused; yet she seemed to have more to say, to which she was unable to give words. In the meantime, Raymond was eloquent. His desire of restoring his lovely friend to her rank in society, and to her lost prosperity, animated him, and he poured forth with energy, all his wishes and intentions on that subject. But he was checked; Evadne exacted a promise, that he should conceal from all her friends her existence in England. "The relatives of the Earl of Windsor," said she haughtily, "doubtless think that I injured him; perhaps the Earl himself would be the first to acquit me, but probably I do not deserve acquittal. I acted then, as I ever must, from impulse. This abode of penury may at least prove the disinterestedness of my conduct. No matter: I do not wish to plead my cause before any of them, not even before your Lordship, had you not first discovered me. The tenor of my actions will prove that I had rather die, than be a mark for scorn - behold the proud Evadne in her tatters! look on the beggar-princess! There is aspic venom in the thought - promise me that my secret shall not be violated by you."

Raymond promised; but then a new discussion ensued. Evadne required another engagement on his part, that he would not without her concurrence enter into any project for her benefit, nor himself offer relief. "Do not degrade me in my own eyes," she said; "poverty has long been my nurse; hard-visaged she is, but honest. If dishonor, or what I conceive to be dishonor, come near me, I am lost." Raymond adduced many arguments and fervent persuasions to overcome her feeling, but she remained unconvinced; and, agitated by the discussion, she wildly and passionately made a solemn vow, to fly and hide herself where he never could discover her, where famine would soon bring death to conclude her woes, if he persisted in his to her disgracing offers. She could support herself, she said. And then she shewed him how, by executing various designs and paintings, she earned a pittance for her support. Raymond yielded for the present. He felt assured, after he had for a while humored her self-will, that in the end friendship and reason would gain the day.

But the feelings that actuated Evadne were rooted in the depths of her being and were such in their growth as he had no means of understanding. Evadne loved Raymond. He was the hero of her imagination, the image carved by love in the unchanged texture of her heart. Seven years ago, in her youthful prime, she had become attached to him; he had served her country against the Turks; he had in her own land acquired that military glory peculiarly dear to the Greeks, since they were still obliged inch by inch to fight for their security. Yet when he returned thence, and first appeared in public life in England, her love did not purchase his, which then vacillated between Perdita and a crown. While he was yet undecided, she had quitted England; the news of his marriage reached her, and her hopes, poorly nurtured blossoms, withered and fell. The glory of life was gone for her; the roseate halo of love, which had imbued every object with its own color, faded; - she was content to take life as it was, and to make the best of leaden-colored reality. She married; and, carrying her restless energy of character with her into new scenes, she turned her thoughts to ambition, and aimed at the title and power of Princess of Wallachia; while her patriotic feelings were soothed by the idea of the good she might do her country, when her husband should be chief of this principality. She lived to find ambition, as unreal a delusion as love. Her intrigues with Russia for the furtherance of her object, excited the jealousy of the Porte, and the animosity of the Greek government. She was considered a traitor by both, the ruin of her husband followed; they avoided death by a timely flight, and she fell from the height of her desires to penury in England. Much of this tale she concealed from Raymond; nor did she confess, that repulse and denial, as to a criminal convicted of the worst of crimes, that of bringing the scythe of foreign despotism to cut away the new springing liberties of her country, would have followed her application to any among the Greeks.

She knew that she was the cause of her husband's utter ruin; and she strung herself to bear the consequences. The reproaches which agony extorted; or worse, cureless, uncomplaining depression, when his mind was sunk in a torpor, not the less painful because it was silent and moveless. She reproached herself with the crime of his death; guilt and its punishments appeared to surround her; in vain she endeavored to allay remorse by the memory of her real integrity; the rest of the world, and she among them, judged of her actions, by their consequences. She prayed for her husband's soul; she conjured the Supreme to place on her head the crime of his self-destruction - she vowed to live to expiate his fault.

In the midst of such wretchedness as must soon have destroyed her, one thought only was matter of consolation. She lived in the same country, breathed the same air as Raymond. His name as Protector was the burthen of every tongue, his achievements, projects, and magnificence, the argument of every story. Nothing is so precious to a woman's heart as the glory and excellence of him she loves; thus, in every horror Evadne reveled in his fame and prosperity. While her husband lived, this feeling was regarded by her as a crime, repressed, repented of. When he died, the tide of love resumed its ancient flow, it deluged her soul with its tumultuous waves, and she gave herself up a prey to its uncontrollable power. But never, O, never, should he see her in her degraded state. Never should he behold her fallen, as she deemed, from her pride of beauty, the poverty-stricken inhabitant of a garret, with a name which had become a reproach, and a weight of guilt on her soul. But though impenetrably veiled from him, his public office permitted her to become acquainted with all his actions, his daily course of life, even his conversation. She allowed herself one luxury, she saw the newspapers every day, and feasted on the praise and actions of the Protector. Not that this indulgence was devoid of accompanying grief. Perdita's name was forever joined with his; their conjugal felicity was celebrated even by the authentic testimony of facts. They were continually together, nor could the unfortunate Evadne read the monosyllable that designated his name, without, at the same time, being presented with the image of her who was the faithful companion of all his labors and pleasures. They, their Excellencies, met her eyes in each line, mingling an evil potion that poisoned her very blood.

It was in the newspaper that she saw the advertisement for the design for a national gallery. Combining with taste her remembrance of the edifices which she had seen in the east, and by an effort of genius enduing them with unity of design, she executed the plan which had been sent to the Protector. She triumphed in the idea of bestowing, unknown and forgotten as she was, a benefit upon him she loved; and with enthusiastic pride looked forward to the accomplishment of a work of hers, which, immortalized in stone, would go down to posterity stamped with the name of Raymond. She awaited with eagerness the return of her messenger from the palace; she listened insatiate to his account of each word, each look of the Protector; she felt bliss in this communication with her beloved, although he knew not to whom he addressed his instructions. The drawing itself became ineffably dear to her. He had seen it, and praised it; it was again retouched by her, each stroke of her pencil was as a chord of thrilling music, and bore to her the idea of a temple raised to celebrate the deepest and most unutterable emotions of her soul. These contemplations engaged her, when the voice of Raymond first struck her ear, a voice, once heard, never to be forgotten; she mastered her gush of feelings and welcomed him with quiet gentleness.

Pride and tenderness now struggled, and at length made a compromise together. She would see Raymond, since destiny had led him to her, and her constancy and devotion must merit his friendship. But her rights with regard to him, and her cherished independence, should not be injured by the idea of interest, or the intervention of the complicated feelings attendant on pecuniary obligation, and the relative situations of the benefactor, and benefited. Her mind was of uncommon strength; she could subdue her sensible wants to her mental wishes, and suffer cold, hunger and misery, rather than concede to fortune a contested point. Alas! that in human nature such a pitch of mental discipline, and disdainful negligence of nature itself, should not have been allied to the extreme of moral excellence! But the resolution that permitted her to resist the pains of privation, sprung from the too great energy of her passions; and the concentrated self-will of which this was a sign, was destined to destroy even the very idol, to preserve whose respect she submitted to this detail of wretchedness.

Their intercourse continued. By degrees Evadne related to her friend the whole of her story, the stain her name had received in Greece, the weight of sin which had accrued to her from the death of her husband. When Raymond offered to clear her reputation, and demonstrate to the world her real patriotism, she declared that it was only through her present sufferings that she hoped for any relief to the stings of conscience; that, in her state of mind, diseased as he might think it, the necessity of occupation was salutary medicine; she ended by extorting a promise that for the space of one month he would refrain from the discussion of her interests, engaging after that time to yield in part to his wishes. She could not disguise to herself that any change would separate her from him; now she saw him each day. His connection with Adrian and Perdita was never mentioned; he was to her a meteor, a companionless star, which at its appointed hour rose in her hemisphere, whose appearance brought felicity, and which, although it set, was never eclipsed. He came each day to her abode of penury, and his presence transformed it to a temple redolent with sweets, radiant with heaven's own light; he partook of her delirium. "They built a wall between them and the world" - Without, a thousand harpies raved, remorse and misery, expecting the destined moment for their invasion. Within, was the peace as of innocence, reckless blindness, deluding joy, hope, whose still anchor rested on placid but unconstant water.

Thus, while Raymond had been wrapped in visions of power and fame, while he looked forward to entire dominion over the elements and the mind of man, the territory of his own heart escaped his notice; and from that unthought of source arose the mighty torrent that overwhelmed his will, and carried to the oblivious sea, fame, hope, and happiness.

CHAPTER VIII

In the meantime, what did Perdita?

During the first months of his Protectorate, Raymond and she had been inseparable; each project was discussed with her, each plan approved by her. I never beheld any one so perfectly happy as my sweet sister. Her expressive eyes were two stars whose beams were love; hope and light-heartedness sat on her cloudless brow. She fed even to tears of joy on the praise and glory of her Lord; her whole existence was one sacrifice to him, and if in the humility of her heart she felt self-complacency, it arose from the reflection that she had won the distinguished hero of the age, and had for years preserved him, even after time had taken from love its usual nourishment. Her own feeling was as entire as at its birth. Five years had failed to destroy the dazzling unreality of passion. Most men ruthlessly destroy the sacred veil, with which the female heart is wont to adorn the idol of its affections. Not so Raymond; he was an enchanter, whose reign was forever undiminished; a king whose power never was suspended: follow him through the details of common life, still the same charm of grace and majesty adorned him; nor could he be despoiled of the innate deification with which nature had invested him. Perdita grew in beauty and excellence under his eye; I no longer recognized my reserved abstracted sister in the fascinating and open-hearted wife of Raymond. The genius that enlightened her countenance, was now united to an expression of benevolence, which gave divine perfection to her beauty.

Happiness is in its highest degree the sister of goodness. Suffering and amiability may exist together, and writers have loved to depict their conjunction; there is a human and touching harmony in the picture. But perfect happiness is an attribute of angels; and those who possess it, appear angelic. Fear has been said to be the parent of religion: even of that religion is it the generator, which leads its votaries to sacrifice human victims at its altars; but the religion which springs from happiness is a lovelier growth; the religion which makes the heart breathe forth fervent thanksgiving, and causes us to pour out the overflowing of the soul before the author of our being; that which is the parent of the imagination and the nurse of poetry; that which bestows benevolent intelligence on the visible mechanism of the world, and makes earth a temple with heaven for its cope. Such happiness, goodness, and religion inhabited the mind of Perdita.

During the five years we had spent together, a knot of happy human beings at Windsor Castle, her blissful lot had been the frequent theme of my sister's conversation. From early habit, and natural affection, she selected me in preference to Adrian or Idris, to be the partner in her overflowing of delight; perhaps, though apparently much unlike, some secret point of resemblance, the offspring of consanguinity, induced this preference. Often at sunset, I have walked with her, in the sober, in shadowed forest paths, and listened with joyful sympathy. Security gave dignity to her passion; the certainty of a full return, left her with no wish unfulfilled. The birth of her daughter, embryo copy of her Raymond, filled up the measure of her content, and produced a sacred and indissoluble tie between them. Sometimes she felt proud that he had preferred her to the hopes of a crown. Sometimes she remembered that she had suffered keen anguish, when he hesitated in his choice. But this memory of past discontent only served to enhance her present joy. What had been hardly won, was now, entirely possessed, doubly dear. She would look at him at a distance with the same rapture, (O, far more exuberant rapture!) that one might feel, who after the perils of a tempest, should find himself in the desired port; she would hasten towards him, to feel more certain in his arms, the reality of her bliss. This warmth of affection, added to the depth of her understanding, and the brilliancy of her imagination, made her beyond words dear to Raymond.

If a feeling of dissatisfaction ever crossed her, it arose from the idea that he was not perfectly happy. Desire of renown, and presumptuous ambition, had characterized his youth. The one he had acquired in Greece; the other he had sacrificed to love. His intellect found sufficient field for exercise in his domestic circle, whose members, all adorned by refinement and literature, were many of them, like himself, distinguished by genius. Yet active life was the genuine soil for his virtues; and he sometimes suffered tedium from the monotonous succession of events in our retirement. Pride made him recoil from complaint; and gratitude and affection to Perdita, generally acted as an opiate to all desire, save that of meriting her love. We all observed the visitation of these feelings, and none regretted them so much as Perdita. Her life consecrated to him, was a slight sacrifice to reward his choice, but was not that sufficient - Did he need any gratification that she was unable to bestow? This was the only cloud in the azure of her happiness.

His passage to power had been full of pain to both. He however attained his wish; he filled the situation for which nature seemed to have moulded him. His activity was fed in wholesome measure, without either exhaustion or satiety; his taste and genius found worthy expression in each of the modes human beings have invented to encage and manifest the spirit of beauty; the goodness of his heart made him never weary of conducing to the well-being of his fellow-creatures; his magnificent spirit, and aspirations for the respect and love of mankind, now received fruition; true, his exaltation was temporary; perhaps it were better that it should be so. Habit would not dull his sense of the enjoyment of power; nor struggles, disappointment and defeat await the end of that which would expire at its maturity. He determined to extract and condense all of glory, power, and achievement, which might have resulted from a long reign, into the three years of his Protectorate.

Raymond was eminently social. All that he now enjoyed would have been devoid of pleasure to him, had it been unparticipated. But in Perdita he possessed all that his heart could desire. Her love gave birth to sympathy; her intelligence made her understand him at a word; her powers of intellect enabled her to assist and guide him. He felt her worth. During the early years of their union, the inequality of her temper, and yet unsubdued self-will which tarnished her character, had been a slight drawback to the fulness of his sentiment. Now that unchanged serenity, and gentle compliance were added to her other qualifications, his respect equaled his love. Years added to the strictness of their union. They did not now guess at, and totter on the pathway, divining the mode to please, hoping, yet fearing the continuance of bliss. Five years gave a sober certainty to their emotions, though it did not rob them of their ethereal nature. It had given them a child; but it had not detracted from the personal attractions of my sister. Timidity, which in her had almost amounted to awkwardness, was exchanged for a graceful decision of manner; frankness, instead of reserve, characterized her physiognomy; and her voice was attuned to thrilling softness. She was now three and twenty, in the pride of womanhood, fulfilling the precious duties of wife and mother, possessed of all her heart had ever coveted. Raymond was ten years older; to his previous beauty, noble mien, and commanding aspect, he now added gentlest benevolence, winning tenderness, graceful and unwearied attention to the wishes of another.

The first secret that had existed between them was the visits of Raymond to Evadne. He had been struck by the fortitude and beauty of the ill-fated Greek; and, when her constant tenderness towards him unfolded itself, he asked with astonishment, by what act of his he had merited this passionate and unrequited love. She was for a while the sole object of his reveries; and Perdita became aware that his thoughts and time were bestowed on a subject unparticipated by her. My sister was by nature destitute of the common feelings of anxious, petulant jealousy. The treasure which she possessed in the affections of Raymond, was more necessary to her being, than the life-blood that animated her veins — more truly than Othello she might say,

> *To be once in doubt,*
> *Is - once to be resolved.*

On the present occasion she did not suspect any alienation of affection; but she conjectured that some circumstance connected with his high place, had occasioned this mystery. She was startled and pained. She began to count the long days, and months, and years which must elapse, before he would be restored to a private station, and unreservedly to her. She was not content that, even for a time, he should practice concealment with her. She often repined; but her trust in the singleness of his affection was undisturbed; and, when they were together, unchecked by fear, she opened her heart to the fullest delight.

Time went on. Raymond, stopping mid-way in his wild career, paused suddenly to think of consequences. Two results presented themselves in the view he took of the future. That his intercourse with Evadne should continue a secret to, or that finally it should be discovered by Perdita. The destitute condition, and highly wrought feelings of his friend prevented him from adverting to the possibility of exiling himself from her. In the first event he had bidden an eternal farewell to open-hearted converse, and entire sympathy with the companion of his life. The veil must be thicker than that invented by Turkish jealousy; the wall higher than the unscalable tower of Vathek, which should conceal from her the workings of his heart and hide from her view the secret of his actions. This idea was intolerably painful to him. Frankness and social feelings were the essence of Raymond's nature; without them his qualities became common-place; without these to spread glory over his intercourse with Perdita, his vaunted exchange of a throne for her love, was as weak and empty as the rainbow hues which vanish when the sun is down. But there was no remedy. Genius, devotion, and courage; the adornments of his mind, and the energies of his soul, all exerted to their uttermost stretch, could not roll back one hair's breadth the wheel of time's chariot; that which had been was written with the adamantine pen of reality, on the everlasting volume of the past; nor could agony and tears suffice to wash out one iota from the act fulfilled.

But this was the best side of the question. What, if circumstance should lead Perdita to suspect, and suspecting to be resolved? The fibers of his frame became relaxed, and cold dew stood on his forehead, at this idea. Many men may scoff at his dread; but he read the future; and the peace of Perdita was too dear to him, her speechless agony too certain, and too fearful, not to unman him. His course was speedily decided upon. If the worst befell; if she learnt the truth, he would neither stand her reproaches, or the anguish of her altered looks. He would forsake her, England, his friends, the scenes of his youth, the hopes of coming time, he would seek another country, and in other scenes begin life again. Having resolved on this, he became calmer. He endeavored to guide with prudence the steeds of destiny through the devious road which he had chosen and bent all his efforts the better to conceal what he could not alter.

The perfect confidence that subsisted between Perdita and him, rendered every communication common between them. They opened each other's letters, even as, until now, the inmost fold of the heart of each was disclosed to the other. A letter came unawares, Perdita read it. Had it contained confirmation; she must have been annihilated. As it was, trembling, cold, and pale, she sought Raymond. He was alone, examining some petitions lately presented. She entered silently, sat on a sofa opposite to him, and gazed on him with a look of such despair, that wildest shrieks and dire moans would have been tame exhibitions of misery, compared to the living incarnation of the thing itself exhibited by her.

At first he did not take his eyes from the papers; when he raised them, he was struck by the wretchedness manifest on her altered cheek; for a moment he forgot his own acts and fears, and asked with consternation — "Dearest girl, what is the matter; what has happened?"

"Nothing," she replied at first; "and yet not so," she continued, hurrying on in her speech; "you have secrets, Raymond; where have you been lately, whom have you seen, what do you conceal from me? — why am I banished from your confidence? Yet this is not it — I do not intend to entrap you with questions — one will suffice - am I completely a wretch?"

With trembling hand, she gave him the paper, and sat white and motionless looking at him while he read it. He recognized the handwriting of Evadne, and the color mounted in his cheeks. With lightning-speed he conceived the contents of the letter; all was now cast on one die; falsehood and artifice were trifles in comparison with the impending ruin. He would either entirely dispel Perdita's suspicions, or quit her forever. "My dear girl," he said, "I have been to blame; but you must pardon me. I was in the wrong to commence a system of concealment; but I did it for the sake of sparing you pain; and each day has rendered it more difficult for me to alter my plan. Besides, I was instigated by delicacy towards the unhappy writer of these few lines."

Perdita gasped: "Well," she cried, "well, go on!"

"That is all - this paper tells all. I am placed in the most difficult circumstances. I have done my best, though perhaps I have done wrong. My love for you is inviolate."

Perdita shook her head doubtingly: "It cannot be," she cried, "I know that it is not. You would deceive me, but I will not be deceived. I have lost you, myself, my life!"

"Do you not believe me?" said Raymond haughtily.

"To believe you," she exclaimed, "I would give up all, and expire with joy, so that in death I could feel that you were true - but that cannot be!"

"Perdita," continued Raymond, "you do not see the precipice on which you stand. You may believe that I did not enter on my present line of conduct without reluctance and pain. I knew that it was possible that your suspicions might be excited; but I trusted that my simple word would cause them to disappear. I built my hope on your confidence. Do you think that I will be questioned, and my replies disdainfully set aside? Do you think that I will be suspected, perhaps watched, cross-questioned, and disbelieved? I am not yet fallen so low; my honor is not yet so tarnished. You have loved me; I adored you. But all human sentiments come to an end. Let our affection expire — but let it not be exchanged for distrust and recrimination. Heretofore we have been friends – lovers - let us not become enemies, mutual spies. I cannot live the object of suspicion - you cannot believe me - let us part!"

"Exactly so," cried Perdita, "I knew that it would come to this! Are we not already parted? Does not a stream, boundless as ocean, deep as vacuum, yawn between us?"

Raymond rose, his voice was broken, his features convulsed, his manner calm as the earthquake-cradling atmosphere, he replied: "I am rejoiced that you take my decision so philosophically. Doubtless you will play the part of the injured wife to admiration. Sometimes you may be stung with the feeling that you have wronged me, but the condolence of your relatives, the pity of the world, the complacency which the consciousness of your own immaculate innocence will bestow, will be excellent balm; — me you will never see more!"

Raymond moved towards the door. He forgot that each word he spoke was false. He personated his assumption of innocence even to self-deception. Have not actors wept, as they portrayed imagined passion? A more intense feeling of the reality of fiction possessed Raymond. He spoke with pride; he felt injured. Perdita looked up; she saw his angry glance; his hand was on the lock of the door. She started up, she threw herself on his neck, she gasped and sobbed; he took her hand, and leading her to the sofa, sat down near her. Her head fell on his shoulder, she trembled, alternate changes of fire and ice ran through her limbs: observing her emotion he spoke with softened accents:

"The blow is given. I will not part from you in anger; - I owe you too much. I owe you six years of unalloyed happiness. But they are passed. I will not live the mark of suspicion, the object of jealousy. I love you too well. In an eternal separation only can either of us hope for dignity and propriety of action. We shall not then be degraded from our true characters. Faith and devotion have hitherto been the essence of our intercourse; - these lost, let us not cling to the seedless husk of life, the unkernelled shell. You have your child, your brother, Idris, Adrian" -

"And you," cried Perdita, "the writer of that letter."

Uncontrollable indignation flashed from the eyes of Raymond. He knew that this accusation at least was false. "Entertain this belief," he cried, "hug it to your heart - make it a pillow to your head, an opiate for your eyes - I am content.

But, by the God that made me, hell is not falser than the word you have spoken!"

Perdita was struck by the impassioned seriousness of his asseverations. She replied with earnestness, "I do not refuse to believe you, Raymond; on the contrary I promise to put implicit faith in your simple word. Only assure me that your love and faith towards me have never been violated; and suspicion, and doubt, and jealousy will at once be dispersed. We shall continue as we have ever done, one heart, one hope, one life."

"I have already assured you of my fidelity," said Raymond with disdainful coldness, "triple assertions will avail nothing where one is despised. I will say no more; for I can add nothing to what I have already said, to what you before contemptuously set aside. This contention is unworthy of both of us; and I confess that I am weary of replying to charges at once unfounded and unkind."

Perdita tried to read his countenance, which he angrily averted. There was so much of truth and nature in his resentment, that her doubts were dispelled. Her countenance, which for years had not expressed a feeling unallied to affection, became again radiant and satisfied. She found it however no easy task to soften and reconcile Raymond. At first, he refused to stay to hear her. But she would not be put off; secure of his unaltered love, she was willing to undertake any labor, use any entreaty, to dispel his anger. She obtained a hearing, he sat in haughty silence, but he listened. She first assured him of her boundless confidence; of this he must be conscious, since but for that she would not seek to detain him. She enumerated their years of happiness; she brought before him past scenes of intimacy and happiness; she pictured their future life; she mentioned their child - tears unbidden now filled her eyes. She tried to disperse them, but they refused to be checked - her utterance was choked. She had not wept before. Raymond could not resist these signs of distress: he felt perhaps somewhat ashamed of the part he acted of the injured man, he who was in truth the injurer. And then he devoutly loved Perdita; the bend of her head, her glossy ringlets, the turn of her form were to him subjects of deep tenderness and admiration; as she spoke, her melodious tones entered his soul; he soon softened towards her, comforting and caressing her, and endeavoring to cheat himself into the belief that he had never wronged her.

Raymond staggered forth from this scene, as a man might do, who had been just put to the torture, and looked forward to when it would be again inflicted. He had sinned against his own honor, by affirming, swearing to, a direct falsehood; true this he had palmed on a woman, and it might therefore be deemed less base - by others - not by him; - for whom had he deceived? - his own trusting, devoted, affectionate Perdita, whose generous belief galled him doubly, when he remembered the parade of innocence with which it had been exacted. The mind of Raymond was not so rough cast, nor had been so rudely handled, in the circumstance of life, as to make him proof to these considerations - on the contrary, he was all nerve; his spirit was as a pure fire, which fades and shrinks from every contagion of foul atmosphere: but now the contagion had become incorporated with its essence, and the change was the more painful. Truth and falsehood, love and hate lost their eternal boundaries, heaven rushed in to mingle with hell; while his sensitive mind, turned to a field for such battle, was stung to madness. He heartily despised himself, he was angry with Perdita, and the idea of Evadne was attended by all that was hideous and cruel. His passions, always his masters, acquired fresh strength, from the long sleep in which love had cradled them, the clinging weight of destiny bent him down; he was goaded, tortured, fiercely impatient of that worst of miseries, the sense of remorse. This troubled state yielded by degrees, to sullen animosity, and depression of spirits. His dependents, even his equals, if in his present post he had any, were startled to find anger, derision, and bitterness in one, before distinguished for suavity and benevolence of manner. He transacted public business with distaste and hastened from it to the solitude which was at once his bane and relief. He mounted a fiery horse, that which had borne him forward to victory in Greece; he fatigued himself with deadening exercise, losing the pangs of a troubled mind in animal sensation.

He slowly recovered himself; yet, at last, as one might from the effects of poison, he lifted his head from above the vapors of fever and passion into the still atmosphere of calm reflection. He meditated on what was best to be done. He was first struck by the space of time that had elapsed, since madness, rather than any reasonable impulse, had regulated his actions. A month had gone by, and during that time he had not seen Evadne. Her power, which was linked to few of the enduring emotions of his heart, had greatly decayed. He was no longer her slave - no longer her lover: he would never see her more, and by the completeness of his return, deserve the confidence of Perdita.

Yet, as he thus determined, fancy conjured up the miserable abode of the Greek girl. An abode, which from noble and lofty principle, she had refused to exchange for one of greater luxury. He thought of the splendor of her situation and appearance when he first knew her; he thought of her life at Constantinople, attended by every circumstance of oriental magnificence; of her present penury, her daily task of industry, her lorn state, her faded, famine-struck cheek. Compassion swelled his breast; he would see her once again; he would devise some plan for restoring her to society, and the enjoyment of her rank; their separation would then follow, as a matter of course.

Again, he thought, how during this long month, he had avoided Perdita, flying from her as from the stings of his own conscience. But he was awake now; all this should be remedied; and future devotion erase the memory of this only blot on the serenity of their life. He became cheerful, as he thought of this, and soberly and resolutely marked out the line of conduct he would adopt. He remembered that he had promised Perdita to be present this very evening (the 19th of October, anniversary of his election as Protector) at a festival given in his honor. Good augury should this festival be of the happiness of future years. First, he would look in on Evadne; he would not stay; but he owed her some account, some compensation for his long and unannounced absence; and then to Perdita, to the forgotten world, to the duties of society, the splendor of rank, the enjoyment of power.

After the scene sketched in the preceding pages, Perdita had contemplated an entire change in the manners and conduct of Raymond. She expected freedom of communication, and a return to those habits of affectionate intercourse which had formed the delight of her life. But Raymond did not join her in any of her avocations. He transacted the business of the day apart from her; he went out, she knew not whither. The pain inflicted by this disappointment was tormenting and keen. She looked on it as a deceitful dream and tried to throw off the consciousness of it; but like the shirt of Nessus, it clung to her very flesh, and ate with sharp agony into her vital principle. She possessed that (though such an assertion may appear a paradox) which belongs to few, a capacity of happiness. Her delicate organization and creative imagination rendered her peculiarly susceptible of pleasurable emotion. The overflowing warmth of her heart, by making love a plant of deep root and stately growth, had attuned her whole soul to the reception of happiness, when she found in Raymond all that could adorn love and satisfy her imagination. But if the sentiment on which the fabric of her existence was founded, became common place through participation, the endless succession of attentions and graceful action snapped by transfer, his universe of love wrested from her, happiness must depart, and then be exchanged for its opposite. The same peculiarities of character rendered her sorrows agonies; her fancy magnified them; her sensibility made her forever open to their renewed impression; love envenomed the heart-piercing sting. There was neither submission, patience, nor self-abandonment in her grief; she fought with it, struggled beneath it, and rendered every pang sharper by resistance. Again, and again the idea recurred, that he loved another. She did him justice; she believed that he felt a tender affection for her; but give a paltry prize to him who in some life-pending lottery has calculated on the possession of tens of thousands, and it will disappoint him more than a blank. The affection and amity of a Raymond might be inestimable; but, beyond that affection, embosomed deeper than friendship, was the indivisible treasure of love. Take the sum in its completeness, and no arithmetic can calculate its price; take from it the smallest portion, give it but the name of parts, separate it into degrees and sections, and like the magician's coin, the valueless gold of the mine, is turned to vilest substance. There is a meaning in the eye of love; a cadence in its voice, an irradiation in its smile, the talisman of whose enchantments one only can possess; its spirit is elemental, its essence single, its divinity an unit. The very heart and soul of Raymond and Perdita had mingled, even as two mountain brooks that join in their descent, and murmuring and sparkling flow over shining pebbles, beside starry flowers; but let one desert its primal course, or be dammed up by choking obstruction, and the other shrinks in its altered banks. Perdita was sensible of the failing of the tide that fed her life. Unable to support the slow withering of her hopes, she suddenly formed a plan, resolving to terminate at once the period of misery, and to bring to an happy conclusion the late disastrous events.

The anniversary was at hand of the exaltation of Raymond to the office of Protector; and it was customary to celebrate this day by a splendid festival. A variety of feelings urged Perdita to shed double magnificence over the scene; yet, as she arrayed herself for the evening gala, she wondered herself at the pains she took, to render sumptuous the celebration of an event which appeared to her the beginning of her sufferings. Woe befall the day, she thought, woe, tears, and mourning betide the hour, that gave Raymond another hope than love, another wish than my devotion; and thrice joyful the moment when he shall be restored to me! God knows, I put my trust in his vows, and believe his asserted faith - but for that, I would not seek what I am now resolved to attain. Shall two years more be thus passed, each day adding to our alienation, each act being another stone piled on the barrier which separates us? No, my Raymond, my only beloved, sole possession of Perdita! This night, this splendid assembly, these sumptuous apartments, and this adornment of your tearful girl, are all united to celebrate your abdication. Once for me, you relinquished the prospect of a crown. That was in days of early love, when I could only hold out the hope, not the assurance of happiness.

Now you have the experience of all that I can give, the heart's devotion, taintless love, and unhesitating subjection to you. You must choose between these and your protectorate. This, proud noble, is your last night! Perdita has bestowed on it all of magnificent and dazzling that your heart best loves - but, from these gorgeous rooms, from this princely attendance, from power and elevation, you must return with to-morrow's sun to our rural abode; for I would not buy an immortality of joy, by the endurance of one more week sister to the last.

Brooding over this plan, resolved when the hour should come, to propose, and insist upon its accomplishment, secure of his consent, the heart of Perdita was lightened, or rather exalted. Her cheek was flushed by the expectation of struggle; her eyes sparkled with the hope of triumph. Having cast her fate upon a die, and feeling secure of winning, she, whom I have named as bearing the stamp of queen of nations on her noble brow, now rose superior to humanity, and seemed in calm power, to arrest with her finger, the wheel of destiny. She had never before looked so supremely lovely.

We, the Arcadian shepherds of the tale, had intended to be present at this festivity, but Perdita wrote to entreat us not to come, or to absent ourselves from Windsor; for she (though she did not reveal her scheme to us) resolved the next morning to return with Raymond to our dear circle, there to renew a course of life in which she had found entire felicity. Late in the evening she entered the apartments appropriated to the festival. Raymond had quitted the palace the night before; he had promised to grace the assembly, but he had not yet returned. Still she felt sure that he would come at last; and the wider the breach might appear at this crisis, the more secure she was of closing it forever.

It was as I said, the nineteenth of October; the autumn was far advanced and dreary. The wind howled; the half bare trees were despoiled of the remainder of their summer ornament; the state of the air which induced the decay of vegetation, was hostile to cheerfulness or hope. Raymond had been exalted by the determination he had made; but with the declining day his spirits declined. First, he was to visit Evadne, and then to hasten to the palace of the Protectorate. As he walked through the wretched streets in the neighborhood of the luckless Greek's abode, his heart smote him for the whole course of his conduct towards her. First, his having entered into any engagement that should permit her to remain in such a state of degradation; and then, after a short wild dream, having left her to drear solitude, anxious conjecture, and bitter, still - disappointed expectation. What had she done the while, how supported his absence and neglect? Light grew dim in these close streets, and when the well-known door was opened, the staircase was shrouded in perfect night. He groped his way up, he entered the garret, he found Evadne stretched speechless, almost lifeless on her wretched bed. He called for the people of the house, but could learn nothing from them, except that they knew nothing. Her story was plain to him, plain and distinct as the remorse and horror that darted their fangs into him. When she found herself forsaken by him, she lost the heart to pursue her usual avocations; pride forbade every application to him; famine was welcomed as the kind porter to the gates of death, within whose opening folds she should now, without sin, quickly repose. No creature came near her, as her strength failed.

If she died, where could there be found on record a murderer, whose cruel act might compare with his? What fiend more wanton in his mischief, what damned soul more worthy of perdition! But he was not reserved for this agony of self-reproach. He sent for medical assistance; the hours passed, spun by suspense into ages; the darkness of the long autumnal night yielded today, before her life was secure. He had her then removed to a more commodious dwelling, and hovered about her, again and again to assure himself that she was safe.

In the midst of his greatest suspense and fear as to the event, he remembered the festival given in his honor, by Perdita; in his honor then, when misery and death were affixing indelible disgrace to his name, honor to him whose crimes deserved a scaffold; this was the worst mockery. Still Perdita would expect him; he wrote a few incoherent words on a scrap of paper, testifying that he was well, and bade the woman of the house take it to the palace, and deliver it into the hands of the wife of the Lord Protector. The woman, who did not know him, contemptuously asked, how he thought she should gain admittance, particularly on a festal night, to that lady's presence? Raymond gave her his ring to ensure the respect of the menials. Thus, while Perdita was entertaining her guests, and anxiously awaiting the arrival of her lord, his ring was brought her; and she was told that a poor woman had a note to deliver to her from its wearer.

The vanity of the old gossip was raised by her commission, which, after all, she did not understand, since she had no suspicion, even now that Evadne's visitor was Lord Raymond. Perdita dreaded a fall from his horse, or some similar accident - till the woman's answers woke other fears. From a feeling of cunning blindly exercised, the officious, if not malignant messenger, did not speak of Evadne's illness; but she garrulously gave an account of Raymond's frequent visits, adding to her narration such circumstances, as, while they convinced Perdita of its truth, exaggerated the unkindness and perfidy of Raymond. Worst of all, his absence now from the festival, his message wholly unaccounted for, except by the disgraceful hints of the woman, appeared the deadliest insult. Again, she looked at the ring, it was a small ruby, almost heart-shaped, which she had herself given him. She looked at the hand-writing, which she could not mistake, and repeated to herself the words - "Do not, I charge you, I entreat you, permit your guests to wonder at my absence:" the while the old crone going on with her talk, filled her ear with a strange medley of truth and falsehood. At length Perdita dismissed her.

The poor girl returned to the assembly, where her presence had not been missed. She glided into a recess somewhat obscured, and leaning against an ornamental column there placed, tried to recover herself. Her faculties were palsied. She gazed on some flowers that stood near in a carved vase: that morning she had arranged them, they were rare and lovely plants; even now all aghast as she was, she observed their brilliant colors and starry shapes. - "Divine infoliations of the spirit of beauty," she exclaimed, "Ye droop not, neither do ye mourn; the despair that clasps my heart, has not spread contagion over you! — Why am I not a partner of your insensibility, a sharer in your calm!"

She paused. "To my task," she continued mentally, "my guests must not perceive the reality, either as it regards him or me. I obey; they shall not, though I die the moment they are gone. They shall behold the antipodes of what is real — for I will appear to live — while I am — dead." It required all her self-command, to suppress the gush of tears self-pity caused at this idea. After many struggles, she succeeded, and turned to join the company.

All her efforts were now directed to the dissembling her internal conflict. She had to play the part of a courteous hostess; to attend to all; to shine the focus of enjoyment and grace. She had to do this, while in deep woe she sighed for loneliness, and would gladly have exchanged her crowded rooms for dark forest depths, or a drear, night-enshadowed heath. But she became gay. She could not keep in the medium, nor be, as was usual with her, placidly content. Every one remarked her exhilaration of spirits; as all actions appear graceful in the eye of rank, her guests surrounded her applaudingly, although there was a sharpness in her laugh, and an abruptness in her sallies, which might have betrayed her secret to an attentive observer. She went on, feeling that, if she had paused for a moment, the checked waters of misery would have deluged her soul, that her wrecked hopes would raise their wailing voices, and that those who now echoed her mirth, and provoked her repartees, would have shrunk in fear from her convulsive despair. Her only consolation during the violence which she did herself, was to watch the motions of an illuminated clock, and internally count the moments which must elapse before she could be alone.

At length the rooms began to thin. Mocking her own desires, she rallied her guests on their early departure. One by one they left her — at length she pressed the hand of her last visitor. "How cold and damp your hand is," said her friend; "you are over fatigued, pray hasten to rest." Perdita smiled faintly — her guest left her; the carriage rolling down the street assured the final departure. Then, as if pursued by an enemy, as if wings had been at her feet, she flew to her own apartment, she dismissed her attendants, she locked the doors, she threw herself wildly on the floor, she bit her lips even to blood to suppress her shrieks, and lay long a prey to the vulture of despair, striving not to think, while multitudinous ideas made a home of her heart; and ideas, horrid as furies, cruel as vipers, and poured in with such swift succession, that they seemed to jostle and wound each other, while they worked her up to madness.

At length she rose, more composed, not less miserable. She stood before a large mirror — she gazed on her reflected image; her light and graceful dress, the jewels that studded her hair, and encircled her beauteous arms and neck, her small feet shod in satin, her profuse and glossy tresses, all were to her clouded brow and woe-begone countenance like a gorgeous frame to a dark tempest-pourtraying picture. "Vase am I," she thought, "vase brimful of despair's direst essence. Farewell, Perdita! farewell, poor girl! never again will you see yourself thus; luxury and wealth are no longer yours; in the excess of your poverty you may envy the homeless beggar; most truly am I without a home! I live on a barren desart, which, wide and interminable, brings forth neither fruit or flower; in the midst is a solitary rock, to which thou, Perdita, art chained, and thou seest the dreary level stretch far away."

She threw open her window, which looked on the palace-garden. Light and darkness were struggling together, and the orient was streaked by roseate and golden rays. One star only trembled in the depth of the kindling atmosphere. The morning air blowing freshly over the dewy plants, rushed into the heated room. "All things go on," thought Perdita, "all things proceed, decay, and perish! When noontide has passed, and the weary day has driven her team to their western stalls, the fires of heaven rise from the East, moving in their accustomed path, they ascend and descend the skiey hill. When their course is fulfilled, the dial begins to cast westward an uncertain shadow; the eye-lids of day are opened, and birds and flowers, the startled vegetation, and fresh breeze awaken; the sun at length appears, and in majestic procession climbs the capitol of heaven. All proceeds, changes and dies, except the sense of misery in my bursting heart.

"Ay, all proceeds and changes: what wonder then, that love has journeyed on to its setting, and that the lord of my life has changed? We call the supernal lights fixed, yet they wander about yonder plain, and if I look again where I looked an hour ago, the face of the eternal heavens is altered. The silly moon and inconstant planets vary nightly their erratic dance; the sun itself, sovereign of the sky, ever and anon deserts his throne, and leaves his dominion to night and winter. Nature grows old, and shakes in her decaying limbs, - creation has become bankrupt! What wonder then that eclipse and death have led to destruction the light of thy life, O Perdita!"

CHAPTER IX

Thus, sad and disarranged were the thoughts of my poor sister, when she became assured of the infidelity of Raymond. All her virtues and all her defects tended to make the blow incurable. Her affection for me, her brother, for Adrian and Idris, was subject as it were to the reigning passion of her heart; even her maternal tenderness borrowed half its force from the delight she had in tracing Raymond's features and expression in the infant's countenance. She had been reserved and even stern in childhood; but love had softened the asperities of her character, and her union with Raymond had caused her talents and affections to unfold themselves; the one betrayed, and the other lost, she in some degree returned to her ancient disposition. The concentrated pride of her nature, forgotten during her blissful dream, awoke, and with its adder's sting pierced her heart; her humility of spirit augmented the power of the venom; she had been exalted in her own estimation, while distinguished by his love: of what worth was she, now that he thrust her from this preferment? She had been proud of having won and preserved him - but another had won him from her, and her exultation was as cold as a water quenched ember.

We, in our retirement, remained long in ignorance of her misfortune. Soon after the festival she had sent for her child, and then she seemed to have forgotten us. Adrian observed a change during a visit that he afterward paid them; but he could not tell its extent or divine the cause. They still appeared in public together and lived under the same roof. Raymond was as usual courteous, though there was, on occasions, an unbidden haughtiness, or painful abruptness in his manners, which startled his gentle friend; his brow was not clouded but disdain sat on his lips, and his voice was harsh. Perdita was all kindness and attention to her lord; but she was silent, and beyond words sad. She had grown thin and pale; and her eyes often filled with tears. Sometimes she looked at Raymond, as if to say - That it should be so! At others her countenance expressed - I will still do all I can to make you happy. But Adrian read with uncertain aim the character of her face and might mistake. - Clara was always with her, and she seemed most at ease, when, in an obscure corner, she could sit holding her child's hand, silent and lonely. Still Adrian was unable to guess the truth; he entreated them to visit us at Windsor, and they promised to come during the following month.

It was May before they arrived: the season had decked the forest trees with leaves, and its paths with a thousand flowers. We had notice of their intention the day before; and, early in the morning, Perdita arrived with her daughter. Raymond would follow soon, she said; he had been detained by business. According to Adrian's account, I had expected to find her sad; but, on the contrary, she appeared in the highest spirits: true, she had grown thin, her eyes were somewhat hollow, and her cheeks sunk, though tinged by a bright glow. She was delighted to see us; caressed our children, praised their growth and improvement; Clara also was pleased to meet again her young friend Alfred; all kinds of childish games were entered into, in which Perdita joined. She communicated her gaiety to us, and as we amused ourselves on the Castle Terrace, it appeared that a happier, less care-worn party could not have been assembled. "This is better, Mamma," said Clara, "than being in that dismal London, where you often cry, and never laugh as you do now."..."Silence, little foolish thing," replied her mother, "and remember any one that mentions London is sent to Coventry for an hour."

Soon after, Raymond arrived. He did not join as usual in the playful spirit of the rest; but, entering into conversation with Adrian and myself, by degrees we seceded from our companions, and Idris and Perdita only remained with the children. Raymond talked of his new buildings; of his plan for an establishment for the better education of the poor; as usual Adrian and he entered into argument, and the time slipped away unperceived.

We assembled again towards evening, and Perdita insisted on our having recourse to music. She wanted, she said, to give us a specimen of her new accomplishment; for since she had been in London, she had applied herself to music, and sang, without much power, but with a great deal of sweetness. We were not permitted by her to select any but light-hearted melodies; and all the Operas of Mozart were called into service, that we might choose the most exhilarating of his airs. Among the other transcendent attributes of Mozart's music, it possesses more than any other that of appearing to come from the heart; you enter into the passions expressed by him, and are transported with grief, joy, anger, or confusion, as he, our soul's master, chooses to inspire. For some time, the spirit of hilarity was kept up; but, at length, Perdita receded from the piano, for Raymond had joined in the trio of , Taci ingiusto core, in Don Giovanni, whose arch entreaty was softened by him into tenderness, and thrilled her heart with memories of the changed past; it was the same voice, the same tone, the self-same sounds and words, which often before she had received, as the homage of love to her — no longer was it that; and this concord of sound with its dissonance of expression penetrated her with regret and despair. Soon after Idris, who was at the harp, turned to that passionate and sorrowful air in Figaro, Porgi, amor, qualche risforo, in which the deserted Countess laments the change of the faithless Almaviva. The soul of tender sorrow is breathed forth in this strain; and the sweet voice of Idris, sustained by the mournful chords of her instrument, added to the expression of the words. During the pathetic appeal with which it concludes, a stifled sob attracted our attention to Perdita, the cessation of the music recalled her to herself, she hastened out of the hall - I followed her. At first, she seemed to wish to shun me; and then, yielding to my earnest questioning, she threw herself on my neck, and wept aloud: - "Once more," she cried, "once more on your friendly breast, my beloved brother, can the lost Perdita pour forth her sorrows. I had imposed a law of silence on myself; and for months I have kept it. I do wrong in weeping now, and greater wrong in giving words to my grief. I will not speak! Be it enough for you to know that I am miserable - be it enough for you to know, that the painted veil of life is rent, that I sit for ever shrouded in darkness and gloom, that grief is my sister, everlasting lamentation my mate!"

I endeavored to console her; I did not question her! but I caressed her, assured her of my deepest affection and my intense interest in the changes of her fortune: "Dear words," she cried, "expressions of love come upon my ear, like the remembered sounds of forgotten music, that had been dear to me. They are vain, I know; how very vain in their attempt to soothe or comfort me. Dearest Lionel, you cannot guess what I have suffered during these long months. I have read of mourners in ancient days, who clothed themselves in sackcloth, scattered dust upon their heads, ate their bread mingled with ashes, and took up their abode on the bleak mountain tops, reproaching heaven and earth aloud with their misfortunes. Why this is the very luxury of sorrow! thus one might go on from day to day contriving new extravagances, reveling in the paraphernalia of woe, wedded to all the appurtenances of despair. Alas! I must forever conceal the wretchedness that consumes me. I must weave a veil of dazzling falsehood to hide my grief from vulgar eyes, smooth my brow, and paint my lips in deceitful smiles - even in solitude I dare not think how lost I am, lest I become insane and rave."

The tears and agitation of my poor sister had rendered her unfit to return to the circle we had left — so I persuaded her to let me drive her through the park; and, during the ride, I induced her to confide the tale of her unhappiness to me, fancying that talking of it would lighten the burthen, and certain that, if there were a remedy, it should be found and secured to her.

Several weeks had elapsed since the festival of the anniversary, and she had been unable to calm her mind, or to subdue her thoughts to any regular train. Sometimes she reproached herself for taking too bitterly to heart, that which many would esteem an imaginary evil; but this was no subject for reason; and, ignorant as she was of the motives and true conduct of Raymond, things assumed for her even a worse appearance, than the reality warranted. He was seldom at the palace; never, but when he was assured that his public duties would prevent his remaining alone with Perdita. They seldom addressed each other, shunning explanation, each fearing any communication the other might make. Suddenly, however, the manners of Raymond changed; he appeared to desire to find opportunities of bringing about a return to kindness and intimacy with my sister. The tide of love towards her appeared to flow again; he could never forget, how once he had been devoted to her, making her the shrine and storehouse wherein to place every thought and every sentiment. Shame seemed to hold him back; yet he evidently wished to establish a renewal of confidence and affection. From the moment Perdita had sufficiently recovered herself to form any plan of action, she had laid one down, which now she prepared to follow. She received these tokens of returning love with gentleness; she did not shun his company; but she endeavored to place a barrier in the way of familiar intercourse or painful discussion, which mingled pride and shame prevented Raymond from surmounting. He began at last to shew signs of angry impatience, and Perdita became aware that the system she had adopted could not continue; she must explain herself to him; she could not summon courage to speak - she wrote thus:

"Read this letter with patience, I entreat you. It will contain no reproaches. Reproach is indeed an idle word: for what should I reproach you?

"Allow me in some degree to explain my feeling; without that, we shall both grope in the dark, mistaking one another; erring from the path which may conduct, one of us at least, to a more eligible mode of life than that led by either during the last few weeks.

"I loved you - I love you - neither anger nor pride dictates these lines, but a feeling beyond, deeper, and more unalterable than either. My affections are wounded; it is impossible to heal them: - cease then the vain endeavor, if indeed that way your endeavors tend. Forgiveness! Return! Idle words are these! I forgive the pain I endure; but the trodden path cannot be retraced.

"Common affection might have been satisfied with common usages. I believed that you read my heart, and knew its devotion, its unalienable fidelity towards you. I never loved any but you. You came the embodied image of my fondest dreams. The praise of men, power and high aspirations attended your career. Love for you invested the world for me in enchanted light; it was no longer the earth I trod — the earth, common mother, yielding only trite and stale repetition of objects and circumstances old and worn out. I lived in a temple glorified by intense sense of devotion and rapture; I walked, a consecrated being, contemplating only your power, your excellence.

> For O, you stood beside me, like my youth,
> Transformed for me the real to a dream,
> Clothing the palpable and familiar
> With golden exhalations of the dawn.

'The bloom has vanished from my life' - there is no morning to this all investing night; no rising to the set-sun of love. In those days the rest of the world was nothing to me: all other men - I never considered nor felt what they were; nor did I look on you as one of them. Separated from them; exalted in my heart; sole possessor of my affections; single object of my hopes, the best half of myself.

"Ah, Raymond, were we not happy? Did the sunshine on any, who could enjoy its light with purer and more intense bliss? It was not - it is not a common infidelity at which I repine. It is the disunion of an whole which may not have parts; it is the carelessness with which you have shaken off the mantle of election with which to me you were invested, and have become one among the many. Dream not to alter this. Is not love a divinity, because it is immortal? Did not I appear sanctified, even to myself, because this love had for its temple my heart? I have gazed on you as you slept, melted even to tears, as the idea filled my mind, that all I possessed lay cradled in those idolized, but mortal lineaments before me. Yet, even then, I have checked thick-coming fears with one thought; I would not fear death, for the emotions that linked us must be immortal.

"And now I do not fear death. I should be well pleased to close my eyes, never more to open them again. And yet I fear it; even as I fear all things; for in any state of being linked by the chain of memory with this, happiness would not return - even in Paradise, I must feel that your love was less enduring than the mortal beatings of my fragile heart, every pulse of which knells audibly,

> The funeral note
> Of love, deep buried, without resurrection.
> No – no - me miserable; for love extinct there is no resurrection!

"Yet I love you. Yet, and forever, would I contribute all I possess to your welfare. On account of a tattling world, for the sake of my - of our child, I would remain by you, Raymond, share your fortunes, partake your counsel. Shall it be thus? We are no longer lovers; nor can I call myself a friend to any; since, lost as I am, I have no thought to spare from my own wretched, engrossing self. But it will please me to see you each day! to listen to the public voice praising you; to keep up your paternal love for our girl; to hear your voice; to know that I am near you, though you are no longer mine.

"If you wish to break the chains that bind us, say the word, and it shall be done - I will take all the blame on myself, of harshness or unkindness, in the world's eye.

"Yet, as I have said, I should be best pleased, at least for the present, to live under the same roof with you. When the fever of my young life is spent; when placid age shall tame the vulture that devours me, friendship may come, love and hope being dead. May this be true? Can my soul, inextricably linked to this perishable frame, become lethargic and cold, even as this sensitive mechanism shall lose its youthful elasticity? Then, with lack-luster eyes, grey hairs, and wrinkled brow, though now the words sound hollow and meaningless, then, tottering on the grave's extreme edge, I may be - your affectionate and true friend,

"PERDITA."

Raymond's answer was brief. What indeed could he reply to her complaints, to her griefs which she jealously paled round, keeping out all thought of remedy. "Notwithstanding your bitter letter," he wrote, "for bitter I must call it, you are the chief person in my estimation, and it is your happiness that I would principally consult. Do that which seems best to you: and if you can receive gratification from one mode of life in preference to another, do not let me be any obstacle. I foresee that the plan which you mark out in your letter will not endure long; but you are mistress of yourself, and it is my sincere wish to contribute as far as you will permit me to your happiness."

"Raymond has prophesied well," said Perdita, "alas, that it should be so! our present mode of life cannot continue long, yet I will not be the first to propose alteration. He beholds in me one whom he has injured even unto death; and I derive no hope from his kindness; no change can possibly be brought about even by his best intentions. As well might Cleopatra have worn as an ornament the vinegar which contained her dissolved pearl, as I be content with the love that Raymond can now offer me."

I own that I did not see her misfortune with the same eyes as Perdita. At all events methought that the wound could be healed; and, if they remained together, it would be so. I endeavored therefore to sooth and soften her mind; and it was not until after many endeavors that I gave up the task as impracticable. Perdita listened to me impatiently, and answered with some asperity: - "Do you think that any of your arguments are new to me? or that my own burning wishes and intense anguish have not suggested them all a thousand times, with far more eagerness and subtlety than you can put into them? Lionel, you cannot understand what woman's love is. In days of happiness I have often repeated to myself, with a grateful heart and exulting spirit, all that Raymond sacrificed for me. I was a poor, uneducated, unbefriended, mountain girl, raised from nothingness by him. All that I possessed of the luxuries of life came from him. He gave me an illustrious name and noble station; the world's respect reflected from his own glory: all this joined to his own undying love, inspired me with sensations towards him, akin to those with which we regard the Giver of life. I gave him love only. I devoted myself to him: imperfect creature that I was, I took myself to task, that I might become worthy of him. I watched over my hasty temper, subdued my burning impatience of character, schooled my self-engrossing thoughts, educating myself to the best perfection I might attain, that the fruit of my exertions might be his happiness. I took no merit to myself for this. He deserved it all—all labor, all devotion, all sacrifice; I would have toiled up a scaleless Alp, to pluck a flower that would please him. I was ready to quit you all, my beloved and gifted companions, and to live only with him, for him. I could not do otherwise, even if I had wished; for if we are said to have two souls, he was my better soul, to which the other was a perpetual slave. One only return did he owe me, even fidelity. I earned that; I deserved it. Because I was mountain bred, unallied to the noble and wealthy, shall he think to repay me by an empty name and station? Let him take them back; without his love they are nothing to me. Their only merit in my eyes was that they were his."

Thus, passionately Perdita ran on. When I adverted to the question of their entire separation, she replied: "Be it so! One day the period will arrive; I know it and feel it. But in this I am a coward. This imperfect companionship, and our masquerade of union, are strangely dear to me. It is painful, I allow, destructive, impracticable. It keeps up a perpetual fever in my veins; it frets my immedicable wound; it is instinct with poison. Yet I must cling to it; perhaps it will kill me soon, and thus perform a thankful office."

In the meantime, Raymond had remained with Adrian and Idris. He was naturally frank; the continued absence of Perdita and myself became remarkable; and Raymond soon found relief from the constraint of months, by an unreserved confidence with his two friends. He related to them the situation in which he had found Evadne. At first, from delicacy to Adrian he concealed her name; but it was divulged in the course of his narrative, and her former lover heard with the most acute agitation the history of her sufferings. Idris had shared Perdita's ill opinion of the Greek; but Raymond's account softened and interested her. Evadne's constancy, fortitude, even her ill-fated and ill-regulated love, were matter of admiration and pity; especially when, from the detail of the events of the nineteenth of October, it was apparent that she preferred suffering and death to any in her eyes degrading application for the pity and assistance of her lover. Her subsequent conduct did not diminish this interest. At first, relieved from famine and the grave, watched over by Raymond with the tenderest assiduity, with that feeling of repose peculiar to convalescence, Evadne gave herself up to rapturous gratitude and love. But reflection returned with health. She questioned him with regard to the motives which had occasioned his critical absence. She framed her enquiries with Greek subtlety; she formed her conclusions with the decision and firmness peculiar to her disposition. She could not divine, that the breach which she had occasioned between Raymond and Perdita was already irreparable: but she knew, that under the present system it would be widened each day, and that its result must be to destroy her lover's happiness, and to implant the fangs of remorse in his heart. From the moment that she perceived the right line of conduct, she resolved to adopt it, and to part from Raymond forever. Conflicting passions, long-cherished love, and self-inflicted disappointment made her regard death alone as sufficient refuge for her woe. But the same feelings and opinions which had before restrained her, acted with redoubled force; for she knew that the reflection that he had occasioned her death, would pursue Raymond through life, poisoning every enjoyment, clouding every prospect. Besides, though the violence of her anguish made life hateful, it had not yet produced that monotonous, lethargic sense of changeless misery which for the most part produces suicide. Her energy of character induced her still to combat with the ills of life; even those attendant on hopeless love presented themselves, rather in the shape of an adversary to be overcome, than of a victor to whom she must submit. Besides, she had memories of past tenderness to cherish, smiles, words, and even tears, to con over, which, though remembered in desertion and sorrow, were to be preferred to the forgetfulness of the grave. It was impossible to guess at the whole of her plan. Her letter to Raymond gave no clue for discovery; it assured him, that she was in no danger of wanting the means of life; she promised in it to preserve herself, and some future day perhaps to present herself to him in a station not unworthy of her. She then bade him, with the eloquence of despair and of unalterable love, a last farewell.

All these circumstances were now related to Adrian and Idris. Raymond then lamented the cureless evil of his situation with Perdita. He declared, notwithstanding her harshness, he even called it coldness, that he loved her. He had been ready once with the humility of a penitent, and the duty of a vassal, to surrender himself to her; giving up his very soul to her tutelage, to become her pupil, her slave, her bondsman. She had rejected these advances; and the time for such exuberant submission, which must be founded on love and nourished by it, was now passed. Still all his wishes and endeavors were directed towards her peace, and his chief discomfort arose from the perception that he exerted himself in vain. If she were to continue inflexible in the line of conduct, she now pursued, they must part. The combinations and occurrences of this senseless mode of intercourse were maddening to him. Yet he would not propose the separation. He was haunted by the fear of causing the death of one or other of the beings implicated in these events; and he could not persuade himself to undertake to direct the course of events, lest, ignorant of the land he traversed, he should lead those attached to the car into irremediable ruin.

After a discussion on this subject, which lasted for several hours, he took leave of his friends, and returned to town, unwilling to meet Perdita before us, conscious, as we all must be, of the thoughts uppermost in the minds of both. Perdita prepared to follow him with her child. Idris endeavored to persuade her to remain. My poor sister looked at the counsellor with affright. She knew that Raymond had conversed with her; had he instigated this request? — was this to be the prelude to their eternal separation? — I have said, that the defects of her character awoke and acquired vigor from her unnatural position. She regarded with suspicion the invitation of Idris; she embraced me, as if she were about to be deprived of my affection also: calling me her more than brother, her only friend, her last hope, she pathetically conjured me not to cease to love her; and with increased anxiety she departed for London, the scene and cause of all her misery.

The scenes that followed, convinced her that she had not yet fathomed the obscure gulph into which she had plunged. Her unhappiness assumed every day a new shape; every day some unexpected event seemed to close, while in fact it led onward, the train of calamities which now befell her.

The selected passion of the soul of Raymond was ambition. Readiness of talent, a capacity of entering into, and leading the dispositions of men; earnest desire of distinction were the awakeners and nurses of his ambition. But other ingredients mingled with these, and prevented him from becoming the calculating, determined character, which alone forms a successful hero. He was obstinate, but not firm; benevolent in his first movements; harsh and reckless when provoked. Above all, he was remorseless and unyielding in the pursuit of any object of desire, however lawless. Love of pleasure, and the softer sensibilities of our nature, made a prominent part of his character, conquering the conqueror; holding him in at the moment of acquisition; sweeping away ambition's web; making him forget the toil of weeks, for the sake of one moment's indulgence of the new and actual object of his wishes. Obeying these impulses, he had become the husband of Perdita: egged on by them, he found himself the lover of Evadne. He had now lost both. He had neither the ennobling self-gratulation, which constancy inspires, to console him, nor the voluptuous sense of abandonment to a forbidden, but intoxicating passion. His heart was exhausted by the recent events; his enjoyment of life was destroyed by the resentment of Perdita, and the flight of Evadne; and the inflexibility of the former, set the last seal upon the annihilation of his hopes. As long as their disunion remained a secret, he cherished an expectation of reawakening past tenderness in her bosom; now that we were all made acquainted with these occurrences, and that Perdita, by declaring her resolves to others, in a manner pledged herself to their accomplishment, he gave up the idea of re-union as futile, and sought only, since he was unable to influence her to change, to reconcile himself to the present state of things. He made a vow against love and its train of struggles, disappointment and remorse, and sought in mere sensual enjoyment, a remedy for the injurious inroads of passion.

Debasement of character is the certain follower of such pursuits. Yet this consequence would not have been immediately remarkable, if Raymond had continued to apply himself to the execution of his plans for the public benefit, and the fulfilling his duties as Protector. But, extreme in all things, given up to immediate impressions, he entered with ardor into this new pursuit of pleasure, and followed up the incongruous intimacies occasioned by it without reflection or foresight. The council-chamber was deserted; the crowds which attended on him as agents to his various projects were neglected. Festivity, and even libertinism, became the order of the day.

Perdita beheld with affright the increasing disorder. For a moment she thought that she could stem the torrent, and that Raymond could be induced to hear reason from her. - Vain hope! The moment of her influence was passed. He listened with haughtiness, replied disdainfully; and, if in truth, she succeeded in awakening his conscience, the sole effect was that he sought an opiate for the pang in oblivious riot. With the energy natural to her, Perdita then endeavored to supply his place. Their still apparent union permitted her to do much; but no woman could, in the end, present a remedy to the increasing negligence of the Protector; who, as if seized with a paroxysm of insanity, trampled on all ceremony, all order, all duty, and gave himself up to license.

Reports of these strange proceedings reached us, and we were undecided what method to adopt to restore our friend to himself and his country, when Perdita suddenly appeared among us. She detailed the progress of the mournful change, and entreated Adrian and myself to go up to London, and endeavor to remedy the increasing evil: - "Tell him," she cried, "tell Lord Raymond, that my presence shall no longer annoy him. That he need not plunge into this destructive dissipation for the sake of disgusting me and causing me to fly. This purpose is now accomplished; he will never see me more. But let me, it is my last entreaty, let me in the praises of his countrymen and the prosperity of England, find the choice of my youth justified."

During our ride up to town, Adrian and I discussed and argued upon Raymond's conduct, and his falling off from the hopes of permanent excellence on his part, which he had before given us cause to entertain. My friend and I had both been educated in one school, or rather I was his pupil in the opinion, that steady adherence to principle was the only road to honor; a ceaseless observance of the laws of general utility, the only conscientious aim of human ambition. But though we both entertained these ideas, we differed in their application. Resentment added also a sting to my censure; and I reprobated Raymond's conduct in severe terms. Adrian was more benign, more considerate. He admitted that the principles that I laid down were the best; but he denied that they were the only ones. Quoting the text, there are many mansions in my father's house, he insisted that the modes of becoming good or great, varied as much as the dispositions of men, of whom it might be said, as of the leaves of the forest, there were no two alike.

We arrived in London at about eleven at night. We conjectured, notwithstanding what we had heard, that we should find Raymond in St. Stephen's: thither we sped. The chamber was full - but there was no Protector; and there was an austere discontent manifest on the countenances of the leaders, and a whispering and busy tattle among the underlings, not less ominous. We hastened to the palace of the Protectorate. We found Raymond in his dining room with six others: the bottle was being pushed about merrily and had made considerable inroads on the understanding of one or two. He who sat near Raymond was telling a story, which convulsed the rest with laughter.

Raymond sat among them, though while he entered into the spirit of the hour, his natural dignity never forsook him. He was gay, playful, fascinating - but never did he overstep the modesty of nature, or the respect due to himself, in his wildest sallies. Yet I own, that considering the task which Raymond had taken on himself as Protector of England, and the cares to which it became him to attend, I was exceedingly provoked to observe the worthless fellows on whom his time was wasted, and the jovial if not drunken spirit which seemed on the point of robbing him of his better self. I stood watching the scene, while Adrian flitted like a shadow in among them, and, by a word and look of sobriety, endeavored to restore order in the assembly. Raymond expressed himself delighted to see him, declaring that he should make one in the festivity of the night.

This action of Adrian provoked me. I was indignant that he should sit at the same table with the companions of Raymond - men of abandoned characters, or rather without any, the refuse of high-bred luxury, the disgrace of their country.

"Let me entreat Adrian," I cried, "not to comply rather join with me in endeavoring to withdraw Lord Raymond from this scene and restore him to other society."

"My good fellow," said Raymond, "this is neither the time nor place for the delivery of a moral lecture: take my word for it that my amusements and society are not so bad as you imagine. We are neither hypocrites or fools - for the rest, 'Dost thou think because thou art virtuous, there shall be no more cakes and ale?'" I turned angrily away: "Verney," said Adrian, "you are very cynical: sit down; or if you will not, perhaps, as you are not a frequent visitor, Lord Raymond will humor you, and accompany us, as we had previously agreed upon, to parliament."

Raymond looked keenly at him; he could read benignity only in his gentle lineaments; he turned to me, observing with scorn my moody and stern demeanor. "Come," said Adrian, "I have promised for you, enable me to keep my engagement. Come with us." - Raymond made an uneasy movement, and laconically replied - "I won't!"

The party in the meantime had broken up. They looked at the pictures, strolled into the other apartments, talked of billiards, and one by one vanished. Raymond strode angrily up and down the room. I stood ready to receive and reply to his reproaches. Adrian leaned against the wall. "This is infinitely ridiculous," he cried, "if you were school-boys, you could not conduct yourselves more unreasonably."

"You do not understand," said Raymond. "This is only part of a system: - a scheme of tyranny to which I will never submit. Because I am Protector of England, am I to be the only slave in its empire? My privacy invaded, my actions censured, my friends insulted? But I will get rid of the whole together. - Be you witnesses," and he took the star, insignia of office, from his breast, and threw it on the table. "I renounce my office; I abdicate my power - assume it who will!" -

"Let him assume it," exclaimed Adrian, "who can pronounce himself, or whom the world will pronounce to be your superior. There does not exist the man in England with adequate presumption. Know yourself, Raymond, and your indignation will cease; your complacency return. A few months ago, whenever we prayed for the prosperity of our country, or our own, we at the same time prayed for the life and welfare of the Protector, as indissolubly linked to it. Your hours were devoted to our benefit, your ambition was to obtain our commendation. You decorated our towns with edifices, you bestowed on us useful establishments, you gifted the soil with abundant fertility. The powerful and unjust cowered at the steps of your judgment-seat, and the poor and oppressed arose like morn-awakened flowers under the sunshine of your protection.

"Can you wonder that we are all aghast and mourn, when this appears changed? But, come, this splenetic fit is already passed; resume your functions; your partisans will hail you; your enemies be silenced; our love, honor, and duty will again be manifested towards you. Master yourself, Raymond, and the world is subject to you."

"All this would be very good sense, if addressed to another," replied Raymond, moodily, "con the lesson yourself, and you, the first peer of the land, may become its sovereign. You the good, the wise, the just, may rule all hearts. But I perceive, too soon for my own happiness, too late for England's good, that I undertook a task to which I am unequal. I cannot rule myself. My passions are my masters, my smallest impulse my tyrant. Do you think that I renounced the Protectorate (and I have renounced it) in a fit of spleen? By the God that lives, I swear never to take up that bauble again; never again to burthen myself with the weight of care and misery, of which that is the visible sign.

"Once I desired to be a king. It was in the hey-day of youth, in the pride of boyish folly. I knew myself when I renounced it. I renounced it to gain - no matter what - for that also I have lost. For many months I have submitted to this mock majesty - this solemn jest. I am its dupe no longer. I will be free.

I have lost that which adorned and dignified my life; that which linked me to other men. Again, I am a solitary man; and I will become again, as in my early years, a wanderer, a soldier of fortune. My friends, for Verney, I feel that you are my friend, do not endeavor to shake my resolve. Perdita, wedded to an imagination, careless of what is behind the veil, whose character is in truth faulty and vile, Perdita has renounced me. With her it was pretty enough to play a sovereign's part; and, as in the recesses of your beloved forest we acted masques, and imagined ourselves Arcadian shepherds, to please the fancy of the moment - so was I content, more for Perdita's sake than my own, to take on me the character of one of the great ones of the earth; to lead her behind the scenes of grandeur, to vary her life with a short act of magnificence and power. This was to be the color, love and confidence the substance of our existence. But we must live, and not act our lives; pursuing the shadow, I lost the reality - now I renounce both.

Adrian, I am about to return to Greece, to become again a soldier, perhaps a conqueror. Will you accompany me? You will behold new scenes; see a new people; witness the mighty struggle there going forward between civilization and barbarism; behold, and perhaps direct the efforts of a young and vigorous population, for liberty and order. Come with me. I have expected you. I waited for this moment; all is prepared; - will you accompany me?"

"I will," replied Adrian. "Immediately?"

"To-morrow if you will."

"Reflect!" I cried.

"Wherefore?" asked Raymond - "My dear fellow, I have done nothing else than reflect on this step the live-long summer; and be assured that Adrian has condensed an age of reflection into this little moment. Do not talk of reflection; from this moment I abjure it; this is my only happy moment during a long interval of time. I must go, Lionel - the Gods will it; and I must. Do not endeavor to deprive me of my companion, the out-cast's friend.

"One word more concerning unkind, unjust Perdita. For a time, I thought that, by watching a complying moment, fostering the still warm ashes, I might relume in her the flame of love. It is colder within her, than a fire left by gypsies in wintertime, the spent embers crowned by a pyramid of snow. Then, in endeavoring to do violence to my own disposition, I made all worse than before. Still I think that time, and even absence, may restore her to me. Remember, that I love her still, that my dearest hope is that she will again be mine. I know, though she does not, how false the veil is which she has spread over the reality - do not endeavor to rend this deceptive covering, but by degrees withdraw it. Present her with a mirror, in which she may know herself; and, when she is an adept in that necessary but difficult science, she will wonder at her present mistake, and hasten to restore to me, what is by right mine, her forgiveness, her kind thoughts, her love."

CHAPTER X

After these events, it was long before we were able to attain any degree of composure. A moral tempest had wrecked our richly freighted vessel, and we, remnants of the diminished crew, were aghast at the losses and changes which we had undergone. Idris passionately loved her brother, and could ill brook an absence whose duration was uncertain; his society was dear and necessary to me - I had followed up my chosen literary occupations with delight under his tutorship and assistance; his mild philosophy, unerring reason, and enthusiastic friendship were the best ingredient, the exalted spirit of our circle; even the children bitterly regretted the loss of their kind playfellow. Deeper grief oppressed Perdita. In spite of resentment, by day and night she figured to herself the toils and dangers of the wanderers. Raymond absent, struggling with difficulties, lost to the power and rank of the Protectorate, exposed to the perils of war, became an object of anxious interest; not that she felt any inclination to recall him, if recall must imply a return to their former union. Such return she felt to be impossible; and while she believed it to be thus, and with anguish regretted that so it should be, she continued angry and impatient with him, who occasioned her misery. These perplexities and regrets caused her to bathe her pillow with nightly tears, and to reduce her in person and in mind to the shadow of what she had been. She sought solitude and avoided us when in gaiety and unrestrained affection we met in a family circle. Lonely musings, interminable wanderings, and solemn music were her only pastimes. She neglected even her child; shutting her heart against all tenderness, she grew reserved towards me, her first and fast friend.

I could not see her thus lost, without exerting myself to remedy the evil - remediless I knew, if I could not in the end bring her to reconcile herself to Raymond. Before he went, I used every argument, every persuasion to induce her to stop his journey. She answered the one with a gush of tears – telling me that to be persuaded - life and the goods of life were a cheap exchange. It was not will that she wanted, but the capacity; again and again she declared, it were as easy to enchain the sea, to put reins on the wind's viewless courses, as for her to take truth for falsehood, deceit for honesty, heartless communion for sincere, confiding love. She answered my reasonings more briefly, declaring with disdain, that the reason was hers; and, until I could persuade her that the past could be unacted, that maturity could go back to the cradle, and that all that was could become as though it had never been, it was useless to assure her that no real change had taken place in her fate. And thus, with stern pride she suffered him to go, though her very heartstrings cracked at the fulfilling of the act, which rent from her all that made life valuable.

To change the scene for her, and even for ourselves, all unhinged by the cloud that had come over us, I persuaded my two remaining companions that it were better that we should absent ourselves for a time from Windsor. We visited the north of England, my native Ullswater, and lingered in scenes dear from a thousand associations. We lengthened our tour into Scotland, that we might see Loch Katrine and Loch Lomond; thence we crossed to Ireland and passed several weeks in the neighborhood of Killarney. The change of scene operated to a great degree as I expected; after a year's absence, Perdita returned in gentler and more docile mood to Windsor. The first sight of this place for a time unhinged her. Here every spot was distinct with associations now grown bitter. The forest glades, the ferny dells, and lawny uplands, the cultivated and cheerful country spread around the silver pathway of ancient Thames, all earth, air, and wave, took up one choral voice, inspired by memory, instinct with plaintive regret.

But my essay towards bringing her to a saner view of her own situation, did not end here. Perdita was still to a great degree uneducated. When first she left her peasant life, and resided with the elegant and cultivated Evadne, the only accomplishment she brought to any perfection was that of painting, for which she had a taste almost amounting to genius. This had occupied her in her lonely cottage, when she quitted her Greek friend's protection. Her pallet and easel were now thrown aside; did she try to paint, thronging recollections made her hand tremble, her eyes fill with tears. With this occupation she gave up almost every other; and her mind preyed upon itself almost to madness.

For my own part, since Adrian had first withdrawn me from my selvatic wilderness to his own paradise of order and beauty, I had been wedded to literature. I felt convinced that however it might have been in former times, in the present stage of the world, no man's faculties could be developed, no man's moral principle be enlarged and liberal, without an extensive acquaintance with books. To me they stood in the place of an active career, of ambition, and those palpable excitements necessary to the multitude. The collation of philosophical opinions, the study of historical facts, the acquirement of languages, were at once my recreation, and the serious aim of my life. I turned author myself. My productions however were sufficiently unpretending; they were confined to the biography of favorite historical characters, especially those whom I believed to have been traduced, or about whom clung obscurity and doubt.

As my authorship increased, I acquired new sympathies and pleasures. I found another and a valuable link to enchain me to my fellow-creatures; my point of sight was extended, and the inclinations and capacities of all human beings became deeply interesting to me. Kings have been called the fathers of their people. Suddenly I became as it were the father of all mankind. Posterity became my heirs. My thoughts were gems to enrich the treasure house of man's intellectual possessions; each sentiment was a precious gift I bestowed on them. Let not these aspirations be attributed to vanity. They were not expressed in words, nor even reduced to form in my own mind; but they filled my soul, exalting my thoughts, raising a glow of enthusiasm, and led me out of the obscure path in which I before walked, into the bright noon-enlightened highway of mankind, making me, citizen of the world, a candidate for immortal honors, an eager aspirant to the praise and sympathy of my fellow men.

No one certainly ever enjoyed the pleasures of composition more intensely than I. If I left the woods, the solemn music of the waving branches, and the majestic temple of nature, I sought the vast halls of the Castle, and looked over wide, fertile England, spread beneath our regal mount, and listened the while to inspiring strains of music. At such times solemn harmonies or spirit-stirring airs gave wings to my lagging thoughts, permitting them, methought, to penetrate the last veil of nature and her God, and to display the highest beauty in visible expression to the understandings of men. As the music went on, my ideas seemed to quit their mortal dwelling house; they shook their pinions and began a flight, sailing on the placid current of thought, filling the creation with new glory, and rousing sublime imagery that else had slept voiceless. Then I would hasten to my desk, weave the new-found web of mind in firm texture and brilliant colors, leaving the fashioning of the material to a calmer moment.

But this account, which might as properly belong to a former period of my life as to the present moment, leads me far afield. It was the pleasure I took in literature, the discipline of mind I found arise from it, that made me eager to lead Perdita to the same pursuits. I began with light hand and gentle allurement; first exciting her curiosity, and then satisfying it in such a way as might occasion her, at the same time that she half forgot her sorrows in occupation, to find in the hours that succeeded a reaction of benevolence and toleration.

Intellectual activity, though not directed towards books, had always been my sister's characteristic. It had been displayed early in life, leading her out to solitary musing among her native mountains, causing her to form innumerous combinations from common objects, giving strength to her perceptions, and swiftness to their arrangement. Love had come, as the rod of the master-prophet, to swallow up every minor propensity. Love had doubled all her excellencies and placed a diadem on her genius. Was she to cease to love? Take the colors and odors from the rose, change the sweet nutriment of mother's milk to gall and poison as easily might you wean Perdita from love. She grieved for the loss of Raymond with an anguish, that exiled all smile from her lips, and trenched sad lines on her brow of beauty. But each day seemed to change the nature of her suffering, and every succeeding hour forced her to alter (if so, I may style it) the fashion of her soul's mourning garb. For a time, music was able to satisfy the cravings of her mental hunger, and her melancholy thoughts renewed themselves in each change of key and varied with every alteration in the strain. My schooling first impelled her towards books; and, if music had been the food of sorrow, the productions of the wise became its medicine. The acquisition of unknown languages was too tedious an occupation, for one who referred every expression to the universe within, and read not, as many do, for the mere sake of filling up time; but who was still questioning herself and her author, molding every idea in a thousand ways, ardently desirous for the discovery of truth in every sentence. She sought to improve her understanding; mechanically her heart and dispositions became soft and gentle under this benign discipline. After a while she discovered, that amidst all her newly acquired knowledge, her own character, which formerly she fancied that she thoroughly understood, became the first in rank among the terrae incognitae, the pathless wilds of a country that had no chart. Erringly and strangely she began the task of self-examination with self-condemnation. And then again, she became aware of her own excellencies, and began to balance with juster scales the shades of good and evil. I, who longed beyond words, to restore her to the happiness it was still in her power to enjoy, watched with anxiety the result of these internal proceedings.

But man is a strange animal. We cannot calculate on his forces like that of an engine; and, though an impulse draw with a forty-horsepower at what appears willing to yield to one, yet in contempt of calculation the movement is not affected. Neither grief, philosophy, nor love could make Perdita think with mildness of the dereliction of Raymond. She now took pleasure in my society; towards Idris she felt and displayed a full and affectionate sense of her worth—she restored to her child in abundant measure her tenderness and care. But I could discover, amidst all her repining's, deep resentment towards Raymond, and an unfading sense of injury, that plucked from me my hope, when I appeared nearest to its fulfilment. Among other painful restrictions, she has occasioned it to become a law among us, never to mention Raymond's name before her. She refused to read any communications from Greece, desiring me only to mention when any arrived, and whether the wanderers were well. It was curious that even little Clara observed this law towards her mother. This lovely child was nearly eight years of age. Formerly she had been a light-hearted infant, fanciful, but gay and childish. After the departure of her father, thought became impressed on her young brow. Children, unadepts in language, seldom find words to express their thoughts, nor could we tell in what manner the late events had impressed themselves on her mind. But certainly, she had made deep observations while she noted in silence the changes that passed around her. She never mentioned her father to Perdita, she appeared half afraid when she spoke of him to me, and though I tried to draw her out on the subject, and to dispel the gloom that hung about her ideas concerning him, I could not succeed. Yet each foreign post-day she watched for the arrival of letters - knew the post mark and watched me as I read. I found her often poring over the article of Greek intelligence in the newspaper.

There is no more painful sight than that of untimely care in children, and it was particularly observable in one whose disposition had heretofore been mirthful. Yet there was so much sweetness and docility about Clara, that your admiration was excited; and if the moods of mind are calculated to paint the cheek with beauty, and endow motions with grace, surely her contemplations must have been celestial; since every lineament was moulded into loveliness, and her motions were more harmonious than the elegant bounding of the fawns of her native forest. I sometimes expostulated with Perdita on the subject of her reserve; but she rejected my counsels, while her daughter's sensibility excited in her a tenderness still more passionate.

After the lapse of more than a year, Adrian returned from Greece.

When our exiles had first arrived, a truce was in existence between the Turks and Greeks; a truce that was as sleep to the mortal frame, signal of renewed activity on waking. With the numerous soldiers of Asia, with all of warlike stores, ships, and military engines, that wealth and power could command, the Turks at once resolved to crush an enemy, which creeping on by degrees, had from their stronghold in the Morea, acquired Thrace and Macedonia, and had led their armies even to the gates of Constantinople, while their extensive commercial relations gave every European nation an interest in their success. Greece prepared for a vigorous resistance; it rose to a man; and the women, sacrificing their costly ornaments, accoutered their sons for the war, and bade them conquer or die with the spirit of the Spartan mother. The talents and courage of Raymond were highly esteemed among the Greeks. Born at Athens, that city claimed him for her own, and by giving him the command of her peculiar division in the army, the commander-in-chief only possessed superior power. He was numbered among her citizens; his name was added to the list of Grecian heroes. His judgment, activity, and consummate bravery justified their choice. The Earl of Windsor became a volunteer under his friend.

"It is well," said Adrian, "to prate of war in these pleasant shades, and with much ill-spent oil make a show of joy, because many thousands of our fellow-creatures leave with pain this sweet air and natal earth. I shall not be suspected of being averse to the Greek cause; I know and feel its necessity; it is beyond every other a good cause. I have defended it with my sword and was willing that my spirit should be breathed out in its defense; freedom is of more worth than life, and the Greeks do well to defend their privilege unto death. But let us not deceive ourselves. The Turks are men; each fiber, each limb is as feeling as our own, and every spasm, be it mental or bodily, is as truly felt in a Turk's heart or brain, as in a Greek's. The last action at which I was present was the taking of --. The Turks resisted to the last, the garrison perished on the ramparts, and we entered by assault. Every breathing creature within the walls was massacred. Think you, amidst the shrieks of violated innocence and helpless infancy, I did not feel in every nerve the cry of a fellow being? They were men and women, the sufferers, before they were Mohammedans, and when they rise turbanless from the grave, in what except their good or evil actions will they be the better or worse than we? Two soldiers contended for a girl, whose rich dress and extreme beauty excited the brutal appetites of these wretches, who, perhaps good men among their families, were changed by the fury of the moment into incarnated evils. An old man, with a silver beard, decrepit and bald, he might be her grandfather, interposed to save her; the battle axe of one of them clove his skull. I rushed to her defense, but rage made them blind and deaf; they did not distinguish my Christian garb or heed my words - words were blunt weapons then, for while war cried "havoc," and murder gave fit echo, how could I -

> *Turn back the tide of ills, relieving wrong*
> *With mild accost of soothing eloquence.*

One of the fellows, enraged at my interference, struck me with his bayonet in the side, and I fell senseless.

"This wound will probably shorten my life, having shattered a frame, weak of itself. But I am content to die. I have learnt in Greece that one man, more or less, is of small import, while human bodies remain to fill up the thinned ranks of the soldiery; and that the identity of an individual may be overlooked, so that the muster roll contain its full numbers. All this has a different effect upon Raymond. He is able to contemplate the ideal of war, while I am sensible only to its realities. He is a soldier, a general. He can influence the blood-thirsty war-dogs, while I resist their propensities vainly. The cause is simple. Burke has said that, 'in all bodies those who would lead, must also, in a considerable degree, follow.' - I cannot follow; for I do not sympathize in their dreams of massacre and glory - to follow and to lead in such a career, is the natural bent of Raymond's mind. He is always successful, and bids fair, at the same time that he acquires high name and station for himself, to secure liberty, probably extended empire, to the Greeks."

Perdita's mind was not softened by this account. He, she thought, can be great and happy without me. Would that I also had a career! Would that I could freight some untried bark with all my hopes, energies, and desires, and launch it forth into the ocean of life - bound for some attainable point, with ambition or pleasure at the helm! But adverse winds detain me on shore; like Ulysses, I sit at the water's edge and weep. But my nerveless hands can neither fell the trees, nor smooth the planks. Under the influence of these melancholy thoughts, she became more than ever in love with sorrow. Yet Adrian's presence did some good; he at once broke through the law of silence observed concerning Raymond. At first, she started from the unaccustomed sound; soon she got used to it and to love it, and she listened with avidity to the account of his achievements. Clara got rid also of her restraint; Adrian and she had been old playfellows; and now, as they walked or rode together, he yielded to her earnest entreaty, and repeated, for the hundredth time, some tale of her father's bravery, munificence, or justice.

Each vessel in the meantime brought exhilarating tidings from Greece. The presence of a friend in its armies and councils made us enter into the details with enthusiasm; and a short letter now and then from Raymond told us how he was engrossed by the interests of his adopted country. The Greeks were strongly attached to their commercial pursuits, and would have been satisfied with their present acquisitions, had not the Turks roused them by invasion. The patriots were victorious; a spirit of conquest was instilled; and already they looked on Constantinople as their own. Raymond rose perpetually in their estimation; but one man held a superior command to him in their armies. He was conspicuous for his conduct and choice of position in a battle fought in the plains of Thrace, on the banks of the Hebrus, which was to decide the fate of Islam. The Mohammedans were defeated, and driven entirely from the country west of this river. The battle was sanguinary, the loss of the Turks apparently irreparable; the Greeks, in losing one man, forgot the nameless crowd strewed upon the bloody field, and they ceased to value themselves on a victory, which cost them - Raymond.

At the battle of Makri he had led the charge of cavalry and pursued the fugitives even to the banks of the Hebrus. His favorite horse was found grazing by the margin of the tranquil river. It became a question whether he had fallen among the unrecognized; but no broken ornament or stained trapping betrayed his fate. It was suspected that the Turks, finding themselves possessed of so illustrious a captive, resolved to satisfy their cruelty rather than their avarice, and fearful of the interference of England, had come to the determination of concealing forever the cold-blooded murder of the soldier they most hated and feared in the squadrons of their enemy.

Raymond was not forgotten in England. His abdication of the Protectorate had caused an unexampled sensation; and, when his magnificent and manly system was contrasted with the narrow views of succeeding politicians, the period of his elevation was referred to with sorrow. The perpetual recurrence of his name, joined to most honorable testimonials, in the Greek gazettes, kept up the interest he had excited. He seemed the favorite child of fortune, and his untimely loss eclipsed the world, and shewed forth the remnant of mankind with diminished luster. They clung with eagerness to the hope held out that he might yet be alive. Their minister at Constantinople was urged to make the necessary perquisitions, and should his existence be ascertained, to demand his release. It was to be hoped that their efforts would succeed, and that though now a prisoner, the sport of cruelty and the mark of hate, he would be rescued from danger and restored to the happiness, power, and honor which he deserved.

The effect of this intelligence upon my sister was striking. She never for a moment credited the story of his death; she resolved instantly to go to Greece. Reasoning and persuasion were thrown away upon her; she would endure no hindrance, no delay. It may be advanced for a truth, that, if argument or entreaty can turn anyone from a desperate purpose, whose motive and end depends on the strength of the affections only, then it is right so to turn them, since their docility shews, that neither the motive nor the end were of sufficient force to bear them through the obstacles attendant on their undertaking. If, on the contrary, they are proof against expostulation, this very steadiness is an omen of success; and it becomes the duty of those who love them, to assist in smoothing the obstructions in their path. Such sentiments actuated our little circle. Finding Perdita immoveable, we consulted as to the best means of furthering her purpose. She could not go alone to a country where she had no friends, where she might arrive only to hear the dreadful news, which must overwhelm her with grief and remorse. Adrian, whose health had always been weak, now suffered considerable aggravation of suffering from the effects of his wound. Idris could not endure to leave him in this state; nor was it right either to quit or take with us a young family for a journey of this description. I resolved at length to accompany Perdita. The separation from my Idris was painful - but necessity reconciled us to it in some degree: necessity and the hope of saving Raymond and restoring him again to happiness and Perdita. No delay was to ensue. Two days after we came to our determination, we set out for Portsmouth, and embarked. The season was May, the weather was without storm; we were promised a prosperous voyage. Cherishing the most fervent hopes, embarked on the waste ocean, we saw with delight the receding shore of Britain, and on the wings of desire outspeed our well filled sails towards the South. The light curling waves bore us onward, and old ocean smiled at the freight of love and hope committed to his charge; it stroked gently its tempestuous plains, and the path was smoothed for us. Day and night the wind right aft, gave steady impulse to our keel - nor did rough gale, or treacherous sand, or destructive rock interpose an obstacle between my sister and the land, which was to restore her to her first beloved,

Her dear heart's confessor—a heart within that heart.

VOL. II.

CHAPTER I

During this voyage, when on calm evenings we conversed on deck, watching the glancing of the waves and the changeful appearances of the sky, I discovered the total revolution that the disasters of Raymond had wrought in the mind of my sister. Were they the same waters of love, which, lately cold and cutting as ice, repelling as that, now loosened from their frozen chains, flowed through the regions of her soul in gushing and grateful exuberance? She did not believe that he was dead, but she knew that he was in danger, and the hope of assisting in his liberation, and the idea of soothing by tenderness the ills that he might have undergone, elevated and harmonized the late jarring element of her being. I was not so sanguine as she as to the result of our voyage. She was not sanguine, but secure; and the expectation of seeing the lover she had banished, the husband, friend, heart's companion from whom she had long been alienated, wrapped her senses in delight, her mind in placidity. It was beginning life again; it was leaving barren sands for an abode of fertile beauty; it was a harbor after a tempest, an opiate after sleepless nights, a happy waking from a terrible dream.

Little Clara accompanied us; the poor child did not well understand what was going forward. She heard that we were bound for Greece, that she would see her father, and now, for the first time, she prattled of him to her mother.

On landing at Athens, we found difficulties increased upon us: nor could the storied earth or balmy atmosphere inspire us with enthusiasm or pleasure, while the fate of Raymond was in jeopardy. No man had ever excited so strong an interest in the public mind; this was apparent even among the phlegmatic English, from whom he had long been absent. The Athenians had expected their hero to return in triumph; the women had taught their children to lisp his name joined to thanksgiving; his manly beauty, his courage, his devotion to their cause, made him appear in their eyes almost as one of the ancient deities of the soil descended from their native Olympus to defend them. When they spoke of his probable death and certain captivity, tears streamed from their eyes; even as the women of Syria sorrowed for Adonis, did the wives and mothers of Greece lament our English Raymond - Athens was a city of mourning.

All these shews of despair struck Perdita with affright. With that sanguine but confused expectation, which desire engendered while she was at a distance from reality, she had formed an image in her mind of instantaneous change, when she should set her foot on Grecian shores. She fancied that Raymond would already be free, and that her tender attentions would come to entirely obliterate even the memory of his mischance. But his fate was still uncertain; she began to fear the worst, and to feel that her soul's hope was cast on a chance that might prove a blank. The wife and lovely child of Lord Raymond became objects of intense interest in Athens. The gates of their abode were besieged, audible prayers were breathed for his restoration; all these circumstances added to the dismay and fears of Perdita.

My exertions were unremitted: after a time, I left Athens, and joined the army stationed at Kishan in Thrace. Bribery, threats, and intrigue soon discovered the secret that Raymond was alive, a prisoner, suffering the most rigorous confinement and wanton cruelties. We put in movement every impulse of policy and money to redeem him from their hands.

The impatience of my sister's disposition now returned on her, awakened by repentance, sharpened by remorse. The very beauty of the Grecian climate, during the season of spring, added torture to her sensations. The unexampled loveliness of the flower-clad earth - the genial sunshine and grateful shade - the melody of the birds - the majesty of the woods - the splendor of the marble ruins - the clear effulgence of the stars by night - the combination of all that was exciting and voluptuous in this transcending land, by inspiring a quicker spirit of life and an added sensitiveness to every articulation of her frame, only gave edge to the poignancy of her grief. Each long hour was counted, and "He suffers" was the burthen of all her thoughts. She abstained from food; she lay on the bare earth, and, by such mimicry of his enforced torments, endeavored to hold communion with his distant pain. I remembered in one of her harshest moments a quotation of mine had roused her to anger and disdain. "Perdita," I had said, "someday you will discover that you have done wrong in again casting Raymond on the thorns of life. When disappointment has sullied his beauty, when a soldier's hardships have bent his manly form, and loneliness made even triumph bitter to him, then you will repent, and regret for the irreparable change

will move In hearts all rocky now, the late remorse of love.

The stinging "remorse of love" now pierced her heart. She accused herself of his journey to Greece - his dangers - his imprisonment. She pictured to herself the anguish of his solitude; she remembered with what eager delight he had in former days made her the partner of his joyful hopes - with what grateful affection he received her sympathy in his cares. She called to mind how often he had declared that solitude was to him the greatest of all evils, and how death itself was to him more full of fear and pain when he pictured to himself a lonely grave. "My best girl," he had said, "relieves me from these phantasies. United to her, cherished in her dear heart, never again shall I know the misery of finding myself alone. Even if I die before you, my Perdita, treasure up my ashes till yours may mingle with mine. It is a foolish sentiment for one who is not a materialist, yet methinks, even in that dark cell, I may feel that my inanimate dust mingles with yours, and thus have a companion in decay." In her resentful mood, these expressions had been remembered with acrimony and disdain; they visited her in her softened hour, taking sleep from her eyes, all hope of rest from her uneasy mind.

Two months passed thus, when at last we obtained a promise of Raymond's release. Confinement and hardship had undermined his health; the Turks feared an accomplishment of the threats of the English government, if he died under their hands; they looked upon his recovery as impossible; they delivered him up as a dying man, willingly making over to us the rites of burial.

He came by sea from Constantinople to Athens. The wind, favorable to him, blew so strongly in shore, that we were unable, as we had at first intended, to meet him on his watery road. The watchtower of Athens was besieged by inquirers, each sail eagerly looked out for; till on the first of May the gallant frigate bore in sight, freighted with treasure more invaluable than the wealth which, piloted from Mexico, the vexed Pacific swallowed, or that was conveyed over its tranquil bosom to enrich the crown of Spain. At early dawn the vessel was discovered bearing in shore; it was conjectured that it would cast anchor about five miles from land. The news spread through Athens, and the whole city poured out at the gate of the Piraeus, down the roads, through the vineyards, the olive woods and plantations of fig-trees, towards the harbor. The noisy joy of the populace, the gaudy colors of their dress, the tumult of carriages and horses, the march of soldiers intermixed, the waving of banners and sound of martial music added to the high excitement of the scene; while round us reposed in solemn majesty the relics of antient time. To our right the Acropolis rose high, spectators of a thousand changes, of ancient glory, Turkish slavery, and the restoration of dear-bought liberty; tombs and cenotaphs were strewed thick around, adorned by ever renewing vegetation; the mighty dead hovered over their monuments, and beheld in our enthusiasm and congregated numbers a renewal of the scenes in which they had been the actors. Perdita and Clara rode in a close carriage; I attended them on horseback. At length we arrived at the harbor; it was agitated by the outward swell of the sea; the beach, as far could be discerned, was covered by a moving multitude, which, urged by those behind toward the sea, again rushed back as the heavy waves with sullen roar burst close to them. I applied my glass, and could discern that the frigate had already cast anchor, fearful of the danger of approaching nearer to a lee shore: a boat was lowered; with a pang I saw that Raymond was unable to descend the vessel's side; he was let down in a chair, and lay wrapped in cloaks at the bottom of the boat.

I dismounted, and called to some sailors who were rowing about the harbor to pull up, and take me into their skiff; Perdita at the same moment alighted from her carriage - she seized my arm -"Take me with you," she cried; she was trembling and pale; Clara clung to her -"You must not," I said, "the sea is rough -he will soon be here - do you not see his boat?" The little bark to which I had beckoned had now pulled up; before I could stop her, Perdita, assisted by the sailors was in it - Clara followed her mother - a loud shout echoed from the crowd as we pulled out of the inner harbor; while my sister at the prow, had caught hold of one of the men who was using a glass, asking a thousand questions, careless of the spray that broke over her, deaf, sightless to all, except the little speck that, just visible on the top of the waves, evidently neared. We approached with all the speed six rowers could give; the orderly and picturesque dress of the soldiers on the beach, the sounds of exulting music, the stirring breeze and waving flags, the unchecked exclamations of the eager crowd, whose dark looks and foreign garb were purely eastern; the sight of temple-crowned rock, the white marble of the buildings glittering in the sun, and standing in bright relief against the dark ridge of lofty mountains beyond; the near roar of the sea, the splash of oars, and dash of spray, all steeped my soul in a delirium, unfelt, unimagined in the common course of common life. Trembling, I was unable to continue to look through the glass with which I had watched the motion of the crew, when the frigate's boat had first been launched. We rapidly drew near, so that at length the number and forms of those within could be discerned; its dark sides grew big, and the splash of its oars became audible: I could distinguish the languid form of my friend, as he half raised himself at our approach.

Perdita's questions had ceased; she leaned on my arm, panting with emotions too acute for tears - our men pulled alongside the other boat. As a last effort, my sister mustered her strength, her firmness; she stepped from one boat to the other, and then with a shriek she sprang towards Raymond, knelt at his side, and gluing her lips to the hand she seized, her face shrouded by her long hair, gave herself up to tears.

Raymond had somewhat raised himself at our approach, but it was with difficulty that he exerted himself even thus much. With sunken cheek and hollow eyes, pale and gaunt, how could I recognize the beloved of Perdita? I continued awe-struck and mute - he looked smilingly on the poor girl; the smile was his. A day of sun-shine falling on a dark valley, displays its before hidden characteristics; and now this smile, the same with which he first spoke love to Perdita, with which he had welcomed the protectorate, playing on his altered countenance, made me in my heart's core feel that this was Raymond.

He stretched out to me his other hand; I discerned the trace of manacles on his bared wrist. I heard my sister's sobs, and thought, happy are women who can weep, and in a passionate caress disburden the oppression of their feelings; shame and habitual restraint hold back a man. I would have given worlds to have acted as in days of boyhood, have strained him to my breast, pressed his hand to my lips, and wept over him; my swelling heart choked me; the natural current would not be checked; the big rebellious tears gathered in my eyes; I turned aside, and they dropped in the sea - they came fast and faster; - yet I could hardly be ashamed, for I saw that the rough sailors were not unmoved, and Raymond's eyes alone were dry from among our crew. He lay in that blessed calm which convalescence always induces, enjoying in secure tranquility his liberty and reunion with her whom he adored. Perdita at length subdued her burst of passion, and rose, - she looked round for Clara; the child frightened, not recognizing her father, and neglected by us, had crept to the other end of the boat; she came at her mother's call. Perdita presented her to Raymond; her first words were: "Beloved, embrace our child!"

"Come hither, sweet one," said her father, "do you not know me?" she knew his voice and cast herself in his arms with half bashful but uncontrollable emotion.

Perceiving the weakness of Raymond, I was afraid of ill consequences from the pressure of the crowd on his landing. But they were awed as I had been, at the change of his appearance. The music died away; the shouts abruptly ended; the soldiers had cleared a space in which a carriage was drawn up. He was placed in it; Perdita and Clara entered with him, and his escort closed round it; a hollow murmur, akin to the roaring of the near waves, went through the multitude; they fell back as the carriage advanced, and fearful of injuring him they had come to welcome, by loud testimonies of joy, they satisfied themselves with bending in a low salaam as the carriage passed; it went slowly along the road of the Piraeus; passed by antique temple and heroic tomb, beneath the craggy rock of the citadel. The sound of the waves was left behind; that of the multitude continued at intervals, suppressed and hoarse; and though, in the city, the houses, churches, and public buildings were decorated with tapestry and banners - though the soldiery lined the streets, and the inhabitants in thousands were assembled to give him hail, the same solemn silence prevailed, the soldiery presented arms, the banners vailed, many a white hand waved a streamer, and vainly sought to discern the hero in the vehicle, which, closed and encompassed by the city guards, drew him to the palace allotted for his abode.

Raymond was weak and exhausted, yet the interest he perceived to be excited on his account, filled him with proud pleasure. He was nearly killed with kindness. It is true, the populace retained themselves; but there arose a perpetual hum and bustle from the throng round the palace, which added to the noise of fireworks, the frequent explosion of arms, the tramp to and fro of horsemen and carriages, to which effervescence he was the focus, retarded his recovery. So we retired awhile to Eleusis, and here rest and tender care added each day to the strength of our invalid. The zealous attention of Perdita claimed the first rank in the causes which induced his rapid recovery; but the second was surely the delight he felt in the affection and good will of the Greeks. We are said to love much those whom we greatly benefit. Raymond had fought and conquered for the Athenians; he had suffered, on their account, peril, imprisonment, and hardship; their gratitude affected him deeply, and he inly vowed to unite his fate for ever to that of a people so enthusiastically devoted to him.

Social feeling and sympathy constituted a marked feature in my disposition. In early youth, the living drama acted around me, drew me heart and soul into its vortex. I was now conscious of a change. I loved, I hoped, I enjoyed; but there was something besides this. I was inquisitive as to the internal principles of action of those around me: anxious to read their thoughts justly, and forever occupied in divining their inmost mind. All events, at the same time that they deeply interested me, arranged themselves in pictures before me. I gave the right place to every personage in the group, the just balance to every sentiment. This undercurrent of thought often soothed me amidst distress, and even agony. It gave ideality to that, from which, taken in naked truth, the soul would have revolted: it bestowed pictorial colors on misery and disease, and not unfrequently relieved me from despair in deplorable changes. This faculty, or instinct, was now roused. I watched the re-awakened devotion of my sister, Clara's timid, but concentrated admiration of her father, and Raymond's appetite for renown, and sensitiveness to the demonstrations of affection of the Athenians. Attentively perusing this animated volume, I was the less surprised at the tale I read on the new-turned page. The Turkish army were at this time besieging Rodosto; and the Greeks, hastening their preparations, and sending each day reinforcements, were on the eve of forcing the enemy to battle. Each people looked on the coming struggle as that which would be to a great degree decisive; as, in case of victory, the next step would be the siege of Constantinople by the Greeks. Raymond, being somewhat recovered, prepared to reassume his command in the army.

Perdita did not oppose herself to his determination. She only stipulated to be permitted to accompany him. She had set down no rule of conduct for herself; but for her life she could not have opposed his slightest wish or do other than acquiesce cheerfully in all his projects. One word, in truth, had alarmed her more than battles or sieges, during which she trusted Raymond's high command would exempt him from danger. That word, as yet it was not more to her, was PLAGUE. This enemy to the human race had begun early in June to raise its serpent-head on the shores of the Nile; parts of Asia, not usually subject to this evil, were infected.

It was in Constantinople; but as each year that city experienced a like visitation, small attention was paid to those accounts which declared more people to have died there already, than usually made up the accustomed prey of the whole of the hotter months. However, it might be, neither plague nor war could prevent Perdita from following her lord or induce her to utter one objection to the plans which he proposed. To be near him, to be loved by him, to feel him again her own, was the limit of her desires. The object of her life was to do him pleasure: it had been so before, but with a difference. In past times, without thought or foresight she had made him happy, being so herself, and in any question of choice, consulted her own wishes, as being one with his. Now she sedulously put herself out of the question, sacrificing even her anxiety for his health and welfare to her resolve not to oppose any of his desires. Love of the Greek people, appetite for glory, and hatred of the barbarian government under which he had suffered even to the approach of death, stimulated him. He wished to repay the kindness of the Athenians, to keep alive the splendid associations connected with his name, and to eradicate from Europe a power which, while every other nation advanced in civilization, stood still, a monument of antique barbarism. Having effected the reunion of Raymond and Perdita, I was eager to return to England; but his earnest request, added to awakening curiosity, and an indefinable anxiety to behold the catastrophe, now apparently at hand, in the long drawn history of Grecian and Turkish warfare, induced me to consent to prolong until the autumn, the period of my residence in Greece.

As soon as the health of Raymond was sufficiently re-established, he prepared to join the Grecian camp, hear Kishan, a town of some importance, situated to the east of the Hebrus; in which Perdita and Clara were to remain until the event of the expected battle. We quitted Athens on the 2nd of June. Raymond had recovered from the gaunt and pallid looks of fever. If I no longer saw the fresh glow of youth on his matured countenance, if care had besieged his brow, "And dug deep trenches in his beauty's field," if his hair, slightly mingled with grey, and his look, considerate even in its eagerness, gave signs of added years and past sufferings, yet there was something irresistibly affecting in the sight of one, lately snatched from the grave, renewing his career, untamed by sickness or disaster. The Athenians saw in him, not as heretofore, the heroic boy or desperate man, who was ready to die for them; but the prudent commander, who for their sakes was careful of his life, and could make his own warrior-propensities second to the scheme of conduct policy might point out.

All Athens accompanied us for several miles. When he had landed a month ago, the noisy populace had been hushed by sorrow and fear; but this was a festival day to all. The air resounded with their shouts; their picturesque costume, and the gay colors of which it was composed, flaunted in the sunshine; their eager gestures and rapid utterance accorded with their wild appearance. Raymond was the theme of every tongue, the hope of each wife, mother or betrothed bride, whose husband, child, or lover, making a part of the Greek army, were to be conducted to victory by him.

Notwithstanding the hazardous object of our journey, it was full of romantic interest, as we passed through the valleys, and over the hills, of this divine country. Raymond was inspirited by the intense sensations of recovered health; he felt that in being general of the Athenians, he filled a post worthy of his ambition;

and, in his hope of the conquest of Constantinople, he counted on an event which would be as a landmark in the waste of ages, an exploit unequalled in the annals of man; when a city of grand historic association, the beauty of whose site was the wonder of the world, which for many hundred years had been the strong hold of the Moslems, should be rescued from slavery and barbarism, and restored to a people illustrious for genius, civilization, and a spirit of liberty. Perdita rested on his restored society, on his love, his hopes and fame, even as a Sybarite on a luxurious couch; every thought was transport, each emotion bathed as it were in a congenial and balmy element.

We arrived at Kishan on the 7th of July. The weather during our journey had been serene. Each day, before dawn, we left our night's encampment, and watched the shadows as they retreated from hill and valley, and the golden splendor of the sun's approach. The accompanying soldiers received, with national vivacity, enthusiastic pleasure from the sight of beautiful nature. The uprising of the star of day was hailed by triumphant strains, while the birds, heard by snatches, filled up the intervals of the music. At noon, we pitched our tents in some shady valley, or embowering wood among the mountains, while a stream prattling over pebbles induced grateful sleep. Our evening march, more calm, was yet more delightful than the morning restlessness of spirit. If the band played, involuntarily they chose airs of moderated passion; the farewell of love, or lament at absence, was followed and closed by some solemn hymn, which harmonized with the tranquil loveliness of evening, and elevated the soul to grand and religious thought. Often all sounds were suspended, that we might listen to the nightingale, while the fireflies danced in bright measure, and the soft cooing of the aziolo spoke of fair weather to the travelers. Did we pass a valley? Soft shades encompassed us, and rocks tinged with beauteous hues. If we traversed a mountain, Greece, a living map, was spread beneath, her renowned pinnacles cleaving the ether, her rivers threading in silver line the fertile land. Afraid almost to breathe, we English travelers surveyed with extasy this splendid landscape, so different from the sober hues and melancholy graces of our native scenery. When we quitted Macedonia, the fertile but low plains of Thrace afforded fewer beauties; yet our journey continued to be interesting. An advanced guard gave information of our approach, and the country people were quickly in motion to do honor to Lord Raymond. The villages were decorated by triumphal arches of greenery by day, and lamps by night; tapestry waved from the windows, the ground was strewed with flowers, and the name of Raymond, joined to that of Greece, was echoed in the Evive of the peasant crowd.

When we arrived at Kishan, we learnt, that on hearing of the advance of Lord Raymond and his detachment, the Turkish army had retreated from Rodosto; but meeting with a reinforcement, they had re-trod their steps. In the meantime, Argyropylo, the Greek commander-in-chief, had advanced, so as to be between the Turks and Rodosto; a battle, it was said, was inevitable. Perdita and her child were to remain at Kishan. Raymond asked me, if I would not continue with them. "Now by the fells of Cumberland," I cried, "by all of the vagabond and poacher that appertains to me, I will stand at your side, draw my sword in the Greek cause, and be hailed as a victor along with you!"

All the plain, from Kishan to Rodosto, a distance of sixteen leagues, was alive with troops, or with the camp-followers, all in motion at the approach of a battle. The small garrisons were drawn from the various towns and fortresses and went to swell the main army. We met baggage wagons, and many females of high and low rank returning to Fairy or Kishan, there to wait the issue of the expected day. When we arrived at Rodosto, we found that the field had been taken, and the scheme of the battle arranged. The sound of firing, early on the following morning, informed us that advanced posts of the armies were engaged. Regiment after regiment advanced, their colors flying and bands playing. They planted the cannon on the tumuli, sole elevations in this level country, and formed themselves into column and hollow square, while the pioneers threw up small mounds for their protection.

These then were the preparations for a battle, nay, the battle itself; far different from anything the imagination had pictured. We read of center and wing in Greek and Roman history; we fancy a spot, plain as a table, and soldiers small as chessmen; and drawn forth, so that the most ignorant of the game can discover science and order in the disposition of the forces. When I came to the reality, and saw regiments file off to the left far out of sight, fields intervening between the battalions, but a few troops sufficiently near me to observe their motions, I gave up all idea of understanding, even of seeing a battle, but attaching myself to Raymond attended with intense interest to his actions. He shewed himself collected, gallant and imperial; his commands were prompt, his intuition of the events of the day to me miraculous. In the meantime the cannon roared; the music lifted up its enlivening voice at intervals; and we on the highest of the mounds I mentioned, too far off to observe the fallen sheaves which death gathered into his storehouse, beheld the regiments, now lost in smoke, now banners and staves peering above the cloud, while shout and clamor drowned every sound.

Early in the day, Argyropylo was wounded dangerously, and Raymond assumed the command of the whole army. He made few remarks, till, on observing through his glass the sequel of an order he had given, his face, clouded for a while with doubt, became radiant. "The day is ours," he cried, "the Turks fly from the bayonet." And then swiftly he dispatched his aides-de-camp to command the horse to fall on the routed enemy. The defeat became total; the cannon ceased to roar; the infantry rallied, and horse pursued the flying Turks along the dreary plain; the staff of Raymond was dispersed in various directions, to make observations, and bear commands. Even I was dispatched to a distant part of the field.

The ground on which the battle was fought, was a level plain - so level, that from the tumuli you saw the waving line of mountains on the wide-stretched horizon; yet the intervening space was unvaried by the least irregularity, save such undulations as resembled the waves of the sea. The whole of this part of Thrace had been so long a scene of contest, that it had remained uncultivated, and presented a dreary, barren appearance. The order I had received, was to make an observation of the direction which a detachment of the enemy might have taken, from a northern tumulus; the whole Turkish army, followed by the Greek, had poured eastward; none but the dead remained in the direction of my side. From the top of the mound, I looked far round - all was silent and deserted.

The last beams of the nearly sunken sun shot up from behind the far summit of Mount Athos; the sea of Marmora still glittered beneath its rays, while the Asiatic coast beyond was half hid in a haze of low cloud. Many a casque, and bayonet, and sword, fallen from unnerved arms, reflected the departing ray;

they lay scattered far and near. From the east, a band of ravens, old inhabitants of the Turkish cemeteries, came sailing along towards their harvest; the sun disappeared. This hour, melancholy yet sweet, has always seemed to me the time when we are most naturally led to commune with higher powers; our mortal sternness departs, and gentle complacency invests the soul. But now, in the midst of the dying and the dead, how could a thought of heaven or a sensation of tranquility possess one of the murderers? During the busy day, my mind had yielded itself a willing slave to the state of things presented to it by its fellow-beings; historical association, hatred of the foe, and military enthusiasm had held dominion over me. Now, I looked on the evening star, as softly and calmly it hung pendulous in the orange hues of sunset. I turned to the corpse-strewn earth; and felt ashamed of my species. So perhaps were the placid skies; for they quickly veiled themselves in mist, and in this change assisted the swift disappearance of twilight usual in the south; heavy masses of cloud floated up from the south east, and red and turbid lightning shot from their dark edges; the rushing wind disturbed the garments of the dead, and was chilled as it passed over their icy forms. Darkness gathered round; the objects about me became indistinct, I descended from my station, and with difficulty guided my horse, so as to avoid the slain.

Suddenly I heard a piercing shriek; a form seemed to rise from the earth; it flew swiftly towards me, sinking to the ground again as it drew near. All this passed so suddenly, that I with difficulty reined in my horse, so that it should not trample on the prostrate being. The dress of this person was that of a soldier, but the bared neck and arms, and the continued shrieks discovered a female thus disguised. I dismounted to her aid, while she, with heavy groans, and her hand placed on her side, resisted my attempt to lead her on. In the hurry of the moment I forgot that I was in Greece, and in my native accents endeavored to soothe the sufferer. With wild and terrific exclamations did the lost, dying Evadne (for it was she) recognize the language of her lover; pain and fever from her wound had deranged her intellects, while her piteous cries and feeble efforts to escape, penetrated me with compassion. In wild delirium she called upon the name of Raymond; she exclaimed that I was keeping him from her, while the Turks with fearful instruments of torture were about to take his life. Then again she sadly lamented her hard fate; that a woman, with a woman's heart and sensibility, should be driven by hopeless love and vacant hopes to take up the trade of arms, and suffer beyond the endurance of man privation, labor, and pain - the while her dry, hot hand pressed mine, and her brow and lips burned with consuming fire.

As her strength grew less, I lifted her from the ground; her emaciated form hung over my arm, her sunken cheek rested on my breast; in a sepulchral voice she murmured: - "This is the end of love! - Yet not the end!" - and frenzy lent her strength as she cast her arm up to heaven: "there is the end! there we meet again. Many living deaths have I borne for thee, O Raymond, and now I expire, thy victim! - By my death I purchase thee - lo! the instruments of war, fire, the plague are my servitors. I dared, I conquered them all, till now! I have sold myself to death, with the sole condition that thou shouldst follow me - Fire, and war, and plague, unite for thy destruction - O my Raymond, there is no safety for thee!"

With an heavy heart I listened to the changes of her delirium; I made her a bed of cloaks; her violence decreased and a clammy dew stood on her brow as the paleness of death succeeded to the crimson of fever, I placed her on the cloaks.

She continued to rave of her speedy meeting with her beloved in the grave, of his death nigh at hand; sometimes she solemnly declared that he was summoned; sometimes she bewailed his hard destiny. Her voice grew feebler, her speech interrupted; a few convulsive movements, and her muscles relaxed, the limbs fell, no more to be sustained, one deep sigh, and life was gone.

I bore her from the near neighborhood of the dead; wrapped in cloaks, I placed her beneath a tree. Once more I looked on her altered face; the last time I saw her she was eighteen; beautiful as poet's vision, splendid as a Sultana of the East - Twelve years had passed; twelve years of change, sorrow and hardship; her brilliant complexion had become worn and dark, her limbs had lost the roundness of youth and womanhood; her eyes had sunk deep,

> *Crushed and o'erworn,*
> *The hours had drained her blood, and filled her brow*
> *With lines and wrinkles.*

With shuddering horror I veiled this monument of human passion and human misery; I heaped over her all of flags and heavy accoutrements I could find, to guard her from birds and beasts of prey, until I could bestow on her a fitting grave. Sadly, and slowly I stemmed my course from among the heaps of slain, and, guided by the twinkling lights of the town, at length reached Rodosto.

CHAPTER II

On my arrival, I found that an order had already gone forth for the army to proceed immediately towards Constantinople; and the troops which had suffered least in the battle were already on their way. The town was full of tumult. The wound, and consequent inability of Argyropylo, caused Raymond to be the first in command. He rode through the town, visiting the wounded, and giving such orders as were necessary for the siege he meditated. Early in the morning the whole army was in motion. In the hurry I could hardly find an opportunity to bestow the last offices on Evadne. Attended only by my servant, I dug a deep grave for her at the foot of the tree, and without disturbing her warrior shroud, I placed her in it, heaping stones upon the grave. The dazzling sun and glare of daylight deprived the scene of solemnity; from Evadne's low tomb, I joined Raymond and his staff, now on their way to the Golden City.

Constantinople was invested, trenches dug, and advances made. The whole Greek fleet blockaded it by sea; on land from the river Kyat Kbanah, near the Sweet Waters, to the Tower of Marmora, on the shores of the Propontis, along the whole line of the ancient walls, the trenches of the siege were drawn. We already possessed Pera; the Golden Horn itself, the city, bastioned by the sea, and the ivy-mantled walls of the Greek emperors was all of Europe that the Muhammadans could call theirs. Our army looked on her as certain prey. They counted the garrison; it was impossible that it should be relieved; each sally was a victory; for, even when the Turks were triumphant, the loss of men they sustained was an irreparable injury. I rode one morning with Raymond to the lofty mound, not far from the Top Kapou, (Cannon-gate), on which Mahmoud planted his standard, and first saw the city. Still the same lofty domes and minarets towered above the verdurous walls, where Constantine had died, and the Turk had entered the city. The plain around was interspersed with cemeteries, Turk, Greek, and Armenian, with their growth of cypress trees; and other woods of more cheerful aspect, diversified the scene. Among them the Greek army was encamped, and their squadrons moved to and fro - now in regular march, now in swift career.

Raymond's eyes were fixed on the city. "I have counted the hours of her life," said he; "one month, and she falls. Remain with me till then; wait till you see the cross on St. Sophia; and then return to your peaceful glades."

"You then," I asked, "still remain in Greece?"

"Assuredly," replied Raymond. "Yet Lionel, when I say this, believe me I look back with regret to our tranquil life at Windsor. I am but half a soldier; I love the renown, but not the trade of war. Before the battle of Rodosto I was full of hope and spirit; to conquer there, and afterwards to take Constantinople, was the hope, the borne, the fulfilment of my ambition. This enthusiasm is now spent, I know not why; I seem to myself to be entering a darksome gulph; the ardent spirit of the army is irksome to me, the rapture of triumph null."

He paused and was lost in thought. His serious mien recalled, by some association, the half-forgotten Evadne to my mind, and I seized this opportunity to make enquiries from him concerning her strange lot. I asked him, if he had ever seen among the troops anyone resembling her; if since he had returned to Greece, he had heard of her?

He started at her name, - he looked uneasily on me. "Even so," he cried, "I knew you would speak of her. Long, long I had forgotten her. Since our encampment here, she daily, hourly visits my thoughts. When I am addressed, her name is the sound I expect in every communication, I imagine that she will form a part. At length you have broken the spell, tell me what you know of her."

I related my meeting with her; the story of her death was told and re-told. With painful earnestness he questioned me concerning her prophecies with regard to him. I treated them as the ravings of a maniac. "No, no," he said, "do not deceive yourself, - me you cannot. She has said nothing but what I knew before – though this is confirmation. Fire, the sword, and plague! They may all be found in yonder city; on my head alone may they fall!"

From this day Raymond's melancholy increased. He secluded himself as much as the duties of his station permitted. When in company, sadness would in spite of every effort steal over his features, and he sat absent and mute among the busy crowd that thronged about him. Perdita rejoined him, and before her he forced himself to appear cheerful, for she, even as a mirror, changed as he changed, and if he were silent and anxious, she solicitously inquired concerning, and endeavored to remove the cause of his seriousness. She resided at the palace of Sweet Waters, a summer seraglio of the Sultan; the beauty of the surrounding scenery, undefiled by war, and the freshness of the river, made this spot doubly delightful. Raymond felt no relief, received no pleasure from any show of heaven or earth. He often left Perdita, to wander in the grounds alone; or in a light shallop he floated idly on the pure waters, musing deeply. Sometimes I joined him; at such times his countenance was invariably solemn, his air dejected. He seemed relieved on seeing me and would talk with some degree of interest on the affairs of the day. There was evidently something behind all this; yet, when he appeared about to speak of that which was nearest his heart, he would abruptly turn away, and with a sigh endeavor to deliver the painful idea to the winds.

It had often occurred, that, when, as I said, Raymond quitted Perdita's drawing-room, Clara came up to me, and gently drawing me aside, said, "Papa is gone; shall we go to him? I dare say he will be glad to see you." And, as accident permitted, I complied with or refused her request. One evening a numerous assembly of Greek chieftains were gathered together in the palace. The intriguing Palli, the accomplished Karazza, the warlike Ypsilanti, were among the principal. They talked of the events of the day; the skirmish at noon; the diminished numbers of the Infidels; their defeat and flight: they contemplated, after a short interval of time, the capture of the Golden City. They endeavored to picture forth what would then happen and spoke in lofty terms of the prosperity of Greece, when Constantinople should become its capital. The conversation then reverted to Asiatic intelligence, and the ravages the plague made in its chief cities; conjectures were hazarded as to the progress that disease might have made in the besieged city.

Raymond had joined in the former part of the discussion. In lively terms he demonstrated the extremities to which Constantinople was reduced; the wasted and haggard, though ferocious appearance of the troops; famine and pestilence was at work for them, he observed, and the infidels would soon be obliged to take refuge in their only hope - submission. Suddenly in the midst of his harangue he broke off, as if stung by some painful thought; he rose uneasily, and I perceived him at length quit the hall, and through the long corridor seek the open air. He did not return; and soon Clara crept round to me, making the accustomed invitation. I consented to her request, and taking her little hand, followed Raymond. We found him just about to embark in his boat, and he readily agreed to receive us as companions. After the heats of the day, the cooling land-breeze ruffled the river, and filled our little sail. The city looked dark to the south, while numerous lights along the near shores, and the beautiful aspect of the banks reposing in placid night, the waters keenly reflecting the heavenly lights, gave to this beauteous river a dower of loveliness that might have characterized a retreat in Paradise. Our single boatman attended to the sail; Raymond steered; Clara sat at his feet, clasping his knees with her arms, and laying her head on them. Raymond began the conversation somewhat abruptly.

"This, my friend, is probably the last time we shall have an opportunity of conversing freely; my plans are now in full operation, and my time will become more and more occupied. Besides, I wish at once to tell you my wishes and expectations, and then never again to revert to so painful a subject. First, I must thank you, Lionel, for having remained here at my request. Vanity first prompted me to ask you: vanity, I call it; yet even in this I see the hand of fate - your presence will soon be necessary; you will become the last resource of Perdita, her protector and consoler. You will take her back to Windsor."

"Not without you," I said. "You do not mean to separate again?"

"Do not deceive yourself," replied Raymond, "the separation at hand is one over which I have no control; most near at hand is it; the days are already counted. May I trust you? For many days I have longed to disclose the mysterious presentiments that weigh on me, although I fear that you will ridicule them. Yet do not, my gentle friend; for, all childish and unwise as they are, they have become a part of me, and I dare not expect to shake them off.

"Yet how can I expect you to sympathize with me? You are of this world; I am not. You hold forth your hand; it is even as a part of yourself; and you do not yet divide the feeling of identity from the mortal form that shapes forth Lionel. How then can you understand me? Earth is to me a tomb, the firmament a vault, shrouding mere corruption. Time is no more, for I have stepped within the threshold of eternity; each man I meet appears a curse, which will soon be deserted of its animating spark, on the eve of decay and corruption.

Cada piedra un piramide levanta, y cada flor costruye un monumento, cada edificio es un sepulcro altivo, cada soldado un esqueleto vivo."
(Each stone raises a pyramid, and each flower builds a monument, each building is a haughty grave, each soldier a living skeleton)

His accent was mournful, - he sighed deeply. "A few months ago," he continued, "I was thought to be dying; but life was strong within me. My affections were human; hope and love were the day-stars of my life. Now - they dream that the brows of the conqueror of the infidel faith are about to be encircled by triumphant laurel; they talk of honorable reward, of title, power, and wealth—all I ask of Greece is a grave. Let them raise a mound above my lifeless body, which may stand even when the dome of St. Sophia has fallen.

"Wherefore do I feel thus? At Rodosto I was full of hope; but when first I saw Constantinople, that feeling, with every other joyful one, departed. The last words of Evadne were the seal upon the warrant of my death. Yet I do not pretend to account for my mood by any particular event. All I can say is, that it is so. The plague I am told is in Constantinople, perhaps I have imbibed its effluvia—perhaps disease is the real cause of my prognostications. It matters little why or wherefore I am affected, no power can avert the stroke, and the shadow of Fate's uplifted hand already darkens me.

To you, Lionel, I entrust your sister and her child. Never mention to her the fatal name of Evadne. She would doubly sorrow over the strange link that enchains me to her, making my spirit obey her dying voice, following her, as it is about to do, to the unknown country."

I listened to him with wonder; but that his sad demeanor and solemn utterance assured me of the truth and intensity of his feelings, I should with light derision have attempted to dissipate his fears. Whatever I was about to reply, was interrupted by the powerful emotions of Clara. Raymond had spoken, thoughtless of her presence, and she, poor child, heard with terror and faith the prophecy of his death. Her father was moved by her violent grief; he took her in his arms and soothed her, but his very soothings were solemn and fearful. "Weep not, sweet child," said he, "the coming death of one you have hardly known. I may die, but in death I can never forget or desert my own Clara. In after sorrow or joy, believe that you father's spirit is near, to save or sympathize with you. Be proud of me and cherish your infant remembrance of me. Thus, sweetest, I shall not appear to die. One thing you must promise, - not to speak to anyone but your uncle, of the conversation you have just overheard. When I am gone, you will console your mother, and tell her that death was only bitter because it divided me from her; that my last thoughts will be spent on her. But while I live, promise not to betray me; promise, my child."

With faltering accents Clara promised, while she still clung to her father in a transport of sorrow. Soon we returned to shore, and I endeavored to obviate the impression made on the child's mind, by treating Raymond's fears lightly. We heard no more of them; for, as he had said, the siege, now drawing to a conclusion, became paramount in interest, engaging all his time and attention.

The empire of the Mohammedans in Europe was at its close. The Greek fleet blockading every port of Stambol, prevented the arrival of succor from Asia; all egress on the side towards land had become impracticable, except to such desperate sallies, as reduced the numbers of the enemy without making any impression on our lines. The garrison was now so much diminished, that it was evident that the city could easily have been carried by storm; but both humanity and policy dictated a slower mode of proceeding. We could hardly doubt that, if pursued to the utmost, its palaces, its temples and store of wealth would be destroyed in the fury of contending triumph and defeat. Already the defenseless citizens had suffered through the barbarity of the Janissaries; and, in time of storm, tumult and massacre, beauty, infancy and decrepitude, would have alike been sacrificed to the brutal ferocity of the soldiers. Famine and blockade were certain means of conquest; and on these we founded our hopes of victory.

Each day the soldiers of the garrison assaulted our advanced posts and impeded the accomplishment of our works. Fireboats were launched from the various ports, while our troops sometimes recoiled from the devoted courage of men who did not seek to live, but to sell their lives dearly. These contests were aggravated by the season: they took place during summer, when the southern Asiatic wind came laden with intolerable heat, when the streams were dried up in their shallow beds, and the vast basin of the sea appeared to glow under the unmitigated rays of the solstitial sun. Nor did night refresh the earth. Dew was denied; herbage and flowers there were none; the very trees drooped; and summer assumed the blighted appearance of winter, as it went forth in silence and flame to abridge the means of sustenance to man. In vain did the eye strive to find the wreck of some northern cloud in the stainless empyrean, which might bring hope of change and moisture to the oppressive and windless atmosphere. All was serene, burning, annihilating. We the besiegers were in the comparison little affected by these evils. The woods around afforded us shade, -the river secured to us a constant supply of water; nay, detachments were employed in furnishing the army with ice, which had been laid up on Haemus, and Athos, and the mountains of Macedonia, while cooling fruits and wholesome food renovated the strength of the laborer's, and made us bear with less impatience the weight of the unrefreshing air. But in the city things wore a different face. The sun's rays were refracted from the pavement and buildings - the stoppage of the public fountains- the bad quality of the food, and scarcity even of that, produced a state of suffering, which was aggravated by the scourge of disease; while the garrison arrogated every superfluity to themselves, adding by waste and riot to the necessary evils of the time. Still they would not capitulate.

Suddenly the system of warfare was changed. We experienced no more assaults; and by night and day we continued our labors unimpeded. Stranger still, when the troops advanced near the city, the walls were vacant, and no cannon was pointed against the intruders. When these circumstances were reported to Raymond, he caused minute observations to be made as to what was doing within the walls, and when his scouts returned, reporting only the continued silence and desolation of the city, he commanded the army to be drawn out before the gates. No one appeared on the walls; the very portals, though locked and barred, seemed unguarded; above, the many domes and glittering crescents pierced heaven; while the old walls, survivors of ages, with ivy-crowned tower and weed-tangled buttress, stood as rocks in an uninhabited waste. From within the city neither shout nor cry, nor aught except the casual howling of a dog, broke the noon-day stillness. Even our soldiers were awed to silence; the music paused; the clang of arms was hushed. Each man asked his fellow in whispers, the meaning of this sudden peace; while Raymond from a height endeavored, by means of glasses, to discover and observe the stratagem of the enemy. No form could be discerned on the terraces of the houses; in the higher parts of the town no moving shadow bespoke the presence of any living being: the very trees waved not and mocked the stability of architecture with like immovability.

The tramp of horses, distinctly heard in the silence, was at length discerned. It was a troop sent by Karazza, the Admiral; they bore dispatches to the

Lord General. The contents of these papers were important. The night before, the watch, on board one of the smaller vessels anchored near the seraglio wall, was roused by a slight splashing as of muffled oars; the alarm was given: twelve small boats, each containing three Janissaries, were descried endeavoring to make their way through the fleet to the opposite shore of Scutari. When they found themselves discovered they discharged their muskets, and some came to the front to cover the others, whose crews, exerting all their strength, endeavored to escape with their light barks from among the dark hulls that environed them. They were in the end all sunk, and, with the exception of two or three prisoners, the crews drowned. Little could be got from the survivors; but their cautious answers caused it to be surmised that several expeditions had preceded this last, and that several Turks of rank and importance had been conveyed to Asia. The men disdainfully repelled the idea of having deserted the defense of their city; and one, the youngest among them, in answer to the taunt of a sailor, exclaimed, "Take it, Christian dogs! take the palaces, the gardens, the mosques, the abode of our fathers - take plague with them; pestilence is the enemy we fly; if she be your friend, hug her to your bosoms. The curse of Allah is on Stambol, share ye her fate."

Such was the account sent by Karazza to Raymond: but a tale full of monstrous exaggerations, though founded on this, was spread by the accompanying troop among our soldiers. A murmur arose, the city was the prey of pestilence; already had a mighty power subjugated the inhabitants; Death had become lord of Constantinople.

I have heard a picture described, wherein all the inhabitants of earth were drawn out in fear to stand the encounter of Death. The feeble and decrepit fled; the warriors retreated, though they threatened even in flight. Wolves and lions, and various monsters of the desert roared against him; while the grim Unreality hovered shaking his spectral dart, a solitary but invincible assailant. Even so was it with the army of Greece. I am convinced, that had the myriad troops of Asia come from over the Propontis, and stood defenders of the Golden City, each and every Greek would have marched against the overwhelming numbers, and have devoted himself with patriotic fury for his country. But here no hedge of bayonets opposed itself, no death-dealing artillery, no formidable array of brave soldiers - the unguarded walls afforded easy entrance - the vacant palaces luxurious dwellings; but above the dome of St. Sophia the superstitious Greek saw Pestilence, and shrunk in trepidation from her influence.

Raymond was actuated by far other feelings. He descended the hill with a face beaming with triumph, and pointing with his sword to the gates, commanded his troops to - down with those barricades — the only obstacles now to completest victory. The soldiers answered his cheerful words with aghast and awe-struck looks; instinctively they drew back, and Raymond rode in the front of the lines:

- "*By my sword I swear,*" *he cried,* "*that no ambush or stratagem endangers you. The enemy is already vanquished; the pleasant places, the noble dwellings and spoil of the city are already yours; force the gate; enter and possess the seats of your ancestors, your own inheritance!*"

A universal shudder and fearful whispering passed through the lines; not a soldier moved. "Cowards!" exclaimed their general, exasperated, "give me a hatchet! I alone will enter! I will plant your standard; and when you see it wave from yon highest minaret, you may gain courage, and rally round it!"

One of the officers now came forward: "General," he said, "we neither fear the courage, nor arms, the open attack, nor secret ambush of the Moslems. We are ready to expose our breasts, exposed ten thousand times before, to the balls and scimitars of the infidels, and to fall gloriously for Greece. But we will not die in heaps, like dogs poisoned in summertime, by the pestilential air of that city - we dare not go against the Plague!"

A multitude of men are feeble and inert, without a voice, a leader; give them that, and they regain the strength belonging to their numbers. Shouts from a thousand voices now rent the air - the cry of applause became universal. Raymond saw the danger; he was willing to save his troops from the crime of disobedience; for he knew, that contention once begun between the commander and his army, each act and word added to the weakness of the former, and bestowed power on the latter. He gave orders for the retreat to be sounded, and the regiments repaired in good order to the camp.

I hastened to carry the intelligence of these strange proceedings to Perdita; and we were soon joined by Raymond. He looked gloomy and perturbed. My sister was struck by my narrative: "How beyond the imagination of man," she exclaimed, "are the decrees of heaven, wondrous and inexplicable!"

"Foolish girl," cried Raymond angrily, "are you like my valiant soldiers, panic-struck? What is there inexplicable, pray, tell me, in so very natural an occurrence? Does not the plague rage each year in Stambol? What wonder, that this year, when as we are told, its virulence is unexampled in Asia, that it should have occasioned double havoc in that city? What wonder then, in time of siege, want, extreme heat, and drought, that it should make unaccustomed ravages? Less wonder far is it, that the garrison, despairing of being able to hold out longer, should take advantage of the negligence of our fleet to escape at once from siege and capture. It is not pestilence - by the God that lives! it is not either plague or impending danger that makes us, like birds in harvest-time, terrified by a scarecrow, abstain from the ready prey — it is base superstition - And thus the aim of the valiant is made the shuttlecock of fools; the worthy ambition of the high-souled, the plaything of these tamed hares! But yet Stambol shall be ours! By my past labors, by torture and imprisonment suffered for them, by my victories, by my sword, I swear - by my hopes of fame, by my former deserts now awaiting their reward, I deeply vow, with these hands to plant the cross on yonder mosque!"

"Dearest Raymond!" interrupted Perdita, in a supplicating accent.

He had been walking to and fro in the marble hall of the seraglio; his very lips were pale with rage, while, quivering, they shaped his angry words - his eyes shot fire - his gestures seemed restrained by their very vehemence. "Perdita," he continued, impatiently, "I know what you would say; I know that you love me, that you are good and gentle; but this is no woman's work - nor can a female heart guess at the hurricane which tears me!"

He seemed half afraid of his own violence, and suddenly quitted the hall: a look from Perdita shewed me her distress, and I followed him. He was pacing the garden: his passions were in a state of inconceivable turbulence. "Am I forever," he cried, "to be the sport of fortune! Must man, the heaven-climber, be forever the victim of the crawling reptiles of his species! Were I as you, Lionel, looking forward to many years of life, to a succession of love-enlightened days, to refined enjoyments and fresh-springing hopes, I might yield, and breaking my General's staff, seek repose in the glades of Windsor. But I am about to die! - nay, interrupt me not - soon I shall die. From the many-peopled earth, from the sympathies of man, from the loved resorts of my youth, from the kindness of my friends, from the affection of my only beloved Perdita, I am about to be removed. Such is the will of fate! Such the decree of the High Ruler from whom there is no appeal: to whom I submit. But to lose all - to lose with life and love, glory also! It shall not be! "I, and in a few brief years, all you, - this panic-struck army, and all the population of fair Greece, will no longer be. But other generations will arise, and ever and for-ever will continue, to be made happier by our present acts, to be glorified by our valor. The prayer of my youth was to be one among those who render the pages of earth's history splendid, who exalt the race of man, and make this little globe a dwelling of the mighty. Alas, for Raymond! the prayer of his youth is wasted — the hopes of his manhood are null!

"From my dungeon in yonder city I cried, soon I will be thy lord! When Evadne pronounced my death, I thought that the title of Victor of Constantinople would be written on my tomb, and I subdued all mortal fear. I stand before its vanquished walls and dare not call myself a conqueror. So, shall it not be! Did not Alexander leap from the walls of the city of the Oxydracae, to shew his coward troops the way to victory, encountering alone the swords of its defenders? Even so will I brave the plague - and though no man follows, I will plant the Grecian standard on the height of St. Sophia."

Reason came unavailing to such high-wrought feelings. In vain I shewed him, that when winter came, the cold would dissipate the pestilential air, and re-store courage to the Greeks. "Talk not of other season than this!" he cried. "I have lived my last winter, and the date of this year, 2092, will be carved upon my tomb. Already do I see," he continued, looking up mournfully, "the borne and precipitate edge of my existence, over which I plunge into the gloomy mystery of the life to come. I am prepared, so that I leave behind a trail of light so radiant, that my worst enemies cannot cloud it. I owe this to Greece, to you, to my surviving Perdita, and to myself, the victim of ambition."

We were interrupted by an attendant, who announced, that the staff of Raymond was assembled in the council-chamber. He requested me in the mean-time to ride through the camp, and to observe and report to him the dispositions of the soldiers; he then left me. I had been excited to the utmost by the proceedings of the day, and now more than ever by the passionate language of Raymond. Alas! for human reason! He accused the Greeks of superstition: what name did he give to the faith he lent to the predictions of Evadne? I passed from the palace of Sweet Waters to the plain on which the encampment lay and found its inhabitants in commotion. The arrival of several with fresh stories of marvels, from the fleet; the exaggerations bestowed on what was already known; tales of old prophecies, of fearful histories of whole regions which had been laid waste during the present year by pestilence, alarmed and occupied the troops. Discipline was lost; the army disbanded itself. Each individual, before a part of a great whole moving only in unison with others, now became resolved into the unit nature had made him and thought of himself only. They stole off at first by ones and twos, then in larger companies, until, unimpeded by the officers, whole battalions sought the road that led to Macedonia.

About midnight I returned to the palace and sought Raymond; he was alone, and apparently composed; such composure, at least, was his as is inspired by a resolve to adhere to a certain line of conduct. He heard my account of the self-dissolution of the army with calmness, and then said, "You know, Verney, my fixed determination not to quit this place, until in the light of day Stambol is confessedly ours. If the men I have about me shrink from following me, others, more courageous, are to be found. Go you before break of day, bear these dispatches to Karazza, add to them your own entreaties that he send me his marines and naval force; if I can get but one regiment to second me, the rest would follow of course. Let him send me this regiment. I shall expect your return by to-morrow noon." Methought this was but a poor expedient; but I assured him of my obedience and zeal. I quitted him to take a few hours rest. With the breaking of morning I was accoutered for my ride. I lingered awhile, desirous of taking leave of Perdita, and from my window observed the approach of the sun. The golden splendor arose, and weary nature awoke to suffer yet another day of heat and thirsty decay. No flowers lifted up their dew-laden cups to meet the dawn; the dry grass had withered on the plains; the burning fields of air were vacant of birds; the cycle alone, children of the sun, began their shrill and deafening song among the cypresses and olives. I saw Raymond's coal-black charger brought to the palace gate; a small company of officers arrived soon after; care and fear was painted on each cheek, and in each eye, unrefreshed by sleep. I found Raymond and Perdita together. He was watching the rising sun, while with one arm he encircled his beloved's waist; she looked on him, the sun of her life, with earnest gaze of mingled anxiety and tenderness. Raymond started angrily when he saw me. "Here still?" he cried. "Is this your promised zeal?"

"Pardon me," I said, "but even as you speak, I am gone."

"Nay, pardon me," he replied, "I have no right to command or reproach, but my life hangs on your departure and speedy return. Farewell!"

His voice had recovered its bland tone, but a dark cloud still hung on his features. I would have delayed; I wished to recommend watchfulness to Perdita, but his presence restrained me. I had no pretense for my hesitation; and on his repeating his farewell, I clasped his outstretched hand; it was cold and clammy. "Take care of yourself, my dear Lord," I said.

"Nay," said Perdita, "that task shall be mine. Return speedily, Lionel." With an air of absence, he was playing with her auburn locks, while she leaned on him; twice I turned back, only to look again on this matchless pair. At last, with slow and heavy steps, I had paced out of the hall, and sprung upon my horse. At that moment Clara flew towards me; clasping my knee she cried, "Make haste back, uncle! Dear uncle, I have such fearful dreams; I dare not tell my mother. Do not be long away!" I assured her of my impatience to return, and then, with a small escort rode along the plain towards the tower of Marmora.

I fulfilled my commission; I saw Karazza. He was somewhat surprised; he would see, he said, what could be done; but it required time; and Raymond had ordered me to return by noon. It was impossible to affect anything in so short a time. I must stay till the next day; or come back, after having reported the present state of things to the general. My choice was easily made. A restlessness, a fear of what was about to betide, a doubt as to Raymond's purposes, urged me to return without delay to his quarters. Quitting the Seven Towers, I rode eastward towards the Sweet Waters. I took a circuitous path, principally for the sake of going to the top of the mount before mentioned, which commanded a view of the city. I had my glass with me. The city basked under the noon-day sun, and the venerable walls formed its picturesque boundary. Immediately before me was the Top Kapou, the gate near which Mahomet had made the breach by which he entered the city.

Trees gigantic and aged grew near; before the gate I discerned a crowd of moving human figures - with intense curiosity I lifted my glass to my eye. I saw Lord Raymond on his charger; a small company of officers had gathered about him; and behind was a promiscuous concourse of soldiers and subalterns, their discipline lost, their arms thrown aside; no music sounded, no banners streamed. The only flag among them was one which Raymond carried; he pointed with it to the gate of the city. The circle round him fell back. With angry gestures he leapt from his horse and seizing a hatchet that hung from his saddlebow, went with the apparent intention of battering down the opposing gate. A few men came to aid him; their numbers increased; under their united blows the obstacle was vanquished, gate, portcullis, and fence were demolished; and the wide sun-lit way, leading to the heart of the city, now lay open before them. The men shrank back; they seemed afraid of what they had already done and stood as if they expected some Mighty Phantom to stalk in offended majesty from the opening. Raymond sprung lightly on his horse, grasped the standard, and with words which I could not hear (but his gestures, being their fit accompaniment, were marked by passionate energy,) he seemed to adjure their assistance and companionship; even as he spoke, the crowd receded from him. Indignation now transported him; his words I guessed were fraught with disdain - then turning from his coward followers, he addressed himself to enter the city alone. His very horse seemed to back from the fatal entrance; his dog, his faithful dog, lay moaning and supplicating in his path - in a moment more, he had plunged the rowels into the sides of the stung animal, who bounded forward, and he, the gateway passed, was galloping up the broad and deserted street.

Until this moment my soul had been in my eyes only. I had gazed with wonder, mixed with fear and enthusiasm. The latter feeling now predominated. I forgot the distance between us: "I will go with thee, Raymond!" I cried; but my eye removed from the glass, I could scarce discern the pigmy forms of the crowd, which about a mile from me surrounded the gate; the form of Raymond was lost. Stung with impatience, I urged my horse with force of spur and loosened reins down the acclivity, that, before danger could arrive, I might be at the side of my noble, godlike friend. A number of buildings and trees intervened, when I had reached the plain, hiding the city from my view. But at that moment a crash was heard. Thunder like it reverberated through the sky, while the air was darkened. A moment more and the old walls again met my sight, while over them hovered a murky cloud; fragments of buildings whirled above, half seen in smoke, while flames burst out beneath, and continued explosions filled the air with terrific thunders. Flying from the mass of falling ruin which leapt over the high walls, and shook the ivy towers, a crowd of soldiers made for the road by which I came; I was surrounded, hemmed in by them, unable to get forward. My impatience rose to its utmost; I stretched out my hands to the men; I conjured them to turn back and save their General, the conqueror of Stambol, the liberator of Greece; tears, aye tears, in warm flow gushed from my eyes - I would not believe in his destruction; yet every mass that darkened the air seemed to bear with it a portion of the martyred Raymond. Horrible sights were shaped to me in the turbid cloud that hovered over the city; and my only relief was derived from the struggles I made to approach the gate. Yet when I effected my purpose, all I could discern within the precincts of the massive walls was a city of fire: the open way through which Raymond had ridden was enveloped in smoke and flame. After an interval the explosions ceased, but the flames still shot up from various quarters; the dome of St. Sophia had disappeared. Strange to say (the result perhaps of the concussion of air occasioned by the blowing up of the city) huge, white thunder clouds lifted themselves up from the southern horizon, and gathered over-head; they were the first blots on the blue expanse that I had seen for months, and amidst this havoc and despair they inspired pleasure. The vault above became obscured, lightning flashed from the heavy masses, followed instantaneously by crashing thunder; then the big rain fell. The flames of the city bent beneath it; and the smoke and dust arising from the ruins was dissipated.

I no sooner perceived an abatement of the flames than, hurried on by an irresistible impulse, I endeavored to penetrate the town. I could only do this on foot, as the mass of ruin was impracticable for a horse. I had never entered the city before, and its ways were unknown to me. The streets were blocked up, the ruins smoking; I climbed up one heap, only to view others in succession; and nothing told me where the center of the town might be, or towards what point Raymond might have directed his course. The rain ceased; the clouds sunk behind the horizon; it was now evening, and the sun descended swiftly the western sky. I scrambled on, until I came to a street, whose wooden houses, half-burnt, had been cooled by the rain, and were fortunately uninjured by the gunpowder. Up this I hurried - until now I had not seen a vestige of man. Yet none of the defaced human forms which I distinguished, could be Raymond; so, I turned my eyes away, while my heart sickened within me. I came to an open space - a mountain of ruin in the midst, announced that some large mosque had occupied the space - and here, scattered about, I saw various articles of luxury and wealth, singed, destroyed - but shewing what they had been in their ruin - jewels, strings of pearls, embroidered robes, rich furs, glittering tapestries, and oriental ornaments, seemed to have been collected here in a pile destined for destruction; but the rain had stopped the havoc midway.

Hours passed, while in this scene of ruin I sought for Raymond. Insurmountable heaps sometimes opposed themselves; the still burning fires scorched me. The sun set; the atmosphere grew dim - and the evening star no longer shone companionless. The glare of flames attested the progress of destruction, while, during mingled light and obscurity, the piles around me took gigantic proportions and weird shapes. For a moment I could yield to the creative power of the imagination, and for a moment was soothed by the sublime fictions it presented to me. The beatings of my human heart drew me back to blank reality. Where, in this wilderness of death, art thou, O Raymond - ornament of England, deliverer of Greece, "hero of unwritten story," where in this burning chaos are thy dear relics strewed? I called aloud for him - through the darkness of night, over the scorching ruins of fallen Constantinople, his name was heard; no voice replied - echo even was mute.

I was overcome by weariness; the solitude depressed my spirits. The sultry air impregnated with dust, the heat and smoke of burning palaces, palsied my limbs. Hunger suddenly came acutely upon me. The excitement which had hitherto sustained me was lost; as a building, whose props are loosened, and whose foundations rock, totters and falls, so when enthusiasm and hope deserted me, did my strength fail. I sat on the sole remaining step of an edifice, which even in its downfall, was huge and magnificent; a few broken walls, not dislodged by gunpowder, stood in fantastic groups, and a flame glimmered at intervals on the summit of the pile. For a time, hunger and sleep contended, till the constellations reeled before my eyes and then were lost. I strove to rise, but my heavy lids closed, my limbs over-wearied, claimed repose - I rested my head on the stone, I yielded to the grateful sensation of utter forgetfulness; and in that scene of desolation, on that night of despair - I slept.

CHAPTER III

The stars still shone brightly when I awoke, and Taurus high in the southern heaven shewed that it was midnight. I awoke from disturbed dreams. Methought I had been invited to Timon's last feast; I came with keen appetite, the covers were removed, the hot water sent up its unsatisfying steams, while I fled before the anger of the host, who assumed the form of Raymond; while to my diseased fancy, the vessels hurled by him after me, were surcharged with fetid vapor, and my friend's shape, altered by a thousand distortions, expanded into a gigantic phantom, bearing on its brow the sign of pestilence. The growing shadow rose and rose, filling, and then seeming to endeavor to burst beyond, the adamantine vault that bent over, sustaining and enclosing the world. The nightmare became torture; with a strong effort I threw off sleep, and recalled reason to her wonted functions. My first thought was Perdita; to her I must return; her I must support, drawing such food from despair as might best sustain her wounded heart; recalling her from the wild excesses of grief, by the austere laws of duty, and the soft tenderness of regret.

The position of the stars was my only guide. I turned from the awful ruin of the Golden City, and, after great exertion, succeeded in extricating myself from its enclosure. I met a company of soldiers outside the walls; I borrowed a horse from one of them and hastened to my sister. The appearance of the plain was changed during this short interval; the encampment was broken up; the relics of the disbanded army met in small companies here and there; each face was clouded; every gesture spoke astonishment and dismay.

With an heavy heart I entered the palace, and stood fearful to advance, to speak, to look. In the midst of the hall was Perdita; she sat on the marble pavement, her head fallen on her bosom, her hair disheveled, her fingers twined busily one within the other; she was pale as marble, and every feature was contracted by agony. She perceived me and looked up enquiringly; her half glance of hope was misery; the words died before I could articulate them; I felt a ghastly smile wrinkle my lips. She understood my gesture; again, her head fell; again her fingers worked restlessly. At last I recovered speech, but my voice terrified her; the hapless girl had understood my look, and for worlds she would not that the tale of her heavy misery should have been shaped out and confirmed by hard, irrevocable words. Nay, she seemed to wish to distract my thoughts from the subject: she rose from the floor: "Hush!" she said, whisperingly; "after much weeping, Clara sleeps; we must not disturb her." She seated herself then on the same ottoman where I had left her in the morning resting on the beating heart of her Raymond; I dared not approach her, but sat at a distant corner, watching her starting and nervous gestures. At length, in an abrupt manner she asked, "Where is he?"

"O, fear not," she continued, "fear not that I should entertain hope! Yet tell me, have you found him? To have him once more in my arms, to see him, however changed, is all I desire. Though Constantinople be heaped above him as a tomb, yet I must find him - then cover us with the city's weight, with a mountain piled above - I care not, so that one grave hold Raymond and his Perdita." Then weeping, she clung to me: "Take me to him," she cried, "unkind Lionel, why do you keep me here? Of myself I cannot find him - but you know where he lies - lead me thither."

At first these agonizing plaints filled me with intolerable compassion. But soon I endeavored to extract patience for her from the ideas she suggested. I related my adventures of the night, my endeavors to find our lost one, and my disappointment. Turning her thoughts this way, I gave them an object which rescued them from insanity. With apparent calmness she discussed with me the probable spot where he might be found and planned the means we should use for that purpose. Then hearing of my fatigue and abstinence, she herself brought me food. I seized the favorable moment and endeavored to awaken in her something beyond the killing torpor of grief. As I spoke, my subject carried me away; deep admiration; grief, the offspring of truest affection, the overflowing of a heart bursting with sympathy for all that had been great and sublime in the career of my friend, inspired me as I poured forth the praises of Raymond.

"Alas, for us," I cried, "who have lost this latest honor of the world! Beloved Raymond! He is gone to the nations of the dead; he has become one of those, who render the dark abode of the obscure grave illustrious by dwelling there. He has journeyed on the road that leads to it and joined the mighty of soul who went before him. When the world was in its infancy death must have been terrible, and man left his friends and kindred to dwell, a solitary stranger, in an unknown country. But now, he who dies finds many companions gone before to prepare for his reception. The great of past ages people it, the exalted hero of our own days is counted among its inhabitants, while life becomes doubly 'the desert and the solitude.'

"What a noble creature was Raymond, the first among the men of our time. By the grandeur of his conceptions, the graceful daring of his actions, by his wit and beauty, he won and ruled the minds of all. Of one only fault he might have been accused; but his death has cancelled that. I have heard him called inconstant of purpose - when he deserted, for the sake of love, the hope of sovereignty, and when he abdicated the Protectorship of England, men blamed his infirmity of purpose. Now his death has crowned his life, and to the end of time it will be remembered, that he devoted himself, a willing victim, to the glory of Greece. Such was his choice: he expected to die. He foresaw that he should leave this cheerful earth, the lightsome sky, and thy love, Perdita; yet he neither hesitated nor turned back, going right onward to his mark of fame. While the earth lasts, his actions will be recorded with praise. Grecian maidens will in devotion strew flowers on his tomb and make the air around it resonant with patriotic hymns, in which his name will find high record."

I saw the features of Perdita soften; the sternness of grief yielded to tenderness - I continued: - "Thus to honor him, is the sacred duty of his survivors. To make his name even as a holy spot of ground, enclosing it from all hostile attacks by our praise, shedding on it the blossoms of love and regret, guarding it from decay, and bequeathing it untainted to posterity. Such is the duty of his friends. A dearer one belongs to you, Perdita, mother of his child. Do you remember in her infancy, with what transport you beheld Clara, recognizing in her the united being of yourself and Raymond; joying to view in this living temple a manifestation of your eternal loves. Even such is she still. You say that you have lost Raymond. O, no! - yet he lives with you and in you there. From him she sprung, flesh of his flesh, bone of his bone - and not, as heretofore, are you content to trace in her downy cheek and delicate limbs, an affinity to Raymond, but in her enthusiastic affections, in the sweet qualities of her mind, you may still find him living, the good, the great, the beloved. Be it your care to foster this similarity - be it your care to render her worthy of him, so that, when she glories in her origin, she takes not shame for what she is."

I could perceive that, when I recalled my sister's thoughts to her duties in life, she did not listen with the same patience as before. She appeared to suspect a plan of consolation on my part, from which she, cherishing her new-born grief, revolted. "You talk of the future," she said, "while the present is all to me. Let me find the earthly dwelling of my beloved; let us rescue that from common dust, so that in times to come men may point to the sacred tomb, and name it his - then to other thoughts, and a new course of life, or what else fate, in her cruel tyranny, may have marked out for me."

After a short repose I prepared to leave her, that I might endeavor to accomplish her wish. In the meantime, we were joined by Clara, whose pallid cheek and scared look shewed the deep impression grief had made on her young mind. She seemed to be full of something to which she could not give words; but, seizing an opportunity afforded by Perdita's absence, she preferred to me an earnest prayer, that I would take her within view of the gate at which her father had entered Constantinople. She promised to commit no extravagance, to be docile, and immediately to return. I could not refuse; for Clara was not an ordinary child; her sensibility and intelligence seemed already to have endowed her with the rights of womanhood. With her therefore, before me on my horse, attended only by the servant who was to re-conduct her, we rode to the Top Kapou. We found a party of soldiers gathered round it. They were listening. "They are human cries," said one: "More like the howling of a dog," replied another; and again, they bent to catch the sound of regular distant moans, which issued from the precincts of the ruined city. "That, Clara," I said, "is the gate, that the street which yestermorn your father rode up." Whatever Clara's intention had been in asking to be brought hither, it was balked by the presence of the soldiers. With earnest gaze she looked on the labyrinth of smoking piles which had been a city, and then expressed her readiness to return home. At this moment a melancholy howl struck on our ears; it was repeated; "Hark!" cried Clara, "he is there; that is Florio, my father's dog." It seemed to me impossible that she could recognize the sound, but she persisted in her assertion till she gained credit with the crowd about. At least it would be a benevolent action to rescue the sufferer, whether human or brute, from the desolation of the town; so, sending Clara back to her home, I again entered Constantinople. Encouraged by the impunity attendant on my former visit, several soldiers who had made a part of Raymond's bodyguard, who had loved him, and sincerely mourned his loss, accompanied me.

It is impossible to conjecture the strange enchainment of events which restored the lifeless form of my friend to our hands. In that part of the town where the fire had most raged the night before, and which now lay quenched, black and cold, the dying dog of Raymond crouched beside the mutilated form of its lord.

At such a time sorrow has no voice; affliction, tamed by it is very vehemence, is mute. The poor animal recognized me, licked my hand, crept close to its lord, and died. He had been evidently thrown from his horse by some falling ruin, which had crushed his head, and defaced his whole person. I bent over the body and took in my hand the edge of his cloak, less altered in appearance than the human frame it clothed. I pressed it to my lips, while the rough soldiers gathered around, mourning over this worthiest prey of death, as if regret and endless lamentation could re-illumine the extinguished spark, or call to its shattered prison-house of flesh the liberated spirit. Yesterday those limbs were worth an universe; they then enshrined a transcendent power, whose intents, words, and actions were worthy to be recorded in letters of gold; now the superstition of affection alone could give value to the shattered mechanism, which, incapable and clod-like, no more resembled Raymond, than the fallen rain is like the former mansion of cloud in which it climbed the highest skies, and gilded by the sun, attracted all eyes, and satiated the sense by its excess of beauty.

Such as he had now become, such as was his terrene vesture, defaced and spoiled, we wrapped it in our cloaks, and lifting the burthen in our arms, bore it from this city of the dead. The question arose as to where we should deposit him. In our road to the palace, we passed through the Greek cemetery; here on a tablet of black marble I caused him to be laid; the cypresses waved high above, their death-like gloom accorded with his state of nothingness. We cut branches of the funereal trees and placed them over him, and on these again his sword. I left a guard to protect this treasure of dust; and ordered perpetual torches to be burned around.

When I returned to Perdita, I found that she had already been informed of the success of my undertaking. He, her beloved, the sole and eternal object of her passionate tenderness, had restored her. Such was the maniac language of her enthusiasm. What though those limbs moved not, and those lips could no more frame modulated accents of wisdom and love! What though like a weed flung from the fruitless sea, he lay the prey of corruption - still that was the form she had caressed, those the lips that meeting hers, had drank the spirit of love from the commingling breath; that was the earthly mechanism of dissoluble clay she had called her own. True, she looked forward to another life; true, the burning spirit of love seemed to her unextinguishable throughout eternity. Yet at this time, with human fondness, she clung to all that her human senses permitted her to see and feel to be a part of Raymond.

Pale as marble, clear and beaming as that, she heard my tale, and enquired concerning the spot where he had been deposited. Her features had lost the distortion of grief; her eyes were brightened, her very person seemed dilated; while the excessive whiteness and even transparency of her skin, and something hollow in her voice, bore witness that not tranquility, but excess of excitement, occasioned the treacherous calm that settled on her countenance. I asked her where he should be buried. She replied, "At Athens; even at the Athens which he loved. Without the town, on the acclivity of Hymettus, there is a rocky recess which he pointed out to me as the spot where he would wish to repose."

My own desire certainly was that he should not be removed from the spot where he now lay. But her wish was of course to be complied with; and I entreated her to prepare without delay for our departure.

Behold now the melancholy train cross the flats of Thrace, and wind through the defiles, and over the mountains of Macedonia, coast the clear waves of the Peneus, cross the Larissean plain, pass the straits of Thermopylae, and ascending in succession Oeta and Parnassus, descend to the fertile plain of Athens. Women bear with resignation these long drawn ills, but to a man's impatient spirit, the slow motion of our cavalcade, the melancholy repose we took at noon, the perpetual presence of the pall, gorgeous though it was, that wrapped the rifled casket which had contained Raymond, the monotonous recurrence of day and night, unvaried by hope or change, all the circumstances of our march were intolerable. Perdita, shut up in herself, spoke little. Her carriage was closed; and, when we rested, she sat leaning her pale cheek on her white cold hand, with eyes fixed on the ground, indulging thoughts which refused communication or sympathy.

We descended from Parnassus, emerging from its many folds, and passed through Livadia on our road to Attica. Perdita would not enter Athens; but reposing at Marathon on the night of our arrival, conducted me on the following day, to the spot selected by her as the treasure house of Raymond's dear remains. It was in a recess near the head of the ravine to the south of Hymettus. The chasm, deep, black, and hoary, swept from the summit to the base; in the fissures of the rock myrtle underwood grew and wild thyme, the food of many nations of bees; enormous crags protruded into the cleft, some beetling over, others rising perpendicularly from it. At the foot of this sublime chasm, a fertile laughing valley reached from sea to sea, and beyond was spread the blue Aegean, sprinkled with islands, the light waves glancing beneath the sun. Close to the spot on which we stood, was a solitary rock, high and conical, which, divided on every side from the mountain, seemed a nature-hewn pyramid; with little labor this block was reduced to a perfect shape; the narrow cell was scooped out beneath in which Raymond was placed, and a short inscription, carved in the living stone, recorded the name of its tenant, the cause and aera of his death.

Everything was accomplished with speed under my directions. I agreed to leave the finishing and guardianship of the tomb to the head of the religious establishment at Athens, and by the end of October prepared for my return to England. I mentioned this to Perdita. It was painful to appear to drag her from the last scene that spoke of her lost one; but to linger here was vain, and my very soul was sick with its yearning to rejoin my Idris and her babes. In reply, my sister requested me to accompany her the following evening to the tomb of Raymond. Some days had passed since I had visited the spot. The path to it had been enlarged, and steps hewn in the rock led us less circuitously than before, to the spot itself; the platform on which the pyramid stood was enlarged, and looking towards the south, in a recess overshadowed by the straggling branches of a wild fig-tree, I saw foundations dug, and props and rafters fixed, evidently the commencement of a cottage; standing on its unfinished threshold, the tomb was at our right-hand, the whole ravine, and plain, and azure sea immediately before us; the dark rocks received a glow from the descending sun, which glanced along the cultivated valley, and dyed in purple and orange the placid waves; we sat on a rocky elevation, and I gazed with rapture on the beauteous panorama of living and changeful colors, which varied and enhanced the graces of earth and ocean.

"Did I not do right," said Perdita, "in having my loved one conveyed hither? Hereafter this will be the cynosure of Greece. In such a spot death loses half its terrors, and even the inanimate dust appears to partake of the spirit of beauty which hallows this region. Lionel, he sleeps there; that is the grave of Raymond, he whom in my youth I first loved; whom my heart accompanied in days of separation and anger; to whom I am now joined forever. Never - mark me - never will I leave this spot. Methinks his spirit remains here as well as that dust, which, uncommunicable though it be, is more precious in its nothingness than aught else widowed earth clasps to her sorrowing bosom. The myrtle bushes, the thyme, the little cyclamen, which peep from the fissures of the rock, all the produce of the place, bear affinity to him; the light that invests the hills participates in his essence, and sky and mountains, sea and valley, are imbued by the presence of his spirit. I will live and die here!

"Go you to England, Lionel; return to sweet Idris and dearest Adrian; return and let my orphan girl be as a child of your own in your house. Look on me as dead; and truly if death be a mere change of state, I am dead. This is another world, from that which late I inhabited, from that which is now your home. Here I hold communion only with the has been, and to come. Go you to England and leave me where alone I can consent to drag out the miserable days which I must still live."

A shower of tears terminated her sad harangue. I had expected some extravagant proposition, and remained silent awhile, collecting my thoughts that I might the better combat her fanciful scheme. "You cherish dreary thoughts, my dear Perdita," I said, "nor do I wonder that for a time your better reason should be influenced by passionate grief and a disturbed imagination. Even I am in love with this last home of Raymond's; nevertheless, we must quit it."

"I expected this," cried Perdita; "I supposed that you would treat me as a mad, foolish girl. But do not deceive yourself; this cottage is built by my order; and here I shall remain, until the hour arrives when I may share his happier dwelling."

"My dearest girl!"

"And what is there so strange in my design? I might have deceived you; I might have talked of remaining here only a few months; in your anxiety to reach Windsor you would have left me, and without reproach or contention, I might have pursued my plan. But I disdained the artifice; or rather in my wretchedness it was my only consolation to pour out my heart to you, my brother, my only friend. You will not dispute with me? You know how willful your poor, misery-stricken sister is. Take my girl with you; wean her from sights and thoughts of sorrow; let infantine hilarity revisit her heart, and animate her eyes; so could it never be, were she near me; it is far better for all of you that you should never see me again. For myself, I will not voluntarily seek death, that is, I will not, while I can command myself; and I can here. But drag me from this country; and my power of self-control vanishes, nor can I answer for the violence my agony of grief may lead me to commit."

"You clothe your meaning, Perdita," I replied, "in powerful words, yet that meaning is selfish and unworthy of you. You have often agreed with me that there is but one solution to the intricate riddle of life; to improve ourselves, and contribute to the happiness of others: and now, in the very prime of life, you desert your principles, and shut yourself up in useless solitude. Will you think of Raymond less at Windsor, the scene of your early happiness? Will you commune less with his departed spirit, while you watch over and cultivate the rare excellence of his child? You have been sadly visited; nor do I wonder that a feeling akin to insanity should drive you to bitter and unreasonable imaginings. But a home of love awaits you in your native England. My tenderness and affection must soothe you; the society of Raymond's friends will be of more solace than these dreary speculations. We will all make it our first care, our dearest task, to contribute to your happiness." Perdita shook her head; "If it could be so," she replied, "I was much in the wrong to disdain your offers. But it is not a matter of choice; I can live here only. I am a part of this scene; each and all its properties are a part of me. This is no sudden fancy; I live by it. The knowledge that I am here, rises with me in the morning, and enables me to endure the light; it is mingled with my food, which else were poison; it walks, it sleeps with me, forever it accompanies me. Here I may even cease to repine and may add my tardy consent to the decree which has taken him from me. He would rather have died such a death, which will be recorded in history to endless time, than have lived to old age unknown, unhonored. Nor can I desire better, than, having been the chosen and beloved of his heart, here, in youth's prime, before added years can tarnish the best feelings of my nature, to watch his tomb, and speedily rejoin him in his blessed repose.

"So much, my dearest Lionel, I have said, wishing to persuade you that I do right. If you are unconvinced, I can add nothing further by way of argument, and I can only declare my fixed resolve. I stay here; force only can remove me. Be it so; drag me away - I return; confine me, imprison me, still I escape, and come here. Or would my brother rather devote the heart-broken Perdita to the straw and chains of a maniac, than suffer her to rest in peace beneath the shadow of His society, in this my own selected and beloved recess?" -

All this appeared to me, I own, methodized madness. I imagined that it was my imperative duty to take her from scenes that thus forcibly reminded her of her loss. Nor did I doubt, that in the tranquility of our family circle at Windsor, she would recover some degree of composure, and in the end, of happiness. My affection for Clara also led me to oppose these fond dreams of cherished grief; her sensibility had already been too much excited; her infant heedlessness too soon exchanged for deep and anxious thought. The strange and romantic scheme of her mother might confirm and perpetuate the painful view of life, which had intruded itself thus early on her contemplation.

On returning home, the captain of the steam packet with whom I had agreed to sail, came to tell me, that accidental circumstances hastened his departure, and that, if I went with him, I must come on board at five on the following morning. I hastily gave my consent to this arrangement, and as hastily formed a plan through which Perdita should be forced to become my companion. I believe that most people in my situation would have acted in the same manner. Yet this consideration does not, or rather did not in after time, diminish the reproaches of my conscience. At the moment, I felt convinced that I was acting for the best, and that all I did was right and even necessary.

I sat with Perdita and soothed her, by my seeming assent to her wild scheme. She received my concurrence with pleasure, and a thousand times over thanked her deceiving, deceitful brother. As night came on, her spirits, enlivened by my unexpected concession, regained an almost forgotten vivacity. I pretended to be alarmed by the feverish glow in her cheek; I entreated her to take a composing draught; I poured out the medicine, which she took docilely from me. I watched her as she drank it. Falsehood and artifice are in themselves so hateful, that, though I still thought I did right, a feeling of shame and guilt came painfully upon me. I left her, and soon heard that she slept soundly under the influence of the opiate I had administered. She was carried thus unconscious on board; the anchor weighed, and the wind being favorable, we stood far out to sea; with all the canvas spread, and the power of the engine to assist, we scudded swiftly and steadily through the chafed element.

It was late in the day before Perdita awoke, and a longer time elapsed before recovering from the torpor occasioned by the laudanum, she perceived her change of situation. She started wildly from her couch and flew to the cabin window. The blue and troubled sea sped past the vessel and was spread shoreless around: the sky was covered by a rack, which in its swift motion shewed how speedily she was borne away. The creaking of the masts, the clang of the wheels, the tramp above, all persuaded her that she was already far from the shores of Greece. -"Where are we?" she cried, "where are we going?" -

The attendant whom I had stationed to watch her, replied, "to England." -

"And my brother?" -

"Is on deck, Madam."

"Unkind! unkind!" exclaimed the poor victim, as with a deep sigh she looked on the waste of waters. Then without further remark, she threw herself on her couch, and closing her eyes remained motionless; so that but for the deep sighs that burst from her, it would have seemed that she slept.

As soon as I heard that she had spoken, I sent Clara to her, that the sight of the lovely innocent might inspire gentle and affectionate thoughts. But neither the presence of her child, nor a subsequent visit from me, could rouse my sister. She looked on Clara with a countenance of woeful meaning, but she did not speak. When I appeared, she turned away, and in reply to my enquiries, only said, "You know not what you have done!" - I trusted that this sullenness betokened merely the struggle between disappointment and natural affection, and that in a few days she would be reconciled to her fate.

When night came on, she begged that Clara might sleep in a separate cabin. Her servant, however, remained with her. About midnight she spoke to the latter, saying that she had had a bad dream, and bade her go to her daughter, and bring word whether she rested quietly. The woman obeyed.

The breeze, that had flagged since sunset, now rose again. I was on deck, enjoying our swift progress. The quiet was disturbed only by the rush of waters as they divided before the steady keel, the murmur of the moveless and full sails, the wind whistling in the shrouds, and the regular motion of the engine. The sea was gently agitated, now shewing a white crest, and now resuming a uniform hue; the clouds had disappeared; and dark ether clipped the broad ocean, in which the constellations vainly sought their accustomed mirror. Our rate could not have been less than eight knots.

Suddenly I heard a splash in the sea. The sailors on watch rushed to the side of the vessel, with the cry - someone gone overboard. "It is not from deck," said the man at the helm, "something has been thrown from the aft cabin." A call for the boat to be lowered was echoed from the deck. I rushed into my sister's cabin; it was empty.

With sails abaft, the engine stopped, the vessel remained unwillingly stationary, until, after an hour's search, my poor Perdita was brought on board. But no care could re-animate her, no medicine causes her dear eyes to open, and the blood to flow again from her pulseless heart. One clenched hand contained a slip of paper, on which was written, "To Athens." To ensure her removal thither and prevent the irrecoverable loss of her body in the wide sea, she had had the precaution to fasten a long shawl round her waist, and again to the stanchions of the cabin window. She had drifted somewhat under the keel of the vessel, and her being out of sight occasioned the delay in finding her. And thus, the ill-starred girl died a victim to my senseless rashness. Thus, in early day, she left us for the company of the dead, and preferred to share the rocky grave of Raymond, before the animated scene this cheerful earth afforded, and the society of loving friends. Thus, in her twenty-ninth year she died; having enjoyed some few years of the happiness of paradise and sustaining a reverse to which her impatient spirit and affectionate disposition were unable to submit. As I marked the placid expression that had settled on her countenance in death, I felt, in spite of the pangs of remorse, in spite of heart-rending regret, that it was better to die so, than to drag on long, miserable years of repining and inconsolable grief. Stress of weather drove us up the Adriatic Gulph; and, our vessel being hardly fitted to weather a storm, we took refuge in the port of Ancona. Here I met Giorgio Palli, the vice-admiral of the Greek fleet, a former friend and warm partisan of Raymond. I committed the remains of my lost Perdita to his care, for the purpose of having them transported to Hymettus, and placed in the cell her Raymond already occupied beneath the pyramid. This was all accomplished even as I wished. She reposed beside her beloved, and the tomb above was inscribed with the united names of Raymond and Perdita.

I then came to a resolution of pursuing our journey to England overland. My own heart was racked by regrets and remorse. The apprehension, that Raymond had departed for ever, that his name, blended eternally with the past, must be erased from every anticipation of the future, had come slowly upon me. I had always admired his talents; his noble aspirations; his grand conceptions of the glory and majesty of his ambition: his utter want of mean passions; his fortitude and daring. In Greece I had learnt to love him; his very waywardness, and self-abandonment to the impulses of superstition, attached me to him doubly; it might be weakness, but it was the antipodes of all that was groveling and selfish. To these pangs were added the loss of Perdita, lost through my own accursed self-will and conceit. This dear one, my sole relation; whose progress I had marked from tender childhood through the varied path of life, and seen her throughout conspicuous for integrity, devotion, and true affection; for all that constitutes the peculiar graces of the female character, and beheld her at last the victim of too much loving, too constant an attachment to the perishable and lost, she, in her pride of beauty and life, had thrown aside the pleasant perception of the apparent world for the unreality of the grave, and had left poor Clara quite an orphan. I concealed from this beloved child that her mother's death was voluntary and tried every means to awaken cheerfulness in her sorrow-stricken spirit.

One of my first acts for the recovery even of my own composure, was to bid farewell to the sea. Its hateful splash renewed again and again to my sense the death of my sister; its roar was a dirge; in every dark hull that was tossed on its inconstant bosom, I imaged a bier, that would convey to death all who trusted to its treacherous smiles. Farewell to the sea! Come, my Clara, sit beside me in this aerial bark; quickly and gently it cleaves the azure serene, and with soft undulation glides upon the current of the air; or, if storm shake its fragile mechanism, the green earth is below; we can descend, and take shelter on the stable continent. Here aloft, the companions of the swift-winged birds, we skim through the unresisting element, fleetly and fearlessly. The light boat heaves not, nor is opposed by death-bearing waves; the ether opens before the prow, and the shadow of the globe that upholds it, shelters us from the noon-day sun. Beneath are the plains of Italy, or the vast undulations of the wave-like Apennines: fertility reposes in their many folds, and woods crown the summits. The free and happy peasant, unshackled by the Austrian, bears the double harvest to the garner; and the refined citizens rear without dread the long-blighted tree of knowledge in this garden of the world. We were lifted above the Alpine peaks, and from their deep and brawling ravines entered the plain of fair France, and after an airy journey of six days, we landed at Dieppe, furled the feathered wings, and closed the silken globe of our little pinnace. A heavy rain made this mode of travelling now incommodious; so, we embarked in a steam-packet, and after a short passage landed at Portsmouth.

A strange story was rife here. A few days before, a tempest-struck vessel had appeared off the town: the hull was parched-looking and cracked, the sails rent, and bent in a careless, un-seamanlike manner, the shrouds tangled and broken. She drifted towards the harbor and was stranded on the sands at the entrance. In the morning the custom-house officers, together with a crowd of idlers, visited her. One only of the crew appeared to have arrived with her. He had got to shore, and had walked a few paces towards the town, and then, vanquished by malady and approaching death, had fallen on the inhospitable beach. He was found stiff, his hands clenched, and pressed against his breast. His skin, nearly black, his matted hair and bristly beard, were signs of a long-protracted misery. It was whispered that he had died of the plague. No one ventured on board the vessel, and strange sights were averred to be seen at night, walking the deck, and hanging on the masts and shrouds. She soon went to pieces; I was shewn where she had been, and saw her disjoined timbers tossed on the waves. The body of the man who had landed, had been buried deep in the sands; and none could tell more, than that the vessel was American built, and that several months before the Fortunatas had sailed from Philadelphia, of which no tidings were afterwards received.

CHAPTER IV

I RETURNED to my family estate in the autumn of the year 2092. My heart had long been with them; and I felt sick with the hope and delight of seeing them again. The district which contained them appeared the abode of every kindly spirit. Happiness, love and peace, walked the forest paths, and tempered the atmosphere. After all the agitation and sorrow, I had endured in Greece, I sought Windsor, as the storm-driven bird does the nest in which it may fold its wings in tranquility.

How unwise had the wanderers been, who had deserted its shelter, entangled themselves in the web of society, and entered on what men of the world call "life," - that labyrinth of evil, that scheme of mutual torture. To live, according to this sense of the word, we must not only observe and learn, we must also feel; we must not be mere spectators of action, we must act; we must not describe, but be subjects of description. Deep sorrow must have been the inmate of our bosoms; fraud must have lain in wait for us; the artful must have deceived us; sickening doubt and false hope must have checkered our days; hilarity and joy, that lap the soul in ecstasy, must at times have possessed us. Who that knows what "life" is, would pine for this feverish species of existence? I have lived. I have spent days and nights of festivity; I have joined in ambitious hopes, and exulted in victory: now, - shut the door on the world, and build high the wall that is to separate me from the troubled scene enacted within its precincts. Let us live for each other and for happiness; let us seek peace in our dear home, near the inland murmur of streams, and the gracious waving of trees, the beauteous vesture of earth, and sublime pageantry of the skies. Let us leave "life," that we may live.

Idris was well content with this resolve of mine. Her native sprightliness needed no undue excitement, and her placid heart reposed contented on my love, the well-being of her children, and the beauty of surrounding nature. Her pride and blameless ambition were to create smiles in all around her, and to shed repose on the fragile existence of her brother. In spite of her tender nursing, the health of Adrian perceptibly declined. Walking, riding, the common occupations of life, overcame him: he felt no pain, but seemed to tremble forever on the verge of annihilation. Yet, as he had lived on for months nearly in the same state, he did not inspire us with any immediate fear; and, though he talked of death as an event most familiar to his thoughts, he did not cease to exert himself to render others happy, or to cultivate his own astonishing powers of mind. Winter passed away; and spring, led by the months, awakened life in all nature. The forest was dressed in green; the young calves frisked on the new-sprung grass; the wind-winged shadows of light clouds sped over the green cornfields; the hermit cuckoo repeated his monotonous all-hail to the season; the nightingale, bird of love and minion of the evening star, filled the woods with song; while Venus lingered in the warm sunset, and the young green of the trees lay in gentle relief along the clear horizon.

Delight awoke in every heart, delight and exultation; for there was peace through all the world; the temple of Universal Janus was shut, and man died not that year by the hand of man.

"Let this last but twelve months," said Adrian; "and earth will become a Paradise. The energies of man were before directed to the destruction of his species: they now aim at its liberation and preservation. Man cannot repose, and his restless aspirations will now bring forth good instead of evil. The favored countries of the south will throw off the iron yoke of servitude; poverty will quit us, and with that, sickness. What may not the forces, never before united, of liberty and peace achieve in this dwelling of man?"

"Dreaming, forever dreaming, Windsor!" said Ryland, the old adversary of Raymond, and candidate for the Protectorate at the ensuing election. "Be assured that earth is not, nor ever can be heaven, while the seeds of hell are natives of her soil. When the seasons have become equal, when the air breeds no disorders, when its surface is no longer liable to blights and droughts, then sickness will cease; when men's passions are dead, poverty will depart. When love is no longer akin to hate, then brotherhood will exist we are very far from that state at present."

"Not so far as you may suppose," observed a little old astronomer, by name Merrival, "the poles precede slowly, but securely; in an hundred thousand years - "

"We shall all be underground," said Ryland.

"The pole of the earth will coincide with the pole of the ecliptic," continued the astronomer, "a universal spring will be produced, and earth become a paradise."

"And we shall of course enjoy the benefit of the change," said Ryland, contemptuously.

"We have strange news here," I observed. I had the newspaper in my hand, and, as usual, had turned to the intelligence from Greece. "It seems that the total destruction of Constantinople, and the supposition that winter had purified the air of the fallen city, gave the Greeks courage to visit its site, and begin to rebuild it. But they tell us that the curse of God is on the place, for everyone who has ventured within the walls has been tainted by the plague; that this disease has spread in Thrace and Macedonia; and now, fearing the virulence of infection during the coming heats, a cordon has been drawn on the frontiers of Thessaly, and a strict quarantine exacted." This intelligence brought us back from the prospect of paradise, held out after the lapse of a hundred thousand years, to the pain and misery at present existent upon earth. We talked of the ravages made last year by pestilence in every quarter of the world; and of the dreadful consequences of a second visitation. We discussed the best means of preventing infection, and of preserving health and activity in a large city thus afflicted - London, for instance. Merrival did not join in this conversation; drawing near Idris, he proceeded to assure her that the joyful prospect of an earthly paradise after an hundred thousand years, was clouded to him by the knowledge that in a certain period of time after, an earthly hell or purgatory, would occur, when the ecliptic and equator would be at right angles. Our party at length broke up; "We are all dreaming this morning," said Ryland, "it is as wise to discuss the probability of a visitation of the plague in our well-governed metropolis, as to calculate the centuries which must escape before we can grow pine-apples here in the open air."

But though it seemed absurd to calculate upon the arrival of the plague in London, I could not reflect without extreme pain on the desolation this evil would cause in Greece. The English for the most part talked of Thrace and Macedonia, as they would of a lunar territory, which, unknown to them, presented no distinct idea or interest to the minds. I had trod the soil. The faces of many of the inhabitants were familiar to me; in the towns, plains, hills, and defiles of these countries, I had enjoyed unspeakable delight, as I journeyed through them the year before. Some romantic village, some cottage, or elegant abode there situated, inhabited by the lovely and the good, rose before my mental sight, and the question haunted me, is the plague there also? - That same invincible monster, which hovered over and devoured Constantinople - that fiend crueler than tempest, less tame than fire, is, alas, unchained in that beautiful country — these reflections would not allow me to rest.

The political state of England became agitated as the time drew near when the new Protector was to be elected. This event excited the more interest, since it was the current report, that if the popular candidate (Ryland) should be chosen, the question of the abolition of hereditary rank, and other feudal relics, would come under the consideration of parliament. Not a word had been spoken during the present session on any of these topics. Everything would depend upon the choice of a Protector, and the elections of the ensuing year. Yet this very silence was awful, shewing the deep weight attributed to the question; the fear of either party to hazard an ill-timed attack, and the expectation of a furious contention when it should begin.

But although St. Stephen's did not echo with the voice which filled each heart, the newspapers teemed with nothing else; and in private companies the conversation however remotely begun, soon verged towards this central point, while voices were lowered and chairs drawn closer. The nobles did not hesitate to express their fear; the other party endeavored to treat the matter lightly. "Shame on the country," said Ryland, "to lay so much stress upon words and frippery; it is a question of nothing; of the new painting of carriage-panels and the embroidery of footmen's coats."

Yet could England indeed doff her lordly trappings, and be content with the democratic style of America? Was the pride of ancestry, the patrician spirit, the gentle courtesies and refined pursuits, splendid attributes of rank, to be erased among us? We were told that this would not be the case; that we were by nature a poetical people, a nation easily duped by words, ready to array clouds in splendor, and bestow honor on the dust. This spirit we could never lose; and it was to diffuse this concentrated spirit of birth, that the new law was to be brought forward. We were assured that, when the name and title of Englishman was the sole patent of nobility, we should all be noble; that when no man born under English sway, felt another his superior in rank, courtesy and refinement would become the birth-right of all our countrymen. Let not England be so far disgraced, as to have it imagined that it can be without nobles, nature's true nobility, who bear their patent in their mien, who are from their cradle elevated above the rest of their species, because they are better than the rest. Among a race of independent, and generous, and well-educated men, in a country where the imagination is empress of men's minds, there needs be no fear that we should want a perpetual succession of the high-born and lordly. That party, however, could hardly yet be considered a minority in the kingdom, who extolled the ornament of the column, "the Corinthian capital of polished society;" they appealed to prejudices without number, to old attachments and young hopes; to the expectation of thousands who might one day become peers; they set up as a scarecrow, the specter of all that was sordid, mechanic and base in the commercial republics.

The plague had come to Athens. Hundreds of English residents returned to their own country. Raymond's beloved Athenians, the free, the noble people of the divinest town in Greece, fell like ripe corn before the merciless sickle of the adversary. Its pleasant places were deserted; its temples and palaces were converted into tombs; its energies, bent before towards the highest objects of human ambition, were now forced to converge to one point, the guarding against the innumerable arrows of the plague.

At any other time, this disaster would have excited extreme compassion among us; but it was now passed over, while each mind was engaged by the coming controversy. It was not so with me; and the question of rank and right dwindled to insignificance in my eyes, when I pictured the scene of suffering Athens. I heard of the death of only sons; of wives and husbands most devoted; of the rending of ties twisted with the heart's fibers, of friend losing friend, and young mothers mourning for their first born; and these moving incidents were grouped and painted in my mind by the knowledge of the persons, by my esteem and affection for the sufferers. It was the admirers, friends, fellow soldiers of Raymond, families that had welcomed Perdita to Greece, and lamented with her the loss of her lord, that were swept away, and went to dwell with them in the undistinguishing tomb.

The plague at Athens had been preceded and caused by the contagion from the East; and the scene of havoc and death continued to be acted there, on a scale of fearful magnitude. A hope that the visitation of the present year would prove the last, kept up the spirits of the merchants connected with these countries; but the inhabitants were driven to despair, or to a resignation which, arising from fanaticism, assumed the same dark hue. America had also received the taint; and were it yellow fever or plague, the epidemic was gifted with a virulence before unfelt. The devastation was not confined to the towns but spread throughout the country; the hunter died in the woods, the peasant in the cornfields, and the fisher on his native waters.

A strange story was brought to us from the East, to which little credit would have been given, had not the fact been attested by a multitude of witnesses, in various parts of the world. On the twenty-first of June, it was said that an hour before noon, a black sun arose: an orb, the size of that luminary, but dark, defined, whose beams were shadows, ascended from the west; in about an hour it had reached the meridian, and eclipsed the bright parent of day. Night fell upon every country, night, sudden, rayless, entire. The stars came out, shedding their ineffectual glimmerings on the light-widowed earth. But soon the dim orb passed from over the sun and lingered down the eastern heaven. As it descended, its dusky rays crossed the brilliant ones of the sun and deadened or distorted them. The shadows of things assumed strange and ghastly shapes. The wild animals in the woods took fright at the unknown shapes figured on the ground. They fled they knew not whither; and the citizens were filled with greater dread, at the convulsion which "shook lions into civil streets;" — birds, strong-winged eagles, suddenly blinded, fell in the market-places, while owls and bats shewed themselves welcoming the early night. Gradually the object of fear sank beneath the horizon, and to the last shot up shadowy beams into the otherwise radiant air. Such was the tale sent us from Asia, from the eastern extremity of Europe, and from Africa as far west as the Golden Coast. Whether this story were true or not, the effects were certain. Through Asia, from the banks of the Nile to the shores of the Caspian, from the Hellespont even to the sea of Oman, a sudden panic was driven. The men filled the mosques; the women, veiled, hastened to the tombs, and carried offerings to the dead, thus, to preserve the living. The plague was forgotten, in this new fear which the black sun had spread; and, though the dead multiplied, and the streets of Ispahan, of Pekin, and of Delhi were strewed with pestilence-struck corpses, men passed on, gazing on the ominous sky, regardless of the death beneath their feet. The Christians sought their churches, - Christian maidens, even at the feast of roses, clad in white, with shining veils, sought, in long procession, the places consecrated to their religion, filling the air with their hymns; while, ever and anon, from the lips of some poor mourner in the crowd, a voice of wailing burst, and the rest looked up, fancying they could discern the sweeping wings of angels, who passed over the earth, lamenting the disasters about to fall on man.

In the sunny clime of Persia, in the crowded cities of China, amidst the aromatic groves of Cashmere, and along the southern shores of the Mediterranean, such scenes had place. Even in Greece the tale of the sun of darkness increased the fears and despair of the dying multitude. We, in our cloudy isle, were far removed from danger, and the only circumstance that brought these disasters at all home to us, was the daily arrival of vessels from the east, crowded with emigrants, mostly English; for the Moslems, though the fear of death was spread keenly among them, still clung together; that, if they were to die (and if they were, death would as readily meet them on the homeless sea, or in far England, as in Persia,) - if they were to die, their bones might rest in earth made sacred by the relics of true believers. Mecca had never before been so crowded with pilgrims; yet the Arabs neglected to pillage the caravans, but, humble and weaponless, they joined the procession, praying Mahomet to avert plague from their tents and deserts.

I cannot describe the rapturous delight with which I turned from political brawls at home, and the physical evils of distant countries, to my own dear home, to the selected abode of goodness and love; to peace, and the interchange of every sacred sympathy. Had I never quitted Windsor, these emotions would not have been so intense; but I had in Greece been the prey of fear and deplorable change; in Greece, after a period of anxiety and sorrow, I had seen depart two, whose very names were the symbol of greatness and virtue. But such miseries could never intrude upon the domestic circle left to me, while, secluded in our beloved forest, we passed our lives in tranquility. Some small change indeed the progress of years brought here; and time, as it is wont, stamped the traces of mortality on our pleasures and expectations. Idris, the most affectionate wife, sister and friend, was a tender and loving mother. The feeling was not with her as with many, a pastime; it was a passion. We had had three children; one, the second in age, died while I was in Greece. This had dashed the triumphant and rapturous emotions of maternity with grief and fear. Before this event, the little beings, sprung from herself, the young heirs of her transient life, seemed to have a sure lease of existence; now she dreaded that the pitiless destroyer might snatch her remaining darlings, as it had snatched their brother. The least illness caused throes of terror; she was miserable if she were at all absent from them; her treasure of happiness she had garnered in their fragile being, and kept forever on the watch, lest the insidious thief should as before steal these valued gems. She had fortunately small cause for fear. Alfred, now nine years old, was an upright, manly little fellow, with radiant brow, soft eyes, and gentle, though independent disposition. Our youngest was yet in infancy; but his downy cheek was sprinkled with the roses of health, and his unwearied vivacity filled our halls with innocent laughter.

Clara had passed the age which, from its mute ignorance, was the source of the fears of Idris. Clara was dear to her, to all. There was so much intelligence combined with innocence, sensibility with forbearance, and seriousness with perfect good-humor, a beauty so transcendent, united to such endearing simplicity, that she hung like a pearl in the shrine of our possessions, a treasure of wonder and excellence.

At the beginning of winter our Alfred, now nine years of age, first went to school at Eton. This appeared to him the primary step towards manhood, and he was proportionably pleased. Community of study and amusement developed the best parts of his character, his steady perseverance, generosity, and well-governed firmness. What deep and sacred emotions are excited in a father's bosom, when he first becomes convinced that his love for his child is not a mere instinct, but worthily bestowed, and that others, less akin, participate his approbation! It was supreme happiness to Idris and myself, to find that the frankness which Alfred's open brow indicated, the intelligence of his eyes, the tempered sensibility of his tones, were not delusions, but indications of talents and virtues, which would "grow with his growth, and strengthen with his strength." At this period, the termination of an animal's love for its offspring, - the true affection of the human parent commences. We no longer look on this dearest part of ourselves, as a tender plant which we must cherish, or a plaything for an idle hour. We build now on his intellectual faculties; we establish our hopes on his moral propensities. His weakness still imparts anxiety to this feeling, his ignorance prevents entire intimacy; but we begin to respect the future man, and to endeavor to secure his esteem, even as if he were our equal. What can a parent have more at heart than the good opinion of his child? In all our transactions with him our honor must be inviolate, the integrity of our relations untainted: fate and circumstance may, when he arrives at maturity, separate us forever - but, as his aegis in danger, his consolation in hardship, let the ardent youth for ever bear with him through the rough path of life, love and honor for his parents.

We had lived so long in the vicinity of Eton, that its population of young folks was well known to us. Many of them had been Alfred's playmates, before they became his schoolfellows. We now watched this youthful congregation with redoubled interest. We marked the difference of character among the boys and endeavored to read the future man in the stripling. There is nothing more lovely, to which the heart more yearns than a free-spirited boy, gentle, brave, and generous. Several of the Etonians had these characteristics; all were distinguished by a sense of honor, and spirit of enterprise; in some, as they verged towards manhood, this degenerated into presumption; but the younger ones, lads a little older than our own, were conspicuous for their gallant and sweet dispositions.

Here were the future governors of England; the men, who, when our ardor was cold, and our projects completed or destroyed forever, when, our drama acted, we doffed the garb of the hour, and assumed the uniform of age, or of more equalizing death; here were the beings who were to carry on the vast machine of society; here were the lovers, husbands, fathers; here the landlord, the politician, the soldier; some fancied that they were even now ready to appear on the stage, eager to make one among the dramatis personae of active life. It was not long since I was like one of these beardless aspirants; when my boy shall have obtained the place I now hold, I shall have tottered into a grey-headed, wrinkled old man. Strange system! riddle of the Sphynx, most awe-striking! that thus man remains, while we the individuals pass away. Such is, to borrow the words of an eloquent and philosophic writer, "the mode of existence decreed to a permanent body composed of transitory parts; wherein, by the disposition of a stupendous wisdom, molding together the great mysterious incorporation of the human race, the whole, at one time, is never old, or middle-aged, or young, but, in a condition of unchangeable constancy, moves on through the varied tenor of perpetual decay, fall, renovation, and progression."

Willingly do I give place to thee, dear Alfred! advance, offspring of tender love, child of our hopes; advance a soldier on the road to which I have been the pioneer! I will make way for thee. I have already put off the carelessness of childhood, the unlined brow, and springy gait of early years, that they may adorn thee. Advance: and I will despoil myself still further for thy advantage. Time shall rob me of the graces of maturity, shall take the fire from my eyes, and agility from my limbs, shall steal the better part of life, eager expectation and passionate love, and shower them in double portion on thy dear head. Advance! avail thyself of the gift, thou and thy comrades; and in the drama you are about to act, do not disgrace those who taught you to enter on the stage, and to pronounce becomingly the parts assigned to you! May your progress be uninterrupted and secure; born during the springtide of the hopes of man, may you lead up the summer to which no winter may succeed!

CHAPTER V

Some disorder had surely crept into the course of the elements, destroying their benignant influence. The wind, prince of air, raged through his kingdom, lashing the sea into fury, and subduing the rebel earth into some sort of obedience.

> *The God sends down his angry plagues from high,*
> *Famine and pestilence in heaps they die.*
> *Again, in vengeance of his wrath he falls*
> *On their great hosts and breaks their tottering walls.*
> *Arrests their navies on the ocean's plain,*
> *And whelms their strength with mountains of the main.*

Their deadly power shook the flourishing countries of the south, and during winter, even, we, in our northern retreat, began to quake under their ill effects.

That fable is unjust, which gives the superiority to the sun over the wind. Who has not seen the lightsome earth, the balmy atmosphere, and basking nature become dark, cold and ungenial, when the sleeping wind has awoken in the east? Or, when the dun clouds thickly veil the sky, while exhaustless stores of rain are poured down, until, the dank earth refusing to imbibe the superabundant moisture, it lies in pools on the surface; when the torch of day seems like a meteor, to be quenched; who has not seen the cloud-stirring north arise, the streaked blue appear, and soon an opening made in the vapors in the eye of the wind, through which the bright azure shines? The clouds become thin; an arch is formed forever rising upwards, till, the universal cope being unveiled, the sun pours forth its rays, re-animated and fed by the breeze.

Then mighty art thou, O wind, to be throne above all other vicegerents of nature's power; whether thou comest destroying from the east, or pregnant with elementary life from the west; thee the clouds obey; the sun is subservient to thee; the shoreless ocean is thy slave! Thou sweepest over the earth, and oaks, the growth of centuries, submit to thy viewless axe; the snowdrift is scattered on the pinnacles of the Alps, the avalanche thunders down their valleys. Thou holdest the keys of the frost, and canst first chain and then set free the streams; under thy gentle governance the buds and leaves are born, they flourish nursed by thee.

Why dost thou howl thus, O wind? By day and by night for four long months thy roaring's have not ceased—the shores of the sea are strewn with wrecks, its keel-welcoming surface has become impassable, the earth has shed her beauty in obedience to thy command; the frail balloon dares no longer sail on the agitated air; thy ministers, the clouds, deluge the land with rain; rivers forsake their banks; the wild torrent tears up the mountain path; plain and wood, and verdant dell are despoiled of their loveliness; our very cities are wasted by thee. Alas, what will become of us? It seems as if the giant waves of ocean, and vast arms of the sea, were about to wrench the deep-rooted island from its center; and cast it, a ruin and a wreck, upon the fields of the Atlantic.

What are we, the inhabitants of this globe, least among the many that people infinite space? Our minds embrace infinity; the visible mechanism of our being is subject to merest accident. Day by day we are forced to believe this. He whom a scratch has disorganized, he who disappears from apparent life under the influence of the hostile agency at work around us, had the same powers as I - I also am subject to the same laws. In the face of all this we call ourselves lords of the creation, wielders of the elements, masters of life and death, and we allege in excuse of this arrogance, that though the individual is destroyed, man continues for ever. Thus, losing our identity, that of which we are chiefly conscious, we glory in the continuity of our species, and learn to regard death without terror. But when any whole nation becomes the victim of the destructive powers of exterior agents, then indeed man shrinks into insignificance, he feels his tenure of life insecure, his inheritance on earth cut off.

I remember, after having witnessed the destructive effects of a fire, I could not even behold a small one in a stove, without a sensation of fear. The mounting flames had curled round the building, as it fell, and was destroyed. They insinuated themselves into the substances about them, and the impediments to their progress yielded at their touch. Could we take integral parts of this power, and not be subject to its operation? Could we domesticate a cub of this wild beast, and not fear its growth and maturity?

Thus, we began to feel, with regard to many-visaged death let loose on the chosen districts of our fair habitation, and above all, with regard to the plague. We feared the coming summer. Nations, bordering on the already infected countries, began to enter upon serious plans for the better keeping out of the enemy. We, a commercial people, were obliged to bring such schemes under consideration; and the question of contagion became matter of earnest disquisition.

That the plague was not what is commonly called contagious, like the scarlet fever, or extinct smallpox, was proved. It was called an epidemic. But the grand question was still unsettled of how this epidemic was generated and increased. If infection depended upon the air, the air was subject to infection. As for instance, a typhus fever has been brought by ships to one sea-port town; yet the very people who brought it there, were incapable of communicating it in a town more fortunately situated. But how are we to judge of airs, and pronounce — in such a city plague will die unproductive; in such another, nature has provided for it a plentiful harvest? In the same way, individuals may escape ninety-nine times, and receive the deathblow at the hundredth; because bodies are sometimes in a state to reject the infection of malady, and at others, thirsty to imbibe it. These reflections made our legislators pause, before they could decide on the laws to be put in force. The evil was so wide-spreading, so violent and immedicable, that no care, no prevention could be judged superfluous, which even added a chance to our escape.

These were questions of prudence; there was no immediate necessity for an earnest caution. England was still secure. France, Germany, Italy and Spain, were interposed, walls yet without a breach, between us and the plague. Our vessels truly were the sport of winds and waves, even as Gulliver was the toy of the

Brobdingnagians; but we on our stable abode could not be hurt in life or limb by these eruptions of nature. We could not fear - we did not. Yet a feeling of awe, a breathless sentiment of wonder, a painful sense of the degradation of humanity, was introduced into every heart. Nature, our mother, and our friend had turned on us a brow of menace. She shewed us plainly, that, though she permitted us to assign her laws and subdue her apparent powers, yet, if she put forth but a finger, we must quake. She could take our globe, fringed with mountains, girded by the atmosphere, containing the condition of our being, and all that man's mind could invent or his force achieve; she could take the ball in her hand, and cast it into space, where life would be drunk up, and man and all his efforts for ever annihilated.

These speculations were rife among us; yet not the less we proceeded in our daily occupations, and our plans, whose accomplishment demanded the lapse of many years. No voice was heard telling us to hold! When foreign distresses came to be felt by us through the channels of commerce, we set ourselves to apply remedies. Subscriptions were made for the emigrants, and merchants bankrupt by the failure of trade. The English spirit awoke to its full activity, and, as it had ever done, set itself to resist the evil, and to stand in the breach which diseased nature had suffered chaos and death to make in the bounds and banks which had hitherto kept them out.

At the commencement of summer, we began to feel, that the mischief which had taken place in distant countries was greater than we had at first suspected. Quito was destroyed by an earthquake. Mexico laid waste by the united effects of storm, pestilence and famine. Crowds of emigrants inundated the west of Europe; and our island had become the refuge of thousands. In the meantime, Ryland had been chosen Protector. He had sought this office with eagerness, under the idea of turning his whole forces to the suppression of the privileged orders of our community. His measures were thwarted, and his schemes interrupted by this new state of things. Many of the foreigners were utterly destitute; and their increasing numbers at length forbade a recourse to the usual modes of relief. Trade was stopped by the failure of the interchange of cargoes usual between us, and America, India, Egypt and Greece. A sudden break was made in the routine of our lives. In vain our Protector and his partisans sought to conceal this truth; in vain, day after day, he appointed a period for the discussion of the new laws concerning hereditary rank and privilege; in vain he endeavored to represent the evil as partial and temporary. These disasters came home to so many bosoms, and, through the various channels of commerce, were carried so entirely into every class and division of the community, that of necessity they became the first question in the state, the chief subjects to which we must turn our attention.

Can it be true, each asked the other with wonder and dismay, that whole countries are laid waste, whole nations annihilated, by these disorders in nature? The vast cities of America, the fertile plains of Hindustan, the crowded abodes of the Chinese, are menaced with utter ruin. Where late the busy multitudes assembled for pleasure or profit, now only the sound of wailing and misery is heard. The air is empoisoned, and each human being inhales death, even while in youth and health, their hopes are in the flower. We called to mind the plague of 1348, when it was calculated that a third of mankind had been destroyed. As yet western Europe was uninfected; would it always be so?

O, yes, it would - Countrymen, fear not! In the still uncultivated wilds of America, what wonder that among its other giant destroyers, Plague should be numbered! It is of old a native of the East, sister of the tornado, the earthquake, and the simoom. Child of the sun, and nursling of the tropics, it would expire in these climes. It drinks the dark blood of the inhabitant of the south, but it never feasts on the pale-faced Celt. If perchance some stricken Asiatic come among us, plague dies with him, uncommunicated and innoxious. Let us weep for our brethren, though we can never experience their reverse. Let us lament over and assist the children of the garden of the earth. Late we envied their abodes, their spicy groves, fertile plains, and abundant loveliness. But in this mortal life extremes are always matched; the thorn grows with the rose; the poison tree and the cinnamon mingle their boughs. Persia, with its cloth of gold, marble halls, and infinite wealth, is now a tomb. The tent of the Arab is fallen in the sands, and his horse spurns the ground unbridled and unsaddled. The voice of lamentation fills the valley of Cashmere; its dells and woods, it's cool fountains, and gardens of roses, are polluted by the dead; in Circassia and Georgia the spirit of beauty weeps over the ruin of its favorite temple - the form of woman.

Our own distresses, though they were occasioned by the fictitious reciprocity of commerce, increased in due proportion. Bankers, merchants, and manufacturers, whose trade depended on exports and interchange of wealth, became bankrupt. Such things, when they happen singly, affect only the immediate parties; but the prosperity of the nation was now shaken by frequent and extensive losses. Families, bred in opulence and luxury, were reduced to beggary. The very state of peace in which we gloried was injurious; there were no means of employing the idle, or of sending any overplus of population out of the country. Even the source of colonies was dried up, for in New Holland, Van Diemen's Land, and the Cape of Good Hope, plague raged. O, for some medicinal vial to purge unwholesome nature, and bring back the earth to its accustomed health!

Ryland was a man of strong intellects and quick and sound decision in the usual course of things, but he stood aghast at the multitude of evils that gathered round us. Must he tax the landed interest to assist our commercial population? To do this, he must gain the favor of the chief land-holders, the nobility of the country; and these were his vowed enemies - he must conciliate them by abandoning his favorite scheme of equalization; he must confirm them in their manorial rights; he must sell his cherished plans for the permanent good of his country, for temporary relief. He must aim no more at the dear object of his ambition; throwing his arms aside, he must for present ends give up the ultimate object of his endeavors. He came to Windsor to consult with us. Every day added to his difficulties; the arrival of fresh vessels with emigrants, the total cessation of commerce, the starving multitude that thronged around the palace of the Protectorate, were circumstances not to be tampered with. The blow was struck; the aristocracy obtained all they wished, and they subscribed to a twelvemonths' bill, which levied twenty per cent on all the rent-rolls of the country. Calm was now restored to the metropolis, and to the populous cities, before driven to desperation; and we returned to the consideration of distant calamities, wondering if the future would bring any alleviation to their excess. It was August; so there could be small hope of relief during the heats. On the contrary, the disease gained virulence, while starvation did its accustomed work. Thousands died unlamented; for beside the yet warm corpse the mourner was stretched, made mute by death.

On the eighteenth of this month news arrived in London that the plague was in France and Italy. These tidings were at first whispered about town; but no one dared express aloud the soul-quailing intelligence. When any one met a friend in the street, he only cried as he hurried on, "You know!" - while the other, with an ejaculation of fear and horror, would answer, - "What will become of us?" At length it was mentioned in the newspapers. The paragraph was inserted in an obscure part: "We regret to state that there can be no longer a doubt of the plague having been introduced at Leghorn, Genoa, and Marseilles." No word of comment followed; each reader made his own fearful one. We were as a man who hears that his house is burning, and yet hurries through the streets, borne along by a lurking hope of a mistake, till he turns the corner, and sees his sheltering roof enveloped in a flame. Before it had been a rumor; but now in words uneraseable, in definite and undeniable print, the knowledge went forth. Its obscurity of situation rendered it the more conspicuous: the diminutive letters grew gigantic to the bewildered eye of fear: they seemed graven with a pen of iron, impressed by fire, woven in the clouds, stamped on the very front of the universe.

The English, whether travelers or residents, came pouring in one great revulsive stream, back on their own country; and with them crowds of Italians and Spaniards. Our little island was filled even to bursting. At first an unusual quantity of specie made its appearance with the emigrants; but these people had no means of receiving back into their hands what they spent among us. With the advance of summer, and the increase of the distemper, rents were unpaid, and their remittances failed them. It was impossible to see these crowds of wretch- ed, perishing creatures, late nurslings of luxury, and not stretch out a hand to save them. As at the conclusion of the eighteenth century, the English unlocked their hospitable store, for the relief of those driven from their homes by political revolution; so now they were not backward in affording aid to the victims of a more wide-spreading calamity. We had many foreign friends whom we eagerly sought out, and relieved from dreadful penury. Our Castle became an asylum for the unhappy. A little population occupied its halls. The revenue of its possessor, which had always found a mode of expenditure congenial to his generous nature, was now attended to more parsimoniously, that it might embrace a wider portion of utility. It was not however money, except partially, but the necessaries of life, that became scarce. It was difficult to find an immediate remedy. The usual one of imports was entirely cut off. In this emergency, to feed the very people to whom we had given refuge, we were obliged to yield to the plough and the mattock our pleasure-grounds and parks. Livestock diminished sensibly in the country, from the effects of the great demand in the market. Even the poor deer, our antlered proteges, were obliged to fall for the sake of worthier pensioners. The labor neces- sary to bring the lands to this sort of culture, employed and fed the off casts of the diminished manufactories.

Adrian did not rest only with the exertions he could make with regard to his own possessions. He addressed himself to the wealthy of the land; he made proposals in parliament little adapted to please the rich; but his earnest pleadings and benevolent eloquence were irresistible. To give up their pleasure-grounds to the agriculturist, to diminish sensibly the number of horses kept for the purposes of luxury throughout the country, were means obvious, but unpleasing. Yet, to the honor of the English be it recorded, that, although natural disinclination made them delay awhile, yet when the misery of their fellow-creatures became glaring, an enthusiastic generosity inspired their decrees. The most luxurious were often the first to part with their indulgencies. As is common in communities, a fashion was set. The high-born ladies of the country would have deemed themselves disgraced if they had now enjoyed, what they before called a necessary, the ease of a carriage. Chairs, as in olden time, and Indian palanquins were introduced for the infirm; but else it was nothing singular to see females of rank going on foot to places of fashionable resort. It was more common, for all who possessed landed property to secede to their estates, attended by whole troops of the indigent, to cut down their woods to erect temporary dwellings, and to portion out their parks, parterres and flower-gardens, to necessitous families. Many of these, of high rank in their own countries, now, with hoe in hand, turned up the soil. It was found necessary at last to check the spirit of sacrifice, and to remind those whose generosity proceeded to lavish waste, that, until the present state of things became permanent, of which there was no likelihood, it was wrong to carry change so far as to make a reaction difficult. Experience demonstrated that in a year or two pestilence would cease; it was well that in the mean time we should not have destroyed our fine breeds of horses, or have utterly changed the face of the ornamented portion of the country.

It may be imagined that things were in a bad state indeed, before this spirit of benevolence could have struck such deep roots. The infection had now spread in the southern provinces of France. But that country had so many resources in the way of agriculture, that the rush of population from one part of it to another, and its increase through foreign emigration, was less felt than with us. The panic struck appeared of more injury, than disease and its natural concomitants.

Winter was hailed, a general and never-failing physician. The embrowning woods, and swollen rivers, the evening mists, and morning frosts, were welcomed with gratitude. The effects of purifying cold were immediately felt; and the lists of mortality abroad were curtailed each week. Many of our visitors left us: those whose homes were far in the south, fled delightfully from our northern winter, and sought their native land, secure of plenty even after their fearful visitation. We breathed again. What the coming summer would bring, we knew not; but the present months were our own, and our hopes of a cessation of pestilence were high.

CHAPTER VI

I have lingered thus long on the extreme bank, the wasting shoal that stretched into the stream of life, dallying with the shadow of death. Thus long, I have cradled my heart in retrospection of past happiness, when hope was. Why not for ever thus? I am not immortal; and the thread of my history might be spun out to the limits of my existence. But the same sentiment that first led me to portray scenes replete with tender recollections, now bids me hurry on. The same yearning of this warm, panting heart, that has made me in written words record my vagabond youth, my serene manhood, and the passions of my soul, makes me now recoil from further delay. I must complete my work.

Here then I stand, as I said, beside the fleet waters of the flowing years, and now away! Spread the sail, and strain with oar, hurrying by dark impending crags, a down steep rapids, even to the sea of desolation I have reached. Yet one moment, one brief interval before I put from shore - once, once again let me fancy myself as I was in 2094 in my abode at Windsor, let me close my eyes, and imagine that the immeasurable boughs of its oaks still shadow me, its castle walls anear. Let fancy portray the joyous scene of the twentieth of June, such as even now my aching heart recalls it.

Circumstances had called me to London; here I heard talk that symptoms of the plague had occurred in hospitals of that city. I returned to Windsor; my brow was clouded, my heart heavy; I entered the Little Park, as was my custom, at the Frogmore gate, on my way to the Castle. A great part of these grounds had been given to cultivation, and strips of potato-land and corn were scattered here and there. The rooks cawed loudly in the trees above; mixed with their hoarse cries I heard a lively strain of music. It was Alfred's birthday. The young people, the Etonians, and children of the neighboring gentry, held a mock fair, to which all the country people were invited. The park was speckled by tents, whose flaunting colors and gaudy flags, waving in the sunshine, added to the gaiety of the scene. On a platform erected beneath the terrace, a number of the younger part of the assembly were dancing. I leaned against a tree to observe them. The band played the wild eastern air of Weber introduced in Abon Hassan; its volatile notes gave wings to the feet of the dancers, while the lookers-on unconsciously beat time. At first the tripping measure lifted my spirit with it, and for a moment my eyes gladly followed the mazes of the dance. The revulsion of thought passed like keen steel to my heart. Ye are all going to die, I thought; already your tomb is built up around you. Awhile, because you are gifted with agility and strength, you fancy that you live: but frail is the "bower of flesh" that encases life; dissoluble the silver cord than binds you to it. The joyous soul, charioted from pleasure to pleasure by the graceful mechanism of well-formed limbs, will suddenly feel the axletree give way, and spring and wheel dissolve in dust. Not one of you, O! fated crowd, can escape - not one! not my own ones! not my Idris and her babes! Horror and misery! Already the gay dance vanished, the green sward was strewn with corpses, the blue air above became fetid with deathly exhalations. Shriek, ye clarions! ye loud trumpets, howl! Pile dirge on dirge; rouse the funereal chords; let the air ring with dire wailing; let wild discord rush on the wings of the wind! Already I hear it, while guardian angels, attendant on humanity, their task achieved, hasten away, and their departure is announced by melancholy strains; faces all unseemly with weeping, forced open my lids; faster and faster many groups of these woe-begone countenances thronged around, exhibiting every variety of wretchedness – well known faces mingled with the distorted creations of fancy. Ashy pale, Raymond and Perdita sat apart, looking on with sad smiles. Adrian's countenance flitted across, tainted by death - Idris, with eyes languidly closed and livid lips, was about to slide into the wide grave. The confusion grew - their looks of sorrow changed to mockery; they nodded their heads in time to the music, whose clang became maddening.

I felt that this was insanity - I sprang forward to throw it off; I rushed into the midst of the crowd. Idris saw me: with light step she advanced; as I folded her in my arms, feeling, as I did, that I thus enclosed what was to me a world, yet frail as the waterdrop which the noon-day sun will drink from the water lily's cup; tears filled my eyes, unwonted to be thus moistened. The joyful welcome of my boys, the soft gratulation of Clara, the pressure of Adrian's hand, contributed to unman me. I felt that they were near, that they were safe, yet methought this was all deceit; - the earth reeled, the firm-enrooted trees moved - dizziness came over me - I sank to the ground.

My beloved friends were alarmed - nay, they expressed their alarm so anxiously, that I dared not pronounce the word plague, that hovered on my lips, lest they should construe my perturbed looks into a symptom, and see infection in my languor. I had scarcely recovered, and with feigned hilarity had brought back smiles into my little circle, when we saw Ryland approach.

Ryland had something the appearance of a farmer; of a man whose muscles and full-grown stature had been developed under the influence of vigorous exercise and exposure to the elements. This was to a great degree the case: for, though a large landed proprietor, yet, being a projector, and of an ardent and industrious disposition, he had on his own estate given himself up to agricultural labors. When he went as ambassador to the Northern States of America, he, for some time, planned his entire migration; and went so far as to make several journeys far westward on that immense continent, for the purpose of choosing the site of his new abode. Ambition turned his thoughts from these designs - ambition, which laboring through various lets and hindrances, had now led him to the summit of his hopes, in making him Lord Protector of England.

His countenance was rough but intelligent - his ample brow and quick grey eyes seemed to look out, over his own plans, and the opposition of his enemies. His voice was stentorian: his hand stretched out in debate, seemed by its gigantic and muscular form, to warn his hearers that words were not his only weapons. Few people had discovered some cowardice and much infirmity of purpose under this imposing exterior. No man could crush a "butterfly on the wheel" with better effect; no man better cover a speedy retreat from a powerful adversary. This had been the secret of his secession at the time of Lord Raymond's election. In the unsteady glance of his eye, in his extreme desire to learn the opinions of all, in the feebleness of his handwriting, these qualities might be obscurely traced, but they were not generally known. He was now our Lord Protector. He had canvassed eagerly for this post. His protectorate was to be distinguished by every kind of innovation on the aristocracy. This his selected task was exchanged for the far different one of encountering the ruin caused by the convulsions of physical nature. He was incapable of meeting these evils by any comprehensive system; he had resorted to expedient after expedient and could never be induced to put a remedy in force, till it came too late to be of use.

Certainly, the Ryland that advanced towards us now, bore small resemblance to the powerful, ironical, seemingly fearless canvasser for the first rank among Englishmen. Our native oak, as his partisans called him, was visited truly by a nipping winter. He scarcely appeared half his usual height; his joints were unknit, his limbs would not support him; his face was contracted, his eye wandering; debility of purpose and dastard fear were expressed in every gesture.

In answer to our eager questions, one word alone fell, as it were involuntarily, from his convulsed lips: The Plague. - "Where?" -"Everywhere - we must fly - all fly - but whither? No man can tell - there is no refuge on earth, it comes on us like a thousand packs of wolves - we must all fly - where shall you go? Where can any of us go?"

These words were syllabled trembling by the iron man. Adrian replied, "Whither indeed would you fly? We must all remain; and do our best to help our suffering fellow-creatures."

"Help!" said Ryland, "there is no help! - great God, who talks of help! All the world has the plague!"

"Then to avoid it, we must quit the world," observed Adrian, with a gentle smile.

Ryland groaned; cold drops stood on his brow. It was useless to oppose his paroxysm of terror: but we soothed and encouraged him, so that after an interval he was better able to explain to us the ground of his alarm. It had come sufficiently home to him. One of his servants, while waiting on him, had suddenly fallen down dead. The physician declared that he died of the plague. We endeavored to calm him - but our own hearts were not calm. I saw the eye of Idris wander from me to her children, with an anxious appeal to my judgment. Adrian was absorbed in meditation. For myself, I own that Ryland's words rang in my ears; all the world was infected; - in what uncontaminated seclusion could I save my beloved treasures, until the shadow of death had passed from over the earth? We sunk into silence: a silence that drank in the doleful accounts and prognostications of our guest. We had receded from the crowd; and ascending the steps of the terrace, sought the Castle. Our change of cheer struck those nearest to us; and, by means of Ryland's servants, the report soon spread that he had fled from the plague in London. The sprightly parties broke up — they assembled in whispering groups. The spirit of gaiety was eclipsed; the music ceased; the young people left their occupations and gathered together. The lightness of heart which had dressed them in masquerade habits, had decorated their tents, and assembled them in fantastic groups, appeared a sin against, and a provocative to, the awful destiny that had laid its palsying hand upon hope and life. The merriment of the hour was an unholy mockery of the sorrows of man. The foreigners whom we had among us, who had fled from the plague in their own country, now saw their last asylum invaded; and, fear making them garrulous, they described to eager listeners the miseries they had beheld in cities visited by the calamity, and gave fearful accounts of the insidious and irremediable nature of the disease.

We had entered the Castle. Idris stood at a window that over-looked the park; her maternal eyes sought her own children among the young crowd. An Italian lad had got an audience about him, and with animated gestures was describing some scene of horror. Alfred stood immoveable before him; his whole attention absorbed. Little Evelyn had endeavored to draw Clara away to play with him; but the Italian's tale arrested her, she crept near, her lustrous eyes fixed on the speaker. Either watching the crowd in the park, or occupied by painful reflection, we were all silent; Ryland stood by himself in an embrasure of the window; Adrian paced the hall, revolving some new and overpowering idea — suddenly he stopped and said: "I have long expected this; could we in reason expect that this island should be exempt from the universal visitation? The evil is come home to us, and we must not shrink from our fate. What are your plans, my Lord Protector, for the benefit of our country?"

"For heaven's love! Windsor," cried Ryland, "do not mock me with that title. Death and disease level all men. I neither pretend to protect nor govern a hospital - such will England quickly become."

"Do you then intend, now in time of peril, to recede from your duties?"

"Duties! speak rationally, my Lord! - when I am a plague-spotted corpse, where will my duties be? Every man for himself! the devil take the Protectorship, say I, if it exposes me to danger!"

"Faint-hearted man!" cried Adrian indignantly - "Your countrymen put their trust in you, and you betray them!"

"I betray them!" said Ryland, "the plague betrays me. Faint-hearted! It is well, shut up in your castle, out of danger, to boast yourself out of fear. Take the Protectorship who will; before God I renounce it!"

"And before God," replied his opponent, fervently, "do I receive it! No one will canvass for this honor now - none envy my danger or labors. Deposit your powers in my hands. Long have I fought with death, and much" (he stretched out his thin hand) "much have I suffered in the struggle. It is not by flying, but by facing the enemy, that we can conquer. If my last combat is now about to be fought, and I am to be worsted - so let it be!"

"But come, Ryland, recollect yourself! Men have hitherto thought you magnanimous and wise, will you cast aside these titles? Consider the panic your departure will occasion. Return to London. I will go with you. Encourage the people by your presence. I will incur all the danger. Shame! shame! if the first magistrate of England be foremost to renounce his duties."

Meanwhile among our guests in the park, all thoughts of festivity had faded. As summer-flies are scattered by rain, so did this congregation, late noisy and happy, in sadness and melancholy murmurs break up, dwindling away apace. With the set sun and the deepening twilight the park became nearly empty. Adrian and Ryland were still in earnest discussion. We had prepared a banquet for our guests in the lower hall of the castle; and thither Idris and I repaired to receive and entertain the few that remained. There is nothing melancholier than a merry-meeting thus turned to sorrow: the gala dresses - the decorations, gay as they might otherwise be, receive a solemn and funereal appearance. If such change be painful from lighter causes, it weighed with intolerable heaviness from the knowledge that the earth's desolator had at last, even as an arch-fiend, lightly over-leaped the boundaries our precautions raised, and at once enthroned himself in the full and beating heart of our country. Idris sat at the top of the half-empty hall. Pale and tearful, she almost forgot her duties as hostess; her eyes were fixed on her children. Alfred's serious air shewed that he still revolved the tragic story related by the Italian boy. Evelyn was the only mirthful creature present: he sat on Clara's lap; and, making matter of glee from his own fancies, laughed aloud. The vaulted roof echoed again his infant tone. The poor mother who had brooded long over, and suppressed the expression of her anguish, now burst into tears, and folding her babe in her arms, hurried from the hall. Clara and Alfred followed. While the rest of the company, in confused murmur, which grew louder and louder, gave voice to their many fears.

The younger part gathered round me to ask my advice; and those who had friends in London were anxious beyond the rest, to ascertain the present extent of disease in the metropolis. I encouraged them with such thoughts of cheer as presented themselves. I told them exceedingly few deaths had yet been occasioned by pestilence, and gave them hopes, as we were the last visited, so the calamity might have lost its most venomous power before it had reached us. The cleanliness, habits of order, and the manner in which our cities were built, were all in our favor. As it was an epidemic, its chief force was derived from pernicious qualities in the air, and it would probably do-little harm where this was naturally salubrious. At first, I had spoken only to those nearest me; but the whole assembly gathered about me, and I found that I was listened to by all. "My friends," I said, "our risk is common; our precautions and exertions shall be common also. If manly courage and resistance can save us, we will be saved. We will fight the enemy to the last. Plague shall not find us a ready prey; we will dispute every inch of ground; and, by methodical and inflexible laws, pile invincible barriers to the progress of our foe. Perhaps in no part of the world has she met with so systematic and determined an opposition. Perhaps no country is naturally so well protected against our invader; nor has nature anywhere been so well assisted by the hand of man. We will not despair. We are neither cowards nor fatalists; but, believing that God has placed the means for our preservation in our own hands, we will use those means to our utmost. Remember that cleanliness, sobriety, and even good-humor and benevolence, are our best medicines."

There was little I could add to this general exhortation; for the plague, though in London, was not among us. I dismissed the guests; therefore, and they went thoughtful, more than sad, to await the events in store for them.

I now sought Adrian, anxious to hear the result of his discussion with Ryland. He had in part prevailed; the Lord Protector consented to return to London for a few weeks; during which time things should be so arranged, as to occasion less consternation at his departure. Adrian and Idris were together. The sadness with which the former had first heard that the plague was in London had vanished; the energy of his purpose informed his body with strength, the solemn joy of enthusiasm and self-devotion illuminated his countenance; and the weakness of his physical nature seemed to pass from him, as the cloud of humanity did, in the ancient fable, from the divine lover of Semele. He was endeavoring to encourage his sister, and to bring her to look on his intent in a less tragic light than she was prepared to do; and with passionate eloquence he unfolded his designs to her.

"Let me, at the first word," he said, "relieve your mind from all fear on my account. I will not task myself beyond my powers, nor will I needlessly seek danger. I feel that I know what ought to be done, and as my presence is necessary for the accomplishment of my plans, I will take especial care to preserve my life.

"I am now going to undertake an office fitted for me. I cannot intrigue, or work a tortuous path through the labyrinth of men's vices and passions; but I can bring patience, and sympathy, and such aid as art affords, to the bed of disease; I can raise from earth the miserable orphan, and awaken to new hopes the shut heart of the mourner. I can enchain the plague in limits and set a term to the misery it would occasion; courage, forbearance, and watchfulness, are the forces I bring towards this great work.

"O, I shall be something now! From my birth I have aspired like the eagle - but, unlike the eagle, my wings have failed, and my vision has been blinded. Disappointment and sickness have hitherto held dominion over me; twin born with me, my would, was forever enchained by the shall not, of these my tyrants. A shepherd-boy that tends a silly flock on the mountains, was more in the scale of society than I. Congratulate me then that I have found fitting scope for my powers. I have often thought of offering my services to the pestilence-stricken towns of France and Italy; but fear of paining you, and expectation of this catastrophe, withheld me. To England and to Englishmen I dedicate myself. If I can save one of her mighty spirits from the deadly shaft; if I can ward disease from one of her smiling cottages, I shall not have lived in vain."

Strange ambition this! Yet such was Adrian. He appeared given up to contemplation, averse to excitement, a lowly student, a man of visions - but afford him worthy theme, and -

> *Like to the lark at break of day arising,*
> *From sullen earth, sings hymns at heaven's gate.*
> *so, did he spring up from listlessness and unproductive thought,*
> *to the highest pitch of virtuous action.*

With him went enthusiasm, the high-wrought resolve, the eye that without blenching could look at death. With us remained sorrow, anxiety, and unendurable expectation of evil. The man, says Lord Bacon, who hath wife and children, has given hostages to fortune. Vain was all philosophical reasoning - vain all fortitude - vain, vain, a reliance on probable good. I might heap high the scale with logic, courage, and resignation - but let one fear for Idris and our children enter the opposite one, and, over-weighed, it kicked the beam.

The plague was in London! Fools that we were not long ago to have foreseen this. We wept over the ruin of the boundless continents of the east, and the desolation of the western world; while we fancied that the little channel between our island and the rest of the earth was to preserve us alive among the dead. It were no mighty leap methinks from Calais to Dover. The eye easily discerns the sister land; they were united once; and the little path that runs between looks in a map but as a trodden footway through high grass. Yet this small interval was to save us: the sea was to rise a wall of adamant - without, disease and misery - within, a shelter from evil, a nook of the garden of paradise — a particle of celestial soil, which no evil could invade - truly we were wise in our generation, to imagine all these things!

But we are awake now. The plague is in London; the air of England is tainted, and her sons and daughters strew the unwholesome earth. And now, the sea, late our defense, seems our prison bound; hemmed in by its gulphs, we shall die like the famished inhabitants of a besieged town. Other nations have a fellowship in death; but we, shut out from all neighborhood, must bury our own dead, and little England become a wide, wide tomb.

This feeling of universal misery assumed concentration and shape, when I looked on my wife and children; and the thought of danger to them possessed my whole being with fear. How could I save them? I revolved a thousand and a thousand plans. They should not die - first I would be gathered to nothingness, ere infection should come anear these idols of my soul. I would walk barefoot through the world, to find an uninfected spot; I would build my home on some wave-tossed plank, drifted about on the barren, shoreless ocean. I would betake me with them to some wild beast's den, where a tiger's cubs, which I would slay, had been reared in health. I would seek the mountain eagle's eirie, and live years suspended in some inaccessible recess of a sea-bounding cliff - no labor too great, no scheme too wild, if it promised life to them. O! ye heartstrings of mine, could ye be torn asunder, and my soul does not spend itself in tears of blood for sorrow! Idris, after the first shock, regained a portion of fortitude. She studiously shut out all prospect of the future and cradled her heart in present blessings. She never for a moment lost sight of her children. But while they in health sported about her, she could cherish contentment and hope. A strange and wild restlessness came over me - the more intolerable, because I was forced to conceal it. My fears for Adrian were ceaseless; August had come; and the symptoms of plague increased rapidly in London. It was deserted by all who possessed the power of removing; and he, the brother of my soul, was exposed to the perils from which all but slaves enchained by circumstance fled. He remained to combat the fiend - his side unguarded, his toils unshared - infection might even reach him, and he die unattended and alone. By day and night these thoughts pursued me. I resolved to visit London, to see him; to quiet these agonizing throes by the sweet medicine of hope, or the opiate of despair.

It was not until I arrived at Brentford, that I perceived much change in the face of the country. The better sort of houses were shut up; the busy trade of the town palsied; there was an air of anxiety among the few passengers I met, and they looked wonderingly at my carriage—the first they had seen pass towards London, since pestilence sat on its high places, and possessed its busy streets. I met several funerals; they were slenderly attended by mourners and were regarded by the spectators as omens of direst import. Some gazed on these processions with wild eagerness - others fled timidly - some wept aloud.

Adrian's chief endeavor, after the immediate succor of the sick, had been to disguise the symptoms and progress of the plague from the inhabitants of London. He knew that fear and melancholy forebodings were powerful assistants to disease; that desponding and brooding care rendered the physical nature of man peculiarly susceptible of infection. No unseemly sights were therefore discernible: the shops were in general open, the concourse of passengers in some degree kept up. But although the appearance of an infected town was avoided, to me, who had not beheld it since the commencement of the visitation, London appeared sufficiently changed. There were no carriages, and grass had sprung high in the streets; the houses had a desolate look; most of the shutters were closed; and there was a ghast and frightened stare in the persons I met, very different from the usual business-like demeanor of the Londoners. My solitary carriage attracted notice, as it rattled along towards the Protectoral Palace - and the fashionable streets leading to it wore a still more dreary and deserted appearance. I found Adrian's anti-chamber crowded - it was his hour for giving audience. I was unwilling to disturb his labors, and waited, watching the ingress and egress of the petitioners. They consisted of people of the middling and lower classes of society, whose means of subsistence failed with the cessation of trade, and of the busy spirit of money-making in all its branches, peculiar to our country. There was an air of anxiety, sometimes of terror in the newcomers, strongly contrasted with the resigned and even satisfied mien of those who had had audience. I could read the influence of my friend in their quickened motions and cheerful faces. Two o'clock struck, after which none were admitted; those who had been disappointed went sullenly or sorrowfully away, while I entered the audience-chamber.

I was struck by the improvement that appeared in the health of Adrian. He was no longer bent to the ground, like an over-nursed flower of spring, that, shooting up beyond its strength, is weighed down even by its own coronal of blossoms. His eyes were bright, his countenance composed, an air of concentrated energy was diffused over his whole person, much unlike its former languor. He sat at a table with several secretaries, who were arranging petitions, or registering the notes made during that day's audience. Two or three petitioners were still in attendance. I admired his justice and patience. Those who possessed a power of living out of London, he advised immediately to quit it, affording them the means of so doing. Others, whose trade was beneficial to the city, or who possessed no other refuge, he provided with advice for better avoiding the epidemic; relieving overloaded families, supplying the gaps made in others by death. Order, comfort, and even health, rose under his influence, as from the touch of a magician's wand.

"I am glad you are come," he said to me, when we were at last alone; "I can only spare a few minutes and must tell you much in that time. The plague is now in progress - it is useless closing one's eyes to the fact - the deaths increase each week. What will come I cannot guess. As yet, thank God, I am equal to the government of the town; and I look only to the present. Ryland, whom I have so long detained, has stipulated that I shall suffer him to depart before the end of this month. The deputy appointed by parliament is dead; another therefore must be named; I have advanced my claim, and I believe that I shall have no competitor. Tonight the question is to be decided, as there is a call of the house for the purpose. You must nominate me, Lionel; Ryland, for shame, cannot shew himself; but you, my friend, will do me this service?

How lovely is devotion! Here was a youth, royally sprung, bred in luxury, by nature averse to the usual struggles of a public life, and now, in time of danger, at a period when to live was the utmost scope of the ambitious, he, the beloved and heroic Adrian, made, in sweet simplicity, an offer to sacrifice himself for the public good. The very idea was generous and noble, - but, beyond this, his unpretending manner, his entire want of the assumption of a virtue, rendered his act ten times more touching. I would have withstood his request; but I had seen the good he diffused; I felt that his resolves were not to be shaken, so, with a heavy heart,

I consented to do as he asked. He grasped my hand affectionately: -"Thank you," he said, "you have relieved me from a painful dilemma, and are, as you ever were, the best of my friends. Farewell - I must now leave you for a few hours. Go you and converse with Ryland. Although he deserts his post in London, he may be of the greatest service in the north of England, by receiving and assisting travelers, and contributing to supply the metropolis with food. Awaken him, I entreat you, to some sense of duty."

Adrian left me, as I afterwards learnt, upon his daily task of visiting the hospitals, and inspecting the crowded parts of London. I found Ryland much altered, even from what he had been when he visited Windsor. Perpetual fear had jaundiced his complexion and shriveled his whole person. I told him of the business of the evening, and a smile relaxed the contracted muscles. He desired to go; each day he expected to be infected by pestilence, each day he was unable to resist the gentle violence of Adrian's detention. The moment Adrian should be legally elected his deputy, he would escape to safety. Under this impression he listened to all I said; and, elevated almost to joy by the near prospect of his departure, he entered into a discussion concerning the plans he should adopt in his own county, forgetting, for the moment, his cherished resolution of shutting himself up from all communication in the mansion and grounds of his estate.

In the evening, Adrian and I proceeded to Westminster. As we went, he reminded me of what I was to say and do, yet, strange to say, I entered the chamber without having once reflected on my purpose. Adrian remained in the coffee-room, while I, in compliance with his desire, took my seat in St. Stephen's. There reigned unusual silence in the chamber. I had not visited it since Raymond's protectorate, a period conspicuous for a numerous attendance of members, for the eloquence of the speakers, and the warmth of the debate. The benches were very empty, those by custom occupied by the hereditary members were vacant; the city members were there - the members for the commercial towns, few landed proprietors, and not many of those who entered parliament for the sake of a career. The first subject that occupied the attention of the house was an address from the Lord Protector, praying them to appoint a deputy during a necessary absence on his part.

A silence prevailed, till one of the members coming to me, whispered that the Earl of Windsor had sent him word that I was to move his election, in the absence of the person who had been first chosen for this office. Now for the first time I saw the full extent of my task, and I was overwhelmed by what I had brought on myself. Ryland had deserted his post through fear of the plague: from the same fear Adrian had no competitor. And I, the nearest kinsman of the Earl of Windsor, was to propose his election. I was to thrust this selected and matchless friend into the post of danger - impossible! the die was cast - I would offer myself as candidate.

The few members who were present, had come more for the sake of terminating the business by securing a legal attendance, than under the idea of a debate. I had risen mechanically - my knees trembled; irresolution hung on my voice, as I uttered a few words on the necessity of choosing a person adequate to the dangerous task in hand. But, when the idea of presenting myself in the room of my friend intruded, the load of doubt and pain was taken from off me. My words flowed spontaneously — my utterance was firm and quick. I adverted to what Adrian had already done - I promised the same vigilance in furthering all his views. I drew a touching picture of his vacillating health; I boasted of my own strength. I prayed them to save even from himself this scion of the noblest family in England. My alliance with him was the pledge of my sincerity, my union with his sister, my children, his presumptive heirs, were the hostages of my truth.

This unexpected turn in the debate was quickly communicated to Adrian. He hurried in and witnessed the termination of my impassioned harangue. I did not see him: my soul was in my words, - my eyes could not perceive that which was; while a vision of Adrian's form, tainted by pestilence, and sinking in death, floated before them. He seized my hand, as I concluded - "Unkind!" he cried, "you have betrayed me!" then, springing forwards, with the air of one who had a right to command, he claimed the place of deputy as his own. He had bought it, he said, with danger, and paid for it with toil. His ambition rested there; and, after an interval devoted to the interests of his country, was I to step in, and reap the profit? Let them remember what London had been when he arrived: the panic that prevailed brought famine, while every moral and legal tie was loosened. He had restored order - this had been a work which required perseverance, patience, and energy; and he had neither slept nor waked but for the good of his country - Would they dare wrong him thus? Would they wrest his hard-earned reward from him, to bestow it on one, who, never having mingled in public life, would come a tyro to the craft, in which he was an adept? He demanded the place of deputy as his right. Ryland had shown that he preferred him. Never before had he, who was born even to the inheritance of the throne of England, never had he asked favor or honor from those now his equals, but who might have been his subjects. Would they refuse him? Could they thrust back from the path of distinction and laudable ambition, the heir of their ancient kings, and heap another disappointment on a fallen house.

No one had ever before heard Adrian allude to the rights of his ancestors. None had ever before suspected that power, or the suffrage of the many, could in any manner become dear to him. He had begun his speech with vehemence; he ended with unassuming gentleness, making his appeal with the same humility, as if he had asked to be the first in wealth, honor, and power among Englishmen, and not, as was the truth, to be the foremost in the ranks of loathsome toils and inevitable death. A murmur of approbation rose after his speech. "Oh, do not listen to him," I cried, "he speaks false - false to himself," - I was interrupted: and, silence being restored, we were ordered, as was the custom, to retire during the decision of the house. I fancied that they hesitated, and that there was some hope for me - I was mistaken - hardly had we quitted the chamber, before Adrian was recalled, and installed in his office of Lord Deputy to the Protector.

We returned together to the palace. "Why, Lionel," said Adrian, "what did you intend? you could not hope to conquer, and yet you gave me the pain of a triumph over my dearest friend."

"This is mockery," I replied, "you devote yourself, - you, the adored brother of Idris, the being, of all the world contains, dearest to our hearts - you devote yourself to an early death. I would have prevented this; my death would be a small evil - or rather I should not die; while you cannot hope to escape."

"As to the likelihood of escaping," said Adrian, "ten years hence the cold stars may shine on the graves of all of us; but as to my peculiar liability to infection, I could easily prove, both logically and physically, that in the midst of contagion I have a better chance of life than you.

"This is my post: I was born for this - to rule England in anarchy, to save her in danger - to devote myself for her. The blood of my forefathers cries aloud in my veins, and bids me be first among my countrymen. Or, if this mode of speech offend you, let me say, that my mother, the proud queen, instilled early into me a love of distinction, and all that, if the weakness of my physical nature and my peculiar opinions had not prevented such a design, might have made me long since struggle for the lost inheritance of my race. But now my mother, or, if you will, my mother's lessons, awaken within me. I cannot lead on to battle; I cannot, through intrigue and faithlessness rear again the throne upon the wreck of English public spirit. But I can be the first to support and guard my country, now that terrific disasters and ruin have laid strong hands upon her.

"That country and my beloved sister are all I have. I will protect the first - the latter I commit to your charge. If I survive, and she be lost, I were far better dead. Preserve her - for her own sake I know that you will — if you require any other spur, think that, in preserving her, you preserve me. Her faultless nature, one sum of perfections, is wrapped up in her affections — if they were hurt, she would droop like an unwatered floweret, and the slightest injury they receive is a nipping frost to her. Already she fears for us. She fears for the children she adores, and for you, the father of these, her lover, husband, protector; and you must be near her to support and encourage her. Return to Windsor then, my brother; for such you are by every tie — fill the double place my absence imposes on you, and let me, in all my sufferings here, turn my eyes towards that dear seclusion, and say - *There is peace.*"

CHAPTER VII

I did proceed to Windsor, but not with the intention of remaining there. I went but to obtain the consent of Idris, and then to return and take my station beside my unequalled friend; to share his labors, and save him, if so, it must be, at the expense of my life. Yet I dreaded to witness the anguish which my resolve might excite in Idris. I had vowed to my own heart never to shadow her countenance even with transient grief, and should I prove recreant at the hour of greatest need? I had begun my journey with anxious haste; now I desired to draw it out through the course of days and months. I longed to avoid the necessity of action; I strove to escape from thought – vainly - futurity, like a dark image in a phantasmagoria, came nearer and nearer, till it clasped the whole earth in its shadow.

A slight circumstance induced me to alter my usual route, and to return home by Egham and Bishopgate. I alighted at Perdita's ancient abode, her cottage; and, sending forward the carriage, determined to walk across the park to the castle. This spot, dedicated to sweetest recollections, the deserted house and neglected garden were well adapted to nurse my melancholy. In our happiest days, Perdita had adorned her cottage with every aid art might bring, to that which nature had selected to favor. In the same spirit of exaggeration, she had, on the event of her separation from Raymond, caused it to be entirely neglected. It was now in ruin: the deer had climbed the broken palings and reposed among the flowers; grass grew on the threshold, and the swinging lattice creaking to the wind, gave signal of utter desertion. The sky was blue above, and the air impregnated with fragrance by the rare flowers that grew among the weeds. The trees moved overhead, awakening nature's favorite melody - but the melancholy appearance of the choked paths, and weed-grown flowerbeds, dimmed even this gay summer scene. The time when in proud and happy security we assembled at this cottage, was gone - soon the present hours would join those past, and shadows of future ones rose dark and menacing from the womb of time, their cradle and their bier. For the first time in my life I envied the sleep of the dead and thought with pleasure of one's bed under the sod, where grief and fear have no power. I passed through the gap of the broken paling - I felt, while I disdained, the choking tears - I rushed into the depths of the forest. O death and change, rulers of our life, where are ye, that I may grapple with you! What was there in our tranquility, that excited your envy - in our happiness, that ye should destroy it? We were happy, loving, and beloved; the horn of Amalthea contained no blessing unshowered upon us, but alas!

la fortuna deidad barbara importuna, oy cadaver y ayer flor, no permanece jamas! Fortune the important barbarian diety,the corpse and flower of yesteryear, never stays!

As I wandered on thus ruminating, a number of country people passed me. They seemed full of careful thought, and a few words of their conversation that reached me, induced me to approach and make further enquiries. A party of people flying from London, as was frequent in those days, had come up the Thames in a boat. No one at Windsor would afford them shelter; so, going a little further up, they remained all night in a deserted hut near Bolter's lock. They pursued their way the following morning, leaving one of their company behind them, sick of the plague. This circumstance once spread abroad, none dared approach within half a mile of the infected neighborhood, and the deserted wretch was left to fight with disease and death in solitude, as he best might. I was urged by compassion to hasten to the hut, for the purpose of ascertaining his situation, and administering to his wants.

As I advanced, I met knots of country-people talking earnestly of this event: distant as they were from the apprehended contagion, fear was impressed on every countenance. I passed by a group of these terrorists, in a lane in the direct road to the hut. One of them stopped me, and, conjecturing that I was ignorant of the circumstance, told me not to go on, for that an infected person lay but at a short distance.

"I know it," I replied, "and I am going to see in what condition the poor fellow is."

A murmur of surprise and horror ran through the assembly. I continued:

"This poor wretch is deserted, dying, succourless; in these unhappy times, God knows how soon any or all of us may be in like want. I am going to do, as I would be done by."

"But you will never be able to return to the Castle - Lady Idris - his children -" in confused speech were the words that struck my ear.

"Do you not know, my friends," I said, "that the Earl himself, now Lord Protector, visits daily, not only those probably infected by this disease, but the hospitals and pest houses, going near, and even touching the sick? yet he was never in better health. You labor under an entire mistake as to the nature of the plague; but do not fear, I do not ask any of you to accompany me, nor to believe me, until I return safe and sound from my patient."

So, I left them, and hurried on. I soon arrived at the hut: the door was ajar. I entered, and one glance assured me that its former inhabitant was no more - he lay on a heap of straw, cold and stiff; while a pernicious effluvia filled the room, and various stains and marks served to shew the virulence of the disorder.

I had never before beheld one killed by pestilence. While every mind was full of dismay at its effects, a craving for excitement had led us to peruse De Foe's account, and the masterly delineations of the author of Arthur Mervyn. The pictures drawn in these books were so vivid, that we seemed to have experienced the results depicted by them. But cold were the sensations excited by words, burning though they were, and describing the death and misery of thousands, compared to what I felt in looking on the corpse of this unhappy stranger. This indeed was the plague. I raised his rigid limbs, I marked the distortion of his face, and the stony eyes lost to perception. As I was thus occupied, chill horror congealed my blood, making my flesh quiver and my hair to stand on end. Half insanely I spoke to the dead. So, the plague killed you, I muttered. How came this? Was the coming painful? You look as if the enemy had tortured, before he murdered you. And now I leapt up precipitately, and escaped from the hut, before nature could revoke her laws, and inorganic words be breathed in answer from the lips of the departed.

On returning through the lane, I saw at a distance the same assemblage of persons which I had left. They hurried away, as soon as they saw me; my agitated mien added to their fear of coming near one who had entered within the verge of contagion.

At a distance from facts one draws conclusions which appear infallible, which yet when put to the test of reality, vanish like unreal dreams. I had ridiculed the fears of my countrymen, when they related to others; now that they came home to myself, I paused. The Rubicon, I felt, was passed; and it behooved me well to reflect what I should do on this hither side of disease and danger. According to the vulgar superstition, my dress, my person, the air I breathed, bore in it mortal danger to myself and others. Should I return to the Castle, to my wife and children, with this taint upon me? Not surely if I were infected; but I felt certain that I was not - a few hours would determine the question - I would spend these in the forest, in reflection on what was to come, and what my future actions were to be. In the feeling communicated to me by the sight of one struck by the plague, I forgot the events that had excited me so strongly in London; new and more painful prospects, by degrees were cleared of the mist which had hitherto veiled them. The question was no longer whether I should share Adrian's toils and danger; but in what manner I could, in Windsor and the neighborhood, imitate the prudence and zeal which, under his government, produced order and plenty in London, and how, now pestilence had spread more widely, I could secure the health of my own family.

I spread the whole earth out as a map before me. On no one spot of its surface could I put my finger and say, here is safety. In the south, the disease, virulent and immedicable, had nearly annihilated the race of man; storm and inundation, poisonous winds and blights, filled up the measure of suffering. In the north it was worse - the lesser population gradually declined, and famine and plague kept watch on the survivors, who, helpless and feeble, were ready to fall an easy prey into their hands.

I contracted my view to England. The overgrown metropolis, the great heart of mighty Britain, was pulseless. Commerce had ceased. All resort for ambition or pleasure was cut off - the streets were grass-grown - the houses empty - the few, that from necessity remained, seemed already branded with the taint of inevitable pestilence. In the larger manufacturing towns, the same tragedy was acted on a smaller, yet more disastrous scale. There was no Adrian to superintend and direct, while whole flocks of the poor were struck and killed. Yet we were not all to die. No truly, though thinned, the race of man would continue, and the great plague would, in after years, become matter of history and wonder. Doubtless this visitation was for extent unexampled - more need that we should work hard to dispute its progress; ere this men have gone out in sport, and slain their thousands and tens of thousands; but now man had become a creature of price; the life of one of them was of more worth than the so called treasures of kings. Look at his thought-endued countenance, his graceful limbs, his majestic brow, his wondrous mechanism - the type and model of this best work of God is not to be cast aside as a broken vessel - he shall be preserved, and his children and his children's children carry down the name and form of man to latest time.

Above all I must guard those entrusted by nature and fate to my especial care. And surely, if among all my fellow-creatures I were to select those who might stand forth examples of the greatness and goodness of man, I could choose no other than those allied to me by the most sacred ties. Some from among the family of man must survive, and these should be among the survivors; that should be my task - to accomplish it my own life were a small sacrifice. There then in that castle - in Windsor Castle, birthplace of Idris and my babes, should be the haven and retreat for the wrecked bark of human society. Its forest should be our world - its garden affords us food; within its walls I would establish the shaken throne of health. I was an outcast and a vagabond when Adrian gently threw over me the silver net of love and civilization and linked me inextricably to human charities and human excellence. I was one, who, though an aspirant after good, and an ardent lover of wisdom, was yet unenrolled in any list of worth, when Idris, the princely born, who was herself the personification of all that was divine in woman, she who walked the earth like a poet's dream, as a carved goddess endued with sense, or pictured saint stepping from the canvas - she, the most worthy, chose me, and gave me herself - a priceless gift.

During several hours I continued thus to meditate, till hunger and fatigue brought me back to the passing hour, then marked by long shadows cast from the descending sun. I had wandered towards Bracknel, far to the west of Windsor. The feeling of perfect health which I enjoyed, assured me that I was free from contagion. I remembered that Idris had been kept in ignorance of my proceedings. She might have heard of my return from London, and my visit to Bolter's Lock, which, connected with my continued absence, might tend greatly to alarm her. I returned to Windsor by the Long Walk, and passing through the town towards the Castle, I found it in a state of agitation and disturbance.

"It is too late to be ambitious," says Sir Thomas Browne. "We cannot hope to live so long in our names as some have done in their persons; one face of Janus holds no proportion to the other." Upon this text many fanatics arose, who prophesied that the end of time was come. The spirit of superstition had birth, from the wreck of our hopes, and antics wild and dangerous were played on the great theatre, while the remaining particle of futurity dwindled into a point in the eyes of the prognosticators. Weak-spirited women died of fear as they listened to their denunciations; men of robust form and seeming strength fell into idiocy and madness, racked by the dread of coming eternity. A man of this kind was now pouring forth his eloquent despair among the inhabitants of Windsor. The scene of the morning, and my visit to the dead, which had been spread abroad, had alarmed the country-people, so they had become fit instruments to be played upon by a maniac.

The poor wretch had lost his young wife and lovely infant by the plague. He was a mechanic; and, rendered unable to attend to the occupation which supplied his necessities, famine was added to his other miseries. He left the chamber which contained his wife and child - wife and child no more, but "dead earth upon the earth" - wild with hunger, watching and grief, his diseased fancy made him believe himself sent by heaven to preach the end of time to the world. He entered the churches and foretold to the congregations their speedy removal to the vaults below. He appeared like the forgotten spirit of the time in the theatres, and bade the spectators go home and die. He had been seized and confined; he had escaped and wandered from London among the neighboring towns, and, with frantic gestures and thrilling words, he unveiled to each their hidden fears, and gave voice to the soundless thought they dared not syllable. He stood under the arcade of the town-hall of Windsor, and from this elevation harangued a trembling crowd.

"Hear, O ye inhabitants of the earth," he cried, "hear thou, all seeing, but most pitiless Heaven! hear thou too, O tempest-tossed heart, which breathes out these words, yet faints beneath their meaning! Death is among us! The earth is beautiful and flower-bedecked, but she is our grave! The clouds of heaven weep for us - the pageantry of the stars is but our funeral torchlight. Grey headed men, ye hoped for yet a few years in your long-known abode - but the lease is up, you must remove - children, ye will never reach maturity, even now the small grave is dug for ye - mothers, clasp them in your arms, one death embraces you!"

Shuddering, he stretched out his hands, his eyes cast up, seemed bursting from their sockets, while he appeared to follow shapes, to us invisible, in the yielding air -"There they are," he cried, "the dead! They rise in their shrouds, and pass in silent procession towards the far land of their doom — their bloodless lips move not - their shadowy limbs are void of motion, while still they glide onwards. We come," he exclaimed, springing forwards, "for what should we wait? Haste, my friends, apparel yourselves in the court-dress of death. Pestilence will usher you to his presence. Why thus long? they, the good, the wise, and the beloved, are gone before. Mothers kiss you last - husbands, protectors no more, lead on the partners of your death! Come, O come! while the dear ones are yet in sight, for soon they will pass away, and we never, never, shall join them more."

From such ravings as these, he would suddenly become collected, and with unexaggerated but terrific words, paint the horrors of the time; describe with minute detail, the effects of the plague on the human frame, and tell heart-breaking tales of the snapping of dear affinities - the gasping horror of despair over the death-bed of the last beloved - so that groans and even shrieks burst from the crowd. One man in particular stood in front, his eyes fixed on the prophet, his mouth open, his limbs rigid, while his face changed to various colors, yellow, blue, and green, through intense fear. The maniac caught his glance and turned his eye on him - one has heard of the gaze of the rattlesnake, which allures the trembling victim till he falls within his jaws. The maniac became composed; his person rose higher; authority beamed from his countenance. He looked on the peasant, who began to tremble, while he still gazed; his knees knocked together; his teeth chattered. He at last fell down in convulsions. "That man has the plague," said the maniac calmly. A shriek burst from the lips of the poor wretch; and then sudden motionlessness came over him; it was manifest to all that he was dead.

Cries of horror filled the place - every one endeavored to effect his escape - in a few minutes the market place was cleared - the corpse lay on the ground; and the maniac, subdued and exhausted, sat beside it, leaning his gaunt cheek upon his thin hand. Soon some people, deputed by the magistrates, came to remove the body; the unfortunate being saw a jailor in each - he fled precipitately, while I passed onwards to the Castle.

Death, cruel and relentless, had entered these beloved walls. An old servant, who had nursed Idris in infancy, and who lived with us more on the footing of a revered relative than a domestic, had gone a few days before to visit a daughter, married, and settled in the neighborhood of London. On the night of her return she sickened of the plague. From the haughty and unbending nature of the Countess of Windsor, Idris had few tender filial associations with her. This good woman had stood in the place of a mother, and her very deficiencies of education and knowledge, by rendering her humble and defenseless, endeared her to us - she was the especial favorite of the children. I found my poor girl, there is no exaggeration in the expression, wild with grief and dread. She hung over the patient in agony, which was not mitigated when her thoughts wandered towards her babes, for whom she feared infection. My arrival was like the newly discovered lamp of a lighthouse to sailors, who are weathering some dangerous point. She deposited her appalling doubts in my hands; she relied on my judgment and was comforted by my participation in her sorrow. Soon our poor nurse expired; and the anguish of suspense was changed to deep regret, which though at first more painful, yet yielded with greater readiness to my consolations. Sleep, the sovereign balm, at length steeped her tearful eyes in forgetfulness.

She slept; and quiet prevailed in the Castle, whose inhabitants were hushed to repose. I was awake, and during the long hours of dead night, my busy thoughts worked in my brain, like ten thousand millwheels, rapid, acute, untamable. All slept - all England slept; and from my window, commanding a wide prospect of the star-illumined country, I saw the land stretched out in placid rest. I was awake, alive, while the brother of death possessed my race. What, if the more potent of these fraternal deities should obtain dominion over it? The silence of midnight, to speak truly, though apparently a paradox, rung in my ears. The solitude became intolerable - I placed my hand on the beating heart of Idris, I bent my head to catch the sound of her breath, to assure myself that she still existed - for a moment I doubted whether I should not awake her; so effeminate an horror ran through my frame. - Great God! would it one day be thus? One day all extinct, save myself, should I walk the earth alone? Were these warning voices, whose inarticulate and oracular sense forced belief upon me?

> Yet I would not call them
> Voices of warning, that announce to us
> Only the inevitable. As the sun,
> Ere it is risen, sometimes paints its image
> In the atmosphere — so often do the spirits
> Of great events stride on before the events,
> And in to-day already walks to-morrow.

CHAPTER VIII

After a long interval, I am again impelled by the restless spirit within me to continue my narration; but I must alter the mode which I have hitherto adopted. The details contained in the foregoing pages, apparently trivial, yet each slightest one weighing like lead in the depressed scale of human afflictions; this tedious dwelling on the sorrows of others, while my own were only in apprehension; this slowly laying bare of my soul's wounds: this journal of death; this long drawn and tortuous path, leading to the ocean of countless tears, awakens me again to keen grief. I had used this history as an opiate; while it described my beloved friends, fresh with life and glowing with hope, active assistants on the scene, I was soothed; there will be a more melancholy pleasure in painting the end of all. But the intermediate steps, the climbing the wall, raised up between what was and is, while I still looked back nor saw the concealed desert beyond, is a labor past my strength. Time and experience have placed me on an height from which I can comprehend the past as a whole; and in this way I must describe it, bringing forward the leading incidents, and disposing light and shade so as to form a picture in whose very darkness there will be harmony.

It would be needless to narrate those disastrous occurrences, for which a parallel might be found in any slighter visitation of our gigantic calamity. Does the reader wish to hear of the pest-houses, where death is the comforter - of the mournful passage of the death-cart -of the insensibility of the worthless, and the anguish of the loving heart - of harrowing shrieks and silence dire - of the variety of disease, desertion, famine, despair, and death? There are many books which can feed the appetite craving for these things; let them turn to the accounts of Boccaccio, De Foe, and Browne. The vast annihilation that has swallowed all things - the voiceless solitude of the once busy earth - the lonely state of singleness which hems me in, has deprived even such details of their stinging reality, and mellowing the lurid tints of past anguish with poetic hues, I am able to escape from the mosaic of circumstance, by perceiving and reflecting back the grouping and combined coloring of the past.

I had returned from London possessed by the idea, with the intimate feeling that it was my first duty to secure, as well as I was able, the well-being of my family, and then to return and take my post beside Adrian. The events that immediately followed on my arrival at Windsor changed this view of things. The plague was not in London alone, it was everywhere - it came on us, as Ryland had said, like a thousand packs of wolves, howling through the winter night, gaunt and fierce. When once disease was introduced into the rural districts, its effects appeared more horrible, more exigent, and more difficult to cure, than in towns. There was a companionship in suffering there, and the neighbors keeping constant watch on each other, and inspired by the active benevolence of Adrian, succor was afforded, and the path of destruction smoothed. But in the country, among the scattered farmhouses, in lone cottages, in fields, and barns, tragedies were acted harrowing to the soul, unseen, unheard, unnoticed. Medical aid was less easily procured, food was more difficult to obtain, and human beings, unwithheld by shame, for they were unbeheld of their fellows, ventured on deeds of greater wickedness, or gave way more readily to their abject fears.

Deeds of heroism also occurred, whose very mention swells the heart and brings tears into the eyes. Such is human nature, that beauty and deformity are often closely linked. In reading history, we are chiefly struck by the generosity and self-devotion that follow close on the heels of crime, veiling with supernal flowers the stain of blood. Such acts were not wanting to adorn the grim train that waited on the progress of the plague.

The inhabitants of Berkshire and Bucks had been long aware that the plague was in London, in Liverpool, Bristol, Manchester, York, in short, in all the more populous towns of England. They were not however the less astonished and dismayed when it appeared among themselves. They were impatient and angry in the midst of terror. They would do something to throw off the clinging evil, and, while in action, they fancied that a remedy was applied. The inhabitants of the smaller towns left their houses, pitched tents in the fields, wandering separate from each other careless of hunger or the sky's inclemency, while they imagined that they avoided the death-dealing disease. The farmers and cottagers, on the contrary, struck with the fear of solitude, and madly desirous of medical assistance, flocked into the towns.

But winter was coming, and with winter, hope. In August, the plague had appeared in the country of England, and during September it made its ravages. Towards the end of October, it dwindled away, and was in some degree replaced by a typhus, of hardly less virulence. The autumn was warm and rainy: the infirm and sickly died off - happier they: many young people flushed with health and prosperity, made pale by wasting malady, became the inhabitants of the grave. The crop had failed, the bad corn, and want of foreign wines, added vigor to disease. Before Christmas half England was under water. The storms of the last winter were renewed; but the diminished shipping of this year caused us to feel less the tempests of the sea. The flood and storms did more harm to continental Europe than to us - giving, as it were, the last blow to the calamities which destroyed it. In Italy, the rivers were unwatched by the diminished peasantry; and, like wild beasts from their lair when the hunters and dogs are afar, did Tiber, Arno, and Po, rush upon and destroy the fertility of the plains. Whole villages were carried away. Rome, and Florence, and Pisa were overflowed, and their marble palaces, late mirrored in tranquil streams, had their foundations shaken by their winter-gifted power. In Germany and Russia, the injury was still more momentous.

But frost would come at last, and with it a renewal of our lease of earth. Frost would blunt the arrows of pestilence and enchain the furious elements; and the land would in spring throw off her garment of snow, released from her menace of destruction. It was not until February that the desired signs of winter appeared. For three days the snow fell, ice stopped the current of the rivers, and the birds flew out from crackling branches of the frost-whitened trees. On the fourth morning all vanished. A south-west wind brought up rain - the sun came out, and mocking the usual laws of nature, seemed even at this early season to burn with solstitial force. It was no consolation, that with the first winds of March the lanes were filled with violets, the fruit trees covered with blossoms, that the corn sprung up, and the leaves came out, forced by the unseasonable heat. We feared the balmy air - we feared the cloudless sky, the flower-covered earth, and delightful woods, for we looked on the fabric of the universe no longer as our dwelling, but our tomb, and the fragrant land smelled to the apprehension of fear like a wide church-yard.

Pisando la tierra dura de continuo el hombre esta y cada passo que da es sobre su sepultura.
Continuously stepping on the hard earth the man is and every step he gives is on his grave.

Yet notwithstanding these disadvantages winter was breathing time; and we exerted ourselves to make the best of it. Plague might not revive with the summer; but if it did, it should find us prepared. It is a part of man's nature to adapt itself through habit even to pain and sorrow. Pestilence had become a part of our future, our existence; it was to be guarded against, like the flooding of rivers, the encroachments of ocean, or the inclemency of the sky. After long suffering and bitter experience, some panacea might be discovered; as it was, all that received infection died - all however were not infected; and it became our part to fix deep the foundations, and raise high the barrier between contagion and the sane; to introduce such order as would conduce to the well-being of the survivors, and as would preserve hope and some portion of happiness to those who were spectators of the still renewed tragedy. Adrian had introduced systematic modes of proceeding in the metropolis, which, while they were unable to stop the progress of death, yet prevented other evils, vice and folly, from rendering the awful fate of the hour still more tremendous. I wished to imitate his example, but men are used to

move all together, if they move at all,

and I could find no means of leading the inhabitants of scattered towns and villages, who forgot my words as soon as they heard them not, and veered with every baffling wind, that might arise from an apparent change of circumstance.
I adopted another plan. Those writers who have imagined a reign of peace and happiness on earth, have generally described a rural country, where each small township was directed by the elders and wise men. This was the key of my design. Each village, however small, usually contains a leader, one among themselves whom they venerate, whose advice they seek in difficulty, and whose good opinion they chiefly value. I was immediately drawn to make this observation by occurrences that presented themselves to my personal experience.

In the village of Little Marlow an old woman ruled the community. She had lived for some years in an alms-house, and on fine Sundays her threshold was constantly beset by a crowd, seeking her advice and listening to her admonitions. She had been a soldier's wife, and had seen the world; infirmity, induced by fevers caught in unwholesome quarters, had come on her before its time, and she seldom moved from her little cot. The plague entered the village; and, while fright and grief deprived the inhabitants of the little wisdom they possessed, old Martha stepped forward and said, "Before now I have been in a town where there was the plague."
"And you escaped?"

"No, but I recovered."

After this Martha was seated more firmly than ever on the regal seat, elevated by reverence and love. She entered the cottages of the sick; she relieved their wants with her own hand; she betrayed no fear and inspired all who saw her with some portion of her own native courage. She attended the markets - she insisted upon being supplied with food for those who were too poor to purchase it. She shewed them how the well-being of each included the prosperity of all. She would not permit the gardens to be neglected, nor the very flowers in the cottage lattices to droop from want of care. Hope, she said, was better than a doctor's prescription, and everything that could sustain and enliven the spirits, of more worth than drugs and mixtures.

It was the sight of Little Marlow, and my conversations with Martha, that led me to the plan I formed. I had before visited the manor houses and gentlemen's seats, and often found the inhabitants actuated by the purest benevolence, ready to lend their utmost aid for the welfare of their tenants. But this was not enough. The intimate sympathy generated by similar hopes and fears, similar experience, and pursuits, was wanting here. The poor perceived that the rich possessed other means of preservation than those which could be partaken of by themselves, seclusion, and, as far as circumstances permitted, freedom from care. They could not place reliance on them but turned with tenfold dependence to the succor and advice of their equals. I resolved therefore to go from village to village, seeking out the rustic archon of the place, and by systematizing their exertions, and enlightening their views, increase both their power and their use among their fellow-cottagers. Many changes also now occurred in these spontaneous regal elections: depositions and abdications were frequent, while, in the place of the old and prudent, the ardent youth would step forward, eager for action, regardless of danger. Often too, the voice to which all listened was suddenly silenced, the helping hand cold, the sympathetic eye closed, and the villagers feared still more the death that had selected a choice victim, shivering in dust the heart that had beat for them, reducing to incommunicable annihilation the mind for ever occupied with projects for their welfare.

Whoever labors for man must often find ingratitude, watered by vice and folly, spring from the grain which he has sown. Death, which had in our younger days walked the earth like "a thief that comes in the night," now, rising from his subterranean vault, girt with power, with dark banner floating, came a conqueror. Many saw, seated above his vice-regal throne, a supreme Providence, who directed his shafts, and guided his progress, and they bowed their heads in resignation, or at least in obedience. Others perceived only a passing casualty; they endeavored to exchange terror for heedlessness, and plunged into licentiousness, to avoid the agonizing throes of worst apprehension. Thus, while the wise, the good, and the prudent were occupied by the labors of benevolence, the truce of winter produced other effects among the young, the thoughtless, and the vicious. During the colder months there was a general rush to London in search of amusement—the ties of public opinion were loosened; many were rich, heretofore poor - many had lost father and mother, the guardians of their morals, their mentors and restraints. It would have been useless to have opposed these impulses by barriers, which would only have driven those actuated by them to more pernicious indulgencies. The theatres were open and thronged; dance and midnight festival were frequented - in many of these decorum was violated, and the evils, which hitherto adhered to an advanced state of civilization, were doubled. The student left his books, the artist his study: the occupations of life were gone, but the amusements remained; enjoyment might be protracted to the verge of the grave. All factitious coloring disappeared - death rose like night, and, protected by its murky shadows the blush of modesty, the reserve of pride, the decorum of prudery were frequently thrown aside as useless veils. This was not universal. Among better natures, anguish and dread, the fear of eternal separation, and the awful wonder produced by unprecedented calamity, drew closer the ties of kindred and friendship. Philosophers opposed their principles, as barriers to the inundation of profligacy or despair, and the only ramparts to protect the invaded territory of human life; the religious, hoping now for their reward, clung fast to their creeds, as the rafts and planks which over the tempest-vexed sea of suffering, would bear them in safety to the harbor of the Unknown Continent. The loving heart, obliged to contract its view, bestowed its overflow of affection in triple portion on the few that remained. Yet, even among these, the present, as an unalienable possession, became all of time to which they dared commit the precious freight of their hopes.

The experience of immemorial time had taught us formerly to count our enjoyments by years, and extend our prospect of life through a lengthened period of progression and decay; the long road threaded a vast labyrinth, and the Valley of the Shadow of Death, in which it terminated, was hid by intervening objects. But an earthquake had changed the scene - under our very feet the earth yawned - deep and precipitous the gulph below opened to receive us, while the hours charioted us towards the chasm. But it was winter now, and months must elapse before we are hurled from our security. We became ephemera, to whom the interval between the rising and setting sun was as a long-drawn year of common time. We should never see our children ripen into maturity, nor behold their downy cheeks roughen, their blithe hearts subdued by passion or care; but we had them now - they lived, and we lived - what more could we desire? With such schooling did my poor Idris try to hush thronging fears, and in some measure succeeded. It was not as in summer-time, when each hour might bring the dreaded fate - until summer, we felt sure; and this certainty, short lived as it must be, yet for a while satisfied her maternal tenderness. I know not how to express or communicate the sense of concentrated, intense, though evanescent transport, that imparadised us in the present hour. Our joys were dearer because we saw their end; they were keener because we felt, to its fullest extent, their value; they were purer because their essence was sympathy - as a meteor is brighter than a star, did the felicity of this winter contain in itself the extracted delights of a long, long life.

How lovely is spring! As we looked from Windsor Terrace on the sixteen fertile counties spread beneath, speckled by happy cottages and wealthier towns, all looked as in former years, heart-cheering and fair. The land was ploughed, the slender blades of wheat broke through the dark soil, the fruit trees were covered with buds, the husbandman was abroad in the fields, the milk-maid tripped home with well-filled pails, the swallows and martins struck the sunny pools with their long, pointed wings, the new dropped lambs reposed on the young grass, the tender growth of leaves:

Lifts its sweet head into the air, and feeds
A silent space with ever sprouting green.

Man himself seemed to regenerate, and feel the frost of winter yield to an elastic and warm renewal of life — reason told us that care and sorrow would grow with the opening year — but how to believe the ominous voice breathed up with pestiferous vapors from fear's dim cavern, while nature, laughing and scattering from her green lap flowers, and fruits, and sparkling waters, invited us to join the gay masque of young life she led upon the scene?

Where was the plague? "Here - everywhere!" one voice of horror and dismay exclaimed, when in the pleasant days of a sunny May the Destroyer of man brooded again over the earth, forcing the spirit to leave its organic chrysalis, and to enter upon an untried life. With one mighty sweep of its potent weapon, all caution, all care, all prudence were levelled low: death sat at the tables of the great, stretched itself on the cottager's pallet, seized the dastard who fled, quelled the brave man who resisted: despondency entered every heart, sorrow dimmed every eye.

Sights of woe now became familiar to me, and were I to tell all of anguish and pain that I witnessed, of the despairing moans of age, and the more terrible smiles of infancy in the bosom of horror, my reader, his limbs quivering and his hair on end, would wonder how I did not, seized with sudden frenzy, dash myself from some precipice, and so close my eyes forever on the sad end of the world. But the powers of love, poetry, and creative fancy will dwell even beside the sick of the plague, with the squalid, and with the dying. A feeling of devotion, of duty, of a high and steady purpose, elevated me; a strange joy filled my heart. In the midst of saddest grief, I seemed to tread air, while the spirit of good shed round me an ambrosial atmosphere, which blunted the sting of sympathy, and purified the air of sighs. If my wearied soul flagged in its career, I thought of my loved home, of the casket that contained my treasures, of the kiss of love and the filial caress, while my eyes were moistened by purest dew, and my heart was at once softened and refreshed by thrilling tenderness.

Maternal affection had not rendered Idris selfish; at the beginning of our calamity she had, with thoughtless enthusiasm, devoted herself to the care of the sick and helpless. I checked her; and she submitted to my rule. I told her how the fear of her danger palsied my exertions, how the knowledge of her safety strung my nerves to endurance. I shewed her the dangers which her children incurred during her absence; and she at length agreed not to go beyond the enclosure of the forest. Indeed, within the walls of the Castle we had a colony of the unhappy, deserted by their relatives, and in themselves helpless, sufficient to occupy her time and attention, while ceaseless anxiety for my welfare and the health of her children, however she strove to curb or conceal it, absorbed all her thoughts, and undermined the vital principle. After watching over and providing for their safety, her second care was to hide from me her anguish and tears. Each night I returned to the Castle and found their repose and love awaiting me. Often, I waited beside the bed of death till midnight, and through the obscurity of rainy, cloudy nights rode many miles, sustained by one circumstance only, the safety and sheltered repose of those I loved. If some scene of tremendous agony shook my frame and fevered my brow, I would lay my head on the lap of Idris, and the tumultuous pulses subsided into a temperate flow - her smile could raise me from hopelessness, her embrace bathe my sorrowing heart in calm peace. Summer advanced, and, crowned with the sun's potent rays, plague shot her unerring shafts over the earth. The nations beneath their influence bowed their heads and died. The corn that sprung up in plenty, lay in autumn rotting on the ground, while the melancholy wretch who had gone out to gather bread for his children, lay stiff and plague-struck in the furrow. The green woods waved their boughs majestically, while the dying were spread beneath their shade, answering the solemn melody with inharmonious cries. The painted birds flitted through the shades; the careless deer reposed unhurt upon the fern—the oxen and the horses strayed from their unguarded stables, and grazed among the wheat, for death fell on man alone.

With summer and mortality grew our fears. My poor love and I looked at each other, and our babes. -"We will save them, Idris," I said, "I will save them. Years hence we shall recount to them our fears, then passed away with their occasion. Though they only should remain on the earth, still they shall live, nor shall their cheeks become pale nor their sweet voices languish." Our eldest in some degree understood the scenes passing around, and at times, he with serious looks questioned me concerning the reason of so vast a desolation. But he was only ten years old; and the hilarity of youth soon chased unreasonable care from his brow. Evelyn, a laughing cherub, a gamesome infant, without idea of pain or sorrow, would, shaking back his light curls from his eyes, make the halls re-echo with his merriment, and in a thousand artless ways attract our attention to his play. Clara, our lovely gentle Clara, was our stay, our solace, our delight. She made it her task to attend the sick, comfort the sorrowing, assist the aged, and partake the sports and awaken the gaiety of the young. She flitted through the rooms, like a good spirit, dispatched from the celestial kingdom, to illumine our dark hour with alien splendor. Gratitude and praise marked where her footsteps had been. Yet, when she stood in unassuming simplicity before us, playing with our children, or with girlish assiduity performing little kind offices for Idris, one wondered in what fair lineament of her pure loveliness, in what soft tone of her thrilling voice, so much of heroism, sagacity and active goodness resided.

The summer passed tediously, for we trusted that winter would at least check the disease. That it would vanish altogether was a hope too dear - too heartfelt, to be expressed. When such a thought was heedlessly uttered, the hearers, with a gush of tears and passionate sobs, bore witness how deep their fears were, how small their hopes. For my own part, my exertions for the public good permitted me to observe more closely than most others, the virulence and extensive ravages of our sightless enemy. A short month has destroyed a village, and where in May the first person sickened, in June the paths were deformed by unburied corpses - the houses tenantless, no smoke arising from the chimneys; and the housewife's clock marked only the hour when death had been triumphant. From such scenes I have sometimes saved a deserted infant - sometimes led a young and grieving mother from the lifeless image of her first born or drawn the sturdy laborer from childish weeping over his extinct family.

July is gone. August must pass, and by the middle of September we may hope. Each day was eagerly counted; and the inhabitants of towns, desirous to leap this dangerous interval, plunged into dissipation, and strove, by riot, and what they wished to imagine to be pleasure, to banish thought and opiate despair.

None but Adrian could have tamed the motley population of London, which, like a troop of unbitted steeds rushing to their pastures, had thrown aside all minor fears, through the operation of the fear paramount. Even Adrian was obliged in part to yield, that he might be able, if not to guide, at least to set bounds to the license of the times. The theatres were kept open; every place of public resort was frequented; though he endeavored so to modify them, as might best quiet the agitation of the spectators, and at the same time prevent a reaction of misery when the excitement was over. Tragedies deep and dire were the chief favorites. Comedy brought with it too great a contrast to the inner despair: when such were attempted, it was not infrequent for a comedian, in the midst of the laughter occasioned by his disproportioned buffoonery, to find a word or thought in his part that jarred with his own sense of wretchedness, and burst from mimic merriment into sobs and tears, while the spectators, seized with irresistible sympathy, wept, and the pantomimic revelry was changed to a real exhibition of tragic passion.

It was not in my nature to derive consolation from such scenes; from theatres, whose buffoon laughter and discordant mirth awakened distempered sympathy, or where fictitious tears and wailings mocked the heart-felt grief within; from festival or crowded meeting, where hilarity sprung from the worst feelings of our nature, or such enthrallment of the better ones, as impressed it with garish and false varnish; from assemblies of mourners in the guise of revelers. Once however I witnessed a scene of singular interest at one of the theatres, where nature overpowered art, as an overflowing cataract will tear away the puny manufacture of a mock cascade, which had before been fed by a small portion of its waters.

I had come to London to see Adrian. He was not at the palace; and, though the attendants did not know whether he had gone, they did not expect him till late at night. It was between six and seven o'clock, a fine summer afternoon, and I spent my leisure hours in a ramble through the empty streets of London; now turning to avoid an approaching funeral, now urged by curiosity to observe the state of a particular spot; my wanderings were instinct with pain, for silence and desertion characterized every place I visited, and the few beings I met were so pale and woe-begone, so marked with care and depressed by fear, that weary of encountering only signs of misery, I began to retread my steps towards home.

I was now in Holborn and passed by a public house filled with uproarious companions, whose songs, laughter, and shouts were more sorrowful than the pale looks and silence of the mourner. Such an one was near, hovering round this house. The sorry plight of her dress displayed her poverty, she was ghastly pale, and continued approaching, first the window and then the door of the house, as if fearful, yet longing to enter. A sudden burst of song and merriment seemed to sting her to the heart; she murmured, "Can he have the heart?" and then mustering her courage, she stepped within the threshold. The landlady met her in the passage; the poor creature asked, "Is my husband here? Can I see George?"

"See him," cried the woman, "yes, if you go to him; last night he was taken with the plague, and we sent him to the hospital."

The unfortunate inquirer staggered against a wall; a faint cry escaped her "O! were you cruel enough," she exclaimed, "to send him there?"

The landlady meanwhile hurried away; but a more compassionate barmaid gave her a detailed account, the sum of which was, that her husband had been taken ill, after a night of riot, and sent by his boon companions with all expedition to St. Bartholomew's Hospital. I had watched this scene, for there was a gentleness about the poor woman that interested me; she now tottered away from the door, walking as well as she could down Holborn Hill; but her strength soon failed her; she leaned against a wall, and her head sunk on her bosom, while her pallid cheek became still more white. I went up to her and offered my services. She hardly looked up - "You can do me no good," she replied, "I must go to the hospital; if I do not die before I get there."

There were still a few hackney-coaches accustomed to stand about the streets, more truly from habit than for use. I put her in one of these and entered with her that I might secure her entrance into the hospital. Our way was short, and she said little; except interrupted ejaculations of reproach that he had left her, exclamations on the unkindness of some of his friends, and hope that she would find him alive. There was a simple, natural earnestness about her that interested me in her fate, especially when she assured me that her husband was the best of men, - had been so, till want of business during these unhappy times had thrown him into bad company. "He could not bear to come home," she said, "only to see our children die. A man cannot have the patience a mother has, with her own flesh and blood."

We were set down at St. Bartholomew's, and entered the wretched precincts of the house of disease. The poor creature clung closer to me, as she saw with what heartless haste they bore the dead from the wards, and took them into a room, whose half-opened door displayed a number of corpses, horrible to behold by one unaccustomed to such scenes. We were directed to the ward where her husband had been first taken, and still was, the nurse said, if alive. My companion looked eagerly from one bed to the other, till at the end of the ward she espied, on a wretched bed, a squalid, haggard creature, writhing under the torture of disease. She rushed towards him, she embraced him, blessing God for his preservation.

The enthusiasm that inspired her with this strange joy, blinded her to the horrors about her; but they were intolerably agonizing to me. The ward was filled with an effluvia that caused my heart to heave with painful qualms. The dead were carried out, and the sick brought in, with like indifference; some were screaming with pain, others laughing from the influence of more terrible delirium; some were attended by weeping, despairing relations, others called aloud with thrilling tenderness or reproach on the friends who had deserted them, while the nurses went from bed to bed, incarnate images of despair, neglect, and death. I gave gold to my luckless companion; I recommended her to the care of the attendants; I then hastened away; while the tormentor, the imagination, busied itself in picturing my own loved ones, stretched on such beds, attended thus. The country afforded no such mass of horrors; solitary wretches died in the open fields; and I have found a survivor in a vacant village, contending at once with famine and disease; but the assembly of pestilence, the banqueting hall of death, was spread only in London. I rambled on, oppressed, distracted by painful emotions - suddenly I found myself before Drury Lane Theatre. The play was Macbeth - the first actor of the age was there to exert his powers to drug with irreflection the auditors; such a medicine I yearned for, so I entered. The theatre was tolerably well filled. Shakespeare, whose popularity was established by the approval of four centuries, had not lost his influence even at this dread period; but was still "Ut magus," the wizard to rule our hearts and govern our imaginations. I came in during the interval between the third and fourth act. I looked round on the audience; the females were mostly of the lower classes, but the men were of all ranks, come hither to forget awhile the protracted scenes of wretchedness, which awaited them at their miserable homes. The curtain drew up, and the stage presented the scene of the witches' cave. The wildness and supernatural machinery of Macbeth was a pledge that it could contain little directly connected with our present circumstances. Great pains had been taken in the scenery to give the semblance of reality to the impossible. The extreme darkness of the stage, whose only light was received from the fire under the cauldron, joined to a kind of mist that floated about it, rendered the unearthly shapes of the witches' obscure and shadowy. It was not three decrepit old hags that bent over their pot throwing in the grim ingredients of the magic charm, but forms frightful, unreal, and fanciful. The entrance of Hecate, and the wild music that followed, took us out of this world. The cavern shape the stage assumed, the beetling rocks, the glare of the fire, the misty shades that crossed the scene at times, the music in harmony with all witch-like fancies, permitted the imagination to revel, without fear of contradiction, or reproof from reason or the heart. The entrance of Macbeth did not destroy the illusion, for he was actuated by the same feelings that inspired us, and while the work of magic proceeded we sympathized in his wonder and his daring, and gave ourselves up with our whole souls to the influence of scenic delusion. I felt the beneficial result of such excitement, in a renewal of those pleasing flights of fancy to which I had long been a stranger. The effect of this scene of incantation communicated a portion of its power to that which followed. We forgot that Malcolm and Macduff were mere human beings, acted upon by such simple passions as warmed our own breasts. By slow degrees however we were drawn to the real interest of the scene. A shudder like the swift passing of an electric shock ran through the house, when Rosse exclaimed, in answer to "Stands Scotland where it did?"

> Alas, poor country.
> Almost afraid to know itself! It cannot
> Be called our mother, but our grave: where nothing,
> But who knows nothing, is once seen to smile.
> Where sighs, and groans, and shrieks that rent the air,
> Are made, not marked, where violent sorrow seems
> A modern extasy: the dead man's knell
> Is there scarce asked, for who, and good men's lives
> Expire before the flowers in their caps,
> Dying, or ere they sicken.

Each word struck the sense, as our life's passing bell; we feared to look at each other, but bent our gaze on the stage, as if our eyes could fall innocuous on that alone. The person who played the part of Rosse, suddenly became aware of the dangerous ground he trod. He was an inferior actor, but truth now made him excellent; as he went on to announce to Macduff the slaughter of his family, he was afraid to speak, trembling from apprehension of a burst of grief from the audience, not from his fellow-mime. Each word was drawn out with difficulty; real anguish painted his features; his eyes were now lifted in sudden horror, now fixed in dread upon the ground. This shew of terror increased ours, we gasped with him, each neck was stretched out, each face changed with the actor's changes - at length while Macduff, who, attending to his part, was unobservant of the high wrought sympathy of the house, cried with well-acted passion:

> *All my pretty ones?*
> *Did you say all? - O hell kite! All?*
> *What! all my pretty chickens, and their dam,*
> *At one fell swoop!*

A pang of tameless grief wrenched every heart, a burst of despair was echoed from every lip. - I had entered into the universal feeling - I had been absorbed by the terrors of Rosse - I re-echoed the cry of Macduff, and then rushed out as from an hell of torture, to find calm in the free air and silent street.

Free the air was not, or the street silent. Oh, how I longed then for the dear soothing's of maternal Nature, as my wounded heart was still further stung by the roar of heartless merriment from the public-house, by the sight of the drunkard reeling home, having lost the memory of what he would find there in oblivious debauch, and by the more appalling salutations of those melancholy beings to whom the name of home was a mockery. I ran on at my utmost speed until I found myself, I knew not how, close to Westminster Abbey, and was attracted by the deep and swelling tone of the organ. I entered with soothing awe the lighted chancel, and listened to the solemn religious chaunt, which spoke peace and hope to the unhappy. The notes, freighted with man's dearest prayers, re-echoed through the dim aisles, and the bleeding of the soul's wounds was staunched by heavenly balm. In spite of the misery I deprecated, and could not understand; in spite of the cold hearths of wide London, and the corpse-strewn fields of my native land; in spite of all the variety of agonizing emotions I had that evening experienced, I thought that in reply to our melodious adjurations, the Creator looked down in compassion and promise of relief; the awful peal of the heaven-winged music seemed fitting voice wherewith to commune with the Supreme; calm was produced by its sound, and by the sight of many other human creatures offering up prayers and submission with me. A sentiment approaching happiness followed the total resignation of one's being to the guardianship of the world's ruler. Alas! with the failing of this solemn strain, the elevated spirit sank again to earth. Suddenly one of the choristers died—he was lifted from his desk, the vaults below were hastily opened—he was consigned with a few muttered prayers to the darksome cavern, abode of thousands who had gone before - now wide yawning to receive even all who fulfilled the funeral rites. In vain I would then have turned from this scene, to darkened aisle or lofty dome, echoing with melodious praise. In the open air alone I found relief; among nature's beauteous works, her God reassumed his attribute of benevolence, and again I could trust that he who built up the mountains, planted the forests, and poured out the rivers, would erect another state for lost humanity, where we might awaken again to our affections, our happiness, and our faith.

Fortunately for me those circumstances were of rare occurrence that obliged me to visit London, and my duties were confined to the rural district which our lofty castle overlooked; and here labor stood in the place of pastime, to occupy such of the country people as were sufficiently exempt from sorrow or disease. My endeavors were directed towards urging them to their usual attention to their crops, and to the acting as if pestilence did not exist. The mower's scythe was at times heard; yet the joyless haymakers after they had listlessly turned the grass, forgot to cart it; the shepherd, when he had sheared his sheep, would let the wool lie to be scattered by the winds, deeming it useless to provide clothing for another winter. At times however the spirit of life was awakened by these employments; the sun, the refreshing breeze, the sweet smell of the hay, the rustling leaves and prattling rivulets brought repose to the agitated bosom, and bestowed a feeling akin to happiness on the apprehensive. Nor, strange to say, was the time without its pleasures. Young couples, who had loved long and hopelessly, suddenly found every impediment removed, and wealth pour in from the death of relatives. The very danger drew them closer. The immediate peril urged them to seize the immediate opportunity; wildly and passionately they sought to know what delights existence afforded, before they yielded to death, and

> *Snatching their pleasures with rough strife*
> *Thorough the iron gates of life,*

they defied the conquering pestilence to destroy what had been, or to erase even from their death-bed thoughts the sentiment of happiness which had been theirs. One instance of this kind came immediately under our notice, where a high-born girl had in early youth given her heart to one of meaner extraction. He was a schoolfellow and friend of her brother's, and usually spent a part of the holidays at the mansion of the duke her father. They had played together as children, been the confidants of each other's little secrets, mutual aids and consolers in difficulty and sorrow. Love had crept in, noiseless, terrorless at first, till each felt their life bound up in the other, and at the same time knew that they must part. Their extreme youth, and the purity of their attachment, made them yield with less resistance to the tyranny of circumstances. The father of the fair Juliet separated them; but not until the young lover had promised to remain absent only till he had rendered himself worthy of her, and she had vowed to preserve her virgin heart, his treasure, till he returned to claim and possess it.

Plague came, threatening to destroy at once the aim of the ambitious and the hopes of love. Long the Duke of L— derided the idea that there could be danger while he pursued his plans of cautious seclusion; and he so far succeeded, that it was not till this second summer, that the destroyer, at one fell stroke, overthrew his precautions, his security, and his life. Poor Juliet saw one by one, father, mother, brothers, and sisters, sicken and die. Most of the servants fled on the first appearance of disease, those who remained were infected mortally; no neighbor or rustic ventured within the verge of contagion. By a strange fatality Juliet alone escaped, and she to the last waited on her relatives, and smoothed the pillow of death. The moment at length came, when the last blow was given to the last of the house: the youthful survivor of her race sat alone among the dead. There was no living being near to soothe her or withdraw her from this hideous company. With the declining heat of a September night, a whirlwind of storm, thunder, and hail, rattled round the house, and with ghastly harmony sung the dirge of her family. She sat upon the ground absorbed in wordless despair, when through the gusty wind and bickering rain she thought she heard her name called. Who could that familiar voice be? Not one of her relations, for they lay glaring on her with stony eyes. Again, her name was syllabled, and she shuddered as she asked herself, am I becoming mad, or am I dying, that I hear the voices of the departed? A second thought passed, swift as an arrow, into her brain; she rushed to the window; and a flash of lightning shewed to her the expected vision, her lover in the shrubbery beneath; joy lent her strength to descend the stairs, to open the door, and then she fainted in his supporting arms.

A thousand times she reproached herself, as with a crime, that she should revive to happiness with him. The natural clinging of the human mind to life and joy was in its full energy in her young heart; she gave herself impetuously up to the enchantment: they were married; and in their radiant features I saw incarnate, for the last time, the spirit of love, of rapturous sympathy, which once had been the life of the world.

I envied them but felt how impossible it was to imbibe the same feeling, now that years had multiplied my ties in the world. Above all, the anxious mother, my own beloved and drooping Idris, claimed my earnest care; I could not reproach the anxiety that never for a moment slept in her heart, but I exerted myself to distract her attention from too keen an observation of the truth of things, of the near and nearer approaches of disease, misery, and death, of the wild look of our attendants as intelligence of another and yet another death reached us; for to the last something new occurred that seemed to transcend in horror all that had gone before. Wretched beings crawled to die under our succoring roof; the inhabitants of the Castle decreased daily, while the survivors huddled together in fear, and, as in a famine-struck boat, the sport of the wild, interminable waves, each looked in the other's face, to guess on whom the death-lot would next fall. All this I endeavored to veil, so that it might least impress my Idris; yet, as I have said, my courage survived even despair: I might be vanquished, but I would not yield.

One day, it was the ninth of September, seemed devoted to every disaster, to every harrowing incident. Early in the day, I heard of the arrival of the aged grandmother of one of our servants at the Castle. This old woman had reached her hundredth year; her skin was shriveled, her form was bent and lost in extreme decrepitude; but as still from year to year she continued in existence, out-living many younger and stronger, she began to feel as if she were to live forever. The plague came, and the inhabitants of her village died. Clinging, with the dastard feeling of the aged, to the remnant of her spent life, she had, on hearing that the pestilence had come into her neighborhood, barred her door, and closed her casement, refusing to communicate with any. She would wander out at night to get food, and returned home, pleased that she had met no one, that she was in no danger from the plague. As the earth became more desolate, her difficulty in acquiring sustenance increased; at first, her son, who lived near, had humored her by placing articles of food in her way: at last he died. But, even though threatened by famine, her fear of the plague was paramount; and her greatest care was to avoid her fellow creatures. She grew weaker each day, and each day she had further to go. The night before, she had reached Datchet; and, prowling about, had found a baker's shop open and deserted. Laden with spoil, she hastened to return, and lost her way. The night was windless, hot, and cloudy; her load became too heavy for her; and one by one she threw away her loaves, still endeavoring to get along, though her hobbling fell into lameness, and her weakness at last into inability to move.

She lay down among the tall corn and fell asleep. Deep in midnight, she was awaked by a rustling near her; she would have started up, but her stiff joints refused to obey her will. A low moan close to her ear followed, and the rustling increased; she heard a smothered voice breathe out, Water, Water! several times; and then again, a sigh heaved from the heart of the sufferer. The old woman shuddered, she contrived at length to sit upright; but her teeth chattered, and her knees knocked together - close, very close, lay a half-naked figure, just discernible in the gloom, and the cry for water and the stifled moan were again uttered. Her motions at length attracted the attention of her unknown companion; her hand was seized with a convulsive violence that made the grasp feel like iron, the fingers like the keen teeth of a trap. -"At last you are come!" were the words given forth - but this exertion was the last effort of the dying - the joints relaxed, the figure fell prostrate, one low moan, the last, marked the moment of death. Morning broke; and the old woman saw the corpse, marked with the fatal disease, close to her; her wrist was livid with the hold loosened by death. She felt struck by the plague; her aged frame was unable to bear her away with sufficient speed; and now, believing herself infected, she no longer dreaded the association of others; but, as swiftly as she might, came to her grand-daughter, at Windsor Castle, there to lament and die. The sight was horrible; still she clung to life and lamented her mischance with cries and hideous groans; while the swift advance of the disease shewed, what proved to be the fact, that she could not survive many hours.

While I was directing that the necessary care should be taken of her, Clara came in; she was trembling and pale; and, when I anxiously asked her the cause of her agitation, she threw herself into my arms weeping and exclaiming - "Uncle, dearest uncle, do not hate me forever! I must tell you, for you must know, that Evelyn, poor little Evelyn" - her voice was choked by sobs. The fear of so mighty a calamity as the loss of our adored infant made the current of my blood pause with chilly horror; but the remembrance of the mother restored my presence of mind. I sought the little bed of my darling; he was oppressed by fever; but I trusted, I fondly and fearfully trusted, that there were no symptoms of the plague. He was not three years old, and his illness appeared only one of those attacks' incident to infancy. I watched him long -his heavy half-closed lids, his burning cheeks and restless twining of his small fingers - the fever was violent, the torpor complete - enough, without the greater fear of pestilence, to awaken alarm. Idris must not see him in this state. Clara, though only twelve years old, was rendered, through extreme sensibility, so prudent and careful, that I felt secure in entrusting the charge of him to her, and it was my task to prevent Idris from observing their absence. I administered the fitting remedies, and left my sweet niece to watch beside him, and bring me notice of any change she should observe.

I then went to Idris, contriving in my way, plausible excuses for remaining all day in the Castle, and endeavoring to disperse the traces of care from my brow. Fortunately, she was not alone. I found Merrival, the astronomer, with her. He was far too long sighted in his view of humanity to heed the casualties of the day and lived in the midst of contagion unconscious of its existence. This poor man, learned as La Place, guileless and unforeseen as a child, had often been on the point of starvation, he, his pale wife and numerous offspring, while he neither felt hunger, nor observed distress. His astronomical theories absorbed him; calculations were scrawled with coal on the bare walls of his garret: a hard-earned

guinea, or an article of dress, was exchanged for a book without remorse; he neither heard his children cry, nor observed his companion's emaciated form, and the
excess of calamity was merely to him as the occurrence of a cloudy night, when he
would have given his right hand to observe a celestial phenomenon. His wife was
one of those wondrous beings, to be found only among women, with affections
not to be diminished by misfortune. Her mind was divided between boundless
admiration for her husband, and tender anxiety for her children - she waited on
him, worked for them, and never complained, though care rendered her life one
long-drawn, melancholy dream.

He had introduced himself to Adrian, by a request he made to observe
some planetary motions from his glass. His poverty was easily detected and relieved. He often thanked us for the books we lent him, and for the use of our
instruments, but never spoke of his altered abode or change of circumstances. His
wife assured us, that he had not observed any difference, except in the absence
of the children from his study, and to her infinite surprise he complained of this
unaccustomed quiet.

He came now to announce to us the completion of his Essay on the Pericy-
clical Motions of the Earth's Axis, and the precession of the equinoctial points. If an
old Roman of the period of the Republic had returned to life, and talked of the impending election of some laurel-crowned consul, or of the last battle with Mithri-
dates, his ideas would not have been more alien to the times, than the conversation
of Merrival. Man, no longer with an appetite for sympathy, clothed his thoughts
in visible signs; nor were there any readers left: while each one, having thrown
away his sword with opposing shield alone, awaited the plague, Merrival talked
of the state of mankind six thousand years hence. He might with equal interest to
us, have added a commentary, to describe the unknown and unimaginable lineaments of the creatures, who would then occupy the vacated dwelling of mankind.
We had not the heart to undeceive the poor old man; and at the moment I came
in, he was reading parts of his book to Idris, asking what answer could be given to
this or that position.

Idris could not refrain from a smile, as she listened; she had already gathered from him that his family was alive and in health; though not apt to forget the
precipice of time on which she stood, yet I could perceive that she was amused
for a moment, by the contrast between the contracted view we had so long taken
of human life, and the seven league strides with which Merrival paced a coming
eternity. I was glad to see her smile, because it assured me of her total ignorance of
her infant's danger: but I shuddered to think of the revulsion that would be occasioned by a discovery of the truth. While Merrival was talking, Clara softly opened
a door behind Idris, and beckoned me to come with a gesture and look of grief. A
mirror betrayed the sign to Idris - she started up. To suspect evil, to perceive that,
Alfred being with us, the danger must regard her youngest darling, to fly across
the long chambers into his apartment, was the work but of a moment. There she
beheld her Evelyn lying fever-stricken and motionless. I followed her and strove
to inspire more hope than I could myself entertain; but she shook her head mournfully. Anguish deprived her of presence of mind; she gave up to me and Clara the
physician's and nurse's parts; she sat by the bed, holding one little burning hand,
and, with glazed eyes fixed on her babe, passed the long day in one unvaried agony. It was not the plague that visited our little boy so roughly; but she could not

listen to my assurances; apprehension deprived her of judgment and reflection; every slight convulsion of her child's features shook her frame - if he moved, she dreaded the instant crisis; if he remained still, she saw death in his torpor, and the cloud on her brow darkened.

The poor little thing's fever increased towards night. The sensation is most dreary, to use no stronger term, with which one looks forward to passing the long hours of night beside a sick bed, especially if the patient be an infant, who cannot explain its pain, and whose flickering life resembles the wasting flame of the watch-light,

> *Whose narrow fire*
> *Is shaken by the wind, and on whose edge*
> *Devouring darkness hovers.*

With eagerness one turns toward the east, with angry impatience one marks the uncheckered darkness; the crowing of a cock, that sound of glee during day-time, comes wailing and untuneable - the creaking of rafters, and slight stir of invisible insect is heard and felt as the signal and type of desolation. Clara, overcome by weariness, had seated herself at the foot of her cousin's bed, and in spite of her efforts slumber weighed down her lids; twice or thrice she shook it off; but at length she was conquered and slept. Idris sat at the bedside, holding Evelyn's hand; we were afraid to speak to each other; I watched the stars - I hung over my child - I felt his little pulse - I drew near the mother - again I receded. At the turn of morning a gentle sigh from the patient attracted me, the burning spot on his cheek faded - his pulse beat softly and regularly - torpor yielded to sleep. For a long time I dared not hope; but when his unobstructed breathing and the moisture that suffused his forehead, were tokens no longer to be mistaken of the departure of mortal malady, I ventured to whisper the news of the change to Idris, and at length succeeded in persuading her that I spoke truth.

But neither this assurance, nor the speedy convalescence of our child could restore her, even to the portion of peace she before enjoyed. Her fear had been too deep, too absorbing, too entire, to be changed to security. She felt as if during her past calm she had dreamed, but was now awake; she was

> *As one*
> *In some lone watchtower on the deep, awakened*
> *From soothing visions of the home, he loves,*
> *Trembling to hear the wrathful billows roar;*

as one who has been cradled by a storm and awakes to find the vessel sinking. Before, she had been visited by pangs of fear - now, she never enjoyed an interval of hope. No smile of the heart ever irradiated her fair countenance; sometimes she forced one, and then gushing tears would flow, and the sea of grief close above these wrecks of past happiness. Still while I was near her, she could not be in utter despair - she fully confided herself to me - she did not seem to fear my death, or revert to its possibility; to my guardianship she consigned the full freight of her anxieties, reposing on my love, as a wind-nipped fawn by the side of a doe, as a wounded nestling under its mother's wing, as a tiny, shattered boat, quivering still, beneath some protecting willow-tree. While I, not proudly as in days of joy, yet tenderly, and with glad consciousness of the comfort I afforded, drew my trembling girl close to my heart, and tried to ward every painful thought or rough circumstance from her sensitive nature.

One other incident occurred at the end of this summer. The Countess of Windsor, Ex-Queen of England, returned from Germany. She had at the beginning of the season quitted the vacant city of Vienna; and, unable to tame her haughty mind to anything like submission, she had delayed at Hamburg, and, when at last she came to London, many weeks elapsed before she gave Adrian notice of her arrival. In spite of her coldness and long absence, he welcomed her with sensibility, displaying such affection as sought to heal the wounds of pride and sorrow, and was repulsed only by her total apparent want of sympathy. Idris heard of her mother's return with pleasure. Her own maternal feelings were so ardent, that she imagined her parent must now, in this waste world, have lost pride and harshness, and would receive with delight her filial attentions. The first check to her duteous demonstrations was a formal intimation from the fallen majesty of England, that I was in no manner to be intruded upon her. She consented, she said, to forgive her daughter, and acknowledge her grandchildren; larger concessions must not be expected.

To me this proceeding appeared (if so, light a term may be permitted) extremely whimsical. Now that the race of man had lost in fact all distinction of rank, this pride was doubly fatuitous; now that we felt a kindred, fraternal nature with all who bore the stamp of humanity, this angry reminiscence of times for ever gone, was worse than foolish. Idris was too much taken up by her own dreadful fears, to be angry, hardly grieved; for she judged that insensibility must be the source of this continued rancor. This was not altogether the fact: but predominant self-will assumed the arms and masque of callous feeling; and the haughty lady disdained to exhibit any token of the struggle she endured; while the slave of pride, she fancied that she sacrificed her happiness to immutable principle.

False was all this - false all but the affections of our nature, and the links of sympathy with pleasure or pain. There was but one good and one evil in the world - life and death. The pomp of rank, the assumption of power, the possessions of wealth vanished like morning mist. One living beggar had become of more worth than a national peerage of dead lords - alas the day! - than of dead heroes, patriots, or men of genius. There was much of degradation in this: for even vice and virtue had lost their attributes - life - life - the continuation of our animal mechanism - was the Alpha and Omega of the desires, the prayers, the prostrate ambition of human race.

CHAPTER IX

Half England was desolate, when October came, and the equinoctial winds swept over the earth, chilling the ardors of the unhealthy season. The summer, which was uncommonly hot, had been protracted into the beginning of this month, when on the eighteenth a sudden change was brought about from summer temperature to winter frost. Pestilence then made a pause in her death-dealing career. Gasping, not daring to name our hopes, yet full even to the brim with intense expectation, we stood, as a ship-wrecked sailor stands on a barren rock islanded by the ocean, watching a distant vessel, fancying that now it nears, and then again that it is bearing from sight. This promise of a renewed lease of life turned rugged natures to melting tenderness, and by contrast filled the soft with harsh and unnatural sentiments. When it seemed destined that all were to die, we were reckless of the how and when - now that the virulence of the disease was mitigated, and it appeared willing to spare some, each was eager to be among the elect, and clung to life with dastard tenacity. Instances of desertion became more frequent; and even murders, which made the hearer sick with horror, where the fear of contagion had armed those nearest in blood against each other. But these smaller and separate tragedies were about to yield to a mightier interest - and, while we were promised calm from infectious influences, a tempest arose wilder than the winds, a tempest bred by the passions of man, nourished by his most violent impulses, unexampled and dire.

A number of people from North America, the relics of that populous continent, had set sail for the East with mad desire of change, leaving their native plains for lands not less afflicted than their own. Several hundred landed in Ireland, about the first of November, and took possession of such vacant habitations as they could find, seizing upon the superabundant food, and the stray cattle. As they exhausted the produce of one spot, they went on to another. At length they began to interfere with the inhabitants, and strong in their concentrated numbers, ejected the natives from their dwellings, and robbed them of their winter store. A few events of this kind roused the fiery nature of the Irish; and they attacked the invaders. Some were destroyed; the major part escaped by quick and well-ordered movements; and danger made them careful. Their numbers ably arranged; the very deaths among them concealed; moving on in good order, and apparently given up to enjoyment, they excited the envy of the Irish. The Americans permitted a few to join their band, and presently the recruits outnumbered the strangers - nor did they join with them, nor imitate the admirable order which, preserved by the Trans-Atlantic chiefs, rendered them at once secure and formidable. The Irish followed their track in disorganized multitudes; each day increasing; each day becoming more lawless. The Americans were eager to escape from the spirit they had roused, and, reaching the eastern shores of the island, embarked for England. Their incursion would hardly have been felt had they come alone; but the Irish, collected in unnatural numbers, began to feel the inroads of famine, and they followed in the wake of the Americans for England also. The crossing of the sea could not arrest their progress. The harbors of the desolate seaports of the west of Ireland were filled with vessels of all sizes, from the man of war to the small fishers' boat, which lay sailor less, and rotting on the lazy deep. The emigrants embarked by hundreds, and unfurling their sails with rude hands, made strange havoc of buoy and cordage. Those who modestly betook themselves to the smaller craft, for the most part achieved their watery journey in safety. Some, in the true spirit of reckless enterprise, went on board a ship of an hundred and twenty guns; the vast hull drifted with the tide out of the bay, and after many hours its crew of landsmen contrived to spread a great part of her enormous canvass - the wind took it, and while a thousand mistakes of the helmsman made her present her head now to one point, and now to another, the vast fields of canvass that formed her sails flapped with a sound like that of a huge cataract; or such as a sea-like forest may give forth when buffeted by an equinoctial north-wind. The portholes were open, and with every sea, which as she lurched, washed her decks, they received whole tons of water. The difficulties were increased by a fresh breeze which began to blow, whistling among the shrouds, dashing the sails this way and that, and rending them with horrid split, and such whir as may have visited the dreams of Milton, when he imagined the winnowing of the arch-fiend's van-like wings, which increased the uproar of wild chaos. These sounds were mingled with the roaring of the sea, the splash of the chafed billows round the vessel's sides, and the gurgling up of the water in the hold. The crew, many of whom had never seen the sea before, felt indeed as if heaven and earth came ruining together, as the vessel dipped her bows in the waves, or rose high upon them. Their yells were drowned in the clamor of elements, and the thunder rivings of their unwieldy habitation - they discovered at last that the water gained on them, and they betook themselves to their pumps; they might as well have labored to empty the ocean by bucketful's.

As the sun went down, the gale increased; the ship seemed to feel her danger, she was now completely water-logged, and presented other indications of settling before she went down. The bay was crowded with vessels, whose crews, for the most part, were observing the uncouth sporting of this huge unwieldy machine - they saw her gradually sink; the waters now rising above her lower decks - they could hardly wink before she had utterly disappeared, nor could the place where the sea had closed over her be at all discerned. Some few of her crew were saved, but the greater part clinging to her cordage and masts went down with her, to rise only when death loosened their hold.

This event caused many of those who were about to sail, to put foot again on firm land, ready to encounter any evil rather than to rush into the yawning jaws of the pitiless ocean. But these were few, in comparison to the numbers who actually crossed. Many went up as high as Belfast to ensure a shorter passage, and then journeying south through Scotland, they were joined by the poorer natives of that country, and all poured with one consent into England.

Such incursions struck the English with affright, in all those towns where there was still sufficient population to feel the change. There was room enough indeed in our hapless country for twice the number of invaders; but their lawless spirit instigated them to violence; they took a delight in thrusting the possessors from their houses; in seizing on some mansion of luxury, where the noble dwellers secluded themselves in fear of the plague; in forcing these of either sex to become their servants and purveyors; till, the ruin complete in one place, they removed their locust visitation to another. When unopposed they spread their ravages wide; in cases of danger they clustered, and by dint of numbers overthrew their weak and despairing foes. They came from the east and the north, and directed their course without apparent motive, but unanimously towards our unhappy metropolis.

Communication had been to a great degree cut off through the paralyzing effects of pestilence, so that the van of our invaders had proceeded as far as Manchester and Derby, before we received notice of their arrival. They swept the country like a conquering army, burning - laying waste - murdering. The lower and vagabond English joined with them. Some few of the Lords Lieutenant who remained, endeavored to collect the militia - but the ranks were vacant, panic seized on all, and the opposition that was made only served to increase the audacity and cruelty of the enemy. They talked of taking London, conquering England - calling to mind the long detail of injuries which had for many years been forgotten. Such vaunts displayed their weakness, rather than their strength—yet still they might do extreme mischief, which, ending in their destruction, would render them at last objects of compassion and remorse.

We were now taught how, in the beginning of the world, mankind clothed their enemies in impossible attributes - and how details proceeding from mouth to mouth, might, like Virgil's ever-growing Rumor, reach the heavens with her brow, and clasp Hesperus and Lucifer with her outstretched hands. Gorgon and Centaur, dragon and iron-hoofed lion, vast sea-monster and gigantic hydra, were but types of the strange and appalling accounts brought to London concerning our invaders. Their landing was long unknown but having now advanced within a hundred miles of London, the country people flying before them arrived in successive troops, each exaggerating the numbers, fury, and cruelty of the assailants. Tumult filled the before quiet streets - women and children deserted their homes, escaping they knew not whither -fathers, husbands, and sons, stood trembling, not for themselves, but for their loved and defenseless relations. As the country people poured into London, the citizens fled southwards - they climbed the higher edifices of the town, fancying that they could discern the smoke and flames the enemy spread around them. As Windsor lay, to a great degree, in the line of march from the west, I removed my family to London, assigning the Tower for their sojourn, and joining Adrian, acted as his Lieutenant in the coming struggle.

We employed only two days in our preparations and made good use of them. Artillery and arms were collected; the remnants of such regiments, as could be brought through many losses into any show of muster, were put under arms, with that appearance of military discipline which might encourage our own party, and seem most formidable to the disorganized multitude of our enemies. Even music was not wanting banners floated in the air, and the shrill fife and loud trumpet breathed forth sounds of encouragement and victory. A practiced ear might trace an undue faltering in the step of the soldiers; but this was not occasioned so much by fear of the adversary, as by disease, by sorrow, and by fatal prognostications, which often weighed most potently on the brave, and quelled the manly heart to abject subjection.

Adrian led the troops. He was full of care. It was small relief to him that our discipline should gain us success in such a conflict; while plague still hovered to equalize the conqueror and the conquered, it was not victory that he desired, but bloodless peace. As we advanced, we were met by bands of peasantry, whose almost naked condition, whose despair and horror, told at once the fierce nature of the coming enemy. The senseless spirit of conquest and thirst of spoil blinded them, while with insane fury they deluged the country in ruin. The sight of the military restored hope to those who fled, and revenge took place of fear. They inspired the soldiers with the same sentiment. Languor was changed to ardor, the slow step converted to a speedy pace, while the hollow murmur of the multitude, inspired by one feeling, and that deadly, filled the air, drowning the clang of arms and sound of music. Adrian perceived the change and feared that it would be difficult to prevent them from wreaking their utmost fury on the Irish. He rode through the lines, charging the officers to restrain the troops, exhorting the soldiers, restoring order, and quieting in some degree the violent agitation that swelled every bosom.

We first came upon a few stragglers of the Irish at St. Albans. They retreated, and, joining others of their companions, still fell back, till they reached the main body. Tidings of an armed and regular opposition recalled them to a sort of order. They made Buckingham their headquarters, and scouts were sent out to ascertain our situation. We remained for the night at Luton. In the morning, a simultaneous movement caused us each to advance. It was early dawn, and the air, impregnated with freshest odor, seemed in idle mockery to play with our banners, and bore onwards towards the enemy the music of the bands, the neighing of the horses, and regular step of the infantry. The first sound of martial instruments that came upon our undisciplined foe, inspired surprise, not unmingled with dread. It spoke of other days, of days of concord and order; it was associated with times when plague was not, and man lived beyond the shadow of imminent fate. The pause was momentary. Soon we heard their disorderly clamor, the barbarian shouts, the untimed step of thousands coming on in disarray. Their troops now came pouring on us from the open country or narrow lanes; a large extent of unenclosed fields lay between us; we advanced to the middle of this, and then made a halt: being somewhat on superior ground, we could discern the space they covered. When their leaders perceived us drawn out in opposition, they also gave the word to halt, and endeavored to form their men into some imitation of military discipline.

The first ranks had muskets; some were mounted, but their arms were such as they had seized during their advance, their horses those they had taken from the peasantry; there was no uniformity, and little obedience, but their shouts and wild gestures showed the untamed spirit that inspired them. Our soldiers received the word, and advanced to quickest time, but in perfect order: their uniform dresses, the gleam of their polished arms, their silence, and looks of sullen hate, were more appalling than the savage clamor of our innumerous foe. Thus coming nearer and nearer each other, the howls and shouts of the Irish increased; the English proceeded in obedience to their officers, until they came near enough to distinguish the faces of their enemies; the sight inspired them with fury: with one cry, that rent heaven and was re-echoed by the furthest lines, they rushed on; they disdained the use of the bullet, but with fixed bayonet dashed among the opposing foe, while the ranks opening at intervals, the matchmen lighted the cannon, whose deafening roar and blinding smoke filled up the horror of the scene. I was beside Adrian; a moment before he had again given the word to halt, and had remained a few yards distant from us in deep meditation: he was forming swiftly his plan of action, to prevent the effusion of blood; the noise of cannon, the sudden rush of the troops, and yell of the foe, startled him: with flashing eyes he exclaimed, "Not one of these must perish!" and plunging the rowels into his horse's sides, he dashed between the conflicting bands. We, his staff, followed him to surround and protect him; obeying his signal, however, we fell back somewhat. The soldiery perceiving him, paused in their onset; he did not swerve from the bullets that passed near him, but rode immediately between the opposing lines. Silence succeeded to clamor; about fifty men lay on the ground dying or dead. Adrian raised his sword in act to speak: "By whose command," he cried, addressing his own troops, "do you advance? Who ordered your attack? Fall back; these misguided men shall not be slaughtered, while I am your general. Sheath your weapons; these are your brothers, commit not fratricide; soon the plague will not leave one for you to glut your revenge upon: will you be more pitiless than pestilence? As you honor me - as you worship God, in whose image those also are created - as your children and friends are dear to you, - shed not a drop of precious human blood."

He spoke with outstretched hand and winning voice, and then turning to our invaders, with a severe brow, he commanded them to lay down their arms: "Do you think," he said, "that because we are wasted by plague, you can overcome us; the plague is also among you, and when ye are vanquished by famine and disease, the ghosts of those you have murdered will arise to bid you not hope in death. Lay down your arms, barbarous and cruel men - men whose hands are stained with the blood of the innocent, whose souls are weighed down by the orphan's cry! We shall conquer, for the right is on our side; already your cheeks are pale - the weapons fall from your nerveless grasp. Lay down your arms, fellow men! brethren! Pardon, succor, and brotherly love await your repentance. You are dear to us, because you wear the frail shape of humanity; each one among you will find a friend and host among these forces. Shall man be the enemy of man, while plague, the foe to all, even now is above us, triumphing in our butchery, crueler than her own?"

Each army paused. On our side the soldiers grasped their arms firmly and looked with stern glances on the foe. These had not thrown down their weapons, more from fear than the spirit of contest; they looked at each other, each wishing to follow some example given him, - but they had no leader. Adrian threw himself from his horse and approaching one of those just slain: "He was a man," he cried, "and he is dead. O quickly bind up the wounds of the fallen - let not one die; let not one more soul escape through your merciless gashes, to relate before the throne of God the tale of fratricide; bind up their wounds - restore them to their friends. Cast away the hearts of tigers that burn in your breasts; throw down those tools of cruelty and hate; in this pause of exterminating destiny, let each man be brother, guardian, and stay to the other. Away with those blood-stained arms and hasten some of you to bind up these wounds."

As he spoke, he knelt on the ground, and raised in his arms a man from whose side the warm tide of life gushed - the poor wretch gasped - so still had either host become, that his moans were distinctly heard, and every heart, late fiercely bent on universal massacre, now beat anxiously in hope and fear for the fate of this one man. Adrian tore off his military scarf and bound it round the sufferer - it was too late - the man heaved a deep sigh, his head fell back, his limbs lost their sustaining power. - "He is dead!" said Adrian, as the corpse fell from his arms on the ground, and he bowed his head in sorrow and awe. The fate of the world seemed bound up in the death of this single man. On either side the bands threw down their arms, even the veterans wept, and our party held out their hands to their foes, while a gush of love and deepest amity filled every heart. The two forces mingling, unarmed and hand in hand, talking only how each might assist the other, the adversaries conjoined; each repenting, the one side their former cruelties, the other their late violence, they obeyed the orders of the General to proceed towards London.

Adrian was obliged to exert his utmost prudence, first to allay the discord, and then to provide for the multitude of the invaders. They were marched to various parts of the southern counties, quartered in deserted villages, - a part were sent back to their own island, while the season of winter so far revived our energy, that the passes of the country were defended, and any increase of numbers prohibited.

On this occasion Adrian and Idris met after a separation of nearly a year. Adrian had been occupied in fulfilling a laborious and painful task. He had been familiar with every species of human misery, and had for ever found his powers inadequate, his aid of small avail. Yet the purpose of his soul, his energy and ardent resolution, prevented any re-action of sorrow. He seemed born anew, and virtue, more potent than Medean alchemy, endued him with health and strength. Idris hardly recognized the fragile being, whose form had seemed to bend even to the summer breeze, in the energetic man, whose very excess of sensibility rendered him more capable of fulfilling his station of pilot in storm-tossed England.

It was not thus with Idris. She was uncomplaining; but the very soul of fear had taken its seat in her heart. She had grown thin and pale, her eyes filled with involuntary tears, her voice was broken and low. She tried to throw a veil over the change which she knew her brother must observe in her, but the effort was ineffectual; and when alone with him, with a burst of irrepressible grief she gave vent to her apprehensions and sorrow. She described in vivid terms the ceaseless care that with still renewing hunger ate into her soul; she compared this gnawing of sleepless expectation of evil, to the vulture that fed on the heart of Prometheus; under the influence of this eternal excitement, and of the interminable struggles she endured to combat and conceal it, she felt, she said, as if all the wheels and springs of the animal machine worked at double rate, and were fast consuming themselves. Sleep was not sleep, for her waking thoughts, bridled by some remains of reason, and by the sight of her children happy and in health, were then transformed to wild dreams, all her terrors were realized, all her fears received their dread fulfilment. To this state there was no hope, no alleviation, unless the grave should quickly receive its destined prey, and she be permitted to die, before she experienced a thousand living deaths in the loss of those she loved. Fearing to give me pain, she hid as best she could the excess of her wretchedness, but meeting thus her brother after a long absence, she could not restrain the expression of her woe, but with all the vividness of imagination with which misery is always replete, she poured out the emotions of her heart to her beloved and sympathizing Adrian.

Her present visit to London tended to augment her state of inquietude, by shewing in its utmost extent the ravages occasioned by pestilence. It hardly preserved the appearance of an inhabited city; grass sprung up thick in the streets; the squares were weed-grown, the houses were shut up, while silence and loneliness characterized the busiest parts of the town. Yet in the midst of desolation Adrian had preserved order; and each one continued to live according to law and custom - human institutions thus surviving as it were divine ones, and while the decree of population was abrogated, property continued sacred. It was a melancholy reflection; and in spite of the diminution of evil produced, it struck on the heart as a wretched mockery. All idea of resort for pleasure, of theatres and festivals had passed away. "Next summer," said Adrian as we parted on our return to Windsor, "will decide the fate of the human race. I shall not pause in my exertions until that time; but, if plague revives with the coming year, all contest with her must cease, and our only occupation be the choice of a grave."

I must not forget one incident that occurred during this visit to London. The visits of Merrival to Windsor, before frequent, had suddenly ceased. At this time where but a hair's line separated the living from the dead, I feared that our friend had become a victim to the all-embracing evil. On this occasion I went, dreading the worst, to his dwelling, to see if I could be of any service to those of his family who might have survived. The house was deserted and had been one of those assigned to the invading strangers quartered in London. I saw his astronomical instruments put to strange uses, his globes defaced, his papers covered with abstruse calculations destroyed. The neighbors could tell me little, till I lighted on a poor woman who acted as nurse in these perilous times. She told me that all the family were dead, except Merrival himself, who had gone mad - mad, she called it, yet on questioning her further, it appeared that he was possessed only by the delirium of excessive grief. This old man, tottering on the edge of the grave, and prolonging his prospect through millions of calculated years, - this visionary who had not seen starvation in the wasted forms of his wife and children, or plague in the horrible sights and sounds that surrounded him - this astronomer, apparently dead on earth, and living only in the motion of the spheres - loved his family with unapparent but intense affection. Through long habit they had become a part of himself; his want of worldly knowledge, his absence of mind and infant guilelessness, made him utterly dependent on them. It was not till one of them died that he perceived their danger; one by one they were carried off by pestilence; and his wife, his helpmate and supporter, more necessary to him than his own limbs and frame, which had hardly been taught the lesson of self-preservation, the kind companion whose voice always spoke peace to him, closed her eyes in death. The old man felt the system of universal nature which he had so long studied and adored, slide from under him, and he stood among the dead, and lifted his voice in curses. - No wonder that the attendant should interpret as phrensy the harrowing maledictions of the grief-struck old man.

I had commenced my search late in the day, a November day, that closed in early with pattering rain and melancholy wind. As I turned from the door, I saw Merrival, or rather the shadow of Merrival, attenuated and wild, pass me, and sit on the steps of his home. The breeze scattered the grey locks on his temples, the rain drenched his uncovered head, he sat hiding his face in his withered hands. I pressed his shoulder to awaken his attention, but he did not alter his position.

"Merrival," I said, "it is long since we have seen you - you must return to Windsor with me - Lady Idris desires to see you, you will not refuse her request - come home with me."

He replied in a hollow voice, "Why deceive a helpless old man, why talk hypocritically to one half crazed? Windsor is not my home; my true home I have found; the home that the Creator has prepared for me."

His accent of bitter scorn thrilled me - "Do not tempt me to speak," he continued, "my words would scare you — in an universe of cowards I dare think - among the church-yard tombs - among the victims of His merciless tyranny I dare reproach the Supreme Evil. How can he punish me? Let him bare his arm and transfix me with lightning - this is also one of his attributes" - and the old man laughed.

He rose, and I followed him through the rain to a neighboring church-yard - he threw himself on the wet earth. "Here they are," he cried, "beautiful creatures - breathing, speaking, loving creatures. She who by day and night cherished the age-worn lover of her youth - they, parts of my flesh, my children - here they are call them, scream their names through the night; they will not answer!" He clung to the little heaps that marked the graves. "I ask but one thing; I do not fear His hell, for I have it here; I do not desire His heaven, let me but die and be laid beside them; let me but, when I lie dead, feel my flesh as it molders, mingle with theirs. Promise," and he raised himself painfully, and seized my arm, "promise to bury me with them."

"So, God help me and mine as I promise," I replied, "on one condition: return with me to Windsor."

"To Windsor!" he cried with a shriek, "Never! - from this place I never go - my bones, my flesh, I myself, are already buried here, and what you see of me is corrupted clay like them. I will lie here, and cling here, till rain, and hail, and lightning and storm, ruining on me, make me one in substance with them below." In a few words I must conclude this tragedy. I was obliged to leave London, and Adrian undertook to watch over him; the task was soon fulfilled; age, grief, and inclement weather, all united to hush his sorrows, and bring repose to his heart, whose beats were agony. He died embracing the sod, which was piled above his breast, when he was placed beside the beings whom he regretted with such wild despair.

I returned to Windsor at the wish of Idris, who seemed to think that there was greater safety for her children at that spot; and because, once having taken on me the guardianship of the district, I would not desert it while an inhabitant survived. I went also to act in conformity with Adrian's plans, which was to congregate in masses what remained of the population; for he possessed the conviction that it was only through the benevolent and social virtues that any safety was to be hoped for the remnant of mankind.

It was a melancholy thing to return to this spot so dear to us, as the scene of a happiness rarely before enjoyed, here to mark the extinction of our species, and trace the deep uneraseable footsteps of disease over the fertile and cherished soil. The aspect of the country had so far changed, that it had been impossible to enter on the task of sowing seed, and other autumnal labors. That season was now gone; and winter had set in with sudden and unusual severity. Alternate frosts and thaws succeeding to floods, rendered the country impassable. Heavy falls of snow gave an arctic appearance to the scenery; the roofs of the houses peeped from the white mass; the lowly cot and stately mansion, alike deserted, were blocked up, their thresholds uncleared; the windows were broken by the hail, while the prevalence of a north-east wind rendered out-door exertions extremely painful. The altered state of society made these accidents of nature, sources of real misery. The luxury of command and the attentions of servitude were lost. It is true that the necessaries of life were assembled in such quantities, as to supply to superfluity the wants of the diminished population; but still much labor was required to arrange these, as it were, raw materials; and depressed by sickness, and fearful of the future, we had not energy to enter boldly and decidedly on any system.

I can speak for myself - want of energy was not my failing. The intense life that quickened my pulses, and animated my frame, had the effect, not of drawing me into the mazes of active life, but of exalting my lowliness, and of bestowing majestic proportions on insignificant objects - I could have lived the life of a peasant in the same way - my trifling occupations were swelled into important pursuits; my affections were impetuous and engrossing passions, and nature with all her changes was invested in divine attributes. The very spirit of the Greek mythology inhabited my heart; I deified the uplands, glades, and streams, I

> *Had sight of Proteus coming from the sea;*
> *And heard old Triton blow his wreathed horn.*

Strange, that while the earth preserved her monotonous course, I dwelt with ever-renewing wonder on her antique laws, and now that with eccentric wheel she rushed into an untried path, I should feel this spirit fade; I struggled with despondency and weariness, but like a fog, they choked me. Perhaps, after the labors and stupendous excitement of the past summer, the calm of winter and the almost menial toils it brought with it, were by natural re-action doubly irksome. It was not the grasping passion of the preceding year, which gave life and individuality to each moment—it was not the aching pangs induced by the distresses of the times. The utter inutility that had attended all my exertions took from them their usual effects of exhilaration, and despair rendered abortive the balm of self-applause - I longed to return to my old occupations, but of what use were they? To read were futile—to write, vanity indeed. The earth, late wide circus for the display of dignified exploits, vast theatre for a magnificent drama, now presented a vacant space, an empty stage - for actor or spectator there was no longer ought to say or hear.

Our little town of Windsor, in which the survivors from the neighboring counties were chiefly assembled, wore a melancholy aspect. Its streets were blocked up with snow - the few passengers seemed palsied, and frozen by the ungenial visitation of winter. To escape these evils was the aim and scope of all our exertions. Families late devoted to exalting and refined pursuits, rich, blooming, and young, with diminished numbers and care-fraught hearts, huddled over a fire, grown selfish and groveling through suffering. Without the aid of servants, it was necessary to discharge all household duties; hands unused to such labor must knead the bread, or in the absence of flour, the statesmen or perfumed courtier must undertake the butcher's office. Poor and rich were now equal, or rather the poor were the superior, since they entered on such tasks with alacrity and experience; while ignorance, inaptitude, and habits of repose, rendered them fatiguing to the luxurious, galling to the proud, disgustful to all whose minds, bent on intellectual improvement, held it their dearest privilege to be exempt from attending to mere animal wants.

But in every change goodness and affection can find field for exertion and display. Among some these changes produced a devotion and sacrifice of self at once graceful and heroic. It was a sight for the lovers of the human race to enjoy; to behold, as in ancient times, the patriarchal modes in which the variety of kindred and friendship fulfilled their duteous and kindly offices. Youths, nobles of the land, performed for the sake of mother or sister, the services of menials with amiable cheerfulness. They went to the river to break the ice, and draw water: they assembled on foraging expeditions, or axe in hand felled the trees for fuel. The females received them on their return with the simple and affectionate welcome known before only to the lowly cottage - a clean hearth and bright fire; the supper ready cooked by beloved hands; gratitude for the provision for to-morrow's meal: strange enjoyments for the high-born English, yet they were now their sole, hard earned, and dearly prized luxuries.

None was more conspicuous for this graceful submission to circumstances, noble humility, and ingenious fancy to adorn such acts with romantic coloring, than our own Clara. She saw my despondency, and the aching cares of Idris. Her perpetual study was to relieve us from labor and to spread ease and even elegance over our altered mode of life. We still had some attendants spared by disease, and warmly attached to us. But Clara was jealous of their services; she would be sole handmaid of Idris, sole minister to the wants of her little cousins; nothing gave her so much pleasure as our employing her in this way; she went beyond our desires, earnest, diligent, and unwearied,

> *Abra was ready ere we called her name,*
> *And though we called another, Abra came.*

It was my task each day to visit the various families assembled in our town, and when the weather permitted, I was glad to prolong my ride, and to muse in solitude over every changeful appearance of our destiny, endeavoring to gather lessons for the future from the experience of the past. The impatience with which, while in society, the ills that afflicted my species inspired me, were softened by loneliness, when individual suffering was merged in the general calamity, strange to say, less afflicting to contemplate. Thus often, pushing my way with difficulty through the narrow snow-blocked town, I crossed the bridge and passed through Eton. No youthful congregation of gallant-hearted boys thronged the portal of the college; sad silence pervaded the busy schoolroom and noisy playground. I extended my ride towards Salt Hill, on every side impeded by the snow. Were those the fertile fields I loved - was that the interchange of gentle upland and cultivated dale, once covered with waving corn, diversified by stately trees, watered by the meandering Thames? One sheet of white covered it, while bitter recollection told me that cold as the winter-clothed earth, were the hearts of the inhabitants. I met troops of horses, herds of cattle, flocks of sheep, wandering at will; here throwing down a hay-rick, and nestling from cold in its heart, which afforded them shelter and food - there having taken possession of a vacant cottage. Once on a frosty day, pushed on by restless unsatisfying reflections, I sought a favorite haunt, a little wood not far distant from Salt Hill. A bubbling spring prattles over stones on one side, and a plantation of a few elms and beeches, hardly deserve, and yet continue the name of wood. This spot had for me peculiar charms. It had been a favorite resort of Adrian; it was secluded; and he often said that in boyhood, his happiest hours were spent here; having escaped the stately bondage of his mother, he sat on the roughhewn steps that led to the spring, now reading a favorite book, now musing, with speculation beyond his years, on the still unrivalled skein of morals or metaphysics. A melancholy foreboding assured me that I should never see this place more; so with careful thought, I noted each tree, every winding of the streamlet and irregularity of the soil, that I might better call up its idea in absence. A robin red-breast dropped from the frosty branches of the trees, upon the congealed rivulet; its panting breast and half-closed eyes shewed that it was dying: a hawk appeared in the air; sudden fear seized the little creature; it exerted its last strength, throwing itself on its back, raising its talons in impotent defense against its powerful enemy. I took it up and placed it in my breast. I fed it with a few crumbs from a biscuit; by degrees it revived; its warm fluttering heart beat against me; I cannot tell why I detail this trifling incident - but the scene is still before me; the snow-clad fields seen through the silvered trunks of the beeches, - the brook, in days of happiness alive with sparkling waters, now choked by ice - the leafless trees fantastically dressed in hoar frost - the shapes of summer leaves imaged by winter's frozen hand on the hard ground - the dusky sky, drear cold, and unbroken silence - while close in my bosom, my feathered nursling lay warm, and safe, speaking its content with a light chirp - painful reflections thronged, stirring my brain with wild commotion - cold and death-like as the snowy fields was all earth - misery-stricken the life-tide of the inhabitants - why should I oppose the cataract of destruction that swept us away? - why string my nerves and renew my wearied efforts - ah, why? But that my firm courage and cheerful exertions might shelter the dear mate, whom I chose in the spring of my life; though the throbbing's of my heart be replete with pain, though my hopes for the future are chill, still while your dear head, my gentlest love, can repose in peace on that heart, and while you derive from its fostering care, comfort, and hope, my struggles shall not cease, - I will not call myself altogether vanquished.

One fine February day, when the sun had reassumed some of its genial power, I walked in the forest with my family. It was one of those lovely winter-days which assert the capacity of nature to bestow beauty on barrenness. The leafless trees spread their fibrous branches against the pure sky; their intricate and pervious tracery resembled delicate sea-weed; the deer were turning up the snow in search of the hidden grass; the white was made intensely dazzling by the sun, and trunks of the trees, rendered more conspicuous by the loss of preponderating foliage, gathered around like the labyrinthine columns of a vast temple; it was impossible not to receive pleasure from the sight of these things. Our children, freed from the bondage of winter, bounded before us, pursuing the deer, or rousing the pheasants and partridges from their coverts. Idris leant on my arm; her sadness yielded to the present sense of pleasure. We met other families on the Long Walk, enjoying like ourselves the return of the genial season. At once, I seemed to awake; I cast off the clinging sloth of the past months; earth assumed a new appearance, and my view of the future was suddenly made clear. I exclaimed, "I have now found out the secret!"

"What secret?"

In answer to this question, I described our gloomy winter-life, our sordid cares, our menial labors: -"This northern country," I said, "is no place for our diminished race. When mankind was few, it was not here that they battled with the powerful agents of nature and were enabled to cover the globe with offspring. We must seek some natural Paradise, some garden of the earth, where our simple wants may be easily supplied, and the enjoyment of a delicious climate compensate for the social pleasures we have lost. If we survive this coming summer, I will not spend the ensuing winter in England; neither I nor any of us."

I spoke without much heed, and the very conclusion of what I said brought with its other thoughts. Should we, any of us, survive the coming summer? I saw the brow of Idris clouded; I again felt that we were enchained to the car of fate, over whose coursers we had no control. We could no longer say, this we will do, and this we will leave undone. A mightier power than the human was at hand to destroy our plans or to achieve the work we avoided. It was madness to calculate upon another winter. This was our last. The coming summer was the extreme end of our vista; and, when we arrived there, instead of a continuation of the long road, a gulph yawned, into which we must of force be precipitated. The last blessing of humanity was wrested from us; we might no longer hope. Can the madman, as he clanks his chains, hope? Can the wretch, led to the scaffold, who when he lays his head on the block, marks the double shadow of himself and the executioner, whose uplifted arm bears the axe, hope? Can the ship-wrecked mariner, who spent with swimming, hears close behind the splashing waters divided by a shark which pursues him through the Atlantic, hope? Such hope as theirs, we also may entertain!

Old fable tells us, that this gentle spirit sprung from the box of Pandora, else crammed with evils; but these were unseen and null, while all admired the inspiriting loveliness of young Hope; each man's heart became her home; she was enthroned sovereign of our lives, here and here-after; she was deified and worshipped, declared incorruptible and everlasting. But like all other gifts of the Creator to Man, she is mortal; her life has attained its last hour. We have watched over her; nursed her flickering existence; now she has fallen at once from youth to decrepitude, from health to unmedicinable disease; even as we spend ourselves in struggles for her recovery, she dies; to all nations the voice goes forth, Hope is dead! We are but mourners in the funeral train, and what immortal essence or perishable creation will refuse to make one in the sad procession that attends to its grave the dead comforter of humanity?

> *Does not the sun call in his light? and day*
> *Like a thin exhalation melt away —*
> *Both wrapping up their beams in clouds to be*
> *Themselves close mourners at this obsequie.*

VOL. III

CHAPTER I

Hear you not the rushing sound of the coming tempest? Do you not behold the clouds open, and destruction lurid and dire pour down on the blasted earth? See you not the thunderbolt fall, and are deafened by the shout of heaven that follows its descent? Feel you not the earthquake and open with agonizing groans, while the air is pregnant with shrieks and wailings, - all announcing the last days of man? No! none of these things accompanied our fall! The balmy air of spring, breathed from nature's ambrosial home, invested the lovely earth, which wakened as a young mother about to lead forth in pride her beauteous offspring to meet their sire who had been long absent. The buds decked the trees, the flowers adorned the land: the dark branches, swollen with seasonable juices, expanded into leaves, and the variegated foliage of spring, bending and singing in the breeze, rejoiced in the genial warmth of the unclouded empyrean: the brooks flowed murmuring, the sea was wakeless, and the promontories that over-hung it were reflected in the placid waters; birds awoke in the woods, while abundant food for man and beast sprung up from the dark ground. Where was pain and evil? Not in the calm air or weltering ocean, not in the woods or fertile fields, nor among the birds that made the woods resonant with song, nor the animals that in the midst of plenty basked in the sunshine. Our enemy, like the Calamity of Homer, trod our hearts, and no sound was echoed from her steps

> *With ills the land is rife, with ills the sea,*
> *Diseases haunt our frail humanity,*
> *Through noon, through night, on casual wing they glide,*
> *Silent, - a voice the power all-wise denied.*

Once man was a favorite of the Creator, as the royal psalmist sang, "God had made him a little lower than the angels and had crowned him with glory and honor. God made him to have dominion over the works of his hands and put all things under his feet." Once it was so; now is man lord of the creation? Look at him - ha! I see plague! She has invested his form, is incarnate in his flesh, has entwined herself with his being, and blinds his heaven-seeking eyes. Lie down, O man, on the flower-strewn earth; give up all claim to your inheritance, all you can ever possess of it is the small cell which the dead require. Plague is the companion of spring, of sunshine, and plenty. We no longer struggle with her. We have forgotten what we did when she was not. Of old navies used to stem the giant ocean-waves betwixt Indus and the Pole for slight articles of luxury. Men made perilous journeys to possess themselves of earth's splendid trifles, gems and gold. Human labor was wasted - human life set at naught. Now life is all that we covet; that this automaton of flesh should, with joints and springs in order, perform its functions, that this dwelling of the soul should be capable of containing its dweller. Our minds, late spread abroad through countless spheres and endless combinations of thought, now retrenched themselves behind this wall of flesh, eager to preserve its well-being only. We were surely sufficiently degraded.

At first the increase of sickness in spring brought increase of toil to such of us, who, as yet spared to life, bestowed our time and thoughts on our fellow creatures. We nerved ourselves to the task: "in the midst of despair we performed the tasks of hope." We went out with the resolution of disputing with our foe. We aided the sick and comforted the sorrowing; turning from the multitudinous dead to the rare survivors, with an energy of desire that bore the resemblance of power, we bade them - live. Plague sat paramount the while and laughed us to scorn.

Have any of you, my readers, observed the ruins of an anthill immediately after its destruction? At first it appears entirely deserted of its former inhabitants; in a little time, you see an ant struggling through the upturned mould; they reappear by twos and threes, running hither and thither in search of their lost companions. Such were we upon earth, wondering aghast at the effects of pestilence. Our empty habitations remained, but the dwellers were gathered to the shades of the tomb.

As the rules of order and pressure of laws were lost, some began with hesitation and wonder to transgress the accustomed uses of society. Palaces were deserted, and the poor man dared at length, unreproved, intrude into the splendid apartments, whose very furniture and decorations were an unknown world to him. It was found, that, though at first the stop put to all circulation of property, had reduced those before supported by the factitious wants of society to sudden and hideous poverty, yet when the boundaries of private possession were thrown down, the products of human labor at present existing were more, far more, than the thinned generation could possibly consume. To some among the poor this was matter of exultation. We were all equal now; magnificent dwellings, luxurious carpets, and beds of down, were afforded to all. Carriages and horses, gardens, pictures, statues, and princely libraries, there were enough of these even to superfluity; and there was nothing to prevent each from assuming possession of his share. We were all equal now; but near at hand was an equality still more levelling, a state where beauty and strength, and wisdom, would be as vain as riches and birth. The grave yawned beneath us all, and its prospect prevented any of us from enjoying the ease and plenty which in so awful a manner was presented to us.

Still the bloom did not fade on the cheeks of my babes; and Clara sprung up in years and growth, unsullied by disease. We had no reason to think the site of Windsor Castle peculiarly healthy, for many other families had expired beneath its roof; we lived therefore without any particular precaution; but we lived, it seemed, in safety. If Idris became thin and pale, it was anxiety that occasioned the change; an anxiety I could in no way alleviate. She never complained, but sleep and appetite fled from her, a slow fever preyed on her veins, her color was hectic, and she often wept in secret; gloomy prognostications, care, and agonizing dread, ate up the principle of life within her. I could not fail to perceive this change. I often wished that I had permitted her to take her own course and engage herself in such labors for the welfare of others as might have distracted her thoughts. But it was too late now. Besides that, with the nearly extinct race of man, all our toils grew near a conclusion, she was too weak; consumption, if so it might be called, or rather the over active life within her, which, as with Adrian, spent the vital oil in the early morning hours, deprived her limbs of strength. At night, when she could leave me unperceived, she wandered through the house, or hung over the couches of her children; and in the day time would sink into a perturbed sleep, while her murmurs and starts betrayed the unquiet dreams that vexed her. As this state of wretchedness became more confirmed, and, in spite of her endeavors at concealment more apparent, I strove, though vainly, to awaken in her courage and hope. I could not wonder at the vehemence of her care; her very soul was tenderness; she trusted indeed that she should not outlive me if I became the prey of the vast calamity, and this thought sometimes relieved her. We had for many years trod the highway of life hand in hand, and still thus linked, we might step within the shades of death; but her children, her lovely, playful, animated children - beings sprung from her own dear side - portions of her own being - depositories of our loves - even if we died, it would be comfort to know that they ran man's accustomed course. But it would not be so; young and blooming as they were, they would die, and from the hopes of maturity, from the proud name of attained manhood, they were cut off forever. Often with maternal affection she had figured their merits and talents exerted on life's wide stage. Alas for these latter days! The world had grown old, and all its inmates partook of the decrepitude. Why talk of infancy, manhood, and old age? We all stood equal sharers of the last throes of time-worn nature. Arrived at the same point of the world's age - there was no difference in us; the name of parent and child had lost their meaning; young boys and girls were level now with men. This was all true; but it was not less agonizing to take the admonition home.

Where could we turn, and not find a desolation pregnant with the dire lesson of example? The fields had been left uncultivated, weeds and gaudy flowers sprung up, - or where a few wheat-fields shewed signs of the living hopes of the husbandman, the work had been left halfway, the ploughman had died beside the plough; the horses had deserted the furrow, and no seedsman had approached the dead; the cattle unattended wandered over the fields and through the lanes; the tame inhabitants of the poultry yard, baulked of their daily food, had become wild - young lambs were dropped in flower-gardens, and the cow stalled in the hall of pleasure. Sickly and few, the country people neither went out to sow nor reap; but sauntered about the meadows, or lay under the hedges, when the inclement sky did not drive them to take shelter under the nearest roof. Many of those who remained, secluded themselves; some had laid up stores which should prevent the necessity of leaving their homes; - some deserted wife and child, and imagined that they secured their safety in utter solitude. Such had been Ryland's plan, and he was discovered dead and half-devoured by insects, in a house many miles from any other, with piles of food laid up in useless superfluity. Others made long journeys to unite themselves to those they loved and arrived to find them dead.

London did not contain above a thousand inhabitants; and this number was continually diminishing. Most of them were country people, come up for the sake of change; the Londoners had sought the country. The busy eastern part of the town was silent, or at most you saw only where, half from cupidity, half from curiosity, the warehouses had been more ransacked than pillaged: bales of rich India goods, shawls of price, jewels, and spices, unpacked, strewed the floors. In some places the possessor had to the last kept watch on his store and died before the barred gates. The massy portals of the churches swung creaking on their hinges, and some few lay dead on the pavement. The wretched female, loveless victim of vulgar brutality, had wandered to the toilet of high-born beauty, and, arraying herself in the garb of splendor, had died before the mirror which reflected to herself alone her altered appearance. Women whose delicate feet had seldom touched the earth in their luxury, had fled in fright and horror from their homes, till, losing themselves in the squalid streets of the metropolis, they had died on the threshold of poverty. The heart sickened at the variety of misery presented; and, when I saw a specimen of this gloomy change, my soul ached with the fear of what might befall my beloved Idris and my babes. Were they, surviving Adrian and myself, to find themselves protectorless in the world? As yet the mind alone had suffered - could I forever put off the time, when the delicate frame and shrinking nerves of my child of prosperity, the nursling of rank and wealth, who was my companion, should be invaded by famine, hardship, and disease? Better die at once - better plunge a poniard in her bosom, still untouched by drear adversity, and then again sheathe it in my own! But no; in times of misery we must fight against our destinies and strive not to be overcome by them. I would not yield, but to the last gasp resolutely defended my dear ones against sorrow and pain; and if I were vanquished at last, it should not be ingloriously. I stood in the gap, resisting the enemy - the impalpable, invisible foe, who had so long besieged us - as yet he had made no breach: it must be my care that he should not, secretly undermining, burst up within the very threshold of the temple of love, at whose altar I daily sacrificed. The hunger of Death was now stung more sharply by the diminution of his food: or was it that before, the survivors being many, the dead were less eagerly counted? Now each life was a gem, each human breathing form of far, O! far more worth than subtlest imagery of sculptured stone; and the daily, nay, hourly decrease visible in our numbers, visited the heart with sickening misery. This summer extinguished our hopes, the vessel of society was wrecked, and the shattered raft, which carried the few survivors over the sea of misery, was riven and tempest toast. Man existed by twos and threes; man, the individual who might sleep, and wake, and perform the animal functions; but man, in himself weak, yet more powerful in congregated numbers than wind or ocean; man, the queller of the elements, the lord of created nature, the peer of demi-gods, existed no longer.

Farewell to the patriotic scene, to the love of liberty and well-earned meed of virtuous aspiration! - farewell to crowded senate, vocal with the councils of the wise, whose laws were keener than the sword blade tempered at Damascus! - farewell to kingly pomp and warlike pageantry; the crowns are in the dust, and the wearers are in their graves! - farewell to the desire of rule, and the hope of victory; to high vaulting ambition, to the appetite for praise, and the craving for the suffrage of their fellows! The nations are no longer! No senate sits in council for the dead; no scion of a time honored dynasty pants to rule over the inhabitants of a charnel house; the general's hand is cold, and the soldier has his untimely grave dug in his native fields, unhonored, though in youth. The marketplace is empty, the candidate for popular favor finds none whom he can represent. To chambers of painted state farewell! - To midnight revelry, and the panting emulation of beauty, to costly dress and birthday shew, to title and the gilded coronet, farewell! Farewell to the giant powers of man, - to knowledge that could pilot the deep-drawing bark through the opposing waters of shoreless ocean, - to science that directed the silken balloon through the pathless air, - to the power that could put a barrier to mighty waters, and set in motion wheels, and beams, and vast machinery, that could divide rocks of granite or marble, and make the mountains plain!

Farewell to the arts, - to eloquence, which is to the human mind as the winds to the sea, stirring, and then allaying it; - farewell to poetry and deep philosophy, for man's imagination is cold, and his enquiring mind can no longer expatiate on the wonders of life, for "there is no work, nor device, nor knowledge, nor wisdom in the grave, whither thou goest!" — to the graceful building, which in its perfect proportion transcended the rude forms of nature, the fretted gothic and massy Saracenic pile, to the stupendous arch and glorious dome, the fluted column with its capital, Corinthian, Ionic, or Doric, the peristyle and fair entablature, whose harmony of form is to the eye as musical concord to the ear! - farewell to sculpture, where the pure marble mocks human flesh, and in the plastic expression of the culled excellencies of the human shape, shines forth the god! - farewell to painting, the high wrought sentiment and deep knowledge of the artists' mind in pictured canvas - to paradisaical scenes, where trees are ever vernal, and the ambrosial air rests in perpetual glow: - to the stamped form of tempest, and wildest uproar of universal nature engaged in the narrow frame, O farewell! Farewell to music, and the sound of song; to the marriage of instruments, where the concord of soft and harsh unites in sweet harmony, and gives wings to the panting listeners, whereby to climb heaven, and learn the hidden pleasures of the eternals! - Farewell to the well-trod stage; a truer tragedy is enacted on the world's ample scene, that puts to shame mimic grief: to high-bred comedy, and the low buffoon, farewell! - Man may laugh no more. Alas! to enumerate the adornments of humanity, shews, by what we have lost, how supremely great man was. It is all over now. He is solitary; like our first parents expelled from Paradise, he looks back towards the scene he has quitted. The high walls of the tomb, and the flaming sword of plague, lie between it and him. Like to our first parents, the whole earth is before him, a wide desert. Unsupported and weak, let him wander through fields where the unreaped corn stands in barren plenty, through copses planted by his fathers, through towns built for his use. Posterity is no more; fame, and ambition, and love, are words void of meaning; even as the cattle that grazes in the field, do thou, O deserted one, lie down at evening-tide, unknowing of the past, careless of the future, for from such fond ignorance alone canst thou hope for ease!

Joy paints with its own colors every act and thought. The happy do not feel poverty - for delight is as a gold-tissued robe and crowns them with priceless gems. Enjoyment plays the cook to their homely fare and mingles intoxication with their simple drink. Joy strews the hard couch with roses and makes labor ease.

Sorrow doubles the burthen to the bent-down back; plants thorns in the unyielding pillow; mingles gall with water; adds saltness to their bitter bread; clothing them in rags, and strewing ashes on their bare heads. To our irremediable distress every small and pelting inconvenience came with added force; we had strung our frames to endure the Atlean weight thrown on us; we sank beneath the added feather chance threw on us, "the grasshopper was a burthen." Many of the survivors had been bred in luxury - their servants were gone, their powers of command vanished like unreal shadows: the poor even suffered various privations; and the idea of another winter like the last, brought affright to our minds.

Was it not enough that we must die, but toil must be added? - must we prepare our funeral repast with labor, and with unseemly drudgery heap fuel on our deserted hearths - must we with servile hands fabricate the garments, soon to be our shroud?

Not so! We are presently to die, let us then enjoy to its full relish the remnant of our lives. Sordid care, avaunt! menial labors, and pains, slight in themselves, but too gigantic for our exhausted strength, shall make no part of our ephemeral existences. In the beginning of time, when, as now, man lived by families, and not by tribes or nations, they were placed in a genial clime, where earth fed them untilled, and the balmy air enwrapped their reposing limbs with warmth more pleasant than beds of down. The south is the native place of the human race; the land of fruits, more grateful to man than the hard-earned Ceres of the north, - of trees, whose boughs are as a palace-roof, of couches of roses, and of the thirst-appeasing grape. We need not there fear cold and hunger.

Look at England! the grass shoots up high in the meadows; but they are dank and cold, unfit bed for us. Corn we have none, and the crude fruits cannot support us. We must seek firing in the bowels of the earth, or the unkind atmosphere will fill us with rheums and aches. The labor of hundreds of thousands alone could make this inclement nook fit habitation for one man. To the south then, to the sun! - where nature is kind, where Jove has showered forth the contents of Amalthea's horn, and earth is garden.

England, late birthplace of excellence and school of the wise, thy children are gone, thy glory faded! Thou, England, wert the triumph of man! Small favor was shewn thee by thy Creator, thou Isle of the North; a ragged canvas naturally, painted by man with alien colors; but the hues he gave are faded, never more to be renewed. So, we must leave thee, thou marvel of the world; we must bid farewell to thy clouds, and cold, and scarcity forever! Thy manly hearts are still, thy tale of power and liberty at its close! Bereft of man, O little isle! the ocean waves will buffet thee, and the raven flap his wings over thee; thy soil will be birthplace of weeds, thy sky will canopy barrenness. It was not for the rose of Persia thou wert famous, nor the banana of the east; not for the spicy gales of India, nor the sugar groves of America; not for thy vines nor thy double harvests, nor for thy vernal airs, nor solstitial sun - but for thy children, their unwearied industry and lofty aspiration. They are gone, and thou goest with them the oft trodden path that leads to oblivion,

> *Farewell, sad Isle, farewell, thy fatal glory*
> *Is summed, cast up, and cancelled in this story.*

CHAPTER II

In the autumn of this year 2096, the spirit of emigration crept in among the few survivors, who, congregating from various parts of England, met in London. This spirit existed as a breath, a wish, a far-off thought, until communicated to Adrian, who imbibed it with ardor, and instantly engaged himself in plans for its execution. The fear of immediate death vanished with the heats of September. Another winter was before us, and we might elect our mode of passing it to the best advantage. Perhaps in rational philosophy none could be better chosen than this scheme of migration, which would draw us from the immediate scene of our woe, and leading us through pleasant and picturesque countries, amuse for a time our despair. The idea once broached; all were impatient to put it in execution.

We were still at Windsor; our renewed hopes medicined the anguish we had suffered from the late tragedies. The death of many of our inmates had weaned us from the fond idea, that Windsor Castle was a spot sacred from the plague; but our lease of life was renewed for some months, and even Idris lifted her head, as a lily after a storm, when a last sunbeam tinges its silver cup. Just at this time Adrian came down to us; his eager looks shewed us that he was full of some scheme. He hastened to take me aside and disclosed to me with rapidity his plan of emigration from England.

To leave England forever! to turn from its polluted fields and groves, and, placing the sea between us, to quit it, as a sailor quits the rock on which he has been wrecked, when the saving ship rides by. Such was his plan.

To leave the country of our fathers, made holy by their graves! - We could not feel even as a voluntary exile of old, who might for pleasure or convenience forsake his native soil; though thousands of miles might divide him, England was still a part of him, as he of her. He heard of the passing events of the day; he knew that, if he returned, and resumed his place in society, the entrance was still open, and it required but the will, to surround himself at once with the associations and habits of boyhood. Not so with us, the remnant. We left none to represent us, none to repeople the desert land, and the name of England died, when we left her,

In vagabond pursuit of dreadful safety.

Yet let us go! England is in her shroud, - we may not enchain ourselves to a corpse. Let us go - the world is our country now, and we will choose for our residence its most fertile spot. Shall we, in these desert halls, under this wintry sky, sit with closed eyes and folded hands, expecting death? Let us rather go out to meet it gallantly: or perhaps - for all this pendulous orb, this fair gem in the sky's diadem, is not surely plague-stricken - perhaps, in some secluded nook, amidst eternal spring, and waving trees, and purling streams, we may find Life. The world is vast, and England, though her many fields and widespread woods seem interminable, is but a small part of her. At the close of a day's march over high mountains and through snowy valleys, we may come upon health, and committing our loved ones to its charge, replant the uprooted tree of humanity, and send to late posterity the tale of the ante-pestilential race, the heroes and sages of the lost state of things. Hope beckons and sorrow urges us, the heart beats high with expectation, and this eager desire of change must be an omen of success. O come! Farewell to the dead! farewell to the tombs of those we loved! - farewell to giant London and the placid Thames, to river and mountain or fair district, birth-place of the wise and good, to Windsor Forest and its antique castle, farewell! themes for story alone are they, - we must live elsewhere.

Such were in part the arguments of Adrian, uttered with enthusiasm and unanswerable rapidity. Something more was in his heart, to which he dared not give words. He felt that the end of time was come; he knew that one by one we should dwindle into nothingness. It was not advisable to wait this sad consummation in our native country; but travelling would give us our object for each day, that would distract our thoughts from the swift-approaching end of things. If we went to Italy, to sacred and eternal Rome, we might with greater patience submit to the decree, which had laid her mighty towers low. We might lose our selfish grief in the sublime aspect of its desolation. All this was in the mind of Adrian; but he thought of my children, and, instead of communicating to me these resources of despair, he called up the image of health and life to be found, where we knew not - when we knew not; but if never to be found, forever and forever to be sought. He won me over to his party, heart and soul.

It devolved on me to disclose our plan to Idris. The images of health and hope which I presented to her, made her with a smile consent. With a smile she agreed to leave her country, from which she had never before been absent, and the spot she had inhabited from infancy; the forest and its mighty trees, the woodland paths and green recesses, where she had played in childhood, and had lived so happily through youth; she would leave them without regret, for she hoped to purchase thus the lives of her children. They were her life; dearer than a spot consecrated to love, dearer than all else the earth contained. The boys heard with childish glee of our removal: Clara asked if we were to go to Athens. "It is possible," I replied, and her countenance became radiant with pleasure. There she would behold the tomb of her parents, and the territory filled with recollections of her father's glory. In silence, but without respite, she had brooded over these scenes. It was the recollection of them that had turned her infant gaiety to seriousness and had impressed her with high and restless thoughts.

There were many dear friends whom we must not leave behind, humble though they were. There was the spirited and obedient steed which Lord Raymond had given his daughter; there was Alfred's dog and a pet eagle, whose sight was dimmed through age. But this catalogue of favorites to be taken with us, could not be made without grief to think of our heavy losses, and a deep sigh for the many things we must leave behind. The tears rushed into the eyes of Idris, while Alfred and Evelyn brought now a favorite rose tree, now a marble vase beautifully carved, insisting that these must go, and exclaiming on the pity that we could not take the castle and the forest, the deer and the birds, and all accustomed and cherished objects along with us. "Fond and foolish ones," I said, "we have lost forever treasures far more precious than these; and we desert them, to preserve treasures to which in comparison they are nothing. Let us not for a moment forget our object and our hope; and they will form a resistless mound to stop the overflowing of our regret for trifles."

The children were easily distracted, and again returned to their prospect of future amusement. Idris had disappeared. She had gone to hide her weakness; escaping from the castle, she had descended to the little park, and sought solitude, that she might there indulge her tears; I found her clinging round an old oak, pressing its rough trunk with her roseate lips, as her tears fell plenteously, and her sobs and broken exclamations could not be suppressed; with surpassing grief I beheld this loved one of my heart thus lost in sorrow! I drew her towards me; and, as she felt my kisses on her eyelids, as she felt my arms press her, she revived to the knowledge of what remained to her. "You are very kind not to reproach me," she said: "I weep, and a bitter pang of intolerable sorrow tears my heart. And yet I am happy; mothers lament their children, wives lose their husbands, while you and my children are left to me. Yes, I am happy, most happy, that I can weep thus for imaginary sorrows, and that the slight loss of my adored country is not dwindled and annihilated in mightier misery. Take me where you will; where you and my children are, there shall be Windsor, and every country will be England to me. Let these tears flow not for myself, happy and ungrateful as I am, but for the dead world - for our lost country - for all of love, and life, and joy, now choked in the dusty chambers of death."

She spoke quickly, as if to convince herself; she turned her eyes from the trees and forest-paths she loved; she hid her face in my bosom, and we - yes, my masculine firmness dissolved - we wept together consolatory tears, and then calm - nay, almost cheerful, we returned to the castle.

The first cold weather of an English October made us hasten our preparations. I persuaded Idris to go up to London, where she might better attend to necessary arrangements. I did not tell her, that to spare her the pang of parting from inanimate objects, now the only things left, I had resolved that we should none of us return to Windsor. For the last time we looked on the wide extent of country visible from the terrace, and saw the last rays of the sun tinge the dark masses of wood variegated by autumnal tints; the uncultivated fields and smokeless cottages lay in shadow below; the Thames wound through the wide plain, and the venerable pile of Eton college, stood in dark relief, a prominent object; the cawing of the myriad rooks which inhabited the trees of the little park, as in column or thick wedge they speeded to their nests, disturbed the silence of evening. Nature was the same, as when she was the kind mother of the human race; now, childless and forlorn, her fertility was a mockery; her loveliness a mask for deformity. Why should the breeze gently stir the trees, man felt not its refreshment? Why did dark night adorn herself with stars - man saw them not? Why are there fruits, or flowers, or streams, man is not here to enjoy them?

Idris stood beside me; her dear hand locked in mine. Her face was radiant with a smile. - "The sun is alone," she said, "but we are not. A strange star, my Lionel, ruled our birth; sadly, and with dismay we may look upon the annihilation of man; but we remain for each other. Did I ever in the wide world seek other than thee? And since in the wide world thou remainest, why should I complain? Thou and nature are still true to me. Beneath the shades of night, and through the day, whose garish light displays our solitude, thou wilt still be at my side, and even Windsor will not be regretted."

I had chosen nighttime for our journey to London, that the change and desolation of the country might be the less observable. Our only surviving servant drove us. We passed down the steep hill and entered the dusky avenue of the Long Walk. At times like these, minute circumstances assume giant and majestic proportions; the very swinging open of the white gate that admitted us into the forest, arrested my thoughts as matter of interest; it was an everyday act, never to occur again! The setting crescent of the moon glittered through the massy trees to our right, and when we entered the park, we scared a troop of deer, that fled bounding away in the forest shades. Our two boys quietly slept; once, before our road turned from the view, I looked back on the castle. Its windows glistened in the moonshine, and its heavy outline lay in a dark mass against the sky - the trees near us waved a solemn dirge to the midnight breeze. Idris leaned back in the carriage; her two hands pressed mine, her countenance was placid, she seemed to lose the sense of what she now left, in the memory of what she still possessed.

My thoughts were sad and solemn, yet not of unmingled pain. The very excess of our misery carried a relief with it, giving sublimity and elevation to sorrow. I felt that I carried with me those I best loved; I was pleased, after a long separation to rejoin Adrian; never again to part. I felt that I quitted what I loved, not what loved me. The castle walls, and long familiar trees, did not hear the parting sound of our carriage-wheels with regret. And, while I felt Idris to be near, and heard the regular breathing of my children, I could not be unhappy. Clara was greatly moved; with streaming eyes, suppressing her sobs, she leaned from the window, watching the last glimpse of her native Windsor.

Adrian welcomed us on our arrival. He was all animation; you could no longer trace in his look of health, the suffering valetudinarian; from his smile and sprightly tones you could not guess that he was about to lead forth from their native country, the numbered remnant of the English nation, into the tenantless realms of the south, there to die, one by one, till the LAST MAN should remain in a voiceless, empty world.

Adrian was impatient for our departure and had advanced far in his preparations. His wisdom guided all. His care was the soul, to move the luckless crowd, who relied wholly on him. It was useless to provide many things, for we should find abundant provision in every town. It was Adrian's wish to prevent all labor; to bestow a festive appearance on this funeral train. Our numbers amounted to not quite two thousand persons. These were not all assembled in London, but each day witnessed the arrival of fresh numbers, and those who resided in the neighboring towns, had received orders to assemble at one place, on the twentieth of November. Carriages and horses were provided for all; captains and under officers chosen, and the whole assemblage wisely organized. All obeyed the Lord Protector of dying England; all looked up to him. His council was chosen, it consisted of about fifty persons. Distinction and station were not the qualifications of their election. We had no station among us, but that which benevolence and prudence gave; no distinction save between the living and the dead. Although we were anxious to leave England before the depth of winter, yet we were detained. Small parties had been dispatched to various parts of England, in search of stragglers; we would not go, until we had assured ourselves that in all human probability we did not leave behind a single human being.

On our arrival in London, we found that the aged Countess of Windsor was residing with her son in the palace of the Protectorate; we repaired to our accustomed abode near Hyde Park. Idris now for the first time for many years saw her mother, anxious to assure herself that the childishness of old age did not mingle with unforgotten pride, to make this high-born dame still so inveterate against me. Age and care had furrowed her cheeks and bent her form; but her eye was still bright, her manners authoritative and unchanged; she received her daughter coldly but displayed more feeling as she folded her grandchildren in her arms. It is our nature to wish to continue our systems and thoughts to posterity through our own offspring. The Countess had failed in this design with regard to her children; perhaps she hoped to find the next remove in birth more tractable. Once Idris named me casually - a frown, a convulsive gesture of anger, shook her mother, and, with voice trembling with hate, she said - "I am of little worth in this world; the young are impatient to push the old off the scene; but, Idris, if you do not wish to see your mother expire at your feet, never again name that person to me; all else I can bear; and now I am resigned to the destruction of my cherished hopes: but it is too much to require that I should love the instrument that providence gifted with murderous properties for my destruction."

This was a strange speech, now that, on the empty stage, each might play his part without impediment from the other. But the haughty Ex-Queen thought as Octavius Caesar and Mark Antony,

We could not stall together
In the whole world.

The period of our departure was fixed for the twenty-fifth of November. The weather was temperate; soft rains fell at night, and by day the wintry sun shone out. Our numbers were to move forward in separate parties, and to go by different routes, all to unite at last at Paris. Adrian and his division, consisting in all of five hundred persons, were to take the direction of Dover and Calais. On the twentieth of November, Adrian and I rode for the last time through the streets of London. They were grass-grown and desert. The open doors of the empty mansions creaked upon their hinges; rank herbage, and deforming dirt, had swiftly accumulated on the steps of the houses; the voiceless steeples of the churches pierced the smokeless air; the churches were open, but no prayer was offered at the altars; mildew and damp had already defaced their ornaments; birds, and tame animals, now homeless, had built nests, and made their lairs in consecrated spots. We passed St. Paul's. London, which had extended so far in suburbs in all direction, had been somewhat deserted in the midst, and much of what had in former days obscured this vast building was removed. Its ponderous mass, blackened stone, and high dome made it look, not like a temple, but a tomb. Methought above the portico was engraved the Hic jacet of England. We passed on eastwards, engaged in such solemn talk as the times inspired. No human step was heard, nor human form discerned. Troops of dogs, deserted of their masters, passed us; and now and then a horse, unbridled and unsaddled, trotted towards us, and tried to attract the attention of those which we rode, as if to allure them to seek like liberty. An unwieldy ox, who had fed in an abandoned granary, suddenly lowed, and shewed his shapeless form in a narrow doorway; everything was desert; but nothing was in ruin. And this medley of undamaged buildings, and luxurious accommodation, in trim and fresh youth, was contrasted with the lonely silence of the unpeopled streets.

Night closed in, and it began to rain. We were about to return homewards, when a voice, a human voice, strange now to hear, attracted our attention. It was a child singing a merry, lightsome air; there was no other sound. We had traversed London from Hyde Park even to where we now were in the Minories, and had met no person, heard no voice nor footstep. The singing was interrupted by laughing and talking; never was merry ditty so sadly timed, never laughter more akin to tears. The door of the house from which these sounds proceeded was open, the upper rooms were illuminated as for a feast. It was a large magnificent house, in which doubtless some rich merchant had lived. The singing again commenced, and rang through the high-roofed rooms, while we silently ascended the staircase. Lights now appeared to guide us; and a long suite of splendid rooms illuminated, made us still more wonder. Their only inhabitant, a little girl, was dancing, waltzing, and singing about them, followed by a large Newfoundland dog, who boisterously jumping on her, and interrupting her, made her now scold, now laugh, now throw herself on the carpet to play with him. She was dressed grotesquely, in glittering robes and shawls fit for a woman; she appeared about ten years of age. We stood at the door looking on this strange scene, till the dog perceiving us barked loudly; the child turned and saw us: her face, losing its gaiety, assumed a sullen expression: she slunk back, apparently meditating an escape. I came up to her, and held her hand; she did not resist, but with a stern brow, so strange in childhood, so different from her former hilarity, she stood still, her eyes fixed on the ground. "What do you do here?" I said gently; "Who are you?" - she was silent, but trembled violently. -"My poor child," asked Adrian, "are you alone?" There was a winning softness in his voice, that went to the heart of the little girl; she looked at him, then snatching her hand from me, threw herself into his arms, clinging round his neck, ejaculating -"Save me! save me!" while her unnatural sullenness dissolved in tears.

"I will save you," he replied, "of what are you afraid? you need not fear my friend, he will do you no harm. Are you alone?"

"No, Lion is with me."

"And your father and mother? -"

"I never had any; I am a charity girl. Everybody is gone, gone for a great, great many days; but if they come back and find me out, they will beat me so!" Her unhappy story was told in these few words: an orphan, taken on pretended charity, ill-treated and reviled, her oppressors had died: unknowing of what had passed around her, she found herself alone; she had not dared venture out, but by the continuance of her solitude her courage revived, her childish vivacity caused her to play a thousand freaks, and with her brute companion she passed a long holiday, fearing nothing but the return of the harsh voices and cruel usage of her protectors. She readily consented to go with Adrian.

In the meantime, while we descanted on alien sorrows, and on a solitude which struck our eyes and not our hearts, while we imagined all of change and suffering that had intervened in these once thronged streets, before, tenantless and abandoned, they became mere kennels for dogs, and stables for cattle: - while we read the death of the world upon the dark fane, and hugged ourselves in the remembrance that we possessed that which was all the world to us - in the meanwhile --

We had arrived from Windsor early in October and had now been in London about six weeks. Day by day, during that time, the health of my Idris declined: her heart was broken; neither sleep nor appetite, the chosen servants of health, waited on her wasted form. To watch her children hour by hour, to sit by me, drinking deep the dear persuasion that I remained to her, was all her pastime. Her vivacity, so long assumed, her affectionate display of cheerfulness, her light-hearted tone and springy gait were gone. I could not disguise to myself, nor could she conceal, her life-consuming sorrow. Still change of scene, and reviving hopes might restore her; I feared the plague only, and she was untouched by that.

I had left her this evening, reposing after the fatigues of her preparations. Clara sat beside her, relating a story to the two boys. The eyes of Idris were closed: but Clara perceived a sudden change in the appearance of our eldest darling; his heavy lids veiled his eyes, an unnatural color burnt in his cheeks, his breath became short. Clara looked at the mother; she slept yet started at the pause the narrator made - Fear of awakening and alarming her, caused Clara to go on at the eager call of Evelyn, who was unaware of what was passing. Her eyes turned alternately from Alfred to Idris; with trembling accents she continued her tale, till she saw the child about to fall starting forward she caught him, and her cry roused Idris. She looked on her son. She saw death stealing across his features; she laid him on a bed, she held drink to his parched lips.

Yet he might be saved. If I were there, he might be saved; perhaps it was not the plague. Without a counsellor, what could she do? stay and behold him die! Why at that moment was I away? "Look to him, Clara," she exclaimed, "I will return immediately."

She inquired among those who, selected as the companions of our journey, had taken up their residence in our house; she heard from them merely that I had gone out with Adrian. She entreated them to seek me: she returned to her child, he was plunged in a frightful state of torpor; again she rushed down stairs; all was dark, desert, and silent; she lost all self-possession; she ran into the street; she called on my name. The pattering rain and howling wind alone replied to her. Wild fear gave wings to her feet; she darted forward to seek me, she knew not where; but, putting all her thoughts, all her energy, all her being in speed only, most misdirected speed, she neither felt, nor feared, nor paused, but ran right on, till her strength suddenly deserted her so suddenly, that she had not thought to save herself. Her knees failed her, and she fell heavily on the pavement. She was stunned for a time; but at length rose, and though sorely hurt, still walked on, shedding a fountain of tears, stumbling at times, going she knew not whither, only now and then with feeble voice she called my name, adding with heart-piercing exclamations, that I was cruel and unkind. Human being there was none to reply; and the inclemency of the night had driven the wandering animals to the habitations they had usurped. Her thin dress was drenched with rain; her wet hair clung round her neck; she tottered through the dark streets; till, striking her foot against an unseen impediment, she again fell; she could not rise; she hardly strove; but, gathering up her limbs, she resigned herself to the fury of the elements, and the bitter grief of her own heart. She breathed an earnest prayer to die speedily, for there was no relief but death. While hopeless of safety for herself, she ceased to lament for her dying child, but shed kindly, bitter tears for the grief I should experience in losing her. While she lay, life almost suspended, she felt a warm, soft hand on her brow, and a gentle female voice asked her, with expressions of tender compassion, if she could not rise? That another human being, sympathetic and kind, should exist near, roused her; half rising, with clasped hands, and fresh springing tears, she entreated her companion to seek for me, to bid me hasten to my dying child, to save him, for the love of heaven, to save him!

The woman raised her; she led her under shelter, she entreated her to return to her home, whither perhaps I had already returned. Idris easily yielded to her persuasions, she leaned on the arm of her friend, she endeavored to walk on, but irresistible faintness made her pause again and again.

Quickened by the increasing storm, we had hastened our return, our little charge was placed before Adrian on his horse. There was an assemblage of persons under the portico of our house, in whose gestures I instinctively read some heavy change, some new misfortune. With swift alarm, afraid to ask a single question, I leapt from my horse; the spectators saw me, knew me, and in awful silence divided to make way for me. I snatched a light, and rushing upstairs, and hearing a groan, without reflection I threw open the door of the first room that presented itself. It was quite dark; but, as I stepped within, a pernicious scent assailed my senses, producing sickening qualms, which made their way to my very heart, while I felt my leg clasped, and a groan repeated by the person that held me. I lowered my lamp, and saw a negro half clad, writhing under the agony of disease, while he held me with a convulsive grasp. With mixed horror and impatience, I strove to disengage myself, and fell on the sufferer; he wound his naked festering arms round me, his face was close to mine, and his breath, death-laden, entered my vitals. For a moment I was overcome, my head was bowed by aching nausea; till, reflection returning, I sprung up, threw the wretch from me, and darting up the staircase, entered the chamber usually inhabited by my family. A dim light shewed me Alfred on a couch; Clara trembling, and paler than whitest snow, had raised him on her arm, holding a cup of water to his lips. I saw full well that no spark of life existed in that ruined form, his features were rigid, his eyes glazed, his head had fallen back. I took him from her, I laid him softly down, kissed his cold little mouth, and turned to speak in a vain whisper, when loudest sound of thunder like cannon could not have reached him in his immaterial abode.

And where was Idris? That she had gone out to seek me, and had not returned, were fearful tidings, while the rain and driving wind clattered against the window and roared round the house. Added to this, the sickening sensation of disease gained upon me; no time was to be lost, if ever I would see her again. I mounted my horse and rode out to seek her, fancying that I heard her voice in every gust, oppressed by fever and aching pain.

I rode in the dark and rain through the labyrinthine streets of unpeopled London. My child lay dead at home; the seeds of mortal disease had taken root in my bosom; I went to seek Idris, my adored, now wandering alone, while the waters were rushing from heaven like a cataract to bathe her dear head in chill damp, her fair limbs in numbing cold. A female stood on the step of a door and called to me as I galloped past. It was not Idris; so I rode swiftly on, until a kind of second sight, a reflection back again on my senses of what I had seen but not marked, made me feel sure that another figure, thin, graceful and tall, stood clinging to the foremost person who supported her. In a minute I was beside the suppliant, in a minute I received the sinking Idris in my arms. Lifting her up, I placed her on the horse; she had not strength to support herself; so I mounted behind her, and held her close to my bosom, wrapping my riding-cloak round her, while her companion, whose well known, but changed countenance, (it was Juliet, daughter of the

Duke of L -) could at this moment of horror obtain from me no more than a passing glance of compassion. She took the abandoned rein and conducted our obedient steed homewards. Dare I avouch it? That was the last moment of my happiness; but I was happy. Idris must die, for her heart was broken: I must die, for I had caught the plague; earth was a scene of desolation; hope was madness; life had married death; they were one; but, thus supporting my fainting love, thus feeling that I must soon die, I reveled in the delight of possessing her once more; again and again I kissed her, and pressed her to my heart.

We arrived at our home. I assisted her to dismount, I carried her upstairs, and gave her into Clara's care, that her wet garments might be changed. Briefly I assured Adrian of her safety and requested that we might be left to repose. As the miser, who with trembling caution visits his treasure to count it again and again, so I numbered each moment, and grudged every one that was not spent with Idris. I returned swiftly to the chamber where the life of my life reposed; before I entered the room I paused for a few seconds; for a few seconds I tried to examine my state; sickness and shuddering ever and anon came over me; my head was heavy, my chest oppressed, my legs bent under me; but I threw off resolutely the swift growing symptoms of my disorder, and met Idris with placid and even joyous looks. She was lying on a couch; carefully fastening the door to prevent all intrusion; I sat by her, we embraced, and our lips met in a kiss long drawn and breathless - would that moment had been my last!

Maternal feeling now awoke in my poor girl's bosom, and she asked: "And Alfred?"

"Idris," I replied, "we are spared to each other, we are together; do not let any other idea intrude. I am happy; even on this fatal night, I declare myself happy, beyond all name, all thought - what would you more, sweet one?"

Idris understood me: she bowed her head on my shoulder and wept. "Why," she again asked, "do you tremble, Lionel, what shakes you thus?"

"Well may I be shaken," I replied, "happy as I am. Our child is dead, and the present hour is dark and ominous. Well may I tremble! but, I am happy, mine own Idris, most happy."

"I understand thee, my kind love," said Idris, "thus - pale as thou art with sorrow at our loss; trembling and aghast, though wouldest assuage my grief by thy dear assurances. I am not happy," (and the tears flashed and fell from under her down-cast lids), "for we are inmates of a miserable prison, and there is no joy for us; but the true love I bear you will render this and every other loss endurable."

"We have been happy together, at least," I said; "no future misery can deprive us of the past. We have been true to each other for years, ever since my sweet princess-love came through the snow to the lowly cottage of the poverty-stricken heir of the ruined Verney. Even now, that eternity is before us, we take hope only from the presence of each other. Idris, do you think, that when we die, we shall be divided?"

"Die! when we die! what mean you? What secret lies hid from me in those dreadful words?"

"Must we not all die, dearest?" I asked with a sad smile.

"Gracious God! are you ill, Lionel, that you speak of death? My only friend, heart of my heart, speak!"

"I do not think," replied I, "that we have any of us long to live; and when the curtain drops on this mortal scene, where, think you, we shall find ourselves?" Idris was calmed by my unembarrassed tone and look; she answered: -"You may easily believe that during this long progress of the plague, I have thought much on death, and asked myself, now that all mankind is dead to this life, to what other life they may have been borne. Hour after hour, I have dwelt on these thoughts, and strove to form a rational conclusion concerning the mystery of a future state. What a scare-crow, indeed, would death be, if we were merely to cast aside the shadow in which we now walk, and, stepping forth into the unclouded sunshine of knowledge and love, revived with the same companions, the same affections, and reached the fulfilment of our hopes, leaving our fears with our earthly vesture in the grave. Alas! the same strong feeling which makes me sure that I shall not wholly die, makes me refuse to believe that I shall live wholly as I do now. Yet, Lionel, never, never, can I love any but you; through eternity I must desire your society; and, as I am innocent of harm to others, and as relying and confident as my mortal nature permits, I trust that the Ruler of the world will never tear us asunder."

"Your remarks are like yourself, dear love," replied I, "gentle and good; let us cherish such a belief and dismiss anxiety from our minds. But, sweet, we are so formed, (and there is no sin, if God made our nature, to yield to what he ordains), we are so formed, that we must love life, and cling to it; we must love the living smile, the sympathetic touch, and thrilling voice, peculiar to our mortal mechanism. Let us not, through security in hereafter, neglect the present. This present moment, short as it is, is a part of eternity, and the dearest part, since it is our own unalienably. Thou, the hope of my futurity, art my present joy. Let me then look on thy dear eyes, and, reading love in them, drink intoxicating pleasure."

Timidly, for my vehemence somewhat terrified her, Idris looked on me. My eyes were bloodshot, starting from my head; every artery beat, methought, audibly, every muscle throbbed, each single nerve felt. Her look of wild affright told me, that I could no longer keep my secret: -"So it is, mine own beloved," I said, "the last hour of many happy ones is arrived, nor can we shun any longer the inevitable destiny. I cannot live long - but, again and again, I say, this moment is ours!"

Paler than marble, with white lips and convulsed features, Idris became aware of my situation. My arm, as I sat, encircled her waist. She felt the palm burn with fever, even on the heart it pressed: -"One moment," she murmured, scarce audibly, "only one moment."

She kneeled, and hiding her face in her hands, uttered a brief, but earnest prayer, that she might fulfil her duty, and watch over me to the last. While there was hope, the agony had been unendurable; - all was now concluded; her feelings became solemn and calm. Even as Epicharis, unperturbed and firm, submitted to the instruments of torture, did Idris, suppressing every sigh and sign of grief, enter upon the endurance of torments, of which the rack and the wheel are but faint and metaphysical symbols.

I was changed; the tight-drawn cord that sounded so harshly was loosened, the moment that Idris participated in my knowledge of our real situation. The perturbed and passion-tossed waves of thought subsided, leaving only the heavy swell that kept right on without any outward manifestation of its disturbance, till it should break on the remote shore towards which I rapidly advanced:

-"It is true that I am sick," I said, "and your society, my Idris is my only medicine; come, and sit beside me."

She made me lie down on the couch, and, drawing a low ottoman near, sat close to my pillow, pressing my burning hands in her cold palms. She yielded to my feverish restlessness, and let me talk, and talked to me, on subjects strange indeed to beings, who thus looked the last, and heard the last, of what they loved alone in the world. We talked of times gone by; of the happy period of our early love; of Raymond, Perdita, and Evadne. We talked of what might arise on this desert earth, if, two or three being saved, it was slowly re-peopled. - We talked of what was beyond the tomb; and, man in his human shape being nearly extinct, we felt with certainty of faith, that other spirits, other minds, other perceptive beings, sightless to us, must people with thought and love this beauteous and imperishable universe.

We talked - I know not how long - but, in the morning I awoke from a painful heavy slumber; the pale cheek of Idris rested on my pillow; the large orbs of her eyes half raised the lids, and shewed the deep blue lights beneath; her lips were unclosed, and the slight murmurs they formed told that, even while asleep, she suffered. "If she were dead," I thought, "what difference? now that form is the temple of a residing deity; those eyes are the windows of her soul; all grace, love, and intelligence are enthroned on that lovely bosom - were she dead, where would this mind, the dearer half of mine, be? For quickly the fair proportion of this edifice would be more defaced, than are the sand-choked ruins of the desert temples of Palmyra."

CHAPTER III

Idris stirred and awoke; alas! she awoke to misery. She saw the signs of disease on my countenance and wondered how she could permit the long night to pass without her having sought, not cure, that was impossible, but alleviation to my sufferings. She called Adrian; my couch was quickly surrounded by friends and assistants, and such medicines as were judged fitting were administered. It was the peculiar and dreadful distinction of our visitation, that none who had been attacked by the pestilence had recovered. The first symptom of the disease was the death-warrant, which in no single instance had been followed by pardon or reprieve. No gleam of hope therefore cheered my friends.

While fever producing torpor, heavy pains, sitting like lead on my limbs, and making my breast heave, were upon me; I continued insensible to everything but pain, and at last even to that. I awoke on the fourth morning as from a dreamless sleep. An irritating sense of thirst, and, when I strove to speak or move, an entire dereliction of power, was all I felt.

For three days and nights Idris had not moved from my side. She administered to all my wants, and never slept nor rested. She did not hope; and therefore, she neither endeavored to read the physician's countenance, nor to watch for symptoms of recovery. All her thought was to attend on me to the last, and then to lie down and die beside me. On the third night animation was suspended; to the eye and touch of all I was dead. With earnest prayer, almost with force, Adrian tried to draw Idris from me. He exhausted every adjuration, her child's welfare and his own. She shook her head, and wiped a stealing tear from her sunk cheek, but would not yield; she entreated to be allowed to watch me that one night only, with such affliction and meek earnestness, that she gained her point, and sat silent and motionless, except when, stung by intolerable remembrance, she kissed my closed eyes and pallid lips, and pressed my stiffening hands to her beating heart.

At dead of night, when, though it was mid-winter, the cock crowed at three o'clock, as herald of the morning change, while hanging over me, and mourning in silent, bitter thought for the loss of all of love towards her that had been enshrined in my heart; her disheveled hair hung over her face, and the long tresses fell on the bed; she saw one ringlet in motion, and the scattered hair slightly stirred, as by a breath. It is not so, she thought, for he will never breathe more. Several times the same thing occurred, and she only marked it by the same reflection; till the whole ringlet waved back, and she thought she saw my breast heave. Her first emotion was deadly fear, cold dew stood on her brow; my eyes half opened; and, re-assured, she would have exclaimed, "He lives!" but the words were choked by a spasm, and she fell with a groan on the floor.

Adrian was in the chamber. After long watching, he had unwillingly fallen into a sleep. He started up, and beheld his sister senseless on the earth, weltering in a stream of blood that gushed from her mouth. Increasing signs of life in me in some degree explained her state; the surprise, the burst of joy, the revulsion of every sentiment, had been too much for her frame, worn by long months of care, late shattered by every species of woe and toil. She was now in far greater danger than I, the wheels and springs of my life, once again set in motion, acquired elasticity from their short suspension. For a long time, no one believed that I should indeed continue to live; during the reign of the plague upon earth, not one person, attacked by the grim disease, had recovered. My restoration was looked on as a deception; every moment it was expected that the evil symptoms would recur with redoubled violence, until confirmed convalescence, absence of all fever or pain, and increasing strength, brought slow conviction that I had recovered from the plague.

The restoration of Idris was more problematical. When I had been attacked by illness, her cheeks were sunk, her form emaciated; but now, the vessel, which had broken from the effects of extreme agitation, did not entirely heal, but was as a channel that drop by drop drew from her the ruddy stream that vivified her heart. Her hollow eyes and worn countenance had a ghastly appearance; her cheekbones, her open fair brow, the projection of the mouth, stood fearfully prominent; you might tell each bone in the thin anatomy of her frame. Her hand hung powerless; each joint lay bare, so that the light penetrated through and through. It was strange that life could exist in what was wasted and worn into a very type of death.

To take her from these heart-breaking scenes, to lead her to forget the world's desolation in the variety of objects presented by travelling, and to nurse her failing strength in the mild climate towards which we had resolved to journey, was my last hope for her preservation. The preparations for our departure, which had been suspended during my illness, were renewed. I did not revive to doubtful convalescence; health spent her treasures upon me; as the tree in spring may feel from its wrinkled limbs the fresh green break forth, and the living sap rise and circulate, so did the renewed vigor of my frame, the cheerful current of my blood, the new-born elasticity of my limbs, influence my mind to cheerful endurance and pleasurable thoughts. My body, late the heavy weight that bound me to the tomb, was exuberant with health; mere common exercises were insufficient for my reviving strength; methought I could emulate the speed of the race-horse, discern through the air objects at a blinding distance, hear the operations of nature in her mute abodes; my senses had become so refined and susceptible after my recovery from mortal disease.

Hope, among my other blessings, was not denied to me; and I did fondly trust that my unwearied attentions would restore my adored girl. I was therefore eager to forward our preparations. According to the plan first laid down, we were to have quitted London on the twenty-fifth of November; and, in pursuance of this scheme, two-thirds of our people - the people - all that remained of England, had gone forward, and had already been some weeks in Paris. First my illness, and subsequently that of Idris, had detained Adrian with his division, which consisted of three hundred persons, so that we now departed on the first of January 2098. It was my wish to keep Idris as distant as possible from the hurry and clamor of the crowd, and to hide from her those appearances that would remind her most forcibly of our real situation. We separated ourselves to a great degree from Adrian, who was obliged to give his whole time to public business. The Countess of Windsor travelled with her son. Clara, Evelyn, and a female who acted as our attendant, were the only persons with whom we had contact. We occupied a commodious carriage, our servant officiated as coachman. A party of about twenty persons preceded us at a small distance. They had it in charge to prepare our halting places and our nightly abode. They had been selected for this service out of a great number that offered, on account of the superior sagacity of the man who had been appointed their leader.

Immediately on our departure, I was delighted to find a change in Idris, which I fondly hoped prognosticated the happiest results. All the cheerfulness and gentle gaiety natural to her revived. She was weak, and this alteration was rather displayed in looks and voice than in acts; but it was permanent and real. My recovery from the plague and confirmed health instilled into her a firm belief that I was now secure from this dread enemy. She told me that she was sure she should recover. That she had a presentiment, that the tide of calamity which deluged our unhappy race had now turned. That the remnant would be preserved, and among them the dear objects of her tender affection; and that in some selected spot we should wear out our lives together in pleasant society. "Do not let my state of feebleness deceive you," she said; "I feel that I am better; there is a quick life within me, and a spirit of anticipation that assures me, that I shall continue long to make a part of this world. I shall throw off this degrading weakness of body, which infects even my mind with debility, and I shall enter again on the performance of my duties. I was sorry to leave Windsor: but now I am weaned from this local attachment; I am content to remove to a mild climate, which will complete my recovery. Trust me, dearest, I shall neither leave you, nor my brother, nor these dear children; my firm determination to remain with you to the last, and to continue to contribute to your happiness and welfare, would keep me alive, even if grim death were nearer at hand than he really is."

I was only half re-assured by these expressions; I could not believe that the over-quick flow of her blood was a sign of health, or that her burning cheeks denoted convalescence. But I had no fears of an immediate catastrophe; nay, I persuaded myself that she would ultimately recover. And thus, cheerfulness reigned in our little society. Idris conversed with animation on a thousand topics. Her chief desire was to lead our thoughts from melancholy reflections; so she drew charming pictures of a tranquil solitude, of a beauteous retreat, of the simple manners of our little tribe, and of the patriarchal brotherhood of love, which would survive the ruins of the populous nations which had lately existed. We shut out from our thoughts the present and withdrew our eyes from the dreary landscape we traversed. Winter reigned in all its gloom. The leafless trees lay without motion against the dun sky; the forms of frost, mimicking the foliage of summer, strewed the ground; the paths were overgrown; the unploughed cornfields were patched with grass and weeds; the sheep congregated at the threshold of the cottage, the horned ox thrust his head from the window. The wind was bleak, and frequent sleet or snowstorms, added to the melancholy appearance wintry nature assumed.

We arrived at Rochester, and an accident caused us to be detained there a day. During that time, a circumstance occurred that changed our plans, and which, alas! in its result changed the eternal course of events, turning me from the pleasant new sprung hope I enjoyed, to an obscure and gloomy desert. But I must give some little explanation before I proceed with the final cause of our temporary alteration of plan and refer again to those times when man walked the earth fearless, before Plague had become Queen of the World.

There resided a family in the neighborhood of Windsor, of very humble pretensions, but which had been an object of interest to us on account of one of the persons of whom it was composed. The family of the Claytons had known better days; but, after a series of reverses, the father died a bankrupt, and the mother heartbroken, and a confirmed invalid, retired with her five children to a little cottage between Eton and Salt Hill. The eldest of these children, who was thirteen years old, seemed at once from the influence of adversity, to acquire the sagacity and principle belonging to a more mature age. Her mother grew worse and worse in health, but Lucy attended on her, and was as a tender parent to her younger brothers and sisters, and in the meantime shewed herself so good-humored, social, and benevolent, that she was beloved as well as honored, in her little neighborhood.

Lucy was besides extremely pretty; so, when she grew to be sixteen, it was to be supposed, notwithstanding her poverty, that she should have admirers. One of these was the son of a country-curate; he was a generous, frank-hearted youth, with an ardent love of knowledge, and no mean acquirements. Though Lucy was untaught, her mother's conversation and manners gave her a taste for refinements superior to her present situation. She loved the youth even without knowing it, except that in any difficulty she naturally turned to him for aid, and awoke with a lighter heart every Sunday, because she knew that she would be met and accompanied by him in her evening walk with her sisters. She had another admirer, one of the headwaiters at the inn at Salt Hill. He also was not without pretensions to urbane superiority, such as he learnt from gentlemen's servants and waiting-maids, who initiating him in all the slang of high life below stairs, rendered his arrogant temper ten times more intrusive. Lucy did not disclaim him - she was incapable of that feeling; but she was sorry when she saw him approach, and quietly resisted all his endeavors to establish an intimacy. The fellow soon discovered that his rival was preferred to him; and this changed what was at first a chance admiration into a passion, whose main springs were envy, and a base desire to deprive his competitor of the advantage he enjoyed over himself.

Poor Lucy's sad story was but a common one. Her lover's father died; and he was left destitute. He accepted the offer of a gentleman to go to India with him, feeling secure that he should soon acquire an independence, and return to claim the hand of his beloved. He became involved in the war carried on there, was taken prisoner, and years elapsed before tidings of his existence were received in his native land. In the meantime, disastrous poverty came on Lucy. Her little cottage, which stood looking from its trellice, covered with woodbine and jessamine, was burnt down; and the whole of their little property was included in the destruction. Whither betake them? By what exertion of industry could Lucy procure them another abode? Her mother nearly bed-ridden, could not survive any extreme of famine-struck poverty. At this time, her other admirer stepped forward, and renewed his offer of marriage. He had saved money and was going to set up a little inn at Datchet. There was nothing alluring to Lucy in this offer, except the home it secured to her mother; and she felt surer of this, since she was struck by the apparent generosity which occasioned the present offer. She accepted it; thus, sacrificing herself for the comfort and welfare of her parent.

It was some years after her marriage that we became acquainted with her. The accident of a storm caused us to take refuge in the inn, where we witnessed the brutal and quarrelsome behavior of her husband, and her patient endurance. Her lot was not a fortunate one. Her first lover had returned with the hope of making her his own, and met her by accident, for the first time, as the mistress of his country inn, and the wife of another. He withdrew despairingly to foreign parts; nothing went well with him; at last he enlisted, and came back again wounded and sick, and yet Lucy was debarred from nursing him. Her husband's brutal disposition was aggravated by his yielding to the many temptations held out by his situation, and the consequent disarrangement of his affairs. Fortunately she had no children; but her heart was bound up in her brothers and sisters, and these his avarice and ill temper soon drove from the house; they were dispersed about the country, earning their livelihood with toil and care. He even shewed an inclination to get rid of her mother - but Lucy was firm here - she had sacrificed herself for her; she lived for her - she would not part with her - if the mother went, she would also go beg bread for her, die with her, but never desert her. The presence of Lucy was too necessary in keeping up the order of the house, and in preventing the whole establishment from going to wreck, for him to permit her to leave him. He yielded the point; but in all accesses of anger, or in his drunken fits, he recurred to the old topic, and stung poor Lucy's heart by opprobrious epithets bestowed on her parent.

A passion however, if it be wholly pure, entire, and reciprocal, brings with it its own solace. Lucy was truly, and from the depth of heart, devoted to her mother; the sole end she proposed to herself in life, was the comfort and preservation of this parent. Though she grieved for the result, yet she did not repent of her marriage, even when her lover returned to bestow competence on her. Three years had intervened, and how, in their penniless state, could her mother have existed during this time? This excellent woman was worthy of her child's devotion. A perfect confidence and friendship existed between them; besides, she was by no means illiterate; and Lucy, whose mind had been in some degree cultivated by her former lover, now found in her the only person who could understand and appreciate her. Thus, though suffering, she was by no means desolate, and when, during fine summer days, she led her mother into the flowery and shady lanes near their abode, a gleam of unmixed joy enlightened her countenance; she saw that her parent was happy, and she knew that this happiness was of her sole creating.

Meanwhile her husband's affairs grew more and more involved; ruin was near at hand, and she was about to lose the fruit of all her labors, when pestilence came to change the aspect of the world. Her husband reaped benefit from the universal misery; but, as the disaster increased, the spirit of lawlessness seized him; he deserted his home to revel in the luxuries promised him in London and found there a grave. Her former lover had been one of the first victims of the disease. But Lucy continued to live for and in her mother. Her courage only failed when she dreaded peril for her parent or feared that death might prevent her from performing those duties to which she was unalterably devoted.

When we had quitted Windsor for London, as the previous step to our final emigration, we visited Lucy, and arranged with her the plan of her own and her mother's removal. Lucy was sorry at the necessity which forced her to quit her native lanes and village, and to drag an infirm parent from her comforts at home, to the homeless waste of depopulate earth; but she was too well disciplined by adversity, and of too sweet a temper, to indulge in repining's at what was inevitable. Subsequent circumstances, my illness and that of Idris, drove her from our remembrance; and we called her to mind at last, only to conclude that she made one of the few who came from Windsor to join the emigrants, and that she was already in Paris. When we arrived at Rochester therefore, we were surprised to receive, by a man just come from Slough, a letter from this exemplary sufferer. His account was, that, journeying from his home, and passing through Datchet, he was surprised to see smoke issue from the chimney of the inn, and supposing that he should find comrades for his journey assembled there, he knocked and was admitted. There was no one in the house but Lucy, and her mother; the latter had been deprived of the use of her limbs by an attack of rheumatism, and so, one by one, all the remaining inhabitants of the country set forward, leaving them alone. Lucy intreated the man to stay with her; in a week or two her mother would be better, and they would then set out; but they must perish, if they were left thus helpless and forlorn. The man said that his wife and children were already among the emigrants, and it was therefore, according to his notion, impossible for him to remain. Lucy, as a last resource, gave him a letter for Idris, to be delivered to her wherever he should meet us. This commission at least he fulfilled, and Idris received with emotion the following letter:

HONOURED LADY,

I am sure that you will remember and pity me, and I dare hope that you will assist me; what other hope have I? Pardon my manner of writing, I am so bewildered. A month ago, my dear mother was deprived of the use of her limbs. She is already better, and in another month would I am sure be able to travel, in the way you were so kind as to say you would arrange for us. But now everybody is gone – everybody - as they went away, each said, that perhaps my mother would be better, before we were quite deserted. But three days ago I went to Samuel Woods, who, on account of his new-born child, remained to the last; and there being a large family of them, I thought I could persuade them to wait a little longer for us; but I found the house deserted. I have not seen a soul since, till this good man came. - What will become of us? My mother does not know our state; she is so ill, that I have hidden it from her.

Will you not send someone to us? I am sure we must perish miserably as we are. If I were to try to move my mother now, she would die on the road; and if, when she gets better, I were able, I cannot guess how, to find out the roads, and get on so many many miles to the sea, you would all be in France, and the great ocean would be between us, which is so terrible even to sailors. What would it be to me, a woman, who never saw it? We should be imprisoned by it in this country, all, all alone, with no help; better die where we are. I can hardly write - I cannot stop my tears - it is not for myself; I could put my trust in God; and let the worst come, I think I could bear it, if I were alone. But my mother, my sick, my dear, dear mother, who never, since I was born, spoke a harsh word to me, who has been patient in many sufferings; pity her, dear Lady, she must die a miserable death if you do not pity her. People speak carelessly of her, because she is old and infirm, as if we must not all, if we are spared, become so; and then, when the young are old themselves, they will think that they ought to be taken care of. It is very silly of me to write in this way to you; but, when I hear her *trying not to groan, and see her look smiling on me to comfort me, when I know she is in pain; and when I think that she does not know the worst, but she soon must; and then she will not complain; but I shall sit guessing at all that she is dwelling upon, of famine and misery - I feel as if my heart must break, and I do not know what I say or do; my mother - mother for whom I have borne much, God preserve you from this fate! Preserve her, Lady, and He will bless you; and I, poor miserable creature as I am, will thank you and pray for you while I live.*

Your unhappy and dutiful servant,

Dec. 30th, 2097. LUCY MARTIN.

This letter deeply affected Idris, and she instantly proposed, that we should return to Datchet, to assist Lucy and her mother. I said that I would without delay set out for that place, but entreated her to join her brother, and there await my return with the children. But Idris was in high spirits, and full of hope. She declared that she could not consent even to a temporary separation from me, but that there was no need of this, the motion of the carriage did her good, and the distance was too trifling to be considered. We could dispatch messengers to Adrian, to inform him of our deviation from the original plan. She spoke with vivacity, and drew a picture after her own dear heart, of the pleasure we should bestow upon Lucy, and declared, if I went, she must accompany me, and that she should very much dislike to entrust the charge of rescuing them to others, who might fulfil it with coldness or inhumanity. Lucy's life had been one act of devotion and virtue; let her now reap the small reward of finding her excellence appreciated, and her necessity assisted, by those whom she respected and honored.

These, and many other arguments, were urged with gentle pertinacity, and the ardor of a wish to do all the good in her power, by her whose simple expression of a desire and slightest request had ever been a law with me. I, of course, consented, the moment that I saw that she had set her heart upon this step. We sent half our attendant troop on to Adrian; and with the other half our carriage took a retrograde course back to Windsor.

I wonder now how I could be so blind and senseless, as thus to risk the safety of Idris; for, if I had eyes, surely I could see the sure, though deceitful, advance of death in her burning cheek and increasing weakness. But she said she was better; and I believed her. Extinction could not be near a being, whose vivacity and intelligence hourly increased, and whose frame was endowed with an intense, and I fondly thought, a strong and permanent spirit of life. Who, after a great disaster, has not looked back with wonder at his inconceivable obtuseness of understanding, that could not perceive the many minute threads with which fate weaves the inextricable net of our destinies, until he is enmeshed completely in it? The crossroads which we now entered upon, were even in a worse state than the long-neglected highways; and the inconvenience seemed to menace the perishing frame of Idris with destruction. Passing through Dartford, we arrived at Hampton on the second day. Even in this short interval my beloved companion grew sensibly worse in health, though her spirits were still light, and she cheered my growing anxiety with gay sallies; sometimes the thought pierced my brain - is she dying? - as I saw her fair fleshless hand rest on mine, or observed the feebleness with which she performed the accustomed acts of life. I drove away the idea, as if it had been suggested by insanity; but it occurred again and again, only to be dispelled by the continued liveliness of her manner.

About mid-day, after quitting Hampton, our carriage broke down: the shock caused Idris to faint, but on her reviving no other ill consequence ensued; our party of attendants had as usual gone on before us, and our coachman went in search of another vehicle, our former one being rendered by this accident unfit for service. The only place near us was a poor village, in which he found a kind of caravan, able to hold four people, but it was clumsy and ill hung; besides this he found a very excellent cabriolet: our plan was soon arranged; I would drive Idris in the latter; while the children were conveyed by the servant in the former. But these arrangements cost time; we had agreed to proceed that night to Windsor, and thither our purveyors had gone: we should find considerable difficulty in getting accommodation, before we reached this place; after all, the distance was only ten miles; my horse was a good one; I would go forward at a good pace with Idris, leaving the children to follow at a rate more consonant to the uses of their cumbrous machine.

Evening closed in quickly, far more quickly than I was prepared to expect. At the going down of the sun it began to snow heavily. I attempted in vain to defend my beloved companion from the storm; the wind drove the snow in our faces; and it lay so high on the ground, that we made but small way; while the night was so dark, that but for the white covering on the ground we should not have been able to see a yard before us. We had left our accompanying caravan far behind us; and now I perceived that the storm had made me unconsciously deviate from my intended route. I had gone some miles out of my way. My knowledge of the country enabled me to regain the right road; but, instead of going, as at first agreed upon, by a cross-road through Stanwell to Datchet, I was obliged to take the way of Egham and Bishopgate. It was certain therefore that I should not be rejoined by the other vehicle, that I should not meet a single fellow-creature till we arrived at Windsor.

The back of our carriage was drawn up, and I hung a pelisse before it, thus, to curtain the beloved sufferer from the pelting sleet. She leaned on my shoulder, growing every moment more languid and feeble; at first she replied to my words of cheer with affectionate thanks; but by degrees she sunk into silence; her head lay heavily upon me; I only knew that she lived by her irregular breathing and frequent sighs. For a moment I resolved to stop, and, opposing the back of the cabriolet to the force of the tempest, to expect morning as well as I might. But the wind was bleak and piercing, while the occasional shuddering of my poor Idris, and the intense cold I felt myself, demonstrated that this would be a dangerous experiment. At length methought she slept - fatal sleep, induced by frost: at this moment I saw the heavy outline of a cottage traced on the dark horizon close to us: "Dearest love," I said, "support yourself but one moment, and we shall have shelter; let us stop here, that I may open the door of this blessed dwelling."

As I spoke, my heart was transported, and my senses swam with excessive delight and thankfulness; I placed the head of Idris against the carriage, and, leaping out, scrambled through the snow to the cottage, whose door was open. I had apparatus about me for procuring light, and that shewed me a comfortable room, with a pile of wood in one corner, and no appearance of disorder, except that, the door having been left partly open, the snow, drifting in, had blocked up the threshold. I returned to the carriage, and the sudden change from light to darkness at first blinded me. When I recovered my sight - eternal God of this lawless world! O supreme Death! I will not disturb thy silent reign, or mar my tale with fruitless exclamations of horror - I saw Idris, who had fallen from the seat to the bottom of the carriage; her head, its long hair pendent, with one arm, hung over the side. - Struck by a spasm of horror, I lifted her up; her heart was pulseless, her faded lips unfanned by the slightest breath.

I carried her into the cottage; I placed her on the bed. Lighting a fire, I chafed her stiffening limbs; for two long hours I sought to restore departed life; and, when hope was as dead as my beloved, I closed with trembling hands her glazed eyes. I did not doubt what I should now do. In the confusion attendant on my illness, the task of interring our darling Alfred had devolved on his grandmother, the Ex-Queen, and she, true to her ruling passion, had caused him to be carried to Windsor, and buried in the family vault, in St. George's Chapel. I must proceed to Windsor, to calm the anxiety of Clara, who would wait anxiously for us - yet I would fain spare her the heart-breaking spectacle of Idris, brought in by me lifeless from the journey. So first I would place my beloved beside her child in the vault, and then seek the poor children who would be expecting me.

I lighted the lamps of my carriage; I wrapped her in furs and placed her along the seat; then taking the reins, made the horses go forward. We proceeded through the snow, which lay in masses impeding the way, while the descending flakes, driving against me with redoubled fury, blinded me. The pain occasioned by the angry elements, and the cold iron of the shafts of frost which buffeted me, and entered my aching flesh, were a relief to me, blunting my mental suffering. The horses staggered on, and the reins hung loosely in my hands. I often thought I would lay my head close to the sweet, cold face of my lost angel, and thus resign myself to conquering torpor. Yet I must not leave her a prey to the fowls of the air; but, in pursuance of my determination place her in the tomb of her forefathers, where a merciful God might permit me to rest also.

The road we passed through Egham was familiar to me; but the wind and snow caused the horses to drag their load slowly and heavily. Suddenly the wind veered from south-west to west, and then again to north-west. As Sampson with tug and strain stirred from their bases the columns that supported the Philistine temple, so did the gale shake the dense vapors propped on the horizon, while the massy dome of clouds fell to the south, disclosing through the scattered web the clear empyrean, and the little stars, which were set at an immeasurable distance in the crystalline fields, showered their small rays on the glittering snow. Even the horses were cheered and moved on with renovated strength. We entered the forest at Bishopgate, and at the end of the Long Walk I saw the Castle, "the proud Keep of Windsor, rising in the majesty of proportion, girt with the double belt of its kindred and coeval towers." I looked with reverence on a structure, ancient almost as the rock on which it stood, abode of kings, theme of admiration for the wise. With greater reverence and, tearful affection I beheld it as the asylum of the long lease of love I had enjoyed there with the perishable, unmatchable treasure of dust, which now lay cold beside me. Now indeed, I could have yielded to all the softness of my nature, and wept; and, womanlike, have uttered bitter plaints; while the familiar trees, the herds of living deer, the sward oft pressed by her fairy-feet, one by one with sad association presented themselves. The white gate at the end of the Long Walk was wide open, and I rode up the empty town through the first gate of the feudal tower; and now St. George's Chapel, with its blackened fretted sides, was right before me. I halted at its door, which was open; I entered, and placed my lighted lamp on the altar; then I returned, and with tender caution I bore Idris up the aisle into the chancel, and laid her softly down on the carpet which covered the step leading to the communion table. The banners of the knights of the garter, and their half-drawn swords, were hung in vain emblazonry above the stalls. The banner of her family hung there, still surmounted by its regal crown. Farewell to the glory and heraldry of England - I turned from such vanity with a slight feeling of wonder, at how mankind could have ever been interested in such things. I bent over the lifeless corpse of my beloved; and, while looking on her uncovered face, the features already contracted by the rigidity of death, I felt as if all the visible universe had grown as soulless, inane, and comfortless as the clay-cold image beneath me. I felt for a moment the intolerable sense of struggle with, and detestation for, the laws which govern the world; till the calm still visible on the face of my dead love recalled me to a more soothing tone of mind, and I proceeded to fulfil the last office that could now be paid her. For her I could not lament, so much I envied her enjoyment of "the sad immunities of the grave."

The vault had been lately opened to place our Alfred therein. The ceremony customary in these latter days had been cursorily performed, and the pavement of the chapel, which was its entrance, having been removed, had not been replaced. I descended the steps and walked through the long passage to the large vault which contained the kindred dust of my Idris. I distinguished the small coffin of my babe. With hasty, trembling hands I constructed a bier beside it, spreading it with the furs and Indian shawls, which had wrapped Idris in her journey thither. I lighted the glimmering lamp, which flickered in this damp abode of the dead; then I bore my lost one to her last bed, decently composing her limbs, and covering them with a mantle, veiling all except her face, which remained lovely and placid. She appeared to rest like one over-wearied, her beauteous eyes steeped in sweet slumber. Yet so it was not - she was dead! How intensely I then longed to lie down beside her, to gaze till death should gather me to the same repose.

But death does not come at the bidding of the miserable. I had lately recovered from mortal illness, and my blood had never flowed with such an even current, nor had my limbs ever been so instinct with quick life, as now. I felt that my death must be voluntary. Yet what more natural than famine, as I watched in this chamber of mortality, placed in a world of the dead, beside the lost hope of my life? Meanwhile as I looked on her, the features, which bore a sisterly resemblance to Adrian, brought my thoughts back again to the living, to this dear friend, to Clara, and to Evelyn, who were probably now in Windsor, waiting anxiously for our arrival.

Methought I heard a noise, a step in the far chapel, which was re-echoed by its vaulted roof, and borne to me through the hollow passages. Had Clara seen my carriage pass up the town, and did she seek me here? I must save her at least from the horrible scene the vault presented. I sprung up the steps, and then saw a female figure, bent with age, and clad in long mourning robes, advance through the dusky chapel, supported by a slender cane, yet tottering even with this support. She heard me, and looked up; the lamp I held illuminated my figure, and the moon-beams, struggling through the painted glass, fell upon her face, wrinkled and gaunt, yet with a piercing eye and commanding brow - I recognized the Countess of Windsor. With a hollow voice she asked, "Where is the princess?"

I pointed to the torn-up pavement: she walked to the spot and looked down into the palpable darkness; for the vault was too distant for the rays of the small lamp I had left there to be discernible.

"Your light," she said. I gave it her; and she regarded the now visible, but precipitous steps, as if calculating her capacity to descend. Instinctively I made a silent offer of my assistance. She motioned me away with a look of scorn, saying in a harsh voice, as she pointed downwards, "There at least I may have her undisturbed."

She walked deliberately down, while I, overcome, miserable beyond words, or tears, or groans, threw myself on the pavement near - the stiffening form of Idris was before me, the death-struck countenance hushed in eternal repose beneath. That was to me the end of all! The day before, I had figured to myself various adventures, and communion with my friends in after time - now I had leapt the interval and reached the utmost edge and borne of life. Thus wrapped in gloom, enclosed, walled up, vaulted over by the omnipotent present, I was startled by the sound of feet on the steps of the tomb, and I remembered her whom I had utterly forgotten, my angry visitant; her tall form slowly rose upwards from the vault, a living statue, instinct with hate, and human, passionate strife: she seemed to me as having reached the pavement of the aisle; she stood motionless, seeking with her eyes alone, some desired object - till, perceiving me close to her, she placed her wrinkled hand on my arm, exclaiming with tremulous accents, "Lionel Verney, my son!" This name, applied at such a moment by my angel's mother, instilled into me more respect than I had ever before felt for this disdainful lady. I bowed my head, and kissed her shriveled hand, and, remarking that she trembled violently, supported her to the end of the chancel, where she sat on the steps that led to the regal stall. She suffered herself to be led, and still holding my hand, she leaned her head back against the stall, while the moon beams, tinged with various colors by the painted glass, fell on her glistening eyes; aware of her weakness, again calling to mind her long cherished dignity, she dashed the tears away; yet they fell fast, as she said, for excuse, "She is so beautiful and placid, even in death. No harsh feeling ever clouded her serene brow; how did I treat her? wounding her gentle heart with savage coldness; I had no compassion on her in past years, does she forgive me now? Little, little does it boot to talk of repentance and forgiveness to the dead, had I during her life once consulted her gentle wishes, and curbed my rugged nature to do her pleasure, I should not feel thus."

Idris and her mother were unlike in person. The dark hair, deep-set black eyes, and prominent features of the Ex-Queen were in entire contrast to the golden tresses, the full blue orbs, and the soft lines and contour of her daughter's countenance. Yet, in latter days, illness had taken from my poor girl the full outline of her face and reduced it to the inflexible shape of the bone beneath. In the form of her brow, in her oval chin, there was to be found a resemblance to her mother; nay in some moods, their gestures were not unlike; nor, having lived so long together, was this wonderful.

There is a magic power in resemblance. When one we love dies, we hope to see them in another state, and half expect that the agency of mind will inform its new garb in imitation of its decayed earthly vesture. But these are ideas of the mind only. We know that the instrument is shivered, the sensible image lies in miserable fragments, dissolved to dusty nothingness; a look, a gesture, or a fashioning of the limbs similar to the dead in a living person, touches a thrilling chord, whose sacred harmony is felt in the heart's dearest recess. Strangely moved, prostrate before this spectral image, and enslaved by the force of blood manifested in likeness of look and movement, I remained trembling in the presence of the harsh, proud, and till now unloved mother of Idris.

Poor, mistaken woman! in her tenderest mood before, she had cherished the idea, that a word, a look of reconciliation from her, would be received with joy, and repay long years of severity. Now that the time was gone for the exercise of such power, she fell at once upon the thorny truth of things, and felt that neither smile nor caress could penetrate to the unconscious state, or influence the happiness of her who lay in the vault beneath. This conviction, together with the remembrance of soft replies to bitter speeches, of gentle looks repaying angry glances; the perception of the falsehood, paltriness and futility of her cherished dreams of birth and power; the overpowering knowledge, that love and life were the true emperors of our mortal state; all, as a tide, rose, and filled her soul with stormy and bewildering confusion. It fell to my lot, to come as the influential power, to allay the fierce tossing of these tumultuous waves. I spoke to her; I led her to reflect how happy Idris had really been, and how her virtues and numerous excellencies had found scope and estimation in her past career. I praised her, the idol of my heart's dear worship, the admired type of feminine perfection. With ardent and overflowing eloquence, I relieved my heart from its burthen, and awoke to the sense of a new pleasure in life, as I poured forth the funeral eulogy. Then I referred to Adrian, her loved brother, and to her surviving child. I declared, which I had before almost forgotten, what my duties were with regard to these valued portions of herself, and bade the melancholy repentant mother reflect, how she could best expiate unkindness towards the dead, by redoubled love of the survivors. Consoling her, my own sorrows were assuaged; my sincerity won her entire conviction.

She turned to me. The hard, inflexible, persecuting woman, turned with a mild expression of face, and said, "If our beloved angel sees us now, it will delight her to find that I do you even tardy justice. You were worthy of her; and from my heart I am glad that you won her away from me. Pardon, my son, the many wrongs I have done you; forget my bitter words and unkind treatment - take me and govern me as you will."

I seized this docile moment to propose our departure from the church.

"First," she said, "let us replace the pavement above the vault."

We drew near to it; "Shall we look on her again?" I asked.

"I cannot," she replied, "and I pray you, neither do you. We need not torture ourselves by gazing on the soulless body, while her living spirit is buried quick in our hearts, and her surpassing loveliness is so deeply carved there, that sleeping or waking she must ever be present to us."

For a few moments, we bent in solemn silence over the open vault. I consecrated my future life, to the embalming of her dear memory; I vowed to serve her brother and her child till death. The convulsive sob of my companion made me break off my internal orisons. I next dragged the stones over the entrance of the tomb and closed the gulph that contained the life of my life. Then, supporting my decrepit fellow-mourner, we slowly left the chapel. I felt, as I stepped into the open air, as if I had quitted a happy nest of repose, for a dreary wilderness, a tortuous path, a bitter, joyless, hopeless pilgrimage.

CHAPTER IV

Our escort had been directed to prepare our abode for the night at the inn, opposite the ascent to the Castle. We could not again visit the halls and familiar chambers of our home, on a mere visit. We had already left for ever the glades of Windsor, and all of coppice, flowery hedgerow, and murmuring stream, which gave shape and intensity to the love of our country, and the almost superstitious attachment with which we regarded native England. It had been our intention to have called at Lucy's dwelling in Datchet, and to have re-assured her with promises of aid and protection before we repaired to our quarters for the night. Now, as the Countess of Windsor and I turned down the steep hill that led from the Castle, we saw the children, who had just stopped in their caravan, at the inn-door. They had passed through Datchet without halting. I dreaded to meet them, and to be the bearer of my tragic story, so while they were still occupied in the hurry of arrival, I suddenly left them, and through the snow and clear moon-light air, hastened along the well-known road to Datchet.

Well known indeed it was. Each cottage stood on its accustomed site; each tree wore its familiar appearance. Habit had gravened uneraseably on my memory, every turn and change of object on the road. At a short distance beyond the Little Park, was an elm half blown down by a storm, some ten years ago; and still, with leafless snow-laden branches, it stretched across the pathway, which wound through a meadow, beside a shallow brook, whose brawling was silenced by frost - that stile, that white gate, that hollow oak tree, which doubtless once belonged to the forest, and which now shewed in the moonlight its gaping rent; to whose fanciful appearance, tricked out by the dusk into a resemblance of the human form, the children had given the name of Falstaff; - all these objects were as well known to me as the cold hearth of my deserted home, and every moss-grown wall and plot of orchard ground, alike as twin lambs are to each other in a stranger's eye, yet to my accustomed gaze bore differences, distinction, and a name. England remained, though England was dead - it was the ghost of merry England that I beheld, under those greenwood shade passing generations had sported in security and ease. To this painful recognition of familiar places, was added a feeling experienced by all, understood by none - a feeling as if in some state, less visionary than a dream, in some past real existence, I had seen all I saw, with precisely the same feelings as I now beheld them - as if all my sensations were a duplex mirror of a former revelation. To get rid of this oppressive sense I strove to imagine change in this tranquil spot - this augmented my mood, by causing me to bestow more attention on the objects which occasioned me pain.

I reached Datchet and Lucy's humble abode - once noisy with Saturday night revelers, or trim and neat on Sunday morning it had borne testimony to the labors and orderly habits of the housewife. The snow lay high about the door, as if it had remained unclosed for many days.

"What scene of death hath Roscius now to act?" I muttered to myself as I looked at the dark casements. At first I thought I saw a light in one of them, but it proved to be merely the refraction of the moon-beams, while the only sound was the crackling branches as the breeze whirred the snowflakes from them - the moon sailed high and unclouded in the interminable ether, while the shadow of the cottage lay black on the garden behind. I entered this by the open wicket, and anxiously examined each window. At length I detected a ray of light struggling through a closed shutter in one of the upper rooms - it was a novel feeling, alas! to look at any house and say there dwells its usual inmate - the door of the house was merely on the latch: so I entered and ascended the moon-lit staircase. The door of the inhabited room was ajar: looking in, I saw Lucy sitting as at work at the table on which the light stood; the implements of needlework were about her, but her hand had fallen on her lap, and her eyes, fixed on the ground, shewed by their vacancy that her thoughts wandered. Traces of care and watching had diminished her former attractions - but her simple dress and cap, her desponding attitude, and the single candle that cast its light upon her, gave for a moment a picturesque grouping to the whole. A fearful reality recalled me from the thought - a figure lay stretched on the bed covered by a sheet - her mother was dead, and Lucy, apart from all the world, deserted and alone, watched beside the corpse during the weary night. I entered the room, and my unexpected appearance at first drew a scream from the lone survivor of a dead nation; but she recognized me, and recovered herself, with the quick exercise of self-control habitual to her. "Did you not expect me?" I asked, in that low voice which the presence of the dead makes us as it were instinctively assume.

"You are very good," replied she, "to have come yourself; I can never thank you sufficiently; but it is too late."

"Too late," cried I, "what do you mean? It is not too late to take you from this deserted place, and conduct you to -"

My own loss, which I had forgotten as I spoke, now made me turn away, while choking grief impeded my speech. I threw open the window, and looked on the cold, waning, ghastly, misshaped circle on high, and the chill white earth beneath - did the spirit of sweet Idris sail along the moon-frozen crystal air? - No, no, a more genial atmosphere, a lovelier habitation was surely hers!

I indulged in this meditation for a moment, and then again addressed the mourner, who stood leaning against the bed with that expression of resigned despair, of complete misery, and a patient sufferance of it, which is far more touching than any of the insane ravings or wild gesticulation of untamed sorrow. I desired to draw her from this spot; but she opposed my wish. That class of persons whose imagination and sensibility have never been taken out of the narrow circle immediately in view, if they possess these qualities to any extent, are apt to pour their influence into the very realities which appear to destroy them, and to cling to these with double tenacity from not being able to comprehend anything beyond. Thus Lucy, in desert England, in a dead world, wished to fulfil the usual ceremonies of the dead, such as were customary to the English country people, when death was a rare visitant, and gave us time to receive his dreaded usurpation with pomp and circumstance - going forth in procession to deliver the keys of the tomb into his conquering hand. She had already, alone as she was, accomplished some of these, and the work on which I found her employed, was her mother's shroud. My heart sickened at such detail of woe, which a female can endure, but which is more painful to the masculine spirit than deadliest struggle, or throes of unutterable but transient agony.

This must not be, I told her; and then, as further inducement, I communicated to her my recent loss, and gave her the idea that she must come with me to take charge of the orphan children, whom the death of Idris had deprived of a mother's care. Lucy never resisted the call of a duty, so she yielded, and closing the casements and doors with care, she accompanied me back to Windsor. As we went, she communicated to me the occasion of her mother's death. Either by some mischance she had got sight of Lucy's letter to Idris, or she had overheard her conversation with the countryman who bore it; however it might be, she obtained a knowledge of the appalling situation of herself and her daughter, her aged frame could not sustain the anxiety and horror this discovery instilled - she concealed her knowledge from Lucy, but brooded over it through sleepless nights, till fever and delirium, swift forerunners of death, disclosed the secret. Her life, which had long been hovering on its extinction, now yielded at once to the united effects of misery and sickness, and that same morning she had died.

After the tumultuous emotions of the day, I was glad to find on my arrival at the inn that my companions had retired to rest. I gave Lucy in charge to the Countess's attendant, and then sought repose from my various struggles and impatient regrets. For a few moments the events of the day floated in disastrous pageant through my brain, till sleep bathed it in forgetfulness; when morning dawned and I awoke, it seemed as if my slumber had endured for years.

My companions had not shared my oblivion. Clara's swollen eyes shewed that she has passed the night in weeping. The Countess looked haggard and wan. Her firm spirit had not found relief in tears, and she suffered the more from all the painful retrospect and agonizing regret that now occupied her. We departed from Windsor, as soon as the burial rites had been performed for Lucy's mother, and, urged on by an impatient desire to change the scene, went forward towards Dover with speed, our escort having gone before to provide horses; finding them either in the warm stables they instinctively sought during the cold weather, or standing shivering in the bleak fields ready to surrender their liberty in exchange for offered corn.

During our ride the Countess recounted to me the extraordinary circumstances which had brought her so strangely to my side in the chancel of St. George's chapel. When last she had taken leave of Idris, as she looked anxiously on her faded person and pallid countenance, she had suddenly been visited by a conviction that she saw her for the last time. It was hard to part with her while under the dominion of this sentiment, and for the last time she endeavored to persuade her daughter to commit herself to her nursing, permitting me to join Adrian. Idris mildly refused, and thus they separated. The idea that they should never again meet grew on the Countess's mind, and haunted her perpetually; a thousand times she had resolved to turn back and join us, and was again and again restrained by the pride and anger of which she was the slave. Proud of heart as she was, she bathed her pillow with nightly tears, and through the day was subdued by nervous agitation and expectation of the dreaded event, which she was wholly incapable of curbing. She confessed that at this period her hatred of me knew no bounds, since she considered me as the sole obstacle to the fulfilment of her dearest wish, that of attending upon her daughter in her last moments. She desired to express her fears to her son, and to seek consolation from his sympathy with, or courage from his rejection of, her auguries.

On the first day of her arrival at Dover she walked with him on the sea beach, and with the timidity characteristic of passionate and exaggerated feeling was by degrees bringing the conversation to the desired point, when she could communicate her fears to him, when the messenger who bore my letter announcing our temporary return to Windsor, came riding down to them. He gave some oral account of how he had left us, and added, that notwithstanding the cheerfulness and good courage of Lady Idris, he was afraid that she would hardly reach Windsor alive. "True," said the Countess, "your fears are just, she is about to expire!"

As she spoke, her eyes were fixed on a tomblike hollow of the cliff, and she saw, she averred the same to me with solemnity, Idris pacing slowly towards this cave. She was turned from her, her head was bent down, her white dress was such as she was accustomed to wear, except that a thin crape-like veil covered her golden tresses and concealed her as a dim transparent mist. She looked dejected, as docilely yielding to a commanding power; she submissively entered and was lost in the dark recess.

"Were I subject to visionary moods," said the venerable lady, as she continued her narrative, "I might doubt my eyes, and condemn my credulity; but reality is the world I live in, and what I saw I doubt not had existence beyond myself. From that moment I could not rest; it was worth my existence to see her once again before she died; I knew that I should not accomplish this, yet I must endeavor. I immediately departed for Windsor; and, though I was assured that we travelled speedily, it seemed to me that our progress was snail-like, and that delays were created solely for my annoyance. Still I accused you and heaped on your head the fiery ashes of my burning impatience. It was no disappointment, though an agonizing pang, when you pointed to her last abode; and words would ill express the abhorrence I that moment felt towards you, the triumphant impediment to my dearest wishes. I saw her, and anger, and hate, and injustice died at her bier, giving place at their departure to a remorse (Great God, that I should feel it!) which must last while memory and feeling endure."

To medicine such remorse, to prevent awakening love and new-born mildness from producing the same bitter fruit that hate and harshness had done, I devoted all my endeavors to soothe the venerable penitent. Our party was a melancholy one; each was possessed by regret for what was remediless; for the absence of his mother shadowed even the infant gaiety of Evelyn. Added to this was the prospect of the uncertain future. Before the final accomplishment of any great voluntary change the mind vacillates, now soothing itself by fervent expectation, now recoiling from obstacles which seem never to have presented themselves before with so frightful an aspect. An involuntary tremor ran through me when I thought that in another day we might have crossed the watery barrier, and have set forward on that hopeless, interminable, sad wandering, which but a short time before I regarded as the only relief to sorrow that our situation afforded.

Our approach to Dover was announced by the loud roaring of the wintry sea. They were borne miles inland by the sound-laden blast, and by their unaccustomed uproar, imparted a feeling of insecurity and peril to our stable abode. At first we hardly permitted ourselves to think that any unusual eruption of nature caused this tremendous war of air and water, but rather fancied that we merely listened to what we had heard a thousand times before, when we had watched the flocks of fleece-crowned waves, driven by the winds, come to lament and die on the barren sands and pointed rocks. But we found upon advancing farther, that Dover was overflowed - many of the houses were overthrown by the surges which filled the streets, and with hideous brawling's sometimes retreated leaving the pavement of the town bare, till again hurried forward by the influx of ocean, they returned with thunder-sound to their usurped station.

Hardly less disturbed than the tempestuous world of waters was the assembly of human beings, that from the cliff fearfully watched its ravings. On the morning of the arrival of the emigrants under the conduct of Adrian, the sea had been serene and glassy, the slight ripples refracted the sunbeams, which shed their radiance through the clear blue frosty air. This placid appearance of nature was hailed as a good augury for the voyage, and the chief immediately repaired to the harbor to examine two steamboats which were moored there. On the following midnight, when all were at rest, a frightful storm of wind and clattering rain and hail first disturbed them, and the voice of one shrieking in the streets, that the sleepers must awake or they would be drowned; and when they rushed out, half clothed, to discover the meaning of this alarm, they found that the tide, rising above every mark, was rushing into the town. They ascended the cliff, but the darkness permitted only the white crest of waves to be seen, while the roaring wind mingled its howling in dire accord with the wild surges. The awful hour of night, the utter inexperience of many who had never seen the sea before, the wailing of women and cries of children added to the horror of the tumult. All the following day the same scene continued. When the tide ebbed, the town was left dry; but on its flow, it rose even higher than on the preceding night. The vast ships that lay rotting in the roads were whirled from their anchorage, and driven and jammed against the cliff, the vessels in the harbor were flung on land like sea-weed, and there battered to pieces by the breakers. The waves dashed against the cliff, which if in any place it had been before loosened, now gave way, and the affrighted crowd saw vast fragments of the near earth fall with crash and roar into the deep. This sight operated differently on different persons. The greater part thought it a judgment of God, to prevent or punish our emigration from our native land. Many were doubly eager to quit a nook of ground now become their prison, which appeared unable to resist the inroads of ocean's giant waves.

When we arrived at Dover, after a fatiguing day's journey, we all required rest and sleep; but the scene acting around us soon drove away such ideas. We were drawn, along with the greater part of our companions, to the edge of the cliff, there to listen to and make a thousand conjectures. A fog narrowed our horizon to about a quarter of a mile, and the misty veil, cold and dense, enveloped sky and sea in equal obscurity. What added to our inquietude was the circumstance that two-thirds of our original number were now waiting for us in Paris, and clinging, as we now did most painfully, to any addition to our melancholy remnant, this division, with the tameless impassable ocean between, struck us with affright. At length, after loitering for several hours on the cliff, we retired to Dover Castle, whose roof sheltered all who breathed the English air, and sought the sleep necessary to restore strength and courage to our worn frames and languid spirits.

Early in the morning Adrian brought me the welcome intelligence that the wind had changed: it had been south-west; it was now north-east. The sky was stripped bare of clouds by the increasing gale, while the tide at its ebb seceded entirely from the town. The change of wind rather increased the fury of the sea, but it altered its late dusky hue to a bright green; and in spite of its unmitigated clamor, its more cheerful appearance instilled hope and pleasure. All day we watched the ranging of the mountainous waves, and towards sunset a desire to decipher the promise for the morrow at its setting, made us all gather with one accord on the edge of the cliff. When the mighty luminary approached within a few degrees of the tempest-tossed horizon, suddenly, a wonder! three other suns, alike burning and brilliant, rushed from various quarters of the heavens towards the great orb; they whirled round it. The glare of light was intense to our dazzled eyes; the sun itself seemed to join in the dance, while the sea burned like a furnace, like all Vesuvius a-light, with flowing lava beneath. The horses broke loose from their stalls in terror - a herd of cattle, panic struck, raced down to the brink of the cliff, and blinded by light, plunged down with frightful yells in the waves below. The time occupied by the apparition of these meteors was comparatively short; suddenly the three mock suns united in one and plunged into the sea. A few seconds afterwards, a deafening watery sound came up with awful peal from the spot where they had disappeared.

Meanwhile the sun, disencumbered from his strange satellites, paced with its accustomed majesty towards its western home. When - we dared not trust our eyes late dazzled, but it seemed that - the sea rose to meet it - it mounted higher and higher, till the fiery globe was obscured, and the wall of water still ascended the horizon; it appeared as if suddenly the motion of earth was revealed to us - as if no longer we were ruled by ancient laws, but were turned adrift in an unknown region of space. Many cried aloud, that these were no meteors, but globes of burning matter, which had set fire to the earth, and caused the vast cauldron at our feet to bubble up with its measureless waves; the day of judgment was come they averred, and a few moments would transport us before the awful countenance of the omnipotent judge; while those less given to visionary terrors, declared that two conflicting gales had occasioned the last phenomenon. In support of this opinion they pointed out the fact that the east wind died away, while the rushing of the coming west mingled its wild howl with the roar of the advancing waters. Would the cliff resist this new battery? Was not the giant wave far higher than the precipice? Would not our little island be deluged by its approach? The crowd of spectators fled. They were dispersed over the fields, stopping now and then, and looking back in terror. A sublime sense of awe calmed the swift pulsations of my heart - I awaited the approach of the destruction menaced, with that solemn resignation which an unavoidable necessity instils. The ocean every moment assumed a more terrific aspect, while the twilight was dimmed by the rack which the west wind spread over the sky. By slow degrees however, as the wave advanced, it took a more mild appearance; some undercurrent of air, or obstruction in the bed of the waters, checked its progress, and it sank gradually; while the surface of the sea became uniformly higher as it dissolved into it. This change took from us the fear of an immediate catastrophe, although we were still anxious as to the final result. We continued during the whole night to watch the fury of the sea and the pace of the driving clouds, through whose openings the rare stars rushed impetuously;

the thunder of conflicting elements deprived us of all power to sleep.

This endured ceaselessly for three days and nights. The stoutest hearts quailed before the savage enmity of nature; provisions began to fail us, though everyday foraging parties were dispersed to the nearer towns. In vain we schooled ourselves into the belief, that there was nothing out of the common order of nature in the strife we witnessed; our disastrous and overwhelming destiny turned the best of us to cowards. Death had hunted us through the course of many months, even to the narrow strip of time on which we now stood; narrow indeed, and buffeted by storms, was our footway overhanging the great sea of calamity

As an unsheltered northern shore
Is shaken by the wintry wave —
And frequent storms for evermore,
(While from the west the loud winds rave,
Or from the east, or mountains hoar)
The struck and tott'ring sandbank lave.

It required more than human energy to bear up against the menaces of destruction that everywhere surrounded us.

After the lapse of three days, the gale died away, the seagull sailed upon the calm bosom of the windless atmosphere, and the last yellow leaf on the topmost branch of the oak hung without motion. The sea no longer broke with fury; but a swell setting in steadily for shore, with long sweep and sullen burst replaced the roar of the breakers. Yet we derived hope from the change, and we did not doubt that after the interval of a few days the sea would resume its tranquility. The sunset of the fourth day favored this idea; it was clear and golden. As we gazed on the purple sea, radiant beneath, we were attracted by a novel spectacle; a dark speck - as it neared, visibly a boat - rode on the top of the waves, every now and then lost in the steep valleys between. We marked its course with eager questionings; and, when we saw that it evidently made for shore, we descended to the only practicable landing place, and hoisted a signal to direct them. By the help of glasses, we distinguished her crew; it consisted of nine men, Englishmen, belonging in truth to the two divisions of our people, who had preceded us, and had been for several weeks at Paris. As countryman was wont to meet countryman in distant lands, did we greet our visitors on their landing, with outstretched hands and gladsome welcome. They were slow to reciprocate our gratulations. They looked angry and resentful; not less than the chafed sea which they had traversed with imminent peril, though apparently more displeased with each other than with us. It was strange to see these human beings, who appeared to be given forth by the earth like rare and inestimable plants, full of towering passion, and the spirit of angry contest. Their first demand was to be conducted to the Lord Protector of England, so they called Adrian, though he had long discarded the empty title, as a bitter mockery of the shadow to which the Protectorship was now reduced. They were speedily led to Dover Castle, from whose keep Adrian had watched the movements of the boat. He received them with the interest and wonder so strange a visitation created. In the confusion occasioned by their angry demands for precedence, it was long before we could discover the secret meaning of this strange scene. By degrees, from the furious declamations of one, the fierce interruptions of another, and the bitter scoffs of a third, we found that they were deputies from our colony at Paris, from three parties there formed, who, each with angry rivalry, tried to attain a superiority over the other two. These deputies had been dispatched by them to Adrian, who had been selected arbiter; and they had journeyed from Paris to Calais, through the vacant towns and desolate country, indulging the while violent hatred against each other; and now they pleaded their several causes with unmitigated party-spirit.

By examining the deputies apart, and after much investigation, we learnt the true state of things at Paris. Since parliament had elected him Ryland's deputy, all the surviving English had submitted to Adrian. He was our captain to lead us from our native soil to unknown lands, our lawgiver and our preserver. On the first arrangement of our scheme of emigration, no continued separation of our members was contemplated, and the command of the whole body in gradual ascent of power had its apex in the Earl of Windsor. But unforeseen circumstances changed our plans for us and occasioned the greater part of our numbers to be divided for the space of nearly two months, from the supreme chief. They had gone over in two distinct bodies; and on their arrival at Paris dissension arose between them.

They had found Paris a desert. When first the plague had appeared, the return of travelers and merchants, and communications by letter, informed us regularly of the ravages made by disease on the continent. But with the increased mortality this intercourse declined and ceased. Even in England itself communication from one part of the island to the other became slow and rare. No vessel stemmed the flood that divided Calais from Dover; or if some melancholy voyager, wishing to assure himself of the life or death of his relatives, put from the French shore to return among us, often the greedy ocean swallowed his little craft, or after a day or two he was infected by the disorder, and died before he could tell the tale of the desolation of France. We were therefore to a great degree ignorant of the state of things on the continent and were not without some vague hope of finding numerous companions in its wide track. But the same causes that had so fearfully diminished the English nation had had even greater scope for mischief in the sister land. France was a blank; during the long line of road from Calais to Paris not one human being was found. In Paris there were a few, perhaps a hundred, who, resigned to their coming fate, flitted about the streets of the capital and assembled to converse of past times, with that vivacity and even gaiety that seldom deserts the individuals of this nation.

The English took uncontested possession of Paris. Its high houses and narrow streets were lifeless. A few pale figures were to be distinguished at the accustomed resort at the Tuileries; they wondered wherefore the islanders should approach their ill-fated city - for in the excess of wretchedness, the sufferers always imagine, that their part of the calamity is the bitterest, as, when enduring intense pain, we would exchange the particular torture we writhe under, for any other which should visit a different part of the frame. They listened to the account the emigrants gave of their motives for leaving their native land, with a shrug almost of disdain - "Return," they said, "return to your island, whose sea breezes, and division from the continent gives some promise of health; if Pestilence among you has slain its hundreds, with us it has slain its thousands. Are you not even now more numerous than we are? - A year ago you would have found only the sick burying the dead; now we are happier; for the pang of struggle has passed away, and the few you find here are patiently waiting the final blow. But you, who are not content to die, breathe no longer the air of France, or soon you will only be a part of her soil."

Thus, by menaces of the sword, they would have driven back those who had escaped from fire. But the peril left behind was deemed imminent by my countrymen; that before them doubtful and distant; and soon other feelings arose to obliterate fear, or to replace it by passions, that ought to have had no place among a brotherhood of unhappy survivors of the expiring world.

The more numerous divisions of emigrants, which arrived first at Paris, assumed a superiority of rank and power; the second party asserted their independence. A third was formed by a sectarian, a self-erected prophet, who, while he attributed all power and rule to God, strove to get the real command of his comrades into his own hands. This third division consisted of fewest individuals, but their purpose was more one, their obedience to their leader more entire, their fortitude and courage more unyielding and active.

During the whole progress of the plague, the teachers of religion were in possession of great power; a power of good, if rightly directed, or of incalculable mischief, if fanaticism or intolerance guided their efforts. In the present instance, a worse feeling than either of these actuated the leader. He was an impostor in the most determined sense of the term. A man who had in early life lost, through the indulgence of vicious propensities, all sense of rectitude or self-esteem; and who, when ambition was awakened in him, gave himself up to its influence unbridled by any scruple. His father had been a Methodist preacher, an enthusiastic man with simple intentions; but whose pernicious doctrines of election and special grace had contributed to destroy all conscientious feeling in his son. During the progress of the pestilence he had entered upon various schemes, by which to acquire adherents and power. Adrian had discovered and defeated these attempts; but Adrian was absent; the wolf assumed the shepherd's garb, and the flock admitted the deception: he had formed a party during the few weeks he had been in Paris, who zealously propagated the creed of his divine mission, and believed that safety and salvation were to be afforded only to those who put their trust in him.

When once the spirit of dissension had arisen, the most frivolous causes gave it activity. The first party, on arriving at Paris, had taken possession of the Tuileries; chance and friendly feeling had induced the second to lodge near to them. A contest arose concerning the distribution of the pillage; the chiefs of the first division demanded that the whole should be placed at their disposal; with this assumption the opposite party refused to comply. When next the latter went to forage, the gates of Paris were shut on them. After overcoming this difficulty, they marched in a body to the Tuileries. They found that their enemies had been already expelled thence by the Elect, as the fanatical party designated themselves, who refused to admit any into the palace who did not first abjure obedience to all except God, and his delegate on earth, their chief. Such was the beginning of the strife, which at length proceeded so far, that the three divisions, armed, met in the Place Vendome, each resolved to subdue by force the resistance of its adversaries. They assembled, their muskets were loaded, and even pointed at the breasts of their so-called enemies. One word had been sufficient; and there the last of mankind would have burthened their souls with the crime of murder and dipped their hands in each other's blood. A sense of shame, a recollection that not only their cause, but the existence of the whole human race was at stake, entered the breast of the leader of the more numerous parties. He was aware, that if the ranks were thinned, no other recruits could fill them up; that each man was as a priceless gem in a kingly crown, which if destroyed, the earth's deep entrails could yield no paragon. He was a young man, and had been hurried on by presumption, and the notion of his high rank and superiority to all other pretenders; now he repented his work, he felt that all the blood about to be shed would be on his head; with sudden impulse therefore he spurred his horse between the bands, and, having fixed a white handkerchief on the point of his uplifted sword, thus demanded parley; the opposite leaders obeyed the signal. He spoke with warmth; he reminded them of the oath all the chiefs had taken to submit to the Lord Protector; he declared their present meeting to be an act of treason and mutiny; he allowed that he had been hurried away by passion, but that a cooler moment had arrived; and he proposed that each party should send deputies to the Earl of Windsor, inviting his interference and offering submission to his decision. His offer was accepted so far, that each leader consented to command a retreat, and moreover agreed, that after the approbation of their several parties had been consulted, they should meet that night on some neutral spot to ratify the truce. At the meeting of the chiefs, this plan was finally concluded upon. The leader of the fanatics indeed refused to admit the arbitration of Adrian; he sent ambassadors, rather than deputies, to assert his claim, not plead his cause.

The truce was to continue until the first of February, when the bands were again to assemble on the Place Vendome; it was of the utmost consequence therefore that Adrian should arrive in Paris by that day, since an hair might turn the scale, and peace, scared away by intestine broils, might only return to watch by the silent dead. It was now the twenty-eighth of January; every vessel stationed near Dover had been beaten to pieces and destroyed by the furious storms I have commemorated. Our journey however would admit of no delay. That very night, Adrian, and I, and twelve others, either friends or attendants, put off from the English shore, in the boat that had brought over the deputies. We all took our turn at the oar; and the immediate occasion of our departure affording us abundant matter for conjecture and discourse, prevented the feeling that we left our native country, depopulate England, for the last time, to enter deeply into the minds of the greater part of our number. It was a serene starlight night, and the dark line of the English coast continued for some time visible at intervals, as we rose on the broad back of the waves. I exerted myself with my long oar to give swift impulse to our skiff; and, while the waters splashed with melancholy sound against its sides, I looked with sad affection on this last glimpse of sea-girt England, and strained my eyes not too soon to lose sight of the castellated cliff, which rose to protect the land of heroism and beauty from the inroads of ocean, that, turbulent as I had lately seen it, required such cyclopean walls for its repulsion. A solitary seagull winged its flight over our heads, to seek its nest in a cleft of the precipice. Yes, thou shalt revisit the land of thy birth, I thought, as I looked invidiously on the airy voyager; but we shall, never more! Tomb of Idris, farewell! Grave, in which my heart lies sepulture, farewell forever!

We were twelve hours at sea, and the heavy swell obliged us to exert all our strength. At length, by mere dint of rowing, we reached the French coast. The stars faded, and the grey morning cast a dim veil over the silver horns of the waning moon - the sun rose broad and red from the sea, as we walked over the sands to Calais. Our first care was to procure horses, and although wearied by our night of watching and toil, some of our party immediately went in quest of these in the wide fields of the unenclosed and now barren plain round Calais. We divided ourselves, like seamen, into watches, and some reposed, while others prepared the morning's repast. Our foragers returned at noon with only six horses—on these, Adrian and I, and four others, proceeded on our journey towards the great city, which its inhabitants had fondly named the capital of the civilized world. Our horses had become, through their long holiday, almost wild, and we crossed the plain round Calais with impetuous speed. From the height near Boulogne, I turned again to look on England; nature had cast a misty pall over her, her cliff was hidden - there was spread the watery barrier that divided us, never again to be crossed; she lay on the ocean plain,

In the great pool a swan's nest.

Ruined the nest, alas! the swans of Albion had passed away forever - an uninhabited rock in the wide Pacific, which had remained since the creation uninhabited, unnamed, unmarked, would be of as much account in the world's future history, as desert England.

Our journey was impeded by a thousand obstacles. As our horses grew tired, we had to seek for others; and hours were wasted, while we exhausted our artifices to allure some of these enfranchised slaves of man to resume the yoke; or as we went from stable to stable through the towns, hoping to find some who had not forgotten the shelter of their native stalls. Our ill success in procuring them, obliged us continually to leave some one of our companions behind; and on the first of February, Adrian and I entered Paris, wholly unaccompanied. The serene morning had dawned when we arrived at Saint Denis, and the sun was high, when the clamor of voices, and the clash, as we feared, of weapons, guided us to where our countrymen had assembled on the Place Vendome. We passed a knot of Frenchmen, who were talking earnestly of the madness of the insular invaders, and then coming by a sudden turn upon the Place, we saw the sun glitter on drawn swords and fixed bayonets, while yells and clamors rent the air. It was a scene of unaccustomed confusion in these days of depopulation. Roused by fancied wrongs, and insulting scoffs, the opposite parties had rushed to attack each other; while the elect, drawn up apart, seemed to wait an opportunity to fall with better advantage on their foes, when they should have mutually weakened each other. A merciful power interposed, and no blood was shed; for, while the insane mob were in the very act of attack, the females, wives, mothers and daughters, rushed between; they seized the bridles; they embraced the knees of the horsemen, and hung on the necks, or enweaponed arms of their enraged relatives; the shrill female scream was mingled with the manly shout, and formed the wild clamor that welcomed us on our arrival.

Our voices could not be heard in the tumult; Adrian however was eminent for the white charger he rode; spurring him, he dashed into the midst of the throng: he was recognized, and a loud cry raised for England and the Protector. The late adversaries, warmed to affection at the sight of him, joined in heedless confusion, and surrounded him; the women kissed his hands, and the edges of his garments; nay, his horse received tribute of their embraces; some wept their welcome; he appeared an angel of peace descended among them; and the only danger was, that his mortal nature would be demonstrated, by his suffocation from the kindness of his friends. His voice was at length heard, and obeyed; the crowd fell back; the chiefs alone rallied round him. I had seen Lord Raymond ride through his lines; his look of victory, and majestic mien obtained the respect and obedience of all: such was not the appearance or influence of Adrian. His slight figure, his fervent look, his gesture, more of deprecation than rule, were proofs that love, unmingled with fear, gave him dominion over the hearts of a multitude, who knew that he never flinched from danger, nor was actuated by other motives than care for the general welfare. No distinction was now visible between the two parties, late ready to shed each other's blood, for, though neither would submit to the other, they both yielded ready obedience to the Earl of Windsor.

One party however remained, cut off from the rest, which did not sympathize in the joy exhibited on Adrian's arrival, or imbibe the spirit of peace, which fell like dew upon the softened hearts of their countrymen. At the head of this assembly was a ponderous, dark-looking man, whose malign eye surveyed with gloating delight the stern looks of his followers. They had hitherto been inactive, but now, perceiving themselves to be forgotten in the universal jubilee, they advanced with threatening gestures: our friends had, as it were in wanton contention, attacked each other; they wanted but to be told that their cause was one, for it to become so: their mutual anger had been a fire of straw, compared to the slow-burning hatred they both entertained for these seceders, who seized a portion of the world to come, there to entrench and encastellated themselves, and to issue with fearful sally, and appalling denunciations, on the mere common children of the earth. The first advance of the little army of the elect reawakened their rage; they grasped their arms, and waited but their leader's signal to commence the attack, when the clear tones of Adrian's voice were heard, commanding them to fall back; with confused murmur and hurried retreat, as the wave ebbs clamorously from the sands it lately covered, our friends obeyed. Adrian rode singly into the space between the opposing bands; he approached the hostile leader, as requesting him to imitate his example, but his look was not obeyed, and the chief advanced, followed by his whole troop. There were many women among them, who seemed more eager and resolute than their male companions. They pressed round their leader, as if to shield him, while they loudly bestowed on him every sacred denomination and epithet of worship. Adrian met them halfway; they halted: "What," he said, "do you seek? Do you require any thing of us that we refuse to give, and that you are forced to acquire by arms and warfare?"

His questions were answered by a general cry, in which the words election, sin, and red right arm of God, could alone be heard.

Adrian looked expressly at their leader, saying, "Can you not silence your followers? Mine, you perceive, obey me."

The fellow answered by a scowl; and then, perhaps fearful that his people should become auditors of the debate he expected to ensue, he commanded them to fall back, and advanced by himself. "What, I again ask," said Adrian, "do you require of us?"

"Repentance," replied the man, whose sinister brow gathered clouds as he spoke. "Obedience to the will of the Most High, made manifest to these his Elected People. Do we not all die through your sins, O generation of unbelief, and have we not a right to demand of you repentance and obedience?"

"And if we refuse them, what then?" his opponent inquired mildly.

"Beware," cried the man, "God hears you, and will smite your stony heart in his wrath; his poisoned arrows fly, his dogs of death are unleashed! We will not perish unrevenged - and mighty will our avenger be, when he descends in visible majesty, and scatters destruction among you."

"My good fellow," said Adrian, with quiet scorn, "I wish that you were ignorant only, and I think it would be no difficult task to prove to you, that you speak of what you do not understand. On the present occasion however, it is enough for me to know that you seek nothing of us; and, heaven is our witness, we seek nothing of you. I should be sorry to embitter by strife the few days that we any of us may have here to live; when there," he pointed downwards, "we shall not be able to contend, while here we need not. Go home or stay; pray to your God in your own mode; your friends may do the like. My orisons consist in peace and good will, in resignation and hope. Farewell!"

He bowed slightly to the angry disputant who was about to reply; and, turning his horse down Rue Saint Honore, called on his friends to follow him. He rode slowly, to give time to all to join him at the Barrier, and then issued his orders that those who yielded obedience to him, should rendezvous at Versailles. In the meantime, he remained within the walls of Paris, until he had secured the safe retreat of all. In about a fortnight the remainder of the emigrants arrived from England, and they all repaired to Versailles; apartments were prepared for the family of the Protector in the Grand Trianon, and there, after the excitement of these events, we reposed amidst the luxuries of the departed Bourbons.

CHAPTER V

After the repose of a few days, we held a council, to decide on our future movements. Our first plan had been to quit our wintry native latitude and seek for our diminished numbers the luxuries and delights of a southern climate. We had not fixed on any precise spot as the termination of our wanderings; but a vague picture of perpetual spring, fragrant groves, and sparkling streams, floated in our imagination to entice us on. A variety of causes had detained us in England, and we had now arrived at the middle of February; if we pursued our original project, we should find ourselves in a worse situation than before, having exchanged our temperate climate for the intolerable heats of a summer in Egypt or Persia. We were therefore obliged to modify our plan, as the season continued to be inclement; and it was determined that we should await the arrival of spring in our present abode, and so order our future movements as to pass the hot months in the icy valleys of Switzerland, deferring our southern progress until the ensuing autumn, if such a season was ever again to be beheld by us.

The castle and town of Versailles afforded our numbers ample accommodation, and foraging parties took it by turns to supply our wants. There was a strange and appalling motley in the situation of these the last of the race. At first, I likened it to a colony, which borne over the far seas, struck root for the first time in a new country. But where was the bustle and industry characteristic of such an assemblage; the rudely constructed dwelling, which was to suffice till a more commodious mansion could be built; the marking out of fields; the attempt at cultivation; the eager curiosity to discover unknown animals and herbs; the excursions for the sake of exploring the country? Our habitations were palaces our food was ready stored in granaries — there was no need of labor, no inquisitiveness, no restless desire to get on. If we had been assured that we should secure the lives of our present numbers, there would have been more vivacity and hope in our councils. We should have discussed as to the period when the existing produce for man's sustenance would no longer suffice for us, and what mode of life we should then adopt. We should have considered more carefully our future plans and debated concerning the spot where we should in future dwell. But summer and the plague were near, and we dared not look forward. Every heart sickened at the thought of amusement; if the younger part of our community were ever impelled, by youthful and untamed hilarity, to enter on any dance or song, to cheer the melancholy time, they would suddenly break off, checked by a mournful look or agonizing sigh from any one among them, who was prevented by sorrows and losses from mingling in the festivity. If laughter echoed under our roof, yet the heart was vacant of joy; and, whenever it chanced that I witnessed such attempts at pastime, they increased instead of diminishing my sense of woe. In the midst of the pleasure-hunting throng, I would close my eyes, and see before me the obscure cavern, where was garnered the mortality of Idris, and the dead lay around, mouldering in hushed repose. When I again became aware of the present hour, softest melody of Lydian flute, or harmonious maze of graceful dance, was but as the demoniac chorus in the Wolf's Glen, and the capering of the reptiles that surrounded the magic circle.

My dearest interval of peace occurred, when, released from the obligation of associating with the crowd, I could repose in the dear home where my children lived. Children I say, for the tenderest emotions of paternity bound me to Clara. She was now fourteen; sorrow, and deep insight into the scenes around her, calmed the restless spirit of girlhood; while the remembrance of her father whom she idolized, and respect for me and Adrian, implanted an high sense of duty in her young heart. Though serious she was not sad; the eager desire that makes us all, when young, plume our wings, and stretch our necks, that we may more swiftly alight tiptoe on the height of maturity, was subdued in her by early experience. All that she could spare of overflowing love from her parents' memory, and attention to her living relatives, was spent upon religion. This was the hidden law of her heart, which she concealed with childish reserve, and cherished the more because it was secret. What faith so entire, what charity so pure, what hope so fervent, as that of early youth? and she, all love, all tenderness and trust, who from infancy had been tossed on the wide sea of passion and misfortune, saw the finger of apparent divinity in all, and her best hope was to make herself acceptable to the power she worshipped. Evelyn was only five years old; his joyous heart was incapable of sorrow, and he enlivened our house with the innocent mirth incident to his years.

The aged Countess of Windsor had fallen from her dream of power, rank and grandeur; she had been suddenly seized with the conviction, that love was the only good of life, virtue the only ennobling distinction and enriching wealth. Such a lesson had been taught her by the dead lips of her neglected daughter; and she devoted herself, with all the fiery violence of her character, to the obtaining the affection of the remnants of her family. In early years the heart of Adrian had been chilled towards her; and, though he observed a due respect, her coldness, mixed with the recollection of disappointment and madness, caused him to feel even pain in her society. She saw this, and yet determined to win his love; the obstacle served the rather to excite her ambition. As Henry, Emperor of Germany, lay in the snow before Pope Leo's gate for three winter days and nights, so did she in humility wait before the icy barriers of his closed heart, till he, the servant of love, and prince of tender courtesy, opened it wide for her admittance, bestowing, with fervency and gratitude, the tribute of filial affection she merited. Her understanding, courage, and presence of mind became powerful auxiliaries to him in the difficult task of ruling the tumultuous crowd, which were subjected to his control, in truth by a single hair.

The principal circumstances that disturbed our tranquility during this interval, originated in the vicinity of the impostor-prophet and his followers. They continued to reside at Paris; but missionaries from among them often visited Versailles - and such was the power of assertions, however false, yet vehemently iterated, over the ready credulity of the ignorant and fearful, that they seldom failed in drawing over to their party some from among our numbers. An instance of this nature coming immediately under our notice, we were led to consider the miserable state in which we should leave our countrymen, when we should, at the approach of summer, move on towards Switzerland, and leave a deluded crew behind us in the hands of their miscreant leader. The sense of the smallness of our numbers, and expectation of decrease, pressed upon us; and, while it would be a subject of congratulation to ourselves to add one to our party, it would be doubly gratifying to rescue from the pernicious influence of superstition and unrelenting tyranny, the victims that now, though voluntarily enchained, groaned beneath it. If we had considered the preacher as sincere in a belief of his own denunciations, or only moderately actuated by kind feeling in the exercise of his assumed powers, we should have immediately addressed ourselves to him, and endeavored with our best arguments to soften and humanize his views. But he was instigated by ambition, he desired to rule over these last stragglers from the fold of death; his projects went so far, as to cause him to calculate that, if, from these crushed remains, a few survived, so that a new race should spring up, he, by holding tight the reins of belief, might be remembered by the post-pestilential race as a patriarch, a prophet, nay a deity; such as of old among the post-diluvians were Jupiter the conqueror, Serapis the lawgiver, and Vishnou the preserver. These ideas made him inflexible in his rule, and violent in his hate of any who presumed to share with him his usurped empire.

It is a strange fact, but incontestable, that the philanthropist, who ardent in his desire to do good, who patient, reasonable and gentle, yet disdains to use other argument than truth, has less influence over men's minds, than he who, grasping and selfish, refuses not to adopt any means, nor awaken any passion, nor diffuse any falsehood, for the advancement of his cause. If this from time immemorial has been the case, the contrast was infinitely greater, now that the one could bring harrowing fears and transcendent hopes into play; while the other had few hopes to hold forth, nor could influence the imagination to diminish the fears which he himself was the first to entertain. The preacher had persuaded his followers, that their escape from the plague, the salvation of their children, and the rise of a new race of men from their seed, depended on their faith in, and their submission to him. They greedily imbibed this belief; and their over-weening credulity even rendered them eager to make converts to the same faith.

How to seduce any individuals from such an alliance of fraud, was a frequent subject of Adrian's meditations and discourse. He formed many plans for the purpose; but his own troop kept him in full occupation to ensure their fidelity and safety; beside which the preacher was as cautious and prudent, as he was cruel. His victims lived under the strictest rules and laws, which either entirely imprisoned them within the Tuileries, or let them out in such numbers, and under such leaders, as precluded the possibility of controversy. There was one among them however whom I resolved to save; she had been known to us in happier days; Idris had loved her; and her excellent nature made it peculiarly lamentable that she should be sacrificed by this merciless cannibal of souls.

This man had between two and three hundred persons enlisted under his banners. More than half of them were women; there were about fifty children of all ages; and not more than eighty men. They were mostly drawn from that which, when such distinctions existed, was denominated the lower rank of society. The exceptions consisted of a few high-born females, who, panic-struck, and tamed by sorrow, had joined him. Among these was one, young, lovely, and enthusiastic, whose very goodness made her a easier victim. I have mentioned her before: Juliet, the youngest daughter, and now sole relic of the ducal house of L -. There are some beings, whom fate seems to select on whom to pour, in unmeasured portion, the vials of her wrath, and whom she bathes even to the lips in misery. Such a one was the ill-starred Juliet. She had lost her indulgent parents, her brothers and sisters, companions of her youth; in one fell swoop they had been carried off from her. Yet she had again dared to call herself happy; united to her admirer, to him who possessed and filled her whole heart, she yielded to the Lethean powers of love, and knew and felt only his life and presence. At the very time when with keen delight she welcomed the tokens of maternity, this sole prop of her life failed, her husband died of the plague. For a time, she had been lulled in insanity; the birth of her child restored her to the cruel reality of things but gave her at the same time an object for whom to preserve at once life and reason. Every friend and relative had died off, and she was reduced to solitude and penury; deep melancholy and angry impatience distorted her judgment, so that she could not persuade herself to disclose her distress to us. When she heard of the plan of universal emigration, she resolved to remain behind with her child, and alone in wide England to live or die, as fate might decree, beside the grave of her beloved. She had hidden herself in one of the many empty habitations of London; it was she who rescued my Idris on the fatal twentieth of November, though my immediate danger, and the subsequent illness of Idris, caused us to forget our hapless friend. This circumstance had however brought her again in contact with her fellow-creatures; a slight illness of her infant, proved to her that she was still bound to humanity by an indestructible tie; to preserve this little creature's life became the object of her being, and she joined the first division of migrants who went over to Paris.

She became an easy prey to the Methodist; her sensibility and acute fears rendered her accessible to every impulse; her love for her child made her eager to cling to the merest straw held out to save him. Her mind, once unstrung, and now tuned by roughest inharmonious hands, made her credulous: beautiful as fabled goddess, with voice of unrivalled sweetness, burning with new lighted enthusiasm, she became a steadfast proselyte, and powerful auxiliary to the leader of the elect. I had remarked her in the crowd, on the day we met on the Place Vendome; and, recollecting suddenly her providential rescue of my lost one, on the night of the twentieth of November, I reproached myself for my neglect and ingratitude, and felt impelled to leave no means that I could adopt untried, to recall her to her better self, and rescue her from the fangs of the hypocrite destroyer.

I will not, at this period of my story, record the artifices I used to penetrate the asylum of the Tuileries, or give what would be a tedious account of my stratagems, disappointments, and perseverance. I at last succeeded in entering these walls and roamed its halls and corridors in eager hope to find my selected convert. In the evening I contrived to mingle unobserved with the congregation, which assembled in the chapel to listen to the crafty and eloquent harangue of their prophet. I saw Juliet near him. Her dark eyes, fearfully impressed with the restless glare of madness, were fixed on him; she held her infant, not yet a year old, in her arms; and care of it alone could distract her attention from the words to which she eagerly listened. After the sermon was over, the congregation dispersed; all quitted the chapel except she whom I sought; her babe had fallen asleep; so she placed it on a cushion, and sat on the floor beside, watching its tranquil slumber.

I presented myself to her; for a moment natural feeling produced a sentiment of gladness, which disappeared again, when with ardent and affectionate exhortation I besought her to accompany me in flight from this den of superstition and misery. In a moment she relapsed into the delirium of fanaticism, and, but that her gentle nature forbade, would have loaded me with execrations. She conjured me, she commanded me to leave her - "Beware, O beware," she cried, "fly while yet your escape is practicable. Now you are safe; but strange sounds and inspirations come on me at times, and if the Eternal should in awful whisper reveal to me his will, that to save my child you must be sacrificed, I would call in the satellites of him you call the tyrant; they would tear you limb from limb; nor would I hallow the death of him whom Idris loved, by a single tear."

She spoke hurriedly, with tuneless voice, and wild look; her child awoke, and, frightened, began to cry; each sob went to the ill-fated mother's heart, and she mingled the epithets of endearment she addressed to her infant, with angry commands that I should leave her. Had I had the means, I would have risked all, have torn her by force from the murderer's den, and trusted to the healing balm of reason and affection. But I had no choice, no power even of longer struggle; steps were heard along the gallery, and the voice of the preacher drew near. Juliet, straining her child in a close embrace, fled by another passage. Even then I would have followed her; but my foe and his satellites entered; I was surrounded and taken prisoner.

I remembered the menace of the unhappy Juliet, and expected the full tempest of the man's vengeance, and the awakened wrath of his followers, to fall instantly upon me. I was questioned. My answers were simple and sincere. "His own mouth condemns him," exclaimed the impostor; "he confesses that his intention was to seduce from the way of salvation our well-beloved sister in God; away with him to the dungeon; to-morrow he dies the death; we are manifestly called upon to make an example, tremendous and appalling, to scare the children of sin from our asylum of the saved."

My heart revolted from his hypocritical jargon: but it was unworthy of me to combat in words with the ruffian; and my answer was cool; while, far from being possessed with fear, methought, even at the worst, a man true to himself, courageous and determined, could fight his way, even from the boards of the scaffold, through the herd of these misguided maniacs. "Remember," I said, "who I am; and be well assured that I shall not die unavenged. Your legal magistrate, the Lord Protector, knew of my design, and is aware that I am here; the cry of blood will reach him, and you and your miserable victims will long lament the tragedy you are about to act."

My antagonist did not deign to reply, even by a look; - "You know your duty," he said to his comrades, -"obey."

In a moment I was thrown on the earth, bound, blindfolded, and hurried away - liberty of limb and sight was only restored to me, when, surrounded by dungeon-walls, dark and impervious, I found myself a prisoner and alone.

Such was the result of my attempt to gain over the proselyte of this man of crime; I could not conceive that he would dare put me to death. -Yet I was in his hands; the path of his ambition had ever been dark and cruel; his power was founded upon fear; the one word which might cause me to die, unheard, unseen, in the obscurity of my dungeon, might be easier to speak than the deed of mercy to act. He would not risk probably a public execution; but a private assassination would at once terrify any of my companions from attempting a like feat, at the same time that a cautious line of conduct might enable him to avoid the enquiries and the vengeance of Adrian.

Two months ago, in a vault more obscure than the one I now inhabited, I had revolved the design of quietly laying me down to die; now I shuddered at the approach of fate. My imagination was busied in shaping forth the kind of death he would inflict. Would he allow me to wear out life with famine; or was the food administered to me to be medicined with death? Would he steal on me in my sleep; or should I contend to the last with my murderers, knowing, even while I struggled, that I must be overcome? I lived upon an earth whose diminished population a child's arithmetic might number; I had lived through long months with death stalking close at my side, while at intervals the shadow of his skeleton-shape darkened my path. I had believed that I despised the grim phantom and laughed his power to scorn.

Any other fate I should have met with courage, nay, have gone out gallantly to encounter. But to be murdered thus at the midnight hour by cold-blooded assassins, no friendly hand to close my eyes, or receive my parting blessing - to die in combat, hate and execration - ah, why, my angel love, didst thou restore me to life, when already I had stepped within the portals of the tomb, now that so soon again I was to be flung back a mangled corpse!

Hours passed - centuries. Could I give words to the many thoughts which occupied me in endless succession during this interval, I should fill volumes. The air was dank, the dungeon-floor mildewed and icy cold; hunger came upon me too, and no sound reached me from without. To-morrow the ruffian had declared that I should die. When would to-morrow come? Was it not already here?

My door was about to be opened. I heard the key turn, and the bars and bolts slowly removed. The opening of intervening passages permitted sounds from the interior of the palace to reach me; and I heard the clock strike one. They come to murder me, I thought; this hour does not befit a public execution. I drew myself up against the wall opposite the entrance; I collected my forces, I rallied my courage, I would not fall a tame prey. Slowly the door receded on its hinges — I was ready to spring forward to seize and grapple with the intruder, till the sight of who it was changed at once the temper of my mind. It was Juliet herself; pale and trembling she stood, a lamp in her hand, on the threshold of the dungeon, looking at me with wistful countenance. But in a moment, she re-assumed her self-possession; and her languid eyes recovered their brilliancy. She said, "I am come to save you, Verney."

"And yourself also," I cried: "dearest friend, can we indeed be saved?"

"Not a word," she replied, "follow me!"

I obeyed instantly. We threaded with light steps many corridors, ascended several flights of stairs, and passed through long galleries; at the end of one she unlocked a low portal; a rush of wind extinguished our lamp; but, in lieu of it, we had the blessed moon-beams and the open face of heaven. Then first Juliet spoke: -"You are safe," she said, "God bless you! - farewell!"

I seized her reluctant hand -"Dear friend," I cried, "misguided victim, do you not intend to escape with me? Have you not risked all in facilitating my flight? and do you think that I will permit you to return, and suffer alone the effects of that miscreant's rage? Never!"

"Do not fear for me," replied the lovely girl mournfully, "and do not imagine that without the consent of our chief you could be without these walls. It is he that has saved you; he assigned to me the part of leading you hither, because I am best acquainted with your motives for coming here, and can best appreciate his mercy in permitting you to depart."

"And are you," I cried, "the dupe of this man? He dreads me alive as an enemy, and dead he fears my avengers. By favoring this clandestine escape, he preserves a shew of consistency to his followers; but mercy is far from his heart. Do you forget his artifices, his cruelty, and fraud? As I am free, so are you. Come, Juliet, the mother of our lost Idris will welcome you, the noble Adrian will rejoice to receive you; you will find peace and love, and better hopes than fanaticism can afford. Come, and fear not; long before day we shall be at Versailles; close the door on this abode of crime - come, sweet Juliet, from hypocrisy and guilt to the society of the affectionate and good."

I spoke hurriedly, but with fervor: and while with gentle violence I drew her from the portal, some thought, some recollection of past scenes of youth and happiness, made her listen and yield to me; suddenly she broke away with a piercing shriek: -"My child, my child! he has my child; my darling girl is my hostage."

She darted from me into the passage; the gate closed between us - she was left in the fangs of this man of crime, a prisoner, still to inhale the pestilential atmosphere which adhered to his demoniac nature; the unimpeded breeze played on my cheek, the moon shone graciously upon me, my path was free. Glad to have escaped, yet melancholy in my very joy, I retraced my steps to Versailles.

CHAPTER VI

Eventful winter passed, winter, the respite of our ills. By degrees the sun, which with slant beams had before yielded the more extended reign to night, lengthened his diurnal journey, and mounted his highest throne, at once the fosterer of earth's new beauty, and her lover. We who, like flies that congregate upon a dry rock at the ebbing of the tide, had played wantonly with time, allowing our passions, our hopes, and our mad desires to rule us, now heard the approaching roar of the ocean of destruction, and would have fled to some sheltered crevice, before the first wave broke over us. We resolved without delay, to commence our journey to Switzerland; we became eager to leave France. Under the icy vaults of the glaciers, beneath the shadow of the pines, the swinging of whose mighty branches was arrested by a load of snow; beside the streams whose intense cold proclaimed their origin to be from the slow-melting piles of congealed waters, amidst frequent storms which might purify the air, we should find health, if in truth health were not herself diseased.

We began our preparations at first with alacrity. We did not now bid adieu to our native country, to the graves of those we loved, to the flowers, and streams, and trees, which had lived beside us from infancy. Small sorrow would be ours on leaving Paris. A scene of shame, when we remembered our late contentions, and thought that we left behind a flock of miserable, deluded victims, bending under the tyranny of a selfish impostor. Small pangs should we feel in leaving the gardens, woods, and halls of the palaces of the Bourbons at Versailles, which we feared would soon be tainted by the dead, when we looked forward to valley's lovelier than any garden, to mighty forests and halls, built not for mortal majesty, but palaces of nature's own, with the Alp of marmoreal whiteness for their walls, the sky for their roof.

Yet our spirits flagged, as the day drew near which we had fixed for our departure. Dire visions and evil auguries, if such things were, thickened around us, so that in vain might men say -

These are their reasons, they are natural,

we felt them to be ominous, and dreaded the future event enchained to them. That the night owl should screech before the noon-day sun, that the hard-winged bat should wheel around the bed of beauty, that muttering thunder should in early spring startle the cloudless air, that sudden and exterminating blight should fall on the tree and shrub, were unaccustomed, but physical events, less horrible than the mental creations of almighty fear. Some had sight of funeral processions, and faces all begrimed with tears, which flitted through the long avenues of the gardens, and drew aside the curtains of the sleepers at dead of night. Some heard wailing and cries in the air; a mournful chaunt would stream through the dark atmosphere, as if spirits above sang the requiem of the human race. What was there in all this, but that fear created other senses within our frames, making us see, hear, and feel what was not? What was this, but the action of diseased imaginations and childish credulity? So might it be; but what was most real, was the existence of these very fears; the staring looks of horror, the faces pale even to ghastliness, the voices struck dumb with harrowing dread, of those among us who saw and heard these things. Of this number was Adrian, who knew the delusion, yet could not cast off the clinging terror. Even ignorant infancy appeared with timorous shrieks and convulsions to acknowledge the presence of unseen powers. We must go in change of scene, in occupation, and such security as we still hoped to find, we should discover a cure for these gathering horrors.

On mustering our company, we found them to consist of fourteen hundred souls, men, women, and children. Until now therefore, we were undiminished in numbers, except by the desertion of those who had attached themselves to the impostor-prophet and remained behind in Paris. About fifty French joined us. Our order of march was easily arranged; the ill success which had attended our division, determined Adrian to keep all in one body. I, with a hundred men, went forward first as purveyor, taking the road of the Cote d'Or, through Auxerre, Dijon, Dole, over the Jura to Geneva. I was to make arrangements, at every ten miles, for the accommodation of such numbers as I found the town or village would receive, leaving behind a messenger with a written order, signifying how many were to be quartered there. The remainder of our tribe was then divided into bands of fifty each, every division containing eighteen men, and the remainder, consisting of women and children. Each of these was headed by an officer, who carried the roll of names, by which they were each day to be mustered. If the numbers were divided at night, in the morning those in the van waited for those in the rear. At each of the large towns before mentioned, we were all to assemble; and a conclave of the principal officers would hold council for the general weal. I went first, as I said, Adrian last. His mother, with Clara and Evelyn under her protection, remained also with him. Thus, our order being determined, I departed. My plan was to go at first no further than Fontainebleau, where in a few days I should be joined by Adrian, before I took flight again further eastward.

My friend accompanied me a few miles from Versailles. He was sad; and, in a tone of unaccustomed despondency, uttered a prayer for our speedy arrival among the Alps, accompanied with an expression of vain regret that we were not already there. "In that case," I observed, "we can quicken our march; why adhere to a plan whose dilatory proceeding you already disapprove?"

"Nay," replied he, "it is too late now. A month ago, and we were masters of ourselves; now, -" he turned his face from me; though gathering twilight had already veiled its expression, he turned it yet more away, as he added -"a man died of the plague last night!"

He spoke in a smothered voice, then suddenly clasping his hands, he exclaimed, "Swiftly, most swiftly advances the last hour for us all; as the stars vanish before the sun, so will his near approach destroy us. I have done my best; with grasping hands and impotent strength, I have hung on the wheel of the chariot of plague; but she drags me along with it, while, like Juggernaut, she proceeds crushing out the being of all who strew the high road of life. Would that it was over - would that her procession achieved, we had all entered the tomb together!"

Tears streamed from his eyes. "Again and again," he continued, "will the tragedy be acted; again I must hear the groans of the dying, the wailing of the survivors; again witness the pangs, which, consummating all, envelope an eternity in their evanescent existence. Why am I reserved for this? Why the tainted weather of the flock, am I not struck to earth among the first? It is hard, very hard, for one of woman born to endure all that I endure!"

Hitherto, with an undaunted spirit, and a high feeling of duty and worth, Adrian had fulfilled his self-imposed task. I had contemplated him with reverence, and a fruitless desire of imitation. I now offered a few words of encouragement and sympathy. He hid his face in his hands, and while he strove to calm himself, he ejaculated, "For a few months, yet for a few months more, let not, O God, my heart fail, or my courage be bowed down; let not sights of intolerable misery madden this half-crazed brain, or cause this frail heart to beat against its prison-bound, so that it burst. I have believed it to be my destiny to guide and rule the last of the race of man, till death extinguish my government; and to this destiny I submit.

"Pardon me, Verney, I pain you, but I will no longer complain. Now I am myself again, or rather I am better than myself. You have known how from my childhood aspiring thoughts and high desires have warred with inherent disease and overstrained sensitiveness, till the latter became victors. You know how I placed this wasted feeble hand on the abandoned helm of human government. I have been visited at times by intervals of fluctuation; yet, until now, I have felt as if a superior and indefatigable spirit had taken up its abode within me or rather incorporated itself with my weaker being. The holy visitant has for a time slept, perhaps to show me how powerless I am without its inspiration. Yet, stay for a while, O Power of goodness and strength, disdain not yet this rent shrine of fleshly mortality, O immortal Capability! While one fellow creature remains to whom aid can be afforded, stay by and prop your shattered, falling engine!"

His vehemence, and voice broken by irrepressible sighs, sunk to my heart; his eyes gleamed in the gloom of night like two earthly stars; and, his form dilating, his countenance beaming, truly it almost seemed as if at his eloquent appeal a more than mortal spirit entered his frame, exalting him above humanity. He turned quickly towards me and held out his hand. "Farewell, Verney," he cried, "brother of my love, farewell; no other weak expression must cross these lips, I am alive again: to our tasks, to our combats with our unvanquished foe, for to the last I will struggle against her."

He grasped my hand, and bent a look on me, more fervent and animated than any smile; then turning his horse's head, he touched the animal with the spur, and was out of sight in a moment.

A man last night had died of the plague. The quiver was not emptied, nor the bow unstrung. We stood as marks, while Parthian Pestilence aimed and shot, insatiated by conquest, unobstructed by the heaps of slain. A sickness of the soul, contagious even to my physical mechanism, came over me. My knees knocked together, my teeth chattered, the current of my blood, clotted by sudden cold, painfully forced its way from my heavy heart. I did not fear for myself, but it was misery to think that we could not even save this remnant. That those I loved might in a few days be as clay-cold as Idris in her antique tomb; nor could strength of body or energy of mind ward off the blow. A sense of degradation came over me. Did God create man, merely in the end to become dead earth in the midst of healthful vegetating nature? Was he of no more account to his Maker, than a field of corn blighted in the ear? Were our proud dreams thus to fade? Our name was written "a little lower than the angels;" and behold, we were no better than ephemera. We had called ourselves the "paragon of animals," and, lo! we were a "quint-essence of dust." We repined that the pyramids had outlasted the embalmed body of their builder. Alas! the mere shepherd's hut of straw we passed on the road, contained in its structure the principle of greater longevity than the whole race of man. How reconcile this sad change to our past aspirations, to our apparent powers!

Sudden an internal voice, articulate and clear, seemed to say: -Thus from eternity, it was decreed: the steeds that bear Time onwards had this hour and this fulfilment enchained to them, since the void brought forth its burthen. Would you read backwards the unchangeable laws of Necessity?

Mother of the world! Servant of the Omnipotent! eternal, changeless Necessity! who with busy fingers sittest ever weaving the indissoluble chain of events! -I will not murmur at thy acts. If my human mind cannot acknowledge that all that is, is right; yet since what is, must be, I will sit amidst the ruins and smile. Truly we were not born to enjoy, but to submit, and to hope.

Will not the reader tire, if I should minutely describe our long-drawn journey from Paris to Geneva? If, day by day, I should record, in the form of a journal, the thronging miseries of our lot, could my hand write, or language afford words to express, the variety of our woe; the hustling and crowding of one deplorable event upon another? Patience, oh reader! whoever thou art, wherever thou dwellest, whether of race spiritual, or, sprung from some surviving pair, thy nature will be human, thy habitation the earth; thou wilt here read of the acts of the extinct race, and wilt ask wonderingly, if they, who suffered what thou findest recorded, were of frail flesh and soft organization like thyself. Most true, they were - weep therefore; for surely, solitary being, thou wilt be of gentle disposition; shed compassionate tears; but the while lend thy attention to the tale, and learn the deeds and sufferings of thy predecessors.

Yet the last events that marked our progress through France were so full of strange horror and gloomy misery, that I dare not pause too long in the narration. If I were to dissect each incident, every small fragment of a second would contain a harrowing tale, whose minutest word would curdle the blood in thy young veins. It is right that I should erect for thy instruction this monument of the foregone race; but not that I should drag thee through the wards of a hospital, nor the secret chambers of the charnel-house. This tale, therefore, shall be rapidly unfolded. Images of destruction, pictures of despair, the procession of the last triumph of death, shall be drawn before thee, swift as the rack driven by the north wind along the blotted splendor of the sky.

Weed-grown fields, desolate towns, the wild approach of riderless horses had now become habitual to my eyes; nay, sights far worse, of the unburied dead, and human forms which were strewed on the road side, and on the steps of once frequented habitations, where,

> Through the flesh that wastes away
> Beneath the parching sun, the whitening bones
> Start forth, and moulder in the sable dust.

Sights like these had become - ah, woe the while! so familiar, that we had ceased to shudder, or spur our stung horses to sudden speed, as we passed them. France in its best days, at least that part of France through which we travelled, had been a cultivated desert, and the absence of enclosures, of cottages, and even of peasantry, was saddening to a traveler from sunny Italy, or busy England. Yet the towns were frequent and lively, and the cordial politeness and ready smile of the wooden-shoed peasant restored good humor to the splenetic. Now, the old woman sat no more at the door with her distaff - the lank beggar no longer asked charity in courtier-like phrase; nor on holidays did the peasantry thread with slow grace the mazes of the dance. Silence, melancholy bride of death, went in procession with him from town to town through the spacious region.

We arrived at Fontainebleau, and speedily prepared for the reception of our friends. On mustering our numbers for the night, three were found missing. When I enquired for them, the man to whom I spoke, uttered the word "plague," and fell at my feet in convulsions; he also was infected. There were hard faces around me; for among my troop were sailors who had crossed the line times un-numbered, soldiers who, in Russia and far America, had suffered famine, cold and danger, and men still sterner-featured, once nightly depredators in our over-grown metropolis; men bred from their cradle to see the whole machine of society at work for their destruction. I looked round and saw upon the faces of all horror and despair written in glaring characters.

We passed four days at Fontainebleau. Several sickened and died, and in the meantime neither Adrian nor any of our friends appeared. My own troop was in commotion; to reach Switzerland, to plunge into rivers of snow, and to dwell in caves of ice, became the mad desire of all. Yet we had promised to wait for the Earl; and he came not. My people demanded to be led forward - rebellion, if so we might call what was the mere casting away of straw-formed shackles, appeared manifestly among them. They would away on the word without a leader. The only chance of safety, the only hope of preservation from every form of indescribable suffering, was our keeping together. I told them this; while the most determined among them answered with sullenness, that they could take care of themselves, and replied to my entreaties with scoffs and menaces.

At length, on the fifth day, a messenger arrived from Adrian, bearing letters, which directed us to proceed to Auxerre, and there await his arrival, which would only be deferred for a few days. Such was the tenor of his public letters. Those privately delivered to me, detailed at length the difficulties of his situation, and left the arrangement of my future plans to my own discretion. His account of the state of affairs at Versailles was brief, but the oral communications of his messenger filled up his omissions and shewed me that perils of the most frightful nature were gathering around him. At first the re-awakening of the plague had been concealed; but the number of deaths increasing, the secret was divulged, and the destruction already achieved, was exaggerated by the fears of the survivors. Some emissaries of the enemy of mankind, the accursed Impostors, were among them instilling their doctrine that safety and life could only be ensured by sub-mission to their chief; and they succeeded so well, that soon, instead of desiring to proceed to Switzerland, the major part of the multitude, weak minded women, and dastardly men, desired to return to Paris, and, by ranging themselves under the banners of the so called prophet, and by a cowardly worship of the principle of evil, to purchase respite, as they hoped, from impending death. The discord and tumult induced by these conflicting fears and passions, detained Adrian. It required all his ardor in pursuit of an object, and his patience under difficulties, to calm and animate such a number of his followers, as might counterbalance the panic of the rest, and lead them back to the means from which alone safety could be derived. He had hoped immediately to follow me; but, being defeated in this intention, he sent his messenger urging me to secure my own troop at such a distance from Versailles, as to prevent the contagion of rebellion from reaching them; promising, at the same time, to join me the moment a favorable occasion should occur, by means of which he could withdraw the main body of the emigrants from the evil influence at present exercised over them.

I was thrown into a most painful state of uncertainty by these communications. My first impulse was that we should all return to Versailles, there to assist in extricating our chief from his perils. I accordingly assembled my troop, and proposed to them this retrograde movement, instead of the continuation of our journey to Auxerre. With one voice they refused to comply. The notion circulated among them was, that the ravages of the plague alone detained the Protector; they opposed his order to my request; they came to a resolve to proceed without me, should I refuse to accompany them. Argument and adjuration were lost on these dastards. The continual diminution of their own numbers, effected by pestilence, added a sting to their dislike of delay; and my opposition only served to bring their resolution to a crisis. That same evening, they departed towards Auxerre. Oaths, as from soldiers to their general, had been taken by them: these they broke. I also had engaged myself not to desert them; it appeared to me inhuman to ground any infraction of my word on theirs. The same spirit that caused them to rebel against me, would impel them to desert each other; and the most dreadful sufferings would be the consequence of their journey in their present unordered and chiefless array. These feelings for a time were paramount; and, in obedience to them, I accompanied the rest towards Auxerre. We arrived the same night at Villeneuve-la-Guiard, a town at the distance of four posts from Fontainebleau.

When my companions had retired to rest, and I was left alone to revolve and ruminate upon the intelligence I received of Adrian's situation, another view of the subject presented itself to me. What was I doing, and what was the object of my present movements? Apparently I was to lead this troop of selfish and lawless men towards Switzerland, leaving behind my family and my selected friend, which, subject as they were hourly to the death that threatened to all, I might never see again. Was it not my first duty to assist the Protector, setting an example of attachment and duty? At a crisis, such as the one I had reached, it is very difficult to balance nicely opposing interests, and that towards which our inclinations lead us, obstinately assumes the appearance of selfishness, even when we meditate a sacrifice. We are easily led at such times to make a compromise of the question; and this was my present resource. I resolved that very night to ride to Versailles; if I found affairs less desperate than I now deemed them, I would return without delay to my troop; I had a vague idea that my arrival at that town, would occasion some sensation more or less strong, of which we might profit, for the purpose of leading forward the vacillating multitude — at least no time was to be lost - I visited the stables, I saddled my favorite horse, and vaulting on his back, without giving myself time for further reflection or hesitation, quitted Villeneuve-la-Guiard on my return to Versailles.

I was glad to escape from my rebellious troop, and to lose sight for a time, of the strife of evil with good, where the former forever remained triumphant. I was stung almost to madness by my uncertainty concerning the fate of Adrian, and grew reckless of any event, except what might lose or preserve my unequalled friend. With a heavy heart, that sought relief in the rapidity of my course, I rode through the night to Versailles. I spurred my horse, who addressed his free limbs to speed, and tossed his gallant head in pride. The constellations reeled swiftly by, swiftly each tree and stone and landmark fled past my onward career. I bared my head to the rushing wind, which bathed my brow in delightful coolness. As I lost sight of Villeneuve-la-Guiard, I forgot the sad drama of human misery; methought it was happiness enough to live, sensitive the while of the beauty of the verdure-clad earth, the star-bespangled sky, and the tameless wind that lent animation to the whole. My horse grew tired - and I, forgetful of his fatigue, still as he lagged, cheered him with my voice, and urged him with the spur. He was a gallant animal, and I did not wish to exchange him for any chance beast I might light on, leaving him never to be refound. All night we went forward; in the morning he became sensible that we approached Versailles, to reach which as his home, he mustered his flagging strength.

The distance we had come was not less than fifty miles, yet he shot down the long Boulevards swift as an arrow; poor fellow, as I dismounted at the gate of the castle, he sunk on his knees, his eyes were covered with a film, he fell on his side, a few gasps inflated his noble chest, and he died. I saw him expire with an anguish, unaccountable even to myself, the spasm was as the wrenching of some limb in agonizing torture, but it was brief as it was intolerable. I forgot him, as I swiftly darted through the open portal, and up the majestic stairs of this castle of victories - heard Adrian's voice - O fool! O woman nurtured, effeminate and contemptible being - I heard his voice, and answered it with convulsive shrieks; I rushed into the Hall of Hercules, where he stood surrounded by a crowd, whose eyes, turned in wonder on me, reminded me that on the stage of the world, a man must repress such girlish ecstasies. I would have given worlds to have embraced him; I dared not - Half in exhaustion, half voluntarily, I threw myself at my length on the ground - dare I disclose the truth to the gentle offspring of solitude? I did so, that I might kiss the dear and sacred earth he trod.

I found everything in a state of tumult. An emissary of the leader of the elect, had been so worked up by his chief, and by his own fanatical creed, as to make an attempt on the life of the Protector and preserver of lost mankind. His hand was arrested while in the act of poignarding the Earl; this circumstance had caused the clamor I heard on my arrival at the castle, and the confused assembly of persons that I found assembled in the Salle d'Hercule. Although superstition and demoniac fury had crept among the emigrants, yet several adhered with fidelity to their noble chieftain; and many, whose faith and love had been unhinged by fear, felt all their latent affection rekindled by this detestable attempt. A phalanx of faithful breasts closed round him; the wretch, who, although a prisoner and in bonds, vaunted his design, and madly claimed the crown of martyrdom, would have been torn to pieces, had not his intended victim interposed. Adrian, springing forward, shielded him with his own person, and commanded with energy the submission of his infuriate friends - at this moment I had entered.

Discipline and peace were at length restored in the castle; and then Adrian went from house to house, from troop to troop, to soothe the disturbed minds of his followers, and recall them to their ancient obedience. But the fear of immediate death was still rife amongst these survivors of a world's destruction; the horror occasioned by the attempted assassination, passed away; each eye turned towards Paris. Men love a prop so well, that they will lean on a pointed poisoned spear; and such was he, the impostor, who, with fear of hell for his scourge, most ravenous wolf, played the driver to a credulous flock.

It was a moment of suspense, that shook even the resolution of the unyielding friend of man. Adrian for one moment was about to give in, to cease the struggle, and quit, with a few adherents, the deluded crowd, leaving them a miserable prey to their passions, and to the worse tyrant who excited them. But again, after a brief fluctuation of purpose, he resumed his courage and resolves, sustained by the singleness of his purpose, and the untried spirit of benevolence which animated him. At this moment, as an omen of excellent import, his wretched enemy pulled destruction on his head, destroying with his own hands the dominion he had erected.

His grand hold upon the minds of men, took its rise from the doctrine inculcated by him, that those who believed in, and followed him, were the remnant to be saved, while all the rest of mankind were marked out for death. Now, at the time of the Flood, the omnipotent repented him that he had created man, and as then with water, now with the arrows of pestilence, was about to annihilate all, except those who obeyed his decrees, promulgated by the ipse dixit prophet. It is impossible to say on what foundations this man built his hopes of being able to carry on such an imposture. It is likely that he was fully aware of the lie which murderous nature might give to his assertions, and believed it to be the cast of a die, whether he should in future ages be reverenced as an inspired delegate from heaven, or be recognized as an impostor by the present dying generation. At any rate he resolved to keep up the drama to the last act. When, on the first approach of summer, the fatal disease again made its ravages among the followers of Adrian, the impostor exultingly proclaimed the exemption of his own congregation from the universal calamity. He was believed; his followers, hitherto shut up in Paris, now came to Versailles. Mingling with the coward band there assembled, they reviled their admirable leader, and asserted their own superiority and exemption.

At length the plague, slow-footed, but sure in her noiseless advance, destroyed the illusion, invading the congregation of the elect, and showering promiscuous death among them. Their leader endeavored to conceal this event; he had a few followers, who, admitted into the arcana of his wickedness, could help him in the execution of his nefarious designs. Those who sickened were immediately and quietly withdrawn, the cord and a midnight-grave disposed of them forever, while some plausible excuse was given for their absence. At last a female, whose maternal vigilance subdued even the effects of the narcotics administered to her, became a witness of their murderous designs on her only child. Mad with horror, she would have burst among her deluded fellow-victims, and, wildly shrieking, have awaked the dull ear of night with the history of the fiend-like crime; when the Impostor, in his last act of rage and desperation, plunged a poignard in her bosom. Thus wounded to death, her garments dripping with her own life-blood, bearing her strangled infant in her arms, beautiful and young as she was, Juliet, (for it was she) denounced to the host of deceived believers, the wickedness of their leader. He saw the aghast looks of her auditors, changing from horror to fury - the names of those already sacrificed were echoed by their relatives, now assured of their loss. The wretch with that energy of purpose, which had borne him thus far in his guilty career, saw his danger, and resolved to evade the worst forms of it - he rushed on one of the foremost, seized a pistol from his girdle, and his loud laugh of derision mingled with the report of the weapon with which he destroyed himself.

They left his miserable remains even where they lay; they placed the corpse of poor Juliet and her babe upon a bier, and all, with hearts subdued to saddest regret, in long procession walked towards Versailles. They met troops of those who had quitted the kindly protection of Adrian and were journeying to join the fanatics. The tale of horror was recounted - all turned back; and thus at last, accompanied by the undiminished numbers of surviving humanity, and preceded by the mournful emblem of their recovered reason, they appeared before Adrian, and again and forever vowed obedience to his commands, and fidelity to his cause.

CHAPTER VII

These events occupied so much time, that June had numbered more than half its days, before we again commenced our long-protracted journey. The day after my return to Versailles, six men, from among those I had left at Villeneuve-la-Guiard, arrived, with intelligence, that the rest of the troop had already proceeded towards Switzerland. We went forward in the same track.

It is strange, after an interval of time, to look back on a period, which, though short in itself, appeared, when in actual progress, to be drawn out interminably. By the end of July, we entered Dijon; by the end of July those hours, days, and weeks had mingled with the ocean of forgotten time, which in their passage teemed with fatal events and agonizing sorrow. By the end of July, little more than a month had gone by, if man's life were measured by the rising and setting of the sun: but, alas! in that interval ardent youth had become grey-haired; furrows deep and uneraseable were trenched in the blooming cheek of the young mother; the elastic limbs of early manhood, paralyzed as by the burthen of years, assumed the decrepitude of age. Nights passed, during whose fatal darkness the sun grew old before it rose; and burning days, to cool whose baleful heat the balmy eve, lingering far in eastern climes, came lagging and ineffectual; days, in which the dial, radiant in its noon-day station, moved not its shadow the space of a little hour, until a whole life of sorrow had brought the sufferer to an untimely grave.

We departed from Versailles fifteen hundred souls. We set out on the eighteenth of June. We made a long procession, in which was contained every dear relationship, or tie of love, that existed in human society. Fathers and husbands, with guardian care, gathered their dear relatives around them; wives and mothers looked for support to the manly form beside them, and then with tender anxiety bent their eyes on the infant troop around. They were sad, but not hopeless. Each thought that someone would be saved; each, with that pertinacious optimism, which to the last characterized our human nature, trusted that their beloved family would be the one preserved.

We passed through France, and found it empty of inhabitants. Some one or two natives survived in the larger towns, which they roamed through like ghosts; we received therefore small increase to our numbers, and such decrease through death, that at last it became easier to count the scanty list of survivors. As we never deserted any of the sick, until their death permitted us to commit their remains to the shelter of a grave, our journey was long, while every day a frightful gap was made in our troop - they died by tens, by fifties, by hundreds. No mercy was shewn by death; we ceased to expect it, and every day welcomed the sun with the feeling that we might never see it rise again.

The nervous terrors and fearful visions which had scared us during the spring, continued to visit our coward troop during this sad journey. Every evening brought its fresh creation of specters; a ghost was depicted by every blighted tree; and appalling shapes were manufactured from each shaggy bush. By degrees these common marvels palled on us, and then other wonders were called into being. Once it was confidently asserted, that the sun rose an hour later than its seasonable time; again, it was discovered that he grew paler and paler; that shadows took an uncommon appearance. It was impossible to have imagined, during the usual calm routine of life men had before experienced, the terrible effects produced by these extravagant delusions: in truth, of such little worth are our senses, when unsupported by concurring testimony, that it was with the utmost difficulty I kept myself free from the belief in supernatural events, to which the major part of our people readily gave credit. Being one sane amidst a crowd of the mad, I hardly dared assert to my own mind, that the vast luminary had undergone no change - that the shadows of night were unthicken by innumerable shapes of awe and terror; or that the wind, as it sung in the trees, or whistled round an empty building, was not pregnant with sounds of wailing and despair. Sometimes realities took ghostly shapes; and it was impossible for one's blood not to curdle at the perception of an evident mixture of what we knew to be true, with the visionary semblance of all that we feared.

Once, at the dusk of the evening, we saw a figure all in white, apparently of more than human stature, flourishing about the road, now throwing up its arms, now leaping to an astonishing height in the air, then turning round several times successively, then raising itself to its full height and gesticulating violently. Our troop, on the alert to discover and believe in the supernatural, made a halt at some distance from this shape; and, as it became darker, there was something appalling even to the incredulous, in the lonely specter, whose gambols, if they hardly accorded with spiritual dignity, were beyond human powers. Now it leapt right up in the air, now sheer over a high hedge, and was again the moment after in the road before us. By the time I came up, the fright experienced by the spectators of this ghostly exhibition, began to manifest itself in the flight of some, and the close huddling together of the rest. Our goblin now perceived us; he approached, and, as we drew reverentially back, made a low bow. The sight was irresistibly ludicrous even to our hapless band, and his politeness was hailed by a shout of laughter; - then, again springing up, as a last effort, it sunk to the ground, and became almost invisible through the dusky night. This circumstance again spread silence and fear through the troop; the more courageous at length advanced, and, raising the dying wretch, discovered the tragic explanation of this wild scene. It was an opera-dancer, and had been one of the troop which deserted from Villeneuve-la-Guiard: falling sick, he had been deserted by his companions; in an access of delirium he had fancied himself on the stage, and, poor fellow, his dying sense eagerly accepted the last human applause that could ever be bestowed on his grace and agility.

At another time we were haunted for several days by an apparition, to which our people gave the appellation of the Black Specter. We never saw it except at evening, when his coal black steed, his mourning dress, and plume of black feathers, had a majestic and awe-striking appearance; his face, one said, who had seen it for a moment, was ashy pale; he had lingered far behind the rest of his troop, and suddenly at a turn in the road, saw the Black Specter coming towards him; he hid himself in fear, and the horse and his rider slowly past, while the moonbeams fell on the face of the latter, displaying its unearthly hue. Sometimes at dead of night, as we watched the sick, we heard one galloping through the town; it was the Black Specter come in token of inevitable death. He grew giant tall to vulgar eyes; an icy atmosphere, they said, surrounded him; when he was heard, all animals shuddered, and the dying knew that their last hour was come. It was Death himself, they declared, come visibly to seize on subject earth, and quell at once our decreasing numbers, sole rebels to his law. One day at noon, we saw a dark mass on the road before us, and, coming up, beheld the Black Specter fallen from his horse, lying in the agonies of disease upon the ground. He did not survive many hours; and his last words disclosed the secret of his mysterious conduct. He was a French noble of distinction, who, from the effects of plague, had been left alone in his district; during many months, he had wandered from town to town, from province to province, seeking some survivor for a companion, and abhorring the loneliness to which he was condemned. When he discovered our troop, fear of contagion conquered his love of society. He dared not join us, yet he could not resolve to lose sight of us, sole human beings who besides himself existed in wide and fertile France; so he accompanied us in the spectral guise I have described, till pestilence gathered him to a larger congregation, even that of Dead Mankind.

It had been well, if such vain terrors could have distracted our thoughts from more tangible evils. But these were too dreadful and too many not to force themselves into every thought, every moment, of our lives. We were obliged to halt at different periods for days together, till another and yet another was consigned as a clod to the vast clod which had been once our living mother. Thus, we continued travelling during the hottest season; and it was not till the first of August, that we, the emigrants, - reader, there were just eighty of us in number, - entered the gates of Dijon.

We had expected this moment with eagerness, for now we had accomplished the worst part of our drear journey, and Switzerland was near at hand. Yet how could we congratulate ourselves on any event thus imperfectly fulfilled? Were these miserable beings, who, worn and wretched, passed in sorrowful procession, the sole remnants of the race of man, which, like a flood, had once spread over and possessed the whole earth? It had come down clear and unimpeded from its primal mountain source in Ararat and grew from a puny streamlet to a vast perennial river, generation after generation flowing on ceaselessly. The same, but diversified, it grew, and swept onwards towards the absorbing ocean, whose dim shores we now reached. It had been the mere plaything of nature, when first it crept out of uncreative void into light; but thought brought forth power and knowledge; and clad with these, the race of man assumed dignity and authority. It was then no longer the mere gardener of earth, or the shepherd of her flocks; "it carried with it an imposing and majestic aspect; it had a pedigree and illustrious ancestors; it had its gallery of portraits, its monumental inscriptions, its records and titles."

This was all over, now that the ocean of death had sucked in the slackening tide, and its source was dried up. We first had bidden adieu to the state of things which having existed many thousand years, seemed eternal; such a state of government, obedience, traffic, and domestic intercourse, as had moulded our hearts and capacities, as far back as memory could reach. Then to patriotic zeal, to the arts, to reputation, to enduring fame, to the name of country, we had bidden farewell. We saw depart all hope of retrieving our ancient state - all expectation, except the feeble one of saving our individual lives from the wreck of the past. To preserve these we had quitted England - England, no more; for without her children, what name could that barren island claim? With tenacious grasp we clung to such rule and order as could best save us; trusting that, if a little colony could be preserved, that would suffice at some remoter period to restore the lost community of mankind.

But the game is up! We must all die; nor leave survivor nor heir to the wide inheritance of earth. We must all die! The species of man must perish; his frame of exquisite workmanship; the wondrous mechanism of his senses; the noble proportion of his godlike limbs; his mind, the enthroned king of these; must perish. Will the earth still keep her place among the planets; will she still journey with unmarked regularity round the sun; will the seasons change, the trees adorn themselves with leaves, and flowers shed their fragrance, in solitude? Will the mountains remain unmoved, and streams still keep a downward course towards the vast abyss; will the tides rise and fall, and the winds fan universal nature; will beasts pasture, birds fly, and fishes swim, when man, the lord, possessor, perceiver, and recorder of all these things, has passed away, as though he had never been? O, what mockery is this! Surely death is not death, and humanity is not extinct; but merely passed into other shapes, unsubjected to our perceptions. Death is a vast portal, a high road to life: let us hasten to pass; let us exist no more in this living death but die that we may live!

We had longed with inexpressible earnestness to reach Dijon, since we had fixed on it, as a kind of station in our progress. But now we entered it with a torpor more painful than acute suffering. We had come slowly but irrevocably to the opinion, that our utmost efforts would not preserve one human being alive. We took our hands therefore away from the long-grasped rudder; and the frail vessel on which we floated, seemed, the government over her suspended, to rush, prow foremost, into the dark abyss of the billows. A gush of grief, a wanton profusion of tears, and vain laments, and overflowing tenderness, and passionate but fruitless clinging to the priceless few that remained, was followed by languor and recklessness.

During this disastrous journey we lost all those, not of our own family, to whom we had particularly attached ourselves among the survivors. It was not well to fill these pages with a mere catalogue of losses; yet I cannot refrain from this last mention of those principally dear to us. The little girl whom Adrian had rescued from utter desertion, during our ride through London on the twentieth of November, died at Auxerre. The poor child had attached herself greatly to us; and the suddenness of her death added to our sorrow. In the morning we had seen her apparently in health - in the evening, Lucy, before we retired to rest, visited our quarters to say that she was dead. Poor Lucy herself only survived, till we arrived at Dijon. She had devoted herself throughout to the nursing the sick and attending the friendless. Her excessive exertions brought on a slow fever, which ended in the dread disease whose approach soon released her from her sufferings. She had throughout been endeared to us by her good qualities, by her ready and cheerful execution of every duty, and mild acquiescence in every turn of adversity. When we consigned her to the tomb, we seemed at the same time to bid a final adieu to those peculiarly feminine virtues conspicuous in her; uneducated and unpretending as she was, she was distinguished for patience, forbearance, and sweetness. These, with all their train of qualities peculiarly English, would never again be revived for us. This type of all that was most worthy of admiration in her class among my countrywomen, was placed under the sod of desert France; and it was as a second separation from our country to have lost sight of her forever.

The Countess of Windsor died during our abode at Dijon. One morning I was informed that she wished to see me. Her message made me remember, that several days had elapsed since I had last seen her. Such a circumstance had often occurred during our journey, when I remained behind to watch to their close the last moments of some one of our hapless comrades, and the rest of the troop past on before me. But there was something in the manner of her messenger, that made me suspect that all was not right. A caprice of the imagination caused me to conjecture that some ill had occurred to Clara or Evelyn, rather than to this aged lady. Our fears, forever on the stretch, demanded a nourishment of horror; and it seemed too natural an occurrence, too like past times, for the old to die before the young. I found the venerable mother of my Idris lying on a couch, her tall emaciated figure stretched out; her face fallen away, from which the nose stood out in sharp profile, and her large dark eyes, hollow and deep, gleamed with such light as may edge a thunder cloud at sun-set. All was shriveled and dried up, except these lights; her voice too was fearfully changed, as she spoke to me at intervals. "I am afraid," said she, "that it is selfish in me to have asked you to visit the old woman again, before she dies: yet perhaps it would have been a greater shock to hear suddenly that I was dead, than to see me first thus."

I clasped her shriveled hand: "Are you indeed so ill?" I asked.

"Do you not perceive death in my face," replied she, "it is strange; I ought to have expected this, and yet I confess it has taken me unaware. I never clung to life, or enjoyed it, till these last months, while among those I senselessly deserted: and it is hard to be snatched immediately away. I am glad, however, that I am not a victim of the plague; probably I should have died at this hour, though the world had continued as it was in my youth."

She spoke with difficulty, and I perceived that she regretted the necessity of death, even more than she cared to confess. Yet she had not to complain of an undue shortening of existence; her faded person shewed that life had naturally spent itself. We had been alone at first; now Clara entered; the Countess turned to her with a smile, and took the hand of this lovely child; her roseate palm and snowy fingers, contrasted with relaxed fibers and yellow hue of those of her aged friend; she bent to kiss her, touching her withered mouth with the warm, full lips of youth. "Verney," said the Countess, "I need not recommend this dear girl to you, for your own sake you will preserve her. Were the world as it was, I should have a thousand sage precautions to impress, that one so sensitive, good, and beauteous, might escape the dangers that used to lurk for the destruction of the fair and excellent. This is all nothing now.

"I commit you, my kind nurse, to your uncle's care; to yours I entrust the dearest relic of my better self. Be to Adrian, sweet one, what you have been to me - enliven his sadness with your sprightly sallies; sooth his anguish by your sober and inspired converse, when he is dying; nurse him as you have done me."

Clara burst into tears; "Kind girl," said the Countess, "do not weep for me. Many dear friends are left to you."

"And yet," cried Clara, "you talk of their dying also. This is indeed cruel - how could I live, if they were gone? If it were possible for my beloved protector to die before me, I could not nurse him; I could only die too."

The venerable lady survived this scene only twenty-four hours. She was the last tie binding us to the ancient state of things. It was impossible to look on her, and not call to mind in their wonted guise, events and persons, as alien to our present situation as the disputes of Themistocles and Aristides, or the wars of the two roses in our native land. The crown of England had pressed her brow; the memory of my father and his misfortunes, the vain struggles of the late king, the images of Raymond, Evadne, and Perdita, who had lived in the world's prime, were brought vividly before us. We consigned her to the oblivious tomb with reluctance; and when I turned from her grave, Janus veiled his retrospective face; that which gazed on future generations had long lost its faculty.

After remaining a week at Dijon, until thirty of our number deserted the vacant ranks of life, we continued our way towards Geneva. At noon on the second day we arrived at the foot of Jura. We halted here during the heat of the day. Here fifty human beings - fifty, the only human beings that survived of the food-teeming earth, assembled to read in the looks of each other ghastly plague, or wasting sorrow, desperation, or worse, carelessness of future or present evil. Here we assembled at the foot of this mighty wall of mountain, under a spreading walnut tree; a brawling stream refreshed the green sward by its sprinkling; and the busy grasshopper chirped among the thyme. We clustered together a group of wretched sufferers. A mother cradled in her enfeebled arms the child, last of many, whose glazed eye was about to close forever. Here beauty, late glowing in youthful luster and consciousness, now wan and neglected, knelt fanning with uncertain motion the beloved, who lay striving to paint his features, distorted by illness, with a thankful smile. There an hard-featured, weather-worn veteran, having prepared his meal, sat, his head dropped on his breast, the useless knife falling from his grasp, his limbs utterly relaxed, as thought of wife and child, and dearest relative, all lost, passed across his recollection. There sat a man who for forty years had basked in fortune's tranquil sunshine; he held the hand of his last hope, his beloved daughter, who had just attained womanhood; and he gazed on her with anxious eyes, while she tried to rally her fainting spirit to comfort him. Here a servant, faithful to the last, though dying, waited on one, who, though still erect with health, gazed with gasping fear on the variety of woe around.

Adrian stood leaning against a tree; he held a book in his hand, but his eye wandered from the pages, and sought mine; they mingled a sympathetic glance; his looks confessed that his thoughts had quitted the inanimate print, for pages more pregnant with meaning, more absorbing, spread out before him. By the margin of the stream, apart from all, in a tranquil nook, where the purling brook kissed the green sward gently, Clara and Evelyn were at play, sometimes beating the water with large boughs, sometimes watching the summer-flies that sported upon it. Evelyn now chased a butterfly - now gathered a flower for his cousin; and his laughing cherub-face and clear brow told of the light heart that beat in his bosom. Clara, though she endeavored to give herself up to his amusement, often forgot him, as she turned to observe Adrian and me. She was now fourteen, and retained her childish appearance, though in height a woman; she acted the part of the tenderest mother to my little orphan boy; to see her playing with him, or attending silently and submissively on our wants, you thought only of her admirable docility and patience; but, in her soft eyes, and the veined curtains that veiled them, in the clearness of her marmoreal brow, and the tender expression of her lips, there was an intelligence and beauty that at once excited admiration and love. When the sun had sunk towards the precipitate west, and the evening shadows grew long, we prepared to ascend the mountain. The attention that we were obliged to pay to the sick, made our progress slow. The winding road, though steep, presented a confined view of rocky fields and hills, each hiding the other, till our farther ascent disclosed them in succession. We were seldom shaded from the declining sun; whose slant beams were instinct with exhausting heat. There are times when minor difficulties grow gigantic - times, when as the Hebrew poet expressively terms it, "the grasshopper is a burthen;" so was it with our ill-fated party this evening. Adrian, usually the first to rally his spirits, and dash foremost into fatigue and hardship, with relaxed limbs and declined head, the reins hanging loosely in his grasp, left the choice of the path to the instinct of his horse, now and then painfully rousing himself, when the steepness of the ascent required that he should keep his seat with better care. Fear and horror encompassed me. Did his languid air attest that he also was struck with contagion? How long, when I look on this matchless specimen of mortality, may I perceive that his thought answers mine? how long will those limbs obey the kindly spirit within? how long will light and life dwell in the eyes of this my sole remaining friend? Thus, pacing slowly, each hill surmounted, only presented another to be ascended; each jutting corner only discovered another, sister to the last, endlessly. Sometimes the pressure of sickness in one among us, caused the whole cavalcade to halt; the call for water, the eagerly expressed wish to repose; the cry of pain, and suppressed sob of the mourner - such were the sorrowful attendants of our passage of the Jura.

Adrian had gone first. I saw him, while I was detained by the loosening of a girth, struggling with the upward path, seemingly more difficult than any we had yet passed. He reached the top, and the dark outline of his figure stood in relief against the sky. He seemed to behold something unexpected and wonderful; for, pausing, his head stretched out, his arms for a moment extended, he seemed to give an All Hail! to some new vision. Urged by curiosity, I hurried to join him. After battling for many tedious minutes with the precipice, the same scene presented itself to me, which had wrapped him in ecstatic wonder.

Nature, or nature's favorite, this lovely earth, presented her most unrivalled beauties in resplendent and sudden exhibition. Below, far, far below, even as it were in the yawning abyss of the ponderous globe, lay the placid and azure expanse of lake Leman; vine-covered hills hedged it in, and behind dark mountains in cone-like shape, or irregular cyclopean wall, served for further defense. But beyond, and high above all, as if the spirits of the air had suddenly unveiled their bright abodes, placed in scale less altitude in the stainless sky, heaven-kissing, companions of the unattainable ether, were the glorious Alps, clothed in dazzling robes of light by the setting sun. And, as if the world's wonders were never to be exhausted, their vast immensities, their jagged crags, and roseate painting, appeared again in the lake below, dipping their proud heights beneath the unruffled waves - palaces for the Naiads of the placid waters. Towns and villages lay scattered at the foot of Jura, which, with dark ravine, and black promontories, stretched its roots into the watery expanse beneath. Carried away by wonder, I forgot the death of man, and the living and beloved friend near me. When I turned, I saw tears streaming from his eyes; his thin hands pressed one against the other, his animated countenance beaming with admiration; "Why," cried he, at last, "Why, oh heart, whisperest thou of grief to me? Drink in the beauty of that scene and possess delight beyond what a fabled paradise could afford."

By degrees, our whole party surmounting the steep, joined us, not one among them, but gave visible tokens of admiration, surpassing any before experienced. One cried, "God reveals his heaven to us; we may die blessed." Another and another, with broken exclamations, and extravagant phrases, endeavored to express the intoxicating effect of this wonder of nature. So we remained awhile, lightened of the pressing burthen of fate, forgetful of death, into whose night we were about to plunge; no longer reflecting that our eyes now and forever were and would be the only ones which might perceive the divine magnificence of this terrestrial exhibition. An enthusiastic transport, akin to happiness, burst, like a sudden ray from the sun, on our darkened life. Precious attribute of woe-worn humanity! that can snatch ecstatic emotion, even from under the very share and harrow, that ruthlessly ploughs up and lays waste every hope.

This evening was marked by another event. Passing through Ferney in our way to Geneva, unaccustomed sounds of music arose from the rural church which stood embosomed in trees, surrounded by smokeless, vacant cottages. The peal of an organ with rich swell awoke the mute air, lingering along, and mingling with the intense beauty that clothed the rocks and woods, and waves around. Music - the language of the immortals, disclosed to us as testimony of their existence - music, "silver key of the fountain of tears," child of love, soother of grief, inspirer of heroism and radiant thoughts, O music, in this our desolation, we had forgotten thee! Nor pipe at eve cheered us, nor harmony of voice, nor linked thrill of string; thou camest upon us now, like the revealing of other forms of being; and transported as we had been by the loveliness of nature, fancying that we beheld the abode of spirits, now we might well imagine that we heard their melodious communings. We paused in such awe as would seize on a pale votarist, visiting some holy shrine at midnight; if she beheld animated and smiling, the image which she worshipped. We all stood mute; many knelt. In a few minutes however, we were recalled to human wonder and sympathy by a familiar strain. The air was Haydn's "New-Created World," and, old and drooping as humanity had become, the world yet fresh as at creation's day, might still be worthily celebrated by such a hymn of praise. Adrian and I entered the church; the nave was empty, though the smoke of incense rose from the altar, bringing with it the recollection of vast congregations, in once thronged cathedrals; we went into the loft. A blind old man sat at the bellows; his whole soul was ear; and as he sat in the attitude of attentive listening, a bright glow of pleasure was diffused over his countenance; for, though his lack-luster eye could not reflect the beam, yet his parted lips, and every line of his face and venerable brow spoke delight. A young woman sat at the keys, perhaps twenty years of age. Her auburn hair hung on her neck, and her fair brow shone in its own beauty; but her drooping eyes let fall fast-flowing tears, while the constraint she exercised to suppress her sobs, and still her trembling, flushed her else pale cheek; she was thin; languor, and alas! sickness, bent her form. We stood looking at the pair, forgetting what we heard in the absorbing sight; till, the last chord struck, the peal died away in lessening reverberations. The mighty voice, inorganic we might call it, for we could in no way associate it with mechanism of pipe or key, stilled its sonorous tone, and the girl, turning to lend her assistance to her aged companion, at length perceived us.

It was her father; and she, since childhood, had been the guide of his darkened steps. They were Germans from Saxony, and, emigrating thither but a few years before, had formed new ties with the surrounding villagers. About the time that the pestilence had broken out, a young German student had joined them. Their simple history was easily divined. He, a noble, loved the fair daughter of the poor musician, and followed them in their flight from the persecutions of his friends; but soon the mighty leveler came with unblunted scythe to mow, together with the grass, the tall flowers of the field. The youth was an early victim. She preserved herself for her father's sake. His blindness permitted her to continue a delusion, at first the child of accident - and now solitary beings, sole survivors in the land, he remained unacquainted with the change, nor was aware that when he listened to his child's music, the mute mountains, senseless lake, and unconscious trees, were, himself excepted, her sole auditors.

The very day that we arrived she had been attacked by symptomatic illness. She was paralyzed with horror at the idea of leaving her aged, sightless father alone on the empty earth; but she had not courage to disclose the truth, and the very excess of her desperation animated her to surpassing exertions. At the accustomed vesper hour, she led him to the chapel; and, though trembling and weeping on his account, she played, without fault in time, or error in note, the hymn written to celebrate the creation of the adorned earth, soon to be her tomb.

We came to her like visitors from heaven itself; her high-wrought courage; her hardly sustained firmness, fled with the appearance of relief. With a shriek she rushed towards us, embraced the knees of Adrian, and uttering but the words, "O save my father!" with sobs and hysterical cries, opened the long-shut floodgates of her woe.

Poor girl! - she and her father now lie side by side, beneath the high walnut-tree where her lover reposes, and which in her dying moments she had pointed out to us. Her father, at length aware of his daughter's danger, unable to see the changes of her dear countenance, obstinately held her hand, till it was chilled and stiffened by death. Nor did he then move or speak, till, twelve hours after, kindly death took him to his brakeless repose. They rest beneath the sod, the tree their monument; - the hallowed spot is distinct in my memory, paled in by craggy Jura, and the far, immeasurable Alps; the spire of the church they frequented still points from out the embosoming trees; and though her hand be cold, still methinks the sounds of divine music which they loved wander about, solacing their gentle ghosts.

CHAPTER VIII

We had now reached Switzerland, so long the final mark and aim of our exertions. We had looked, I know not wherefore, with hope and pleasing expectation on her congregation of hills and snowy crags, and opened our bosoms with renewed spirits to the icy Biz, which even at Midsummer used to come from the northern glacier laden with cold. Yet how could we nourish expectation of relief? Like our native England, and the vast extent of fertile France, this mountain-embowered land was desolate of its inhabitants. Nor bleak mountain-top, nor snow-nourished rivulet; not the ice-laden Biz, nor thunder, the tamer of contagion, had preserved them - why therefore should we claim exemption?

Who was there indeed to save? What troop had we brought fit to stand at bay, and combat with the conqueror? We were a failing remnant, tamed to mere submission to the coming blow. A train half dead, through fear of death - a hopeless, unresisting, almost reckless crew, which, in the tossed bark of life, had given up all pilotage, and resigned themselves to the destructive force of ungoverned winds. Like a few furrows of unreaped corn, which, left standing on a wide field after the rest is gathered to the garner, are swiftly borne down by the winter storm. Like a few straggling swallows, which, remaining after their fellows had, on the first unkind breath of passing autumn, migrated to genial climes, were struck to earth by the first frost of November. Like a stray sheep that wanders over the sleet-beaten hillside, while the flock is in the pen, and dies before morning-dawn. Like a cloud, like one of many that were spread in impenetrable woof over the sky, which, when the shepherd north has driven its companions "to drink Antipodean noon," fades and dissolves in the clear ether - Such were we!

We left the fair margin of the beauteous lake of Geneva, and entered the Alpine ravines; tracing to its source the brawling Arve, through the rock-bound valley of Servox, beside the mighty waterfalls, and under the shadow of the inaccessible mountains, we travelled on; while the luxuriant walnut-tree gave place to the dark pine, whose musical branches swung in the wind, and whose upright forms had braved a thousand storms - till the verdant sod, the flowery dell, and shrubbery hill were exchanged for the sky-piercing, untrodden, seedless rock, "the bones of the world, waiting to be clothed with everything necessary to give life and beauty." Strange that we should seek shelter here! Surely, if, in those countries where earth was wont, like a tender mother, to nourish her children, we had found her a destroyer, we need not seek it here, where stricken by keen penury she seems to shudder through her stony veins. Nor were we mistaken in our conjecture. We vainly sought the vast and ever moving glaciers of Chamounix, rifts of pendant ice, seas of congelated waters, the leafless groves of tempest-battered pines, dells, mere paths for the loud avalanche, and hill-tops, the resort of thunder-storms. Pestilence reigned paramount even here. By the time that day and night, like twin sisters of equal growth, shared equally their dominion over the hours, one by one, beneath the ice-caves, beside the waters springing from the thawed snows of a thousand winters, another and yet another of the remnant of the race of Man, closed their eyes forever to the light.

Yet we were not quite wrong in seeking a scene like this, whereon to close the drama. Nature, true to the last, consoled us in the very heart of misery. Sublime grandeur of outward objects soothed our hapless hearts and were in harmony with our desolation. Many sorrows have befallen man during his checkered course; and many a woe-stricken mourner has found himself sole survivor among many. Our misery took its majestic shape and coloring from the vast ruin, that accompanied and made one with it. Thus on lovely earth, many a dark ravine contains a brawling stream, shadowed by romantic rocks, threaded by mossy paths — but all, except this, wanted the mighty back-ground, the towering Alps, whose snowy capes, or bared ridges, lifted us from our dull mortal abode, to the palaces of Nature's own.

This solemn harmony of event and situation regulated our feelings and gave as it were fitting costume to our last act. Majestic gloom and tragic pomp attended the decease of wretched humanity. The funeral procession of monarchs of old, was transcended by our splendid shews. Near the sources of the Arveiron we performed the rites for, four only excepted, the last of the species. Adrian and I, leaving Clara and Evelyn wrapped in peaceful unobserving slumber, carried the body to this desolate spot, and placed it in those caves of ice beneath the glacier, which rive and split with the slightest sound, and bring destruction on those within the clefts - no bird or beast of prey could here profane the frozen form. So, with hushed steps and in silence, we placed the dead on a bier of ice, and then, departing, stood on the rocky platform beside the river springs. All hushed as we had been, the very striking of the air with our persons had sufficed to disturb the repose of this thawless region; and we had hardly left the cavern, before vast blocks of ice, detaching themselves from the roof, fell, and covered the human image we had deposited within. We had chosen a fair moonlight night, but our journey thither had been long, and the crescent sank behind the western heights by the time we had accomplished our purpose. The snowy mountains and blue glaciers shone in their own light. The rugged and abrupt ravine, which formed one side of Mont Anvert, was opposite to us, the glacier at our side; at our feet Arveiron, white and foaming, dashed over the pointed rocks that jutted into it, and, with whirring spray and ceaseless roar, disturbed the stilly night. Yellow lightnings played around the vast dome of Mont Blanc, silent as the snow-clad rock they illuminated; all was bare, wild, and sublime, while the singing of the pines in melodious murmurings added a gentle interest to the rough magnificence. Now the riving and fall of icy rocks clave the air; now the thunder of the avalanche burst on our ears. In countries whose features are of less magnitude, nature betrays her living powers in the foliage of the trees, in the growth of herbage, in the soft purling of meandering streams; here, endowed with giant attributes, the torrent, the thunder-storm, and the flow of massive waters, display her activity. Such the churchyard, such the requiem, such the eternal congregation, that waited on our companion's funeral!

Nor was it the human form alone which we had placed in this eternal sepulcher, whose obsequies we now celebrated. With this last victim Plague vanished from the earth. Death had never wanted weapons wherewith to destroy life, and we, few and weak as we had become, were still exposed to every other shaft with which his full quiver teemed. But pestilence was absent from among them. For seven years it had had full sway upon earth; she had trod every nook of our spacious globe; she had mingled with the atmosphere, which as a cloak enwraps all our fellow-creatures - the inhabitants of native Europe - the luxurious Asiatic - the swarthy African and free American had been vanquished and destroyed by her. Her barbarous tyranny came to its close here in the rocky vale of Chamounix.

Still recurring scenes of misery and pain, the fruits of this distemper, made no more a part of our lives - the word plague no longer rung in our ears - the aspect of plague incarnate in the human countenance no longer appeared before our eyes. From this moment I saw plague no more. She abdicated her throne and despoiled herself of her imperial scepter among the ice rocks that surrounded us. She left solitude and silence co-heirs of her kingdom.

My present feelings are so mingled with the past, that I cannot say whether the knowledge of this change visited us, as we stood on this sterile spot. It seems to me that it did; that a cloud seemed to pass from over us, that a weight was taken from the air; that henceforth we breathed more freely and raised our heads with some portion of former liberty. Yet we did not hope. We were impressed by the sentiment, that our race was run, but that plague would not be our destroyer. The coming time was as a mighty river, down which a charmed boat is driven, whose mortal steersman knows, that the obvious peril is not the one he needs fear, yet that danger is nigh; and who floats awe-struck under beetling precipices, through the dark and turbid waters - seeing in the distance yet stranger and ruder shapes, towards which he is irresistibly impelled. What would become of us? O for some Delphic oracle, or Pythian maid, to utter the secrets of futurity! O for some Oedipus to solve the riddle of the cruel Sphynx! Such Oedipus was I to be - not divining a word's juggle, but whose agonizing pangs, and sorrow-tainted life were to be the engines, wherewith to lay bare the secrets of destiny, and reveal the meaning of the enigma, whose explanation closed the history of the human race.

Dim fancies, akin to these, haunted our minds, and instilled feelings not unallied to pleasure, as we stood beside this silent tomb of nature, reared by these lifeless mountains, above her living veins, choking her vital principle. "Thus, are we left," said Adrian, "two melancholy blasted trees, where once a forest waved. We are left to mourn, and pine, and die. Yet even now we have our duties, which we must string ourselves to fulfil: the duty of bestowing pleasure where we can, and by force of love, irradiating with rainbow hues the tempest of grief. Nor will I repine if in this extremity we preserve what we now possess. Something tells me, Verney, that we need no longer dread our cruel enemy, and I cling with delight to the oracular voice. Though strange, it will be sweet to mark the growth of your little boy, and the development of Clara's young heart. In the midst of a desert world, we are everything to them; and, if we live, it must be our task to make this new mode of life happy to them. At present this is easy, for their childish ideas do not wander into futurity, and the stinging craving for sympathy, and all of love of which our nature is susceptible, is not yet awake within them: we cannot guess what will happen then, when nature asserts her indefeasible and sacred powers; but, long before that time, we may all be cold, as he who lies in yonder tomb of ice. We need only provide for the present, and endeavor to fill with pleasant images the inexperienced fancy of your lovely niece. The scenes which now surround us, vast and sublime as they are, are not such as can best contribute to this work. Nature is here like our fortunes, grand, but too destructive, bare, and rude, to be able to afford delight to her young imagination. Let us descend to the sunny plains of Italy. Winter will soon be here, to clothe this wilderness in double desolation; but we will cross the bleak hill-tops, and lead her to scenes of fertility and beauty, where her path will be adorned with flowers, and the cheery atmosphere inspire pleasure and hope."

In pursuance of this plan we quitted Chamonix on the following day. We had no cause to hasten our steps; no event was transacted beyond our actual sphere to enchain our resolves, so we yielded to every idle whim, and deemed our time well spent, when we could behold the passage of the hours without dismay. We loitered along the lovely Vale of Servox; passed long hours on the bridge, which, crossing the ravine of Arve, commands a prospect of its pine-clothed depths, and the snowy mountains that wall it in. We rambled through romantic Switzerland; till, fear of coming winter leading us forward, the first days of October found us in the valley of La Maurine, which leads to Cenis. I cannot explain the reluctance we felt at leaving this land of mountains; perhaps it was, that we regarded the Alps as boundaries between our former and our future state of existence, and so clung fondly to what of old we had loved. Perhaps, because we had now so few impulses urging to a choice between two modes of action, we were pleased to preserve the existence of one, and preferred the prospect of what we were to do, to the recollection of what had been done. We felt that for this year danger was past; and we believed that, for some months, we were secured to each other. There was a thrilling, agonizing delight in the thought - it filled the eyes with misty tears, it tore the heart with tumultuous heavings; frailer than the "snow fall in the river," were we each and all - but we strove to give life and individuality to the meteoric course of our several existences, and to feel that no moment escaped us unenjoyed. Thus, tottering on the dizzy brink, we were happy. Yes! as we sat beneath the toppling rocks, beside the waterfalls, near

Forests, ancient as the hills,

And folding sunny spots of greenery, where the chamois grazed, and the timid squirrel laid up its hoard - descanting on the charms of nature, drinking in the while her unalienable beauties - we were, in an empty world, happy.

Yet, O days of joy - days, when eye spoke to eye, and voices, sweeter than the music of the swinging branches of the pines, or rivulet's gentle murmur, answered mine - yet, O days replete with beatitude, days of loved society - days unutterably dear to me forlorn - pass, O pass before me, making me in your memory forget what I am. Behold, how my streaming eyes blot this senseless paper - behold, how my features are convulsed by agonizing throes, at your mere recollection, now that, alone, my tears flow, my lips quiver, my cries fill the air, unseen, unmarked, unheard! Yet, O yet, days of delight! let me dwell on your long-drawn hours!

As the cold increased upon us, we passed the Alps, and descended into Italy. At the uprising of morn, we sat at our repast, and cheated our regrets by gay sallies or learned disquisitions. The live-long day we sauntered on, still keeping in view the end of our journey, but careless of the hour of its completion. As the evening star shone out, and the orange sunset, far in the west, marked the position of the dear land we had forever left, talk, thought enchaining, made the hours fly - O that we had lived thus forever and forever! Of what consequence was it to our four hearts, that they alone were the fountains of life in the wide world? As far as mere individual sentiment was concerned, we had rather be left thus united together, than if, each alone in a populous desert of unknown men, we had wandered truly companionless till life's last term. In this manner, we endeavored to console each other; in this manner, true philosophy taught us to reason.

It was the delight of Adrian and me to wait on Clara, naming her the little queen of the world, ourselves her humblest servitors. When we arrived at a town, our first care was to select for her its most choice abode; to make sure that no harrowing relic remained of its former inhabitants; to seek food for her, and minister to her wants with assiduous tenderness. Clara entered into our scheme with childish gaiety. Her chief business was to attend on Evelyn; but it was her sport to array herself in splendid robes, adorn herself with sunny gems, and ape a princely state. Her religion, deep and pure, did not teach her to refuse to blunt thus the keen sting of regret; her youthful vivacity made her enter, heart and soul, into these strange masquerades.

We had resolved to pass the ensuing winter at Milan, which, as being a large and luxurious city, would afford us choice of homes. We had descended the Alps and left far behind their vast forests and mighty crags. We entered smiling Italy. Mingled grass and corn grew in her plains, the unpruned vines threw their luxuriant branches around the elms. The grapes, overripe, had fallen on the ground, or hung purple, or burnished green, among the red and yellow leaves. The ears of standing corn winnowed to emptiness by the spendthrift winds; the fallen foliage of the trees, the weed-grown brooks, the dusky olive, now spotted with its blackened fruit; the chestnuts, to which the squirrel only was harvest-man; all plenty, and yet, alas! all poverty, painted in wondrous hues and fantastic groupings this land of beauty. In the towns, in the voiceless towns, we visited the churches, adorned by pictures, master-pieces of art, or galleries of statues — while in this genial clime the animals, in new found liberty, rambled through the gorgeous palaces, and hardly feared our forgotten aspect. The dove-colored oxen turned their full eyes on us, and paced slowly by; a startling throng of silly sheep, with pattering feet, would start up in some chamber, formerly dedicated to the repose of beauty, and rush, huddling past us, down the marble staircase into the street, and again in at the first open door, taking unrebuked possession of hallowed sanctuary, or kingly council-chamber. We no longer started at these occurrences, nor at worse exhibition of change — when the palace had become a mere tomb, pregnant with fetid stench, strewn with the dead; and we could perceive how pestilence and fear had played strange antics, chasing the luxurious dame to the dank fields and bare cottage; gathering, among carpets of Indian woof, and beds of silk, the rough peasant, or the deformed half-human shape of the wretched beggar.

We arrived at Milan and stationed ourselves in the Vice-Roy's palace. Here we made laws for ourselves, dividing our day, and fixing distinct occupations for each hour. In the morning we rode in the adjoining country, or wandered through the palaces, in search of pictures or antiquities. In the evening we assembled to read or to converse. There were few books that we dared read; few, that did not cruelly deface the painting we bestowed on our solitude, by recalling combinations and emotions never more to be experienced by us. Metaphysical disquisition; fiction, which wandering from all reality, lost itself in self-created errors; poets of times so far gone by, that to read of them was as to read of Atlantis and Utopia; or such as referred to nature only, and the workings of one particular mind; but most of all, talk, varied and ever new, beguiled our hours.

While we paused thus in our onward career towards death, time held on its accustomed course. Still and for ever did the earth roll on, enthroned in her atmospheric car, speeded by the force of the invisible coursers of never-erring necessity. And now, this dewdrop in the sky, this ball, ponderous with mountains, lucent with waves, passing from the short tyranny of watery Pisces and the frigid Ram, entered the radiant demesne of Taurus and the Twins. There, fanned by vernal airs, the Spirit of Beauty sprung from her cold repose; and, with winnowing wings and soft pacing feet, set a girdle of verdure around the earth, sporting among the violets, hiding within the springing foliage of the trees, tripping lightly down the radiant streams into the sunny deep. "For lo! winter is past, the rain is over and gone; the flowers appear on the earth, the time of the singing of birds is come, and the voice of the turtle is heard in our land; the fig tree putteth forth her green figs, and the vines, with the tender grape, give a good smell." Thus, was it in the time of the ancient regal poet; thus was it now.

Yet how could we miserable hail the approach of this delightful season? We hoped indeed that death did not now as heretofore walk in its shadow; yet, left as we were alone to each other, we looked in each other's faces with enquiring eyes, not daring altogether to trust to our presentiments, and endeavoring to divine which would be the hapless survivor to the other three. We were to pass the summer at the lake of Como, and thither we removed as soon as spring grew to her maturity, and the snow disappeared from the hill tops. Ten miles from Como, under the steep heights of the eastern mountains, by the margin of the lake, was a villa called the Pliniana, from its being built on the site of a fountain, whose periodical ebb and flow is described by the younger Pliny in his letters. The house had nearly fallen into ruin, till in the year 2090, an English nobleman had bought it, and fitted it up with every luxury. Two large halls, hung with splendid tapestry, and paved with marble, opened on each side of a court, of whose two other sides one overlooked the deep dark lake, and the other was bounded by a mountain, from whose stony side gushed, with roar and splash, the celebrated fountain. Above, underwood of myrtle and tufts of odorous plants crowned the rock, while the star-pointing giant cypresses reared themselves in the blue air, and the recesses of the hills were adorned with the luxuriant growth of chestnut-trees. Here we fixed our summer residence. We had a lovely skiff, in which we sailed, now stemming the midmost waves, now coasting the over-hanging and craggy banks, thick sown with evergreens, which dipped their shining leaves in the waters, and were mirrored in many a little bay and creek of waters of translucent darkness. Here orange plants bloomed, here birds poured forth melodious hymns; and here, during spring, the cold snake emerged from the clefts, and basked on the sunny terraces of rock.

Were we not happy in this paradisiacal retreat? If some kind spirit had whispered forgetfulness to us, methinks we should have been happy here, where the precipitous mountains, nearly pathless, shut from our view the far fields of desolate earth, and with small exertion of the imagination, we might fancy that the cities were still resonant with popular hum, and the peasant still guided his plough through the furrow, and that we, the world's free denizens, enjoyed a voluntary exile, and not a remediless cutting off from our extinct species.

Not one among us enjoyed the beauty of this scenery so much as Clara. Before we quitted Milan, a change had taken place in her habits and manners. She lost her gaiety, she laid aside her sports, and assumed an almost vestal plainness of attire. She shunned us, retiring with Evelyn to some distant chamber or silent nook; nor did she enter into his pastimes with the same zest as she was wont, but would sit and watch him with sadly tender smiles, and eyes bright with tears, yet without a word of complaint. She approached us timidly, avoided our caresses, nor shook off her embarrassment till some serious discussion or lofty theme called her for a while out of herself. Her beauty grew as a rose, which, opening to the summer wind, discloses leaf after leaf till the sense aches with its excess of loveliness. A slight and variable color tinged her cheeks, and her motions seemed attuned by some hidden harmony of surpassing sweetness. We redoubled our tenderness and earnest attentions. She received them with grateful smiles, that fled swift as sunny beam from a glittering wave on an April day.

Our only acknowledged point of sympathy with her, appeared to be Evelyn. This dear little fellow was a comforter and delight to us beyond all words. His buoyant spirit, and his innocent ignorance of our vast calamity, were balm to us, whose thoughts and feelings were over-wrought and spun out in the immensity of speculative sorrow. To cherish, to caress, to amuse him was the common task of all. Clara, who felt towards him in some degree like a young mother, gratefully acknowledged our kindness towards him. To me, O! to me, who saw the clear brows and soft eyes of the beloved of my heart, my lost and ever dear Idris, reborn in his gentle face, to me he was dear even to pain; if I pressed him to my heart, methought I clasped a real and living part of her, who had lain there through long years of youthful happiness.

It was the custom of Adrian and myself to go out each day in our skiff to forage in the adjacent country. In these expeditions we were seldom accompanied by Clara or her little charge, but our return was an hour of hilarity. Evelyn ransacked our stores with childish eagerness, and we always brought some new-found gift for our fair companion. Then too we made discoveries of lovely scenes or gay palaces, whither in the evening we all proceeded. Our sailing expeditions were most divine, and with a fair wind or transverse course we cut the liquid waves; and, if talk failed under the pressure of thought, I had my clarinet with me, which awoke the echoes, and gave the change to our careful minds. Clara at such times often returned to her former habits of free converse and gay sally; and though our four hearts alone beat in the world, those four hearts were happy.

One day, on our return from the town of Como, with a laden boat, we expected as usual to be met at the port by Clara and Evelyn, and we were somewhat surprised to see the beach vacant. I, as my nature prompted, would not prognosticate evil, but explained it away as a mere casual incident. Not so Adrian. He was seized with sudden trembling and apprehension, and he called to me with vehemence to steer quickly for land, and, when near, leapt from the boat, half falling into the water; and, scrambling up the steep bank, hastened along the narrow strip of garden, the only level space between the lake and the mountain. I followed without delay; the garden and inner court were empty, so was the house, whose every room we visited. Adrian called loudly upon Clara's name, and was about to rush up the near mountain-path, when the door of a summer-house at the end of the garden slowly opened, and Clara appeared, not advancing towards us, but leaning against a column of the building with blanched cheeks, in a posture of utter despondency. Adrian sprang towards her with a cry of joy and folded her delightedly in his arms. She withdrew from his embrace, and, without a word, again entered the summerhouse. Her quivering lips, her despairing heart refused to afford her voice to express our misfortune. Poor little Evelyn had, while playing with her, been seized with sudden fever, and now lay torpid and speechless on a little couch in the summerhouse.

For a whole fortnight we unceasingly watched beside the poor child, as his life declined under the ravages of a virulent typhus. His little form and tiny lineaments encaged the embryo of the world-spanning mind of man. Man's nature, brimful of passions and affections, would have had a home in that little heart, whose swift pulsations hurried towards their close. His small hand's fine mechanism, now flaccid and unbent, would in the growth of sinew and muscle, have achieved works of beauty or of strength. His tender rosy feet would have trod in firm manhood the bowers and glades of earth - these reflections were now of little use: he lay, thought and strength suspended, waiting unresisting the final blow.

We watched at his bedside, and when the access of fever was on him, we neither spoke nor looked at each other, marking only his obstructed breath and the mortal glow that tinged his sunken cheek, the heavy death that weighed on his eyelids. It is a trite evasion to say, that words could not express our long drawn agony; yet how can words image sensations, whose tormenting keenness throw us back, as it were, on the deep roots and hidden foundations of our nature, which shake our being with earth-quake-throe, so that we leave to confide in accustomed feelings which like mother-earth support us, and cling to some vain imagination or deceitful hope, which will soon be buried in the ruins occasioned by the final shock. I have called that period a fortnight, which we passed watching the changes of the sweet child's malady - and such it might have been — at night, we wondered to find another day gone, while each particular hour seemed endless. Day and night were exchanged for one another uncounted; we slept hardly at all, nor did we even quit his room, except when a pang of grief seized us, and we retired from each other for a short period to conceal our sobs and tears. We endeavored in vain to abstract Clara from this deplorable scene. She sat, hour after hour, looking at him, now softly arranging his pillow, and, while he had power to swallow, administered his drink. At length the moment of his death came: the blood paused in its flow - his eyes opened, and then closed again: without convulsion or sigh, the frail tenement was left vacant of its spiritual inhabitant.

I have heard that the sight of the dead has confirmed materialists in their belief. I ever felt otherwise. Was that my child - that moveless decaying inanimation? My child was enraptured by my caresses; his dear voice clothed with meaning articulations his thoughts, otherwise inaccessible; his smile was a ray of the soul, and the same soul sat upon its throne in his eyes. I turn from this mockery of what he was. Take, O earth, thy debt! freely and forever I consign to thee the garb thou didst afford. But thou, sweet child, amiable and beloved boy, either thy spirit has sought a fitter dwelling, or shrined in my heart, thou livest while it lives.

We placed his remains under a cypress, the upright mountain being scooped out to receive them. And then Clara said, "If you wish me to live, take me from hence. There is something in this scene of transcendent beauty, in these trees, and hills and waves, that forever whisper to me, leave thy cumbrous flesh, and make a part of us. I earnestly entreat you to take me away."

So on the fifteenth of August we bade adieu to our villa, and the embowering shades of this abode of beauty; to calm bay and noisy waterfall; to Evelyn's little grave we bade farewell! and then, with heavy hearts, we departed on our pilgrimage towards Rome.

CHAPTER IX

Now - soft awhile - have I arrived so near the end? Yes! it is all over now - a step or two over those new made graves, and the wearisome way is done. Can I accomplish my task? Can I streak my paper with words capacious of the grand conclusion? Arise, black Melancholy! quit thy Cimmerian solitude! Bring with thee murky fogs from hell, which may drink up the day; bring blight and pestiferous exhalations, which, entering the hollow caverns and breathing places of earth, may fill her stony veins with corruption, so that not only herbage may no longer flourish, the trees may rot, and the rivers run with gall - but the everlasting mountains be decomposed, and the mighty deep putrefy, and the genial atmosphere which clips the globe, lose all powers of generation and sustenance. Do this, sad visaged power, while I write, while eyes read these pages.

And who will read them? Beware, tender offspring of the re-born world - beware, fair being, with human heart, yet untamed by care, and human brow, yet unploughed by time - beware, lest the cheerful current of thy blood be checked, thy golden locks turn grey, thy sweet dimpling smiles be changed to fixed, harsh wrinkles! Let not day look on these lines, lest garish day waste, turn pale, and die. Seek a cypress grove, whose moaning boughs will be harmony befitting; seek some cave, deep embowered in earth's dark entrails, where no light will penetrate, save that which struggles, red and flickering, through a single fissure, staining thy page with grimmest livery of death.

There is a painful confusion in my brain, which refuses to delineate distinctly succeeding events. Sometimes the irradiation of my friend's gentle smile comes before me; and methinks its light spans and fills eternity - then, again, I feel the gasping throes -

We quitted Como, and in compliance with Adrian's earnest desire, we took Venice in our way to Rome. There was something to the English peculiarly attractive in the idea of this wave-encircled, island-enthroned city. Adrian had never seen it. We went down the Po and the Brenta in a boat; and, the days proving intolerably hot, we rested in the bordering palaces during the day, travelling through the night, when darkness made the bordering banks indistinct, and our solitude less remarkable; when the wandering moon lit the waves that divided before our prow, and the night-wind filled our sails, and the murmuring stream, waving trees, and swelling canvass, accorded in harmonious strain. Clara, long overcome by excessive grief, had to a great degree cast aside her timid, cold reserve, and received our attentions with grateful tenderness. While Adrian with poetic fervor discoursed of the glorious nations of the dead, of the beauteous earth and the fate of man, she crept near him, drinking in his speech with silent pleasure. We banished from our talk, and as much as possible from our thoughts, the knowledge of our desolation. And it would be incredible to an inhabitant of cities, to one among a busy throng, to what extent we succeeded. It was as a man confined in a dungeon, whose small and grated rift at first renders the doubtful light more sensibly obscure, till, the visual orb having drunk in the beam, and adapted itself to its scantiness, he finds that clear noon inhabits his cell. So, we, a simple triad on empty earth, were multiplied to each other, till we became all in all. We stood like trees, whose roots are loosened by the wind, which support one another, leaning and clinging with increased fervor while the wintry storms howl. Thus, we floated down the widening stream of the Po, sleeping when the cycle sang, awake with the stars. We entered the narrower banks of the Brenta and arrived at the shore of the Laguna at sunrise on the sixth of September. The bright orb slowly rose from behind its cupolas and towers and shed its penetrating light upon the glassy waters. Wrecks of gondolas, and some few uninjured ones, were strewed on the beach at Fusina. We embarked in one of these for the widowed daughter of ocean, who, abandoned and fallen, sat forlorn on her propping isles, looking towards the far mountains of Greece. We rowed lightly over the Laguna and entered Canale Grande. The tide ebbed sullenly from out the broken portals and violated halls of Venice: sea weed and sea monsters were left on the blackened marble, while the salt ooze defaced the matchless works of art that adorned their walls, and the sea gull flew out from the shattered window. In the midst of this appalling ruin of the monuments of man's power, nature asserted her ascendancy, and shone more beauteous from the contrast. The radiant waters hardly trembled, while the rippling waves made many sided mirrors to the sun; the blue immensity, seen beyond Lido, stretched far, unencumbered by boat, so tranquil, so lovely, that it seemed to invite us to quit the land strewn with ruins, and to seek refuge from sorrow and fear on its placid extent.

We saw the ruins of this hapless city from the height of the tower of San Marco, immediately under us, and turned with sickening hearts to the sea, which, though it be a grave, rears no monument, discloses no ruin. Evening had come apace. The sun set in calm majesty behind the misty summits of the Apennines, and its golden and roseate hues painted the mountains of the opposite shore. "That land," said Adrian, "tinged with the last glories of the day, is Greece." Greece! The sound had a responsive chord in the bosom of Clara. She vehemently reminded us that we had promised to take her once again to Greece, to the tomb of her parents. Why go to Rome? what should we do at Rome? We might take one of the many vessels to be found here, embark in it, and steer right for Albania.

I objected the dangers of ocean, and the distance of the mountains we saw, from Athens; a distance which, from the savage uncultivation of the country, was almost impassable. Adrian, who was delighted with Clara's proposal, obviated these objections. The season was favorable; the north-west that blew would take us transversely across the gulph; and then we might find, in some abandoned port, a light Greek caique, adapted for such navigation, and run down the coast of the Morea, and, passing over the Isthmus of Corinth, without much land-travelling or fatigue, find ourselves at Athens. This appeared to me wild talk; but the sea, glowing with a thousand purple hues, looked so brilliant and safe; my beloved companions were so earnest, so determined, that, when Adrian said, "Well, though it is not exactly what you wish, yet consent, to please me" - I could no longer refuse. That evening we selected a vessel, whose size just seemed fitted for our enterprise; we bent the sails and put the rigging in order, and reposing that night in one of the city's thousand palaces, agreed to embark at sunrise the following morning.

When winds that move not its calm surface, sweep
The azure sea, I love the land no more.
The smiles of the serene and tranquil deep
Tempt my unquiet mind —

Thus, said Adrian, quoting a translation of Moschus's poem, as in the clear morning light, we rowed over the Laguna, past Lido, into the open sea - I would have added in continuation,

But when the roar
Of ocean's gray abyss resounds, and foam
Gathers upon the sea, and vast waves burst —

But my friends declared that such verses were evil augury; so, in cheerful mood we left the shallow waters, and, when out at sea, unfurled our sails to catch the favorable breeze. The laughing morning air filled them, while sun-light bathed earth, sky and ocean - the placid waves divided to receive our keel, and playfully kissed the dark sides of our little skiff, murmuring a welcome; as land receded, still the blue expanse, most waveless, twin sister to the azure empyrean, afforded smooth conduct to our bark. As the air and waters were tranquil and balmy, so were our minds steeped in quiet. In comparison with the unstained deep, funereal earth appeared a grave, its high rocks and stately mountains were but monuments, its trees the plumes of a hearse, the brooks and rivers brackish with tears for departed man. Farewell to desolate towns - to fields with their savage intermixture of corn and weeds - to ever multiplying relics of our lost species. Ocean, we commit ourselves to thee - even as the patriarch of old floated above the drowned world, let us be saved, as thus we betake ourselves to thy perennial flood.

Adrian sat at the helm; I attended to the rigging, the breeze right aft filled our swelling canvas, and we ran before it over the untroubled deep. The wind died away at noon; its idle breath just permitted us to hold our course. As lazy, fair-weather sailors, careless of the coming hour, we talked gaily of our coasting voyage, of our arrival at Athens. We would make our home of one of the Cyclades, and there in myrtle-groves, amidst perpetual spring, fanned by the wholesome sea-breezes - we would live long years in beatific union - Was there such a thing as death in the world?

The sun passed its zenith and lingered down the stainless floor of heaven. Lying in the boat, my face turned up to the sky, I thought I saw on its blue white, marbled streaks, so slight, so immaterial, that now I said - They are there - and now, It is a mere imagination. A sudden fear stung me while I gazed; and, starting up, and running to the prow, - as I stood, my hair was gently lifted on my brow - a dark line of ripples appeared to the east, gaining rapidly on us - my breathless remark to Adrian, was followed by the flapping of the canvas, as the adverse wind struck it, and our boat lurched - swift as speech, the web of the storm thickened overhead, the sun went down red, the dark sea was strewed with foam, and our skiff rose and fell in its increasing furrows.

Behold us now in our frail tenement, hemmed in by hungry, roaring waves, buffeted by winds. In the inky east two vast clouds, sailing contrary ways, met; the lightning leapt forth, and the hoarse thunder muttered. Again, in the south, the clouds replied, and the forked stream of fire running along the black sky, shewed us the appalling piles of clouds, now met and obliterated by the heaving waves. Great God! And we alone - we three - alone – alone - sole dwellers on the sea and on the earth, we three must perish! The vast universe, its myriad worlds, and the plains of boundless earth which we had left - the extent of shoreless sea around - contracted to my view - they and all that they contained, shrunk up to one point, even to our tossing bark, freighted with glorious humanity.

A convulsion of despair crossed the love-beaming face of Adrian, while with set teeth he murmured, "Yet they shall be saved!" Clara, visited by a human pang, pale and trembling, crept near him - he looked on her with an encouraging smile - "Do you fear, sweet girl? O, do not fear, we shall soon be on shore!"

The darkness prevented me from seeing the changes of her countenance; but her voice was clear and sweet, as she replied, "Why should I fear? neither sea nor storm can harm us, if mighty destiny or the ruler of destiny does not permit. And then the stinging fear of surviving either of you, is not here—one death will clasp us undivided."

Meanwhile we took in all our sails, save a gib; and, as soon as we might without danger, changed our course, running with the wind for the Italian shore. Dark night mixed everything; we hardly discerned the white crests of the murderous surges, except when lightning made brief noon, and drank the darkness, shewing us our danger, and restoring us to double night. We were all silent, except when Adrian, as steersman, made an encouraging observation. Our little shell obeyed the rudder miraculously well, and ran along on the top of the waves, as if she had been an offspring of the sea, and the angry mother sheltered her endangered child.

I sat at the prow, watching our course; when suddenly I heard the waters break with redoubled fury. We were certainly near the shore - at the same time I cried, "About there!" and a broad lightning filling the concave, shewed us for one moment the level beach ahead, disclosing even the sands, and stunted, ooze-sprinkled beds of reeds, that grew at high water mark. Again, it was dark, and we drew in our breath with such content as one may, who, while fragments of volcano-hurled rock darken the air, sees a vast mass ploughing the ground immediately at his feet. What to do we know not - the breakers here, there, everywhere, encompassed us - they roared, and dashed, and flung their hated spray in our faces. With considerable difficulty and danger, we succeeded at length in altering our course, and stretched out from shore. I urged my companions to prepare for the wreck of our little skiff, and to bind themselves to some oar or spar which might suffice to float them. I was myself an excellent swimmer - the very sight of the sea was wont to raise in me such sensations, as a huntsman experiences, when he hears a pack of hounds in full cry; I loved to feel the waves wrap me and strive to overpower me; while I, lord of myself, moved this way or that, in spite of their angry buffetings. Adrian also could swim - but the weakness of his frame prevented him from feeling pleasure in the exercise or acquiring any great expertness. But what power could the strongest swimmer oppose to the overpowering violence of ocean in its fury? My efforts to prepare my companions were rendered nearly futile - for the roaring breakers prevented our hearing one another speak, and the waves, that broke continually over our boat, obliged me to exert all my strength in lading the water out, as fast as it came in. The while darkness, palpable and rayless, hemmed us round, dissipated only by the lightning; sometimes we beheld thunderbolts, fiery red, fall into the sea, and at intervals vast spouts stooped from the clouds, churning the wild ocean, which rose to meet them; while the fierce gale bore the rack onwards, and they were lost in the chaotic mingling of sky and sea. Our gunwales had been torn away, our single sail had been rent to ribbands, and borne down the stream of the wind. We had cut away our mast, and lightened the boat of all she contained - Clara attempted to assist me in heaving the water from the hold, and, as she turned her eyes to look on the lightning, I could discern by that momentary gleam, that resignation had conquered every fear. We have a power given us in any worst extremity, which props the else feeble mind of man, and enables us to endure the most savage tortures with a stillness of soul which in hours of happiness we could not have imagined. A calm, more dreadful in truth than the tempest, allayed the wild beatings of my heart - a calm like that of the gamester, the suicide, and the murderer, when the last die is on the point of being cast - while the poisoned cup is at the lips, - as the death-blow is about to be given.

Hours passed thus - hours which might write old age on the face of beard-less youth, and grizzle the silky hair of infancy - hours, while the chaotic uproar continued, while each dread gust transcended in fury the one before, and our skiff hung on the breaking wave, and then rushed into the valley below, and trembled and spun between the watery precipices that seemed most to meet above her. For a moment the gale paused, and ocean sank to comparative silence - it was a breathless interval; the wind which, as a practiced leaper, had gathered itself up before it sprung, now with terrific roar rushed over the sea, and the waves struck our stern. Adrian exclaimed that the rudder was gone; - "We are lost," cried Clara, "Save yourselves - O save yourselves!" The lightning shewed me the poor girl half buried in the water at the bottom of the boat; as she was sinking in it Adrian caught her up, and sustained her in his arms. We were without a rudder - we rushed prow foremost into the vast billows piled up a-head - they broke over and filled the tiny skiff; one scream I heard - one cry that we were gone, I uttered; I found myself in the waters; darkness was around. When the light of the tempest flashed, I saw the keel of our upset boat close to me - I clung to this, grasping it with clenched hand and nails, while I endeavored during each flash to discover any appearance of my companions. I thought I saw Adrian at no great distance from me, clinging to an oar; I sprung from my hold, and with energy beyond my human strength, I dashed aside the waters as I strove to lay hold of him. As that hope failed, instinctive love of life animated me, and feelings of contention, as if a hostile will combat with mine. I breasted the surges, and flung them from me, as I would the opposing front and sharpened claws of a lion about to slash my bosom. When I had been beaten down by one wave, I rose on another, while I felt bitter pride curl my lip.

Ever since the storm had carried us near the shore, we had never attained any great distance from it. With every flash I saw the bordering coast; yet the prog-ress I made was small, while each wave, as it receded, carried me back into ocean's far abysses. At one moment I felt my foot touch the sand, and then again I was in deep water; my arms began to lose their power of motion; my breath failed me un-der the influence of the strangling waters - a thousand wild and delirious thoughts crossed me: as well as I can now recall them, my chief feeling was, how sweet it would be to lay my head on the quiet earth, where the surges would no longer strike my weakened frame, nor the sound of waters ring in my ears - to attain this repose, not to save my life, I made a last effort - the shelving shore suddenly presented a footing for me. I rose, and was again thrown down by the breakers - a point of rock to which I was enabled to cling, gave me a moment's respite; and then, taking advantage of the ebbing of the waves, I ran forwards - gained the dry sands, and fell senseless on the oozy reeds that sprinkled them.

I must have lain long deprived of life; for when first, with a sickening feeling, I unclosed my eyes, the light of morning met them. Great change had taken place meanwhile: grey dawn dappled the flying clouds, which sped onwards, leaving visible at intervals vast lakes of pure ether. A fountain of light arose in an increasing stream from the east, behind the waves of the Adriatic, changing the grey to a roseate hue, and then flooding sky and sea with aerial gold.

A kind of stupor followed my fainting; my senses were alive, but memory was extinct. The blessed respite was short - a snake lurked near me to sting me into life - on the first retrospective emotion I would have started up, but my limbs refused to obey me; my knees trembled, the muscles had lost all power. I still believed that I might find one of my beloved companions cast like me, half alive, on the beach; and I strove in every way to restore my frame to the use of its animal functions. I wrung the brine from my hair; and the rays of the risen sun soon visited me with genial warmth. With the restoration of my bodily powers, my mind became in some degree aware of the universe of misery, henceforth to be its dwelling. I ran to the water's edge, calling on the beloved names. Ocean drank in, and absorbed my feeble voice, replying with pitiless roar. I climbed a near tree: the level sands bounded by a pine forest, and the sea clipped round by the horizon, was all that I could discern. In vain I extended my researches along the beach; the mast we had thrown overboard, with tangled cordage, and remnants of a sail, was the sole relic land received of our wreck. Sometimes I stood still and wrung my hands. I accused earth and sky - the universal machine and the Almighty power that misdirected it. Again, I threw myself on the sands, and then the sighing wind, mimicking a human cry, roused me to bitter, fallacious hope. Assuredly if any little bark or smallest canoe had been near, I should have sought the savage plains of ocean, found the dear remains of my lost ones, and clinging round them, have shared their grave.

The day passed; thus, each moment contained eternity; although when hour after hour had gone by, I wondered at the quick flight of time. Yet even now I had not drunk the bitter potion to the dregs; I was not yet persuaded of my loss; I did not yet feel in every pulsation, in every nerve, in every thought, that I remained alone of my race, - that I was the *LAST MAN*.

The day had clouded over, and a drizzling rain set in at sunset. Even the eternal skies weep, I thought; is there any shame then, that mortal man should spend himself in tears? I remembered the ancient fables, in which human beings are described as dissolving away through weeping into ever-gushing fountains. Ah! that so it was; and then my destiny would be in some sort akin to the watery death of Adrian and Clara. Oh! grief is fantastic; it weaves a web on which to trace the history of its woe from every form and change around; it incorporates itself with all living nature; it finds sustenance in every object; as light, it fills all things, and, like light, it gives its own colors to all.

I had wandered in my search to some distance from the spot on which I had been cast, and came to one of those watchtowers, which at stated distances line the Italian shore. I was glad of shelter, glad to find a work of human hands, after I had gazed so long on nature's drear barrenness; so, I entered, and ascended the rough winding staircase into the guardroom. So far was fate kind, that no harrowing vestige remained of its former inhabitants; a few planks laid across two iron trestles, and strewed with the dried leaves of Indian corn, was the bed presented to me; and an open chest, containing some half moldered biscuit, awakened an appetite, which perhaps existed before, but of which, until now, I was not aware. Thirst also, violent and parching, the result of the seawater I had drank, and of the exhaustion of my frame, tormented me. Kind nature had gifted the supply of these wants with pleasurable sensations, so that I - even I! - was refreshed and calmed, as I ate of this sorry fare, and drank a little of the sour wine which half-filled a flask left in this abandoned dwelling. Then I stretched myself on the bed, not to be disdained by the victim of shipwreck. The earthy smell of the dried leaves was balm to my sense after the hateful odor of seaweed. I forgot my state of loneliness. I neither looked backward nor forward; my senses were hushed to repose; I fell asleep and dreamed of all dear inland scenes, of hay-makers, of the shepherd's whistle to his dog, when he demanded his help to drive the flock to fold; of sights and sounds peculiar to my boyhood's mountain life, which I had long forgotten.

I awoke in a painful agony - for I fancied that ocean, breaking its bounds, carried away the fixed continent and deep rooted mountains, together with the streams I loved, the woods, and the flocks - it raged around, with that continued and dreadful roar which had accompanied the last wreck of surviving humanity. As my waking sense returned, the bare walls of the guard room closed round me, and the rain pattered against the single window. How dreadful it is, to emerge from the oblivion of slumber, and to receive as a good morrow the mute wailing of one's own hapless heart - to return from the land of deceptive dreams, to the heavy knowledge of unchanged disaster! - Thus, was it with me, now, and forever! The sting of other griefs might be blunted by time; and even mine yielded sometimes during the day, to the pleasure inspired by the imagination or the senses; but I never look first upon the morning-light but with my fingers pressed tight on my bursting heart, and my soul deluged with the interminable flood of hopeless misery. Now I awoke for the first time in the dead world - I awoke alone - and the dull dirge of the sea, heard even amidst the rain, recalled me to the reflection of the wretch I had become. The sound came like a reproach, a scoff - like the sting of remorse in the soul - I gasped - the veins and muscles of my throat swelled, suffocating me. I put my fingers to my ears, I buried my head in the leaves of my couch, I would have dived to the center to lose hearing of that hideous moan.

But another task must be mine - again I visited the detested beach - again I vainly looked far and wide - again I raised my unanswered cry, lifting up the only voice that could ever again force the mute air to syllable the human thought.

What a pitiable, forlorn, disconsolate being I was! My very aspect and garb told the tale of my despair. My hair was matted and wild - my limbs soiled with salt ooze; while at sea, I had thrown off those of my garments that encumbered me, and the rain drenched the thin summer-clothing I had retained - my feet were bare, and the stunted reeds and broken shells made them bleed - the while,

I hurried to and fro, now looking earnestly on some distant rock which, islanded in the sands, bore for a moment a deceptive appearance - now with flashing eyes reproaching the murderous ocean for its unutterable cruelty.

For a moment I compared myself to that monarch of the waste -Robinson Crusoe. We had been both thrown companionless - he on the shore of a desolate island: I on that of a desolate world. I was rich in the so-called goods of life. If I turned my steps from the near barren scene, and entered any of the earth's million cities, I should find their wealth stored up for my accommodation - clothes, food, books, and a choice of dwelling beyond the command of the princes of former times - every climate was subject to my selection, while he was obliged to toil in the acquirement of every necessary, and was the inhabitant of a tropical island, against whose heats and storms he could obtain small shelter. - Viewing the question thus, who would not have preferred the Sybarite enjoyments I could command, the philosophic leisure, and ample intellectual resources, to his life of labor and peril? Yet he was far happier than I: for he could hope, nor hope in vain - the destined vessel at last arrived, to bear him to countrymen and kindred, where the events of his solitude became a fire-side tale. To none could I ever relate the story of my adversity, no hope had I. He knew that, beyond the ocean which begird his lonely island, thousands lived whom the sun enlightened wherl it shone also on him: beneath the meridian sun and visiting moon, I alone bore human features; I alone could give articulation to thought; and, when I slept, both day and night were unbeheld of any. He had fled from his fellows and was transported with terror at the print of a human foot. I would have knelt down and worshipped the same. The wild and cruel Caribbean, the merciless Cannibal - or worse than these, the uncouth, brute, and remorseless veteran in the vices of civilization, would have been to me a beloved companion, a treasure dearly prized - his nature would be kin to mine; his form cast in the same mold; human blood would flow in his veins; a human sympathy must link us forever. It cannot be that I shall never behold a fellow being more! - never! - never! - not in the course of years! - Shall I wake, and speak to none, pass the interminable hours, my soul, islanded in the world, a solitary point, surrounded by vacuum? Will day follow day endlessly thus? - No! no! a God rules the world - providence has not exchanged its golden scepter for an aspic's sting. Away! let me fly from the ocean-grave, let me depart from this barren nook, paled in, as it is, from access by its own desolateness; let me tread once again the paved towns; step over the threshold of man's dwellings, and most certainly I shall find this thought a horrible vision - a maddening, but evanescent dream.

I entered Ravenna, (the town nearest to the spot whereon I had been cast), before the second sun had set on the empty world; I saw many living creatures; oxen, and horses, and dogs, but there was no man among them; I entered a cottage, it was vacant; I ascended the marble stairs of a palace, the bats and the owls were nestled in the tapestry; I stepped softly, not to awaken the sleeping town: I rebuked a dog, that by yelping disturbed the sacred stillness; I would not believe that all was as it seemed - The world was not dead, but I was mad; I was deprived of sight, hearing, and sense of touch; I was laboring under the force of a spell, which permitted me to behold all sights of earth, except its human inhabitants; they were pursuing their ordinary labors. Every house had its inmate; but I could not perceive them. If I could have deluded myself into a belief of this kind, I should have been far more satisfied. But my brain, tenacious of its reason, refused to lend itself to such imaginations - and though I endeavored to play the antic to myself, I knew that I, the offspring of man, during long years one among many - now remained sole survivor of my species.

The sun sank behind the western hills; I had fasted since the preceding evening, but, though faint and weary, I loathed food, nor ceased, while yet a ray of light remained, to pace the lonely streets. Night came on and sent every living creature but me to the bosom of its mate. It was my solace, to blunt my mental agony by personal hardship - of the thousand beds around, I would not seek the luxury of one; I lay down on the pavement, - a cold marble step served me for a pillow - midnight came; and then, though not before, did my wearied lids shut out the sight of the twinkling stars, and their reflex on the pavement near. Thus, I passed the second night of my desolation.

CHAPTER X

I AWOKE in the morning, just as the higher windows of the lofty houses received the first beams of the rising sun. The birds were chirping, perched on the windows sills and deserted thresholds of the doors. I awoke, and my first thought was, Adrian and Clara are dead. I no longer shall be hailed by their good-morrow - or pass the long day in their society. I shall never see them more. The ocean has robbed me of them - stolen their hearts of love from their breasts and given over to corruption what was dearer to me than light, or life, or hope.

I was an untaught shepherd-boy when Adrian deigned to confer on me his friendship. The best years of my life had been passed with him. All I had possessed of this world's goods, of happiness, knowledge, or virtue—I owed to him. He had, in his person, his intellect, and rare qualities, given a glory to my life, which without him it had never known. Beyond all other beings he had taught me, that goodness, pure and single, can be an attribute of man. It was a sight for angels to congregate to behold, to view him lead, govern, and solace, the last days of the human race.

My lovely Clara also was lost to me - she who last of the daughters of man, exhibited all those feminine and maiden virtues, which poets, painters, and sculptors, have in their various languages strove to express. Yet, as far as she was concerned, could I lament that she was removed in early youth from the certain advent of misery? Pure she was of soul, and all her intents were holy. But her heart was the throne of love, and the sensibility her lovely countenance expressed, was the prophet of many woes, not the less deep and drear, because she would have forever concealed them.

These two wondrously endowed beings had been spared from the universal wreck, to be my companions during the last year of solitude. I had felt, while they were with me, all their worth. I was conscious that every other sentiment, regret, or passion had by degrees merged into a yearning, clinging affection for them. I had not forgotten the sweet partner of my youth, mother of my children, my adored Idris; but I saw at least a part of her spirit alive again in her brother; and after, that by Evelyn's death I had lost what most dearly recalled her to me; I enshrined her memory in Adrian's form, and endeavored to confound the two dear ideas. I sound the depths of my heart and try in vain to draw thence the expressions that can typify my love for these remnants of my race. If regret and sorrow came athwart me, as well it might in our solitary and uncertain state, the clear tones of Adrian's voice, and his fervent look, dissipated the gloom; or I was cheered unaware by the mild content and sweet resignation Clara's cloudless brow and deep blue eyes expressed. They were all to me - the suns of my benighted soul repose in my weariness - slumber in my sleepless woe. Ill, most ill, with disjointed words, bare and weak, have I expressed the feeling with which I clung to them. I would have wound myself like ivy inextricably round them, so that the same blow might destroy us. I would have entered and been a part of them - so that

> *If the dull substance of my flesh were thought,*
> *even now I had accompanied them to their new and incommunicable abode.*

Never shall I see them more. I am bereft of their dear converse - bereft of sight of them. I am a tree rent by lightning; never will the bark close over the bared fibers - never will their quivering life, torn by the winds, receive the opiate of a moment's balm. I am alone in the world - but that expression yet was less pregnant with misery, than that Adrian and Clara are dead.

The tide of thought and feeling rolls on forever the same, though the banks and shapes around, which govern its course, and the reflection in the wave, vary. Thus, the sentiment of immediate loss in some sort decayed, while that of utter, irremediable loneliness grew on me with time. Three days I wandered through Ravenna - now thinking only of the beloved beings who slept in the oozy caves of ocean - now looking forward on the dread blank before me; shuddering to make an onward step - writhing at each change that marked the progress of the hours. For three days I wandered to and fro in this melancholy town. I passed whole hours in going from house to house, listening whether I could detect some lurking sign of human existence. Sometimes I rang at a bell; it tinkled through the vaulted rooms, and silence succeeded to the sound. I called myself hopeless, yet still I hoped; and still disappointment ushered in the hours, intruding the cold, sharp steel which first pierced me, into the aching festering wound. I fed like a wild beast, which seizes its food only when stung by intolerable hunger. I did not change my garb, or seek the shelter of a roof, during all those days. Burning heats, nervous irritation, a ceaseless, but confused flow of thought, sleepless nights, and days instinct with a frenzy of agitation, possessed me during that time.

As the fever of my blood increased, a desire of wandering came upon me. I remember that the sun had set on the fifth day after my wreck, when, without purpose or aim, I quitted the town of Ravenna. I must have been very ill. Had I been possessed by more or less of delirium, that night had surely been my last; for, as I continued to walk on the banks of the Mantone, whose upward course I followed, I looked wistfully on the stream, acknowledging to myself that its pellucid waves could medicine my woes forever, and was unable to account to myself for my tardiness in seeking their shelter from the poisoned arrows of thought, that were piercing me through and through. I walked a considerable part of the night, and excessive weariness at length conquered my repugnance to the availing myself of the deserted habitations of my species. The waning moon, which had just risen, shewed me a cottage, whose neat entrance and trim garden reminded me of my own England. I lifted up the latch of the door and entered. A kitchen first presented itself, where, guided by the moon beams, I found materials for striking a light. Within this was a bed room; the couch was furnished with sheets of snowy whiteness; the wood piled on the hearth, and an array as for a meal, might almost have deceived me into the dear belief that I had here found what I had so long sought - one survivor, a companion for my loneliness, a solace to my despair. I steeled myself against the delusion; the room itself was vacant: it was only prudent, I repeated to myself, to examine the rest of the house. I fancied that I was proof against the expectation; yet my heartbeat audibly, as I laid my hand on the lock of each door, and it sunk again, when I perceived in each the same vacancy. Dark and silent they were as vaults; so I returned to the first chamber, wondering what sightless host had spread the materials for my repast, and my repose. I drew a chair to the table and examined what the viands were of which I was to partake. In truth it was a death feast! The bread was blue and moldy; the cheese lay a heap of dust. I did not dare examine the other dishes; a troop of ants passed in a double line across the table cloth; every utensil was covered with dust, with cobwebs, and myriads of dead flies: these were objects each and all betokening the fallaciousness of my expectations.

Tears rushed into my eyes; surely this was a wanton display of the power of the destroyer. What had I done, that each sensitive nerve was thus to be anatomized? Yet why complain more now than ever? This vacant cottage revealed no new sorrow - the world was empty; mankind was dead - I knew it well - why quarrel therefore with an acknowledged and stale truth? Yet, as I said, I had hoped in the very heart of despair, so that every new impression of the hard-cut reality on my soul brought with it a fresh pang, telling me the yet unstudied lesson, that neither change of place nor time could bring alleviation to my misery, but that, as I now was, I must continue, day after day, month after month, year after year, while I lived. I hardly dared conjecture what space of time that expression implied. It is true, I was no longer in the first blush of manhood; neither had I declined far in the vale of years - men have accounted mine the prime of life: I had just entered my thirty-seventh year; every limb was as well knit, every articulation as true, as when I had acted the shepherd on the hills of Cumberland; and with these advantages I was to commence the train of solitary life. Such were the reflections that ushered in my slumber on that night.

The shelter, however, and less disturbed repose which I enjoyed, restored me the following morning to a greater portion of health and strength, than I had experienced since my fatal shipwreck. Among the stores I had discovered on searching the cottage the preceding night, was a quantity of dried grapes; these refreshed me in the morning, as I left my lodging and proceeded towards a town which I discerned at no great distance. As far as I could divine, it must have been Forli. I entered with pleasure its wide and grassy streets. All, it is true, pictured the excess of desolation; yet I loved to find myself in those spots which had been the abode of my fellow creatures. I delighted to traverse street after street, to look up at the tall houses, and repeat to myself, once they contained beings similar to myself - I was not always the wretch I am now. The wide square of Forli, the arcade around it, its light and pleasant aspect cheered me. I was pleased with the idea, that, if the earth should be again peopled, we, the lost race, would, in the relics left behind, present no contemptible exhibition of our powers to the newcomers.

I entered one of the palaces and opened the door of a magnificent saloon. I started - I looked again with renewed wonder. What wild-looking, unkempt, half-naked savage was that before me? The surprise was momentary.

I perceived that it was I myself whom I beheld in a large mirror at the end of the hall. No wonder that the lover of the princely Idris should fail to recognize himself in the miserable object there portrayed. My tattered dress was that in which I had crawled half alive from the tempestuous sea. My long and tangled hair hung in elf locks on my brow - my dark eyes, now hollow and wild, gleamed from under them - my cheeks were discolored by the jaundice, which (the effect of misery and neglect) suffused my skin, and were half hid by a beard of many days' growth.

Yet why should I not remain thus, I thought; the world is dead, and this squalid attire is a fitter mourning garb than the foppery of a black suit. And thus, methinks, I should have remained, had not hope, without which I do not believe man could exist, whispered to me, that, in such a plight, I should be an object of fear and aversion to the being, preserved I knew not where, but I fondly trusted, at length, to be found by me. Will my readers scorn the vanity, that made me attire myself with some care, for the sake of this visionary being? Or will they forgive the freaks of a half-crazed imagination? I can easily forgive myself - for hope, however vague, was so dear to me, and a sentiment of pleasure of so rare occurrence, that I yielded readily to any idea, that cherished the one, or promised any recurrence of the former to my sorrowing heart. After such occupation, I visited every street, alley, and nook of Forli. These Italian towns presented an appearance of still greater desolation, than those of England or France. Plague had appeared here earlier - it had finished its course and achieved its work much sooner than with us. Probably the last summer had found no human being alive, in all the track included between the shores of Calabria and the northern Alps. My search was utterly vain, yet I was not despondent. Reason methought was on my side; and the chances were by no means contemptible, that there should exist in some part of Italy a survivor like myself - of a wasted, depopulate land. As therefore I rambled through the empty town, I formed my plan for future operations. I would continue to journey on towards Rome. After I should have satisfied myself, by a narrow search, that I left behind no human being in the towns through which I passed, I would write up in a conspicuous part of each, with white paint, in three languages, that "Verney, the last of the race of Englishmen, had taken up his abode in Rome."

In pursuance of this scheme, I entered a painter's shop, and procured myself the paint. It is strange that so trivial an occupation should have consoled, and even enlivened me. But grief renders one childish, despair fantastic. To this simple inscription, I merely added the adjuration, "Friend, come! I wait for thee! - Deh, vieni! ti aspetto!" On the following morning, with something like hope for my companion, I quitted Forli on my way to Rome. Until now, agonizing retrospect, and dreary prospects for the future, had stung me when awake, and cradled me to my repose. Many times, I had delivered myself up to the tyranny of anguish — many times I resolved a speedy end to my woes; and death by my own hands was a remedy, whose practicability was even cheering to me. What could I fear in the other world? If there were a hell, and I were doomed to it, I should come an adept to the sufferance of its tortures - the act was easy, the speedy and certain end of my deplorable tragedy. But now these thoughts faded before the newborn expectation. I went on my way, not as before, feeling each hour, each minute, to be an age instinct with incalculable pain.

As I wandered along the plain, at the foot of the Apennines - through their valleys, and over their bleak summits, my path led me through a country which had been trodden by heroes, visited and admired by thousands. They had, as a tide, receded, leaving me blank and bare in the midst. But why complain? Did I not hope? - so I schooled myself, even after the enlivening spirit had really deserted me, and thus I was obliged to call up all the fortitude I could command, and that was not much, to prevent a recurrence of that chaotic and intolerable despair, that had succeeded to the miserable shipwreck, that had consummated every fear, and dashed to annihilation every joy.

I rose each day with the morning sun and left my desolate inn. As my feet strayed through the unpeopled country, my thoughts rambled through the universe, and I was least miserable when I could, absorbed in reverie, forget the passage of the hours. Each evening, in spite of weariness, I detested to enter any dwelling, there to take up my nightly abode - I have sat, hour after hour, at the door of the cottage I had selected, unable to lift the latch, and meet face to face blank desertion within. Many nights, though autumnal mists were spread around, I passed under an ilex - many times I have supped on arbutus berries and chestnuts, making a fire, gypsy-like, on the ground - because wild natural scenery reminded me less acutely of my hopeless state of loneliness. I counted the days, and bore with me a peeled willow-wand, on which, as well as I could remember, I had notched the days that had elapsed since my wreck, and each night I added another unit to the melancholy sum.

I had toiled up a hill which led to Spoleto. Around was spread a plain, encircled by the chestnut covered Apennines. A dark ravine was on one side, spanned by an aqueduct, whose tall arches were rooted in the dell below, and attested that man had once deigned to bestow labor and thought here, to adorn and civilize nature. Savage, ungrateful nature, which in wild sport defaced his remains, protruding her easily renewed, and fragile growth of wildflowers and parasite plants around his eternal edifices. I sat on a fragment of rock and looked round. The sun had bathed in gold the western atmosphere, and in the east the clouds caught the radiance, and budded into transient loveliness. It set on a world that contained me alone for its inhabitant. I took out my wand - I counted the marks. Twenty-five were already traced - twenty-five days had already elapsed, since human voice had gladdened my ears, or human countenance met my gaze. Twenty-five long, weary days, succeeded by dark and lonesome nights, had mingled with foregone years, and had become a part of the past - the never to be recalled - a real, undeniable portion of my life - twenty-five long, long days.

Why this was not a month! - Why talk of days - or weeks - or months - I must grasp years in my imagination, if I would truly picture the future to myself - three, five, ten, twenty, fifty anniversaries of that fatal epoch might elapse - every year containing twelve months, each of more numerous calculation in a diary, than the twenty-five days gone by - Can it be? Will it be? - We had been used to look forward to death tremulously - wherefore, but because its place was obscure. But more terrible, and far more obscure, was the unveiled course of my lone futurity. I broke my wand; I threw it from me. I needed no recorder of the inch and barley-corn growth of my life, while my unquiet thoughts created other divisions, than those ruled over by the planets - and, in looking back on the age that had elapsed since I had been alone, I disdained to give the name of days and hours to the throes of agony which had in truth portioned it out.

I hid my face in my hands. The twitter of the young birds going to rest, and their rustling among the trees, disturbed the still evening-air - the crickets chirped - the aziolo cooed at intervals. My thoughts had been of death - these sounds spoke to me of life. I lifted up my eyes - a bat wheeled round - the sun had sunk behind the jagged line of mountains, and the paly, crescent moon was visible, silver white, amidst the orange sunset, and accompanied by one bright star, prolonged thus the twilight. A herd of cattle passed along in the dell below, untended, towards their watering place - the grass was rustled by a gentle breeze, and the olive-woods, mellowed into soft masses by the moonlight, contrasted their sea-green with the dark chestnut foliage. Yes, this is the earth; there is no change - no ruin - no rent made in her verdurous expanse; she continues to wheel round and round, with alternate night and day, through the sky, though man is not her adorner or inhabitant. Why could I not forget myself like one of those animals, and no longer suffer the wild tumult of misery that I endure? Yet, ah! what a deadly breach yawns between their state and mine! Have not they companions? Have not they each their mate — their cherished young, their home, which, though unexpressed to us, is, I doubt not, endeared and enriched, even in their eyes, by the society which kind nature has created for them? It is I only that am alone - I, on this little hill top, gazing on plain and mountain recess - on sky, and its starry population, listening to every sound of earth, and air, and murmuring wave, - I only cannot express to any companion my many thoughts, nor lay my throbbing head on any loved bosom, nor drink from meeting eyes an intoxicating dew, that transcends the fabulous nectar of the gods. Shall I not then complain? Shall I not curse the murderous engine which has mowed down the children of men, my brethren? Shall I not bestow a malediction on every other of nature's offspring, which dares live and enjoy, while I live and suffer?

Ah, no! I will discipline my sorrowing heart to sympathy in your joys; I will be happy, because ye are so. Live on, ye innocents, nature's selected darlings; I am not much unlike to you. Nerves, pulse, brain, joint, and flesh, of such am I composed, and ye are organized by the same laws. I have something beyond this, but I will call it a defect, not an endowment, if it leads me to misery, while ye are happy. Just then, there emerged from a near copse two goats and a little kid, by the mother's side; they began to browse the herbage of the hill. I approached near to them, without their perceiving me; I gathered a handful of fresh grass and held it out; the little one nestled close to its mother, while she timidly withdrew. The male stepped forward, fixing his eyes on me: I drew near, still holding out my lure, while he, depressing his head, rushed at me with his horns. I was a very fool; I knew it, yet I yielded to my rage. I snatched up a huge fragment of rock; it would have crushed my rash foe. I poised it - aimed it - then my heart failed me. I hurled it wide of the mark; it rolled clattering among the bushes into dell. My little visitants, all aghast, galloped back into the covert of the wood; while I, my very heart bleeding and torn, rushed down the hill, and by the violence of bodily exertion, sought to escape from my miserable self.

No, no, I will not live among the wild scenes of nature, the enemy of all that lives. I will seek the towns - Rome, the capital of the world, the crown of man's achievements. Among its storied streets, hallowed ruins, and stupendous remains of human exertion, I shall not, as here, find everything forgetful of man; trampling on his memory, defacing his works, proclaiming from hill to hill, and vale to vale, - by the torrents freed from the boundaries which he imposed - by the vegetation liberated from the laws which he enforced - by his habitation abandoned to mildew and weeds, that his power is lost, his race annihilated forever.

I hailed the Tiber, for that was as it were an unalienable possession of humanity. I hailed the wild Campagna, for every rood had been trod by man; and its savage uncultivation, of no recent date, only proclaimed more distinctly his power, since he had given an honorable name and sacred title to what else would have been a worthless, barren track. I entered Eternal Rome by the Porta del Popolo and saluted with awe its time-honored space. The wide square, the churches near, the long extent of the Corso, the near eminence of Trinita de' Monti appeared like fairy work, they were so silent, so peaceful, and so very fair. It was evening; and the population of animals which still existed in this mighty city, had gone to rest; there was no sound, save the murmur of its many fountains, whose soft monotony was harmony to my soul. The knowledge that I was in Rome, soothed me; that wondrous city, hardly more illustrious for its heroes and sages, than for the power it exercised over the imaginations of men. I went to rest that night; the eternal burning of my heart quenched, - my senses tranquil.

The next morning, I eagerly began my rambles in search of oblivion. I ascended the many terraces of the garden of the Colonna Palace, under whose roof I had been sleeping; and passing out from it at its summit, I found myself on Monte Cavallo. The fountain sparkled in the sun; the obelisk above pierced the clear dark-blue air. The statues on each side, the works, as they are inscribed, of Phidias and Praxiteles, stood in undiminished grandeur, representing Castor and Pollux, who with majestic power tamed the rearing animal at their side. If those illustrious artists had in truth chiseled these forms, how many passing generations had their giant proportions outlived! and now they were viewed by the last of the species they were sculptured to represent and deify. I had shrunk into insignificance in my own eyes, as I considered the multitudinous beings these stone demigods had outlived, but this after-thought restored me to dignity in my own conception. The sight of the poetry eternized in these statues, took the sting from the thought, arraying it only in poetic ideality.

I repeated to myself, - I am in Rome! I behold, and as it were, familiarly converse with the wonder of the world, sovereign mistress of the imagination, majestic and eternal survivor of millions of generations of extinct men. I endeavored to quiet the sorrows of my aching heart, by even now taking an interest in what in my youth I had ardently longed to see. Every part of Rome is replete with relics of ancient times. The meanest streets are strewed with truncated columns, broken capitals - Corinthian and Ionic, and sparkling fragments of granite or porphyry. The walls of the most penurious dwellings enclose a fluted pillar or ponderous stone, which once made part of the palace of the Caesars; and the voice of dead time, in still vibrations, is breathed from these dumb things, animated and glorified as they were by man.

I embraced the vast columns of the temple of Jupiter Stator, which survives in the open space that was the Forum, and leaning my burning cheek against its cold durability, I tried to lose the sense of present misery and present desertion, by recalling to the haunted cell of my brain vivid memories of times gone by. I rejoiced at my success, as I figured Camillus, the Gracchi, Cato, and last the heroes of Tacitus, which shine meteors of surpassing brightness during the murky night of the empire; - as the verses of Horace and Virgil, or the glowing periods of Cicero thronged into the opened gates of my mind, I felt myself exalted by long forgotten enthusiasm. I was delighted to know that I beheld the scene which they behold - the scene which their wives and mothers, and crowds of the unnamed witnessed, while at the same time they honored, applauded, or wept for these matchless specimens of humanity. At length, then, I had found a consolation. I had not vainly sought the storied precincts of Rome - I had discovered a medicine for my many and vital wounds.

I sat at the foot of these vast columns. The Coliseum, whose naked ruin is robed by nature in a verdurous and glowing veil, lay in the sunlight on my right. Not far off, to the left, was the Tower of the Capitol. Triumphal arches, the falling walls of many temples, strewed the ground at my feet. I strove, I resolved, to force myself to see the Plebeian multitude and lofty Patrician forms congregated around; and, as the Diorama of ages passed across my subdued fancy, they were replaced by the modern Roman; the Pope, in his white stole, distributing benedictions to the kneeling worshippers; the friar in his cowl; the dark-eyed girl, veiled by her mezzera; the noisy, sun-burnt rustic, leading his herd of buffaloes and oxen to the Campo Vaccino. The romance with which, dipping our pencils in the rainbow hues of sky and transcendent nature, we to a degree gratuitously endow the Italians, replaced the solemn grandeur of antiquity. I remembered the dark monk, and floating figures of "The Italian," and how my boyish blood had thrilled at the description. I called to mind Corinna ascending the Capitol to be crowned, and, passing from the heroine to the author, reflected how the Enchantress Spirit of Rome held sovereign sway over the minds of the imaginative, until it rested on me - sole remaining spectator of its wonders.

I was long wrapped by such ideas; but the soul wearies of constant flight; and, stooping from its wheeling circuits round and round this spot, suddenly it fell ten thousand fathom deep, into the abyss of the present— into self-knowledge—into tenfold sadness. I roused myself - I cast off my waking dreams; and I, who just now could almost hear the shouts of the Roman throng, and was hustled by countless multitudes, now beheld the desert ruins of Rome sleeping under its own blue sky; the shadows lay tranquilly on the ground; sheep were grazing untended on the Palatine, and a buffalo stalked down the Sacred Way that led to the Capitol. I was alone in the Forum; alone in Rome; alone in the world. Would not one living man - one companion in my weary solitude, be worth all the glory and remembered power of this time-honored city? Double sorrow - sadness, bred in Cimmerian caves, robed my soul in a mourning garb. The generations I had conjured up to my fancy, contrasted more strongly with the end of all - the single point in which, as a pyramid, the mighty fabric of society had ended, while I, on the giddy height, saw vacant space around me.

From such vague laments I turned to the contemplation of the minutiae of my situation. So far, I had not succeeded in the sole object of my desires, the finding a companion for my desolation. Yet I did not despair. It is true that my inscriptions were set up for the most part, in insignificant towns and villages; yet, even without these memorials, it was possible that the person, who like me should find himself alone in a depopulate land, should, like me, come to Rome. The slenderer my expectation was, the more I chose to build on it, and to accommodate my actions to this vague possibility.

It became necessary therefore, that for a time I should domesticate myself at Rome. It became necessary, that I should look my disaster in the face - not playing the school-boy's part of obedience without submission; enduring life, and yet rebelling against the laws by which I lived.

Yet how could I resign myself? Without love, without sympathy, without communion with any, how could I meet the morning sun, and with it trace its oft repeated journey to the evening shades? Why did I continue to live - why not throw off the weary weight of time, and with my own hand, let out the fluttering prisoner from my agonized breast? - It was not cowardice that withheld me; for the true fortitude was to endure; and death had a soothing sound accompanying it, that would easily entice me to enter its demesne. But this I would not do. I had, from the moment I had reasoned on the subject, instituted myself the subject to fate, and the servant of necessity, the visible laws of the invisible God - I believed that my obedience was the result of sound reasoning, pure feeling, and an exalted sense of the true excellence and nobility of my nature. Could I have seen in this empty earth, in the seasons and their change, the hand of a blind power only, most willingly would I have placed my head on the sod and closed my eyes on its loveliness forever. But fate had administered life to me, when the plague had already seized on its prey - she had dragged me by the hair from out the strangling waves - by such miracles she had bought me for her own; I admitted her authority, and bowed to her decrees. If, after mature consideration, such was my resolve, it was doubly necessary that I should not lose the end of life, the improvement of my faculties, and poison its flow by repinings without end. Yet how cease to repine, since there was no hand near to extract the barbed spear that had entered my heart of hearts? I stretched out my hand, and it touched none whose sensations were responsive to mine. I was girded, walled in, vaulted over, by seven-fold barriers of loneliness. Occupation alone, if I could deliver myself up to it, would be capable of affording an opiate to my sleepless sense of woe. Having determined to make Rome my abode, at least for some months, I made arrangements for my accommodation - I selected my home. The Colonna Palace was well adapted for my purpose. Its grandeur - its treasure of paintings, its magnificent halls were objects soothing and even exhilarating.

I found the granaries of Rome well stored with grain, and particularly with Indian corn; this product requiring less art in its preparation for food, I selected as my principal support. I now found the hardships and lawlessness of my youth turn to account. A man cannot throw off the habits of sixteen years. Since that age, it is true, I had lived luxuriously, or at least surrounded by all the conveniences civilization afforded. But before that time, I had been "as uncouth a savage, as the wolf-bred founder of old Rome" - and now, in Rome itself, robber and shepherd propensities, similar to those of its founder, were of advantage to its sole inhabitant. I spent the morning riding and shooting in the Campagna - I passed long hours in the various galleries - I gazed at each statue and lost myself in a reverie before many a fair Madonna or beauteous nymph. I haunted the Vatican and stood surrounded by marble forms of divine beauty. Each stone deity was possessed by sacred gladness, and the eternal fruition of love. They looked on me with unsympathizing complacency, and often in wild accents I reproached them for their supreme indifference - for they were human shapes, the human form divine was manifest in each fairest limb and lineament. The perfect molding brought with it the idea of color and motion; often, half in bitter mockery, half in self-delusion, I clasped their icy proportions, and, coming between Cupid and his Psyche's lips, pressed the unconceiving marble.

I endeavored to read. I visited the libraries of Rome. I selected a volume, and, choosing some sequestered, shady nook, on the banks of the Tiber, or opposite the fair temple in the Borghese Gardens, or under the old pyramid of Cestius, I endeavored to conceal me from myself, and immerse myself in the subject traced on the pages before me. As if in the same soil you plant nightshade and a myrtle tree, they will each appropriate the mold, moisture, and air administered, for the fostering their several properties - so did my grief find sustenance, and power of existence, and growth, in what else had been divine manna, to feed radiant meditation. Ah! while I streak this paper with the tale of what my so named occupations were - while I shape the skeleton of my days - my hand trembles - my heart pants, and my brain refuses to lend expression, or phrase, or idea, by which to image forth the veil of unutterable woe that clothed these bare realities. O, worn and beating heart, may I dissect thy fibers, and tell how in each unmitigable misery, sadness dire, repinings, and despair, existed? May I record my many ravings - the wild curses I hurled at torturing nature - and how I have passed days shut out from light and food - from all except the burning hell alive in my own bosom?
I was presented, meantime, with one other occupation, the one best fitted to discipline my melancholy thoughts, which strayed backwards, over many a ruin, and through many a flowery glade, even to the mountain recess, from which in early youth I had first emerged.

During one of my rambles through the habitations of Rome, I found writing materials on a table in an author's study. Parts of a manuscript lay scattered about. It contained a learned disquisition on the Italian language; one page an unfinished dedication to posterity, for whose profit the writer had sifted and selected the niceties of this harmonious language - to whose everlasting benefit he bequeathed his labors.

I also will write a book, I cried—for whom to read? - to whom dedicated? And then with silly flourish (what so capricious and childish as despair?) I wrote, DEDICATION TO THE ILLUSTRIOUS DEAD. SHADOWS, ARISE, AND READ YOUR FALL! BEHOLD THE HISTORY OF THE LAST MAN.

Yet, will not this world be re-peopled, and the children of a saved pair of lovers, in some to me unknown and unattainable seclusion, wandering to these prodigious relics of the ante-pestilential race, seek to learn how beings so wondrous in their achievements, with imaginations infinite, and powers godlike, had departed from their home to an unknown country?

I will write and leave in this most ancient city, this "world's sole monument," a record of these things. I will leave a monument of the existence of Verney, the Last Man. At first, I thought only to speak of plague, of death, and last, of desertion; but I lingered fondly on my early years and recorded with sacred zeal the virtues of my companions. They have been with me during the fulfilment of my task. I have brought it to an end - I lift my eyes from my paper—again they are lost to me. Again, I feel that I am alone.

A year has passed since I have been thus occupied. The seasons have made their wonted round and decked this eternal city in a changeful robe of surpassing beauty. A year has passed; and I no longer guess at my state or my prospects - loneliness is my familiar, sorrow my inseparable companion. I have endeavored to brave the storm - I have endeavored to school myself to fortitude - I have sought to imbue myself with the lessons of wisdom. It will not do. My hair has become nearly grey — my voice, unused now to utter sound, comes strangely on my ears. My person, with its human powers and features, seem to me a monstrous excrescence of nature. How express in human language a woe human being until this hour never knew! How give intelligible expression to a pang none but I could ever understand! - No one has entered Rome. None will ever come. I smile bitterly at the delusion I have so long nourished, and still more, when I reflect that I have exchanged it for another as delusive, as false, but to which I now cling with the same fond trust.

Winter has come again; and the gardens of Rome have lost their leaves - the sharp air comes over the Campagna, and has driven its brute inhabitants to take up their abode in the many dwellings of the deserted city - frost has suspended the gushing fountains - and Trevi has stilled her eternal music. I had made a rough calculation, aided by the stars, by which I endeavored to ascertain the first day of the new year. In the old out-worn age, the Sovereign Pontiff was used to go in solemn pomp and mark the renewal of the year by driving a nail in the gate of the temple of Janus. On that day I ascended St. Peter's, and carved on its topmost stone the aera 2100, last year of the world!

My only companion was a dog, a shaggy fellow, half water and half shepherd's dog, whom I found tending sheep in the Campagna. His master was dead, but nevertheless he continued fulfilling his duties in expectation of his return. If a sheep strayed from the rest, he forced it to return to the flock, and sedulously kept off every intruder. Riding in the Campagna I had come upon his sheep-walk, and for some time observed his repetition of lessons learned from man, now useless, though unforgotten. His delight was excessive when he saw me. He sprung up to my knees; he capered round and round, wagging his tail, with the short, quick bark of pleasure: he left his fold to follow me, and from that day has never neglected to watch by and attend on me, shewing boisterous gratitude whenever I caressed or talked to him. His pattering steps and mine alone were heard, when we entered the magnificent extent of nave and aisle of St. Peter's. We ascended the myriad steps together, when on the summit I achieved my design, and in rough figures noted the date of the last year. I then turned to gaze on the country, and to take leave of Rome. I had long determined to quit it, and I now formed the plan I would adopt for my future career, after I had left this magnificent abode.

A solitary being is by instinct a wanderer, and that I would become. A hope of amelioration always attends on change of place, which would even lighten the burthen of my life. I had been a fool to remain in Rome all this time: Rome noted for Malaria, the famous caterer for death. But it was still possible, that, could I visit the whole extent of earth, I should find in some part of the wide extent a survivor. Methought the seaside was the most probable retreat to be chosen by such a one. If left alone in an inland district, still they could not continue in the spot where their last hopes had been extinguished; they would journey on, like me, in search of a partner for their solitude, till the watery barrier stopped their further progress.

To that water - cause of my woes, perhaps now to be their cure, I would betake myself. Farewell, Italy! - farewell, thou ornament of the world, matchless Rome, the retreat of the solitary one during long months! - to civilized life - to the settled home and succession of monotonous days, farewell! Peril will now be mine; and I hail her as a friend - death will perpetually cross my path, and I will meet him as a benefactor; hardship, inclement weather, and dangerous tempests will be my sworn mates. Ye spirits of storm, receive me! ye powers of destruction, open wide your arms, and clasp me forever! if a kinder power have not decreed another end, so that after long endurance I may reap my reward, and again feel my heart beat near the heart of another like to me.

Tiber, the road, which is spread by nature's own hand, threading her continent, was at my feet, and many a boat was tethered to the banks. I would with a few books, provisions, and my dog, embark in one of these and float down the current of the stream into the sea; and then, keeping near land, I would coast the beauteous shores and sunny promontories of the blue Mediterranean, pass Naples, along Calabria, and would dare the twin perils of Scylla and Charybdis; then, with fearless aim, (for what had I to lose?) skim ocean's surface towards Malta and the further Cyclades. I would avoid Constantinople, the sight of whose well-known towers and inlets belonged to another state of existence from my present one; I would coast Asia Minor, and Syria, and, passing the seven-mouthed Nile, steer northward again, till losing sight of forgotten Carthage and deserted Lybia, I should reach the pillars of Hercules. And then - no matter where - the oozy caves, and soundless depths of ocean may be my dwelling, before I accomplish this long-drawn voyage, or the arrow of disease find my heart as I float singly on the weltering Mediterranean; or, in some place I touch at, I may find what I seek - a companion; or if this may not be - to endless time, decrepit and grey headed - youth already in the grave with those I love - the lone wanderer will still unfurl his sail, and clasp the tiller - and, still obeying the breezes of heaven, forever round another and another promontory, anchoring in another and another bay, still ploughing seedless ocean, leaving behind the verdant land of native Europe, adown the tawny shore of Africa, having weathered the fierce seas of the Cape, I may moor my worn skiff in a creek, shaded by spicy groves of the odorous islands of the far Indian ocean.

These are wild dreams. Yet since, now a week ago, they came on me, as I stood on the height of St. Peter's, they have ruled my imagination. I have chosen my boat and laid in my scant stores. I have selected a few books; the principal are Homer and Shakespeare - But the libraries of the world are thrown open to me - and in any port I can renew my stock. I form no expectation of alteration for the better; but the monotonous present is intolerable to me. Neither hope nor joy are my pilots—restless despair and fierce desire of change lead me on. I long to grapple with danger, to be excited by fear, to have some task, however slight or voluntary, for each day's fulfilment. I shall witness all the variety of appearance, that the elements can assume - I shall read fair augury in the rainbow - menace in the cloud - some lesson or record dear to my heart in everything. Thus around the shores of deserted earth, while the sun is high, and the moon waxes or wanes, angels, the spirits of the dead, and the ever-open eye of the Supreme, will behold the tiny bark, freighted with Verney - the *LAST MAN.*

THE END

THE END

The Masque of the Red Death

By Edgar Allan Poe

About the Author

Edgar Allan Poe (1809 – 1849) was an American writer, poet, editor, and literary critic. Poe is best known for his poetry and short stories, particularly his tales of mystery and the macabre. He is widely regarded as a central figure of Romanticism in the United States and of American literature as a whole, and he was one of the country's earliest practitioners of the short story. He is also generally considered the inventor of the detective fiction genre and is further credited with contributing to the emerging genre of science fiction. Poe was the first well-known American writer to earn a living through writing alone, resulting in a financially difficult life and career. Poe and his works influenced literature around the world, as well as specialized fields such as cosmology and cryptography. He and his work appear throughout popular culture in literature, music, films, and television. The Mystery Writers of America present an annual award known as the Edgar Award for distinguished work in the mystery genre. He died in Baltimore on 7 October 1849, at age forty. The cause of his death is unknown .

The "Red Death" had long devastated the country. No pestilence had ever been so fatal, or so hideous. Blood was its Avatar and its seal—the redness and the horror of blood. There were sharp pains, and sudden dizziness, and then profuse bleeding at the pores, with dissolution. The scarlet stains upon the body and especially upon the face of the victim, were the pest ban which shut him out from the aid and from the sympathy of his fellowmen. And the whole seizure, progress and termination of the disease, were the incidents of half an hour.

But the Prince Prospero was happy and dauntless and sagacious. When his dominions were half depopulated, he summoned to his presence a thousand hale and light-hearted friends from among the knights and dames of his court, and with these retired to the deep seclusion of one of his castellated abbeys. This was an extensive and magnificent structure, the creation of the prince's own eccentric yet august taste. A strong and lofty wall girdled it in. This wall had gates of iron. The courtiers, having entered, brought furnaces and massy hammers and welded the bolts. They resolved to leave means neither of ingress nor egress to the sudden impulses of despair or of frenzy from within. The abbey was amply provisioned. With such precautions the courtiers might bid defiance to contagion. The external world could take care of itself. In the meantime, it was folly to grieve, or to think. The prince had provided all the appliances of pleasure. There were buffoons, there were improvisatori, there were ballet-dancers, there were musicians, there was Beauty, there was wine. All these and security were within. Without was the "Red Death".

It was towards the close of the fifth or sixth month of his seclusion, and while the pestilence raged most furiously abroad, that the Prince Prospero entertained his thousand friends at a masked ball of the most unusual magnificence.

It was a voluptuous scene, that masquerade. But first let me tell of the rooms in which it was held. These were seven - an imperial suite. In many palaces, however, such suites form a long and straight vista, while the folding doors slide back nearly to the walls on either hand, so that the view of the whole extent is scarcely impeded. Here the case was very different, as might have been expected from the duke's love of the bizarre. The apartments were so irregularly disposed that the vision embraced but little more than one at a time. There was a sharp turn at every twenty or thirty yards, and at each turn a novel effect. To the right and left, in the middle of each wall, a tall and narrow Gothic window looked out upon a closed corridor which pursued the windings of the suite. These windows were of stained glass whose color varied in accordance with the prevailing hue of the decorations of the chamber into which it opened. That at the eastern extremity was hung, for example in blue - and vividly blue were its windows. The second chamber was purple in its ornaments and tapestries, and here the panes were purple. The third was green throughout, and so were the casements. The fourth was furnished and lighted with orange—the fifth with white—the sixth with violet. The seventh apartment was closely shrouded in black velvet tapestries that hung all over the ceiling and down the walls, falling in heavy folds upon a carpet of the same material and hue. But in this chamber only, the color of the windows failed to correspond with the decorations. The panes here were scarlet - a deep blood color. Now in no one of the seven apartments was there any lamp or candelabrum, amid the profusion of golden ornaments that lay scattered to and fro or depended from the roof. There was no light of any kind emanating from lamp or candle within the suite of chambers. But in the corridors that followed the suite, there stood, opposite to each window, a heavy tripod, bearing a brazier of fire, that projected its rays through the tinted glass and so glaringly illumined the room. And thus, were produced a multitude of gaudy and fantastic appearances. But in the western or black chamber the effect of the fire-light that streamed upon the dark hangings through the blood-tinted panes, was ghastly in the extreme, and produced so wild a look upon the countenances of those who entered, that there were few of the company bold enough to set foot within its precincts at all.

It was in this apartment, also, that there stood against the western wall, a gigantic clock of ebony. Its pendulum swung to and fro with a dull, heavy, monotonous clang; and when the minute-hand made the circuit of the face, and the hour was to be stricken, there came from the brazen lungs of the clock a sound which was clear and loud and deep and exceedingly musical, but of so peculiar a note and emphasis that, at each lapse of an hour, the musicians of the orchestra were constrained to pause, momentarily, in their performance, to harken to the sound; and thus the waltzers perforce ceased their evolutions; and there was a brief disconcert of the whole gay company; and, while the chimes of the clock yet rang, it was observed that the giddiest grew pale, and the more aged and sedate passed their hands over their brows as if in confused reverie or meditation. But when the echoes had fully ceased, a light laughter at once pervaded the assembly; the musicians looked at each other and smiled as if at their own nervousness and folly, and made whispering vows, each to the other, that the next chiming of the clock should produce in them no similar emotion; and then, after the lapse of sixty minutes, (which embrace three thousand and six hundred seconds of the Time that flies,) there came yet another chiming of the clock, and then were the same disconcert and tremulousness and meditation as before.

But, in spite of these things, it was a gay and magnificent revel. The tastes of the duke were peculiar. He had a fine eye for colors and effects. He disregarded the decora of mere fashion. His plans were bold and fiery, and his conceptions glowed with barbaric luster. There are some who would have thought him mad. His followers felt that he was not. It was necessary to hear and see and touch him to be sure that he was not.

He had directed, in great part, the movable embellishments of the seven chambers, upon occasion of this great fête; and it was his own guiding taste which had given character to the masqueraders. Be sure they were grotesque. There were many glares and glitter and piquancy and phantasm - much of what has been since seen in "Hernani". There were arabesque figures with unsuited limbs and appointments. There were delirious fancies such as the madman fashions. There were much of the beautiful, much of the wanton, much of the bizarre, something of the terrible, and not a little of that which might have excited disgust. To and fro in the seven chambers there stalked, in fact, a multitude of dreams. And these - the dreams - writhed in and about taking hue from the rooms and causing the wild music of the orchestra to seem as the echo of their steps. And, anon, there strikes the ebony clock which stands in the hall of the velvet. And then, for a moment, all is still, and all is silent save the voice of the clock. The dreams are stiff-frozen as they stand. But the echoes of the chime die away - they have endured but an instant - and a light, half-subdued laughter floats after them as they depart. And now again the music swells, and the dreams live, and writhe to and fro more merrily than ever, taking hue from the many tinted windows through which stream the rays from the tripods. But to the chamber which lies most westwardly of the seven, there are now none of the maskers who venture; for the night is waning away; and there flows a ruddier light through the blood-colored panes; and the blackness of the sable drapery appalls; and to him whose foot falls upon the sable carpet, there comes from the near clock of ebony a muffled peal more solemnly emphatic than any which reaches their ears who indulged in the more remote gaieties of the other apartments.

But these other apartments were densely crowded, and in them beat feverishly the heart of life. And the revel went whirlingly on, until at length there commenced the sounding of midnight upon the clock. And then the music ceased, as I have told; and the evolutions of the waltzers were quieted; and there was an uneasy cessation of all things as before. But now there were twelve strokes to be sounded by the bell of the clock; and thus, it happened, perhaps, that more of thought crept, with more of time, into the meditations of the thoughtful among those who reveled. And thus too, it happened, perhaps, that before the last echoes of the last chime had utterly sunk into silence, there were many individuals in the crowd who had found leisure to become aware of the presence of a masked figure which had arrested the attention of no single individual before. And the rumor of this new presence having spread itself whisperingly around, there arose at length from the whole company a buzz, or murmur, expressive of disapprobation and surprise - then, finally, of terror, of horror, and of disgust.

In an assembly of phantasms such as I have painted, it may well be supposed that no ordinary appearance could have excited such sensation. In truth the masquerade license of the night was nearly unlimited; but the figure in question had out-Heroded Herod and gone beyond the bounds of even the prince's indefinite decorum. There are chords in the hearts of the most reckless which cannot be touched without emotion. Even with the utterly lost, to whom life and death are equally jests, there are matters of which no jest can be made. The whole company, indeed, seemed now deeply to feel that in the costume and bearing of the stranger neither wit nor propriety existed. The figure was tall and gaunt, and shrouded from head to foot in the habiliments of the grave. The mask which concealed the visage was made so nearly to resemble the countenance of a stiffened corpse that the closest scrutiny must have had difficulty in detecting the cheat. And yet all this might have been endured, if not approved, by the mad revelers around. But the mummer had gone so far as to assume the type of the Red Death. His vesture was dabbled in blood - and his broad brow, with all the features of the face, was besprinkled with the scarlet horror.

When the eyes of the Prince Prospero fell upon this spectral image (which, with a slow and solemn movement, as if more fully to sustain its role, stalked to and fro among the waltzers) he was seen to be convulsed, in the first moment with a strong shudder either of terror or distaste; but, in the next, his brow reddened with rage.

"Who dares," - he demanded hoarsely of the courtiers who stood near him -"who dares insult us with this blasphemous mockery? Seize him and unmask him

- that we may know whom we have to hang, at sunrise, from the battlements!"
It was in the eastern or blue chamber in which stood the Prince Prospero as he
uttered these words. They rang throughout the seven rooms loudly and clearly,
for the prince was a bold and robust man, and the music had become hushed at
the waving of his hand.

It was in the blue room where stood the prince, with a group of pale courtiers by his side. At first, as he spoke, there was a slight rushing movement of this
group in the direction of the intruder, who at the moment was also near at hand,
and now, with deliberate and stately step, made closer approach to the speaker.
But from a certain nameless awe with which the mad assumptions of the mummer
had inspired the whole party, there were found none who put forth hand to seize
him; so that, unimpeded, he passed within a yard of the prince's person; and,
while the vast assembly, as if with one impulse, shrank from the centers of the
rooms to the walls, he made his way uninterruptedly, but with the same solemn
and measured step which had distinguished him from the first, through the blue
chamber to the purple - through the purple to the green - through the green to the
orange - through this again to the white - and even thence to the violet, ere a decided movement had been made to arrest him. It was then, however, that the Prince
Prospero, maddening with rage and the shame of his own momentary cowardice,
rushed hurriedly through the six chambers, while none followed him on account
of a deadly terror that had seized upon all. He bore aloft a drawn dagger, and had
approached, in rapid impetuosity, to within three or four feet of the retreating figure, when the latter, having attained the extremity of the velvet apartment, turned
suddenly and confronted his pursuer. There was a sharp cry - and the dagger
dropped gleaming upon the sable carpet, upon which, instantly afterwards, fell
prostrate in death the Prince Prospero. Then, summoning the wild courage of despair, a throng of the revelers at once threw themselves into the black apartment,
and, seizing the mummer, whose tall figure stood erect and motionless within
the shadow of the ebony clock, gasped in unutterable horror at finding the grave
cerements and corpse-like mask, which they handled with so violent a rudeness,
untenanted by any tangible form.

And now was acknowledged the presence of the Red Death. He had come
like a thief in the night. And one by one dropped the revelers in the blood-be-
dewed halls of their revel and died each in the despairing posture of his fall. And
the life of the ebony clock went out with that of the last of the gay. And the flames
of the tripods expired. And Darkness and Decay and the Red Death held illimit-
able dominion overall.

THE SCARLET PLAGUE

By Jack London

About the Author

John Griffith London (born John Griffith Chaney;1876 – 1916) was an American novelist, journalist, and social activist. A pioneer in the world of commercial magazine fiction, he was one of the first writers to become a worldwide celebrity and earn a large fortune from writing. He was also an innovator in the genre that would later become known as science fiction.

His most famous works include *The Call of the Wild* and *White Fang*, both set in the Klondike Gold Rush, as well as the short stories "To Build a Fire", "An Odyssey of the North", and "Love of Life". He also wrote about the South Pacific in stories such as "The Pearls of Parlay", and "The Heathen".

London was part of the radical literary group "The Crowd" in San Francisco and a passionate advocate of unionization, workers' rights, socialism, and eugenics. He wrote several works dealing with these topics, such as his dystopian novel *The Iron Heel*, his non-fiction exposé *The People of the Abyss*, *The War of the Classes*, and *Before Adam*.

THE SCARLET PLAGUE

CHAPTER I

The way led along upon what had once been the embankment of a railroad. But no train had run upon it for many years. The forest on either side swelled up the slopes of the embankment and crested across it in a green wave of trees and bushes. The trail was as narrow as a man's body and was no more than a wild-animal runway. Occasionally, a piece of rusty iron, showing through the forest-mold, advertised that the rail and the ties still remained. In one place, a ten-inch tree, bursting through at a connection, had lifted the end of a rail clearly into view. The tie had evidently followed the rail, held to it by the spike long enough for its bed to be filled with gravel and rotten leaves, so that now the crumbling, rotten timber thrust itself up at a curious slant. Old as the road was, it was manifest that it had been of the mono-rail type.

An old man and a boy travelled along this runway. They moved slowly, for the old man was very old, a touch of palsy made his movements tremulous, and he leaned heavily upon his staff. A rude skullcap of goatskin protected his head from the sun. From beneath this fell a scant fringe of stained and dirty-white hair. A visor, ingeniously made from a large leaf, shielded his eyes, and from under this he peered at the way of his feet on the trail. His beard, which should have been snow-white, but which showed the same weather-wear and camp-stain as his hair, fell nearly to his waist in a great tangled mass. About his chest and shoulders hung a single, mangy garment of goatskin. His arms and legs, withered and skinny, betokened extreme age, as well as did their sunburn and scars and scratches betoken long years of exposure to the elements.

The boy, who led the way, checking the eagerness of his muscles to the slow progress of the elder, likewise wore a single garment - a ragged-edged piece of bear-skin, with a hole in the middle through which he had thrust his head. He could not have been more than twelve years old. Tucked coquettishly over one ear was the freshly severed tail of a pig. In one hand he carried a medium-sized bow and an arrow.

On his back was a quiver full of arrows. From a sheath hanging about his neck on a thong, projected the battered handle of a hunting knife. He was as brown as a berry, and walked softly, with almost a catlike tread. In marked contrast with his sunburned skin were his eyes - blue, deep blue, but keen and sharp as a pair of gimlets. They seemed to bore into aft about him in a way that was habitual. As he went along, he smelled things, as well, his distended, quivering nostrils carrying to his brain an endless series of messages from the outside world. Also, his hearing was acute, and had been so trained that it operated automatically. Without conscious effort, he heard all the slight sounds in the apparent quiet - heard, and differentiated, and classified these sounds - whether they were of the wind rustling the leaves, of the humming of bees and gnats, of the distant rumble of the sea that drifted to him only in lulls, or of the gopher, just under his foot, shoving a pouchful of earth into the entrance of his hole.

Suddenly he became alertly tense. Sound, sight, and odor had given him a simultaneous warning. His hand went back to the old man, touching him, and the pair stood still. Ahead, at one side of the top of the embankment, arose a crackling sound, and the boy's gaze was fixed on the tops of the agitated bushes. Then a large bear, a grizzly, crashed into view, and likewise stopped abruptly, at sight of the humans. He did not like them and growled querulously. Slowly the boy fitted the arrow to the bow, and slowly he pulled the bowstring taut. But he never removed his eyes from the bear.

The old man peered from under his green leaf at the danger and stood as quietly as the boy. For a few seconds this mutual scrutinizing went on; then, the bear betraying a growing irritability, the boy, with a movement of his head, indicated that the old man must step aside from the trail and go down the embankment. The boy followed, going backward, still holding the bow taut and ready. They waited till a crashing among the bushes from the opposite side of the embankment told them the bear had gone on. The boy grinned as he led back to the trail.

"A big un, Granser," he chuckled.

The old man shook his head.

"They get thicker every day," he complained in a thin, undependable falsetto. "Who'd have thought I'd live to see the time when a man would be afraid of his life on the way to the Cliff House. When I was a boy, Edwin, men and women and little babies used to come out here from San Francisco by tens of thousands on a nice day. And there weren't any bears then. No, sir. They used to pay money to look at them in cages, they were that rare."

"What is money, Granser?"

Before the old man could answer, the boy recollected and triumphantly shoved his hand into a pouch under his bearskin and pulled forth a battered and tarnished silver dollar. The old man's eyes glistened, as he held the coin close to them.

"I can't see," he muttered. "You look and see if you can make out the date, Edwin."

The boy laughed.

"You're a great Granser," he cried delightedly, "always making believe them little marks mean something."

The old man manifested an accustomed chagrin as he brought the coin back again close to his own eyes.

"2012," he shrilled, and then fell to cackling grotesquely. "That was the year Morgan the Fifth was appointed President of the United States by the Board of Magnates. It must have been one of the last coins minted, for the Scarlet Death came in 2013. Lord! Lord! - think of it! Sixty years ago, and I am the only person alive today that lived in those times. Where did you find it, Edwin?"

The boy, who had been regarding him with the tolerant curiousness one accords to the prattling's of the feeble-minded, answered promptly.

"I got it off of Hoo-Hoo. He found it when we was herdin' goats down near San José last spring. Hoo-Hoo said it was money. Ain't you hungry, Granser?"

The ancient caught his staff in a tighter grip and urged along the trail, his old eyes shining greedily.

"I hope Har-Lip 's found a crab... or two," he mumbled. "They're good eating, crabs, mighty good eating when you've no more teeth and you've got grandsons that love their old grandsire and make a point of catching crabs for him. When I was a boy -"

But Edwin, suddenly stopped by what he saw, was drawing the bowstring on a fitted arrow. He had paused on the brink of a crevasse in the embankment. An ancient culvert had here washed out, and the stream, no longer confined, had cut a passage through the fill. On the opposite side, the end of a rail projected and overhung. It showed rustily through the creeping vines which overran it. Beyond, crouching by a bush, a rabbit looked across at him in trembling hesitancy. Fully fifty feet was the distance, but the arrow flashed true; and the transfixed rabbit, crying out in sudden fright and hurt, struggled painfully away into the brush. The boy himself was a flash of brown skin and flying fur as he bounded down the steep wall of the gap and up the other side. His lean muscles were springs of steel that released into graceful and efficient action. A hundred feet beyond, in a tangle of bushes, he overtook the wounded creature, knocked its head on a convenient tree-trunk, and turned it over to Granser to carry.

"Rabbit is good, very good," the ancient quavered, "but when it comes to a toothsome delicacy, I prefer crab. When I was a boy -"

"Why do you say so much that ain't got no sense?" Edwin impatiently interrupted the other's threatened garrulousness.

The boy did not exactly utter these words, but something that remotely resembled them and that was more guttural and explosive and economical of qualifying phrases. His speech showed distant kinship with that of the old man, and the latter's speech was approximately an English that had gone through a bath of corrupt usage.

"What I want to know," Edwin continued, "is why you call crab 'toothsome delicacy'? Crab is crab, ain't it? No one I never heard calls it such funny things."

The old man sighed but did not answer, and they moved on in silence. The surf grew suddenly louder, as they emerged from the forest upon a stretch of sand dunes bordering the sea. A few goats were browsing among the sandy hillocks, and a skin-clad boy, aided by a wolfish-looking dog that was only faintly reminiscent of a collie, was watching them. Mingled with the roar of the surf was a continuous, deep-throated barking or bellowing, which came from a cluster of jagged rocks a hundred yards out from shore. Here huge sea-lions hauled themselves up to lie in the sun or battle with one another. In the immediate foreground arose the smoke of a fire, tended by a third savage-looking boy. Crouched near him were several wolfish dogs similar to the one that guarded the goats.

***

The old man accelerated his pace, sniffing eagerly as he neared the fire.

"Mussels!" he muttered ecstatically. "Mussels! And ain't that a crab, Hoo-Hoo? Ain't that a crab? My, my, you boys are good to your old grandsire."

Hoo-Hoo, who was apparently of the same age as Edwin, grinned.

"All you want, Granser. I got four."

The old man's palsied eagerness was pitiful. Sitting down in the sand as quickly as his stiff limbs would let him, he poked a large rock-mussel from out of the coals. The heat had forced its shells apart, and the meat, salmon-colored, was thoroughly cooked. Between thumb and forefinger, in trembling haste, he caught the morsel and carried it to his mouth. But it was too hot, and the next moment was violently ejected. The old man spluttered with the pain, and tears ran out of his eyes and down his cheeks.

The boys were true savages, possessing only the cruel humor of the savage. To them the incident was excruciatingly funny, and they burst into loud laughter. Hoo-Hoo danced up and down, while Edwin rolled gleefully on the ground. The boy with the goats came running to join in the fun.

"Set 'em to cool, Edwin, set 'em to cool," the old man besought, in the midst of his grief, making no attempt to wipe away the tears that still flowed from his eyes. "And cool a crab, Edwin, too. You know your grandsire likes crabs."

From the coals arose a great sizzling, which proceeded from the many mussels bursting open their shells and exuding their moisture. They were large shellfish, running from three to six inches in length. The boys raked them out with sticks and placed them on a large piece of driftwood to cool.

"When I was a boy, we did not laugh at our elders; we respected them."

The boys took no notice, and Granser continued to babble an incoherent flow of complaint and censure. But this time he was more careful and did not burn his mouth. All began to eat, using nothing but their hands and making loudmouth noises and lip-smacking. The third boy, who was called Hare-Lip, slyly deposited a pinch of sand on a mussel the ancient was carrying to his mouth; and when the grit of it bit into the old fellow's mucous membrane and gums, the laughter was again uproarious. He was unaware that a joke had been played on him, and spluttered and spat until Edwin, relenting, gave him a gourd of fresh water with which to wash out his mouth.

"Where's them crabs, Hoo-Hoo?" Edwin demanded. "Granser's set upon having a snack."

Again, Granser's eyes burned with greediness as a large crab was handed to him. It was a shell with legs and all complete, but the meat had long since departed. With shaky fingers and babblings of anticipation, the old man broke off a leg and found it filled with emptiness.

"The crabs, Hoo-Hoo?" he wailed. "The crabs?"

"I was fooling Granser. They ain't no crabs! I never found one."

The boys were overwhelmed with delight at sight of the tears of senile disappointment that dribbled down the old man's cheeks. Then, unnoticed, Hoo-Hoo replaced the empty shell with a fresh-cooked crab. Already dismembered, from the cracked legs the white meat sent forth a small cloud of savory steam. This attracted the old man's nostrils, and he looked down in amazement.

The change of his mood to one of joy was immediate. He snuffled and muttered and mumbled, making almost a croon of delight, as he began to eat. Of this the boys took little notice, for it was an accustomed spectacle. Nor did they notice his occasional exclamations and utterances of phrases which meant nothing to them, as, for instance, when he smacked his lips and champed his gums while muttering: "Mayonnaise! Just think - mayonnaise! And it's sixty years since the last was ever made! Two generations and never a smell of it! Why, in those days it was served in every restaurant with crab."

***

When he could eat no more, the old man sighed, wiped his hands on his naked legs, and gazed out over the sea. With the content of a full stomach, he waxed reminiscent.

"To think of it! I've seen this beach alive with men, women, and children on a pleasant Sunday. And there weren't any bears to eat them up, either. And right up there on the cliff was a big restaurant where you could get anything you wanted to eat. Four million people lived in San Francisco then. And now, in the whole city and county there aren't forty all told. And out there on the sea were ships and ships always to be seen, going in for the Golden Gate or coming out. And airships in the air - dirigibles and flying machines. They could travel two hundred miles an hour. The mail contracts with the New York and San Francisco Limited demanded that for the minimum. There was a chap, a Frenchman, I forget his name, who succeeded in making three hundred; but the thing was risky, too risky for conservative persons. But he was on the right clew, and he would have managed it if it hadn't been for the Great Plague. When I was a boy, there were men alive who remembered the coming of the first airplanes, and now I have lived to see the last of them, and that sixty years ago."

The old man babbled on, unheeded by the boys, who were long accustomed to his garrulousness, and whose vocabularies, besides, lacked the greater portion of the words he used. It was noticeable that in these rambling soliloquies his English seemed to recrudesce into better construction and phraseology. But when he talked directly with the boys it lapsed, largely, into their own uncouth and simpler forms.

"But there weren't many crabs in those days," the old man wandered on. "They were fished out, and they were great delicacies. The open season was only a month long, too. And now crabs are accessible the whole year around. Think of it - catching all the crabs you want, any time you want, in the surf of the Cliff House beach!"

A sudden commotion among the goats brought the boys to their feet. The dogs about the fire rushed to join their snarling fellow who guarded the goats, while the goats themselves stampeded in the direction of their human protectors. A half dozen forms, lean and gray, glided about on the sand hillocks and faced the bristling dogs. Edwin arched an arrow that fell short. But Hare-Lip, with a sling such as David carried into battle against Goliath, hurled a stone through the air that whistled from the speed of its flight. It fell squarely among the wolves and caused them to slink away toward the dark depths of the eucalyptus forest.

The boys laughed and lay down again in the sand, while Granser sighed ponderously. He had eaten too much, and, with hands clasped on his paunch, the fingers interlaced, he resumed his maunderings.

"'The fleeting systems lapse like foam,'" he mumbled what was evidently a quotation. "That's it - foam, and fleeting. All man's toil upon the planet was just so much foam. He domesticated the serviceable animals, destroyed the hostile ones, and cleared the land of its wild vegetation. And then he passed, and the flood of primordial life rolled back again, sweeping his handiwork away - the weeds and the forest inundated his fields, the beasts of prey swept over his flocks, and now there are wolves on the Cliff House beach." He was appalled by the thought. "Where four million people disported themselves, the wild wolves roam to-day, and the savage progeny of our loins, with prehistoric weapons, defend themselves against the fanged despoilers. Think of it! And all because of the Scarlet Death - " The adjective had caught Hare-Lip's ear.

"He's always saying that" he said to Edwin. "What is scarlet?"

"'The scarlet of the maples can shake me like the cry of bugles going by,'" the old man quoted.

"It's red," Edwin answered the question. "And you don't know it because you come from the Chauffeur Tribe. They never did know nothing, none of them. Scarlet is red - I know that."

"Red is red, ain't it?" Hare-Lip grumbled. "Then what's the good of gettin' cocky and calling it scarlet?"

"Granser, what for do you always say so much what nobody knows?" he asked. "Scarlet ain't anything, but red is red. Why don't you say red, then?"

"Red is not the right word," was the reply. "The plague was scarlet. The whole face and body turned scarlet in an hour's time. Don't I know? Didn't I see enough of it? And I am telling you it was scarlet because - well, because it was scarlet. There is no other word for it."

"Red is good enough for me," Hare-Lip muttered obstinately. "My dad calls red red, and he ought to know. He says everybody died of the Red Death."

"Your dad is a common fellow, descended from a common fellow," Granser retorted heatedly. "Don't I know the beginnings of the Chauffeurs? Your grandsire was a chauffeur, a servant, and without education. He worked for other persons. But your grandmother was of good stock, only the children did not take after her. Don't I remember when I first met them, catching fish at Lake Temescal?"

"What is education?" Edwin asked.

"Calling red scarlet," Hare-Lip sneered, then returned to the attack on Granser. "My dad told me, an' he got it from his dad afore he croaked, that your wife was a Santa Rosan, an' that she was sure no account. He said she was a hash-slinger before the Red Death, though I don't know what a hash-slinger is. You can tell me, Edwin."

But Edwin shook his head in token of ignorance.

"It is true, she was a waitress," Granser acknowledged. "But she was a good woman, and your mother was her daughter. Women were very scarce in the days after the Plague. She was the only wife I could find, even if she was a hash-slinger, as your father calls it. But it is not nice to talk about our progenitors that way."

"Dad says that the wife of the first Chauffeur was a lady -"

"What's a lady?" Hoo-Hoo demanded.

"A lady 's a Chauffeur squaw," was the quick reply of Hare-Lip.

"The first Chauffeur was Bill, a common fellow, as I said before," the old man expounded; "but his wife was a lady, a great lady. Before the Scarlet Death she was the wife of Van Worden. He was President of the Board of Industrial Magnates and was one of the dozen men who ruled America. He was worth one billion, eight hundred million dollars - coins like you have there in your pouch, Edwin. And then came the Scarlet Death, and his wife became the wife of Bill, the first Chauffeur. He used to beat her, too. I have seen it myself."

Hoo-Hoo, lying on his stomach and idly digging his toes in the sand, cried out and investigated, first, his toenail, and next, the small hole he had dug. The other two boys joined him, excavating the sand rapidly with their hands till there lay three skeletons exposed. Two were of adults, the third being that of a part-grown child. The old man hudged along on the ground and peered at the find.

"Plague victims," he announced. "That's the way they died everywhere in the last days. This must have been a family, running away from the contagion and perishing here on the Cliff House beach. They - what are you doing, Edwin?"

This question was asked in sudden dismay, as Edwin, using the back of his hunting knife, began to knock out the teeth from the jaws of one of the skulls.

"Going to string 'em," was the response.

The three boys were now hard at it; and quite a knocking and hammering arose, in which Granser babbled on unnoticed.

"You are true savages. Already has begun the custom of wearing human teeth. In another generation you will be perforating your noses and ears and wearing ornaments of bone and shell. I know. The human race is doomed to sink back farther and farther into the primitive night ere again it begins its bloody climb upward to civilization. When we increase and feel the lack of room, we will proceed to kill one another. And then I suppose you will wear human scalp-locks at your waist, as well—as you, Edwin, who are the gentlest of my grandsons, have already begun with that vile pigtail. Throw it away, Edwin, boy; throw it away."

"What a gabble the old geezer makes," Hare-Lip remarked, when, the teeth all extracted, they began an attempt at equal division.

They were very quick and abrupt in their actions, and their speech, in moments of hot discussion over the allotment of the choicer teeth, was truly a gabble. They spoke in monosyllables and short jerky sentences that was more a gibberish than a language. And yet, through it ran hints of grammatical construction, and appeared vestiges of the conjugation of some superior culture. Even the speech of Granser was so corrupt that were it put down literally it would be almost so much nonsense to the reader. This, however, was when he talked with the boys.

When he got into the full swing of babbling to himself, it slowly purged itself into pure English. The sentences grew longer and were enunciated with a rhythm and ease that was reminiscent of the lecture platform.

"Tell us about the Red Death, Granser," Hare-Lip demanded, when the teeth affair had been satisfactorily concluded.

"The Scarlet Death," Edwin corrected.

"An' don't work all that funny lingo on us," Hare-Lip went on. "Talk sensible, Granser, like a Santa Rosan ought to talk. Other Santa Rosans don't talk like you."

CHAPTER II

The old man showed pleasure in being thus called upon. He cleared his throat and began.

"Twenty or thirty years ago my story was in great demand. But in these days nobody seems interested - "

"There you go!" Har-Lip cried hotly. "Cut out the funny stuff and talk sensible. What's interested? You talk like a baby that don't know how."

"Let him alone," Edwin urged, "or he'll get mad and won't talk at all. Skip the funny places. We'll catch on to some of what he tells us."

"Let her go, Granser," Hoo-Hoo encouraged; for the old man was already maundering about the disrespect for elders and the reversion to cruelty of all humans that fell from high culture to primitive conditions.

The tale began.

"There were very many people in the world in those days. San Francisco alone held four millions -"

"What is millions?" Edwin interrupted.

Granser looked at him kindly.

"I know you cannot count beyond ten, so I will tell you. Hold up your two hands. On both of them you have altogether ten fingers and thumbs. Very well. I now take this grain of sand - you hold it, Hoo-Hoo." He dropped the grain of sand into the lad's palm and went on. "Now that grain of sand stands for the ten fingers of Edwin. I add another grain. That's ten more fingers. And I add another, and another, and another, until I have added as many grains as Edwin has fingers and thumbs. That makes what I call one hundred. Remember that word - one hundred. Now I put this pebble in Har-Lip's hand. It stands for ten grains of sand, or ten tens of fingers, or one hundred fingers. I put in ten pebbles. They stand for a thousand fingers. I take a mussel-shell, and it stands for ten pebbles, or one hundred grains of sand, or one thousand fingers...." And so on, laboriously, and with much reiteration, he strove to build up in their minds a crude conception of numbers. As the quantities increased, he had the boys holding different magnitudes in each of their hands. For still higher sums, he laid the symbols on the log of driftwood; and for symbols he was hard put, being compelled to use the teeth from the skulls for millions, and the crab-shells for billions. It was here that he stopped, for the boys were showing signs of becoming tired.

"There were four million people in San Francisco - four teeth."

The boys' eyes ranged along from the teeth and from hand to hand, down through the pebbles and sand-grains to Edwin's fingers. And back again they ranged along the ascending series in the effort to grasp such inconceivable numbers.

"That was a lot of folks, Granser," Edwin at last hazarded.

"Like sand on the beach here, like sand on the beach, each grain of sand a man, or woman, or child. Yes, my boy, all those people lived right here in San

Francisco. And at one time or another all those people came out on this very beach - more people than there are grains of sand. More - more - more. And San Francisco was a noble city. And across the bay - where we camped last year, even more people lived, clear from Point Richmond, on the level ground and on the hills, all the way around to San Leandro - one great city of seven million people. -Seven teeth... there, that's it, seven million."

Again, the boys' eyes ranged up and down from Edwin's fingers to the teeth on the log.

"The world was full of people. The census of 2010 gave eight billion for the whole world - eight crab-shells, yes, eight billion. It was not like today. Mankind knew a great deal more about getting food. And the more food there was, the more people there were. In the year 1800, there were one hundred and seventy million in Europe alone. One hundred years later - a grain of sand, Hoo-Hoo - one hundred years later, at 1900, there were five hundred million in Europe - five grains of sand, Hoo-Hoo, and this one tooth. This shows how easy was the getting of food, and how men increased. And in the year 2000 there were fifteen hundred million in Europe. And it was the same all over the rest of the world. Eight crab-shells there, yes, eight billion people were alive on the earth when the Scarlet Death began.

"I was a young man when the Plague came - twenty-seven years old; and I lived on the other side of San Francisco Bay, in Berkeley. You remember those great stone houses, Edwin, when we came down the hills from Contra Costa? That was where I lived, in those stone houses. I was a professor of English literature."

I Was a Professor of English Literature 054

Much of this was over the heads of the boys, but they strove to comprehend dimly this tale of the past.

"What was them stone houses for?" Har-Lip queried.

"You remember when your dad taught you to swim?" The boy nodded. "Well, in the University of California - that is the name we had for the houses - we taught young men and women how to think, just as I have taught you now, by sand and pebbles and shells, to know how many people lived in those days. There was very much to teach. The young men and women we taught were called students. We had large rooms in which we taught. I talked to them, forty or fifty at a time, just as I am talking to you now. I told them about the books other men had written before their time, and even, sometimes, in their time -"

"Was that all you did? -just talk, talk, talk?" Hoo-Hoo demanded. "Who hunted your meat for you? and milked the goats? and caught the fish?"

"A sensible question, Hoo-Hoo, a sensible question. As I have told you, in those days food-getting was easy. We were very wise. A few men got the food for many men. The other men did other things. As you say, I talked. I talked all the time, and for this food was given me - much food, fine food, beautiful food, food that I have not tasted in sixty years and shall never taste again. I sometimes think the most wonderful achievement of our tremendous civilization was food - its inconceivable abundance, its infinite variety, its marvelous delicacy. O my grandsons, life was life in those days, when we had such wonderful things to eat."

This was beyond the boys, and they let it slip by, words and thoughts, as a mere senile wandering in the narrative.

"Our food-getters were called freemen. This was a joke. We of the ruling classes owned all the land, all the machines, everything. These food-getters were our slaves. We took almost all the food they got, and left them a little so that they might eat, and work, and get us more food -"

"I'd have gone into the forest and got food for myself," Harelip announced; "and if any man tried to take it away from me, I'd have killed him."

The old man laughed.

"Did I not tell you that we of the ruling class owned all the land, all the forest, everything? Any food-getter who would not get food for us, him we punished or compelled to starve to death. And very few did that. They preferred to get food for us, and make clothes for us, and prepare and administer to us a thousand - a mussel-shell, Hoo-Hoo - a thousand satisfactions and delights. And I was Professor Smith in those days - Professor James Howard Smith. And my lecture courses were very popular - that is, very many of the young men and women liked to hear me talk about the books other men had written.

"And I was very happy, and I had beautiful things to eat. And my hands were soft, because I did no work with them, and my body was clean all over and dressed in the softest garments -

"He surveyed his mangy goat-skin with disgust.

"We did not wear such things in those days. Even the slaves had better garments. And we were most clean. We washed our faces and hands often every day. You boys never wash unless you fall into the water or go swimming."

"Neither do you Granzer," Hoo-Hoo retorted.

***

"I know, I know, I am a filthy old man, but times have changed. Nobody washes these days, there are no conveniences. It is sixty years since I have seen a piece of soap.

"You do not know what soap is, and I shall not tell you, for I am telling the story of the Scarlet Death. You know what sickness is. We called it a disease. Very many of the diseases came from what we called germs. Remember that word - germs. A germ is a very small thing. It is like a woodtick, such as you find on the dogs in the spring of the year when they run in the forest. Only the germ is very small. It is so small that you cannot see it -"

***

Hoo-Hoo began to laugh.

"You're a queer un, Granser, talking about things you can't see. If you can't see 'em, how do you know they are? That's what I want to know. How do you know anything you can't see?"

"A good question, a very good question, Hoo-Hoo. But we did see — some of them. We had what we called microscopes and ultra-microscopes and we put them to our eyes and looked through them, so that we saw things larger than they really were, and many things we could not see without the microscopes at all. Our best ultra-microscopes could make a germ look forty thousand times larger. A mussel-shell is a thousand fingers like Edwin's. Take forty mussel-shells, and by as many times larger was the germ when we looked at it through a microscope. And after that, we had other ways, by using what we called moving pictures, of making the forty-thousand-times germ many, many thousand times larger still. And thus, we saw all these things which our eyes of themselves could not see. Take a grain of sand. Break it into ten pieces. Take one piece and break it into ten. Break one of those pieces into ten, and one of those into ten, and one of those into ten, and one of those into ten, and do it all day, and maybe, by sunset, you will have a piece as small as one of the germs." The boys were openly incredulous. Harelip sniffed and sneered and Hoo-Hoo snickered, until Edwin nudged them to be silent.

"The woodtick sucks the blood of the dog, but the germ, being so very small, goes right into the blood of the body, and there it has many children. In those days there would be as many as a billion - a crab-shell, please - as many as that crab-shell in one man's body. We called germs micro-organisms. When a few million, or a billion, of them were in a man, in all the blood of a man, he was sick. These germs were a disease. There were many different kinds of them - more different kinds than there are grains of sand on this beach. We knew only a few of the kinds. The micro-organic world was an invisible world, a world we could not see, and we knew very little about it. Yet we did know something. There was the bacillus anthracis; there was the micrococcus; there was the Bacterium termo, and the Bacterium lactis - that's what turns the goat milk sour even to this day, Harelip; and there were Schizomycetes without end. And there were many others...."

Here the old man launched into a disquisition on germs and their natures, using words and phrases of such extraordinary length and meaninglessness, that the boys grinned at one another and looked out over the deserted ocean till they forgot the old man was babbling on.

"But the Scarlet Death, Granser," Edwin at last suggested.

Granser recollected himself, and with a start tore himself away from the rostrum of the lecture-hall, where, to another world audience, he had been expounding the latest theory, sixty years gone, of germs and germ-diseases.

"Yes, yes, Edwin; I had forgotten. Sometimes the memory of the past is very strong upon me, and I forget that I am a dirty old man, clad in goatskin, wandering with my savage grandsons who are goatherds in the primeval wilderness. 'The fleeting systems lapse like foam,' and so lapsed our glorious, colossal civilization. I am Granser, a tired old man. I belong to the tribe of Santa Rosans. I married into that tribe. My sons and daughters married into the Chauffeurs, the Sacramen-tos, and the Palo-Altos. You, Harelip, are of the Chauffeurs. You, Edwin, are of the Sacramentos. And you, Hoo-Hoo, are of the Palo-Altos. Your tribe takes its name from a town that was near the seat of another great institution of learning. It was called Stanford University. Yes, I remember now. It is perfectly clear. I was telling you of the Scarlet Death. Where was I in my story?"

"You was telling about germs, the things you can't see but which make men sick," Edwin prompted.

"Yes, that's where I was. A man did not notice at first when only a few of these germs got into his body. But each germ broke in half and became two germs, and they kept doing this very rapidly so that in a short time there were many millions of them in the body. Then the man was sick. He had a disease, and the disease was named after the kind of a germ that was in him. It might be measles, it might be influenza, it might be yellow fever; it might be any of thousands and thousands of kinds of diseases.

"Now this is the strange thing about these germs. There were always new ones coming to live in men's bodies. Long and long and long ago, when there were only a few men in the world, there were few diseases. But as men increased and lived closely together in great cities and civilizations, new diseases arose, new kinds of germs entered their bodies. Thus, were countless millions and billions of human beings killed. And the more thickly men packed together, the more terrible were the new diseases that came to be. Long before my time, in the middle ages, there was the Black Plague that swept across Europe. It swept across Europe many times. There was tuberculosis, that entered into men wherever they were thickly packed. A hundred years before my time there was the bubonic plague. And in Africa was the sleeping sickness. The bacteriologists fought all these sicknesses and destroyed them, just as you boys fight the wolves away from your goats or squash the mosquitoes that light on you. The bacteriologists -"

"But Granser, what is a what-you-call-it?" Edwin interrupted.

"You, Edwin, are a goatherd. Your task is to watch the goats. You know a great deal about goats. A bacteriologist watches germs. That's his task, and he knows a great deal about them. So, as I was saying, the bacteriologists fought with the germs and destroyed them - sometimes. There was leprosy, a horrible disease. A hundred years before I was born, the bacteriologists discovered the germ of leprosy. They knew all about it. They made pictures of it. I have seen those pictures. But they never found a way to kill it. But in 1984, there was the Pantoblast Plague, a disease that broke out in a country called Brazil and that killed millions of people. But the bacteriologists found it out, and found the way to kill it, so that the Pantoblast Plague went no farther. They made what they called a serum, which they put into a man's body and which killed the pantoblast germs without killing the man. And in 1910, there was Pellagra, and also the hookworm. These were easily killed by the bacteriologists. But in 1947 there arose a new disease that had never been seen before. It got into the bodies of babies of only ten months old or less, and it made them unable to move their hands and feet, or to eat, or anything; and the bacteriologists were eleven years in discovering how to kill that particular germ and save the babies.

"In spite of all these diseases, and of all the new ones that continued to arise, there were more and more men in the world. This was because it was easy to get food. The easier it was to get food, the more men there were; the more men there were, the more thickly were they packed together on the earth; and the more thickly they were packed, the more new kinds of germs became diseases. There were warnings. Soldervetzsky, as early as 1929, told the bacteriologists that they had no guaranty against some new disease, a thousand times more deadly than any they knew, arising and killing by the hundreds of millions and even by the billion. You see, the micro-organic world remained a mystery to the end. They knew there was such a world, and that from time to time armies of new germs emerged from it to kill men.

"And that was all they knew about it. For all they knew, in that invisible micro-organic world there might be as many different kinds of germs as there are grains of sand on this beach. And also, in that same invisible world it might well be that new kinds of germs came to be. It might be there that life originated -the 'abysmal fecundity,' Soldervetzsky called it, applying the words of other men who had written before him...."

It was at this point that Harelip rose to his feet, an expression of huge contempt on his face.

"Granser," he announced, "you make me sick with your gabble. Why don't you tell about the Red Death? If you ain't going to, say so, an' we'll start back for camp."

The old man looked at him and silently began to cry. The weak tears of age rolled down his cheeks and all the feebleness of his eighty-seven years showed in his grief-stricken countenance.

"Sit down," Edwin counselled soothingly. "Granser's all right. He's just gettin' to the Scarlet Death, ain't you, Granser? He's just goin' to tell us about it right now. Sit down, Harelip. Go ahead, Granser."

CHAPTER III

The old man wiped the tears away on his grimy knuckles and took up the tale in a tremulous, piping voice that soon strengthened as he got the swing of the narrative.

"It was in the summer of 2013 that the Plague came. I was twenty-seven years old, and well do I remember it. Wireless dispatches -"

Har-Lip spat loudly his disgust, and Granser hastened to make amends.

"We talked through the air in those days, thousands and thousands of miles. And the word came of a strange disease that had broken out in New York. There were seventeen million people living then in that noblest city of America. Nobody thought anything about the news. It was only a small thing. There had been only a few deaths. It seemed, though, that they had died very quickly, and that one of the first signs of the disease was the turning red of the face and all the body. Within twenty-four hours came the report of the first case in Chicago. And on the same day, it was made public that London, the greatest city in the world, next to Chicago, had been secretly fighting the plague for two weeks and censoring the news dispatches - that is, not permitting the word to go forth to the rest of the world that London had the plague.

"It looked serious, but we in California, like everywhere else, were not alarmed. We were sure that the bacteriologists would find a way to overcome this new germ, just as they had overcome other germs in the past. But the trouble was the astonishing quickness with which this germ destroyed human beings, and the fact that it inevitably killed any human body it entered. No one ever recovered. There was the old Asiatic cholera, when you might eat dinner with a well man in the evening, and the next morning, if you got up early enough, you would see him being hauled by your window in the death-cart. But this new plague was quicker than that - much quicker.

"From the moment of the first signs of it, a man would be dead in an hour. Some lasted for several hours. Many died within ten or fifteen minutes of the appearance of the first signs.

"The heart began to beat faster and the heat of the body to increase. Then came the scarlet rash, spreading like wildfire over the face and body. Most persons never noticed the increase in heat and heartbeat, and the first they knew was when the scarlet rash came out. Usually, they had convulsions at the time of the appearance of the rash. But these convulsions did not last long and were not very severe. If one lived through them, he became perfectly quiet, and only did he feel a numbness swiftly creeping up his body from the feet. The heels became numb first, then the legs, and hips, and when the numbness reached as high as his heart he died. They did not rave or sleep. Their minds always remained cool and calm up to the moment their heart numbed and stopped. And another strange thing was the rapidity of decomposition. No sooner was a person dead than the body seemed to fall to pieces, to fly apart, to melt away even as you looked at it. That was one of the reasons the plague spread so rapidly. All the billions of germs in a corpse were so immediately released.

"And it was because of all this that the bacteriologists had so little chance in fighting the germs. They were killed in their laboratories even as they studied the germ of the Scarlet Death. They were heroes. As fast as they perished, others stepped forth and took their places. It was in London that they first isolated it. The news was telegraphed everywhere. Trask was the name of the man who succeeded in this, but within thirty hours he was dead. Then came the struggle in all the laboratories to find something that would kill the plague germs. All drugs failed. You see, the problem was to get a drug, or serum, that would kill the germs in the body and not kill the body. They tried to fight it with other germs, to put into the body of a sick man germs that were the enemies of the plague germs -"

"And you can't see these germ-things, Granser," Harelip objected, "and here you gabble, gabble, gabble about them as if they was anything, when they're nothing at all. Anything you can't see, ain't, that's what. Fighting things that ain't with things that ain't! They must have been all fools in them days. That's why they croaked. I ain't goin' to believe in such rot, I tell you that."

Granser promptly began to weep, while Edwin hotly took up his defense.

"Look here, Har-Lip, you believe in lots of things you can't see."

Har-lip shook his head.

"You believe in dead men walking about. You never seen one dead man walk about."

"I tell you I seen 'em, last winter, when I was wolf-hunting with dad."

"Well, you always spit when you cross running water," Edwin challenged.

"That's to keep off bad luck," was Harelip's defense.

"You believe in bad luck?"

"Sure."

"An' you ain't never seen bad luck," Edwin concluded triumphantly. "You're just as bad as Granser and his germs. You believe in what you don't see. Go on, Granser."

Har-lip, crushed by this metaphysical defeat, remained silent, and the old man went on. Often and often, though this narrative must not be clogged by the details, was Granser's tale interrupted while the boys squabbled among themselves. Also, among themselves they kept up a constant, low-voiced exchange of explanation and conjecture, as they strove to follow the old man into his unknown and vanished world.

"The Scarlet Death broke out in San Francisco. The first death came on a Monday morning. By Thursday they were dying like flies in Oakland and San Francisco. They died everywhere - in their beds, at their work, walking along the street. It was on Tuesday that I saw my first death - Miss Collbran, one of my students, sitting right there before my eyes, in my lecture-room. I noticed her face while I was talking. It had suddenly turned scarlet. I ceased speaking and could only look at her, for the first fear of the plague was already on all of us and we knew that it had come. The young women screamed and ran out of the room. So did the young men run out, all but two. Miss Collbran's convulsions were very mild and lasted less than a minute. One of the young men fetched her a glass of water. She drank only a little of it, and cried out:

"'My feet! All sensation has left them.'

"After a minute she said, 'I have no feet. I am unaware that I have any feet. And my knees are cold. I can scarcely feel that I have knees.'

"She lay on the floor, a bundle of notebooks under her head. And we could do nothing. The coldness and the numbness crept up past her hips to her heart, and when it reached her heart, she was dead. In fifteen minutes, by the clock - I timed it - she was dead, there, in my own classroom, dead. And she was a very beautiful, strong, healthy young woman. And from the first sign of the plague to her death only fifteen minutes elapsed. That will show you how swift was the Scarlet Death.

Yet in those few minutes I remained with the dying woman in my classroom, the alarm had spread over the university; and the students, by thousands, all of them, had deserted the lecture-room and laboratories. When I emerged, on my way to make report to the President of the Faculty, I found the university deserted. Across the campus were several stragglers hurrying for their homes. Two of them were running.

President Hoag, I found in his office, all alone, looking very old and very gray, with a multitude of wrinkles in his face that I had never seen before. At the sight of me, he pulled himself to his feet and tottered away to the inner office, banging the door after him and locking it. You see, he knew I had been exposed, and he was afraid. He shouted to me through the door to go away. I shall never forget my feelings as I walked down the silent corridors and out across that deserted campus. I was not afraid. I had been exposed, and I looked upon myself as already dead. It was not that, but a feeling of awful depression that impressed me. Everything had stopped. It was like the end of the world to me - my world. I had been born within sight and sound of the university. It had been my predestined career. My father had been a professor there before me, and his father before him. For a century and a half had this university, like a splendid machine, been running steadily on. And now, in an instant, it had stopped. It was like seeing the sacred flame die down on some thrice-sacred altar. I was shocked, unutterably shocked.

"When I arrived home, my housekeeper screamed as I entered, and fled away. And when I rang, I found the housemaid had likewise fled. I investigated. In the kitchen I found the cook on the point of departure. But she screamed, too, and in her haste dropped a suitcase of her personal belongings and ran out of the house and across the grounds, still screaming. I can hear her scream to this day. You see, we did not act in this way when ordinary diseases smote us. We were always calm over such things and sent for the doctors and nurses who knew just what to do. But this was different. It struck so suddenly, and killed so swiftly, and never missed a stroke. When the scarlet rash appeared on a person's face, that person was marked by death. There was never a known case of a recovery.

"I was alone in my big house. As I have told you often before, in those days we could talk with one another over wires or through the air. The telephone bell rang, and I found my brother talking to me. He told me that he was not coming home for fear of catching the plague from me, and that he had taken our two sisters to stop at Professor Bacon's home. He advised me to remain where I was and wait to find out whether or not I had caught the plague.

"To all of this I agreed, staying in my house and for the first time in my life attempting to cook. And the plague did not come out on me. By means of the telephone I could talk with whomsoever I pleased and get the news. Also, there were the newspapers, and I ordered all of them to be thrown up to my door so that I could know what was happening with the rest of the world.

"New York City and Chicago were in chaos. And what happened with them was happening in all the large cities. A third of the New York police were dead. Their chief was also dead, likewise the mayor. All law and order had ceased. The bodies were lying in the streets un-buried. All railroads and vessels carrying food and such things into the great city had ceased running's and mobs of the hungry poor were pillaging the stores and warehouses. Murder and robbery and drunkenness were everywhere. Already the people had fled from the city by millions - at first the rich, in their private motor-cars and dirigibles, and then the great mass of the population, on foot, carrying the plague with them, themselves starving and pillaging the farmers and all the towns and villages on the way.

"The man who sent this news, the wireless operator, was alone with his instrument on the top of a lofty building. The people remaining in the city - he estimated them at several hundred thousand - had gone mad from fear and drink, and on all sides of him great fires were raging. He was a hero, that man who staid by his post - an obscure newspaperman, most likely.

"For twenty-four hours, he said, no transatlantic airships had arrived, and no more messages were coming from England. He did state, though, that a message from Berlin - that's in Germany — announced that Hoffmeyer, a bacteriologist of the Metchnikoff School, had discovered the serum for the plague. That was the last word, to this day, that we of America ever received from Europe. If Hoffmeyer discovered the serum, it was too late, or otherwise, long ere this, explorers from Europe would have come looking for us. We can only conclude that what happened in America happened in Europe, and that, at the best, some several score may have survived the Scarlet Death on that whole continent.

"For one day longer, the dispatches continued to come from New York. Then they, too, ceased. The man who had sent them, perched in his lofty building, had either died of the plague or been consumed in the great conflagrations he had described as raging around him. And what had occurred in New York had been duplicated in all the other cities. It was the same in San Francisco, and Oakland, and Berkeley. By Thursday, the people were dying so rapidly that their corpses could not be handled, and dead bodies lay everywhere. Thursday night the panicked outrush for the country began. Imagine, my grandsons, people, thicker than the salmon-run you have seen on the Sacramento river, pouring out of the cities by millions, madly over the country, in vain attempt to escape the ubiquitous death. You see, they carried the germs with them. Even the airships of the rich, fleeing for mountain and desert fastnesses, carried the germs.

"Hundreds of these airships escaped to Hawaii, and not only did they bring the plague with them, but they found the plague already there before them. This we learned, by the dispatches, until all order in San Francisco vanished, and there were no operators left at their posts to receive or send. It was amazing, astounding, this loss of communication with the world. It was exactly as if the world had ceased, been blotted out. For sixty years that world has no longer existed for me. I know there must be such places as New York, Europe, Asia, and Africa; but not one word has been heard of them - not in sixty years. With the coming of the Scarlet Death the world fell apart, absolutely, irretrievably. Ten thousand years of culture and civilization passed in the twinkling of an eye, 'lapsed like foam.'

"I was telling about the airships of the rich. They carried the plague with them and no matter where they fled, they died. I never encountered but one survivor of any of them - Mungerson. He was afterwards a Santa Rosan, and he married my eldest daughter. He came into the tribe eight years after the plague. He was then nineteen years old, and he was compelled to wait twelve years more before he could marry. You see, there were no unmarried women, and some of the older daughters of the Santa Rosans were already bespoken. So, he was forced to wait until my Mary had grown to sixteen years. It was his son, Gimp-Leg, who was killed last year by the mountain lion.

"Mungerson was eleven years old at the time of the plague. His father was one of the Industrial Magnates, a very wealthy, powerful man. It was on his airship, the Condor, that they were fleeing, with all the family, for the wilds of British Columbia, which is far to the north of here. But there was some accident, and they were wrecked near Mount Shasta. You have heard of that mountain. It is far to the north. The plague broke out amongst them, and this boy of eleven was the only survivor. For eight years he was alone, wandering over a deserted land and looking vainly for his own kind. And at last, travelling south, he picked up with us, the Santa Rosans.

"But I am ahead of my story. When the great exodus from the cities around San Francisco Bay began, and while the telephones were still working, I talked with my brother. I told him this flight from the cities was insanity, that there were no symptoms of the plague in me, and that the thing for us to do was to isolate ourselves and our relatives in some safe place. We decided on the Chemistry Building, at the university, and we planned to lay in a supply of provisions, and by force of arms to prevent any other persons from forcing their presence upon us after we had retired to our refuge.

"All this being arranged, my brother begged me to stay in my own house for at least twenty-four hours more, on the chance of the plague developing in me. To this I agreed, and he promised to come for me next day. We talked on over the details of the provisioning and the defending of the Chemistry Building until the telephone died. It died in the midst of our conversation. That evening there were no electric lights, and I was alone in my house in the darkness. No more newspapers were being printed, so I had no knowledge of what was taking place outside.

"I heard sounds of rioting and of pistol shots, and from my windows I could see the glare of the sky of some conflagration in the direction of Oakland. It was a night of terror. I did not sleep a wink. A man - why and how I do not know - was killed on the sidewalk in front of the house. I heard the rapid reports of an automatic pistol, and a few minutes later the wounded wretch crawled up to my door, moaning and crying out for help. Arming myself with two automatics, I went to him. By the light of a match I ascertained that while he was dying of the bullet wounds, at the same time the plague was on him. I fled indoors, whence I heard him moan and cry out for half an hour longer.

"In the morning, my brother came to me. I had gathered into a handbag what things of value I purposed taking, but when I saw his face, I knew that he would never accompany me to the Chemistry Building. The plague was on him. He intended shaking my hand, but I went back hurriedly before him.

"'Look at yourself in the mirror,' I commanded.

"He did so, and at sight of his scarlet face, the color deepening as he looked at it, he sank down nervelessly in a chair.

"'My God!' he said. 'I've got it. Don't come near me. I am a dead man.'

"Then the convulsions seized him. He was two hours in dying, and he was conscious to the last, complaining about the coldness and loss of sensation in his feet, his calves, his thighs, until at last it was his heart and he was dead.

"That was the way the Scarlet Death slew. I caught up my handbag and fled. The sights in the streets were terrible. One stumbled on bodies everywhere. Some were not yet dead. And even as you looked, you saw men sink down with the death fastened upon them. There were numerous fires burning in Berkeley, while Oakland and San Francisco were apparently being swept by vast conflagrations. The smoke of the burning filled the heavens, so that the midday was as a gloomy twilight, and, in the shifts of wind, sometimes the sun shone through dimly, a dull red orb. Truly, my grandsons, it was like the last days of the end of the world.

"There were numerous stalled motor cars, showing that the gasoline and the engine supplies of the garages had given out. I remember one such car. A man and a woman lay back dead in the seats, and on the pavement near it were two more women and a child. Strange and terrible sights there were on every hand. People slipped by silently, furtively, like ghosts - white-faced women carrying infants in their arms; fathers leading children by the hand; singly, and in couples, and in families - all fleeing out of the city of death. Some carried supplies of food, other's blankets and valuables, and there were many who carried nothing.

"There was a grocery store - a place where food was sold. The man to whom it belonged - I knew him well - a quiet, sober, but stupid and obstinate fellow, was defending it. The windows and doors had been broken in, but he, inside, hiding behind a counter, was discharging his pistol at a number of men on the sidewalk who were breaking in. In the entrance were several bodies - of men, I decided, whom he had killed earlier in the day. Even as I looked on from a distance, I saw one of the robbers break the windows of the adjoining store, a place where shoes were sold, and deliberately set fire to it. I did not go to the groceryman's assistance. The time for such acts had already passed. Civilization was crumbling, and it was each for himself."

CHAPTER IV

I went away hastily, down a cross-street, and at the first corner I saw another ragedy. Two men of the working class had caught a man and a woman with two children and were robbing them. I knew the man by sight, though I had never been introduced to him. He was a poet whose verses I had long admired. Yet I did not go to his help, for at the moment I came upon the scene there was a pistol shot, and I saw him sinking to the ground. The woman screamed, and she was felled with a fist-blow by one of the brutes. I cried out threateningly, whereupon they discharged their pistols at me, and I ran away around the corner. Here I was blocked by an advancing conflagration. The buildings on both sides were burning, and the street was filled with smoke and flame. From somewhere in that murk came a woman's voice calling shrilly for help. But I did not go to her. A man's heart turned to iron amid such scenes, and one heard all too many appeals for help.

"Returning to the corner, I found the two robbers were gone. The poet and his wife lay dead on the pavement. It was a shocking sight. The two children had vanished - whither I could not tell. And I knew, now, why it was that the fleeing persons I encountered slipped along so furtively and with such white faces. In the midst of our civilization, down in our slums and labor-ghettos, we had bred a race of barbarians, of savages; and now, in the time of our calamity, they turned upon us like the wild beasts they were and destroyed us. And they destroyed themselves as well.

"They inflamed themselves with strong drink and committed a thousand atrocities, quarreling and killing one another in the general madness. One group of workingmen I saw, of the better sort, who had banded together, and, with their women and children in their midst, the sick and aged in litters and being carried, and with a number of horses pulling a truck-load of provisions, they were fighting their way out of the city. They made a fine spectacle as they came down the street through the drifting smoke, though they nearly shot me when I first appeared in their path. As they went by, one of their leaders shouted out to me in apologetic explanation. He said they were killing the robbers and looters on sight, and that they had thus banded together as the only-means by which to escape the prowlers.

"It was here that I saw for the first time what I was soon to see so often. One of the marching men had suddenly shown the unmistakable mark of the plague. Immediately those about him drew away, and he, without a remonstrance, stepped out of his place to let them pass on. A woman, most probably his wife, attempted to follow him. She was leading a little boy by the hand. But the husband commanded her sternly to go on, while others laid hands on her and restrained her from following him. This I saw, and I saw the man also, with his scarlet blaze of face, step into a doorway on the opposite side of the street. I heard the report of his pistol and saw him sink lifeless to the ground.

"After being turned aside twice again by advancing fires, I succeeded in getting through to the university. On the edge of the campus I came upon a party of university folk who were going in the direction of the Chemistry Building. They were all family men, and their families were with them, including the nurses and the servants. Professor Badminton greeted me, I had difficulty in recognizing him. Somewhere he had gone through flames, and his beard was singed off. About his head was a bloody bandage, and his clothes were filthy.

"He told me he had prowlers, and that his brother had been killed the previous night, in the defense of their dwelling.

"Midway across the campus, he pointed suddenly to Mrs. Swinton's face. The unmistakable scarlet was there. Immediately all the other women set up a screaming and began to run away from her. Her two children were with a nurse, and these also ran with the women. But her husband, Doctor Swinton, remained with her.

"'Go on, Smith,' he told me. 'Keep an eye on the children. As for me, I shall stay with my wife. I know she is as already dead, but I can't leave her. Afterwards, if I escape, I shall come to the Chemistry Building, and do you watch for me and let me in.'

"I left him bending over his wife and soothing her last moments, while I ran to overtake the party. We were the last to be admitted to the Chemistry Building. After that, with our automatic rifles we maintained our isolation. By our plans, we had arranged for a company of sixty to be in this refuge. Instead, every one of the numbers originally planned had added relatives and friends and whole families until there were over four hundred souls. But the Chemistry Building was large, and, standing by itself, was in no danger of being burned by the great fires that raged everywhere in the city.

"A large quantity of provisions had been gathered, and a food committee took charge of it, issuing rations daily to the various families and groups that arranged themselves into messes. A number of committees were appointed, and we developed a very efficient organization. I was on the committee of defense, though for the first day no prowlers came near. We could see them in the distance, however, and by the smoke of their fires knew that several camps of them were occupying the far edge of the campus. Drunkenness was rife, and often we heard them singing ribald songs or insanely shouting. While the world crashed to ruin about them and all the air was filled with the smoke of its burning, these low creatures gave rein to their bestiality and fought and drank and died. And after all, what did it matter? Everybody died anyway, the good and the bad, the efficient and the weaklings, those that loved to live and those that scorned to live. They passed. Everything passed.

"When twenty-four hours had gone by and no signs of the plague were apparent, we congratulated ourselves and set about digging a well. You have seen the great iron pipes which in those days carried water to all the city-dwellers. We feared that the fires in the city would burst the pipes and empty the reservoirs. So, we tore up the cement floor of the central court of the Chemistry Building and dug a well. There were many young men, undergraduates, with us, and we worked night and day on the well. And our fears were confirmed. Three hours before we reached water, the pipes went dry.

"A second twenty-four hours passed, and still the plague did not appear among us. We thought we were saved. But we did not know what I afterwards decided to be true, namely, that the period of the incubation of the plague germs in a human's body was a matter of a number of days. It slew so swiftly when once it manifested itself, that we were led to believe that the period of incubation was equally swift. So, when two days had left us unscathed, we were elated with the idea that we were free of the contagion.

"But the third day disillusioned us. I can never forget the night preceding it. I had charge of the night guards from eight to twelve, and from the roof of the building I watched the passing of all man's glorious works. So terrible were the local conflagrations that all the sky was lighted up. One could read the finest print in the red glare. All the world seemed wrapped in flames. San Francisco spouted smoke and fire from a score of vast conflagrations that were like so many active volcanoes. Oakland, San Leandro, Haywards - all were burning; and to the northward, clear to Point Richmond, other fires were at work. It was an awe-inspiring spectacle. Civilization, my grandsons, civilization was passing in a sheet of flame and a breath of death. At ten o'clock that night, the great powder magazines at Point Pinole exploded in rapid succession. So terrific were the concussions that the strong building rocked as in an earthquake, while every pane of glass was broken. It was then that I left the roof and went down the long corridors, from room to room, quieting the alarmed women and telling them what had happened.

"An hour later, at a window on the ground floor, I heard pandemonium break out in the camps of the prowlers. There were cries and screams, and shots from many pistols. As we afterward conjectured, this fight had been precipitated by an attempt on the part of those that were well to drive out those that were sick. At any rate, a number of the plague-stricken prowlers escaped across the campus and drifted against our doors. We warned them back, but they cursed us and discharged a fusillade from their pistols. Professor Merryweather, at one of the windows, was instantly killed, the bullet striking him squarely between the eyes. We opened fire in turn, and all the prowlers fled away with the exception of three. One was a woman. The plague was on them and they were reckless. Like foul fiends, there in the red glare from the skies, with faces blazing, they continued to curse us and fire at us. One of the men I shot with my own hand. After that the other man and the woman, still cursing us, lay down under our windows, where we were compelled to watch them die of the plague.

"The situation was critical. The explosions of the powder magazines had broken all the windows of the Chemistry Building, so that we were exposed to the germs from the corpses. The sanitary committee was called upon to act, and it responded nobly. Two men were required to go out and remove the corpses, and this meant the probable sacrifice of their own lives, for, having performed the task, they were not to be permitted to reenter the building. One of the professors, who was a bachelor, and one of the undergraduates volunteered. They bade good-bye to us and went forth. They were heroes. They gave up their lives that four hundred others might live. After they had performed their work, they stood for a moment, at a distance, looking at us wistfully. Then they waved their hands in farewell and went away slowly across the campus toward the burning city.

"And yet it was all useless. The next morning the first one of us was smitten with the plague - a little nurse-girl in the family of Professor Stout. It was no time for weak-kneed, sentimental policies. On the chance that she might be the only one, we thrust her forth from the building and commanded her to be gone.

"She went away slowly across the campus, wringing her hands and crying pitifully. We felt like brutes, but what were we to do? There were four hundred of us, and individuals had to be sacrificed.

"In one of the laboratories three families had domiciled themselves, and that afternoon we found among them no less than four corpses and seven cases of the plague in all its different stages.

"Then it was that the horror began. Leaving the dead lie, we forced the living ones to segregate themselves in another room. The plague began to break out among the rest of us, and as fast as the symptoms appeared, we sent the stricken ones to these segregated rooms. We compelled them to walk there by themselves, so as to avoid laying hands on them. It was heartrending. But still the plague raged among us, and room after room was filled with the dead and dying. And so, we who were yet clean retreated to the next floor and to the next, before this sea of the dead, that, room by room and floor by floor, inundated the building.

"The place became a charnel house, and in the middle of the night the survivors fled forth, taking nothing with them except arms and ammunition and a heavy store of tinned foods. We camped on the opposite side of the campus from the prowlers, and, while some stood guard, others of us volunteered to scout into the city in quest of horses, motor cars, carts, and wagons, or anything that would carry our provisions and enable us to emulate the banded workingmen I had seen fighting their way out to the open country.

"I was one of these scouts; and Doctor Hoyle, remembering that his motor car had been left behind in his home garage, told me to look for it. We scouted in pairs, and Dombey, a young undergraduate, accompanied me. We had to cross half a mile of the residence portion of the city to get to Doctor Hoyle's home. Here the buildings stood apart, in the midst of trees and grassy lawns, and here the fires had played freaks, burning whole blocks, skipping blocks and often skipping a single house in a block. And here, too, the prowlers were still at their work. We carried our automatic pistols openly in our hands, and looked desperate enough, forsooth, to keep them from attacking us. But at Doctor Hoyle's house the thing happened. Untouched by fire, even as we came to it the smoke of flames burst forth.

"The miscreant who had set fire to it staggered down the steps and out along the driveway. Sticking out of his coat pockets were bottles of whiskey, and he was very drunk. My first impulse was to shoot him, and I have never ceased regretting that I did not. Staggering and maundering to himself, with bloodshot eyes, and a raw and bleeding slash down one side of his bewhiskered face, he was altogether the most nauseating specimen of degradation and filth I had ever encountered. I did not shoot him, and he leaned against a tree on the lawn to let us go by. It was the most absolute, wanton act. Just as we were opposite him, he suddenly drew a pistol and shot Dombey through the head. The next instant I shot him. But it was too late. Dombey expired without a groan, immediately. I doubt if he even knew what had happened to him.

"Leaving the two corpses, I hurried on past the burning house to the garage, and there found Doctor Hoyle's motor car. The tanks were filled with gasoline, and it was ready for use. And it was in this car that I threaded the streets of the ruined city and came back to the survivors on the campus. The other scouts returned, but none had been so fortunate. Professor Fairmead had found a Shetland pony, but the poor creature, tied in a stable and abandoned for days, was so weak from want of food and water that it could carry no burden at all. Some of the men were for turning it loose, but I insisted that we should lead it along with us, so that, if we got out of food, we would have it to eat.

"There were forty-seven of us when we started, many being women and children. The President of the Faculty, an old man to begin with, and now hopelessly broken by the awful happenings of the past week, rode in the motor car with several young children and the aged mother of Professor Fairmead. Wathope, a young professor of English, who had a grievous bullet-wound in his leg, drove the car. The rest of us walked, Professor Fairmead leading the pony.

"It was what should have been a bright summer day, but the smoke from the burning world filled the sky, through which the sun shone murkily, a dull and lifeless orb, blood-red and ominous. But we had grown accustomed to that blood-red sun. With the smoke it was different. It bit into our nostrils and eyes, and there was not one of us whose eyes were not bloodshot. We directed our course to the southeast through the endless miles of suburban residences, travelling along where the first swells of low hills rose from the flat of the central city. It was by this way, only, that we could expect to gain the country.

"Our progress was painfully slow. The women and children could not walk fast. They did not dream of walking, my grandsons, in the way all people walk to-day. In truth, none of us knew how to walk. It was not until after the plague that I learned really to walk. So it was that the pace of the slowest was the pace of all, for we dared not separate on account of the prowlers. There were not so many now of these human beasts of prey. The plague had already well diminished their numbers, but enough still lived to be a constant menace to us. Many of the beautiful residences were untouched by fire, yet smoking ruins were everywhere. The prowlers, too, seemed to have got over their insensate desire to burn, and it was more rarely that we saw houses freshly on fire.

"Several of us scouted among the private garages in search of motor cars and gasoline. But in this we were unsuccessful. The first great flights from the cities had swept all such utilities away. Calgan, a fine young man, was lost in this work. He was shot by prowlers while crossing a lawn. Yet this was our only casualty, though, once, a drunken brute deliberately opened fire on all of us. Luckily, he fired wildly, and we shot him before he had done any hurt.

"At Fruitvale, still in the heart of the magnificent residence section of the city, the plague again smote us. Professor Fair-mead was the victim. Making signs to us that his mother was not to know, he turned aside into the grounds of a beautiful mansion. He sat down forlornly on the steps of the front veranda, and I, having lingered, waved him a last farewell. That night, several miles beyond Fruitvale and still in the city, we made camp. And that night we shifted camp twice to get away from our dead. In the morning there were thirty of us. I shall never forget the President of the Faculty. During the morning's march his wife, who was walking, betrayed the fatal symptoms, and when she drew aside to let us go on, he insisted on leaving the motor car and remaining with her. There was quite a discussion about this, but in the end, we gave in. It was just as well, for we knew not which ones of us, if any, might ultimately escape.

"That night, the second of our march, we camped beyond Haywards in the first stretches of country. And in the morning, there were eleven of us that lived. Also, during the night, Wathope, the professor with the wounded leg, deserted us in the motor car. He took with him his sister and his mother and most of our tinned provisions. It was that day, in the afternoon, while resting by the wayside, that I saw the last airship I shall ever see. The smoke was much thinner here in the country, and I first sighted the ship drifting and veering helplessly at an elevation of two thousand feet. What had happened I could not conjecture, but even as we looked, we saw her bow dip down lower and lower. Then the bulk-heads of the various gas-chambers must have burst, for, quite perpendicular, she fell like a plummet to the earth.

"And from that day to this I have not seen another airship. Often and often, during the next few years, I scanned the sky for them, hoping against hope that somewhere in the world civilization had survived. But it was not to be. What happened with us in California must have happened with everybody everywhere.

"Another day, and at Niles there were three of us. Beyond Niles, in the middle of the highway, we found Wathope. The motor car had broken down, and there, on the rugs which they had spread on the ground, lay the bodies of his sister, his mother, and himself.

"Wearied by the unusual exercise of continual walking, that night I slept heavily. In the morning I was alone in the world. Canfield and Parsons, my last companions, were dead of the plague. Of the four hundred that sought shelter in the Chemistry Building, and of the forty-seven that began the march, I alone remained - I and the Shetland pony. Why this should be so there is no explaining. I did not catch the plague, that is all. I was immune. I was merely the one lucky man in a million - just as every survivor was one in a million, or, rather, in several millions, for the proportion was at least that."

CHAPTER V

"For two days I sheltered in a pleasant grove where there had been no deaths. In those two days, while badly depressed and believing that my turn would come at any moment, nevertheless I rested and recuperated. So did the pony. And on the third day, putting what small store of tinned provisions I possessed on the pony's back, I started on across a very lonely land. Not a live man, woman, or child, did I encounter, though the dead were everywhere. Food, however, was abundant. The land then was not as it is now. It was all cleared of trees and brush, and it was cultivated. The food for millions of mouths was growing, ripening, and going to waste. From the fields and orchards, I gathered vegetables, fruits, and berries. Around the deserted farmhouses I got eggs and caught chickens. And frequently I found supplies of tinned provisions in the storerooms.

"A strange thing was what was taking place with all the domestic animals. Everywhere they were going wild and preying on one another. The chickens and ducks were the first to be destroyed, while the pigs were the first to go wild, followed by the cats. Nor were the dogs long in adapting themselves to the changed conditions. There was a veritable plague of dogs. They devoured the corpses, barked and howled during the nights, and in the daytime slunk about in the distance. As the time went by, I noticed a change in their behavior. At first, they were apart from one another, very suspicious and very prone to fight. But after a not very long while they began to come together and run in packs. The dog, you see, always was a social animal, and this was true before ever he came to be domesticated by man. In the last days of the world before the plague, there were many, many very different kinds of dogs - dogs without hair and dogs with warm fur, dogs so small that they would make scarcely a mouthful for other dogs that were as large as mountain lions. Well, all the small dogs, and the weak types, were killed by their fellows. Also, the very large ones were not adapted for the wildlife and bred out. As a result, the many different kinds of dogs disappeared, and there remained, running in packs, the medium-sized wolfish dogs that you know to-day."

"But the cats don't run in packs, Granser," Hoo-Hoo objected.

"The cat was never a social animal. As one writer in the nineteenth century said, the cat walks by himself. He always walked by himself, from before the time he was tamed by man, down through the long ages of domestication, to to-day when once more he is wild.

"The horses also went wild, and all the fine breeds we had degenerated into the small mustang horse you know to-day. The cows likewise went wild, as did the pigeons and the sheep. And that a few of the chickens survived you know yourself. But the wild chicken of to-day is quite a different thing from the chickens we had in those days.

"But I must go on with my story. I travelled through a deserted land. As the time went by, I began to yearn more and more for human beings. But I never found one, and I grew lonelier and lonelier. I crossed Livermore Valley and the mountains between it and the great valley of the San Joaquin. You have never seen that valley, but it is very large, and it is the home of the wild horse. There are great droves there, thousands and tens of thousands. I revisited it thirty years after, so I know. You think there are lots of wild horses down here in the coast valleys, but they are as nothing compared with those of the San Joaquin. Strange to say, the cows, when they went wild, went back into the lower mountains. Evidently, they were better able to protect themselves there.

"In the country districts the ghouls and prowlers had been less in evidence, for I found many villages and towns untouched by fire. But they were filled by the pestilential dead, and I passed by without exploring them. It was near Lathrop that, out of my loneliness, I picked up a pair of collie dogs that were so newly free that they were urgently willing to return to their allegiance to man. These collies accompanied me for many years, and the strains of them are in those very dogs there that you boys have to-day. But in sixty years the collie strain has worked out. These brutes are more like domesticated wolves than anything else." Harelip rose to his feet, glanced to see that the goats were safe, and looked at the sun's position in the afternoon sky, advertising impatience at the prolixity of the old man's tale. Urged to hurry by Edwin, Granser went on.

"There is little more to tell. With my two dogs and my pony, and riding a horse I had managed to capture, I crossed the San Joaquin and went on to a wonderful valley in the Sierras called Yosemite. In the great hotel there I found a prodigious supply of tinned provisions. The pasture was abundant, as was the game, and the river that ran through the valley was full of trout. I remained there three years in an utter loneliness that none but a man who has once been highly civilized can understand. Then I could stand it no more. I felt that I was going crazy. Like the dog, I was a social animal and I needed my kind. I reasoned that since I had survived the plague, there was a possibility that others had survived. Also, I reasoned that after three years the plague germs must all be gone, and the land be clean again.

"With my horse and dogs and pony, I set out. Again, I crossed the San Joaquin Valley, the mountains beyond, and came down into Livermore Valley. The change in those three years was amazing. All the land had been splendidly tilled, and now I could scarcely recognize it, 'such was the sea of rank vegetation that had overrun the agricultural handiwork of man. You see, the wheat, the vegetables, and orchard trees had always been cared for and nursed by man, so that they were soft and tender. The weeds and wild bushes and such things, on the contrary, had always been fought by man, so that they were tough and resistant. As a result, when the hand of man was removed, the wild vegetation smothered and destroyed practically all the domesticated vegetation. The coyotes were greatly increased, and it was at this time that I first encountered wolves, straying in twos and threes and small packs down from the regions where they had always persisted.

"It was at Lake Temescal, not far from the one-time city of Oakland, that I came upon the first live human beings. Oh, my grandsons, how can I describe to you my emotion, when, astride my horse and dropping down the hillside to the lake, I saw the smoke of a campfire rising through the trees. Almost did my heart stop beating. I felt that I was going crazy. Then I heard the cry of a babe - a human babe. And dogs barked, and my dogs answered. I did not know but what I was the one human alive in the whole world. It could not be true that here were others - smoke, and the cry of a babe.

"Emerging on the lake, there, before my eyes, not a hundred yards away, I saw a man, a large man. He was standing on an out jutting rock and fishing. I was overcome. I stopped my horse. I tried to call out but could not. I waved my hand. It seemed to me that the man looked at me, but he did not appear to wave. Then I laid my head on my arms there in the saddle. I was afraid to look again, for I knew it was an hallucination, and I knew that if I looked the man would be gone. And so precious was the hallucination, that I wanted it to persist yet a little while. I knew, too, that as long as I did not look it would persist.

"Thus, I remained, until I heard my dogs snarling, and a man's voice. What do you think the voice said? I will tell you. It said: 'Where in hell did you come from??'

"Those were the words, the exact words. That was what your other grandfather said to me, Har-lip, when he greeted me there on the shore of Lake Temescal fifty-seven years ago. And they were the most ineffable words I have ever heard. I opened my eyes, and there he stood before me, a large, dark, hairy man, heavy-jawed, slant-browed, fierce-eyed. How I got off my horse I do not know. But it seemed that the next I knew I was clasping his hand with both of mine and crying. I would have embraced him, but he was ever a narrow-minded, suspicious man, and he drew away from me. Yet did I cling to his hand and cry."

Granser's voice faltered and broke at the recollection, and the weak tears streamed down his cheeks while the boys looked on and giggled.

"Yet did I cry," he continued, "and desire to embrace him, though the Chauffeur was a brute, a perfect brute - the most abhorrent man I have ever known. His name was... strange, how I have forgotten his name. Everybody called him Chauffeur — it was the name of his occupation, and it stuck. That is how, to this day, the tribe he founded is called the Chauffeur Tribe.

"He was a violent, unjust man. Why the plague germs spared him I can never understand. It would seem, in spite of our old metaphysical notions about absolute justice, that there is no justice in the universe. Why did he live? - an iniquitous, moral monster, a blot on the face of nature, a cruel, relentless, bestial cheat as well. All he could talk about was motor cars, machinery, gasoline, and garages — and especially, and with huge delight, of his mean pilfering's and sordid swindling's of the persons who had employed him in the days before the coming of the plague. And yet he was spared, while hundreds of millions, yea, billions, of better men were destroyed.

"I went on with him to his camp, and there I saw her, Vesta, the one woman. It was glorious and... pitiful. There she was, Vesta Van Warden, the young wife of John Van Warden, clad in rags, with marred and scarred and toil-calloused hands, bending over the campfire and doing scullion work - she, Vesta, who had been born to the purple of the greatest baronage of wealth the world had ever known. John Van Warden, her husband, worth one billion, eight hundred million and President of the Board of Industrial Magnates, had been the ruler of America. Also, sitting on the International Board of Control, he had been one of the seven men who ruled the world. And she herself had come of equally noble stock. Her father, Philip Saxon, had been President of the Board of Industrial Magnates up to the time of his death. This office was in process of becoming hereditary and had Philip Saxon had a son that son would have succeeded him. But his only child was Vesta, the perfect flower of generations of the highest culture this planet has ever produced. It was not until the engagement between Vesta and Van Warden took place, that Saxon indicated the latter as his successor. It was, I am sure, a political marriage. I have reason to believe that Vesta never really loved her husband in the mad passionate way of which the poets used to sing. It was more like the marriages that obtained among crowned heads in the days before they were displaced by the Magnates.

"And there she was, boiling fish-chowder in a soot-covered pot, her glorious eyes inflamed by the acrid smoke of the open fire. Hers was a sad story. She was the one survivor in a million, as I had been, as the Chauffeur had been. On a crowning eminence of the Alameda Hills, overlooking San Francisco Bay, Van Warden had built a vast summer palace. It was surrounded by a park of a thousand acres. When the plague broke out, Van Warden sent her there. Armed guards patrolled the boundaries of the park, and nothing entered in the way of provisions or even mail matter that was not first fumigated. And yet did the plague enter, killing the guards at their posts, the servants at their tasks, sweeping away the whole army of retainers — or, at least, all of them who did not flee to die elsewhere. So it was that Vesta found herself the sole living person in the palace that had become a charnel house.

"Now the Chauffeur had been one of the servants that ran away. Returning, two months afterward, he discovered Vesta in a little summer pavilion where there had been no deaths and where she had established herself. He was a brute. She was afraid, and she ran away and hid among the trees. That night, on foot, she fled into the mountains - she, whose tender feet and delicate body had never known the bruise of stones nor the scratch of briars. He followed, and that night he caught her. He struck her. Do you understand? He beat her with those terrible fists of his and made her his slave. It was she who had to gather the firewood, build the fires, cook, and do all the degrading camp-labor - she, who had never performed a menial act in her life. These things he compelled her to do, while he, a proper savage, elected to lie around camp and look on. He did nothing, absolutely nothing, except on occasion to hunt meat or catch fish."

"Good for Chauffeur," Harelip commented in an undertone to the other boys. "I remember him before he died. He was a corker. But he did things, and he made things go. You know, Dad married his daughter, an' you ought to see the way he knocked the spots outa Dad. The Chauffeur was a son-of-a-gun. He made us kids stand around. Even when he was croaking, he reached out for me, once, an' laid my head open with that long stick he kept always beside him."

Harelip rubbed his bullet head reminiscently, and the boys returned to the old man, who was maundering ecstatically about Vesta, the squaw of the founder of the Chauffeur Tribe.

"And so, I say to you that you cannot understand the awfulness of the situation. The Chauffeur was a servant, understand, a servant. And he cringed, with bowed head, to such as she. She was a lord of life, both by birth and by marriage. The destinies of millions, such as he, she carried in the hollow of her pink-white hand. And, in the days before the plague, the slightest contact with such as he would have been pollution. Oh, I have seen it. Once, I remember, there was Mrs.

Goldwin, wife of one of the great magnates. It was on a landing stage, just as she was embarking in her private dirigible, that she dropped her parasol. A servant picked it up and made the mistake of handing it to her - to her, one of the greatest royal ladies of the land! She shrank back, as though he were a leper, and indicated her secretary to receive it. Also, she ordered her secretary to ascertain the creature's name and to see that he was immediately discharged from service. And such a woman was Vesta Van Warden. And her the Chauffeur beat and made his slave.

"– Bill - that was it, Bill, the Chauffeur. That was his name. He was a wretched, primitive man, wholly devoid of the finer instincts and chivalrous promptings of a cultured soul. No, there is no absolute justice, for to him fell that wonder of womanhood, Vesta Van Warden. The grievous-ness of this you will never understand, my grandsons; for you are yourselves primitive little savages, unaware of aught else but savagery. Why should Vesta not have been mine? I was a man of culture and refinement, a professor in a great university. Even so, in the time before the plague, such was her exalted position, she would not have deigned to know that I existed. Mark, then, the abysmal degradation to which she fell at the hands of the Chauffeur. Nothing less than the destruction of all mankind had made it possible that I should know her, look in her eyes, converse with her, touch her hand - ay, and love her and know that her feelings toward me were very kindly. I have reason to believe that she, even she, would have loved me, there being no other man in the world except the Chauffeur. Why, when it destroyed eight billion souls, did not the plague destroy just one more man, and that man the Chauffeur?

"Once, when the Chauffeur was away fishing, she begged me to kill him. With tears in her eyes she begged me to kill him. But he was a strong and violent man, and I was afraid. Afterwards, I talked with him. I offered him my horse, my pony, my dogs, all that I possessed, if he would give Vesta to me. And he grinned in my face and shook his head. He was very insulting. He said that in the old days he had been a servant, had been dirt under the feet of men like me and of women like Vesta, and that now he had the greatest lady in the land to be servant to him and cook his food and nurse his brats. 'You had your day before the plague,' he said; 'but this is my day, and a damned good day it is. I wouldn't trade back to the old times for anything.' Such words he spoke, but they are not his words. He was a vulgar, low-minded man, and vile oaths fell continually from his lips.

"Also, he told me that if he caught me making eyes at his woman, he'd wring my neck and give her a beating as well. What was I to do? I was afraid. He was a brute. That first night, when I discovered the camp, Vesta and I had great talk about the things of our vanished world. We talked of art, and books, and poetry; and the Chauffeur listened and grinned and sneered. He was bored and angered by our way of speech which he did not comprehend, and finally he spoke up and said: 'And this is Vesta Van Warden, one-time wife of Van Warden the Magnate - a high and stuck-up beauty, who is now my squaw. Eh, Professor Smith, times is changed, times is changed. Here, you, woman, take off my moccasins, and lively about it. I want Professor Smith to see how well I have you trained.'

"I saw her clench her teeth, and the flame of revolt rise in her face. He drew back his gnarled fist to strike, and I was afraid, and sick at heart. I could do nothing to prevail against him. So, I got up to go, and not be witness to such indignity. But the Chauffeur laughed and threatened me with a beating if I did not stay and behold. And I sat there, perforce, by the campfire on the shore of Lake

Temescal, and saw Vesta, Vesta Van Warden, kneel and remove the moccasins of that grinning, hairy, apelike human brute.

"- Oh, you do not understand, my grandsons. You have never known anything else, and you do not understand.

"'Halter-broke and bridle-wise,' the Chauffeur gloated, while she performed that dreadful, menial task. 'A trifle balky at times, Professor, a trifle balky; but a clout alongside the jaw makes her as meek and gentle as a lamb.'

"And another time he said: 'We've got to start all over and replenish the earth and multiply. You're handicapped, Professor. You ain't got no wife, and we're up against a regular Garden-of-Eden proposition. But I ain't proud. I'll tell you what, Professor.' He pointed at their little infant, barely a year old. 'There's your wife, though you'll have to wait till she grows up. It's rich, ain't it? We're all equals here, and I'm the biggest toad in the splash. But I ain't stuck up - not I. I do you the honor, Professor Smith, the very great honor of betrothing to you my and Vesta Van Warden's daughter. Ain't it cussed bad that Van Warden ain't here to see?'"

CHAPTER VI

"**I** lived three weeks of infinite torment there in the Chauffeur's camp. And then, one day, tiring of me, or of what to him was my bad effect on Vesta, he told me that the year before, wandering through the Contra Costa Hills to the Straits of Carquinez, across the Straits he had seen a smoke. This meant that there were still other human beings, and that for three weeks he had kept this inestimably precious information from me. I departed at once, with my dogs and horses, and journeyed across the Contra Costa Hills to the Straits. I saw no smoke on the other side, but at Port Costa discovered a small steel barge on which I was able to embark my animals. Old canvas which I found served me for a sail, and a southerly breeze fanned me across the Straits and up to the ruins of Vallejo. Here, on the outskirts of the city, I found evidences of a recently occupied camp.

"Many clam-shells showed me why these humans had come to the shores of the Bay. This was the Santa Rosa Tribe, and I followed its track along the old railroad right of way across the salt marshes to Sonoma Valley. Here, at the old brickyard at Glen Ellen, I came upon the camp. There were eighteen souls all told. Two were old men, one of whom was Jones, a banker. The other was Harrison, a retired pawnbroker, who had taken for wife the matron of the State Hospital for the Insane at Napa. Of all the persons of the city of Napa, and of all the other towns and villages in that rich and populous valley, she had been the only-survivor. Next, there were the three young men - Cardiff and Hale, who had been farmers, and Wainwright, a common day-laborer. All three had found wives. To Hale, a crude, illiterate farmer, had fallen Isadore, the greatest prize, next to Vesta, of the women who came through the plague. She was one of the world's most noted singers, and the plague had caught her at San Francisco. She has talked with me for hours at a time, telling me of her adventures, until, at last, rescued by Hale in the Mendocino Forest Reserve, there had remained nothing for her to do but become his wife. But Hale was a good fellow, in spite of his illiteracy. He had a keen sense of justice and right-dealing, and she was far happier with him than was Vesta with the Chauffeur.

"The wives of Cardiff and Wainwright were ordinary women, accustomed to toil with strong constitutions - just the type for the wild new life which they were compelled to live. In addition, were two adult idiots from the feeble-minded home at El-dredge, and five or six young children and infants born after the formation of the Santa Rosa Tribe. Also, there was Bertha. She was a good woman, Harelip, in spite of the sneers of your father. Her I took for wife. She was the mother of your father, Edwin, and of yours, Hoo-Hoo. And it was our daughter, Vera, who married your father, Harelip - your father, Sandow, who was the oldest son of Vesta Van Warden and the Chauffeur.

"And so, it was that I became the nineteenth member of the Santa Rosa Tribe. There were only two outsiders added after me. One was Mungerson, descended from the Magnates, who wandered alone in the wilds of Northern California for eight years before he came south and joined us. He it was who waited twelve years more before he married my daughter, Mary. The other was Johnson, the man who founded the Utah Tribe. That was where he came from, Utah, a country that lies very far away from here, across the great deserts, to the east. It was not until twenty-seven years after the plague that Johnson reached California. In all that Utah region he reported but three survivors, himself one, and all men. For many years these three men lived and hunted together, until, at last, desperate, fearing that with them the human race would perish utterly from the planet, they headed westward on the possibility of finding women survivors in California. Johnson alone came through the great desert, where his two companions died. He was forty-six years old when he joined us, and he married the fourth daughter of Isadore and Hale, and his eldest son married your aunt, Harelip, who was the third daughter of Vesta and the Chauffeur. Johnson was a strong man, with a will of his own. And it was because of this that he seceded from the Santa Rosans and formed the Utah Tribe at San José. It is a small tribe—there are only nine in it; but, though he is dead, such was his influence and the strength of his breed, that it will grow into a strong tribe and play a leading part in the recivilization of the planet.

"There are only two other tribes that we know of—the Los Angelitos and the Carmelitos. The latter started from one man and woman. He was called Lopez, and he was descended from the ancient Mexicans and was very black. He was a cowherd in the ranges beyond Carmel, and his wife was a maidservant in the great Del Monte Hotel. It was seven years before we first got in touch with the Los Ange-litos. They have a good country down there, but it is too warm. I estimate the present population of the world at between three hundred and fifty and four hundred—provided, of course, that there are no scattered little tribes elsewhere in the world. If there be such, we have not heard from them. Since Johnson crossed the desert from Utah, no word nor sign has come from the East or anywhere else. The great world which I knew in my boyhood and early manhood is gone. It has ceased to be. I am the last man who was alive in the days of the plague and who knows the wonders of that far-off time. We, who mastered the planet—its earth, and sea, and sky - and who were as very gods, now live in primitive savagery along the water courses of this California country.

"But we are increasing rapidly - your sister, Harelip, already has four children. We are increasing rapidly and making ready for a new climb toward civilization. In time, pressure of population will compel us to spread out, and a hundred generations from now we may expect our descendants to start across the Sierras, oozing slowly along, generation by generation, over the great continent to the colonization of the East—a new Aryan drift around the world.

"But it will be slow, very slow; we have so far to climb. We fell so hopelessly far. If only one physicist or one chemist had survived! But it was not to be, and we have forgotten everything. The Chauffeur started working in iron. He made the forge which we use to this day. But he was a lazy man, and when he died, he took with him all he knew of metals and machinery. What was I to know of such things? I was a classical scholar, not a chemist. The other men who survived were not educated. Only two things did the Chauffeur accomplish - the brewing of strong drink and the growing of tobacco. It was while he was drunk, once, that he killed Vesta. I firmly believe that he killed Vesta in a fit of drunken cruelty though he always maintained that she fell into the lake and was drowned.

"And, my grandsons, let me warn you against the medicine-men. They call themselves doctors, travestying what was once a noble profession, but in reality, they are medicine-men, devil-devil men, and they make for superstition and darkness. They are cheats and liars. But so debased and degraded are we, that we believe their lies. They, too, will increase in numbers as we increase, and they will strive to rule us. Yet are they liars and charlatans. Look at young Cross-Eyes, posing as a doctor, selling charms against sickness, giving good hunting, exchanging promises of fair weather for good meat and skins, sending the death-stick, performing a thousand abominations. Yet I say to you, that when he says he can do these things, he lies. I, Professor Smith, Professor James Howard Smith, say that he lies. I have told him so to his teeth. Why has he not sent me the death-stick? Because he knows that with me it is without avail. But you, Harelip, so deeply are you sunk in black superstition that did you awake this night and find the death-stick beside you, you would surely die. And you would die, not because of any virtues in the stick, but because you are a savage with the dark and clouded mind of a savage.

"The doctors must be destroyed, and all that was lost must be discovered over again. Wherefore, earnestly, I repeat unto you certain things which you must remember and tell to your children after you. You must tell them that when water is made hot by fire, there resides in it a wonderful thing called steam, which is stronger than ten thousand men and which can do all man's work for him. There are other very useful things. In the lightning flash resides a similarly strong servant of man, which was of old his slave and which some day will be his slave again.

"Quite a different thing is the alphabet. It is what enables me to know the meaning of fine markings, whereas you boys know only rude picture-writing. In that dry cave on Telegraph Hill, where you see me often go when the tribe is down by the sea, I have stored many books. In them is great wisdom. Also, with them, I have placed a key to the alphabet, so that one who knows picture-writing may also know print. Someday men will read again; and then, if no accident has befallen my cave, they will know that Professor James Howard Smith once lived and saved for them the knowledge of the ancients.

"There is another little device that men inevitably will rediscover. It is called gunpowder. It was what enabled us to kill surely and at long distances. Certain things which are found in the ground, when combined in the right proportions, will make this gunpowder. What these things are, I have forgotten, or else I never knew. But I wish I did know. Then would I make powder, and then would I certainly kill Cross-Eyes and rid the land of superstition -"

"After I am man-grown I am going to give Cross-Eyes all the goats, and meat, and skins I can get, so that he'll teach me to be a doctor," Hoo-Hoo asserted. "And when I know, I'll make everybody else sit up and take notice. They'll get down in the dirt to me, you bet."

The old man nodded his head solemnly, and murmured:

"Strange it is to hear the vestiges and remnants of the complicated Aryan speech falling from the lips of a filthy little skin-clad savage. All the world is topsy-turvy. And it has been topsy-turvy ever since the plague."

"You won't make me sit up," Harelip boasted to the would-be medicine-man. "If I paid you for a sending of the death-stick and it didn't work, I'd bust

- 519 -

in your head—understand, you Hoo-Hoo, you?"

"I'm going to get Granser to remember this here gunpowder stuff," Edwin said softly, "and then I'll have you all on the run. You, Harelip, will do my fighting for me and get my meat for me, and you, Hoo-Hoo, will send the death-stick for me and make everybody afraid. And if I catch Harelip trying to bust your head, Hoo-Hoo, I'll fix him with that same gunpowder. Granser ain't such a fool as you think, and I'm going to listen to him and someday I'll be boss over the whole bunch of you."

The old man shook his head sadly, and said:

"The gunpowder will come. Nothing can stop it - the same old story over and over. Man will increase, and men will fight. The gunpowder will enable men to kill millions of men, and in this way only, by fire and blood, will a new civilization, in some remote day, be evolved. And of what profit will it be? Just as the old civilization passed, so will the new. It may take fifty thousand years to build, but it will pass. All things pass. Only remain cosmic force and matter, ever in flux, ever acting and reacting and realizing the eternal types - the priest, the soldier, and the king. Out of the mouths of babes comes the wisdom of all the ages. Some will fight, some will rule, some will pray; and all the rest will toil and suffer sore while on their bleeding carcasses is reared again, and yet again, without end, the amazing beauty and surpassing wonder of the civilized state. It were just as well that I destroyed those cave-stored books - whether they remain or perish, all their old truths will be discovered, their old lies lived and handed down. What is the profit -"

Harelip leaped to his feet, giving a quick glance at the pasturing goats and the afternoon sun.

"Gee!" he muttered to Edwin, "The old geezer gets more long-winded every day. Let's pull for camp."

While the other two, aided by the dogs, assembled the goats and started them for the trail through the forest, Edwin stayed by the old man and guided him in the same direction. When they reached the old right of way, Edwin stopped suddenly and looked back. Harelip and Hoo-Hoo and the dogs and the goats passed on. Edwin was looking at a small herd of wild horses which had come down on the hard sand. There were at least twenty of them, young colts and yearlings and mares, led by a beautiful stallion which stood in the foam at the edge of the surf, with arched neck and bright wild eyes, sniffing the salt air from off the sea.

"What is it?" Granser queried.

"Horses," was the answer. "First time I ever seen 'em on the beach. It's the mountain lions getting thicker and thicker and driving 'em down."

The low sun shot red shafts of light, fan-shaped, up from a cloud-tumbled horizon. And close at hand, in the white waste of shore-lashed waters, the sea-lions, bellowing their old primeval chant, hauled up out of the sea on the black rocks and fought and loved.

"Come on, Granser," Edwin prompted. And old man and boy, skin-clad and barbaric, turned and went along the right of way into the forest in the wake of the goats.

THE END

Section 130

Katrinka Manderly

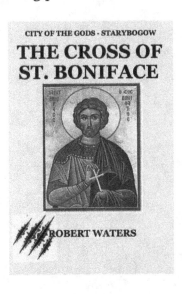